Renegade

Also by L. Timmel Duchamp

Alanya to Alanya

The Grand Conversation

Love's Body, Dancing in Time

The Red Rose Rages (Bleeding)

Renegade

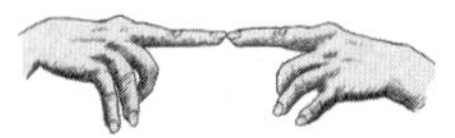

Book Two of the Marq'ssan Cycle

by L. Timmel Duchamp

Aqueduct Press, PO Box 95787
Seattle, WA 98145-2787
www.aqueductpress.com

ISBN: 1-933500-04-2
978-1-933500-04-1
First Edition, First Printing, June 2006

COVER ACKNOWLEDGEMENTS
Cover Design by Lynne Jensen Lampe
Cover photos Ocotillo, Sunset, Prisoner: © Royalty-Free/CORBIS
Cover photo of Emma Goldman speaking in Union Square, © Bettmann/CORBIS collection
Cover photo of Red Square, Courtesy University of Washington Libraries Special Collections, UWC0121
Book Design by Kathryn Wilham

Fingers Touching by Lori Hillard

Printed in the USA
14 13 12 11 10 09 08 07 06 1 2 3 4 5

This book was set in a digital version of Monotype Walbaum, available through AGFA Monotype. The original typeface was designed by Justus Erich Walbaum.

For Kathryn Wilham and Shira Broschat

For we are abandoned, like children lost in the wood. When you stand before me, and look at me, what do you know of the pains that are in me, and what do I know of yours? And if I were to prostrate myself before you, and weep and talk, would you know any more about me than you know about hell when someone tells you that it is hot and fearsome? For this reason alone we human beings should stand before one another with as much respect, as much sympathy, and as much love as if we were standing before the gates of hell.

— Franz Kafka

Chapter One

[i]

It had been a tough, sometimes desperate year, but for many in the Pacific Northwest Free Zone in the summer of 2177, life had become comfortable enough to bathe the future in a glow of rosy expectations. Among these numbered Martha Greenglass.

Lulled by the steady drone of the bus's tires on the asphalt, the chatter of the other women buzzing in the background, Martha drowsed in the heat. She jerked into awareness only when she felt the bus slow to a halt. She opened her eyes and blinked; the bus, she saw, was swinging onto the country road that would carry them northwest from Sedro Woolley.

"Man," Jess said. "Will I be glad to get back to Seattle."

Martha woke to full alert. She looked at Jess and sent her a silent warning to watch her mouth. She said, "You mean you aren't visiting the Whidbey settlement first?" Jess seemed oblivious of the need to be careful of how she talked on their trips away from Seattle. A few words more and she might have dropped some careless remark that any number of the women on the bus— including the teenagers— would have heard, likely been offended by, and spread around Bellingham when they returned there later. In Martha's opinion, a woman over the age of thirty should understand such things and not need to be steered away from careless blunders by someone four years younger.

"I thought you knew I was going straight back to Seattle, Martha," Jess was saying. "There's so much work waiting for us already, a side trip to Whidbey would just—"

"Yeah," Martha said, deliberately interrupting. "I've got so much to do that I should be getting back now, too. But I have to say, I'm looking forward to having a weekend on Farley's farm." It had been three weeks since she'd seen Louise.

"I guess it'll be pretty quiet there." Jess had never been to Farley's before. In fact, Jess had probably never spent so much as a day in any rural or semi-rural place before she'd moved to Seattle. Hadn't she once said that before coming to Seattle she'd been outside of L.A. only three times in her life— twice to New York City and once to Houston?

"Quiet it won't be," Martha said. "Wait until you see it. It's enough to make a nonviolent anarchist go gray. They've set aside several acres for weapons training, you know. It's not just aikido and karate." As soon as the words were out of her mouth Martha wondered if *she* had just been indiscreet. And then she mocked herself for being paranoid. Every soul on the bus was going to Farley's, and once there they'd see all that soon enough for themselves. Besides, if anybody had spies out looking for such things, they'd already know about Farley's.

The bus pulled off the main road onto a rutted single-lane dirt track. "Boy, we *are* out in the sticks." Jess looked faintly appalled by the flat expanse of fields planted in corn and soybeans. "This must be the flattest land I've seen in the entire Free Zone." Her brow wrinkled, and she reached for the emery board she kept in her shirt pocket and went to work touching up her already perfect manicure.

"Hey, Jess. That's why they call it the Skagit Flats." Martha winked at the woman two seats up and across the aisle who kept looking back at them and was unsuccessfully trying to conceal a smile at Jess's city-slicker remarks.

They jounced past fields being worked by women. Martha peered at the plants and decided that what the women were handpicking must be cherry tomatoes. Cherry tomatoes could not be harvested by machine— at least not by the machines the people in the Northwest Free Zone had available to them. A couple of the teenagers, nudging one another and pointing, giggled, probably because they had never seen women working shirtless before. Martha's lips curved into a small, privately amused smile. Within the week they themselves would likely be working shirtless and would think no more about it, except perhaps later to regret the conventions when they were back home in Bellingham.

The bus crunched up the long, thinly graveled drive and parked at the end of the row of vehicles lining one side of the wide, thickly graveled area in which the driveway ended. The women in the bus slipped on backpacks to which they had tied bulky items like sleeping bags, guitars, and tennis rackets. Jess examined her nails one last time and put the emery board back in her pocket. Neither she nor Martha made a move to retrieve their packs.

Martha's breath caught in her throat as she sighted Louise rounding the corner of the barn; she watched Louise tramp toward the bus, then momentarily lost sight of her. And then Louise was inside, standing at the front of the bus, holding up her hand for quiet. "Greetings, women. Welcome to Farley's." She spoke in a clear, well-projected voice. All chatter ceased, though backpacks still rustled and creaked. "My name is Louise Simon. Feel free to ask me anything you think I can tell you. But for now, I want you to listen up. Those who are here for one week belong to Group A, those here for two weeks to Group B, and those here for a month to Group C. So what I want all of you to do when you get off the bus is to organize yourselves into those groupings as quickly and efficiently as you can." Louise stepped off the bus, and the chatter resumed.

Martha watched the women file to the front and debark and wondered how they would do at this their first test. Louise and the other trainers made a point of not giving the women taking the workshops explicit instructions (such as: "everyone in Group A stand on the right side of the bus," and so on). "This isn't kindergarten," Louise liked to say when some of the workshoppers inevitably asked why she wasn't more explicit— and thus more efficient. Martha conjectured that given Bellingham's development of a hierarchical so-called democracy since the withdrawal of Executive forces, a leader would swiftly emerge who would tell everyone what to do. She toyed with laying a bet with Jess— only to realize that doing so would be tactless and that Jess wouldn't know what she was talking about, anyway.

When everyone else had gotten off, Martha and Jess moved into the aisle and put on their own packs. Alighting from the bus, Martha flashed Louise a broad grin, and Louise— her lips pressed together, her eyes dancing— nodded. Martha moved off to the side to watch.

Jess hung back. "What are we waiting for?"

"Go on into the house, Jess. I want to say hello to Louise first."

Jess grinned. "Right. Pretty dumb of me to forget about your, ah, vested interest in stopping here." Stooped under the weight of her backpack, she staggered toward the house. Before this trip Jess had never worn a pack in her life.

The people from Bellingham eventually divided themselves into three groups, but only after five minutes of wrangling and a successful takeover by a woman Martha judged to be about Louise's age, who stood with the group that would be taking the month-long course. Louise gave each group directions for finding their dorms and suggested they unpack, change into loose clothing, and start warming up, mentioning jogging and yoga as possible activities. She then turned to Martha. As Martha had seen happen before, Louise's turning her back on the women disconcerted them. Several stared fixedly after Louise as she moved toward Martha.

Louise took Martha's arm, pulled her around to the other side of the bus out of sight of the others, and— notwithstanding the encumbering backpack— folded her into a tight, sweaty bear-hug that loosened into a tongue-tangling kiss. "I missed you, Martha," Louise said into Martha's ear when she came up for breath. Her hand brushed over the curve of Martha's breast.

Martha inhaled Louise's smell and rubbed her face against Louise's. "I missed you too." She hardly noticed what she was saying because her cunt was practically melting.

"The cabin's finished now— come see."

Arms linked, they set off around the corner of the house in the opposite direction from which the Bellingham people were heading, toward the large stand of trees bordering the river. Martha tried to get a grip, tried to take an interest in all the changes since her last visit.

Louise and the other trainers had begun building two single-room cabins six months earlier. Their lack of organization and time had made Martha wonder if they would ever get the cabins finished. But Martha crowed when she saw the A-frame nestled in the dazzlingly sunlit clearing that had been carved out of the thick grove of cedar, hemlock, and Douglas fir. “Hey, it’s even got windows! And solar panels— which must mean you’ve got electricity! That does it, Louise. I’ll come stay with you here any time.” On Martha’s previous visits, wanting privacy, they had slept in a tent they had pitched in the grove, slathered with insect repellent to keep the mosquitoes at bay. *This* night would be both comfortable and sweet.

Louise flung open the heavy wooden door and stepped back to let Martha enter first. “Oh,” Martha said in wonder. The cabin had a fireplace, a cozy bed-alcove, bookshelves along one wall, a hooked rug with a pair of rockers set before the fireplace, floor cushions, a small refrigerator and hot-plate, a sink… Clearly, if she chose to, Louise could live independently from the others. Martha squeezed her hand. “I love it, Louise. It’s perfect!”

Louise smiled proudly. “Take off your backpack, woman, and stay a while.”

Martha’s eyes scanned the room. “Is there by any chance a toilet?” Her bladder felt stretched to its absolute limit, and all the sexual excitement wasn’t helping.

Louise chuckled. “One of the workshop people who happened to be a plumber noticed what a rough time we were having with the plumbing and installed it for us. I’ve promised to give her follow-up lessons for years to come.” Louise stepped into the bed-alcove and whipped aside the curtain from a place Martha had thought must be a closet. “Voilà, Madame.”

“What more could a woman ask for?” Martha dropped her backpack and propped it against the wall beside the bed.

“What more indeed?”

[ii]

Half an hour into the monthly meeting of the Combined Governing Council of the University of Washington, Kay Zeldin excused herself and left. As the Council’s liaison with the Co-op’s Steering Committee, she had been obliged to put in an appearance; but she knew that the other members of the Council would not appreciate her taking an active role in its business. The chair had a reasonable grasp of the Steering Committee's concerns. And Kay had too many meetings to attend as it was.

Walking from Suzallo Library to Padelford Hall, she cast a wary eye around her— at the young woman propped against the thick, venerable trunk of a cedar, a book open on her knees; at the lovers entwined on the grass in front of the Hub, oblivious to everything but one another; at the service-tech pushing a cart brimming with individually-wrapped rolls of toilet paper in the direction of Savery Hall, belting out *La Donna é mobile.* Everyone she laid eyes on looked content, if not happy. But although the clarity of the air and the sun's radiance made the sky and trees a brilliant feast for the eyes, the beauty of the moment did nothing to ease Kay's fear of being watched. She never for an instant forgot that even in the Pacific Northwest Free Zone her safety could not be assured. Sedgewick might send a thousand Security operatives to Seattle to run ten thousand agents, and no one would lift a finger to stop them.

The Free Zone did not keep people out.

Kay stepped inside Padelford and paused for a few seconds to let her light-dazzled eyes adjust. She chose the stairs over the elevator as safer. When she emerged from the stairwell on the fourth floor, she listened to the quiet and noted that every door on her corridor was shut except the one directly across from her office. Nothing unusual about that, of course.

Outside her office, she knelt on the linoleum and checked the dark brown thread she had left stretched from the lower hinge across the door to the staple she'd embedded in the doorframe so that the slightest movement of the door would break the thread. Over the months, this practice had become just one part of her daily routine. So that afternoon when Kay found a short portion of the thread on the floor and the rest of it missing, she stared at it in disbelief. But slowly the possible implications of the broken thread sank in, and her mouth went dry. Rising to her feet, she glanced up and down the corridor. *This is the opening move I knew would eventually come. I know it is. It's a wonder it's taken them so long.* Kay folded her arms tightly over her chest and reviewed her movements on leaving her office two hours earlier. She was confident that she had not broken the thread when pulling it through the staple, confident that it had been whole and secure when she'd finished the set-up. Her eidetic memory never failed her; she had no reason to doubt its accuracy now.

Kay knocked on the open door of the office opposite. Her thin, bearded colleague glanced up from his monitor, then frowned. "Kay, what is it? Are you all right?"

"Have you had your door open for long, Mike? And if so, did you happen to see anyone lurking outside my office, or even entering it?"

He gave her an odd look. Of speculation, she supposed— or of remembering something in her damned book. "I've been here about forty minutes, I guess. And no, I've seen no one hanging around in the hall, much less entering your office."

Kay pulled her personal handset from her rucksack and speed-dialed Campus Security. "Captain Morrison, please," she said. "This is Professor Kay Zeldin. Tell him it's urgent."

After a short delay, Morrison's voice came over the line. "Professor Zeldin? Lew Morrison here. How can I help you?"

"I have reason to believe someone has made an unauthorized entry into my office, Captain. And I'm concerned that they may have left me an unpleasant surprise. Is your explosives expert available?"

"She's on call. If this is the scenario you warned us about, I'll give her a buzz and have her run right over. In the meantime, we'll want to start evacuating the building at once. You can help us do that by pulling the fire alarm. And we'll give the fire department a heads-up ourselves."

Evacuate *all* of Padelford? She couldn't imagine even Sedgewick's goons using that much power to take out one thin human target. But Kay said, "I'll do that at once." She switched off her phone and looked at Mike. "The head of Campus Security has just requested me to pull the fire alarm in order to get Padelford evacuated." The words left her throat choked up. Brusquely, almost angrily, Kay worked to clear her throat. "It may be a false alarm, but we can't take any chances. I know

what we're up against, Mike. And I know that they wouldn't care if others were killed besides me."

Mike's eyebrows rose, and Kay saw something like disquiet flicker in his eyes. She wondered if he was thinking that the department shouldn't have let her come back, after all. But he said only, "It sounds a little extreme, but I'm sure they're right, that it's best to play it safe."

While Mike packed his rucksack, Kay walked up the hall and around the corner to the nearest alarm box. She studied the set-up, then took the small hammer attached by a cable to the side of the box, used it to break the glass covering the alarm, and pulled the lever. All over the building bells clanged. It's lucky, Kay thought, that it's summer, when the building's population is relatively sparse.

As she joined the people filing down the stairs to the first floor, she considered the situation with a modicum of detachment. It was possible that someone was lurking inside her office, lying in wait for her— in which case the fire alarm would send them flying and they'd make another attempt to waylay her in the near future. But it was also possible that they'd booby-trapped her office with explosives— with timed explosives, explosives triggered to go off at the sound of her voice, explosives wired to a desk drawer, explosives wired to the door. In her gut, Kay believed this the most likely scenario. The SIC had a long history of taking out enemies beyond US jurisdiction with bloody— and dramatic— bomb blasts.

Warning that the bomb squad was on the way, Kay urged everyone milling around the front of the building to stand on the other side of the street. "Who would bomb Padelford?" a Comparative Studies professor said to Kay. "Is it a disgruntled student?" a graduate student asked. "Did you actually *see* the bomb?"

A fire truck arrived just as three Campus Security vehicles pulled up with sirens blaring and lights flashing. A few minutes later, a small unmarked van parked behind the Campus Security vehicles, and a service-tech in khaki pants and tunic got out, leading a German shepherd on a leash. Relieved to escape the barrage of questions she felt com-

pelled to stonewall, Kay led Dora Mink and her dog into the building and up the stairs as she explained about the thread.

The dog sniffed at Kay's door and at the crack below it. Mink told Kay that the door was "probably clean." Kay hated that "probably." "Please move back," she said, "and let me unlock it. In the event that it isn't clean, there's no point in more than one of us getting it."

The other woman raised her eyebrows, but took her dog a couple of yards down the hall and waited for Kay to open the door. "I really do think it's safe," she said.

Kay unlocked the deadbolt and nudged the door open. When nothing happened, she opened it wide. On first, cursory inspection, everything looked just as she had left it. She stood back and let Mink and her dog inspect the room.

Mink watched her dog nose about the office, then said, "I don't believe there are any explosives in here, Professor. It might have been a common, garden-variety thief, you know. I'd check to see if anything has been taken."

Kay panned her gaze around the cramped little room jammed with file cabinets and bookshelves. She supposed she should feel relieved that she'd raised a false alarm. And maybe embarrassed for having caused such a ruckus. But she still felt anxious. She didn't want to turn into a paranoiac, shrilly crying wolf, and yet she knew that if she didn't exercise the greatest caution and vigilance—

Oh.

Yes. There it was, propped against the monitor. One purple envelope with her name written on it. It had been inscribed by hand in thick black ink. She knew that high spidery handwriting; she knew it well. Kay stared at it, and gooseflesh rose all over her body. She had just *known* they had been here. She had *felt* the intrusion.

"What is it?"

Kay pointed to the envelope. "They've left a calling card."

"Let Simeon check it out first." Mink brought the dog forward. "It's probably alright, or Simeon would have noticed it, but still, it's better not to take chances."

The dog showed no interest in the envelope. Mink said, "We're done here. I'm going to give the all-clear so that people can be allowed back into the building."

"Thanks very much," Kay said, suddenly overwhelmed by the awareness that she would have to face the envelope alone. She shook Mink's hand, and the expert and her dog went around the corner to the elevator. Drenched now in a cold sweat, Kay shivered in the stuffy warmth of the office. She could not stop staring at the envelope. It looked so sinister propped against the monitor that she wondered why she hadn't noticed it at once.

"Professor?"

Kay turned. The raspy tenor sounded familiar.

The stocky, visibly middle-aged man wore a Campus Security uniform; his pepper-and-salt nappy hair had been trimmed close to his bullet-shaped skull. "Lew Morrison." He offered his hand, and she shook it. "Do you need any additional assistance?"

Kay exchanged a long look with Morrison. "Let me open the envelope the intruder left before I answer your question." She rubbed her arms, to try to warm them, and sat down at the desk. She drew a deep breath, steeled herself for something terrible, and reached out and picked up the envelope. The purple, tissue-thin paper shook in her hand as she studied it. Only her name had been written on the outside. The envelope itself was plain, lacking the embossed logo usual to such stationary. She slipped her index finger under the flap, tore the envelope jaggedly across the top, and pulled out the single sheet of purple paper.

The note was unsigned but handwritten:

> Zeldin: If you are interested in S.M.'s welfare, cooperate with us. You will be contacted in due course.

Kay's throat closed. She refolded the page and jammed it back into the envelope. She stared down at it until she got her face under control. Then she met Morrison's sharp brown gaze. "Thank you, Captain Morrison, but I find I don't need your help after all." She laid

the envelope on the desk and stood up. "I can't tell you how greatly I appreciate your coming to my assistance. I assume you know why I'm so jumpy?"

His eyes glinted. "Like everyone else in the Free Zone, I read your book, Professor," he said. "If even half of what you wrote is true—"

"Every word is true," Kay said fiercely. "Every word."

His head tilted, and she suspected he didn't believe her. "I don't know," he said. "Some of it's a little unbelievable. Like that stuff you wrote about what those men get done to themselves. I asked the head of the Medical School about it, and he said it was possible. But it sure is hard to believe."

"We're fortunate not to have those people running our lives now," Kay said as she always did, anxious to preserve the hostility against the Executive that she feared would fade into indifference and leave them vulnerable to resubjugation.

"I guess. Though life's gotten a tad rough around here, any way you look at it."

"The people living in the rest of the country aren't having a picnic, you know."

"Yeah, I guess." He held out his hand, on which Kay now saw he wore a small diamond pinky ring. "Well, Professor, if there is ever anything I can do for you, don't hesitate to call on me."

For the second time, Kay shook his hand. Service-techs, she thought, believed that hand-shaking demonstrated social equality. And inspired confidence and trust besides. "I appreciate that, Captain," she said in a tone that carefully blended the earnest with the rueful. "Unfortunately, it seems all too likely I'll be needing your help again. Considering the enemies I have."

"Well, as I said, any time. That's what Campus Security is here for."

Kay closed the door after him and sat down at her desk. Bitterly she stared at the purple; its very presence in her office violated her. She put her hands to her face and slumped down in the chair. She had been expecting them to use Scott to blackmail her, had been surprised they hadn't done it months ago. But she'd thought it would be

Military who would be doing the blackmailing. Surely it was Military Scott had been working for. Could Sedgewick somehow have gotten control of Scott? Or had the day arrived that the two factions had achieved rapprochement or had at least become trusting enough to do deals with one another?

Sedgewick's note raised many questions, but it also sent a pointed message. Whoever had penetrated her office and delivered the purple meant her to understand that she wasn't safe.

She sat motionless for a long time, locked into a mind-numbed, stupid dread. It was almost five o'clock when she returned to her senses. Slowly she stood up and looked around her office, trying to see it as an intruder would have.

As she packed her rucksack it occurred to her that they might have penetrated her apartment, too. Would she have to go through this trauma every time she returned to either home or office? She strapped on the rucksack and wheeled her bicycle into the hall, where she propped it against the wall while she fastened a new length of brown thread between the door and its frame. Everywhere she went now she would know she was a sitting duck. Sedgewick had likely assigned an entire team to her case.

If they wanted to they could shoot her while she was bicycling around Seattle. All it would take would be a single well-placed sniper. But they weren't at that place yet. The note talked about "cooperating." And about her being contacted "in due course." Very Sedgewickian, that phrase.

She could hardly wait.

[iii]

The car jerked at a forty-five degree angle off the highway onto the twisty, sharply descending tarmac. Allison closed her eyes in exhaustion. Almost there. Never had she thought to see the day when landing at Monterey would be such an ordeal. In some ways the gauntlet at that dinky little airport had been worse to run than the one at LAX. Things had changed so drastically since her last trip to the States that she felt bereft, poignantly nostalgic for the image of

home she had been carrying inside her, homesick for what apparently no longer existed.

Frank pulled the car up to the front door. "I'll bring your luggage in right away, Madam, after I put this thing in the garage," he said as she swung her travel-weary legs out of the car.

The front door opened. Vivien Whittier catapulted down the steps and flung her arms around Allison. "You're actually here," she said. "My baby!"

Allison kissed her mother's cheek. "Yes, Mother. Bloodied but unbowed."

Vivien drew back in alarm to examine at her. "Bloodied, Allison?"

"Just a figure of speech." She extricated herself from her mother's embrace. "You can't begin to imagine what it's been like."

"Oh, foreign travel is so exhausting," Vivien said, as if that generalization covered everything. She took Allison's arm and led her into the house.

Allison declined to let the subject drop. "It wasn't the foreign part of the trip that was grueling."

"This way, dear," Vivien said, steering Allison to the back of the house.

"They kept me hung up at the Monterey Airport for a good hour and a half while they debated my bona fides. With service like that, I'm not surprised the airport was empty." Allison stopped to stare at the view of the ocean through the double-glazed windows spanning the thirty-foot length of the room. Peace. There would be peace here. Even if the price of it was her mother and Jocelyn Poole's company.

"Allison," Vivien said insistently.

Allison dragged her gaze from the window. "Yes?" she said— and saw her. For a moment she couldn't speak.

"You do remember Elizabeth Weatherall, dear?"

Even if she hadn't had occasional job contact with Elizabeth, Allison could never not remember Elizabeth Weatherall.

"Hello, stranger," Elizabeth said. A smile warmed the sea blue eyes.

Allison's mouth gushed with saliva. She swallowed a couple of times and smiled back. "Elizabeth, hello. How are you?"

"All right, I guess. You, though, from all appearances, have a terrific case of jet lag."

"More like a surfeit of officious morons making life difficult for weary travelers. Did you come in through LAX?" Allison said, thinking to compare war stories.

Elizabeth shook her lovely golden head. "No, I flew nonstop from Denver."

Allison flushed. Of course Elizabeth wouldn't travel on a public or even semiprivate airline. "Well," she said, trying to overcome her idiot awkwardness. "LAX is crammed to the gills with armed guards, with a few grimly bean-counting officials sprinkled in for good measure, and almost no travelers. Bizarre, going through that." Allison shoved her hands into her pockets and leaned her shoulder against the window. "And because I was carrying my personal weapons they made me jump through any number of security hoops. Some of the people at LAX were downright unfriendly."

Elizabeth said, "Yes, well considering it's a bi-factional site, it would have to be heavily guarded and contain an equal number of officials from both sides. That place is a bloodbath waiting to happen. Those kinds of sites unnerve me. It seems to me we're just asking for trouble. But the powers that be..."

Allison snorted— and then coughed in an attempt to conceal the snort after the fact. Who did Elizabeth think she was kidding, talking about "the powers that be" as though she, Elizabeth, weren't among them?

"Is there anything I can get you, dear?" Vivien said. "Some tea?"

Allison considered. "A long dip in the Jacuzzi will fix me up fine. And then maybe a nap." She had a couple of bottles in her luggage. She could sneak a drink in her room.

Vivien said, all maternal approval, "That sounds very therapeutic, dear. If there's anything you want, don't hesitate to ask the staff. Dinner will be at eight."

Allison glanced at her watch and saw with shock that it was already four-thirty. Where had the day gone? "That sounds fine, Mother." She walked to the door, then turned. "See you later, Elizabeth."

Elizabeth smiled. "Yes. And after dinner we shall talk."

[iv]

During dinner Allison let Vivien, Elizabeth, and Jocelyn do most of the talking, though when called upon she offered a few spare descriptions of post-Blanket Europe. How could it be, Allison wondered, staring at that perfect aristocratic profile, that Elizabeth Weatherall continued to maintain contact with her mother after all these years? Having been bosom buddies in boarding school and college hardly seemed reason enough for two such different women to carry on a forty-year relationship. Had she underestimated her mother? Perhaps Elizabeth saw something in Vivien Whittier that she, Vivien's daughter, could not. But Allison had to admit that part of the reason she found their compatibility incredible was the difference in the lives they had chosen for themselves. Elizabeth— ambitious, energetic, astute— had chosen to be career-line and had driven straight to the top of what executive women could achieve; while Vivien had chosen the maternal-line— preferring security, leisure, emotional ties. What did they think of one another? Throughout the meal, Allison's gaze moved back and forth between them, watching Elizabeth's fingers tear at her roll, deftly, gracefully, ruthlessly, watching Vivien taking delicate, modest bites of fish, as though eating in public verged on the indelicate.

You must be careful, dear, the female nature tends toward wild uncontrollability, and that is why you must never never allow yourself a sexual interest in anyone who is not very definitely your inferior. Only in such relationships can one be certain that one will not lose oneself in a kind of madness. I know of what I speak, dear... I have seen those things happen, and the resulting devastation to executive society and to the women themselves... You must promise me, Allison, never to become sexually involved with another executive. It is the rule, dear, though it is never spoken of except from mother to daughter...

How long ago it seemed that her mother had spoken those words to her. And now they echoed in her head. Because of Elizabeth?

After three courses of light conversation and gossip Allison began to find the non-mention of the current state of affairs almost eerie. What she most wanted to know was what the situation in the States was in general, and here in particular. Obviously Security had control of this strip of the coast, or she and Elizabeth wouldn't be sitting here dining in unconcerned tranquility. But what were things like— in the cities, for instance? European newspaper reports on the subject had been vague and infrequent. Was it as violent here as it was in Europe? Something inhibited Allison from asking: she sensed that a pointed question would be the equivalent of brandishing a grenade and threatening to pull its pin. But then her mother had always pretended nothing existed outside her own small world.

"Do you know, I've eaten so much I think I'd like to walk along the shore," Elizabeth said when they had finished dessert. "Allison, would you care to join me?"

Under the light of the full moon they picked their way around the stacks of driftwood littering the length of beach stretching between the two rocky promontories marking the borders of the property. As they walked Allison marveled at the calmness, so utterly different from the strain of hanging on she had constantly experienced while overseas. The worst had been the excising of her controller a year and a half ago. She should have gotten over that by now, but she hadn't. In times like these members of one's operational team were occasionally killed, as was to be expected. But when one's *controller*— the person in charge, the person pulling all the strings— was excised, that was something different. And worse, when one knew that people supposedly joined with one against the opposition had done the excising...

"We have a job for you," Elizabeth said, breaking into Allison's thoughts.

Allison stopped; despite the darkness, she strained to see into Elizabeth's eyes. "A job? Here?"

"In the States. Not here in Big Sur, but in Seattle."

Seattle. Allison had once lived in Seattle.

"Do you remember any of your professors at the University of Washington?"

"That was thirteen years ago. I suppose so. Anyone in particular?"

"Kay Zeldin. European history."

Allison concentrated and conjured up the image of a woman seated at the head of a seminar table. "I have a vague memory of taking a seminar with her," Allison said. "Something to do with perceptions of the East-West conflict in European politics in the mid- and late-twentieth century."

"Not bad," Elizabeth said. "Your job will involve her. Specifically, you will be handling her."

"Fascinating." Allison muttered this below her breath, too low for Elizabeth to hear over the roar of the surf— and then remembered. "Good *god!* Kay Zeldin! I never made the connection with my professor. Isn't she the one who wrote that scabrous book about the Executive's response to the Marq'ssan invasion?"

In the moonlight Allison saw Elizabeth's mouth curve into an enigmatic smile she could not begin to interpret. "She's the one. I wasn't thinking— I should have realized that the entire American intelligence community— Military and Security alike— would have read that book by now."

Allison grew uncomfortable. If she remembered correctly, Elizabeth herself figured in it. "It was something of a scandal," Allison said apologetically.

"Yes. And scandals are always irresistible, especially to those who know the principals involved."

Allison listened for a moment to the roar of the surf and savored the tiny drops of spray the wind flung against her skin. The setting was so beautiful and romantic. One of her first sexual experiences had taken place on this beach. But there was nothing beautiful or romantic about this conversation. She bit her lip, then said, knowing she skirted the edge of what Elizabeth would permit her, "In light of that book, I'm a little confused, Elizabeth. How am I to handle Zeldin if she's with *them*?"

Elizabeth stared out at the churning moonlit water. "We are compelling her cooperation." Her voice was cold. "Your controller will do the compelling. You need not know all the particulars involved, but one of our leading priorities is to locate and either capture or excise the Marq'ssan. They are the sole obstacle to our getting this country under control. I believe the divisiveness between Security and Military would vanish if the Marq'ssan themselves vanished. But certainly the Pacific Northwest Free Zone would collapse without them."

Elizabeth moved to a mammoth log of driftwood and perched on it. Allison, quite a bit shorter than Elizabeth, had some trouble boosting herself up beside her. "That's quite a goal," Allison said. She looked at Elizabeth. "But perhaps you should know, I've never before handled someone hostile. Wouldn't it be better if someone with that kind of experience—"

Elizabeth interrupted her. "But the point is that your controller will be the coercer, not you, Allison. In fact, we're expecting you to make a sympathetic contact for Zeldin. You see, in the first place she tends to identify with women, and in the second place I'm going to tell you a lot about her psychological makeup so that you'll be able to handle her with the utmost subtlety and sophistication."

Allison stared at Elizabeth but could make out little of her face, for a cloud had drifted in front of the moon. "You mean I'm supposed to befriend her while the controller comes on with rough stuff?" Allison's heart sank. So this was why Elizabeth was here, this was why she'd been called home from Europe?

"Something like that. You'll have to be subtle, though. Zeldin is extremely clever. I'd suggest, for instance, that you drop heavily disguised intimations that you personally have problems with the controller— while on the explicit level displaying the utmost loyalty to him. Do you see the sort of thing I'm talking about?"

"Yes," Allison said, afraid that she did. *Mind-fucking and psychological treachery.* "What will my cover be? Since I'll be in enemy territory."

"Ah. Your cover," Elizabeth repeated with a grin in her voice. "You'll get yourself outfitted like a service-tech, cross over the border,

and hitch up to Seattle. Once there you'll make contact with your CAT, but you'll tell the locals you meet that you've heard all about the Free Zone and just had to move there, to get out of executive territory— and let them think you come from an area run by Military. Lots of people have been migrating to the Free Zone, you know, in spite of border-post security. You'll be one of many. You'll say you were a word-processor for a Dowsanto facility, that you haven't had work since the Blanket."

"You don't think Zeldin will remember me?"

Elizabeth said, "It doesn't matter whether she remembers you or not: she won't have any choice in being run by your CAT."

"Elizabeth, may I ask about something that's puzzling me?"

"Of course you may ask."

Allison held her face rigid. One may ask but not always get an answer: that was the rule. "You have been saying 'we.' Who is it who's ordering all this— ordering me back from Europe, ordering me to Seattle. I mean," Allison said, suddenly breathless, "who is your superior now?" The rumors, oh the rumors about whether Sedgewick was alive or dead or active or retired... There had been nothing but rumors for the last year and a half, nothing but rumors since Scanlon and Percy had been excised.

"Your security clearance isn't up to that kind of information," Elizabeth said. "Just accept that I have the authority to give you orders. And I might point out that the less an operative knows about what is going on inside Security, the better. If you were captured that'd be the first sort of thing either Military or the Free Zone people would try to get out of you."

Allison swallowed. "Understood," she said.

"But one name you do need to know, and that's your controller's. You'll be working for Henry Lauder."

The beach's damp chill crept into Allison's heart. Worse and worse. "Henry Lauder," she said. "Is that as in Mr. Clean?"

Elizabeth chuckled. "The very same, Allison."

So. This was a very big deal. A very big dirty deal. The thought of working for Mr. Clean scared her half to death. She had heard about

him, of course. What Company operative had not? But he had always been safely away on the deepest secret and the most critical of Covert Action operations. With Mr. Clean on the job they might well expect to take the Marq'ssan. One way or another.

"I'm getting chilly," Elizabeth said. "Shall we go in?"

"Yes," Allison said. "I think I'd like to have a fire." And a drink. Yes, a drink here in her mother's house: what decent self-respecting executive woman would drink alcohol? as her mother would say if she knew. But then she couldn't be that decent or self-respecting, could she, or they wouldn't be assigning her to Mr. Clean's CAT.

Turning their backs on the ocean, they trudged up the sandy wooden steps back to the house. Allison wished she had never left Vienna.

Chapter Two

[i]

Waking, Martha breathed in the deliciously intimate essence of Louise and the pervasive forest-like fragrance of fresh pine needles. She slid her arm over the sheet to touch Louise's skin lightly with the backs of her fingers, and her pleasure intensified.

"You're awake, love?" Louise's voice skimmed lightly over the surface of the silence.

"Is it very early?"

Louise chuckled. "No. It's already six-thirty. I'm about to get up and make us some coffee."

"It's nice waking here like this." Martha rolled onto her side to snuggle closer to Louise's hard-muscled back. She nuzzled Louise's shoulder and cupped both palms over Louise's breasts. "Wouldn't it be fun to wake up this way every morning? Together, I mean?"

"Instead of our only ever getting to snatch a few stolen moments... Funny how the more we get things moving in the Free Zone, the less time we have for one another. Each of us making our rounds, doing the things we've decided we have to do. You going around setting up production, making trade deals, and generally soothing the waters, me teaching self-defense skills and organizing women's patrols, in Seattle, here, and everywhere else I'm wanted. We're like footloose wanderers, love."

"But this *feels* like your home," Martha said of the cabin. The basement apartment in Belltown just didn't have the same kind of feel to it.

"Mine and several other women's," Louise said. "But you're right, there's something personal and stable about this place. And some of my things are here, just as some of the others' things are here. There's some of each of us here so that we all can feel it's a base of sorts, if not home."

Louise rolled to face Martha, and their breasts touched. "You don't think you can change your order of rounds and go to Whidbey Island with me?" Martha asked wistfully. Louise's fingers stroked her stomach. "Mmmm, you don't know how much I like having my stomach stroked."

"Yes, I do," Louise said. "But I really can't go to Whidbey now, love. There's a pod-load of women Magyyt's bringing from Boston to our camp in the Cascades. I have to be there for the next two or three weeks."

"Oh, I heard about that group," Martha said, remembering. "Apparently that series of videos the women of the Boston Collective made about the Zone is getting around and making women want to move here."

"But these women say they want to return home after they've finished the course and traveled around the Zone for a month or two—they're not permanently migrating, but preparing themselves."

"It's exciting, so many women pouring into the Zone. All these video-makers, musicians, writers, artists, architects wanting to design Free Zone structures... There's so much movement and flux, I never know what I'm going to find from one town to the next. I suppose though the scary thing is not knowing whether we'll be able to feed everyone when winter comes."

"The scary thing in my opinion is that some of the people that are pouring in are agents of the Executive." Louise rolled over and out of bed. Martha groaned in complaint. "You can't have me and coffee at the same time," Louise said. "I think there's a physical *law* explaining that impossibility, that applies even to anarchists."

Martha opened her eyes to watch her naked lover make coffee on the other side of the room. At forty-five Louise's body was tough, wiry, well-muscled, and tanned. Martha admired that body tremendously, but regretted that Louise now kept her hair clipped nearly to stubble— for reasons to do with "the liabilities of hair in combat situ-

ations," a phrase Louise had used to Martha a half-year past to speak to her dismay.

"You believe most of the people moving here are infiltrators?"

Louise spooned three scoops of coffee beans into the grinder. "Some of them certainly are. And we know they're also doing what Kay Zeldin calls 'penetrating'— that is, they're targeting certain groups and subverting and recruiting them. The men who keep publicly making trouble do it in a somewhat orchestrated fashion, haven't you noticed? And the sabotage attacks— who do you think is behind them?"

Waiting for the racket of the grinder to cease, Martha stared at the dazzle of sunlight striking the single flat, interior wall of the cabin and puzzled over the forms of the shadows trembling and swaying in it. They must be leaves, she had decided by the time the grinder cut out. She said, "If we could prove it, the Marq'ssan would have a reason to retaliate against the Executive. Otherwise your accusations amount to mere speculation. How do you know these men aren't just frustrated at our not allowing them to participate on our otherwise open committees? Any woman in the Zone can attend the Steering Committee meetings if she wants to— but absolutely no men. I think we're going to have to change that policy."

Louise let rip a loud hoot. "Oh right. And then before we know what's hit us, they'll have taken over. I know that, you know that, we all know that: which is the reason that every time the subject's brought up it's dropped. All those men can think about is restoring money to our economy, reinstituting the police force, and stopping us from emptying the godawful prisons." Louise's voice rose. "What they would do if they got control of things would be to bring back the Executive again. You know it, and I know it. I don't see why you persist in your illusions about their being able to learn from us. *They* don't see it that way!"

"No need to shout, Louise. I'm just asking what we can do to deal with the male alienation so rife all over the Zone."

"Not all over the Zone, Martha. There are lots of places in the Zone where they're still running things."

"But they'll have to change. Women are running away from those places. They'll lose all their women if they don't change."

"Maybe. And then it will be boys against girls. Is that what you're saying?"

Martha stared up at the rough log ceiling. "I don't know. I guess I'm confused about it. I never know what we're doing, or even what we *should* be doing. All this is so new, so different, that if I try to think about it I start to feel like I'm drowning."

Louise finished setting up the coffee in the filter and returned to bed. "So don't think about it," she said. "Just keep moving on, doing what you have to do. When the time comes that you don't know what you have to do, *then* think about it. Leave the thinking to our heavy-duty analysts."

Martha said, "I'm not sure that's a good idea. We should all be analysts. We have to take responsibility for ourselves. That's what anarchism is all about."

Martha knew by the way she held her jaw that Louise was gritting her teeth. "You still feel you belong back with your organization, don't you." It was an accusation of disloyalty. Perhaps personal, but certainly political.

The kettle, boiling, filled their ears with a piercing scream, and Louise got out of bed again. Why did Louise have to refer anything she didn't like Martha saying back to Martha's past? It hurt when she did that. Did Louise feel threatened by her past? Or was it her principles that Louise didn't like? But she, Martha, didn't fuss about Louise's decision to carry firearms around with her, though it upset her deeply. She kept quiet about it because she knew she had no right to dictate to Louise, no right to expect her to become exactly like herself. That they could accept one another's differences had always seemed an important part of their relationship. Yet increasingly Louise made these comments about her past.

Louise returned with two cups of coffee. "Here you are, love." She handed Martha a cup that she recognized as having been made there on the farm.

Martha inhaled the steam. "It smells wonderful." She would drop the subject for now. But she promised herself she would try to discuss this problem with Louise before she left the farm on the morrow. The problem was too potentially destructive to be allowed to slide.

[ii]

Kay wadded a few string bags into her empty rucksack, slipped the rucksack onto her back, and set up the electronic as well as the hand-arranged precautions she customarily made when leaving her apartment. As always she wore a holstered S&W .38 strapped to her belt under a knee-length armored vest. She had no illusions that they had not found out where she lived. Though she kept her place of residence relatively secret and moved every few months, she knew that they could have traced her movements home however conscientiously and routinely she took twisty roundabout routes. There was no way she could conceal her whereabouts from specialists if they were willing to devote a lot of resources to her case. It was only a matter of time before the threatened "contact" was made.

The gorgeous August day, the blue glitter of Elliott Bay, lifted Kay's spirits. I'm still alive and kicking, still living without constraint in Seattle, still at liberty, she exulted. She sauntered along First Avenue, her eyes scanning the street, and reviewed the assessment she had spent half the night formulating: she didn't know if Scott was still alive, and she didn't know that Security in particular had him. Military might have him and in fact was likely to, since Military had been rounding up technologists and scientists at the time Scott had been whisked away on his mysterious special project. And even if Security did have him, there was no way of knowing whether Sedgewick were involved. At any link along the way a bluff could have been set up. Kay also doubted that Sedgewick could be running Security now. The note left in her office could simply be his reaching out from his professional grave to frighten her, a gesture with no real power behind it. No doubt he still had friends owing him, upon whom he could call for such nasty little favors.

She knew she must search out the penetrators and infiltrators and unmask them for what they were. Previously she had refused to think

about how Security and Military must both have agents crawling all over the Zone— or rather, she had admitted that they were probably around and had taken personal precautions. But she had not seriously considered their ability to undermine the Zone. Reminded now of the likelihood of operations and case officers at work there, she knew they must be doing their damnedest.

Kay reckoned her personal future lay tied up with the Zone's. After the things she had done, there could be no going back. Nor did she have any desire to go back, not even to turn the clock backwards to a time before the Blanket— except during those difficult moments when the ache for Scott broke through the walls she had erected around her emotions, and she castigated herself for having thrown away the life they had shared.

At Virginia, Kay turned right and began the steep descent down the block, digging her toes in at each step, glancing sidelong to see which pedestrians followed her. Ridiculous! Kay told herself. Anyone on that street on a Saturday morning was likely to be heading for the Market. That three people were following her meant nothing!

At the bottom of Virginia, Kay merged into the crowds milling around the tables and booths set up in the worn brick street and the old market buildings. Cheeses, vegetables, fruit, pottery, photography, wooden utensils, ancient dishes and cutlery, newly made as well as used clothing, on and on the array of goods stretched before her. Bright crimson and gold caught Kay's eye: she smiled at the sight of cut flowers. That they had gotten to the point where people were bringing flowers into the city's markets offered Kay a hopeful augur for the future of the Zone. At this time last year the Market had a been painful place to be, so meager, so desperate, so unlike what it had once been. But now in August, the month when truck-farms and gardens were yielding their annual profusion, when so many people could now eat fresh food in the summer, at least, the Market projected festivity. That this scene was being repeated in neighborhoods all over the city and not just here on this traditional site also excited Kay. Before the Blanket the Pike Place Market stalls had been mainly for professionals and executives, while service-techs had come to "window shop" and

buy trinkets, bread, cider, and the many snacks the Market specialized in, and listen to street musicians and look at and brush shoulders with those actually living the Good Life the vid displayed.

The smell of seafood lured Kay, and she stared wistfully at the rainbow trout and fillets of black cod and halibut, and especially at the whole crabs arranged in rows on their frigid beds of ice. But she settled on the small, shapely mussels gleaming indigo: she would get a couple dozen of them to steam, for they had become safe and plentiful since the Marq'ssan had cleaned up Puget Sound. Kay had a sufficient amount of trading units credited to her account to buy fish, but she had developed a reluctance to live too extravagantly, aware as she was of the likely tenuous nature of the Co-op's survival in the coming year. She didn't know if it was guilt or only her understanding of how the system was working that made her careful in spending the barter credits with which she was so generously paid for her committee work. And it wasn't as if she were sacrificing herself by settling for tubefood.

But the mussels...what else should she serve with them? Pasta would be simple and fast, and with fresh vegetables, reasonably toothsome... So mussels first... Then pasta... And fresh fruit for dessert. And then espresso. Oh, and a bottle of a local wine. It would be a respectable meal to offer a guest in one's home.

Kay discussed the price of mussels with the teenaged girl in charge of them and came to an agreement with her. She and the girl entered the transaction into the terminal, each in turn pressing their thumb to the identification plate, and Kay stowed the plastic sack of mussels in her rucksack. Aware of the need to get the mussels home and into water, she hurried through her vegetable and pasta purchases. Last, she entered the building in which the bakery she usually patronized was located. In front of the bakery's counter paced two women carrying signs advising a boycott of the bakery. Kay took one look at the signs and turned away. She knew she should stop and read the signs before honoring the boycott, but she hated to take the time to do it and knew that she generally approved of the boycotts when she knew the reasoning behind them. The people who incurred boycotts were

usually guilty of unfair labor or marketing practices, or some sort of corruption or turpitude. In one instance a group of women had effected one against a sandal-maker because the man was a known rapist. Kay suspected it was only a matter of time before the exercise of boycott power got out of hand, and people would have to make their choices more responsibly. Still, she returned to the street and found a table where bread was being sold and made her trade there.

As usual she took a roundabout way home. For the first time, though, she avoided slipping through alleys. Getting trapped in an alley with a gang of Security thugs would leave her vulnerable and place her in a situation in which no passersby would be around to help her. After the book had come out the Women's Patrol had offered her a constant escort, but she had declined. Unwilling to live perpetually under guard, Kay felt that if she could not take care of herself she might as well cross the border and turn herself in. Instead, she developed the habit of working out with some of the Women's Patrol and went every few months to Farley's farm for refresher courses. Most of that had become routine. But she felt a different sort of threat now, something at once vaguer and more specific. After having wrestled most of the night with the question of whether she should show someone the purple, she had decided to keep quiet until she knew more. She would wait and see, and try to live as normally as possible. To do otherwise would be to admit that the purple had the power to interfere with her freedom— and her life.

[iii]

Laura Park arrived at Farley's just before lunch. "I almost called first," she said, "but I was positive you would be here today." They hugged; and after Laura had greeted everyone in the kitchen, she and Martha wandered off to chat. Martha fancied a look in Jess's eyes suggesting a desire— no, a perceived right— to join them, but ignored it. She was developing a thicker skin these days.

"So," Laura said as they walked along the edge of a field planted with corn. "How did it go in Bellingham?"

"All right, but only barely. We're going to have trouble there."

"What do you mean? I thought that was one of the mellowest places in the Zone."

"It's their democracy stuff," Martha said, peering about as though expecting to see a Bellingham woman popping out from behind one of the wind-breaking trees they were passing.

"Why should that bother us?"

"Well, they're rigid in certain ways already. Everything they do has to be voted on. And so they have men running everything— since with the vote the men find it easy to dominate right down the line. They've elected a mayor and chief of police and tax collector and so on and so forth. They're getting very upset about the trade system, say we can't survive without money-credit, and they're even more upset about our letting convicts out of prison." Martha chuckled as she remembered one of the occasions on which she had stood before a town hall crowd and fielded questions.

Laura gave her a look. "What's so funny about that?"

"One of the times I discussed how the prison system had never protected women and how women are safer now than they were two years ago when the executives were running things when no woman was ever safe anywhere at any time, well practically the whole audience of women started talking to me and to each other in a kind of fever of excitement; they essentially agreed with me and said they were willing to try something new. The men got pissed as hell and came on really belligerent and violent. After about fifteen minutes of chaos that was getting pretty damned acrimonious, one of the women stood up and yelled something about how violently the men were coming on for no good reason at all, since although no one in that hall had threatened their physical safety, some of them were acting out in a physically threatening way. To which one of the men said, 'Yeah, well that's why we need prisons.' And the woman who had made the comment about the men's violence said, 'Then you'll have to be the first to go, man.' That sent the women off into laughter. But for a minute or so I thought a couple of the men were going to jump that woman and beat her to a pulp."

Laura looked pained. "I have a feeling we're in for some rough times. We're going to *have* to find a way to come to terms with the men, you know."

"Yeah," Martha said. "I do know." They approached an empty, fenced-in pasture. "How about sitting over there?" Martha pointed at a big maple at the other end of the pasture.

Martha climbed the fence, and then Laura handed Martha her briefcase to hold while she climbed over. On the other side Laura took her briefcase back and they walked slowly across the field. "Our three-cornered trade deal with Cameroon and Argentina went through, thanks to Tyln and Leleynl," Laura said.

Martha stopped. "Laura! That means we are really on our way! All we need is to work out a few more deals like that and we won't have to worry about getting through the winter!" Martha touched Laura's hand. "I don't know how you do it!"

"It's all so complicated, especially without using money-credit." She gazed into the middle distance and sighed. "You know, even I have my doubts. Survival is more important than anything else." Sunlight gleamed in the straight, smooth, crow-black hair framing her sharp-featured ivory face.

Martha could never agree with such an attitude. She said, "That kind of survival we can get anywhere, and I'm not sure I'm willing to settle for it now, even if there were nothing better."

"Not everyone feels that money-credit is such an evil, Martha. They say that with our barter-credit system many of the same problems will crop up, only in new forms."

"Well I think we should try it," Martha said with deep conviction. This was one of those things she had spent the last ten years of her life thinking about and discussing. Her conviction ran too deep to be easily shaken.

They chose a spot half in and half out of the shade and sat cross-legged, their denim knees a few inches apart. "Venn called me yesterday," Laura said.

"The arrangement with the paper mills is holding up I hope?" Martha had worked so hard to arrange the labor and materials and equipment for the Co-op's publishing venture that the thought of any part of it breaking down was painful. That had been one of her first big projects to coordinate, and in the process she had learned certain elementary things the hard way.

"Not to worry. Everything's going smoothly. In fact, it's going so smoothly, and we're doing so well marketing our books outside the Zone, that Venn has proposed we take on several new projects. Her idea is that since there's such a demand everywhere for anything to do with the breakaway societies and analyses of what happened during the first weeks following the Blanket, that we might try publishing a whole series— a lot of it in translation. That way we'd be bringing food and materials into the Zone while at the same time exporting our politics and ideology. There's almost no publishing on paper to speak of in the US now, and in most places censorship is pretty tight. Venn thinks such projects would pay for themselves."

"She has specific projects in mind?"

"You remember that women's assembly in Chile last fall?" Martha had wanted to go, but hadn't felt she could afford the time off since everything had been so shaky in the Zone. "Well Venn wants to put together a bilingual edition of some of the reports, speeches, manifestoes, and proposals made at the assembly. Most of the editorial work has already been done on it, though Venn thinks it needs a bit more commentary explaining some of the background for North American readers. And then there are several analyses being done on how the governments reacted to having to deal through women, and more of that sort of thing. For instance, a study of the coup and subsequent authoritarian regime in Poland with a discussion of the position of women before, during, and after. She'd like to get those into print."

Martha said, "None of it will sell as well as Kay's book. But Venn's probably right about expanding." Martha pushed her hair away from her face and tucked it behind her ears. "And it won't be easy to coordinate."

"It won't be as difficult as it was the first time around. You already have the contacts. Frankly, I'm pretty excited about it. We're doing a good international trade with Kay's book, you know."

"I may not be crazy about Kay Zeldin, but I have to admit she's done a lot to help the Zone."

"And is doing more." Laura's tone was crisp. "She's volunteered to go on a head-hunting expedition, to find or replace some of the technologists and scientists the Executive spirited away during the Blanket."

"No shit!" Martha was shocked. "They'll kill her if they get their hands on her. How does she think she can get away with running around outside the Zone without getting caught?"

"She apparently knows something about making clandestine moves," Laura said drily.

"It's true we need such professionals. Who should know better than you and I? We still haven't got most of our processor-driven technology fixed up." Martha met Laura's gaze. "I suppose she feels she has to prove something. She's never been comfortable around most of us." Martha paused, then laughed shortly. "What am I saying? I mean she and I have never been comfortable, and it took me a long time before I could trust her. Between her involvement with those creepy executives and her being a professor, I guess I don't find her easy."

"She agrees with you about one thing at least," Laura said. Martha's eyebrows lifted. "She thinks men have to be brought into the up-front decision-making processes, not just be included as consultants. She says our popular support will erode in the coming year if we don't."

"It's obvious, isn't it?"

"But Martha, look what happens all over the Zone when men are allowed equal participation! They either plunge into a gang mentality, an executive mentality, or a paterfamilias mentality. Remember that time we tried to let them participate in the Steering Committee meeting? Hardly any women got to talk at all. And they wanted to nominate a leadership and create an authority structure and instead of dealing with the issues and problems on the agenda they dragged us into faction fights and adopted intimidating postures and language. I can't see going through that again. We might as well give up as do that."

"I know," Martha said. "I know. But there has to be some way we can work things out with the men. If we can't, we're going to be in a hell of a mess. Because they wouldn't have the same scruples we would in an all-out hostile situation."

"How do you know?" Laura cleared her throat with a sardonic flourish, raised her thin black eyebrows, and titled her head to one side. "Obviously *some* of us don't have those scruples. Look at the Night Patrol. Most of us believe but don't say out loud that it's drastically reduced the rate of assaults against women in Seattle, and much as we deplore its violent and vigilante tactics, we benefit by it and aren't going out of our way to find and confront the women responsible. How do we— even you and I, Martha— know what we're capable of? We've never been tested that way before."

Martha laced and unlaced her fingers, compulsively, rhythmically. "That sounds so negative, Laura. Are you saying you don't think the Zone is going to survive as a place we might want to live in?" Martha watched a striking, elegant black and white striped bug crawl up a blade of grass.

"That's not what I'm saying at all! I just think we have to start paying attention to this particular problem. We can't ignore it. It won't go away by itself. I personally believe we'll find a way— but only if we try. You know?"

Martha said, "And Louise has been warning me that we have to worry about people coming in from the outside to destroy us. Fuck it. Here I was feeling so high because it's August in the Pacific Northwest and the crops are good and the fishing safe and people are working together. I wish somebody else could think about all this negative stuff."

"Those days are past, Martha," Laura said gently. "From now on each and every one of us is responsible for what happens and doesn't happen. We *all* have to be thinking."

Laura was only saying what Martha already knew. But because she wasn't feeling confident, she said, "The Marq'ssan do that, but they aren't human."

"Well I just wanted to get you to start discussing it with other people. So. Should we review my trade deals first, or your coordinations?"

"Let's start with your deals," Martha said. "I could use the good news."

Laura pulled a file out of her briefcase; her eyes narrowed in concentration, and she began describing the women she had talked to in Argentina on the first stop of her trip. Martha relaxed and savored the brush of the breeze ruffling her hair, the strong smell of grass rising from the ground, the warmth of the air. Before long she felt again as if they knew what they were doing and could count on one another and themselves. They didn't need executives to feed them, shelter them, clothe them, run their industries, control them, govern them. Laura Park offered living proof of that, as did she, Martha, and Louise, Lenore, Kay, Farley, and all the others. Taken altogether, they were stronger than any single problem that might dog them, as long as they continued to work together and believe and care. The Zone was there to stay.

[iv]

Estrella Camarena sat at the table in the dining nook in the kitchen, sipping a Free Zone Sauvignon Blanc as Kay steamed the mussels and whisked together a butter-lemon-mustard sauce in a little pan over the second of her two burners. They talked mostly in English, for Kay's Spanish was a peculiar mixture of Castilian Spanish and Italian. When the mussels opened, Kay slid them into a bowl and washed the steamer, filled it with fresh water, and returned it to the burner.

While they ate the tender, succulent morsels dipped in the sauce with a densely-textured, crusty white sour-dough, Estrella described the structures and shapes of the international economic situation since the collapse of the world monetary system a year and a half before. "You must understand, Kay, that although the US government is in shambles and there is a civil war raging over most of North America, the majority of the governments of the world have managed to hold on in one way or another. A few have fallen, true, but only to be replaced by military dictatorships. The exceptions are rare and have been accomplished with Marq'ssan assistance." Estrella popped the mussel

she had been swirling in the sauce into her mouth. "So sweet," she said when she had swallowed. "For flavor I generally prefer clams, but mussels are so tender, and their shells so beautiful." Estrella beamed through the thick heavy lenses that covered half of her face. "The color of your eyes, my friend."

"They aren't always this sweet, but this is a good time of year for them," Kay said. She drank some wine. "Estrella, let me ask you this. Do you conclude from the circumstances you've been describing that most governments are recovering and will soon be where they were before the Blanket? Because if that's so," Kay rushed on before Estrella could answer, "the executives in the US will be recovering, too, since most of them have holdings in multinational corporations."

Estrella waved her fork. "That I cannot say. I doubt that there *can* be a quick recovery. And things may never return to what they were. In fact, it's likely that they'll take another direction. But I would not be at all surprised if North American executives fared well. My government, for instance, would not think of overturning the present disposition of stockholding and property arrangements in Chile. When they have managed to set up a new monetary system, it will be such property and stock arrangements that will determine everything anew. Even if the executives should lose every cent, they'll still have hard capital and stocks. Whereas ordinary souls, if they lose their money-credit, will be in sad straits. So few people own their living quarters in the US. And where do money-paying jobs come from? Do you see what I'm saying?"

"But all the civil disruptions? Won't that affect distribution of goods?"

Estrella shrugged. "I doubt it."

Kay wiped her lips with her napkin. "Well executives can't collect rent in the Free Zone at least. No one can collect rent here— there's no money in the first place, and there's no means of evicting people in the second."

"That may change."

"What do you mean? How could that change?"

"First, landlords could ask for the assignment of goods or labor credits— in the way you do your trading in the markets and arrange wages for labor. Second, landlords could simply hire a force of men to do their evictions for them."

Kay, smiling, shook her head. "You don't think people would stand by and let their neighbors be thrown out onto the street? If one landlord could do it to one tenant, then everyone would be imperiled! No, that's one thing you haven't understood about Seattle yet— here at least most people have begun to see common interests they must protect as a preventive measure to protecting their own interests. It's a fascinating transformation, Estrella. I thought that was why you came to study the Zone's economy?"

"I'm intrigued that you have gotten this far without money-credit." The Chilean sipped her wine. "That is what I came to study, though I'm beginning to see it's a bit more complex than merely studying the flow of barter by reading printouts recording transactions or talking to the trading partners you now have scattered all over the globe. You realize, I hope, that after a bit of time people here may get tired of sporadic shortages, tired of the status quo, and wish for wider access to goods. They may *demand* money. To travel, and so on."

Kay left the table to sauté the vegetables for the pasta. "What makes you think those things will not be worked out in our future? We have toilet paper while many places in the US do not. There's also a certain charm in not paying taxes— in not putting money into executives' pockets. Those attractions may outweigh any other desires that might seem unattainable."

"I can see I will have to come back here again and again, to make new assessments. For a longitudinal study, if you will." Estrella helped herself to another mussel. "A not unpleasant prospect."

"What, to watch the rise and fall of a fascinating historical phenomenon?" Kay jibed as she added sliced peppers to the garlic sizzling in the hot olive oil.

"Oh, I hope not, Kay, truly. But the most difficult part of the study may be coping with a certain amount of confusion. For instance, no one can give me any idea what the population of the Zone is, not the

crudest approximation. There are no estimates of how many people have left, how many have come in. One would think simply on the basis of food imports there would be *some* idea of it."

Kay stirred the peppers and turned down the heat. "We've made it a policy to follow the universal standard of guaranteeing adequate nutrition to all people here— though we don't offer just tubefood, except when we must, as last January we had to."

"You realize that standard has been abandoned in most places now?" Estrella said. "In the US, for one."

"I'd heard something like that."

"You aren't afraid of being flooded with hungry refugees?"

Kay added julienned zucchini, diced tomato, chopped basil leaves, and pine nuts. "Estrella, we have no choice. What we have chosen to set up here doesn't allow us to do anything but accept whoever comes, unless they are malicious troublemakers. And even then we haven't formulated a policy to identify potential troublemakers and keep them out. And as frightening as some of the possibilities are, I don't think we can do anything else but accept what you call refugees. If problems arise, we will find a way of dealing with them: even if it requires demanding an extension of the Zone."

Kay crouched low to take the spinach leaves and plastic sack of fresh pasta from the small refrigerator. Glancing up, she caught an *aha!* expression creasing Estrella's forehead and opening her mouth in the beginnings of a grin. "Then you are breeding revolution here," Estrella said.

Kay stirred the spinach into the vegetables. "I never said *that.*" The thought that Estrella would probably write an account of this conversation for her government flickered in Kay's mind and provoked the suspicion that Estrella might be working for one of the US factions' intelligence services. Kay lifted the lid from the steamer and— carefully pulling the strands apart— dropped the fettuccine into the boiling water. Would she always be suspecting almost everyone she talked to? Was such suspicion her problem, stemming from her own sordid background, or was it reasonable, given her knowledge of the people who wanted to destroy the Zone?

Kay drained the pasta and tossed it with the vegetable mixture and grated cheese, then replaced the bowl of empty mussel shells and the dish of sauce with the bowl of pasta. "Have you been into the southern part of the Zone yet?" Kay asked as she served the pasta.

"Not yet, but I am looking forward to it. One hears a great deal about those Oregonians. One suspects they will not be as eager to welcome outsiders as you who live in Seattle are."

Kay sighed. It seemed as though no subject was neutral in these crazy days. Everything had become political, absolutely everything. If she so chose, even a discussion of this meal and the provenance of each of its ingredients could be taken as political. And then it occurred to Kay that everything had always existed within a political context— they just hadn't troubled to realize it. They had no choice now, though, but to pay attention to such things.

Chapter Three

[i]

Allison gazed down at the mountains. "And all that out there," she said to Elizabeth, using the restricted channel on the headset. "Is it all under Security's control?"

Elizabeth's laugh in Allison's earphones had a weird edge to it. "Good god, Allison. Surely you must have realized that precious little of any of the areas outside the cities are in either faction's *control.* The people who own them may or may not have the firepower to hang onto them. But for the most part it's all up for grabs. Just look at that land down there: who in the hell could control such a spread when everything— and I mean *everything*— is up for grabs?"

The anxieties soothed by two days spent at her mother's resurfaced, intensified. "But you said something about agricultural areas...?"

"Military has most of Iowa, Illinois, and Kansas under control. And we have a healthy chunk of Californian farmlands. And that's about it. For the rest, we scrabble over the cities. But the cities— well, you'll see. Take Oakland. We've barricaded most of it off, with a border guard to let the few people who have jobs outside pass in and out, and to let in what supplies can be spared. San Francisco itself is now composed of islands of heavily guarded enclaves between which people move chiefly by air. It's not a pretty picture you've come home to, Allison. With the economy mostly nonfunctional now it's almost impossible to do anything."

"But isn't there a plan to fix the economy?" Allison was shocked. Things weren't that bad in Europe.

Elizabeth leveled a long, cool look at her. "It's not a good idea to ask those kinds of questions," she said. "Let me put it this way. The single most important thing— next to resurrecting our defense

capabilities and, of course, intimately connected with defense— is getting communication and other satellites back in the sky. But while others— friends and enemies alike— are busily preparing to do just that, we, caught up in our internecine chaos, have no time or resources we can spare for such essentials. So you see, Allison, it is best if you don't speak of these things at all." Elizabeth glanced around at the other people with them in the helicopter. "Until we executives can get ourselves under control, there is no attempting anything beyond raw survival."

Allison ran her tongue over her parched lips. "But my assignment?"

Elizabeth's eyes widened. "Ah. Yes. Well, let me say that that operation is special. And that in certain respects it may generally contribute to a solution of the greater problem...which need not concern you. You are required only to look to your own duties, not to the larger issues involved."

The heavily armored helicopter landed without incident at the San Jose airport. A car accompanied by police escort took them directly from the helicopter to station headquarters in San Jose, bypassing airport security. Allison reflected that Elizabeth had probably never set foot inside an airport for the last year and a half and consequently would have little idea of what an ordeal travel could be.

As they moved at a fast clip through the station's corridors, Elizabeth issued orders that were meekly accepted and fired off questions that were instantly answered. This, too, shocked Allison: she could not remember ever seeing a woman in this kind of control, at least not over Security people. The Northern California supervisor himself came out of his office to meet Elizabeth. He apologized for a variety of minor matters, mumbling that without communication links or anything approaching an operating budget— but here Elizabeth cut him off, and Allison wondered under what sort of conditions Security was trying to operate. The level of chaos... Yet there were certainly plenty of people visibly at work for Security. Allison had gotten no farther than these observations when Elizabeth sent her off with a pair of female service-techs assigned to transform her appearance into the consummate image of a service-tech, which make-over Elizabeth had decided to leave until after Allison's departure from her mother's house in order to spare Vivien the mental anguish it would inevitably cause.

While the girls cut and permed her hair, Allison casually questioned them about life in the Bay area. Everything was boring, they said. No films to see, no concerts, no VR parlors, no cable vid— only local productions— and those only available of course to people who had generators or recharging power in their homes, which most people did not. Things like cosmetics and new clothing were scarce, and the strict curfew coincided with sundown. Even food was boring: almost nothing available at prices they could afford but tubefood, although they (unlike most people) had real paying jobs. Though Allison tried to steer them into talking about things Elizabeth had darkly hinted at, they deftly avoided anything to do with order and security. The subject was apparently taboo.

When they had finished with her hair and had made her up and given her intricate instructions for how to make herself up, Allison changed into tight black denim jeans and a slinky, parrot green shirt. Staring in the mirror, she hardly recognized herself. She took a step forward but froze when she saw in the mirror how the lines of her body visibly moved. She couldn't wear such clothing! Surely it wasn't necessary. If she couldn't dress as a professional (and it had never been made clear to her why she must have a service-tech cover), surely she could dress as a service-tech in another age group. All her past service-tech disguises had tended to be as young men or older women. Though the older age groups wore garish synthetic materials, at least they were allowed the grace of loose, non-revealing styles.

"Ms. Weatherall said we were to take you to her when you were all fixed up," the one with the bright blue feathers in her ears— Joy? Was that her name?— said. "She's probably in the top boss's office."

Allison resigned herself to the embarrassment of walking through the corridors in such a get-up. The embarrassment was pointless, she thought. With one look Elizabeth would realize she couldn't adopt this kind of cover and that they'd have to come up with something else.

As they led her through the corridors, however, no one so much as glanced at her. It dawned on her that to the professionals and executives passing them in the hall she was indistinguishable from the two service-techs walking beside her! It was amazing! What about her walk? *She* didn't slink around, swaying her hips like those two did. Shouldn't her erect posture and smooth stride signal a difference? Could clothing, makeup, and hairstyle alone effect a change in outward appearance?

Dawson's personal assistant confirmed that Ms. Weatherall was in the Supervisor's office and waved them through. The two executives impatiently looked up from their discussion when they saw the three apparent service-techs standing before them, and then an odd expression crossed Elizabeth's face. "Allison! Good lord I never imagined— !" She shook her head and bit her lip to stifle the grin Allison knew was dying to break out of control. "Look at you! I mean…" And with a half-suppressed gurgle she strangled whatever it was she had been about to say.

"You must see I can't carry off this cover," Allison said grumpily. "Maybe if I were an *older* service-tech, say in her forties?"

"No, Bennett." Elizabeth had recovered herself. "This will be perfect. No one would ever guess you're an executive. Right, Dawson?" Elizabeth glanced sidelong at the Northern California supervisor. Allison wondered if Dawson had noticed Elizabeth's use of her first name.

He shrugged with obvious distaste. "How should I know? Why don't you ask *them*?" He flicked his gaze at Allison's creators.

Elizabeth said, "Good idea. Well, girls, what do you think?"

They looked at each other, at Allison, and then at Elizabeth. "She doesn't walk right," Sheena said.

"And if she talks," Joy added, "she'll be easily spotted. Unless she's going to be the bookworm type?"

Elizabeth studied Allison with an openly critical eye. "Hmmm. But she doesn't *look* the bookworm type, does she," she said slyly.

To Allison's annoyance, she felt a flush spreading upward from her chest, covering, she imagined, not only her neck and face but her entire scalp as well.

"Slang won't be the answer," Elizabeth mused. "Too superficial a use of colloquialism without changing basic speech patterns is always a dead giveaway... We'll have to consider this problem a bit more carefully. But for now I think it's more important for you to come with me into the projection room where we can give you a close briefing. As it happens we have a whole special collection of slides and videos of the contact you'll be handling." Elizabeth nodded at the service-techs. "You did a good job, girls. You can return to your regular tasks now." When they had gone, Elizabeth said, "For inconvenient situations where you wish to refer to Zeldin, use 'Dahlia,' her cryptonym."

So that was why it was called Operation Dahlia. Since Zeldin was the centerpiece of the operation, aptly enough they'd named it for her.

"You needn't accompany us, Dawson," Elizabeth said. "Just get on with the things we were talking about." Elizabeth took Allison's arm and steered her to the door. "I can't get over it, Allison. I simply can't get over it. Do you have any idea what you're going to be in for?"

Allison opened the door and nodded glumly. "I can just about guess." It was atrocious, this self-consciousness, this exposure, this attention to her sexuality. And the strangest part of it was that Elizabeth's palpable sexual awareness of her wasn't at all elating or exciting. It only made her anxious. She wondered whether perhaps the taboo weren't natural and necessary after all.

[ii]

Martha perched on the sun-heated rock and sipped the half-liter of water. She had always loved stopping at Deception Pass to sit by the water at the edge of the quiet woods, even in the days when the racket of Navy planes had intruded. Now that the planes had disappeared, nothing disturbed the stillness of the trees, the gentle lapping of the water, the deep blue of the sky. She watched a blue heron, stealthy and focused, fish. The couple picnicking further down the beach, the lone gray-haired man sitting silently fishing on the other side of the pile of rocks over which Martha had climbed, might as well be on another planet. It seemed to her that on a day like this places like Deception Pass should be swarming with city people. Yet from all

she could tell, Seattle people did not leave town very often anymore, though she had no way of knowing whether her subjective sense of that was accurate. Even if she could assume that it was accurate, she was at a loss to interpret it. This was the case for most things now, as though a post-Blanket common sense had not yet taken root in her mind, while the old system was remote, irrelevant, dead. She could no longer be sure anything made sense, even when other people insisted that one particular interpretation explained the way something was. Insight had become kaleidoscopic and suspect to the charge of being hallucinatory. As though two plus two might not necessarily make four all of the time.

Martha planned to spend a week on Whidbey before finally returning to Seattle with only a brief stop at Farley's to drop off the car and catch a bus back. She had been away almost since the last Steering Committee meeting. The indefiniteness of most of what she had done this trip sometimes afflicted her with an anxious feeling of aimlessness, for she could point to little in the way of actual accomplishment: as though she had done nothing but talk at people everywhere she went— or else help them to build castles in the air. Though Martha believed that talking and fantasizing were necessary stages in the work she had undertaken, she often had to remind herself that it wasn't really a matter of castles in the air— she could see that at least some of the projects dreamed up *did* come to fruition and that unless she encouraged people to dream verbally about what they might be able to do, very little might actually get done. The new reality was that every endeavor had to spring from the personal initiatives of individuals without the usual sorts of institutional motivations forcing them on, supporting them, furnishing them with the psychological illusions of authority and stability to prop them up. How many people were there who could in such fragmented circumstances pull any of these projects together single-handed? Apparently so few that more and more communities and groups and individuals were calling on Martha's committee. The committee had developed contacts and by now had a passing acquaintance with mediation and negotiation. "If you supply that for so-and-so, we can arrange to supply this for you," Martha was always saying.

Often everything seemed hopelessly confused and disorganized. Yet most of the parties involved were so pleased just to be getting their projects moving that they didn't balk at the details as Martha and Laura and the other coordinators arranged them. Martha suspected, though, that once the Zone had achieved a degree of stability they would grow dissatisfied. But then she would remember Laura's suggestion: once they got to that stage, they wouldn't need the committee at all and would be able to work things out among themselves.

That day seemed very far off.

Since the Blanket life seemed to have become ever more confusing. Not that there hadn't previously been confusion. But the machinelike orderliness of most everyday things, the certainties, the way so many things had been taken care of and thus had never entered one's mind— food, water, and power, for instance...the lack of such certainties could be upsetting and always increased the sense of confusion. People suffered bouts of panic. Martha herself had had a couple of bad times, but someone had always been there to reassure her. Some people, though, were thoroughly and constantly frightened— many of whom had moved out of the Zone, craving the security they thought the US government could offer them. Others not sufficiently unsettled to fly to the accustomed governmental structures indulged tendencies ranging from compulsiveness to the armed authoritarianism found in many of the small communities in the eastern part of the Zone.

Martha checked her watch and returned to her vehicle. Beatrice would be expecting her for lunch. It would be good to sit at the long communal table with most of the members of the New Sweetwater Settlement. They would clamor for her news and would in turn tell her of how things were going on Whidbey Island. That was one of the most interesting aspects of these trips— acting as a messenger along an ever-expanding network that passed the sort of data never available on vid or in the newspapers. And that kind of news was the news that counted now, in the Free Zone at least. No one in the Zone

cared about the latest mouthings of the State Department or Security Services or whom President Stoddard had eaten lunch with. Martha believed that even if by some miracle national vid were restored, people would not be interested in the old cable news programs.

This thought— Martha started the single-seater— pleased her greatly. It *proved*, she thought, that the Marq'ssan had changed everything.

[iii]

Beatrice wiped her sleeve over her sweaty forehead and peeled off her gloves. "Jackie's almost finished building my loom," she said, wrinkling her nose at the big vats of dye and the wool lots soaking in them. "Soon I'll be getting to the good part of the work. Do you know how long it's been since I've sat at a loom, Martha?"

Martha did know: it had been since the Blanket. Out of nothing more than malice ODS men had broken up every loom Beatrice had had at the original Sweetwater Settlement in Colorado. "That's a dynamite shade of purple," Martha said, pointing at one of the vats.

"Purely vegetable," Beatrice said automatically. Martha grinned; Beatrice grinned back. "Hey, Martha. I haven't seen you in three months and you stand there like a stranger!"

They hugged, and the faint dis-ease Martha had felt on first coming into the barn dissipated. Beatrice was Beatrice. "It must be about lunch time," Beatrice said, glancing at Martha's wrist.

Martha checked her watch. "Yep. It's quarter to one."

"Your timing is perfect. We have a few minutes before lunch will be on the table— in case you want to see how the loom is going?" The invitation ended as a question, as though it had suddenly occurred to Beatrice that Martha might not be interested.

"Of course I'd like to see it." Beatrice led Martha into the next room. "Wow. It looks finished to me. What still needs to be done?"

Beatrice gave her an amused look. "Tell me something, Martha. Have you ever even *seen* a loom?"

Martha laughed. "No, this is the first one."

Beatrice shook her head. "Tsk tsk. The deprived life some people lead."

Martha thought of how often she found Jess's ignorance alternately amusing and dismaying, and winced. To people like the Sweetwaters she probably seemed just as bad as Jess.

Beatrice pointed out various parts of the loom, including pieces lying as yet unattached on Jackie's workbench, and noted things that still had to be done. Unable to imagine what all these pieces of wood had to do with blankets and rugs and sweaters, Martha could not work up much enthusiasm, though she strove— as she did when out on coordinating jobs— to appear interested. But she would rather have gone out to look at the sheep and be shown the wool-making process again.

Apparently satisfied that Martha now had some idea of what the loom would look like when finished, Beatrice took her into the house for lunch. "I thought that must be your car, Martha." Lee patted the chair beside her. "Come sit here and tell me all the places you've been the last few months."

"She's got to tell everybody, Lee," Ariadne said. "We're all starved for news here."

"And gossip," Willow said, carrying in platters of bread and raw vegetables. Willow and Susan together lugged an enormous kettle to the table and set it before Beatrice. "Do the honors with the soup, will you, Beatrice?"

While Beatrice ladled out the soup, the rest of the Sweetwater Settlement trickled in and seated themselves. Two of them, Martha noticed, wore loose gray cotton tunics marked with rainbow armpatches over their jeans. She couldn't remember their names. In fact, she wasn't sure if she remembered having seen them before at all. Martha had never gotten to know all the Sweetwater people personally, for some of them she saw only at the meals she took there. The bread, cheese, and vegetables circulated. Martha exclaimed at the cheese: "Is this *brie*? Where did you get it?"

"Somebody down in Coupeville makes it. We were able to arrange a trade," Lee said.

"That must mean your relations with Coupeville have improved."

"Somewhat. There are a few folks who will talk to us now."

That was progress, Martha thought as she took her first swallow of soup: potato and yogurt base with chunks of cucumber and lots of fresh dill. Maybe some sour cream, too? She liked it, like many of the things she had started eating for the first time in the last year and a half. The communal types of people who lived out in the country certainly ate differently from people like her, who had lived in the city all their lives, subsisting mostly on tubefood.

"Have you seen any of the Marq'ssan lately?" Martha inquired.

"I saw Magyyt at the last Steering Committee meeting," Beatrice said. Martha had seen Magyyt there too. "She said something about spending a lot of time in South America."

"I'd heard that," Martha said. "Still, she does a lot of buzzing around between there and here. Helping with trade deals and such. I was just curious whether you'd seen her lately." Martha had an insatiable desire to hear anything she could about the Marq'ssan. Sometimes she fantasized being Magyyt's assistant, "buzzing around" here and there with her, taking on special projects.

"So come on, Martha, give: where have you come from this time?"

Martha grinned at Willow. "I've spent the last few days at Farley's on vacation. But before that I spent two weeks in Bellingham."

"Ah, the heart of the New Democracy," Ariadne said acidly.

"The LRD was prepared to work with us at the time of the Withdrawal," Martha said, trying not to sound defensive. "We didn't have enough other contacts, and none of the other people organizing in Bellingham were prepared to step into the vacuum."

"Yeah, and I just bet the result is that the men are running the show there. Right?"

Martha said, "Give them a chance, Ariadne. Just because they have male participation doesn't mean the men are running things."

"It will." Ariadne's eyes flashed. "I mean look. They have *government* and a hierarchy and all that garbage. We all know what that means."

Martha sighed. She was getting totally fed up with these political discussions about men. She had thought that at Sweetwater, at least— where there never had been men— she wouldn't have to talk about this. Martha said, "We're in unknown territory. We *can't* really know what anything means. Not yet. Besides, what does it matter to you whether they have a democracy— even a male-run democracy— in Bellingham? You're here, not there. Sweetwater doesn't have to have anything to do with Bellingham if it doesn't choose to."

Ariadne clicked her tongue in disgust. "Whether that's true or not— and I'm not saying it is— it's certainly true that all that male-run stuff is sickening. If you ask me, women should have nothing to do with men!"

Martha fingered her water glass and wished somebody else would say something. What was wrong? She'd never run into this kind of adamant intolerance here before. "Is there something I don't know about that makes you say that?"

Ariadne clicked her tongue again but said nothing. Martha began to wonder if they were all recalling her bisexuality with less than enthusiasm. "Has something happened here at Sweetwater?" Martha stared across the table at Beatrice.

Beatrice picked up a piece of broccoli, only to return it to her plate. "Not at Sweetwater," she said. Her gaze met Martha's. "You're planning to go over to the Way Station, aren't you?"

"Yes. Tomorrow or the day after, depending on how everything schedules out with all the people I need to talk to."

"Then you'll see for yourself. About the men running things, I mean."

"Has there been trouble between them and Sweetwater?"

Beatrice glanced at Lee. Martha turned her head to look at Lee, seated directly on her right, and said, "Lee?"

"Unpleasantness," Lee said. "I don't know if I'd call it trouble. Let's just say there's been some unpleasantness. And that there might be trouble in the future. Some of the men over there—" Lee broke off.

Martha turned her head and caught Beatrice shaking her head at Lee. "Look," she said evenly. "I don't think it's fair of you to be dropping dark hints only to leave me hanging."

"It's better if you see for yourself," Beatrice said. "And then we'll tell you our side of it."

So there was definitely some kind of hostility— enough that there were stories with "sides."

"I can just imagine what those bastards will say, too," Ariadne said angrily.

"Martha isn't stupid, Ariadne."

"Thanks," Martha said drily. "I was beginning to wonder at my own denseness." Realizing she would get no more from them on the subject, Martha concentrated on her soup and left them to find a way to rescue the foundered conversation. She had forgotten how annoying Beatrice could be.

Which just went to show how selective her memory was.

[iv]

Kay panned her gaze over all of Red Square, as much to see if Otto or Meredith had arrived as to spot any SIC types keeping her under observation. Yes, there was Otto Fenichel, sitting on the library steps. Kay strode across the Square toward him, but catching a glimpse of Rainier out of the corner of her eye, paused to look at it. The fountain deliberately planned to be viewed with Rainier from this very vantage point shot water into the air well below the mountain's fairy-castle grandeur floating high in the air above it. The rose garden surrounding the fountain had been recreated through the initiative and care of a variety of individuals. Standing quietly in the midst of this academic tranquility, Kay almost managed to believe that everything was fine, that everything would work out, that this peacefulness and the best qualities of the humans around her could not be destroyed, neither deliberately nor through indirection, happenstance, or ineptitude. But the moment passed when the movement of someone stepping back into the shadows of Kane Hall's concrete portico caught her attention. Was that the whine of a camera lens zooming in or out? Kay pressed her lips together and moved quickly toward Otto.

Otto looked up from the yellow pad on which he had been writing and smiled. "Kay, you're looking well." He rose to his feet and held out his hand, and Kay shook it. "Your life of excitement must agree with you."

Kay laughed. "Mostly committee work, Otto, and you know what that's like." Kay noted the tan on his bald crown and wondered whether he had problems with sunburn. As she pictured him hiking in the Cascades, she flashed on an image of him spreading sunscreen over his entire face and head.

"Committee work has at times been almost enough to send me into the arms of private industry," he said.

"Yes," Kay said. "As Scott often pointed out to me, at Boeing they seldom made you attend committee meetings, just gave you orders and rules to follow and bean-counters to kowtow to. While in academic life one must go to committee meetings to make the rules and orders to be wrangled over and changed every other year."

Otto's shrug was huge and genial. "And so now the rules have to be determined all over again— entirely from scratch. A new idea of the university, is what they're saying." The eagletine lines of Otto's face sharpened. "But will it really be new?" He shrugged again, this time in dismissal. "I'll believe it when I see it."

"This may be one of the only public universities left on the continent." Kay glanced again around Red Square. "There's Meredith Wolfson." She waved until Meredith saw them.

The deterioration visible in Meredith's face shocked Kay. Was it the effect of worry and strain, or was this what happened when people of a certain age missed their scheduled longevity treatments? Should she, Kay, expect to age dramatically when she missed her next scheduled treatment— as she surely would— in only eleven months? Meredith looked as if she had aged twenty years!

"Hello, Kay." Meredith shook her hand and pecked Otto on the cheek. "You're looking very fit, Otto. Getting into the mountains, are you?"

"I can take my work with me, you know. Or at least some of it."

Meredith laughed shortly. "While I'm tied down to my now primitive lab day and night. I have a cot in there in a little cubbyhole. It's pathetic. This is the first time I've been outdoors in forty-eight hours."

"Interested in a cup of coffee?" Kay asked, anxious to move from wide-open Red Square into a more private space.

Otto's forehead creased. "I thought the idea was to escape our offices?"

"We can do that and have coffee, too," Kay said. "I belong to a cafe co-op."

"Cafe co-op?" Meredith repeated. "What on earth is a cafe co-op?"

Kay chuckled. "It's a Free Zone version of a club. It was started last winter by a social psychology graduate student who thought the university community needed a cafe. Everyone who joins contributes materials and labor of varying amounts. One part of the arrangement is that we can bring in guests as we like."

Otto and Meredith exchanged a *what next?* look. "I'm game," Otto said. "Though it doesn't sound like *you*, Kay."

"It's over on Brooklyn." Kay started them on a westward course. Was the man who had been leaning against the concrete support in front of Kane Hall following them? Halfway across Red Square. Kay halted and turned, ostensibly to take a last look at Rainier. The man was no longer there. Kay's eyes made a quick sweep of the Square but failed to light on the suspected observer.

They resumed their course past the undergraduate library and onto the pedestrian overpass. "I wonder," Meredith said, looking down at the street below so empty of cars, "whether they'll get the mass-auto system working before all the street structures deteriorate past usability."

Kay glanced sidelong at Meredith. "That's not a priority, you know. We can survive without it. I agree it would be nice to have the system working. But at this point I think we have to concentrate on the essentials."

"A few of the European cities have *their* mass-auto systems working," Meredith said.

"They also have intact governments and something approaching economies," Otto said. "And may I further point out that life is not entirely pleasant in those places. I for one wouldn't enjoy living cheek by jowl with the military. And you know, Meredith, that you and I would probably be locked away underground or in a camp somewhere, following orders."

"While instead I can be locked away here following my own orders," Meredith said sarcastically.

"You don't think there's a difference?" Otto queried. "Nobody's making you lock yourself up in that lab, you know."

Did the two of them always scrap like this? Kay had known them separately but had seldom seen them together, though she knew they had known one another for longer than she had known either of them. How had they met? Wasn't there something about Otto's spouse having dated Meredith's spouse in graduate school? And then after Meredith had married Joe Kline she had met Cecile Glade and had become Cecile's closest friend...that was what Scott had told Kay, if she remembered correctly. And now both Joe Kline and Cecile Glade were "missing." The three of them had a great deal in common. They could start a society of the spouses of the missing, Kay thought bitterly.

"Here it is," she said, gesturing her guests through the open door. Otto and Meredith went in; Kay glanced over her shoulder. The spook did not trouble even to look away. Either he did not care whether she made him, or he wanted her to. Kay realized that her situation must be nearing crisis.

"Hi, Wilson," Kay greeted the man behind the worn oak counter. She turned to Otto and Meredith. "Is drip all right, or would you prefer espresso?" They both agreed on drip coffee and bran muffins. "Sit anywhere you like," Kay said, handing Meredith her satchel. She set mugs out on a tray, poured coffee into them, and wrapped a few bran muffins in a napkin and put them into a basket, then scribbled an entry in the ledger lying on the counter and carried the tray to the window table where Meredith and Otto sat swapping work stories. Kay sat facing the window. Her observer— in clear view across the street— stood leaning against the old red brick apartment building opposite the cafe. Kay thought of the gun riding her hip and hoped he wouldn't approach while she was around uninvolved people.

"So are you still planning to go through with this head-hunting trip of yours?" Otto said bluntly.

"It is essential."

"But the question is, will you find many scientists and technologists out there," Meredith said. "Perhaps most of them have disappeared, like ours."

You mean like our spouses, Kay thought. "But there are thousands of them," she said. "They can't all have disappeared— and the disappeared must be *somewhere*."

"No, they haven't all disappeared," Otto said. "Take me. But as a pure mathematician, I'm not in a category identified among the useful. Obviously the government simply picked up people they had listed in certain academic and industrial categories. And hence they missed me. Unless they asked my colleagues or went through the journal literature or scrutinized my CV, they wouldn't have had an easy way to know what other things besides differential geometry I know something about. Also, I never applied to the NSF for grants in my extra-specialty interests. Can you imagine it, they probably had a system cataloguing people in the sciences by fields. And then when the time came, they simply pulled the ones they wanted."

"And it must have been in print or in a hardened data archive, underground somewhere," Kay added. She still, after all this time, had no idea precisely what areas of data collection had escaped damage from the EMP. At one time she had believed that nothing had escaped damage, but it had become obvious that that had not been the case. There had been so many things she had not known even when she had been mixing in the highest executive circles.

Meredith pulled a large manila envelope from her briefcase. "This is for you, Kay." She opened the envelope and drew out a thick sheaf of paper. "Otto and I have asked around and have compiled this list. Where they're known we've included spouses names— in case there are disappearances."

Kay glanced reflexively out the window. "Meredith, for reasons I don't want to explain now, I would prefer picking that up from you right before I leave town. I don't think it's safe with me just now."

Meredith gave her a narrow, searching look. "What do you mean, not safe?"

"I have reason to believe that some intelligence agents are interested in me."

"Here? In *Seattle*?" Meredith sounded at first incredulous, and then disturbed.

"You can guess why. So when it comes time to leave town, I'll throw them off and pick up this list from you."

"I also have an assortment of yellow plastic for you," Meredith said, looking pointedly around the room. "I don't know whether the accounts will have been closed or not, or what plastic money is worth now. But several people have contributed their plastic, two of them from outside the Zone."

Kay swallowed. "That will be the hardest part, avoiding being caught by retinal or thumbprint or voice scanners... That and surviving in a plastic-money system. Though I've heard that there's a thriving black market operating almost everywhere. And people willing to take plastic without bio-verification of identity."

"How do you think you're going to find them, Kay?" Otto quietly asked.

Them: Scott, Cecile, and Joe. "I will talk to people. People on your list. And see if I can't find someone who has either returned from wherever they took the missing, or who has heard rumors or has suspicions about where. I'm resourceful in such things," Kay said more confidently than she felt. She saw from their faces that they believed her claim to be an experienced intelligence expert. It was an absurd claim, but they wouldn't know that.

It would be better for everyone, of course, if they had full confidence in her ability to take on the search. Better for her, too. For if they believed in her, she might believe in herself and not be quite so frightened.

"Should we be offering to go with you?" Otto said.

"The Zone needs you here— both of you— more than running around risking your necks," Kay said.

Meredith lightly touched Kay's arm. "Maybe you shouldn't go either, Kay. If it's that risky."

"Being here is risky for me, too. I'd have to hide out in another country to be absolutely safe, and there's no way I'm going to do that. It's just something I have to live with." Or die with, Kay added to herself.

Meredith and Otto stared down at their empty cups.

Kay got up to fetch the coffee pot. It was time to change the subject. She would ask Otto how the university's new processing system was coming. And then she would arrange a contact with Meredith, after which they could return to their offices...

Assuming, of course, that the observer across the street did not interfere.

Chapter Four

[i]

The barracks and officers' housing— all that remained of the US Naval Air Station formerly at Oak Harbor— had not been pulled down after The Withdrawal. In the Free Zone, at least, one could no longer afford to turn up one's nose at facilities already standing. While few of the groups settling on Whidbey even considered living in them, the Science Center had claimed some of the barracks on the assumption that it hardly mattered where they set up shop since all institutional structures looked and felt the same. The Science Center had been the sole resident of the base until the people who had started the "Way Station" (as they called it) had shown up and declared the townhouses that had been used as officers' quarters perfect for their needs. Now Martha wandered through rows of these abandoned-looking townhouses in search of it.

Rounding the corner of one of these buildings, Martha spotted a bearded dark-haired man, naked from the waist up, pushing an old rusted hand mower through the grass. He saw her and stared. "Looking for something?" he asked, not smiling, his eyes tracking her every move. His face, a dark beet red, streamed with sweat.

"Looking for the Whidbey Way Station," Martha said.

"Then you've come to the right place. Who sent you?"

"I'm Martha Greenglass. From the Co-op. I was asked by the Way Station to come."

He dropped his hands from the mower's handlebars. "Then you'd better come in. I'm John Doyle. Glad you could finally see your way to come by."

Was he being sarcastic? Martha had no way of gauging. His face seemed to have only one expression— watchfulness.

John Doyle turned his back on Martha, and she saw that a sharp-featured tattoo of a bald eagle extended from the nape of the man's neck down past the waist of his jeans, its eyes and beak a glorious fury of instinctive cruelty. Martha followed him around the side of the next townhouse and wished he would stand still long enough for her to take a closer look. But he led her, without pause, through the first of the building's four front doors. Martha said, "It might be a good idea to put a sign up."

John Doyle said nothing. He preceded her into a shag-carpeted room crowded with chrome-framed furniture and glass tables. "Have a seat and I'll tell the others you're here," he said, then went back out the door.

Martha looked around the room. She had never been given this kind of reception before. The Way Station had invited her. She never went unless asked, for her committee did not impose itself on groups or individuals. Yet this guy made her feel as though she were intruding at the same time he acted as though she were tardy in responding to a summons issued by an authority. What exactly was it the Sweetwater women had said about the Way Station? Martha could not remember anything specific.

After about ten minutes John Doyle returned with four other men and two women. He named all the people following him into the room and suggested that Martha sit down. Martha caught only the women's names— Isabelle and Paula. The men blurred into an anonymous group, except, of course, for John Doyle himself. Martha seated herself in one of the two upholstered chairs; feeling oddly exposed, she held her briefcase in her lap. The women were dressed in long skirts, the men in jeans and blue denim tunics (including John Doyle, who had donned a tunic since leaving Martha alone in the room). Martha panned her gaze over their faces as they settled themselves around the oval glass coffee table. Into a long uncomfortable silence she said, "What is it our committee can do for you? Do you have your project pretty well sketched out, or is it in the first stages of planning?" At first she found herself looking at Paula while she talked, but when she

saw Paula stealing sidelong looks at John Doyle, she uneasily moved her gaze to his face.

"The people at the Science Center said to talk to you," John Doyle said.

"Yes?"

"We want access to the stuff that can change our DNA so we can have children," he said. "The people at the Science Center said they wouldn't do anything like that without arranging it through you. That's what we want."

Martha was flabbergasted. "Well, uh, I don't know what to say." "I mean, I don't know anything about the injections. That was always handled by the Department of Health, and they kept that stuff pretty secret. Do the Science Center people think they can manufacture whatever it is they inject people with to restore the missing chromosomes?" Martha wondered if she had it right. Wasn't it a chromosome or enzymes or something like that that was deleted at birth?

"They wouldn't talk to us about it," he said. "So we don't know whether they were giving us the runaround or whether they don't know how to do it. But we came to the Free Zone because we want to have families. The Co-op has an obligation here. There are millions of people who want children, and with the Department of Health gone, no one at all in the Free Zone can have them, unless you people do something about it."

Martha's uneasiness intensified as she imagined millions of people having babies in the Free Zone, millions of people flocking to the Free Zone to have babies, and the Co-op somehow struggling to feed so many new, crying mouths...

"I don't understand what it is you want *me* to do," Martha said. "Do you want me to talk to the Science Center people? Is that it?"

"Look. You people are the government," John Doyle said testily. "And therefore—"

"Wait." Martha held up her hand. "Let's be clear about one thing. We are not a government. Don't call us that. In no way can we be considered a government. We don't collect taxes or police people or pass

laws or do any of the stuff that governments do. You're confused if you think we're a government."

"You bitches in Seattle are running everything, aren't you?"

Martha drew a deep breath and fought to keep her voice steady. "I don't know what you mean by 'running everything,'" she said. "A few of us are trying to coordinate things, trying to make sure everyone has enough food and potable water to live. I wouldn't call that *running everything*."

John Doyle crossed his arms over his chest. "You've got the power," he said.

Martha looked at the others and found their eyes all fixed on John Doyle's face. She cleared her throat. "All of you want to have children?" she asked, anxious to bring the others into the conversation.

"All of us," John Doyle said. The others nodded but did not speak.

"Look," Martha said into the uncomfortable silence. "I'll talk to the Science Center people for you. But if they can't help you, I don't know what to suggest. I mean, I haven't heard of anybody giving those injections."

"Isn't there anything left from the Department of Health in the Free Zone?"

Martha shook her head. "Every government agency destroyed its papers and materials during The Withdrawal. They didn't want us having anything we might be able to use."

John Doyle sneered. "Likely story."

Martha got to her feet. There seemed little point in drawing the unpleasantness out any further. "I'll talk to the Science Center people and get back to you."

"When?"

"By the end of the week." Martha knew she would hate coming back to talk to these people. Or rather to John Doyle (since none of the others had said a word to her). But if she said she would return, return she must.

[ii]

Allison checked her watch. Her back, neck, and shoulders ached. The boredom she had expected, but who would have thought sitting

in front of a terminal all day could be so exhausting and muscle-wrecking? She would rather wait on tables (which she had done for some of her past covers). At least it was for only two days and merely practice and background to make her cover more convincing. An executive could go nuts in such a job. *She* certainly wasn't cut out for it. And the damned technical terms: knowing nothing about chemistry, she had had to scrutinize each term carefully before typing it, literally subvocalizing every letter in the long strings of unpronounceable mush. Worse, she was realizing how thin her cover would be. It might be true that one no longer needed an implant to work as a word processor, that one could use a keyboard for inputting text. But whoever had decided on this particular cover for her had been lacking in imagination and hadn't understood that cultural differences even more than physical masquerade and self-control could trip one up. She herself could see now how easy it would be to blow this cover through a trivial slip.

Heavy male hands descended onto her shoulders. Allison stiffened. These asshole sub-execs made her itch to teach them manners. If this jerk, the idiot chemist's budding apprentice, had any idea who she was, he'd be scared shitless to lay a finger on her or say anything but "Yes madam" and jump to. A crushing remark or a simple flip across the room would suffice to put him in his place, but the day's assignment was to preserve her cover at all cost and to practice proper service-tech behavior. Which meant she was supposed to pretend she didn't mind being pawed and condescended to by the male sub-execs who got off on it. All female service-techs had to put up with it, which meant that in any service-tech cover she would have to put up with it, too.

What particularly exasperated her was the sub-execs' conviction that as educated professionals they were far above everyone else. That chemist, for instance, with his "Doctor" title walked around as if he were a god among filthy pitiful mortals existing only to serve his every whim, and his cretinous assistant, leaning against the back of her chair now, running on about how he and his chemist were so brilliant, about how the world could not survive without him— both acted like beings

immeasurably more superior than their subordinates. Allison would like to get a look at their living conditions. Consider, for instance, their clothing: neither of them managed to dress in trousers and tunics that fit properly! And it was ten to one against their being allowed to procreate, too. So much for their inflated self-esteem. They acted among their staff as though they didn't have to answer to the executives supervising them, which was pretense. Or was it self-delusion? What did they do when they came up against their own limitations in the world? Pretend they could do whatever they wanted?

"How's it going, honey?" the jerk said, his lips practically touching her ear. "I hope you're almost done. Dr. Rosenthal wants me to proofread that report before you leave tonight."

Allison tried to turn in her chair. "But Dr. Graham," she said, barely restraining herself from throwing off his hands. She squirmed and twisted in her seat in order to face him without dislodging his hands (which supposedly would have violated the situational norm) and then wished she hadn't, for his face was bent so far forward that she had to draw back to avoid it. "It's almost the end of my shift. I have only one paragraph left. Can't I make the corrections in the morning?"

"Sorry, but he's got to have them done tonight— the report is due on an executive's desk by nine a.m."

Ah, so that's how they dealt with their limitations— they made others pay through the nose when they faced them: dumping it on the service-techs, giving them the stuff at the last minute and letting them suffer for it. "But I have an appointment at six," Allison said, imagining Elizabeth waiting for her to show and getting irritated at the delay.

He leered. "Too bad. You'll just have to stay. If you'd been here longer you might have been able to get someone else to do it for you, but since you don't know anybody here yet who can help you out..."

"I can't stay," Allison said.

The leer changed to a scowl. "Now look, Maggie." His voice took a chill. "You've only been here a single day. If you want the job, you'll stay. Unless you think you can find another?" This last was said sarcastically— obviously to remind her that there were almost no jobs in the city available for service-techs. When she didn't answer, he patted her shoulder. "Now you just finish that paragraph and get the report into hardcopy and bring it over to my cubicle. The sooner you get it to me, the sooner it'll get proofed and the sooner you can get out of here." After a final pat he sauntered off, past the other word processors (all of whom were clearing off their desks preparatory to leaving for the day), and out into the corridor.

Allison slammed her fingers into the keys, setting up a racket as she typed. She wouldn't stay. It would be just too bad if Elizabeth expected her to come and sit here and take this shit for another day. She would finish that paragraph and print the report and leave it sitting on her cleared-off desk. And then she would leave. *Tant pis* for them. Let the assholes make the corrections themselves. It was not her problem. And meeting Elizabeth on time was far more important than keeping the job for another day. Anyway, she was practically paralyzed from the physical strain. She doubted she could stand another eight hours of it.

Signing out at the guard post among the stragglers of service-techs quitting for the day, Allison exited the A.B. Corp. complex, her shirking undetected. A faint uneasiness crept over her as she thought of how irritated Elizabeth would be at her unilateral decision to end this phase of her training, and she flushed with annoyance at finding herself in a predicament resembling the sort of double-bind into which executive schoolgirls always seemed to fall. Alone of all the service-techs, Allison headed for the garage where she had parked her freewheeling auto. She felt male executive eyes frowning at her as she pulled out her blue plastic and inserted it into the intake slot. Damn these clothes and hair, she thought again, and knew that the auto had been a mistake. But how else to get to where she had to go? The only mass-transit available would not take her to that section of San Jose. And since this was only a training exercise, the total congruity of the cover was as yet unimportant.

When two minutes later Allison was punching her destination into the auto's processor, one of a pair of male executives rapped on her window and asked to see her photo ID. She glared at them but

pulled out her Security badge and flashed it in their faces. Low-level administrators, she thought scornfully. The pair exchanged a glance, directed brief nods at her, and retreated. No doubt they'd fantasize something truly bizarre over their preprandial martinis. Allison snorted and eased the auto onto the down-ramp. There was no getting around it: being back in the States was detestable. How in the hell was she going to learn to like living here again? Whenever she saw people like those lower-echelon execs, she wanted to kick them into action. Everything was so out of control, so barbaric...and it was the fault of all the execs living in the States— they had blown it on a scale previously unknown. They had given new meaning to the word *failure.* And why couldn't they pull it together? Simply because they were too busy fighting one another, like savages competing for a pile of bones left by the jackals and vultures. What was the fucking *point*?

Following every turn indicated by the processor to the letter (as per Elizabeth's warning about straying into high-risk areas), Allison repeated this question over and over until *what is the fucking point* had lost all semantic meaning. She hoped Elizabeth would continue being open-minded about her drinking alcohol, for if ever she needed a drink, it was now.

[iii]

Martha added the new lists to her main file for the Science Center, then slid the file back into her briefcase. "Now that we've finished with our business, there's something I need to talk to you about," she said. "It's to do with the people at the Way Station."

Gina and Max exchanged looks. Max cleared his throat. "They came over here about a month ago, Martha," he said cautiously.

"They— no, I mean John Doyle, since none of the others said a word— John Doyle said he'd talked with somebody over here. It seems he's interested in fertility restoration."

"*Interested* isn't a strong enough word to describe John Doyle's state of mind," Gina said. "The man is obsessed. And the word I'd use in relation to him is *demanding*. He *demands* we restore his and his disciples' fertility."

"Disciples?"

Gina nodded vigorously. "Damned straight they're disciples. I wouldn't know what else to call them. Followers, acolytes…"

"You're saying the Way Station is a cult center?"

"That's what I'm saying."

Martha looked at Max. "What about you, Max? Is that what you think?"

Max's shaggy eyebrows knit together, and he sighed. "I'm afraid so, Martha. More people are pouring into that place every week, and all of them are either like John Doyle or John Doyle's disciples. They don't believe in high-tech, for one thing— they're all back to the earth, no electricity, no electronics. We offered to help them repair the solar tech already set up in those buildings they've taken over, but they didn't want that. It seems they prefer to burn fossil fuels. So I told them what would happen if everyone in the Free Zone relied on fossil fuels for their heating and cooking and so on, and Doyle told me to fuck myself, that the day would come in our lifetimes that the population would be so decimated that no one would have to worry about such things. But the centerpiece of their program is procreation on a large scale. They have all sorts of theories already mapping out their social rules for child-raising and procreating, all sorts of plans for populating the Free Zone with their kind. In short, Martha, they're dangerous."

Martha bit her lip. "You agree with Max, Gina?"

"From what Max told me, yes. I was, you see, excluded from most of the conversation Max had with Doyle. Doyle didn't want any women in on the discussion."

Max winked at Gina. "Don't worry, love, you didn't miss a thing. It was boring as hell."

"Doyle asked me to talk to you, to get you to do what they want," Martha said.

Max laughed. "Not a chance in hell. In the first place, we don't know how to do it. We don't have any human fertility specialists here, or even any geneticists. Most of the latter were drafted by the government in the first weeks after the Blanket."

"What about in the rest of the Zone?"

"Listen to me, Martha," Gina said, her voice and face intense and serious. "Before you go around looking for the answer to that question, you'd better do some thinking about this. Suppose, just suppose we could restore fertility on demand. Would we really want to do it? Consider. We don't have any facilities for children, we don't have simple things like nano-filters, without which a substantial number of newborns would probably die of some form of cancer within the first six months, we have barely enough food to go around now, and on top of that we don't have the medical facilities for doing essential things for everyone. Do we really want to open that can of worms? And do we really want wild-eyed religious fanatics migrating to the Zone so that they can have dozens of children apiece? Do you see what I'm getting at, Martha?"

"But...shouldn't people have the right to make that kind of decision for themselves? Isn't that the sort of thing we objected to the government controlling?"

Gina slumped down in her chair and tucked in her chin. "My god. Think about it. Think about it *practically*. At least consider a moratorium. Say five years, long enough for us to get on our feet. Think of how stretched and meager our resources are."

Another morass threatening to pull them down: that's what this fertility issue was. Martha could feel it, feel its threat, its pull. "What should I tell John Doyle?"

"Tell him to fuck himself," Max said, and the three of them laughed.

"How about a beer, Martha?" Gina asked. "We've got at least a year's supply of it because of various jobs we've been doing for people on the Island. It's good dark stuff."

"Thanks," Martha said. "If you'll have one with me."

Gina's dark blue eyes twinkled. "Sure, I'll have one with you. And then I can take you around to see how the clinic is coming along." She left the room.

Max pushed his chair back from the table."`I've got to get back to work. But I'm going to give you a piece of advice first, Martha."

Martha's eyebrows lifted.

"Don't let John Doyle take an inch. Because if you do, he'll take a mile, and then a light year. That's the kind of maniac he is."

"Oh great," Martha said. "That's great advice to give someone whose standard operating procedure is negotiation."

"Complicates matters, doesn't it."

"Yeah."

Max rose to his feet. "Well, maybe there are some people you should just ignore. Maybe some people aren't fit for negotiation."

Martha stared at him. "Do you really believe that?"

He shoved both hands into his pockets. "Yep. I really do. Well, so long. Hope you can get all that stuff on the list for us. It's all essentials, you know."

"Yes, I know," Martha said. "I'll do my best."

Max nodded at her and ambled out the door. Martha glanced around the room. How could they stand living in these barracks without even trying to disguise what they were? They'd been here for a year now, and hardly anything had changed, except that the plastic walls had gotten grimier since no one bothered to do any cleaning except in the labs and the clinic.

Gina returned with the beer. "Max went back to work?"

Martha nodded.

"Good." Gina pushed one of Farley's pottery mugs across the table to Martha.

Martha sipped the beer. "Why do you say that?" She used the back of a finger to wipe the foam off her upper lip.

"Because now you can tell me what's going on in the great, wide world. That rag they put out in Coupeville doesn't say anything one couldn't pick up from one's neighbors. While you have been gallivanting all over the Zone."

Martha laughed. "It looks like Martha Greenglass has replaced com-satellites and satellite dishes, both."

Gina grinned. "I like that. Martha Greenglass, com-satellite. In her own orbit, swinging erratically around the Zone, both receiving and broadcasting as she goes. Better watch out, or you'll be in trouble with John Doyle. I'm sure he thinks satellite dishes are the devil's tools."

Martha's smile faded. "I hope he can't make serious trouble. I wouldn't want him for an enemy. He gives me the creeps."

"Who, John Doyle, or the devil?" Gina asked flippantly. When Martha didn't reply, Gina said, "Okay, change of subject. Tell me where you've been since your last visit here."

"Did you know I went to the northeast corner of the Zone last month?" Martha said, reaching back several legs of her trip before Bellingham. "Up near Colville, where they have a settlement tradition. They're way ahead of us up there, they've been doing for years some of the things we've just started trying to do." Martha was determined to revive the positive mood the last two weeks had been eroding.

"And to think I thought Colville was the back of beyond," Gina said.

"Oh, it is the back of beyond. But now the whole Free Zone is the back of beyond."

Gina laughed. "Is that how you think of it?"

"Sure. We'll sink into oblivion. Don't you think? Once the newness of the thing has passed, I mean."

Gina snorted. "Dream on, Martha. There are only six Free Zones on the whole planet, and they're magnets of distrust and curiosity."

"Yes, but we won't be walking in step with the rest of the world."

"You really think that?" Gina stared down into her mug; after a few long seconds, she looked up and gave Martha a rueful smile. "You're in for a rude awakening some day, my friend."

Martha glared at her. "Why? Because I believe the Free Zone can function partially independently from the rest of the world?"

Gina lifted the mug to her lips. "Yup," she said after she had swallowed. "The world is too small, too closely bound."

"Even without satellites and other communications technology?"

"It's only a matter of time before all that is restored. You don't believe they won't rebuild everything the Marq'ssan destroyed?" Her gaze locked with Martha's, and she shook her head. "Drink your beer, Martha, and tell me about Colville."

Martha drank her beer. She hated Gina's cynicism. Was everyone like that? Did no one really believe the Free Zone would survive as a place different from the rest of the world? Or as a desirable place not overrun by John Doyle types? She set her empty mug on the table and conjured up a picture of one of the most comfortable of the Colville settlements. It *would* work. The Free Zone *would* work. And no John Doyle would spoil it, either. She, Martha Greenglass, would personally see to that.

[iv]

They flew by helicopter back to the house they had stayed in the night before, near Santa Cruz, Elizabeth had said, a house surrounded by acres and acres of vineyards. Allison looked forward to drinking more of the wine produced by those vineyards. "You know, Elizabeth," she said as the chopper settled onto the driveway. "I think that given the choice I'd rather starve than work as a word processor. Or if I did work as a word processor I'd turn into an alcoholic or suicide."

Elizabeth snapped shut her attaché case. "There are worse fates than life as a word processor."

"It's not so much the physical stress," Allison said, "as the degradation. I mean, those men are horrible. They smell, for one thing— as most sub-execs do, of course, but they hang over one, forcing themselves on one, constantly pawing and touching and hovering. And then their lord-of-the-earth attitudes— especially in the professional males." Allison shuddered. "I realize most word processors are morons. But is it really necessary for male professionals to adopt such a contemptuous tone? Consider what they themselves are, Elizabeth!"

"Shall we?" Elizabeth removed her headset and rose from her seat.

Allison unbuckled her seat belt and removed her own headset. Rising, she caught one of Elizabeth's gorillas staring at her tightly-garbed body. She glared at him. "Oh, my aching shoulders," she grumbled as she bent to grab her attaché case from under the seat. But of course no one heard her complaint over the racket the chopper made.

Elizabeth was already alighting. Hurrying to catch up with her, Allison wondered again about the house. Did Elizabeth own it? Nestled in the hills, it was rather rustic and isolated, but tolerably comfortable. All the facilities were operational, but then if it belonged to Elizabeth or some other upper-echelon Security person, they would

be. If it hadn't been for Elizabeth's intervention, Vivien Whittier's house would still be without solar power and probably household processors, too. The estate was well-guarded and well-worked; from the sky at 6:45 that morning Allison had looked down and seen people working in the fields. Considering conditions elsewhere, the house and its grounds seemed a marvel of order and control.

Elizabeth led the way into the house. "You know, Allison, it's not their fault that they smell. They have no choice about using chemically scented water."

"That's the least of it," Allison said. "What really bothers me is all that contempt and contact."

"Let's bathe and change into something comfortable before you make your report," Elizabeth said.

Thank God. It would be a relief to get out of the binding, tacky clothes. All the time she wore them she had the nagging feeling that eyes were staring at her body, drawn by the disgustingly clinging cloth. For a moment she remembered Elizabeth's gorillas and knew they were probably staring at her from behind at that very second. Briefly she considered whirling around to see, but decided to ignore it. They weren't worth the trouble.

"Zita," Elizabeth greeted the service-tech when she opened the door for them. "Ms. Bennett will want a glass of wine with her bath, which she will be taking now."

Allison went into her room and stripped off the offensive clothing. Elizabeth never forgot details. It was wonderful. She would have been reluctant to ask for herself since it was not, after all, her house.

While she bathed and sipped the wine Zita brought her, Allison speculated about how Elizabeth would take the news of her having cut short the training assignment. She would probably be annoyed, Allison decided, but not angry. If her controller had been anyone other than Elizabeth, she would be more worried. But mulling over the facts, she told herself that Elizabeth would have been far more annoyed if Allison had stayed at the A.B. Corp and kept her and the chopper waiting.

Refreshed by the bath, Allison dried and perfumed herself with pleasure. If it weren't for her service-tech hairstyle she would now be herself, completely and entirely. The best covers were the ones that could either be shed for a few hours or that fit one's rank and preferred life-style. Her cover in Vienna had been entirely agreeable— an undisguised executive, working as an aide to the ambassador while in reality a communications specialist for the Company. Her situation years earlier in Rome had been similar. The only non-executive covers she had ever taken on had been for short-term operations. But it seemed likely that the special operation she had been assigned to would be both long-term and disagreeable. Working for Henry Lauder: what *would* that be like?

Allison stared at herself in the mirror: ludicrous, that hairstyle with her flowing silk gown. Like a service-tech disguising herself as an executive! It embarrassed her to be spending so much time with Elizabeth while looking so tacky. Though at least she had scrubbed the cosmetics from her face...

Allison found Elizabeth curled up in a large basket chair on the back terrace, reading reports. "It's beautiful here," Allison said as she stretched out on the chaise lounge. "Peaceful, too. If I were you, I might want to spend all my time here, especially now."

Elizabeth closed the file she had been working on and set it on the table between them. "That particular temptation isn't open to me. This isn't my house."

"Oh," Allison said, wondering again whose house it was. "I think if I were to have my own house, I'd like one like this. Away from the hordes. Quiet. Pleasant. Relatively simple. I bet one doesn't even need to worry about the efficacy of one's filter out here."

"I don't know. I suppose it would be nice to have this kind of house. I can't say I've thought much about it, since the whole thing is so financially out of the question."

This surprised Allison. While Elizabeth, like Allison, did not come from a particularly well-off family, Elizabeth did, however, have one of the most important positions a career-line woman might ever hope to achieve. Upper-echelon Company people had always profited

handsomely from Company proprietaries, and in fact for many of them the income accruing from the proprietaries was their major source of wealth. Allison had never been given stock or invited to purchase it when the proprietaries were formed, but she assumed that that was because she was not among the inner circle of Company people. If anyone could be said to be of that "inner circle," surely Elizabeth must be. How then could it be so "financially out of the question" for her?

Zita appeared with a tray, set a tall glass of grapefruit juice down on the table, and asked Allison if she wanted another glass of wine. Allison said she did. Zita poured wine into a fresh glass, then left the bottle on the table when she went back into the house.

"Tonight I'll brief you on the CAT you'll be joining and on the general intelligence situation in the Free Zone," Elizabeth said. "And tomorrow evening, after your final day of cover preparation, I'll brief you on your travel situation. And then the morning after that we'll take you up to that place near the border and drop you. You should be sufficiently prepared by then. I've already told Lauder to be expecting you four days from now. My latest communication from him leads me to think the sooner you get on the job, the better."

Allison swallowed a good mouthful of wine, then took the plunge. "We'd better forget about my returning to that job tomorrow."

Elizabeth frowned. "You need another day, Allison. You'll find it will make all the difference—"

"It's not my reluctance, but their reluctance to have me back," Allison said, without even noticing she was interrupting.

Elizabeth's eyebrows shot up. "You'd better clarify that."

"One of them told me I had to stay late," Allison said. "And that if I didn't stay I could forget the job. So the choice was either to keep you waiting for god knows how long, or to walk out and have them fire me. Since I didn't have any means of contacting you, and since I had no way of knowing what you had planned for me this evening, I decided to walk."

"Let's be clear. You took it on yourself to disobey orders," Elizabeth said coldly.

Allison flushed. "But if I had stayed I would have been disobeying orders. I had to use my own judgment to decide which order I would disobey and which I would obey, since they were mutually exclusive."

"And if the job hadn't been so disagreeable? Don't tell me your aversion to the situation didn't have something to do with your choice."

"I don't think it did!" Allison drew a deep breath. "Since I had no way of judging the significance of my missing my meeting with you, though I did understand the significance of the job, I decided that meeting you might be more critical than keeping the job. That's how I chose."

Elizabeth shook her head. "I don't like all these signs of temperament. Part of the reason for that job was to give you some practice at the kind of control you'll need for dealing with the emotions such situations evoke in executives. All we know now is that you haven't yet been able to cope with the kinds of interactions service-techs ordinarily experience. Instead you're all indignant about sub-exec odors and being physically handled. Don't you understand that you're supposed to convey the impression that you're not only comfortable getting sexual attention, but that you enjoy it?"

"Enjoy it?" Allison said, stupefied. "Surely they don't enjoy it? Getting pinched and tickled and stroked like that? It's so degrading!"

"Haven't you done any service-tech management at all, Allison?"

Allison gnawed at her lower lip. "A little, but not much. In the field one doesn't need a secretary, for instance, and anyway most of the service-techs are men, and one certainly doesn't want to pinch or stroke them."

"Well take it from me, when dealing with word processors, for instance, it's absolutely necessary to do this as a sort of lubrication." Elizabeth's sea blue eyes bored into Allison's. "I mean there you are, an executive, giving them orders all the time, and either they'll resent you or be terrified of you— or both— unless you can find a way of smoothing them down around the edges, of making some kind of emotional contact. I haven't once had a service-tech work for me who hasn't been terrified of Sedgewick. He doesn't bother with any of that, just gives his orders, occasionally says something cutting when the

work isn't up to his expectations. Consequently he'd be the last person in the world to be able to manage female service-techs. So don't complain at the treatment you got today. Considering how you were dressed, your manager probably thought that was the best way of handling you."

"I don't believe that," Allison said. "He was getting some kind of power-trip out of it. And believe me, I was far from sending him inviting signals. You know how I feel about men."

Elizabeth shook her head. "Your clothing, your hair— *they* were sending him signals. Don't you see?"

Allison lifted her glass. "It's all obnoxious, that's what I see," she said before taking another sip of wine.

"Only to you. Not to them. But that's the sort of thing I wanted you to understand and gain control of. It's possible, you see, for you to use it in reverse, if you're enough in control, for you'll be an executive dealing with sub-execs, even if they don't know it."

"I'll do my best," Allison said.

Elizabeth's mouth twisted. "Damned straight you will. So no more complaints. Clear?"

"Understood," Allison responded.

"Now I'll give you a profile of your CAT," Elizabeth said briskly. "As you know, Henry Lauder is controller. He's highly experienced, as you've probably heard. His father's a Senator. He has connections in the State Department but has loyally chosen to stick with Security. Perhaps you've heard that ten years ago he was offered the position of director of East European operations; but he turned it down— to stay in the field. His deputy controller is Mark Goodwin. Goodwin's specialties are communications and political education. He's worked with Lauder for eight years. His father is Secretary of Communications and Transportation, and is in the Booth contingent. The other executive on the team besides you is Joshua Morgan. He's an electronics specialist, twenty-eight years old. And he's a product of Wilton." Elizabeth paused to meet Allison's gaze. "He's sexually active— with men." Allison opened her mouth to ask, but Elizabeth answered before she could speak: "Yes, he's been fixed. But the behavioral mod at Wilton

was directed toward women, and Wilton..." Allison had heard of other cases. "And then there are three others. David Hughes, an economics expert, is an analyst. A professional. Also professional is Maureen Babcock, an explosives specialist. She has a PhD in chemistry from the University of Illinois. And then there's a service-tech, Dana Pickens." Elizabeth lifted her glass to her lips.

"How long has the team been working together?"

Elizabeth swallowed the sip she had taken, and Allison, watching, found herself fascinated by the smoothness of Elizabeth's long, graceful throat. "Seven months." She set down the glass. "On other projects than Operation Dahlia. They've set up a good solid network there. As you'll see, there are a lot of men disaffected with the Free Zone. But then the people running the Free Zone don't want to give the men any power. You can imagine how that goes over." Elizabeth smiled sourly. "It's been easy pickings. Harder, though, is infiltrating the inner circles of the women running the Free Zone. But then," Elizabeth said with a nod to Allison, "that's part of the reason you're joining the team."

Allison nodded back.

Zita came out onto the terrace. "Dinner is served, Ms. Weatherall."

Elizabeth rose. "Shall we continue this over dinner? I'm famished."

Allison stood up, caught Zita's eye, and indicated the wine. "I'll have the rest with dinner," she said.

Allison followed Elizabeth into the house. This would probably be one of the last decent meals she would have in months. She was certain the Free Zone was probably the American equivalent of Siberia— a bleak prospect for someone as attached to the Good Life as she was.

Chapter Five

[i]

Kay said a quick "hello, how're you doing?" to the service-tech cleaning the tile in the women's room and shut herself into the stall. Busy ticking off the list of things she had to do before leaving the Free Zone that night, an (unconcerned) recognition of how odd it was to see a janitor in the women's room at eleven o'clock in the morning barely rippled the surface of her thoughts. At another time she would probably have taken certain precautions. But since she did not, when Kay left the stall and went to the towel-wipe dispenser to clean her hands, she was unprepared when the service-tech came up behind her and jammed a gun into her back. "Don't do anything stupid, Zeldin," the service-tech said. She snatched the satchel off Kay's shoulder and slid it onto her own, and with her free hand patted Kay down, found the gun in her belt holster, detached the holstered gun from the belt, and dropped it into the satchel.

Kay watched it all in the mirror, as though it were happening to someone else. But the rush of blood pounded so loudly in her ears she could hardly hear the other woman's voice when she next spoke.

"We're going to walk, you a few paces ahead of me, down the stairs and out to the loading dock," the service-tech said. "You'll keep your hands at your sides, at all times visible. Don't think the presence of bystanders will save you. Play it cool, Zeldin, and no one will get hurt. Try anything tricky, and my weapon will go off. I'm going to be carrying it in my hand under the rag. Clear?"

Kay ignored the formula. "What happens after we get to the loading dock?"

"You don't need to know that. Now let's get out of here before somebody else comes in and I'm forced to do something regrettable."

Kay didn't doubt this woman might shoot a bystander. Her cold gray eyes had a businesslike dullness to them.

As they descended the stairs, Kay watched for an opportunity to break free. Twice they passed colleagues with whom she exchanged brief greetings and nods; but because of her awareness of the service-tech's stated indifference to the safety of bystanders, these encounters only made her more cautious.

When they reached the loading dock, the woman ordered her into a large panel van, which had been backed up against it. A man in executive dress stood near one of the open rear doors. The sight of the van was like a fist squeezing her heart. Lake Washington lay spread out below; the sky was so clear, the air so sharp, that not only Rainier, but much of the range flanking it to the east and west stood clearly exposed. Irrationally, Kay wanted to protest that the two realities— the van representing capture and the mountains and lake, so breathtakingly beautiful, could not co-exist. Kay knew that once she was inside that van her chances of escape would drop sharply.

The service-tech jabbed the gun into her back and urged her forward. Kay glanced around the dock. She knew they could have killed her any number of times before now, so she felt fairly confident that they had orders to take her alive. And she could see no bystanders in the vicinity. So she counted silently to three, whirled, and swept her fist up into her captor's gun arm, then leaped down off the dock onto the asphalt and made a desperate dash for the street.

Footsteps pounded behind her. Kay wished desperately for the gun the woman had taken from her. She took hope from the fact that they hadn't immediately shot at her. Several yards short of the street, though, Kay felt a sting in the back of her neck, followed by a lurching rush. She dropped to the pavement. Seconds later she heard the vehicle's quiet approach. And then the service-tech and the executive were heaving her limp, motionless body into the back of the van.

Lying with her limbs tangled just as they'd dumped her, Kay tried to concentrate on the turns the van made. She soon lost her sense of direction, however, and switched her attention to the executive's dressing-down of the service-tech, which the service-tech took in

silence. When the executive had sufficiently vented his spleen, he dropped into silence. Kay grew wildly frustrated at her inability to talk, move, or even blink her eyelids. She supposed she was lucky she could still breathe, though her breaths were shallow and her heart sluggish, making her lightheaded and sickeningly weak. The drive went on for a long time. She knew that the apparent length of the drive might be a ruse to fool her; nevertheless, she judged it likely that wherever they were going lay outside Seattle.

When the van stopped and the engine cut out, the executive spoke again. "We have her, under paralytic. Is the house clear?" Kay did not hear the response; she assumed it came through an earphone. "Okay, Pickens," he said to the service-tech. "We can take her in now."

The doors groaned open. Her captors were rough and indifferent in their handling of her as they pulled her down onto the pavement and— gripping her painfully under the armpits— dragged her to what looked like the back door of a white stucco house. Unable to turn her head (which had flopped to one side), she saw little of the house and its surroundings. Her captors cursed her for their toil the entire way. By the time they had finished pulling her into the house and down a long hall to a room where they deposited her on the carpeted floor, her armpits were throbbing and burning. "Christ she's heavy," the executive said. "If you hadn't screwed up, Pickens, we wouldn't have had to go through this. And now we'll have to wait for the drug to wear off before she can be interrogated." Kay watched a pair of shoes and trouser cuffs move out of her line of vision. "You'll keep her company, Pickens— we're taking no more chances. Clear?"

"Understood," the service-tech responded.

Kay heard a rustle, followed by the sliding shut of a door, electronic by the whirring sound of it. It must be a restored smart house, she thought. Besides the carpeting, Kay saw only the baseboard across the room. Since the service-tech neither talked nor moved again, Kay eventually lapsed into unpleasant speculation about what they intended to do to her.

After an incalculable length of time, the door slid open. Kay's attention returned to her sensory perceptions, and she noticed that her arm, pinned under the weight of her collapsed body, had fallen asleep.

Two pairs of shoes appeared before her. "Put her in a chair so I can see her face." The voice, thick and scratchy, sounded male. Two pairs of hands took hold of, lifted, and dragged her across the room to an armchair. Kay imaged herself as a giant doll being arranged and propped up for some make-believe exercise of childish fantasy. But when she saw the tall stout executive with silver hair and steely blue eyes sitting on the sofa opposite, the image vanished. "So this is the infamous Zeldin." He turned his head toward someone Kay could not see. "Doesn't look that impressive to me." His frigid eyes examined Kay. "I'm so disappointed. One always expects genius mastermind villains to look the part. This is the bitch who single-handedly precipitated this bloody civil war, the bitch who helped the aliens bring down the Executive? She looks like a fucking academic. Nothing like taking the glamour off the word *renegade*." He shook his head sadly. "But then if she'd looked the part maybe she couldn't have pulled it off." He turned his head again. "How long before the drug wears off, Mark?"

"At least two more hours, maybe three," a soft tenor voice replied.

The silver-haired executive nodded. "And then how long before we can administer the loquazene?"

"Depends on whether she's eaten or drunk anything. I'd say to be safe, at least eight hours from the time she resumes voluntary movement."

The silver-haired executive got to his feet. "Put her in the spare bedroom then. But keep her under constant surveillance. I don't want any fuck-ups with her." The executive gave Kay one last look over his shoulder. "We'll be talking, Zeldin." He moved out of her line of sight, and Kay heard the door slide open and close.

"Pickens, help me get her into the bedroom," the tenor voice said. Hands grabbed Kay from behind, yanked her upright and dragged her to the door. Trying not to think about the drug they had mentioned, Kay looked at whatever she could see on their progress through the house. But her vision was blurred. For some reason her eyes had started leaking.

She hoped her keepers wouldn't notice.

[ii]

Having finished her work on Whidbey two days ahead of schedule, Martha returned to Seattle on Friday afternoon instead of Sunday evening, her thoughts warmed by an image of Louise's pleasure at her unexpected arrival. When she reached the Belltown apartment they shared, though, she found it empty. She reminded herself that it was unlikely Louise would be home in the middle of the day and quelled her disappointment by revising her fantasy to an image of Louise's being delightfully surprised at finding Martha there when she got home in the evening.

After downing a bottle of water, Martha took everything out of her backpack, sorting the dirty clothes from the clean and putting away the small number of personal items she had carried around the Zone with her. While she worked she made a mental list of all the people and places she wanted to visit in the next few days— after she and Louise had shared their traditional reunion, of course.

Arms full of toilet articles, Martha stood on tiptoe to slide the shampoo onto the top shelf of the cabinet in the bathroom. Her toothbrush dropped from the jumble onto the floor. She put the other items she had been juggling in the cabinet, then bent down to retrieve the toothbrush. She found it near a large plastic garbage sack. Through the clear plastic she could see clothing that had originally been navy blue, now dark-splotched and thickly stained. A rust-colored substance crusted and wetly beaded the inside of the sack. Up close, she thought she smelled blood.

Martha backed slowly out of the bathroom. She knew it couldn't be Louise's Women's Patrol clothing, for the Women's Patrol wore gray with rainbow patches. So the clothing couldn't have been from some sort of accident Louise had been involved in while on Women's Patrol duty. Martha told herself there must be a perfectly reasonable explanation. Louise would explain it when she got in. She had no reason to be upset, blood was a perfectly natural substance. Perhaps Louise had found someone injured and for some reason had taken their clothes. And yet Martha did feel upset because she could think of no reason for Louise to have taken someone else's bloodied clothes home.

She shut the bathroom door and went back into the main room of the apartment. She hoped Louise would get home soon. Unexplained mysteries always stressed her out.

[iii]

Kay closed her eyes without thinking about it. Two seconds later, it dawned on her that the drug must be wearing off. She worked to clear her throat and successfully swallowed. A host of small tortured frustrations sloughed away as she assuaged various itches and cramps and other minor discomforts.

"So it's wearing off."

Kay turned her head; she looked at Pickens and made eye-contact. "Listen. Tell whoever's running this operation that I'm prepared to talk without the loquazene." Kay struggled to clear her throat of its thick coating of phlegm. "Tell him I don't respond well to drugs. Will you do that for me?"

"I can tell him, but I doubt he'll be impressed." The service-tech moved to the bed and whipped a pair of handcuffs out of her tunic pocket. "We can't take any chances with you." She snapped one of the cuffs around Kay's left wrist and the other to the bedframe.

The cuffs made Kay claustrophobic, reminding her of a past experience she would prefer not to remember. She tried to resign herself to them. Perhaps she would only have to tolerate them until Pickens had talked to the silver-haired executive.

Pickens pulled a handset out of her pocket, duly reported the change in Kay's status, and requested relief.

As Pickens reported, Kay realized she had lost a certain advantage by speaking to her captors. But it had been a quarter of a century since she'd been trained to deal with capture by the enemy. Since she had in fact broken silence, she decided she might as well try to get what she could out of the operation's flunkies. "Why must I be cuffed?" she asked when Pickens folded up the handset and put it back in her pocket.

"I have my orders." Naturally. A service-tech would carry little weight in an operation like this.

A white male professional came into the room, and Pickens left. "I'm David Hughes." He offered Kay his hand. Kay considered the

hand he offered. Why not? There was no point in making a personal enemy out of someone she might conceivably manipulate. But even as she shook hands she wondered about the psychological function of such civility. SIC officers in these sorts of circumstances did nothing without purpose. "I'm the analyst of the team," Hughes said, dropping into the chair Pickens had vacated.

"They take analysts into the field?" Kay asked, incredulous.

He smiled, and Kay was surprised to find that the smile warmed his hazel eyes. "Into this kind of field, yes."

"This kind of field," Kay said. "I suppose that refers to the Zone?"

Hughes's eyebrows shot up. "My god you're quick!"

Kay tried to stifle the nervous laugh that popped out, and it came out as a snort. "Why am I cuffed, do you know?"

"I'm just an analyst."

Right, Kay thought, just an analyst. No one was "just" anything in the Company.

"I found your book fascinating," he said.

Kay's lips twisted in derision.

"But you know I was baffled by it, too. There's a real mystery to you. You never do say exactly why you went renegade." He said the word easily, seemingly without rancor or severity. "I mean, there you were, sitting exceedingly pretty, Sedgewick's favorite, rapidly advancing— oh yes, everyone knew that, even if you didn't go into it in the book, and besides, it's easy to read between the lines, why else would you have been given the level of access you had— a solid professional with all the reasons in the world— material, moral, social, professional— to do everything you could to help defeat the enemy. And then you switch sides midcourse." His eyebrows danced in seeming perplexity. "Nobody switches sides simply because they don't like their side's tactics. But that's the only reason you gave for your treachery. It's lame, Zeldin. Until getting a look at how you've fared since then, I thought the terrorists must have promised you a great deal, a lot of power and money. But if they did, they haven't kept their promise."

Kay's mind labored: there was something here that she might be able to run with, but she wasn't sure what it was. It would be pointless

to say something scathing about how despicable the Executive regime was, how loathsome the Company. So she smiled at him— amiably and enigmatically, she hoped. "Maybe, maybe not. Why should I bare my soul to you?"

In spite of herself Kay found the warmth of his smile seductive. She laughed at this, fully aware that she must be careful not to let him charm her. It was risible, their sending him in here like this. Surely they hadn't so underestimated her. Or had they? "Oh, I wouldn't expect you to bare your soul to me," he said lightly. "But I guess we'll find out the answers to such mysteries a few hours from now."

That chilled her. "I don't believe you have any kind of drug that could get at that sort of thing," she said scornfully. "The unconscious or whatever it is that speaks under the drug is somewhat infantile, Hughes. You only get very literalist sorts of answers, which means the questioning has to be explicit and direct. I doubt you'll learn much about my motivations."

"You probably know more about such things than I do. I'm only an analyst—" he flashed her a wry grin— "and not one of the psychological ilk, either."

How fucking ingenuous can you get? Deliberately Kay broke eye-contact. "I'm dying of thirst," she said, looking past his right ear into the middle distance. "May I have some water? The taste of that drug is horrible."

He wagged his finger at her, as though scolding a child. "Come on, Zeldin. You know you can't have anything to eat or drink now."

"At least let me wash out my mouth." He didn't answer. Kay shifted, trying to ease the prickling in her left arm. "What are you an analyst of?"

"You know. You were an analyst, weren't you? Among other things, I mean," he amended.

"So you claim to be just sitting around analyzing data about the Free Zone. And all you're doing here is collecting information."

Hughes leaned forward. "You have a lot of gall asking me such questions. You don't have any kind of security clearance whatsoever now."

False indignation, or the real thing? Kay wondered. "What does that have to do with it? Anyway, why should you ask me questions and expect answers? You're enemy intelligence on our territory. Your presence in the Free Zone is illicit." What an absurd exchange: as though either of them could claim the right to determine and name the rules of the game. Since they had captured her they would think it their prerogative to declare the rules. But Kay wasn't about to cede that psychological advantage to them— yet.

"The very existence of the Free Zone is illicit," Hughes said. "By the Constitution of the United States, it has no legal right to exist."

"What do we do next?" Kay said. "Stick out our tongues and insult one another's parentage? Get into an 'is not/is so' rally?"

Hughes looked earnestly into her eyes. "How can such a civilized intelligent woman be working for anarchy? I don't get it." He shook his head. "Did they blackmail you? Was that it?"

Kay rolled onto her side and faced the wall. "Is that woman going to fetch your controller or not?"

"I can't believe you'd rather talk to him than to me," Hughes said. "I wouldn't have thought he was your type."

"And you are?"

"He has this thing about traitors. You'll see what I mean."

"He's the one with silver hair?"

Hughes did not answer. Kay wracked her brain for another question that might lead to something interesting. "How long have you been in the Free Zone?" she asked at random.

"You know I'm not going to give you classified information, Zeldin. Why bother asking? I suggest that if you're not interested in really talking to me that we simply not talk. Eight hours is a long time for sustaining this sort of non-conversation."

Kay lay quietly. According to her watch, it was two-thirty. Sorben was supposed to pick her up at midnight. That would not happen now, of course. She tried not to speculate about their ultimate plans for her once they had finished interrogating her.

After about fifteen minutes Kay rolled onto her back and stared at Hughes. "Am I going to be allowed to piss?" she asked at her most abrasive.

"I can't do anything until Pickens gets back," Hughes said in the voice of one trying to reason with a child.

"And of course you have no idea when that is," Kay said sarcastically.

"Of course."

Kay closed her eyes. To avoid confronting her frustrations and fears, she returned to considering how best to convince them not to drug her and possibly to free her, though she had little hope of the latter. The important thing was to keep them from demoralizing her for as long as she could manage. It must mean something that they were trying to cast Hughes in the role of prisoner's friend. Why bother if they were simply going to drug, interrogate, and kill her?

"Tell me something, Zeldin," Hughes said after another long silence.

Kay opened her eyes.

"That Chilean economist you had over for lunch. Who do you think she's working for?"

"How would I know a thing like that? I don't even specially know that she's working for anyone besides herself. Maybe she's honest. It sometimes happens, you know."

Hughes smirked at her. "Really, Zeldin. Can you be that naïve? You can just about bet that almost any outsider in the Twilight Zone— which is what *we* call it— is working for someone. This has got to be one of the most haunted spots on earth right now."

"But why? Nothing's going on here. Nobody's building weapons systems or doing anything of conceivable interest to the rest of the world. Why should governments be throwing away scarce resources by sending their spooks here?"

"Come off it, Zeldin. You're not *that* naive."

"All I'm saying is, we're no threat to anyone here. We're just struggling to get by."

"You're rather free with the collective pronoun. So you consider yourself one of them?"

Kay raised her eyebrows at him. "Them?"

"So all talk between us is to be a fencing match?"

"You surely aren't making idle conversation to pass the time," Kay said. "In your own words, I'm not *that* naive."

"Touché, Madame."

The conversation lapsed. Kay pondered Hughes's eagerness to inform her that they knew about things like whom she ate lunch with in her own apartment and to make her believe that the Free Zone was crawling with foreign intelligence agents. Letting her know they'd had her under surveillance was for sheer intimidation. They'd begun their intimidation campaign with the delivery of that purple to her office and had continued it by letting her make her trackers.

A little before three-thirty Kay heard the sliding door open; she rolled onto her back to face it. Pickens stood in the doorway and stared at her. "You got your wish, Zeldin. He says he'll see you." She looked at Hughes. "He wants us to take her downstairs."

Downstairs? Kay didn't like the sound of that.

Hughes looked puzzled. "To the cellar? But why? I thought—" He glanced at Kay.

She recognized that look and saw that they were playing her. Right. "I want to piss first," she said flatly.

"Nothing in my orders about a stop at the bathroom," Pickens said.

"Oh, hell, Pickens, why not?" Hughes said.

Kay clamped her jaw tight and forced herself to keep quiet. She would not play their game if she could help it.

"Then you take the responsibility for it. I've already gotten into enough damned trouble because of her."

Hughes said, all ease and good-will, "No problem. I'll take responsibility for the entire enormity of the thing." He winked at Kay and unlocked the cuff attached to the bedframe.

When Kay sat up, her head swam. "Wait a second," she said. "I'm a little dizzy." Pickens and Hughes stood waiting, watching. Did they really think she would try something, that she was strong enough even to think of it? What was it they had been told about her? Slowly she got to her feet and swayed before catching her balance. Hughes pulled her right arm behind her back and cuffed her free wrist to the one already cuffed. "Is that necessary?" Kay said. "I won't be able to walk properly, I'm so dizzy and weak."

"Sorry, Zeldin. Orders is orders," Hughes said. "You know the drill."

Hughes grasped her right arm, Pickens her left, and the three of them walked to the door. Hughes pressed his thumb against the small touch-sensitive square panel beside the door. The door slid open. Pickens went out first, then Kay with Hughes behind her. In the hallway they resumed formation until they came to the bathroom, where Pickens thumbed the door open and shoved Kay in. She did not close the door, which Kay thought must be simple nastiness.

"I'm sorry you got into trouble because of me," Kay said while she labored to produce a minuscule amount of urine. She refrained from pointing out that anyone would have tried to run, since doing so might make Pickens angrier through its implication that Pickens should have expected it.

Pickens reacted with anger to the apology anyway. "It's none of your fucking business," she said, crossing her arms over her chest.

As they propelled her down the hallway and along another that branched off from it, Kay concentrated on seeing as much of the house as she could. At the end of the second hallway they halted before a closed door. Hughes pressed his thumb on the plate, and the door opened, revealing stairs. Suddenly worrying that she might never leave the basement alive, she hesitated. "Go on, Zeldin." Hughes's hand on her back exerted pressure. The steps looked so steep Kay wished her hands were free to grab hold of the stair rail. Nerving herself forward, she negotiated the narrow steps as carefully as she could with Pickens and Hughes following close behind, forcing her down without pause. At the bottom of the steps Kay found herself standing at one end of a long gray room flooded by overhead fluorescent lighting. She blinked and turned to Hughes. "Go on," he said.

Dread cramped her stomach as she advanced toward the gray steel door at the far end of the room. When they reached the door, Hughes's thumb opened it. Hughes's— and not Pickens's— thumb had opened

every door they passed on the journey from the room upstairs. Kay supposed that at least some of the doors were keyed to recognize only certain thumbs.

Three rooms later, Kay confronted the silver-haired man, now smoking a cigar, and another man in executive dress, brown-eyed, brown-haired, bearded, with longish hair and an impressive hawk nose. Kay appraised the two men, wondering which of them was the controller.

"You wanted to talk to me, Zeldin?" the silver-haired executive said, glancing at Kay but letting his eyes immediately stray off to the side.

Curious, Kay turned her head to see what was so riveting to the executive— and gasped. A noose made of black electrical cord hung from a hook in the ceiling, a sight chilling and stark under the harsh fluorescent lights.

"That's for you, Zeldin," the executive said. Kay looked again at the executive, and his flat blue eyes stared back at her. "I've agreed to wait— so that you can be interrogated first. But my desire is to do it now. Can't stomach renegades."

"I would be of more use to you alive than dead," Kay said. Her throat and mouth had gone so dry it pained her to speak. "I'm well-connected in the Free Zone. I could help you take it back under control."

Her offer cut no ice with *him*. "Yeah, and then we'd only have to give it up again when the Marq'ssan resumed zapping us."

Kay dry-swallowed and struggled to generate some saliva. "I could help you dispose of the Marq'ssan," she said. "It wouldn't be easy, but I have the contacts with them that you would need to do it. Otherwise you'll never have a chance against them."

He took the cigar out of his mouth. "About seventeen years ago I found out that one of my men was working for the SFS. To get him I had to put more than a dozen people at the highest risk. But I'll tell you this, Zeldin: I took him down."

"She's right, sir," Hughes said. "She's the best chance we'll ever have to get the Marq'ssan."

Kay thought that she understood the game. Her heart slowed to a merely moderately hard gallop.

"That may very well be," said the other executive. Kay recognized his voice as one that had spoken upstairs in the first room into which they had taken her. "But you know she's not to be trusted. There's no way she can be controlled. Letting her loose enough to work for us would simply give her the opportunity to run. Or to organize something new against us— with the Marq'ssan to help."

"Perhaps," Hughes said softly, "but she hasn't told anyone yet about the purple we left her or even about our surveillance of her. And you know she made us."

How could Hughes be so sure of these things, Kay thought, unless they had been extensively and thoroughly bugging her? She shivered.

"Why should we trust you, Zeldin?" the dark-haired executive demanded. "You're a known enemy of the Executive. It's obvious that hatred for the Executive motivated your treachery. Nowhere have you suggested any other reason for it. Why should we believe you'll work with us?"

Kay needed her sharpest thinking, but her brain seemed fuzzy, sluggish, out of synch. "I don't like how things have turned out," she said slowly, focusing her attention on the dark-haired executive. "It's frustrating to me, the way they run— or rather don't run— the Free Zone. And it's clear that as the world recovers from the crisis, the Free Zone will have to develop in a way that I won't be able to tolerate— unless they can get themselves organized. But they're opposed to organization."

"If you're so crazy about hanging with the winners, why did you betray the Executive, Zeldin?" the silver-haired executive said.

"But they weren't winners. They were mismanaging everything they were doing. You know damned well the civil war would have broken out whether I had gone renegade or not. Sedgewick was as crazy as a—" Without warning, the executive's fist shot out and slammed into Kay's jaw. She reeled dizzily backwards, her head fairly exploding with pain. Only Hughes's quick hold on her shoulders kept her from falling.

"Goddam sub-exec bitch," the executive said, "you keep your mouth shut about Sedgewick. Or next time you'll end up with your jaw wired shut."

Kay, gasping for breath, eyed the executive and wondered at his vehemence. She was positive it wasn't assumed as a part of the game: the flush on his face, the glitter in his previously dead eyes implied a deep emotional response he wasn't bothering to control, unusual in a mature executive.

The dark-haired executive broke the tense silence. "Why don't you let us deal with her, Henry?" he said. "You don't have to make a decision yet. Maybe we can clarify things during the interrogation."

The situation was clear: she, Kay, was supposed to offer a degree of cooperativeness that would allow Hughes and this other executive to persuade their controller to put her to work for them. But would the controller kill her anyway? Clearly, he wanted to. The others, she thought, had no intention of killing her but wanted only to intimidate her. Kay's thoughts spun in circles. She *was* intimidated. She *was* playing their game.

The controller chewed his cigar, apparently considering. "All right, Mark," he said. "I'll leave her to you. I assume you think you can get something out of her before you administer the drug?"

The dark-haired executive said, "It's worth a try, isn't it?"

Kay held her breath as the controller passed within inches of her, but he did not so much as glance at her. When she heard the door behind her slide open then closed, she let out her breath in relief.

The dark-haired executive looked at Hughes. "What do you suggest?"

Hughes took his hand from Kay's back. "I suggest we all sit down and chat. Pickens can be the stenographer as well as attend to the recording." Hughes's fingers squeezed Kay's right arm. "Zeldin's civilized," he said.

The executive gestured toward the long table on the other side of the room. "Okay. We'll all sit down at the table." He bowed slightly from the waist. "After you, Zeldin."

Kay walked tensely past the noose, giving it a wide berth, and set her mind to persuading them to give her water. If she got them to do that they would have to wait at least another eight hours before they could give her the drug. By then it would be too late for them to ambush Sorben. Preventing that was now the best she could hope for.

Chapter Six

[i]

Speaking into the terminal's mike in the slow, toneless voice essential for flawless stenography, Pickens, per Hughes's instructions, ordered a print-out of what Hughes claimed was a surveillance log covering the last two weeks of Kay's life.

"I don't know how I'm going to talk for long without water," Kay said as they waited. "Whether conscious or under your damned drug, my throat will only take so much before giving out."

"Don't press your luck, Zeldin," the executive said.

"I'm already hoarse."

The printer whirred somewhere out of Kay's line of sight. "The log," Pickens said, handing several sheets of flimsy to the executive. "Do you want me to input a transcript as you go?"

"Yes. And then afterwards you can check your version against the recording."

The executive glanced over the log, then slid it across the table to Kay. "Read that over," he said.

Kay was surprised. She had thought he wanted the log to assist him in his interrogation. Using the hand they had uncuffed, she moved the flimsies closer and stared down at the top sheet. She noticed that beside the record of every phone call and conversation that took place in her office or apartment was a notation in parentheses— *(tr)*, and deduced that the *(tr)* indicated that a transcript had been made. Other conversations, for instance the one that had taken place at her cafe co-op on Brooklyn, lacked that notation. She saw that they had even transcribed her conversations with Colin, a recent sexual partner. Why bother? Such detailed surveillance was extraordinary. Surely they wouldn't go to such lengths if their ultimate purpose in capturing her were to kill

her. Kay glanced up and found the executive's eyes on her. Quickly she looked down again at the paper, annoyed and self-conscious. She thumbed through the flimsies and moved her eyes over the print. A fast skim now would enable her to recall any of it she wished later. As she skimmed, she became aware of notations suggesting that someone outside the Company had also been observing her. She itched to stop and ask about it but forced herself to finish skimming everything they had given her. They would probably take the flimsies from her once she began talking.

When she finished, Kay tilted her head to one side and regarded the executive through eyes narrowed with derision. "You people are such fools," she said. She let some of her anger at their having spied, drugged, kidnapped, and exercised their usual sadistic techniques on her trickle into her consciousness. "Such fools to spend this kind of time, money, and energy on watching me. What the fuck do you think you have to gain? Haven't you learned anything yet about the Free Zone? Or about me? You'd think with all the observation the Company has made of me over the last decade they'd finally get certain things straight. Killing me out of spite is one thing. But this?" She flicked the flimsies with her fingernail. "You're not only nuts, you're incompetent."

"Nice try, Zeldin," the executive said in a voice almost as toneless as that required for stenographic input. He retrieved the flimsies and pulled a fountain pen out of his pocket. "Allow me to call your attention to certain details of this log." He went through the flimsies and underlined certain entries, then slid them back to her.

Kay checked the places he had marked on the top sheet and found they all noted instances of surveillance by some other party or parties. She looked at him. "Yes, I noticed those entries. You could of course have simply invented them. But for the sake of argument I'll agree that any number of people are watching me. Why should that make your choosing to peep on my sex life any more comprehensible to me? Perhaps they're watching me because *you're* watching me."

Hughes chuckled. Kay turned in her chair to look at his face. "You're amazing, Zeldin," he said, grinning broadly. "I can't remember ever finding a subject in your position so cynically underestimating us. As though you truly believe us incompetent."

Kay returned her gaze to the executive. "I suppose you are going to see to it that I understand the point of your showing me the log? Apart, that is, from vaunting your prowess at surveillance, which is about the only thing the SIC does well."

The executive's face remained blank, but Kay thought she detected a slight tightening around his eyes. "Oh, I wouldn't say that," he came back with after about five seconds. "I wouldn't say that at all. I can think of other things we're good at."

An unpleasant sensation lightly brushed the nape of Kay's neck, as though a sharp draft of cold air had crept up behind her. In her mind's eye she visualized the noose hanging two yards behind her. "Are all your interrogations this lucid?" she said, barely keeping her voice level.

"Very well, Zeldin. I'll spell it out. We know, and apparently several other interested parties know as well, that you are from time to time in personal contact with the aliens. On July third, for instance, you met with the one known as Magyyt. Though we were unable to see or hear your meeting with her, you made numerous references to the meeting in several of the conversations we do have transcriptions of. And we know there's a strong likelihood you were planning a meeting with a Marq'ssan in the very near future, perhaps even in the next few days. That access in itself is enough to justify any amount of expenditure by any intelligence agency on tracking you." He leaned back in his chair and fiddled with the ring on his right index finger; his hooded eyes remained fixed on Kay's face.

Kay tried to see where this line might be leading. "There are other people who have contact with the Marq'ssan," she said.

"Naturally. But we don't know who they are, do we. Or at least not yet." He smiled briefly. "And as all intelligence organizations must know, you're someone with whom it is likely one can do business."

Kay could hear the blood rushing through her eardrums; her voice came out nearly breathless: "Just what the hell do you mean by that?"

"Everyone knows a renegade can't be trusted," the executive said softly. "Those who double are almost always without any real sense of loyalty."

"Don't be so quick to make assumptions about Zeldin," Hughes said. Kay twisted around to look at him. He nodded at her. "I think it's a little more complex than that. Zeldin's psychology is very complicated, perhaps even involuted. Right, Zeldin?"

Kay turned back to the executive, determined to ignore Hughes's contribution to the farce. "So what?" she said flatly. "What do you want?"

The executive smiled. "The Marq'ssan of course."

Kay smiled back. "If I give you the Marq'ssan, what do *I* get out of it?"

The executive looked at Hughes. "What is it she wants, Hughes, seeing you're so tuned in on Zeldin's psychology?"

"Two things," Hughes said. Kay kept her eyes on the executive's face. "She wants her spouse's safety. And she wants power."

The executive's gaze met Kay's, and she recoiled. "Is that what you want, Zeldin?"

"I don't believe Security has Scott Moore."

"Oh, we have him, Zeldin, we have him."

Kay's throat grew tighter; she felt as though she were choking. "No. I think Military has him. I've thought that all along. Security never recruited him for an R & D project."

"Security has him."

"Prove it."

"You know the satellites are out,"' the executive said. "There's no way we can prove it to your satisfaction without taking you to the site of his internment."

"Internment?" Kay said. "Are you saying he isn't involved in an R & D program? That you're holding him just to be holding him?"

"I'm not telling you anything," the executive said. "Everything to do with Scott Moore is classified information. And you're not cleared for reading the public newspapers."

"He hasn't been mistreated, Zeldin," Hughes said.

Kay's left hand gripped the edge of the chair arm it was cuffed to. "I don't think we are going to be able to do business together," she said evenly. "I can't take anything you say on faith, and consequently you will not be able to trust me."

"We don't have to trust you," the executive said. "As I said, only a fool would trust someone already known to have doubled."

"Then we're at an impasse."

"It would seem so. I guess we'll have to settle for the original plan." His voice had a ring of finality to it, as though he had expected before they had even started that they would end at an impasse.

"No!" Kay said. "There must be something we can work out!"

Neither Hughes nor the executive said anything.

"I can tell you things about the Marq'ssan," Kay said.

"Go ahead, Zeldin. We're listening."

"Not until we work something out."

He shrugged as though he were completely indifferent. "The ball's in your court."

Kay struggled against her growing conviction that they would kill her after questioning her under the drug. But no. That couldn't be it, no matter the bastard controller's lust for hanging her. They had invested too much in her to so easily discard her. They were bluffing. They had to be bluffing.

They four of them sat in silence that grew louder and louder the longer it held. "Nothing to say?"' the executive said perhaps five minutes into the silence. Kay did not reply. "That settles it. Hughes, you and Pickens will take her back upstairs until it's time." The executive pushed his chair back and rose to his feet. He looked for a long time at Kay, then walked away from the table. She listened to his steps cross the room, slow, deliberate, and final. The door slid open and closed.

"You blew it, Zeldin," Hughes said softly.

Kay did not answer. She was afraid he was right.

[ii]

Martha had been pacing from one end of the room to the other for more than an hour when she finally heard Louise's key in the lock. She turned and faced the door as it opened and watched Louise walk

in. Louise halted when she saw Martha; her eyes widened. "Martha! You weren't supposed to be coming home today, were you?" She did not seem pleased at the surprise.

Diane came in behind Louise. "Martha!" Diane exclaimed in consternation. And then, as if realizing how impolite that sounded, she added, "Hi. How's it going?"

Martha looked from Diane back to Louise. "I got through on Whidbey Island early and thought I'd surprise you. But that wasn't a very good idea, was it."

Louise moved toward Martha. "But it's a wonderful surprise, love! Of course I'm glad you're home early!" She opened her arms to fold Martha into a hug, but Martha stepped back. "What's wrong?" Louise said, reaching to touch Martha's face and stopping mid-motion.

"What's going on here, Louise? Why are you and Diane acting so strange?"

Louise and Diane looked at one another. "Just knocked a little off balance, I guess," Diane said.

Martha said, "I'm glad at least to see you're all right."

Louise's brow furrowed. "All right? You haven't been worrying about me, have you, love? You know none of us has been seriously hurt since the Women's Patrol was formed. There's really no reason for you to—"

"That's not what I'm talking about," Martha said, needing now to ask Louise about the bloody sack, Diane or no Diane. Martha looked at Diane. "Will you excuse us for a minute, Diane? And will you come into the bathroom with me, Louise?"

"Um, look," Diane said, "maybe I should go out for a few minutes. I know you two haven't gotten to see one another much lately. And besides, there's something else I should be doing..." Martha wondered what that look of purpose Diane was broadcasting to Louise signified.

"Thanks, Di," Louise said thoughtfully. "I think that's an excellent idea."

Diane nodded at Martha and went back out the door.

Martha's gaze locked with Louise's. "All right," Louise said. "Will you now please tell me what's going on?"

"Me tell you?" Martha said. "That's pretty good, turning it around like that. Two strange things happen, both to do with you, and *you* ask *me* what's going on?"

"*What* strange things?"

"First I find a garbage sack full of bloodied clothing in our bathroom, and then you and Diane come home, and the two of you act like conspirators. I don't know what to think, Louise. Though I'm glad I finally decided that the sack didn't necessarily mean you had been hurt— or worse."

Louise went to the couch. "Let's sit down." She patted the cushion beside her.

"You sit if you like. But I'm wound up tight. All I want is for you to tell me what that sack of bloody clothes is doing in our bathroom."

Louise looked Martha in the eye. "What do you think?"

Martha shrugged. "At first I thought they might be the clothes of someone hurt you had had to help. But then I realized it was unlikely that you would bring them here."

Louise stared at the floor. "I think you already know, Martha." She wet her lips. "You *should* know. I essentially told you about it when it started."

Martha's pulse thudded in her ears. "Started? When *what* started?"

Louise raised her gaze. "When the Night Patrol started. You heard me say it needed to be started in Seattle. It was just after the Blanket, when we were all sitting around in the dark in that studio in Pioneer Square." Louise's eyes went nearly black with intensity. "Remember?"

Martha stared at Louise, not believing she was hearing her correctly. "What are you saying? You're not saying that you—" she broke off and shook her head. "No. I don't believe it."

"I helped start the Night Patrol," Louise said. "I didn't think you would be here today, so I agreed to keep the clothes until we could burn them. We were going to do that tonight."

"No," Martha said, pleading. "No. You wouldn't do that, Louise, would you?"

"We've talked about the Night Patrol before, Martha. You know why."

Martha shook her head. "That's different, saying you didn't want to stop them. That's different from actually doing the killing yourself. You're saying you *kill* people, Louise."

"Rapists," Louise said. "I kill rapists. Only rapists. I kill men who don't deserve to be alive."

Martha sank to her knees, physically borne to the ground by the weight of Louise's words. "You don't have the right to decide who deserves to be alive!" Martha cried. "No one has that right!"

"Let's be clear, Martha. You don't approve of a lot of what I do. But you accept it."

"Not this." Martha realized she was crying. "I don't accept this." She wiped her running nose on her sleeve. "It makes me sick, Louise. Do you have any idea of how sick I feel? I'm about ready to vomit, thinking of that sack in the bathroom, thinking of what you do."

Tears brimmed in Louise's eyes. "I feel sick too, dear. I feel sick that this has happened. I knew you couldn't understand. I don't want you to feel this way, but I don't know what we can do to help it. It's all those years of brainwashing by Walt Jennings. His influence is stronger in you than anything I can say, stronger than your love. I always knew that, that's why I didn't tell you outright. But I thought that somewhere inside, you knew. Because I essentially told you any number of times."

Martha shook her head, back and forth, back and forth. "No. No you never told me. I didn't listen to you that way because I trusted you, Louise."

"Oh, Martha," Louise said sadly.

"I can't stay here," Martha whispered. "I can't stay here now." She blundered to the table and grabbed the small rucksack she had seemingly without reason loaded with a few things while waiting for Louise to return. Blinking against her tears, Martha stumbled to the door. She had to get out of there, she couldn't stay. Even the sound of Louise's voice calling her name made her sick.

[iii]

Hughes and Pickens returned Kay to the basement at nine-thirty p.m., to the same room in which they had questioned her, where a reclining chair and a variety of medical equipment had been set up. After strapping her into the chair a blonde professional woman unbuttoned Kay's tunic and fastened EKG receptors to her chest while Pickens wrapped the self-inflating blood pressure cuff around her upper left arm. "This isn't necessary," Kay said to Hughes, still hoping she could persuade them to refrain from administering the drug.

He shook his head. "It's too late, Zeldin. You had your chance with Goodwin. And you blew it. He's not going to change his mind now. You had all afternoon to work something out with us."

The blonde wrapped a tourniquet around Kay's upper right arm and began preparing the IV. Listening to the fast, erratic beeps, Kay grew self-conscious at their being able to hear the fear in her now public pulse. "Why don't you just try asking me your questions first, before drugging me. And then if you're dissatisfied—"

"Lauder's getting impatient. Goodwin's getting impatient. We're all getting impatient," Hughes said.

Kay heard the door slide open. "Ready to go, Babcock?" the dark-haired executive's voice asked. Kay sensed him standing directly behind her chair.

"Yes, sir. I'm ready to start the drip."

"And you, Pickens. You have all your equipment functioning?"

"Yes, sir."

"Excellent. Then let's go for it."

Wanting to make an appeal to Goodwin, Kay tried to twist in the chair, but Hughes pressed her back. "Sit still, Zeldin."

Kay tasted the drug in her mouth, felt it seeping into her body. Her vision blurred, and then she lost consciousness.

[iv]

For hours Martha sat at the edge of Lake Washington staring into the water. When she noticed it was getting dark, she pulled herself out of the trance-state she had slipped into. Her bicycle still stood propped against the tree where she had left it; her rucksack lay on the

ground beside her. No one had taken advantage of her daze to rob her. Martha smiled grimly. Louise taught the women in her classes that one should not sit dazed in a public park with one's back unguarded. But then Louise had always said Martha's problem was trustfulness and naiveté.

Martha got to her feet and stretched her cramped legs and arms. It was still and beautiful here, the water quiet and soothing. She hated to go. But she had never been naive enough to hang out in the park after dark. Louise hadn't had to teach her that.

She strapped on her rucksack, retrieved her bike, and wheeled it over the grass. When she reached the pavement, she mounted and rode west, away from the lake toward the setting sun, which scorched the sky below the Olympics a burnt orange and thick wine red. She stopped at the first data kiosk she came to and used the phone to call Jeannie Meadows to ask her if she could crash on her couch, then got back on her bike and headed for Fremont. She hoped the batteries in her light held out. She had not recharged them for weeks.

[v]

Kay woke from inky, dreamless unconsciousness into darkness. She realized she was lying (handcuffed) on a hard, vibrating surface. She stirred, then felt the fingers pressing lightly against her throat below her right ear. "She's coming around," a male voice said. The fingers left her throat.

"Where am I?" Kay said through a dry throat, frightened and uncomprehending.

"You can remove the oxygen now," the male voice said. Kay felt a touch somewhere below her nose and above her lip. "We were administering the loquazene, Zeldin. Remember?" Kay's memory flooded back. She thought the voice must be Goodwin's. "And now we're returning to your apartment. So that we can be there to meet your Marq'ssan contact when she comes to get you."

Kay groaned as she realized she must have told them everything about her trip and about the Marq'ssan. The thought was almost more than she could bear. She searched for mitigation. Perhaps, she told herself, it was too late… Sorben would probably not wait more than

an hour or so for her... "What time is it?" she asked, trying to keep any trace of hope out of her voice.

"It's not yet eleven-fifteen. We cut the interrogation short so that we could make it in time. We'll continue it later, after we've taken care of the Marq'ssan."

Marq'ssan could not be captured, as they must have found out from her. But if they managed to kill Sorben in an ambush, catastrophe would result, and only five Marq'ssan would be left. Kay realized that they must have gotten that from her, too. How confident that must have made them, discovering there were only six Marq'ssan on the entire planet.

Irritated by the handcuffs, hungry, dizzy, thirsty, Kay shifted. It was bad enough, the extent to which her privacy had been invaded by detailed surveillance. But their questioning her and her not even remembering— that was an obscenity unmatched by all the rest. Who had listened to her talk? Pickens, Hughes, Goodwin, and that blonde professional who had controlled the medical technology. At the very least. But of course many others would hear the recordings or read the transcripts, transcripts as invasive as the ones they had made of her personal, private conversations. "You're fools," Kay said through her teeth, her voice hoarse almost to the point of unintelligibility. "You'll end up bringing down the wrath of other Marq'ssan on you. You have no idea of the scale of retaliation your stupidity is going to trigger."

"Then you should be happy, Zeldin, since you're such a destroyer," Goodwin said.

Kay pressed her lips together. There was no point in talking. She'd already said too much. And her anger could not touch them— not this crew.

The van lurched; Kay strove to brace herself against its side. It made another turn, and another, and stopped.

Goodwin spoke in a low, calm voice. "You'll have a gun in your back the entire time, Zeldin. So don't try anything. I'll be walking next to you, holding your arm. If you are stopped by someone you know, you'll give them the impression I'm a new lover, and if you have to you can introduce me as Mark. No last name. But unless such an

encounter requires it, you won't do more than nod or say good evening or whatever it is you usually say in such cases. Do you understand, Zeldin? If you try anything, you'll get someone else shot. And I think you'd agree that that would be unfortunate. Clear?"

Despair had swallowed her anger. "Understood."

"No fuss, no one gets hurt," Goodwin said smoothly.

"How should I explain the person holding a gun in my back?" Kay asked ironically.

"If anyone comes into sight, Pickens will drop back and carry her weapon under her scarf. She's not blind, Zeldin. The distance doesn't matter."

"Then why must she walk with that thing pressed into my back at all?"

"It's an effective reminder, don't you agree?"

The doors to the van were opened. Kay was pulled out and made to stand on the pavement, and her handcuffs removed. She rubbed her wrists. She had a chance now; she might still manage to run and hide and keep Sorben from walking into the trap.

They moved toward the building at a brisk pace. Inside, the doors to the service elevator stood open. Her captors, tightly circling Kay, pushed in. She stared at the blonde, the only one of the four she had not gotten much of a look at. The blonde must have been the driver...unless someone else had driven and was still sitting in the van with the motor running. Yes, that seemed more likely. Then the blonde must have been riding shotgun. Kay thought it must have been she who had opened the rear doors.

They reached Kay's apartment without having encountered anyone. Goodwin grabbed Kay's right hand and forced her thumb onto the plate beside the door, then inserted her yellow plastic into the intake slot. Her window of opportunity had just about slammed shut. They pushed her into the main room. Pickens and the blonde closed the draperies and turned on a few lights.

"May I have some water now?"

"Where do you keep it?" Goodwin asked.

"In a closet in the kitchen."

"Get her a bottle, Pickens," Goodwin said.

Kay drank it straight down, almost without pause. But the half-liter failed to quench her thirst.

"And now we'll resume the handcuffs," Goodwin said.

"Can't we wait until just before midnight?"

But Goodwin took the cuffs from Hughes and bound Kay's wrists behind her back. "You and I will wait behind the door, Zeldin," Goodwin said. "When she knocks, I'll open it for you, and you'll show your face. Since I'll have a weapon in your back, you won't try to do anything to warn her. Clear?"

Kay turned away from Goodwin without answering. Her anger was foremost again. And she was debating her own courage.

Goodwin grabbed her shoulder and spun her around. "I asked you a question, Zeldin." His fingers dug into her chin, forcing her to look at him.

"I heard, damn you." Kay glared at him. "Your threat is crystal clear. But what's the difference between your killing me here or hanging me there? Come to think of it, I'd rather go here in my own apartment, and by gunshot, than there in your sickening basement by hanging, which by all historical accounts is very unpleasant. I've got nothing to lose."

"We're giving you a second chance, bitch," Goodwin said. "Apart from which I should think you'd like to postpone your own death, whether it's inevitable or not. You don't know yet what we might still manage to work out. After all, we had only just begun your interrogation when we had to stop to take advantage of the timely information you gave us."

Kay, pouring hatred into her gaze, stared into his cold, dark eyes. "You think I'm going to let you use me more than this?" she said softly. "Maybe you're making a mistake. Ever think of that? Maybe I will manage to warn her. So you'll kill me, but then you won't have me to use. And then she'll get away from you, but know you. And *then* you'll be in a mess. Because the Marq'ssan never let these sorts of things pass without retaliation."

Goodwin's eyes blazed with fury. "Shooting you doesn't necessarily mean killing you, Zeldin." His words flew at her like a hail

of sharp, icy pellets. "There are places on your spine where a bullet won't kill, but merely render you a quadriplegic for the rest of your undoubtedly short life."

Shivers rippled over Kay; her teeth clenched at the sudden chill striking deep into her body.

Goodwin nodded. "Yes. I thought you would see my point." He released her chin, turned her around, and pushed her toward the door. "We'll start waiting now. The alien may be early."

Kay tried to think, but her mind had gone stupid. All that came to her were images: of a bullet-damaged spine on an x-ray flimsy, of herself opening the door to Sorben while Goodwin pressed the barrel of his gun into her spine, of Sorben being shot and crumpling to the floor, her field shifting and revealing whatever it was that Marq'ssan looked like. Someone had once said they looked like reptiles, but Magyyt had told Kay they were mammals, though not exactly human-looking. What would a dead Marq'ssan look like? The muscles in Kay's arms tremored. Sorben dead. The thought was unbearable. Sorben and Magyyt should have gone while they had the chance. Kay saw now that their deaths at the hands of people like these had been inevitable, only a matter of time. How terrible that she was to be the instrument for bringing about one of those deaths.

The wait seemed interminable. When Kay finally heard the knock on the door, her breath came in ragged choking gasps. "Control yourself," Goodwin whispered in her ear. He jabbed the barrel of his gun into her spine. Kay closed her eyes and tried to still her breathing. "All right," he whispered. "I'm going to open the door now. Remember what I said— unless you desire a more permanent experience of paralysis than you tasted this afternoon." His hand moved past her and flipped open the locks, took hold of the doorknob, and pulled the door ajar.

"Sorben," Kay whispered, peering around the door. But she did not see the Marq'ssan in the hallway. In fact she saw nothing in the hallway, for the hall lights had been turned off. Kay drew a shallow, shaky breath. Had Sorben overheard Goodwin's remarks to her?

The lights in the apartment went out. Swearing half under his breath, Goodwin savagely kicked the door open. "I said nothing to warn her," Kay said, fearful he would shoot her now out of frustration.

He slammed Kay back into the wall, and she cried out at the pain she took in her elbow. "Hughes and Pickens," he hissed, "get out in the hallway: Hughes to the left, Pickens to the right— and find her." Kay heard them rush past and heard Goodwin speak again, presumably into his transmitter: "We're having problems up here. The alien has given us the slip. I want everyone on the doors ready for her when she comes out. Clear?"

Three *understoods* were given in rapid succession. Kay wondered how many people they had on this operation besides those in the van. How had they organized it so quickly? About half a second after the third *understood* had been uttered, the door to the hallway slammed shut. "Who closed the door?" Goodwin called out. "Babcock? Are you there?"

Kay edged along the wall, hoping the lights would not come on again. She might be able to elude them for a while at least, perhaps until someone heard the commotion and decided to investigate or call the Women's Patrol.

"Yes, sir," Babcock responded. The thin beam of a flashlight moved out of the kitchen.

"Did *you* shut the door?"

"No, sir."

"Why the fuck haven't you got the lights working?"

"I found the circuit panel, sir, but re-setting the switches had no effect. I don't know what's caused the blackout. Maybe it's a generator problem."

"No. It was too timely. Keep trying, Babcock. Shit. It's Morgan we need here, not a damned chemist."

"Sorry, sir."

"Goddam it, Zeldin," Goodwin said menacingly. "Where are you? I know you didn't get out the door. It wasn't possible. You would have had to get by me."

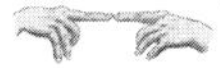

Kay stood very still. She would crawl behind the couch, she decided. The couch was good cover. If only there were a way she could get some kind of a weapon first. She thought longingly of the .45 in the drawer of her bedside table.

"What the hell?" Goodwin cried. "My god, what, how—" There was a thud and a confusion of footsteps. "Babcock, give me your weapon!"

"Keep hold of my hand," Sorben said softly, her lips brushing Kay's ear. The Marq'ssan took her hand. Kay's spirit leaped with hope, sending a surge of adrenalin through her body. "We're going to get out of here before the others get back."

"I can't find my weapon, sir!"

Kay moved as Sorben directed her. She heard the door snick open; they kept walking and turned, and Kay knew they must be in the hallway. "The pod is on the roof," Sorben whispered. She led Kay into the dark stairwell. "I had to disable the lights."

"There'll probably be someone on the roof ready to grab us," Kay said.

"It doesn't matter. Remember the last time?"

Kay remembered and knew it was unlikely that anyone would see them, especially not at night when Sorben's powers of camouflage were greatest.

As Sorben had predicted, they made it to the pod undetected. The Marq'ssan destructured the handcuffs and Kay strapped herself in. The pod lifted, and Kay looked at Sorben in the dawning interior light. She said, "They wanted to kill you, you know."

"Not kill me," Sorben said, "but capture me."

"Capture you?" Kay said blankly. "But— but they couldn't have!"

Sorben shrugged. "You know that, but they apparently did not. I distinctly heard one of them remind another that they were not to risk killing me. Who were they, Kay?"

"SIC officers," Kay said.

"Oh," Sorben said. "Them again."

"Yes, them. They're still trying."

"Then we'll have to do something about that, won't we," Sorben said matter-of-factly.

Kay sighed in contentment. She liked the sound of that "we." It lifted a tremendous burden from her that she hadn't known she had been shouldering. "Yes," she said. "I think we will."

Chapter Seven

[i]

Allison rode a fruit truck into Seattle. This last leg of her trip proved far less demanding than earlier hitches because the driver, a Honduran man who had been in the Yakima Valley on a migrant work permit at the time of the Blanket, took only the slightest notice of her. He spoke little to her and unlike one other of the male drivers she had gotten rides with had expressed no sexual interest in her. Allison thus felt secure enough to doze for most of the road through the Cascades as one lively salsa tune after another poured out of the cab's home-made speakers. She had gotten little sleep since being dropped over the border in Southeastern Oregon and craved a bath and bed. She only hoped her controller wouldn't insist on debriefing her the second she walked through the door.

The driver dropped her near the Mercer Street exit on I-5, leaving her to walk along the edge of the roadway through the tunnel that comprised the major portion of the exit ramp. Once on the surface she easily located a data kiosk. But then, realizing she faced a difficulty she hadn't anticipated, she stood staring at both the terminal and the phone, stymied. Plastic would not work, and she had no credit in the Free Zone. How could she make the call she needed to make to let the station know she had arrived?

Experimenting, she donned the phone's headset and punched in the number. The outside speaker produced a mechanical instruction to either specify collect or give the necessary trade-credit authorization by thumbprint. Allison specified collect. "Collect from whom?" the speaker's mechanical voice queried. "From Bennett," Allison said.

Almost immediately she heard a rhythmic buzz through the headset's speaker. After her brief taste of the state of communications tech in California, such a high level of efficiency surprised her. Her call was accepted and she was told to hold. After about thirty seconds a male voice spoke: "Have you been in touch with the anesthesiologist lately?"

Allison thought for a couple of seconds. "Yes," she replied. "In fact I sent her a bouquet of flowers. She has a passion for dahlias."

"And they cost the earth." She heard a distinct grumble in the voice. "Where are you, Bennett?"

"Just off the I-5 Mercer Street exit."

"Ninety-five minutes from now, northeast corner of Mercer and Queen Anne Avenue North. Just keep moving west, Bennett. The walk is under half an hour." He broke the connection, and Allison replaced the headset. Something had gone wrong with Zeldin and he was warning her to expect trouble. With Lauder? Or with other interested parties? She would have to move with extra care.

It was Sunday but didn't *feel* like it. Allison sighed: oh for one of those lovely Sundays in Vienna with Margarete. Less than a month ago they'd enjoyed one. But that was another world, forever lost.

Allison slipped on her pack and made a final check of the street. She caught no one lingering, spotted no familiar postures or gaits. It was time to move on.

[ii]

Martha drew a deep breath, picked up the phone, and tapped in the number. When Louise did not answer, Martha admitted to herself that she was relieved. Though she would have forced herself to go even if Louise had been there, she much preferred packing with Louise out. Of course, by the time she had walked there Louise might have come home. But that was unlikely. Louise had probably gone out for the day, or might even be out of town— on Women's Patrol business.

Or on Night Patrol business.

"I'll be back for my bicycle tomorrow," Martha said to Jeannie. "Thanks again for letting me crash here."

"If Louise calls, do you want your whereabouts kept secret?" Jeannie asked. Martha had told her she and Louise had had a "serious, irreconcilable quarrel."

"Not necessary." Martha attempted a smile. "I'm sure Louise will be as interested in avoiding me as I am in avoiding her."

"Take care, Martha. I'll probably be home by seven."

They hugged, and Martha set off for Belltown. It occurred to her that if she had followed her original timetable she would have just been getting into Seattle now. She would not have stumbled on Louise's involvement with the Night Patrol, and she and Louise would still be together. Thinking about this, Martha decided that despite the pain it had brought her, she couldn't regret her new knowledge of Louise. She would eventually have found out. Better sooner than later; better this than some other way. And to think that Louise had believed that she, Martha, had known all along…

Martha stared at the Cascades, sharp against the intensely blue sky. What a waste of beautiful weather. Rain would have been infinitely more suited to her mood.

[iii]

Facing fifty-five minutes to kill before the arranged contact, Allison chose to hang out at the Seattle Center. Despite its familiar architecture, it bore surprisingly little resemblance to the site she remembered, which had been all sleazy game arcades, food courts, and virtual-reality parlors the last time she'd seen it. The game arcades had gone, and the many vendors' booths and tables and musicians performing gave it a market-fair atmosphere. Eavesdropping on two women bargaining, Allison recalled the reports she had read about Seattle's "neo-barter economy" (as one analyst termed it). The range of items being sold surprised her. She recalled the San Jose service-techs' lamentations about clothing and cosmetics and wondered at the disparity. Of course none of it was anything that Allison would personally care to wear. Yet it did offer some choice for service-techs.

After ten or so minutes of wandering through the Seattle Center, Allison noticed that about only half of the women around her were dressed as she was, although the women differently appareled were also clearly service-techs. They wore loose-fitting garments of comfortable fabrics, rough cotton or cotton-blend weaves, including denim, which Allison associated with service-tech dress, but not tightly

binding. Seeing this alternative service-tech style, Allison grew increasingly uncomfortable with her own appearance and began to feel she looked as though she were deliberately trying to draw attention to her sexuality by wearing such clothes in a place where there were alternatives. Perhaps she would be able to wear some of the more comfortable-looking clothes herself. Unless the women wearing them had some special background not assimilable to her cover?

At the north end of the Seattle Center Allison came upon a chamber orchestra performing Bach in the open air. A sign requesting donations stood propped beside a terminal, but no one seemed to pay attention to her arrival or her sitting on the grass. Allison had often gone to open-air concerts in European parks, but never without forking over a hefty admission charge (which price had usually included an elegantly packed picnic basket). She had not expected concerts in public parks in American cities, much less free concerts in a place like Seattle. And Bach? What were all these service-techs doing listening to *Bach?* Allison leaned back on her hands and let herself be drawn into the concerto, the tempo of which felt a little fast to her ear. The remaining movements flew by, eating up time and soothing her irritability. And when the concert ended, Allison stood up, hefted her pack onto her back, and headed for the intersection to verify her precontact security.

She was in place when the minivan pulled up at the arranged corner fifteen minutes later. The driver released the passenger door, and Allison climbed in. "Get into the back please, Ms. Bennett," the woman said, "so no one will see you." Allison dropped onto the plush bench behind the driver's seat, confident that the driver's head-rest would conceal her from windshield-view. "By the way, I'm Dana Pickens," the woman said as they pulled away from the curb.

"Hi, Dana. Good to meet you. Call me Allison if you like."

Dana spoke after about a minute of silence. "You'll find things a little tense today."

"I gather that something's gone wrong with Operation Dahlia?"

"We lost Dahlia."

"*Lost* her? In what sense do you mean *lost?*"

"We captured her on Friday, but it was decided that night on only an hour's notice to throw together an operation for capturing an alien. It flopped, and Dahlia escaped."

Allison wished she could see the service-tech's face. "I can't say this sounds like anything I was briefed on."

The minivan sped up the ramp and entered the interstate. "Frankly, things around here aren't in general like anything you'd expect. But you'll have to judge that for yourself. I'm new with this team. Maybe I just don't understand. Or maybe I plain don't fit."

Allison didn't like the tone of that. Lauder had such a fantastic reputation it seemed unlikely he'd be so inept as to allow the development of disaffection in team service-techs.

At the Edmonds exit they left the interstate and headed west. "What beautiful country," Allison said of the blue sky, mountains, and green pines surrounding them. "I can't remember ever seeing so many trees in one place."

"The Pacific Northwest is full of forests," Dana said. "Something to do with the wind, I guess. It rarely blows west here, which means they didn't get hit with as much of those pollutions that have wiped out trees in most other places. They've got other pollutions, of course, but not those."

"Which means this area has a resource in high demand," Allison said thoughtfully.

"Right. After the Withdrawal the executives were run out of the lumber facilities and the workers in those industries took them over. They do business through the Zone Co-op."

"You seem fairly up on the subject."

"You think someone like me wouldn't be able to understand things like that?"

"Not at all," Allison said, noting the sensitivity. "I was just wondering why you should be up on these particular details. So economically oriented."

"We have an analyst on the team who is endlessly fascinated by Twilight Zone economics," Dana said. "And he's about the only person who talks to me."

"Oh," Allison said. More sensitivity. She would have to make Dana her special assignment. It sounded as though Lauder might have some serious problems.

Dana turned the minivan onto a narrow, winding road and after about three kilometers took an even narrower road that forked to the right. After another half a kilometer, the van halted at a gatehouse. This visible evidence that executive enclaves still existed in the Free Zone gave Allison a lift. The guard quickly passed them through the gate, and Allison saw that the road on the other side of the gatehouse was wider, smoother, straighter. "Almost there," Dana said.

"Are most of the houses in here occupied?"

"No. About ninety percent are empty. What executive in his right mind would want to live in the Twilight Zone? The ones here now are all here for a purpose. Mainly running holding operations."

Of course. They needed to keep as much property as possible guarded and out of the hands of marauders— for when the Zone fell. This kind of property, the places hidden away and well-guarded, would be the easiest to protect. Looting seemed unlikely at industrial facilities taken over by workers, which meant those facilities would probably be intact when the Executive had gotten the area under control again. But private residences? One could not imagine them being left alone. Revolutionaries had a history of spoiling private property for sheer spite.

The van stopped at an electronic barrier. Dana waited. After ten seconds the van's terminal chimed. Dana drove up a long wooded driveway, past the house to the garage. "We're here," she said, poking her head around her seat to look at Allison.

"Thank god," Allison said. "I'm dying for a bath."

Dana laughed. "Women executives are so predictable."

Allison returned the service-tech's smile and noticed how attractive the otherwise dour and sallow face became in the smile's glow. This assignment might not be so bad, after all.

[iv]

Martha stuffed her backpack as full as she could get it and tied miscellaneous articles onto the frame. How many trips would she

have to make, carrying her things this way? But without a car or public transport this was really the only way to do it. Each trip back would increase the risk of running into Louise. But that couldn't be helped.

Martha was almost at the point of lifting the pack onto her back when there was a knock on the door. Reluctantly she opened it— and stared, speechless with astonishment.

"Hey, Martha. How're you doing?"

Martha stepped back to let the Marq'ssan in. "Okay, I guess." Sorben crossed the threshold, and Martha closed the door.

Sorben gave her a searching look. "Anything you'd like to talk about?"

Martha hesitated. Sorben would understand her revulsion at Louise's activities. But it might not be right to tell her. It seemed like tattling to an authority, for Sorben would regard the matter as gravely as Martha did, and Sorben was a sort of mentor to them all. "It's personal," Martha said, feeling disingenuous. "I'm moving out. Louise and I have an irreconcilable difference."

"Sorry to hear that," Sorben said. "Still, these things happen. And you and Louise are very different."

"Want to sit down?" Martha asked but suddenly aware of the oddity of Sorben's dropping in, added, "Is this a social visit, or is there something you wanted to discuss?"

The Marq'ssan sat down on the couch, pulled her legs up, and crossed them. "I came to see Louise. But it concerns you just as much as it does Louise, in that it concerns everyone in the Free Zone."

Martha took the armchair. "What is it?"

"It seems there are numerous spies from various governments hanging around this Free Zone. And those from the Security faction of the Executive are making particular trouble in Seattle. Friday morning they abducted Kay Zeldin."

Martha took the news like a punch to the gut. "No shit!" She stared at Sorben and tried to think. She couldn't help recalling what those people had done to Susan for doubling. "What are we going to do?"

"Don't worry, Kay's safe now. They administered some sort of "truth" drug and discovered I was going to be picking her up at her apartment Friday at midnight. So they tried to set a trap to capture me. Naturally I foiled it and freed Kay."

Martha let out her breath. "They tried to capture *you?* Sorben, what are we going to do? I've always been afraid they'd go after you and Magyyt and the others. They know that without you around—"

"Don't be absurd, Martha. If you think about it, you'll realize they might be able to kill us— if we're not careful— but they could never capture us."

Martha drew a deep breath. "Yes, I suppose— well, yeah, you would know about that. I'm never sure about you Marq'ssan, you know." Never sure of what they could or could not do. "But if they set out to kill you—"

"Don't worry about *us*, Martha," Sorben said. "It's the Free Zone that needs your concern. Kay thinks they must have a fairly large contingent here. They had her under surveillance for at least a month before they abducted her. And their surveillance was so close that they had transcripts of many of her conversations."

Martha clasped her arms around herself. "It's like having ODS around again."

"I think we may want to root them out. And perhaps the others, as well."

"*What* others?"

"Those working for other governments— perhaps also with some of the same aims."

Martha wailed. "But *why*? Don't they have enough problems without worrying about us? We aren't harming anyone! Why should they even care?"

"The very existence of Free Zones are a threat to all governments, Martha," Sorben said drily.

"Oh," Martha said. "Of *course*. Before the Free Zone came into existence they could just laugh off the notion of anarchy as idealistic hogwash. And now we're trying to do the things they said were fairy

tales. But...still— things are so rough, it seems absurd of them to worry about us."

"Perhaps it's easier to oppose the Free Zone than to restore order in their own as yet undisputed territories."

"This is all we need." Martha sighed. "There are already so many other things to cope with. It's enough to make a person tired."

"Such as?"

Martha told Sorben about John Doyle's cult and about the growing pressure from men demanding "equal" power with women. But all Sorben said was, "These things were to be expected. Perhaps by the time you work them out you will have come to some critical understanding and be on your way to making your own structures. We Marq'ssan had similar problems in our history. They are nothing to get tired or discouraged over. I'm sure you'll work it out— provided you aren't distracted by the Executive's troublemakers."

"So what are we going to do about them? And how will you protect Kay? We've always known they would be gunning for her."

"That's what I wanted to talk to Louise about. I want to get the Women's Patrol in on this."

"What, to have a counter-espionage group?"

Sorben looked surprised. "I hadn't thought of that."

"Well, I don't think it's a good idea. We could be warped by such a structure," Martha said.

Sorben smiled. "If that's how you feel, you need to discuss it openly with others. And perhaps go so far as to organize a counter-strategy."

"No," Martha said quickly, imagining endless painful meetings with Louise. "I'm too busy as it is."

"Then maybe you can recommend someone who shares your perspective."

"I'll give it some thought," Martha said.

Sorben unfolded her legs and rose to her feet. "I have to be going. To Farley's next, I think. I want to get a lot of people thinking creatively and constructively about this."

"Be careful how you put it," Martha said. "We don't want to get sucked into a war mentality."

When Sorben had gone, Martha shifted the pack onto her back and then, taking hold of the doorknob, stood transfixed with amazement. She, Martha, had given a Marq'ssan advice! And Sorben hadn't mocked or snubbed her. The thought elated, then frightened her.

Get a grip, woman, she told herself as she went out into the hall. The pack was heavy and her destination was Eastlake. She had no business standing around dreaming while wearing a fifty-pound pack on her back. It was time to move on.

[v]

Staring into the bottom of her empty glass, Allison strained the limits of her peripheral vision trying to read Lauder's face without looking directly at him. She said, "I suppose it's possible she's already left town and started on the trip she had planned."

"Either that or she's out looking for us. And all six aliens with her," Goodwin said.

"Unlikely," Allison said.

"What do you know that we don't?"

The level of irritation among these executive males was uncomfortably high. It seemed to Allison that Lauder and Goodwin were close to losing it. And the younger one, Morgan, sat sardonically quiet as though none of it mattered. Allison said, "It seems to me that if she were out looking for you she'd be in obvious places hoping to have you pick up her trail. She'd be luring you to her. But since she's not, either she's hiding out from you in fear, or she's left town. And if she has six aliens at her disposal, she's not likely to be that fearful, is she." Goodwin's brow furrowed: Allison thought he might finally be taking her seriously. She risked a quick, open glance at Lauder. Lauder's eyes had glazed over. Allison wondered if he habitually drank this much scotch in one sitting.

After a long silence Goodwin spoke. "You might be right, Bennett. Part of the reason the operation went awry was our miscalculation of her psychology. She was supposed to be easily intimidated. That's what we were told from above. If we'd had any idea of how difficult she would be to manage, we would never have tried to pull off that

midnight operation on such short notice. And we would have taken our time with her."

Lauder, who hadn't said anything since they'd cleared the dinner away and started the conference, startled Allison by saying, "We should have excised the damned bitch while we had the chance."

"Orders, Henry," Goodwin reminded their controller. "We had our orders, and they were explicit about keeping her more or less intact. Somebody upstairs has something specific in mind for her."

Lauder slopped a few more fingers of scotch into his glass. "I'm aware of that, Mark. But sometimes it's best to ignore orders."

Goodwin glanced at Allison, as though at an outsider. To them she *was* an outsider. It would be a long time before they'd trust her as a team player. "But the point now is to find her," Goodwin said. "It might actually be easier if she's left the Twilight Zone than if she's still here. If she's in Security territory and she passes any kind of scanner, she's had it. If her purpose in traveling is to recruit scientists and to find her spouse, she'll be primarily engaged with professionals. Which means she won't find it easy to avoid scanners."

"Couldn't she be fed a false lead about where her spouse is?" Allison asked.

"That might be good bait, but how will you get the lead to her?"

Allison shrugged. "Circulate rumors among the scientists she's trying to recruit."

Goodwin stroked his beard. "That's a possibility." He looked at Lauder. "What do you think, Henry?" Allison wondered if he seriously expected an answer.

"Go ahead," Lauder said. "It's worked in other situations. She's not *that* smart."

"And in the meantime, we'll keep beating the bushes for her in Seattle," Goodwin said. "And you, Bennett, will get yourself established. At the very least you should get yourself on one of their committees and attend their Steering Committee meeting. Which is three weeks from now. Zeldin will probably be back for that meeting, too. All the leaders attend these meetings and probably at least one alien will be there."

Allison poured more wine into her glass. Because Zeldin wasn't there to be handled, her assignment had changed in emphasis. In the morning she would be leaving the enclave and returning to Seattle to make contact with the women who were running things— to live among them, to get work among them, and to sit on their committees. It would be uncomfortable and strenuous living in constant alienated cover, but the rewards would be immense if she could manage to infiltrate the leaders' circle. But no more baths, no more twenty-year-old wines with dinner. If they had managed Zeldin properly when they had her, this new assignment wouldn't even be necessary. Allison wondered how Elizabeth would take the news of the fuck-up. Would heads roll? Allison doubted that Lauder's would be among them if they did.

"Do you think it will be possible to run Zeldin once we've recovered her?" Allison queried.

Goodwin's eyes smoldered. "There's no one who can't be run."

Allison saw he was serious. She sipped her wine. "Have you read her book?" she said softly, hoping Lauder wouldn't hear.

"That's why I'm so sure of her," Goodwin said.

Allison did not follow that at all. "I must have missed something when I read it," she said. But she had read it before she'd known about the assignment, solely out of curiosity. She could have missed any number of things.

"I'll discuss it with you another time," Goodwin said. Allison wondered if she was imagining Goodwin's eyes flicking meaningly at Lauder.

Allison looked at Morgan. "What's your opinion, Morgan?"

He looked surprised. "*My* opinion? I only saw her for about an hour sum total. And she wasn't talking much then. I did see her attempt to break when we were trying to load her into the van. Based on that, I'd say she's tough. She didn't seem at all fazed by the fact that two of us had weapons aimed directly at her. But then I hit her with a paralytic, and she became just another piece of meat." He snorted. "It's a nuisance having to paint the maxi-van just because she eyeballed it. *My* take is that it wouldn't surprise me if *she* were hunting

us while keeping low herself. To take us by surprise. To sic the aliens on us all at once. Why would she put herself up as bait if she thinks she can find us anyway?"

"Morgan thinks we should have implanted a tracer subcutaneously while we had her under," Goodwin said. His tone of voice was openly snide and sneering. "He thinks gadgetry conquers all. Whether it's practical or not."

Did they always bicker this way? Or was this simply the effect of demoralization following a major setback?

"But then Morgan's main purpose in life is getting hold of alien technology." Allison took another sip of wine. How much longer would this "conference" drag on?

"That about covers it for now, wouldn't you say, Henry?" Goodwin asked, looking at the controller.

"Yeah." Lauder's speech was slurring and mumbled. "That about covers it." He stared at Allison. "Unless you have any questions, Bennett?"

Allison shook her head. "No, sir." She had no questions for Lauder, certainly, though she had a few each for Goodwin and Morgan—but separately.

"Then you can go." His dismissal of her was the clearest and most controlled thing he had said or done all evening. Allison rose from the table, nodded at the men, and left the room. Now what? Would the three of them sit and drink until they were semi-comatose? Allison glided through the house to her room. The slackness was appalling. No wonder the Executive had fallen into the mess it was in: if many men of Lauder's caliber had gone down the tubes, it would be a miracle if the whole damned country didn't fall to the aliens.

Lying in bed between cool cotton sheets, it occurred to Allison that that could really, actually happen. But she did not pursue this negative thought. Instead she closed her eyes, subvocalized the syllable, and dropped instantly into sleep.

[vi]

"I can't say I'm surprised," Laura said when Martha had finished telling her what Sorben had said. "But frankly, I think spies and assas-

sins are less a threat than our other problems." Laura poured tea into her cup. "More for you, Martha?"

Martha shook her head. She didn't care for many herb teas, and this bedtime mixture she found especially loathsome. "The Birth Limitation issue at least is clear," she said.

Laura's silky black eyebrows rose. "It is?"

"Isn't it?" Martha said. "It's clear that we have no business telling people whether they can reproduce or not. If we aren't a government, that makes it all the less our business, though most of us have always argued that such a thing is no government's business, anyway. Deliberately altering people's bodies is an intolerable invasion of privacy. The only question I see is to what extent any of us needs to be involved in undoing this mechanism of control. As far as I can make out, I don't think we have the specific obligation. If someone wants to take on such a project, that's something else. But I don't see it as anyone's business to decide who, what, or when."

"Martha, Martha, what about practicalities?" Laura tapped her finger against her cup. "This *has* been a public issue and a governmentally controlled concern. I'm not sure it's as easy as you make it out to be. What about the medical problems? And the problem of feeding a soaring population? And the problem of religious fundamentalists and other cultie types taking over the Zone if this is the only place on the continent where they can procreate at will?"

Martha pushed her cup, still half-full of the smelly, yellow tea, toward the center of the table. "I don't think we should be thinking in such terms. We've taken what many have called a non-practical approach to disbanding the legal system and other important institutions. I don't see why we have to start playing at government in this one concern merely because it seems practical. Most people said breaking up the Seattle Police Department was the most dangerous thing we could do. They called it impractical idealism. Well, some people are changing their minds now. By the same token, the procreation issue may seem impossible to you looking at it from a conventional perspective. But I think that if we let things take their course we'll be able to deal with whatever problems arise. We can *handle* this cultie

business. I don't like having to talk to people like John Doyle, but he doesn't frighten me."

"He frightens me," Laura said.

Martha searched Laura's dark, almond-shaped eyes. "You're serious," she said. "He really does frighten you? And you haven't even met him."

"His type frightens me. Doesn't it scare you when one person does all the talking for everyone around him?"

"I can think of things more scary than John Doyle," Martha said.

"What about demands for equal power for men?" Laura asked. "I suppose you consider that a minor problem, too."

"It's probably a more serious problem than the procreation issue. I think the first step is clear, though: we have got to get some talking going. I don't mean bringing men into Steering Committee meetings, but forming some sort of mediating structure that will help us work on this problem together. I don't hold with the separatist ideas I've been hearing around. Those ideas frighten me, Laura, more than John Doyle ever could. We don't need that kind of polarization. Men against women, that sort of thing, will end up getting us killed. While we could probably deal with the men if they organized a violent takeover, I don't know how many women we'd lose if they organized something not so overtly violent. My guess is that most women in the Zone sympathize with the men and think the exclusion is unfair."

"Most women," Laura repeated. "You mean the ones who aren't involved in the committees, the ones who aren't participating." Her teeth worried at her lower lip. "That suggests something in itself, doesn't it."

Martha nodded. "I think that's a problem potentially greater than any of the others we've been discussing."

"Let's hope the Executive's spies don't understand that," Laura said drily.

"Hah. They're too busy trying to capture Marq'ssan."

Laura grinned. "A nice harmless occupation."

Martha pushed back her chair and stood up. "I'm for bed," she said. "I'm reporting to the committee tomorrow, which means I'll need to be clearheaded." She yawned. "Do I need to be specially quiet when I go upstairs?"

"Only Lena gets up at the crack of dawn, and she's a sound sleeper. There's no need to walk around on tiptoe. Just don't sing or yell."

"Then good-night, Laura."

"Good-night, Martha. Sleep well."

Martha quietly shut the door to the kitchen and went up the stairs to her new room. She would read before trying to sleep. After two nights of near-sleeplessness she should find it easy to drop off. Though she doubted that she would.

Chapter Eight

[i]

Kay followed Glen Boren into the dark alley. Why so much slinking around? No one had required it of her in Madison, and to all apparent appearances, Champaign-Urbana, though squarely in the middle of Military Territory and effectively cut off from the rest of the world, was under less real surveillance than Madison, where Security forces controlled the city and capitol and university campuses with a nervously clenched fist. Was Boren paranoid? Or did he simply not trust most of the people in his community? In Madison many of the people she had met were rebellious at Security's heavy-handed authority. Were people in Champaign-Urbana collaborators, either contented or timid, who would inform on their neighbors at the faintest suggestion of trouble?

They left the alley to enter the yard of a rambling old house shimmering palely in the moonlight. Kay sniffed the air and recognized the smell of tomato plants.

Boren halted. "Nan lives on the top floor. You can see her light." He pointed to a small, third-floor window, which showed light behind its shade. "We'll take the back stairs. Nod at anyone we might happen to pass." He looked her over. "It probably won't matter if anyone sees you in this house. But to be on the safe side, we had better not talk until we're inside Nan's room."

They went up the steps and into the house; their feet clattered and shuffled on the bare wood. A weak naked bulb at the top of the stairwell barely revealed the decrepit stained paper patching the walls. What was a mathematician doing living in such ruin? Surely she could afford something better?

The stuffiness of the stairwell almost choked Kay. Of course it was bound to be hot in Illinois in August. But the heat had gotten trapped in the stale, airless space, surely needlessly considering the tightly closed windows they were passing. At the top of the stairs the hallway, graced with a mottled, ratty, mildewed-smelling carpet, stretched the length of the house. Boren stopped before the first of the hallway's three doors and knocked. After about fifteen seconds the door opened outward, scraping with difficulty over the filthy rug. The door, Kay thought, must have warped long ago.

Dark bleak eyes in a thin sunken face stared out at them. "Come in," the woman whispered; and she stepped back. Boren and Kay entered, and the woman shut the door and fastened several bolts and chains to lock it. The bolts and chains disturbed Kay more than anything she had seen that night.

They sat on battered furniture that looked as though it had been shredded by cat claws. Kay had hoped for a breath of air once they had escaped the stairwell, but the room seemed just as stuffy and hot. Discrete drops of sweat continually formed between her breasts and trickled down her abdomen; already she could smell the perspiration wetting the fabric under her arms. She craved water and hoped this woman would offer them some.

"This is Kay Zeldin, Nan," Boren said in a low voice. "She's a historian, from Seattle. You may remember she was involved in the initial negotiations with the aliens?" The woman shrugged her painfully scrawny shoulders. Boren looked at Kay. "Zeldin, this is Nan Ramosh." Boren looked at Ramosh. "Your name was on a list Zeldin has." At the mathematician's look of alarm, Boren rushed on, "A list of scientists and spouses of scientists who are missing."

Intense fear and hostility settled into the other woman's face and posture. "Take me off your list," she whispered harshly. "Are you trying to get me in trouble?"

Kay said, "They have my spouse somewhere," she said. "He...he's an electrical engineer. And I don't know if he's alive or dead."

The other woman made a choking sound which could have been either a sob or a laugh. "What do you want with me?"

"I want to find the missing," Kay said softly. She leaned forward, suddenly desperate to make contact with this woman. "Keeping quiet and doing nothing won't help. I'm going to look until I find them. They must be somewhere. The Executive wouldn't have rounded them all up and discarded them: they're too valuable, especially now that the country's technology is in a shambles. Electrical engineers and other scientists are essential to the government's recovering power."

Though her gaze never moved from Kay's, the mathematician seemed inaccessible. She said, "There will be no recovery for anything. We must not think in such terms, for all that is lost. All that can be hoped for is bare survival."

The dingy hot gloom of the room, the glare of the naked bulb dangling from a cord in the ceiling, pressed on Kay, tempting her with the thought that this woman might be correct. But an image of the Pike Place Market as Kay had seen it two weeks earlier wafted into her mind like a breath of air. Flowers, people were vending flowers in the Pike Place Market. Ramosh's notion of bare survival was a nightmare: and like a nightmare its truth wasn't necessarily the apparent one the dreamer first perceived. Kay said. "I know that's not so. I've seen new life. In Seattle we have gone beyond accepting such limitations."

Ramosh's mouth twisted in derision. "So you are one of the crazy dreamers who believe they can start a new world." Her voice neatly categorized Kay. "I've read about your 'Free Zone.' How long will it be before you discover what fools you are? Either the aliens have deluded you or you have deluded yourselves— and will be forced by the rest of the world to come to terms with reality." At Kay's lifting her hand in protest, Ramosh said, "No, no, I don't say you are necessarily the aliens' dupe. But it hardly matters which is the case. Reality will catch up with you."

"Reality being the Executive?"

The other woman shrugged.

"What do you think of the Executive Plan now?" Kay asked. Though she had not noticed it at first, the room smelled rank, fetid even, as though the air were weighted down with disease-bearing spores. A compulsion to gag gripped her throat.

"The Executive Plan has become irrelevant," Ramosh said. "As any sort of long-term program must. The point now is restoring order, keeping people fed and from killing one another." She stared down at the floor, then looked up swiftly to catch Kay staring at her face. "Have you heard about life in Chicago and its environs? Only the executives can do something about that." Her mouth twisted with disdain, probably for Kay's look of disgust. "That's what your aliens have done. They've created the chaos in which people not only starve but routinely assault and kill one another."

"And you of course think your own situation infinitely better." Kay glanced around the squalid room with its dirt-encrusted wallpaper, its stained upholstery, its slimy matted olive shag rug. "Living a privileged professional life."

"I choose to live here," Ramosh snapped. "I voluntarily gave up my apartment. No one forces me to live here."

Kay looked at Boren. "A nice pleasant place to live. I guess I'd give up a comfortable, clean, well-secured apartment for a room like this any day. It's obvious that the service-techs have been living better than us all along. Why—"

"Stop it!" Ramosh cried. Instantly she clapped her hand over her mouth in alarm and looked nervously around the room as though expecting to encounter a suddenly-aroused hostile presence. "You have no right saying such things to me," she whispered. "You don't know anything about me. How dare you come in here and criticize and endanger me like this!"

Kay recoiled from the whispered vehemence. "I'm sorry, Ramosh," she whispered back. "But I had no idea my mere talking to you would put you in danger. My general idea was that it was I who would be endangered, not you. Whom do you fear? And why are we whispering?"

Ramosh looked at Boren. "Why, Glen? Why did you bring her here?"

Kay wondered why he hadn't warned her. He had greeted Kay easily enough, one historian to another, as though little had changed since the last AHA conference two years ago, had looked at her list and said, "Sure, I can put you in touch with these people." He had

explained that Nan Ramosh fell into both categories of persons Kay was interested in contacting. But he had said nothing to warn her of Ramosh's likely hostility to such an approach.

"I think you should talk to her, Nan. You can't go on like this. You're destroying yourself. And you know they'll find you eventually."

"What did you tell her?"

He shook his head. "I told her nothing. But I think you should let her help you."

Ramosh's gaze darted to Kay's face, then back to Boren's. "No," she said. "When they catch me, they catch me. John won't be endangered even when that happens. In fact, he'll be safer than he is now. How do I know they aren't punishing him for my crime?"

"You mean you'd rather risk being killed or put in a camp than going somewhere free?" Boren said incredulously.

"Free? What do you know about what goes on in the so-called Free Zone? She's feeding you lies."

"This woman has been my colleague for years," Boren said, gesturing toward Kay. "I know her well enough to be sure of certain things about her." Kay doubted he would continue to think that after he had read the copy of her book she had given him. "It comes down to simple survival, Nan. Either you live or you die. If you stay here, you'll die. I guess you don't really believe that, though. Otherwise you'd be desperate to escape."

Her dark eyes blazed. "I have friends here," she hissed. "Whereas I wouldn't have any resources if I left. Consider that!"

"How long do you think your friends will be able to help you?" Boren shot back. Kay noted the lightning flash of fear in Ramosh's face that vanished as suddenly as it had appeared. "And how long is it before someone stops you and scans you or asks to see your plastic?" Boren continued. "How long before someone else in this house attracts the Military police? Don't kid yourself, Nan." Boren's voice had become angry, hard, grating. "It's only a matter of time."

Ramosh's head dropped into her hands. Kay looked away from the sight of the painful paroxysms wracking the mathematician's body and wished Boren would go to her and put his arms around her and comfort her. But she understood that he must think this attack his best strategy for deploying his concern. After a long time, Ramosh sat up, and Kay saw that her eyes were dry but fervid. "You mean I'm endangering all of you," she said to Boren. "That's really what's happened." The words jerked out of her breathless, erratic, stammering. "Eventually they'll try to get me through you. When they find out who my friends are, they'll go after you, hound you, follow you, until they find me. Mine is a crime they won't allow to pass. They'll have to find me. You're right: it's only a matter of time. Perhaps the best thing for me to do is to turn myself in. Then no one else will be hurt."

Kay struggled against impatience; she reminded herself that the stress Ramosh had been living under had likely taken a heavy toll. "Am I to understand that you don't regard the Free Zone as an alternative?" she asked. When Ramosh did not answer, Kay looked at Boren. "Does she think we're worse than the Executive?"

Ramosh glared at Kay. "The so-called Free Zone may have an edge now since the aliens who destroyed everything decent and plunged us into chaos are helping those who betrayed humanity. You may not be so much deceiving me as deluded in your own perceptions, Zeldin." She leaned forward. "Do you know what I think is happening?"

Trying not to draw back from Ramosh's glazed, bleak stare, Kay shook her head. The room had been suffocating to begin with, but the mathematician's intensity felt like a hand clutching at Kay's throat, threatening to strangle her. The urge to flight pressed on her nerves.

"The aliens are collecting the humans they intend to rule through," Ramosh stated in a flat staccato whisper. "They have nearly destroyed all existing governments. Under the weight of terrible adversity the remnants of order are breaking down, and desperate from hunger and violence and the ravages of the breakdown, the general population is growing increasingly vulnerable to the control of a new rule. You yourself, Zeldin, possibly unwittingly, are recruiting cadre for this new rule. The aliens think that humanity, finally admitting defeat, will accept their rule with open arms." A dry humorless laugh rasped in her throat. "But the aliens have miscalculated. They don't understand human psychology. Some of us will never give in, no matter

how terrible things become. We are indomitable. Thus rather than sell out to the aliens for whatever paradise you think to promise me, I would rather live like this. Or in a detention camp. For I still retain a sense of loyalty to my species and civilization."

Ramosh's bitterness and intensity, her very victim-ness, struck such chords of pathos and fear in Kay that she sat almost numb in speechless paralysis.

"For god's sake, Nan, you don't believe all that nonsense the government has been putting out?" Boren exclaimed. "It's propaganda, it's all preposterous disinformation! If the aliens had wanted to rule the earth they would never have gone about it in such a clumsy, indirect way! They would have taken over during that first year! They could have wiped out a whole city as easily as they wiped out the satellites and nuclear weapons! But they didn't!" Boren rose to his feet and went to the window. Lifting the shade a fraction, he peered out into the night. After half a minute he returned to the couch. "Nan, your real enemy is Military. You've got to get out of here. Go somewhere else, not necessarily the Free Zone. But you can't stay here."

"It's not possible to go anywhere else!" Ramosh's voice grew shrill with alarm. "At least here my friends make it possible for me to live without plastic."

Kay clasped her sweaty hands over her cotton-clad knees and cleared her throat. She would try another tack. "Who owns this house?" she asked.

Ramosh looked puzzled. "What do you mean?"

"Do you own it yourself? Or do any of the other people living here own it?"

Ramosh's stare was suspicious, but she said, "Of course none of us owns it. Would people who had to live in a dump like this own real estate?"

"Then who does?"

Ramosh shrugged. "I've got no idea. We each pay rent to an agency that handles all the business details pertaining to this house for the owner."

"How do you pay? By plastic? Or through some other means?"

"My friends pay for me, using their plastic, of course." Ramosh said. "Any other way would be illegal."

Kay met Ramosh's burning dark eyes. "Did you know that ninety percent of all real estate in this country is owned by executives?"

"I don't believe that!"

"It's true. It's almost certain that this house is owned by an executive." When the other woman did not respond, Kay said, "In Seattle almost no one pays rent. In most cases there's no one to pay rent to since the executives owned almost everything and have for the most part gone, leaving the real estate for all practical purposes ownerless. Oh, in a few places the executives have left armed guards whom they employ to keep squatters out. But mostly there's no rent and no ownership. None of us realized how big a share of the pie the executives really had." Kay smiled. "How many professionals do you know who own their own apartment or house? Or own real estate they rent out to others?"

Ramosh's eyes flickered. "That's a red herring. The real point is that the aliens managed to crash the world economic system and in some places have succeeded so well in their disruptions that all respect for private property has vanished along with respect for public order and decency."

Kay looked at Boren. "You didn't tell me she's an executive-lover."

"Just someone who appreciated the Good Life before the aliens came and ruined everything," Ramosh said irritably.

Kay wiped the sweat from her nose and cheeks. She couldn't last much longer in here. The conversation felt in some way insane, distorted, bizarre. What was it they had been talking about? "The missing scientists," Kay said, realizing that here was the real crux that had somehow slipped from her mind. "The missing scientists: what did the Executive do with them, and why did they take them in the first place?"

Ramosh's face closed down. Kay waited for her to speak, but in vain.

The silence drove Kay to speak again. "Don't you see, Ramosh? Don't you see that it's the Executive that has a nefarious purpose!

Several thousands of people have disappeared, and no one knows where or why! My spouse told me he couldn't tell me the reason, just that he'd been recruited for some project Washington wanted set up. Why hasn't anyone seen these people since they were first spirited away?" Kay's voice cracked with emotion. Softly, she said, "Maybe they've killed them all, Ramosh. Maybe they're all dead. Maybe—"

"No!" Ramosh shrieked, her voice shocking after the suppressed, hushed ferocity of the last half hour. She stood on frail legs and pointed to the door. "Get out of here. Now."

Kay rose and went to the door: she could not get out of the room fast enough. "Contact Boren if you change your mind," she said as she fumbled with the bolts and chains locking the door.

What was her "crime?" Kay wondered as she and Boren sped down the stairs. What emotional and physical extremity had driven Ramosh into such a twisted and defeated state of mind?

When they reached the bottom of the stairs and escaped into the open, Kay gulped in great breaths of the hot, humid air, perceiving it as refreshing rather than muggy. A half hour in that room upstairs had been enough to make almost any air outside its confines seem salubrious. The Free Zone, she was beginning to think, would look like paradise when she returned to it. And people said Champaign-Urbana was one of the better places in this country to be!

Kay began to dread the rest of her trip.

[ii]

Martha gasped when a certain, entirely unexpected bespectacled face bent over her in the twilight. The bicycle pump dropped from her hands and clattered onto the pavement.

"Sorry. I didn't mean to startle you," he said.

Martha hadn't seen Walter Jennings in over a year. How strange, then, to meet him in a part of town she did not associate with him. She straightened up. "I get a little nervous when I'm out in the streets alone at night," she said apologetically. "How have you been?"

"I'm glad I've run into you, Martha. It's been a long time." He paused. "As it turns out, I was just going to an address someone said

you were likely to be at. But then I saw you— I was sure it was you from half a block away. Did you get a flat?"

"You were looking for me?" Martha said warily. She tried to make out his eyes, but his glasses reflected what remained of the light back at her, and she couldn't see past the glare.

Walt dragged the toe of his right boot around and around in a pattern of small spiraling circles over the gritty pavement. "You see, I heard... I heard about your breakup with Louise. And I was wondering..." His head shifted enough that the glare no longer shielded his eyes. Martha felt sick. "But that was stupid of me, wasn't it," he said bitterly.

Martha moved her hand toward his arm but stopped when she realized her touch would not comfort him and that in fact she wanted to touch him because it would comfort herself to do so, though she did not understand why this was so. "I'm sorry, Walt. But it wasn't because of Louise that I decided to go. I told you then, but you never did believe me. I couldn't live with you now. I just couldn't."

"But why not, Martha? If it's not Louise, who is it?"

Martha stooped to retrieve the pump. "There is no one in the sense you mean. The reason is me. I need to be myself. Which means being by myself in a certain sense. I don't know how to explain it. Except that I don't think I'll ever be able to live with a man again."

"You mean you've had a conversion experience and men turn you off," Walt said flatly. "That damned bitch. She's ruined you for good, hasn't she."

Ruined her? What was he talking about? "Look, we can't talk if you're going to say things like that. I'm sexually attracted to both men and women, if that's what you mean. Just as I always was." Martha wondered if he believed her. Did it matter if he didn't? When he failed to respond, she went on. "But I don't want to live day in and day out with a man. There are too many problems, and I'm not cut out to handle them. Just leave it at that, okay?"

"You mean you'll go to bed with men but not give them the time of day? That you think of men as sex objects but not worth talking to?"

Martha grew impatient. First he complained that she wasn't physically attracted to men, and now he complained at her saying she was! "I'm giving you the time of day right now, aren't I?" she said.

"Right!" Walt snorted. "Sure. You're giving me the time of day alright. I can see that, Martha. Some anarchist you turned out to be! You women claim you don't have a government, but you're running things all the same. No man is good enough to even walk into your Steering Committee meeting, which is really the government after all, admit it, Martha."

"Don't be absurd." Martha flattened her fingers against the aluminum tube they held. "The Steering Committee is not a government. We don't tax, we don't print money, and we don't exercise police powers. Sure, we distribute food and we help organize and facilitate projects when people ask us to. But that's something very different from government. And you know damned well why men aren't allowed into the Steering Committee! Every time we've tried it they've disrupted the meeting, tried to take over, tried to dominate all discussion and even tried psychological manipulation through covert threats of violence!"

Martha realized she was shouting.

"So you say!" Walt was shouting now, too. "Well let me tell you this, Madam Executive: the only reason you can keep men from power-sharing is the Marq'ssan. Once they go, you Queen Bees will see just how powerful you are. If it weren't for the aliens—"

"If it weren't for the aliens," Martha said, "you and I would be in jail somewhere, in one of their camps! Or we'd be dead! Probably the latter! If you don't like the Free Zone, leave! No one's forcing you to stay!" Martha jammed the pump into its holder on the cross bar and wheeled her bike to face the proper direction.

Walt shoved his fists into his pockets. "You've gotten worse, Martha. I don't know why I thought you would have smartened up. When I heard you'd had the sense to leave Louise I thought you'd finally understood. Obviously I was wrong."

Martha mounted her bicycle and pedaled furiously away. There was no point in trying to talk to Walter Jennings. No point at all.

The man was hopeless.

[iii]

"You see," Glen Boren said, pouring Kay a glass of bootleg whiskey, "once they evacuated the students, the only people left were the faculty and staff of the University and local branches of the chemical industries. We're effectively isolated— you know how sparsely populated farmlands are. People aren't necessary. Or should I say, they *weren't* necessary. Unfortunately, like most processor-based technology, farming robotics are on the blink now. Which means most of us around here, whatever our professions, have to perform rudimentary farm labor. Which is really beside the point. We were discussing isolation." Boren sipped the whiskey that was so sharp and burning it brought tears to Kay's eyes whenever she swallowed it. "Yes. Since there's almost no power available for private consumption, we're stuck here, with no way out. Military controls all the roads. They're very careful to do so because agricultural production has become one of their first priorities."

"All right," Kay said, "I see why you haven't tried to leave. But all this service-labor you people are doing: I don't understand it! Why aren't they using your professional expertise now that they most need it? Surely it's inefficient to be using you the way peasants once used oxen and mules!"

Boren tapped the side of his glass lightly, with a fingernail. "I don't think they know *how* to use us. The infrastructure isn't there. We're down to concentrating on basic things like food and water. And there's a deep fear of disorder overriding everything else."

"But why not use professionals to organize the reconstruction of the infrastructure!" Kay exclaimed. "That's obviously what has to be done!"

Boren sipped more of the rotgut whiskey. "Surely you must have noticed everything's in chaos," he said drily. "The thing to do now is to keep one's mouth shut and do as one's told. Precisely because we're professionals— and thus high on the scale of valued persons— we're being given these jobs before service-techs are. Which means we won't be going as heavily into debt to the government. Which

also means we're paying taxes. We're earning wages, Zeldin. And thus we're fortunate."

"What about Nan Ramosh?" Kay asked. "How does she live? I assume she doesn't have the good fortune to be sent out into the fields?"

"Her friends feed her," Boren said shortly. "And she gets a share of the garden belonging to the house she lives in."

"I see." Kay swallowed more of the fiery liquor and managed not to cough. "By the way, just why did you take me to see her? Why didn't you tell me when you saw her name on the list that she wasn't likely to respond positively?"

Boren drooped in sudden depression; his lower lip flopped loosely downward, his moist eyes darkened, and his thick fringe of eyelashes blinked as if in bewilderment. "I thought that when she heard your offer she would jump at it. I thought it would bring her to her senses." He paused. "If she goes on like this much longer, she'll crack."

Kay judged that Ramosh had already cracked. For a moment, the memory of the miasmic ambience of Ramosh's room and Ramosh's harsh bleakness overwhelmed her, making her skin crawl and prickle. "What is her crime?" Kay asked.

Boren said, "I can't talk about it. The fewer people who know any of the details of Nan's situation, the better. I can assure you, though, that it is nothing you would judge her harshly for. The only pertinent fact is that if Military catches her they will undoubtedly send her to a camp or execute her."

"What are these camps you keep talking about? Not the ones they're presumably keeping scientists in."

"Military has set up detention camps. Anyone who catches their attention negatively is put in these camps. Unless they're killed. In that way they've 'cleaned out' the people they considered potential troublemakers in Champaign-Urbana. Known radicals, known criminal offenders, and people who are at the bottom. Or people who won't work when told to. You might say they're catch-all places."

"So that's why everyone I've talked to here has been anxious not to be identified with me," Kay said thoughtfully. "I take it there's no due process involved in these detentions."

Boren laughed. "Due process? Lady, we're under permanent martial law. Whoever heard of due process under martial law?" His gaze met hers, then slewed away.

"Where do they get such weird ideas about the Marq'ssan?" Kay asked. "Is vid working around here?"

Boren heaved himself to his feet and went into the living room. He returned to the kitchen with a thin issue of *Time*. Kay hadn't known *Time* had resumed publishing. "Here," he said, handing her the magazine. "Page through it and you'll see where the weird ideas come from."

The cover of the magazine featured a Military figure with the caption **General Anthony O'Leary: The Rising Star in the East.** "This is done by Military? Or Security?" Kay asked, wondering whether *Time* was distributed in Military-controlled sectors only.

Boren shrugged. "How should I know? I thought they were all the same, Military and Security. What does it matter who produces it? It's propaganda."

Kay stared at Boren in disbelief. "Is it possible you don't know there are two factions of the Executive warring against one another for control of this country?"

He looked puzzled. "What do you mean, two factions warring against one another? *What* two factions?"

Kay rubbed her face, needing to feel the sharp friction burn her skin. She was beginning to feel as if she were in a dream— or rather a nightmare. "You mean you don't know that Military and Security are fighting a civil war? How can you possibly be ignorant of such a major fact? It's inconceivable that you don't know!"

He stared at her, dumbfounded. After perhaps a minute he said, "Let me get this straight. You say there's a civil war going on, in this country, right now. And that it's between two factions of the Executive?"

"That's what I'm saying. I think you'd better read my book, Boren. It describes in detail how the thing got started— a year ago last March. It's incredible that they could keep this from you. Or that they would even want to keep it from you!"

He looked dazed. "We're so cut off from everything here. People leave, sure, but they don't come back. And no one comes here from outside, except Military people. And now, you."

Even in Madison they had known about the war. They apparently sent people to detention camps there, too, but didn't keep such tight control of information, and the surrounding countryside was in no one's control: Security held Madison, and held it tightly, but not Wisconsin at large. Sorben had had to transport her from Madison to Champaign because Military's tight control over Illinois' farmlands put travel to Champaign-Urbana via ground transportation out of the question.

"What a damned fool I've been!" Boren said suddenly. He covered his eyes with his hand. Uncomfortable at being a witness to her colleague's distressed weeping, Kay opened the magazine. Angrily she read what little text had been provided on the glossy page, angrily she glared at the photographs of executives— both "civilian" and uniformed— high in the Military establishment.

Boren's voice drew her attention from the magazine: "All this time I've been kidding myself. What fairy tales people like me can tell themselves and believe! I, Boren the cynic, so far above the silly fools who believe the propaganda we're being fed, who conform seemingly willingly to any directive handed down from above. I thought I was superior to them because I criticized Military to myself, I made jokes about Military to my friends and colleagues. I, Boren, was not taken in. Oh no, not me! But all the while of course I did every damned thing they told me to do without *too* much protest. How bold of me to deconstruct the motives of the Military in their manipulation of us! Yet I still let them manipulate me! How enlightened of me to realize that everything they said about the aliens and the Free Zone were lies! I, Boren, could see through their every piece of hocus-pocus. Hah! As if that mattered!" He grabbed his glass and tossed back the rest of the liquor in it. "I get drunk every damned night, Zeldin," he said. The nakedness of his eyes disturbed Kay, making her shiver in the muggy heat. "But it took hearing myself tell you about how things work here before I could realize the true level of my own complicity. I'm just as

scared of the threat of their camps as anyone else in this town. But I was ego-protective enough to need to hide my own terror from myself." He seized the bottle and refilled his glass.

"Come to the Free Zone," Kay said quietly.

Boren paused with his glass halfway to his mouth. "Go with you? Run away? No. I have to find my self-respect. I'll stay here and fight." When Kay opened her mouth to protest, he added, "Besides, I have to be here in case they send Nicole home. If I left, it would be an absolute certainty I'd never see her again. I can't throw away the minute possibility that they might send her back."

"I understand," Kay said. And she did. But when it came to Scott...she knew for certain they would never send him home. Not only was home the Free Zone, but home was with Kay Zeldin. And that made all the difference in the world where any executive decision about Scott Moore was concerned. No, if she ever wanted to see him again, she would have to find him. And that was assuming he was still alive.

Chapter Nine

[i]

Martha didn't need to look at her engagement book to be reminded that the entire morning and part of the afternoon had been left free for meeting with Venn, for she had gone to sleep the night before thinking about the meeting. Although she liked Venn and got along well with her, Venn's professional background made Martha just uncomfortable enough to endow their interactions with small awkwardnesses and occasional misunderstandings. It seemed to Martha that each time they met they talked at cross-purposes at least once. Venn did not patronize Martha (at least not in any way Martha could perceive). Nor did she dominate their discussions: since their meetings always had a business orientation, Martha naturally led the way, while Venn frequently offered wry acknowledgment of Martha's abilities and of the Rainbow Press's reliance on those abilities. Yet hesitations and pauses opened wide, uncomfortable chasms between them, and Venn— once they got talking and she lost her initial shyness— spoke in complicated sentences and used words Martha was not sure she understood. At such times Venn grew almost glib and would ramble off the subject. Later, when their business had been completed and they were confronted with the need to get Martha on her way without embarrassing abruptness, Venn's stumbling, hesitant inarticulateness would return. After the third or fourth meeting in which this happened, Martha began to suspect that these symptoms did not simply mark an affliction of shyness in Venn, but rather a sort of self-conscious awareness of Martha's difference in background, as though she couldn't talk without falling into involuted sentences and spilling out the contents of her extensive vocabulary and did not believe she could talk naturally to Martha without putting Martha off.

This suspicion not only riled Martha, but also embarrassed her. Sometimes she wanted to ask Venn outright if her suspicion was correct. But when she was with Venn, she couldn't find a trace of condescension in Venn's face, words, or voice. When Venn was awkward, she seemed to be trying hard, and when she wasn't awkward the problem didn't exist. Thus while in Venn's presence, Martha tended to dismiss her suspicions as a sort of paranoia stemming from an inferiority complex about her education and social background.

Martha carried her morning cup of coffee back up to her room and gulped it while she packed her briefcase. The meeting was scheduled for eight-thirty, and the Rainbow Press had its offices on Capitol Hill. If she pedaled like mad she might make it on time. Not that it would matter if she arrived a few minutes late. Martha's "job" was entirely self-directed, and Venn was not the type of person whose feathers would be ruffled by a slight tardiness. Still, Martha liked to keep herself disciplined. If she sloughed off with the little things, she might end up falling down on the big ones, and worrying about that happening was necessary now that she was her own boss.

[ii]

Staring out at the passing scenery, Allison wondered what lay beyond the mass of fog— or was it low-hanging cloud?— obscuring everything but the hillsides of lushly verdant fir. She welcomed the mixture of green and silvery gray after so many days of clear blue skies and sun. But though she liked the change, Allison wished it hadn't happened on the day she had been ordered north. She would have liked to have seen whatever mountains were visible in this part of the state.

Dana did not talk much while she drove, leaving Allison free to speculate about why Central had designated her as the team member to report to their contact with the outside and to figure out how to keep her cover intact. When Allison had pointed out to Dana how difficult it would be for her to explain an absence, especially if they happened to have finally found a permanent job for her that very day, Dana had said that that had been taken into consideration. She was the only one of them living out in the open. All the other team members'

Free Zone contacts were of a less continuous and vulnerable character. They made occasional prearranged contacts with their assets but always kept the station's location and the full range of their contacts undisclosed and isolated. Allison alone was not recruiting and running assets. So why disturb the only deep cover on the team? Allison could not help remembering Elizabeth's annoyance at her decision to blow her training cover in order to meet her at the appointed time.

"Is this place we're going to the usual site for contact?" Allison asked Dana.

"No." Dana kept her eyes on the road. "This is the first time we're using this place. It belongs to an admiral. I gather he used the place a couple of times a year. But since Security took on the responsibility of protecting the residences of high-echelon executives, it's hung onto this place. There's still a shitload of valuables in it, though such things are gradually being evacuated— in case we end up losing control of the enclave." Dana shot a quick look at Allison, then returned her eyes to the road. "You can be damned sure people in Bellingham are aware of the enclave. I suppose it's a good thing we got this van repainted before having to bring it here. Still, we may have to repaint it again afterwards— if there's reason to suspect our going there is noticed. Our contact will be coming by sea. The house accesses Puget Sound."

"Where are contacts usually made?"

"Mostly in Vancouver, BC. Twice on the Olympic Peninsula— but that proved too inconvenient for us because it's such a long drive." Dana left the interstate via an exit just north of Bellingham. "I gather they've brought us a lot of electronic hardware and arms this time. Which is why we're using the maxi-van." Dana consulted the vehicle's terminal for directions and identified their location on the monitor for Allison. "Not far now. Thank god we have processors again in our vehicles. It's still possible, of course, to get lost since without a satellite relay the processors can't track our progress. But at least we have decent mapping."

"Do you think we might get lost?" Allison said, trying not to worry, wondering how far the van could go before its battery would need recharging.

Dana laughed. "Not a chance. Puget Sound is a landmark impossible to miss!"

Dana got them there without so much as a single wrong turn. But when they stopped at the gate and had to show their Security ID to the armed sentry, a new anxiety smote Allison. The guard's glance at her— a look that plainly expressed amazement that her face matched her ID— reminded her of the ugly clothes and of the chemical odor she had acquired living under cover. She should have gotten Dana to stop at the Edmonds house on the way up so that she could at least have bathed, even if she had to continue wearing the clothing and makeup. But it was too late now: she would have to swallow her embarrassment and meet the contact as she was.

The electronically controlled gate swung open, and Dana drove slowly past the gatehouse and along the curving tree-lined drive. "Nice, isn't it," she said. "And to think this place was hardly ever used, even before the aliens invaded." The trees gave way to hedges; a glass and cedar house came into sight. "Ooh, the grounds must be gorgeous in April when the rhododendrons are in flower."

Allison smiled at Dana's enthusiasm. The whole setup reminded her of her mother's house.

Dana parked the van on the north side of the house. Allison glimpsed the sea between the trees and wished for a walk at the edge of the water though she knew it was unlikely there would be a beach to walk on and knew, too, it wouldn't be as lovely as the ocean. Even so, it would be quiet and calm. The lack of privacy over the last two weeks had begun to gnaw at her nerves.

A service-tech (whom the guard had obviously notified of their arrival) held the side-door open for them and led Allison through the kitchen. Dana did not follow, but stayed in the kitchen when the service-tech took Allison to the back of the house to a large room lined with windows overlooking the water. Surveying the room from the threshold, Allison was again reminded of her mother's house.

"So there you are."

Startled to hear Elizabeth's voice, Allison looked around and found her in the far corner, near the back windows, surrounded by a coffee

cup and thermoflask, bottles of water, manila folders, yellow pads, and a terminal. "Elizabeth! I thought—"

Elizabeth smiled. "You thought you were meeting some drab courier-type."

Allison grinned and moved forward. "Well, yes. I couldn't understand why I of all the others was supposed to come." She halted a couple of feet from where Elizabeth sat. "There may be problems with my cover—"

"Yes," Elizabeth said, "I know. But I have my reasons. Are you sick of sitting?"

Allison shrugged. "The drive wasn't too bad."

"Would you like to take a walk before we sit down with our yellow pads?"

"I'd love to," Allison responded, pleased. "But first, point me in the direction of the nearest bathroom, please."

Elizabeth stood up, put her hands on Allison's shoulders, and rotated Allison's body until she faced an unobtrusive door set in the east wall. Allison chuckled (even as her cheeks grew rosy). She hadn't expected to be taken so literally. Away from Elizabeth, she always forgot her quirky sense of humor.

[iii]

In Security-held Ann Arbor, Lynn Garvey, an old graduate school friend of Meredith Wolfson, told Kay horror stories about Detroit—a place outside any executive control whatsoever. They perched on stools at a vacant bench in Garvey's lab, fanning themselves with pieces of paper folded in half. According to Garvey, Security had evacuated all executives from the city and its nearest suburbs more than a year before— thus plunging Ann Arbor's civilians into an apparently permanent state of fear. As a result, she said, most people in Ann Arbor were pro-Security and wished for more, not less, Security forces occupying the area. When Kay asked Garvey her opinion of why Security bothered with Ann Arbor, Garvey pointed out that key industries that the Executive would not want to lose were located in and around the University.

"Do you know if they've got any of them running?" Kay asked.

"As a matter of fact," Garvey said slowly, subjecting Kay to hard, penetrating scrutiny, "I do. At least one of the silicon-production facilities is in operation. And a couple of the drug factories."

Kay swallowed the last drops of tepid water in her glass and wished again it had come with ice. "I suppose that shouldn't surprise me," she said. The Free Zone was having trouble setting up the manufacture of silicon, which they very much needed. "But how do you know?" Kay asked. "Don't they keep such things secret?"

"It's hard to keep something like that secret in a place like this. You think they should be afraid Military will send a fleet of helicopter gunships to wipe out any industry they put into operation?"

"Is it always this hot here in the summer?" Kay asked, envious of the other woman's sleeveless shirt and shorts.

"In the old days the lab was air-conditioned in the summer," Garvey said. "If we were sitting in the shade under a tree somewhere, sipping iced tea and catching the breeze, it wouldn't be so bad. But I thought this would be the best place for meeting some of the others."

"What kind of biology do you do?"

"Before everything crashed I was in a group of twelve— physiologists, bioengineers, and biochemists— working on developing a more sophisticated blood filter. Since pure water is so expensive, we were trying to see if we could find a way to circumvent the need for such a high level of purity. One of the chemists had the idea that— Oh, Fred," Garvey greeted the short, duck-like man heading for the bench along the far wall. "Do you have a minute? I'd like to introduce you to Kay Zeldin."

The man swerved from the intended trajectory of his path to come over to them.

"Kay Zeldin, meet Fred Schoevelkor, one of the physiologists who was working on the filter project." Schoevelkor held out his hand, and Kay shook it. "Fred, Zeldin is a historian from Seattle." At the mention of Seattle, Schoevelkor's entire body arrested, then after a second or two relaxed. "Her spouse, an electrical engineer, was recruited for a project a year ago last March, and she hasn't seen him since. She's discovered that a lot of people in the sciences seem to be missing under

similar circumstances. And she's trying to find out what happened to them." Lynn Garvey paused. "She's also offering to transport to the Free Zone anyone interested in going there to work. She says that at the minimum she can assure food and housing and projects on which to work." Kay could not tell whether Garvey's tone was ironic or not: she had one of those voices gifted with such dryness that one's initial response was to suspect facetiousness behind every utterance.

"Is it just that you haven't heard from your spouse, or that you really don't have any idea where he is?"

Kay said, "He told me he was going to work on a special project 'for the Washington boys,' as he put it. I haven't seen or heard from him since. I know of at least one hundred other science people who are also missing. They tend to be electrical engineers, bioengineers, gene-engineers, robotics specialists, physicists, and applied mathematicians."

Schoevelkor nodded soberly and looked oddly even more duck-like than when he'd been waddling across the room. "I've heard of something like that," he said.

"You know of specific instances of people missing?"

Schoevelkor's eyes swiveled toward Garvey. Garvey shrugged. Schoevelkor looked back at Kay. "Yes. So does Lynn. There's hardly anyone in the University community who doesn't. We were thinking when they started up some of the local industries that they might be returning some of the people who have been missing. But it didn't happen."

"Did anyone ask the government about it?"

He smiled, as though at a joke. "Sure. But the executive running things in Ann Arbor had nothing constructive to say. Said he'd put forward an inquiry, but that since the country was at war no one should expect to hear anything until it was over." He snorted, and the noise was so much like a quack that Kay had to smile, too. "I wonder if that's some kind of code? Or a joke? I never did figure out what it meant besides 'don't ask.' But then I've always tried to steer clear of executives except at grant-renewal time."

"So I guess I'm not going to learn anything in Ann Arbor."

Schoevelkor leaned against the bench. Kay wondered why he didn't pull up a stool and sit with them. "You might talk to the one person I've heard of who's come back," Schoevelkor said casually.

"You *know* someone who's come back!"

"Oh yes, I do indeed. Someone who's come back to work on some kind of project they've got started here. Something classified, I suspect, since it's not general knowledge what it is."

"Can I meet this person? And when did he or she get back?" Kay grew elated with hope.

"She," Schoevelkor said. "Her name is Nadine Morris. She's an electrical engineer. And she got back last week."

"My god!"

He patted Garvey's shoulder. "Lynn can tell you all about it. Nadine lives in her building."

Kay stared at Garvey: why the *fuck* had she been holding back?

Garvey seemed unperturbed at Kay's scrutiny. "I'm not a good judge of character, Zeldin, and I've only just met you," she said. "You may be a friend of Meredith Wolfson, but I don't know you. I thought I'd let Fred decide. He reads character very well." She smiled. "And I guess you rate."

Kay found this exceedingly strange but let it pass. She was too excited to think about anything besides her upcoming meeting with Nadine Morris. This was her first solid lead. More important, this was the first indication she had gotten that any of the missing were still alive. Even if Nadine Morris could tell Kay nothing about Scott, Kay would still feel she had learned something positive.

"Tell me about the Free Zone," Schoevelkor invited. "Is it true there are women vigilantes who go around killing men they suspect of rape?"

Kay wondered if Security allowed *Time* to circulate in places under their control, or whether they had similar stories about the Free Zone in other publications. "Do you know the history of the Night Patrol?" Kay said, hoping to minimize the damage by placing the vigilantes in historical perspective.

"Is that what they're called?" Garvey asked. Fascination peeped through her look of disapproval.

Kay dipped into her satchel and pulled out a copy of her book. "It's all in here." She handed the book to Garvey.

Garvey stared at the book jacket. "You wrote this?"

"About a year ago. It was published in January."

"Published!" Garvey and Schoevelkor repeated simultaneously.

A grin broke out on Kay's face: of course, that would be the thing that got to them. "Published in the Free Zone," Kay said. "The publishing of books is a priority there," she added sententiously.

The biologists stared at one another, then looked back at Kay. "Do they by any chance have any science going on over there?" Schoevelkor said.

A nibble at her bait: encouraging, considering this was her first day in Ann Arbor. But of course the important thing was to talk to Nadine Morris.

"There's this island that used to belong more or less to the Navy," Kay said, sensing he would find the Whidbey Science Center alluring. "But of course the Navy evacuated its people at the time of the Withdrawal of all government functions from Washington and Oregon. It was last fall that a bunch of scientists decided they'd like the peace and quiet of the island to live and work on..."

It was like hooking sophomores on the long-term, medium-term, and short-term causes of World War One. One only had to tell it as a fascinating story to capture their attention until they were too hooked to back out from the intricacies of analysis they had been seduced into. Surely the Night Patrol could mean nothing to people living only a few miles from the place Detroit had become. And when she showed them a hologram of the Science Center on Whidbey (and holograms of other parts of the island), they would forget about the Night Patrol altogether. How could anyone, however propagandized by *Time* and its ilk, associate violence with such a peaceful, isolated place?

[iv]

"That at least is going all right, then," Elizabeth said when Allison had reported on her progress in deep cover. "Unless there's a break on Zeldin, you'll continue as you've been doing. It's critical that

you attend the Steering Committee meeting. I've ordered that you be wired for it." Elizabeth flipped over the pages in the yellow tablet she had been taking notes on until a fresh page lay blank before her. She looked up from the tablet, tilted her head to one side, and directed a close speculative stare into Allison's face. "And now, Allison, it's time to level with me."

Allison's stomach fluttered. What could Elizabeth mean? "I don't understand."

"You're holding back."

Allison swallowed. "I wouldn't do that!" Allison could feel her cheeks heating.

"I've pored over your team's reports. There's a lot missing from them when it comes to their bungling Zeldin's handling. I want to know what happened."

"But I wasn't there! I didn't get into Seattle until Sunday afternoon." Was it possible Elizabeth thought she had gotten into Seattle before Sunday, that there was something being covered up involving her, Allison?

"I know that," Elizabeth said. "But you spent some time being briefed by Lauder, and I imagine you also spent some time talking to the little service-tech. Am I right?"

Elizabeth's smile flashed out, then vanished.

Allison floundered in the dilemma: Elizabeth wanted her to report on her team members. On her *controller*. It was something that was never done, except in the most extreme circumstances. In the ordinary course of things, all Allison's written reports would go only to Lauder, and very occasionally— in certain special instances— to Lauder's immediate superior in the chain of command. Allison suddenly understood why Elizabeth had ordered that she be the one to make contact.

"Come on, Allison," Elizabeth said. "Why the hell do you think I called you out of Vienna to join that team?" When Allison didn't answer, Elizabeth said, softly, "I thought you were loyal to *me*, Allison. Was I wrong?" Her gaze held Allison's irresistibly— demanding.

"You don't trust Lauder?" Allison whispered.

"That's not the question here. Though I do want your considered opinion on how he's handling the team. The question is whether we trust one another. You and I, Allison. The question is whether you're loyal to me."

How could she not be loyal to Elizabeth? Elizabeth had been her mentor, had made so many things possible to the daughter of a non-entity like Mason Bennett. Elizabeth had seen to it that she had gone to Stanford and for a few years to graduate school before starting work for the Company, and had then (Allison felt sure, though she didn't know for a fact) had her assigned to the post in Rome and later promoted and transferred to Vienna. It was Elizabeth who constantly helped Vivien Whittier in dozens of small ways without ever being asked. Allison, aside from her deep affection for Elizabeth, owed her.

And now Elizabeth was calling in the debt.

It came down to a conflict of loyalties. At bottom, Allison knew there could be no question of which loyalty took precedence. "If you ask this of me, Elizabeth, I can answer only one way: there can be no question about my loyalty to you." Allison blinked back the tears that sprang into her eyes. "If I have to compromise myself for it, then so be it."

Smiling, Elizabeth put down her pen and took Allison's hand. "You needn't worry about repercussions, Allison. I'll take care of everything. If it should prove necessary for Lauder or Goodwin to find out, I will see to it that the damage is controlled and contained." She squeezed Allison's fingers. "*I* am controlling *them.*"

Allison wondered again about Elizabeth's position, about her role in Security. In the past, Elizabeth had stayed in the Chief's office, never going out of D.C., always operating behind the scenes. Her power and influence had never before been explicitly visible to Allison.

Elizabeth patted Allison's hand and released it and again took up her pen. "Now tell me, Allison, what the hell is going on with that team."

Allison considered carefully. She began with a qualification: "You must bear in mind that I was in that house for less than twenty-four hours. And that since then I've had contact twice with the service-tech— the two times she provided my transport and our negligible contact on Friday, arranging a meet with Goodwin to report on my progress. And of course the meeting with Goodwin itself. That's the sum total of my contact with the team. It's not that much to go on."

"Granted," Elizabeth said. "But nevertheless you've formed some opinions."

Was Elizabeth suspicious simply because the team had fucked up? "When I arrived on the Sunday, it was the day after they'd lost Zeldin," Allison said. "After dinner, Lauder called an executive meeting. Or rather Goodwin called it for Lauder. We sat around the table, the four of us alone, the sub-execs ordered to keep away unless called. I found what followed pretty strange— but I wrote some of it off to my not being familiar with these types of people. As you know, my contact with CATs has been minimal. Code ops keeps one somewhat isolated, and code and standard intelligence-collection ops have made up the bulk of my assignments." Elizabeth nodded— patiently, Allison thought, rebuking herself for taking so long to get to the point. "Lauder may already have been drunk when he got to the table. He ate very little and drank heavily. And after dinner when we sat in conference, he drank a good three-quarters of a fifth of scotch before my very eyes. Goodwin ran the conference. Whenever Goodwin considered Lauder's authorization necessary he would address Lauder, and Lauder would routinely agree. The only point Lauder seemed to care much about was excising Zeldin. He said they should have simply killed her when they had the chance. And each time Goodwin reminded him of their orders. Elizabeth, what is it? Are you all right?"

The blood had drained from Elizabeth's face; her eyes loomed large and dark against the pallor of her skin. She passed a hand over her face. "My god, if they had killed her—!"

Allison sprang out of her chair and snatched up a bottle of water. She poured out a glass and handed it to Elizabeth. Allison noted a sheen of sweat dampening her chalk-gray face. "I'm all right," Elizabeth said. But she accepted the glass and drained it. "It's clear," she said, "that I must personally supervise Zeldin's interrogation and re-recruitment when she is found. The very possibility that someone might disobey orders and kill her—" She broke off, seemingly overwhelmed by emotion. But color was returning to her face.

"What is it?" Allison asked. "What is so important about Zeldin? Certainly not the contact with the aliens? There are plenty of other people we could get onto, and perhaps more easily, who have that contact."

Elizabeth set the glass on the table flanking her chair. "That's only a minor part of it. Zeldin's value is far greater than that."

"I don't understand," Allison said.

"Tell me, why do you think Lauder is so hot to kill Zeldin?" Elizabeth said sharply.

Allison shrugged. "My impression is that he has this thing about killing anyone who doubles."

"I'm going to have to look into this. Is it possible Lauder has some personal ax to grind? Either about Zeldin or about something for which he blames her personally?"

"All I know is that the subject seemed to unhinge him. And that it was the only thing he was interested in during the entire meeting. The rest of the time he just sat and drank."

Elizabeth thought for a while before she spoke again. Devoured by curiosity, Allison watched her face. Why had she gotten so upset? Zeldin must be important in some undisclosed way. Either she knew something, or she was needed as a hostage, or there was some special operation that only Zeldin could perform. These were the only possibilities Allison could imagine.

"Before we continue," Elizabeth said, "let's discuss our current practical arrangements. I'd like to think a bit about a few things and then talk to you more after I've done so. Is it going to be impossibly inconvenient to your cover for you to spend the night here?"

Allison considered. "I can't really say. I suspect that if being gone the day doesn't blow my cover, neither will staying out the night. I can probably imply that I got caught up in a spur-of-the-moment sexual fling if I stay the night. What do you think?"

Elizabeth's mouth curved upward in a slow smile. "Very good," she murmured. Something in Elizabeth's face brought heat into Allison's cheeks. "And of course it is the obvious thing. Waiting around to be called for a job can get to be very boring. In such circumstances indulgence in sexual adventures is perfectly understandable." Elizabeth stared down at the still-blank fresh yellow page. "Good. Then let us move on. You say Goodwin seemed to be running things. Did you have the sense that this is something that happens frequently?" Elizabeth looked up. "And how was Morgan responding— with the resentment of someone not used to taking orders from Goodwin, or as though it were commonplace? And Lauder: did he even notice that Goodwin was in control?"

"I think it must have seemed perfectly natural to the others that Goodwin was in control," Allison said decisively. "But it seemed odd to me because of my expectations about Lauder."

Elizabeth jotted something on her yellow pad. "Now let's get down to what you've deduced about how or why they bungled it."

Allison's mouth twisted in a slight, wry smile. "I think it might be so simple as their underestimating her. They thought she would be easily intimidated. And they underestimated her intelligence."

Elizabeth sighed. "The same old story. That's been one of the problems with Zeldin all along. I probably shouldn't have left the team's briefing on Zeldin to Wedgewood. It's obvious we need a new approach. Which is why I'm more than ever convinced you should be the one to handle her, Allison. Along the lines we discussed when I first briefed you on her."

"If you're not going to kill her and you want to run her, I suppose that may be true. Though Goodwin expressed the opinion that Zeldin could be easily run with an escalation of intimidation."

Elizabeth scribbled on her yellow pad. "It's a blindness they have," she said.

Allison knew without asking who the "they" were to whom Elizabeth referred. As though hearing something illicit from someone privileged enough to get away with speaking it while she, the listener, might not be privileged enough to acknowledge much less comment on it, Allison picked up her own pen and pad and stared down at its blank yellow page. There were some things better left unsaid. That

was one of the more important things Vivien had taught her, and taught her well.

Chapter Ten

[i]

Martha and Venn halted work a few minutes after one and took their sack-lunches out to the front porch. "So what's new, Martha?" Venn asked as she twisted the cap off her half-liter bottle of water.

Martha laughed. "You too, Venn? But that's silly. I bet you know more about what's going on in the Free Zone than I do." She opened the plastic tub of bean salad, the main course of her lunch.

"I've been hearing disturbing things," Venn said. "And what I'm hearing gives me some concern about the next Steering Committee meeting."

Martha forked two red kidneys, a garbanzo, and a sliver of carrot. The smell of olive oil and garlic filled her nostrils. "How so?"

"Everyone's talking about those cult people on Whidbey. Though that's clearly not all of it, still, I'd say your run-in with them is symptomatic of larger problems." Venn took a long swallow of water.

"And how would you describe these larger problems?" Martha asked cautiously. When discussing matters as tricky as this, it was something of a strain talking in Venn's language, taking pains to complete her sentences, to be careful of her diction.

Venn gave her a wry look. "Martha, you've turned into the deftest of politicians. You know that?"

Martha didn't like this, but she sensed that Venn meant it as a tempered compliment, not an insult. "I'm nothing like a politician," she said. "Or I hope I'm not. I'm just trying to go carefully with such delicate matters." Martha looked down at her bean salad and forked another bite. "And somehow I feel they *are* delicate. People have strong feelings about these things. Which means that an issue like

this could tear the Free Zone apart." Martha looked at Venn. "So. Tell me what you think the larger problems are."

Venn gestured as she swallowed the bite of sandwich she had been chewing. "I think it all comes down to the problem of men. How to deal with them, how much power to share with them, and how we're going to deal with reproduction issues— which in the past, before the government changed the game, were always linked with issues involving sex and sexuality."

Martha eyed what she could see of the egg salad in Venn's sandwich and wondered if it had curry in it. She thought she could smell a hint of curry in the air. "Really? How do you figure that?"

Venn's eyes narrowed in concentration. "I don't exactly understand it myself. But before Birth Limitation went into effect, decisions about reproduction were in a certain sense left to individuals— the decision-making was still political— influenced in fact by a variety of things, but with certain notorious exceptions occasioned by racist hatred, the government didn't determine outright who could or could not have children, or how many. Even back then religious groups were very hot on the subject. But it seems that women had different ideas about bearing children then. It was still wrapped up with economic and status considerations, true, but in a different way. The main point is that women were constrained by most of the social, economic, moral, and legal conventions surrounding childbearing and child-raising. I think we have to be careful not to fall into that kind of a morass again through leaving the initiative up to the religious cult types.

"Sure, government shouldn't be saying who may or may not bear children. But we have to be careful that the religious groups don't come up with new rules and regulations and political manipulations of reproduction." Venn took another swallow of water and offered a thin smile. "I guess I've made a muddle trying to explain it. It's so complicated I don't know how to talk about it."

"But you've studied it," Martha said.

Venn nodded as she chewed another mouthful of her sandwich.

"Maybe," Martha said, not understanding what Venn was talking about but intuiting that it was important, "— maybe it would be

a good idea for you to write and publish a pamphlet elaborating on what you just told me. It's the kind of thing we need to be thinking of when we come to make decisions concerning these problems. It would be a good idea, too, for you to present some kind of report to the Steering Committee. I'd help you get it on the agenda of the next meeting, if you could be ready by then." Martha bit into the first of the three Yakima Valley plums she had packed and groaned at the rush of flavor dancing on her tongue.

"Lord, Martha, I've never done any public speaking, you know. And as for writing a pamphlet... I'm just a reading addict at heart, you know." She quirked her eyebrows askew in apparent self-doubt.

Martha licked the plum juice from her lips. "I'm doing all kinds of things I wasn't trained to do. I think you have to consider how important it is to bring some of what you know to people's attention. You have a contribution to make. And so really it's up to you to make it."

Venn bit her lip. She looked distinctly underwhelmed. "You put it so, well, so practically, Martha. Okay. Let me work on the pamphlet first. If I can find a way to get my concerns down on paper, then I'll go ahead with reporting to the Steering Committee."

"Good," Martha said, wondering what Venn's now-speculative stare was all about. "I won't arrange anything definite for the meeting but reserve a tentative slot for you. How's that?"

Venn laughed, making the deep lines around her mouth and eyes crinkle. "You mean you're committing me but providing me with a bolt-hole for escape should I turn lazy or coward."

"What do *you* think we should do about the men?" Martha asked.

"Oh, the men," Venn said. She narrowed her eyes and took a moment to consider. "We're going to have to find a way to make them see their stake in the Free Zone. But as for how we actually do that..."

Martha listened intently to Venn's suggestions as she finished eating her plums. She hardly knew why it had become necessary for her to collect such opinions, but it had. She wondered, for a moment, whether she had any opinions of her own, now that so many others'

were stashed away in her head. And she decided that the question was essentially meaningless in a place like the Free Zone.

[ii]

Lynn Garvey warned Kay that it might be difficult to get hold of Nadine Morris. Nevertheless, Garvey found Morris at home when she phoned the latter's apartment in the early afternoon. Garvey merely asked if she could drop in to talk with her about a matter of importance; she did not mention Kay. Morris suggested Garvey come by within the hour since she was intending to return to her lab at four.

As they walked the few blocks to Garvey and Morris's apartment complex, Kay asked Garvey how well she knew Nadine Morris.

"That's an odd question," Garvey said. "Not your asking it, precisely, but for me to try answering. I used to lunch with Nadine— before the crash— once or twice a month. And occasionally we met at dinner parties, since some of our acquaintances were mutual. So I suppose I know the usual things one knows about people. I have a sense of her, of what her personality is, of what her frustrations and contentments are, and I know quite a bit about her childhood and her first marriage and its breakup, though very little about her second marriage. Somewhere in there perhaps one could make a judgment as to how well one knows another person, I suppose. In this case, we weren't the closest that friends can be. Yet we were more than acquaintances."

"And now?" Kay asked. "Have you seen her much since she's been back? Has all that changed? Has *she* changed?"

Garvey looked at Kay. "You ask a lot of questions, Kay. You haven't even met the woman! And you don't know me. You're getting rather personal, don't you think?"

Kay flushed. Garvey was correct in her reaction: the problem was that she, Kay, was acting like a spy. "Sorry," she said. "I don't know why I'm so curious. I suppose it has something to do with Scott. Maybe wondering what Scott would be like after more than a year away in unknown circumstances."

Though Kay really did not know why she had asked those questions, she did not believe that wondering about Scott had anything to

do with her inquisitiveness. She felt vaguely ashamed of using him as an excuse.

"Here we are," Garvey said as they approached a sprawling building constructed of irregularly proportioned steel and glass boxes seemingly arranged at random. Garvey used her yellow plastic to open the electronic door, then led the way through thickly carpeted halls, past several thumb-lock access doors, to the northeast corner of the building. They halted outside an unmarked numberless door and Garvey spoke through an intercom to identify herself. Kay wondered at the building's restored technology. Nowhere else outside the Free Zone that she had visited had professionals enjoyed restored processor functions in their living or working spaces. Why here?

The door slid open, and Garvey entered; Kay followed, and the door slid shut. "I've brought you a visitor," Garvey said to a tall thin woman with cinnamon red hair styled in a short, fluffed frizz.

"So I see," Morris said in a dry, coolly ironic voice. A voice in tone very like Garvey's, Kay thought.

"This is Kay Zeldin, Nadine. She's from Seattle. She's interested in finding out what has happened to some of the science people who were recruited on government projects during the first days of the crash."

Morris held out her hand. "Pleased to meet you, Kay Zeldin." She shook Kay's hand. "Do you mind my asking the reason for your interest?"

Kay held Morris's cool blue gaze. "My spouse was one of those recruited," she said evenly. "I have no idea where he is or whether he's still alive. This is the case for other people I know. I'm investigating on their behalf as well as on my own."

Morris led them into the living room: "Let's sit down." Kay chose a chair near the windows and noted that although processor functions had been restored, the apartment was apparently without air-conditioning, for the three-ply windows had been opened. "I don't know, you see, how helpful I can be," Morris said. "There's no reason to believe that what I know must necessarily pertain to others' experience."

Kay nodded. "I understand that. You were recruited to work on a government project that March a year and half ago?"

"That's close enough," Morris said.

Kay thought Morris's face looked guarded. "And what happened? Where did you go?"

"I was taken with others from Ann Arbor to a place deep underground. A place where none of the processors or other electronic equipment had been damaged. There were hundreds of us there, all science people. It was quite extraordinary."

Kay's pulse quickened; she rubbed her sweaty palms on her trousers. "Do you have any idea where this place was?"

Morris shrugged. "Not really. Just that it was somewhere in the mountains. I think the place must have been *inside* a mountain. Most of the levels weren't below sea-level— that I know because altitude is a factor that sometimes must be controlled for." She shook her head. "It was so impressive, at least at first, because it was such a massive, well-equipped place. With everything in it running beautifully."

"If I gave you a list of missing people, would you look at it and tell me whether you know any of the people on it to have been there?"

"Of course," Morris said. "I don't see what harm that could do."

Kay, digging the correct file folder out of her satchel, looked up. "Harm?" she blankly repeated. "Harm to whom?"

"There is the matter of security," Morris said. "One must be careful. And I think I heard Lynn say you are from Seattle? You could be working for the aliens for all I know. I will only help you to the extent that I judge I won't be doing harm." Kay held out the five pages listing missing scientists. Morris met her gaze again. "I can see that you must be very worried about your spouse," she said softly, taking the list. "I'm not unsympathetic. But I also don't want to abet the aliens in anything they might be angling for. I imagine they are highly interested in knowing what the missing scientists have been working on." She looked at the list. "Shall I mark with pencil the ones I know to have been where I was?"

Kay's heart pounded. "Please do."

Morris slipped a Cross pencil out of her pocket. Kay counted each time she made a mark with the pencil. And according to Kay's count,

by the time Morris had gone through the five pages, she had made thirty-five marks.

When Morris handed the list back to Kay, Kay immediately turned to page three. She cried out when she saw the dash by Scott's name. "Scott Moore was there?"

"Yes. For the entire time I was."

"Oh my god, oh my god. Then he's alive?"

"As far as I know," Morris said. "I last saw him maybe two weeks ago. I was sent back here just last week, you know."

"Are they sending any others home?" Kay asked, blinking her brimming eyes.

Morris shrugged. "I have no idea."

"But if they've finished their projects— ?"

"Don't ask me about projects, Zeldin," Morris said sharply.

"But do you think they might send others home?"

"I don't know. I don't know what to tell you. I don't think I can tell you anything more than I already have. Except that Scott Moore, the last time I saw him, was alive and perfectly healthy. That's all."

"What did you see of its location when you left the place?" Kay asked.

Morris shook her head. "It was night. I saw nothing."

"But you know this place is in the mountains, and underground."

"That's my educated guess."

Kay had to be satisfied with that. She thanked Morris for her help and left with Garvey. Unless they had killed him to spite her, Scott Moore was still alive. Now it was only a matter of searching out precise information about the underground place in the mountains— and rescuing him.

[iii]

Allison and Elizabeth lay on the mat, their arms and legs extended, sweating and panting. "I never would have guessed you were so good," Allison said, still gasping for breath. "My image of the desk-bound Elizabeth Weatherall is shattered."

Elizabeth, also breathing hard, grinned. "I work out almost every day. But it looks as though I've got something to learn from you. I'm

going to want you to teach me that lovely little move you made when I thought I was connecting and then found myself staggering forward off balance."

Elizabeth was generous to say so, Allison thought. It was obvious she was in no way in Elizabeth's class.

When their breathing had quieted, they got up and Elizabeth showed Allison to her room. She waved at the box lying on the bed. "That's for you," she said. "I imagine you have nothing with you. Enjoy your bath."

Allison opened the box to discover a silk lounging gown and a vial of the perfume Mason Bennett had had designed for her for her twenty-first birthday. Allison sighed with pleasure: Elizabeth thought of everything. How wonderful it was working for her.

She bathed, perfumed, and dressed herself in Elizabeth's gift. Newly confident and feeling her "real" self, she wandered through most of the house before finding Elizabeth in the kitchen giving Dana instructions about loading the van with the ammunition, office supplies, and electronic paraphernalia requested by Joshua Morgan.

"Oh, I almost forgot, Ms. Weatherall," Dana said when Elizabeth finished. "Mr. Goodwin asked me to give you this." Dana pulled an envelope out of her pocket and handed it to Elizabeth.

Elizabeth drew Allison into the long windowed room overlooking the water. "Let's sit in here, shall we? It's my favorite room in this house, which is otherwise not to my taste."

Allison agreed with Elizabeth's assessment: whoever had decorated for the Admiral had had a pretentiously baroque taste bordering on the garish. Such a simple architectural style could not support so much gilt and scrolling and clutter.

As Elizabeth settled in her chair, she said, "I made a good choice with that gown. The color flatters your skin tone." She opened the envelope Dana had given her, and three Security badges fell into her lap. Elizabeth picked up one of the badges. "Oh for the birthing fuck." She handled each of them in turn. "They must have found these in Zeldin's apartment."

Hoping to get a closer look, Allison leaned over the arm of her chair toward Elizabeth. "What are they?" she said, not certain that Elizabeth would tell her.

"The badges Zeldin, Sedgewick, and I were wearing when Zeldin and the aliens abducted us from Security Central." The flatness in her voice suggested shock. "I'd forgotten about the badges," she said. "And so we learn that Zeldin kept them. As souvenirs? Or for some other reason?"

Elizabeth laid the badges on the table between her chair and Allison's. Allison stared at them. She said, "I never realized Zeldin had been given such a high security clearance." She looked at Elizabeth, but Elizabeth's face revealed nothing.

"The clearance on that badge is classified information, Allison," Elizabeth said, watching her. "Don't repeat it to anyone. Clear?"

"Understood." But Elizabeth's order stoked her curiosity about Zeldin. The woman and the Company's interest in her posed a mystery equal to any Allison had ever stumbled upon.

[iv]

Allison drank down the last drops of the lovely Margaux Elizabeth had invited her to loot from the Admiral's wine cellar, then leaned forward and stretched to set the empty glass onto the fireplace's slate apron. She loved that the evening was cool enough here for a fire. She wished the day would never end. The fire, the wine, the silk against her skin, and best of all Elizabeth's eyes glowing like deep tropical seas warming her surrounding her filling her with excited eager affection and pleasure— these were the sorts of gifts one only ever got in dreams. Allison had never enjoyed another evening as she was enjoying this one; but she had never had Elizabeth all to herself, had never had Elizabeth seated on cushions beside her, occasionally taking up some new point or question as it occurred to her, more often sitting quietly, staring into the fire, sharing smiles with Allison.

"And another thing," Elizabeth said, her voice a murmur barely rising above the hiss of the flames. "I'll especially instruct Lauder that you are to be present during the weekly executive meetings. Dana can fetch you from town. The reason for the instruction will be obvious—

your infiltration is of far greater significance just now than the penetration efforts being coordinated by the others. Recruiting and training a paramilitary force isn't much use at the present since the aliens would make a deployment of it extravagantly costly. However," Elizabeth said, looking puzzled, "I'm wondering why the aliens haven't retaliated yet over our capture of Zeldin. I was certain they'd do something really nasty in response." Elizabeth leaned a bit to the right, and through two sets of sleeves Allison could feel the light pressure of Elizabeth's arm, the touch of which instantly sensitized Allison's skin. She closed her eyes for a moment as a wave of giddiness overwhelmed her. "But then they haven't done anything about the com satellite the French launched last week, either. Is it possible they've withdrawn, do you think?" Before Allison could answer, Elizabeth said, "Forget I said that, Allison. You're not supposed to know about that launch."

Allison smiled. How many times had Elizabeth said that this evening? But though Allison enjoyed receiving Elizabeth's confidences, she worried about remembering which things she was supposed to know and which she was not. It would be all too easy in an executive conference to use whatever came into her head to aid in analysis or persuasion.

Again they lapsed into silence. Acutely aware of Elizabeth's arm brushing her own, Allison stared for a long time into the fire, savoring Elizabeth's nearness. She could feel the end of the evening approach; and the aching desire heavy in her limbs seemed to squeeze her heart as the moment of loss drew closer and closer. "Oh, Elizabeth," she murmured, "I've so loved spending this day with you like this. I wish…I wish it would go on and on."

Elizabeth's arm slid around Allison's waist; wave after wave of sensation diffused through Allison's body. Elizabeth leaned into Allison and said low in her throat, her lips almost touching Allison's ear, "That's how I feel too, darling."

Trembling, Allison turned her face to Elizabeth's and was overcome by her first inhalation of Elizabeth's scent. She closed her eyes so to sense Elizabeth in dark warmth. Their lips brushed intoxicatingly, and Allison's arms encircled Elizabeth. Elizabeth's mouth pressed against Allison's, her tongue slipped between Allison's lips and lightly

swept the gum above her teeth. Sensing the necessity of restraining the violence of her response, Allison waited for Elizabeth's gentle, lingeringly slow lead. She knew she couldn't bear it if they were to stop now; she was so afraid Elizabeth would draw back, separate, abandon her. But then Elizabeth's fingers slid between the folds of Allison's labia, and Allison's body shuddered as she fell into the hot dark vortex Elizabeth wove between them, and Allison knew that Elizabeth would not pull back now.

When they lay naked caressing and kissing, the wonder of it overcame her— Elizabeth so beautiful, the ever untouchable, playing here with her, her long lithe golden-downed body responsive to Allison's desire— like the kind of dream one wanted to prolong and then remember and remember and remember. "You're so beautiful, so beautiful, so beautiful," Allison chanted, making Elizabeth smile and murmur tender things until at length Allison's fingers lips and tongue drew from Elizabeth only inarticulate responses. Later, with Elizabeth's tongue in her vulva spreading ripples, shimmering waves, and shudders, Allison forgot the other's beauty, aware only of pleasure, desire, sensation.

When they had had enough Allison lay exhausted with her head on Elizabeth's belly, her hand on Elizabeth's thigh as Elizabeth stroked her hair.

"Vivien would kill me for this if she knew," was the first thing Elizabeth said.

Allison thought about how her mother would react if she found out. "No," she said, "I'd be the one she'd kill. She'd know that *I* was the one who seduced *you*."

Elizabeth laughed. "Seduced! When in fact neither of us seduced the other, sweetie. It just happened. Which is a first for me." Elizabeth kissed the top of Allison's head. Allison swelled with elation at the thought that for Elizabeth what they were sharing was new. "But you know," Elizabeth went on, "we have to keep this a secret between us. No one would understand. And since I am the oldest, and presumably the most experienced—" Elizabeth chuckled again— "and also your working superior, I most certainly am the one to be held to blame."

"I've wanted you for so long, Elizabeth." Allison needed to say it. "Ever since I can remember. I've always loved you, Elizabeth."

"Ssh." Elizabeth's fingers pressed against Allison's lips, and Allison kissed them. After a long silence, Elizabeth continued, "You see, darling, it's very complicated now with us. We will have to be oh so careful. If anyone were to find out— you can imagine, can't you, what would be said and what would have to happen. If there's one thing I've learned in all the years working for Sedgewick, it's that when one breaks the rules one must above all be careful not to be caught— while at the same time being careful to go on protecting the very rules one breaks. And of course be prepared for exposure and its consequences. We shall have to think very carefully about this."

Only after Elizabeth had finished speaking did Allison realize that Elizabeth did not see their intimacy as one evening's impulse and aberration. Elizabeth was talking as though they would go on this way, as though they needn't stop. Allison pressed herself against Elizabeth ecstatically. "Elizabeth," she gurgled her delight, "Elizabeth!" The sweetness was almost painful in its intensity.

"But right now you're not thinking about anything, darling, are you." Elizabeth fairly purred.

Allison laughed. "Oh yes I am. I'm thinking about one thing."

Elizabeth rolled Allison over and bent her head over Allison's breast. The touch of Elizabeth's tongue and teeth on the nipple made the pulse in her vulva start up again. "Then we'll have to do something about that, won't we," she said, lifting her head to look into Allison's eyes.

Allison gripped Elizabeth's long hard waist and slid her hands down to the hard, sharp hip bones and dug her fingers in hard. Elizabeth always knew everything. She had always been perfect. And now she was her very own perfect lover.

Chapter Eleven

[i]

It was dark when Sorben landed the pod near the Boulder campus. Kay, unstrapping, said, just to make conversation, "I hope you'll be able to duplicate all the lab equipment we promised the biologists and chemists." She and Sorben had spent most of the day moving newly recruited scientists to Whidbey Island.

Sorben said, "That part is easy. What *I'm* wondering, Kay, is what you're going to do if your hunch is right about that facility in the mountains."

Kay fingered the handle of her satchel. "Why, I thought," she said— then halted at the warning she saw in Sorben's eyes. She swallowed. "I thought you and Magyyt and Tyln might help me rescue Scott and the others."

Sorben's head moved slowly from side to side, back and forth, and despite her human form looked profoundly alien in the off-ness of the movement. "No, Kay. It isn't possible. There can be no question of such a rescue."

"But why not?" A sudden suspicion crawled into her thoughts. "Oh, I see!" she said angrily. "It's because Scott is a man! That's it, isn't it! If it were a woman I was going in after, that would be something else altogether." She glared at the Marq'ssan. "Am I right?"

"Wrong," Sorben said flatly. "You're in every way *wrong*. All human life matters to Marq'ssan. The reason is that we can't do it. *Can't*, Kay. We can't go into places like that. You said the electronics there were reported to be undamaged after the Blanket. That means it's a heavily shielded place. And if it's that heavily shielded, it's no safe place for Marq'ssan to be. And know this, Kay Zeldin: I am not suicidal. Nor is Magyyt or Tyln. We would soon die in a place like that,

and we would almost immediately lose what you humans like to call our 'powers.' Which means our presence would be unhelpful."

Kay spoke almost through her teeth. "I don't believe that. Just being there with the pod would be helpful." The slow, deliberate way Sorben again shook her head made Kay furious. "Just what the hell is your thing about men, anyway? And why aren't there any men among you? Do you keep your males subordinated the way human males of regressive cultures keep females subordinated?"

Sorben rolled her eyes. "Kay Zeldin, sometimes you are as exasperating as an adolescent of any species can be! In the first place, gender isn't an appropriate distinction for most things to do with Marqeuei and Marq'ssan. May I point out that you have no way of knowing whether any of us are male or female: we have not told you our sex, nor will we ever do so. We all assume human female form for good reasons, which you of all people should be able to deduce and understand. Your eagerness to find your world's weaknesses duplicated in us distresses me."

Kay sank down onto the flight couch. Sorben looked as close to upset as she had ever seen a Marq'ssan be. "I'm sorry," she said, trying to understand. "I'm sorry I accused you of being that kind of oppressor. Of course it was ridiculous. But I'm at my wit's end, Sorben. I have every reason to believe Scott is in that place— the description Nadine Morris gave me combined with the memory of the mountain facility mentioned in Sedgewick's files..." Kay looked at Sorben. "What am I going to do? Give up?"

"I don't know, Kay," Sorben said. "I think you're going to have to find another way to go about this. Surely if we think about it we should be able to find some way to force them to release those people."

Bitterly, Kay said: "I should have wrung Scott's whereabouts out of Sedgewick when I had the chance."

"Oh? And how do you think you could have done that?" Sorben folded her arms over her chest. "Certainly he wouldn't have given the information to you willingly. And second, you didn't even know at the time that he had anything to do with Scott's assignment."

"Maybe so, but if I *had* known I would have gotten it out of him, one way or another!" Kay's hand clenched into a fist. "Considering everything that's happened, I think, on balance, it would have been best if I'd killed Sedgewick and Weatherall when I had the chance. Since I wouldn't be in fear for my life now if I had."

Sorben looked appalled. "On *balance*? It's revenge you want, isn't it. You're so angry, Kay."

Angry? More like just wishing she could make them leave her the fuck alone. "Not revenge," Kay said. "But these people are taking a damned good shot at ruining my life. If they had died that day, no one would have known of my part in it." But then she probably wouldn't have been able to write the book or expose Security's Operation Scapegoat over vid as she had. And there was also the small matter of what committing murder would have done to her.

"I see anger in your face and body, I hear it in your voice," Sorben said. "The word *Sedgewick* almost chokes you every time you utter it."

Kay searched in her satchel for a bottle of water. "Maybe so, Sorben. But don't I have a right to be angry? It's not as though it's all in the past. They're still fucking with me!" She found the water and pulled off the cap and drank from the bottle. And realized how stupid it was to talk about having rights to feeling an emotion.

Sorben's eyes were sad. "Don't go to that place, Kay. Your transmitter probably won't work there. I suggest you call me when you've finished talking to the people at the university here. And then return to Seattle and think about what to do next."

"I can't see myself returning to Seattle yet," Kay said. "I've only begun my trip."

"Can it be you're planning to not attend the Steering Committee meeting?"

"That's almost two weeks away."

"Yes. But you will want to return to Seattle well before it. There'll be serious issues on the agenda you'll want to discuss with others before the meeting."

A reluctant smile lifted the edges of Kay's lips. "So much advice, Sorben."

She nodded. "I thought you needed it."

Kay got to her feet and prepared to leave the pod. She could not recall a single instance in which any Marq'ssan had offered her advice. The significance of Sorben's doing so now did not escape her.

[ii]

Allison, waking to rain-muffled darkness, burrowed deeper into her sleeping bag. From the rustling sounds she heard Verna make getting up, dressing, and straightening and zipping her bag, Allison knew that if she wanted to sit at the breakfast table with the others she would have to get up soon. Here in the Free Zone one picked up the most intelligence at meals. And besides, she had to be out early this morning— the Labor Exchange had come up with a job possibility for her and her interview was at nine. She was so sick of temp work that she hoped she got it.

But how delightful to lie in the dark listening to the rain with images of Elizabeth hovering in one's thoughts, a secret hoard of which even a reminder was a delight— and guilty pleasure. She could look backwards, could retrace not only every word spoken, but even Elizabeth's every inflection and touch and facial expression, each one of which lay clear and vivid in her mind like a film she could screen again and again and again. Or she could look forward and imagine the next meeting. In Vancouver, probably. Perhaps after the Steering Committee meeting. Or possibly somewhere else. A long-shot, Elizabeth had said, but she might arrange for her to come to make a "special report" at whatever place Elizabeth might be at the time.

And where was Elizabeth now? She could be any place under Security's control. Elizabeth traveled much of the time these days, weaving in and out of HQ— which was currently somewhere in Colorado, in the mountains. Elizabeth had told her that most of Virginia and Maryland belonged to Military. Already Allison had learned a great deal from her.

Elizabeth trusted her.

Shivering, Allison dressed and used the disgusting chemical toilet common to service-tech existence. It was the hygienic details of service-tech life that she most detested. She might manage to get used to the clothing— especially the sorts of things the women in the Free Zone had begun wearing— the hairstyles, and even the makeup and the food. (Actually, the food in this house at least wasn't bad.) But using blue water showers and towel-wipes was horrible. She wondered that the chemicals necessary for these things hadn't run out. But then they were still cheaper and more easily produced than potable water. Somehow the women running the Free Zone had managed to keep the supply flowing.

Every other person living in the house was already seated at the table when Allison entered the dining room. "Morning," Verna said, all bouncy energy and cheer. Ms. Perky, Allison named her in the privacy of her own mind. "I was beginning to think you were going to sleep in. It's tempting on mornings like this, for sure."

Ms. Perky tempted to sleep in? Impossible! Allison mustered a smile and poured coffee into the only unclaimed mug. At least they drank coffee out of non-biodegradable mugs. But then coffee mugs didn't require washing after every use. "I have an interview this morning for a job," she said. "Otherwise I might indeed have been tempted." She heard herself say "indeed" and kicked herself for the slip out of cover. She was her own worst enemy before coffee.

"With the Rainbow Press, isn't it?" Jenny said.

Allison nodded and took her first sip of the scorched, muddy brew.

"Cool," Jenny said. "I've heard Venn's totally okay to work for."

Allison registered the thud of the paper hitting the front door. "There's the *Rainbow Times*," Micki said unnecessarily as she pushed back from the table.

The arrival of the paper during breakfast was one of the big moments of the day. While they ate the women took turns reading it out loud so that they could all have the paper with their breakfast. And of course they insisted on embellishing every damned article with comments, wisecracks, and discussion. Sometimes this irritated Allison almost to the point of an outburst. Fortunately, though, her years of training held her steady enough that she never did reach critical mass.

Allison listened to Micki first open and then close the front door. Half a second later came the sound of Micki whooping. "Hallelujah!" she shouted. "Hallelujah!" She burst into the dining room. "Ladies, would you take a *look* at this headline!" she shrieked, holding up the newspaper for all to see.

Large inky block capitals declared **MARQ'SSAN ZAP BOSTON MUNITIONS.** Allison's stomach hollowed. All around her the women shrieked and shouted and crowed with triumph. Ms. Perky especially was ecstatic, for before the Blanket she had been part of the Boston Collective, which she had described to Allison as an anti-Executive organization of women, mainly African-American, working to overthrow Security's control of Boston. Verna had come to Seattle to observe and participate in the Co-operative's projects as preparation for the time following Boston's projected liberation. As she did of the other women in the house, Allison doubted Verna could be recruited and run. Her CAT's estimation of the Free Zone situation hewed close to the Company's experiences with foreign agents and made no allowances for the differences in the Free Zone types they had to deal with.

Isn't it wonderful!" gushed the woman sitting on Allison's left. "Just think, Boston may be freed now!"

Acutely aware that she was the only one in the room not exulting and celebrating, Allison tried to smile. "Maybe. But I doubt that the loss of weapons and ammunition will be enough to liberate Boston."

The elation shining out of Verna's velvety dark eyes did not dim, but she said, clearly uncomprehending of what Allison could mean, "Why do you say that? Without weapons they can't hold Boston. That's a fact!"

Allison nodded. "That's probably true," she said. "But those forces holding Boston are only one of two powerful factions with weapons. As far as I can see, what is most likely to happen is that Military forces will attack and rout Security forces. And what good will that do anyone? It'll just be a change of regime. And maybe some people will get killed in the process. Especially if Military employs air-strikes."

The women fell silent. Their smiles faded; their eyes dulled. The silence that expanded among them made Allison wonder if she'd just exposed herself. She began to think about what she would do in the next five minutes if that were the case.

After about half a minute Micki said to Allison, "You have an awfully negative way of looking at things." Her eyes narrowed. "Anyway, it might not work out that way. It doesn't have to, you know."

Allison stared down into her oatmeal. "Why don't you read the story, Micki. You're right, I might be wrong." She looked up and half-smiled in what she hoped looked like apology. "Sorry to be such a downer. I guess I'm a born pessimist."

Micki picked up the newspaper and began reading in a flat, detached voice, as though what she was reading held no more than academic interest. The details the newspaper provided mainly concerned the Marq'ssan's reason for the raid— namely, retaliation against Security forces for their capture of Kay Zeldin and their attempt to abduct Sorben I Sorben. The newspaper said little about the situation in Boston. Could Elizabeth be in Boston now, attempting to keep Military from taking it? For the first time, fear of the factional conflict crept into Allison's consciousness, fear that harm could come to Elizabeth. She did not fear for herself— she was such a minor player Military would never consider it worth their while excising her. But Elizabeth— Elizabeth constituted a visible target, one nearly as significant as Sedgewick himself.

"I would have liked to have seen their faces when they realized what was happening," the woman on Allison's left said when Micki had finished. "Poof! And suddenly the warehouse is gone. Just like that!" The woman snapped her fingers.

The very thought of it cheered the others. For several minutes they giggled over and fantasized about the "special powers" of the Marq'ssan. This time Allison forced herself to join in the laughter and gleeful speculations. It surprised— and relieved— her that none of them initiated a discussion on the presence of covert action teams in the Free Zone. But that part of the story seemed to have escaped their attention. After a decent interval, Allison finished her coffee and pushed away from the table. "I'd better be going," she said to Verna. "It's a good walk."

"You have the map I printed out for you?" Verna asked.

Allison nodded.

"Then good luck," Verna said. "See you tonight?"

Allison raised her eyebrows and shrugged. "I don't know for sure yet, but I think I might be out tonight."

Ms. Perky grinned. "Meeting your new friend?"

Allison nodded sheepishly. "I hope so."

As she left the dining room she felt their eyes on her back. For a moment she thought anxiously of the Biretta and her blue plastic in the false bottom of her backpack. But closing the front door behind her, she chided herself for worrying. They wouldn't go through her things unless their suspicions were full-blown, and even then unless they had a scanner or a metal detector they wouldn't be likely to find the compartment concealing the Biretta and executive plastic. And apart from her own words and behavior, the only other thing that could give her away was her Security ID, which she carried sewn into an easy-access pocket hidden behind the right breast pocket in her denim jacket. She must believe she was safe, or she would give herself away— presuming she hadn't done so already. She really needed to discipline her control more effectively. One more incident like that and they likely *would* make her.

[iii]

Martha thanked Jess again, hung up the phone, and crossed *flyers* off her list. She knew that she could count on Jess to see to it that the flyers were printed and distributed. It was only layouts that Jess couldn't be trusted with (besides out-of-town assignments). Next on Martha's list was *Rainbow Times*. She picked up the handset and punched in the *Rainbow Times*'s number. As she had expected, she was given the choice to leave a message or have her call put into a queue. She hung up. It would be best to walk over. The *Rainbow Times* had its offices only a few blocks away in the Pike Place Market.

Martha donned her rain hat and was snapping closed her parka when the phone chirped. Being the only one in the office, she picked up the handset, slid the message pad closer, and grabbed a pen. "Martha Greenglass."

"Hey, Martha! It's Geneva. I'm so glad to find you in the office! We urgently need to meet. Would you be able to do lunch today?"

"Let me check my calendar," Martha said, digging her engagement book out of her rucksack. "What is it that's so urgent?" She flipped the book open to the second week in September.

"Your call for a committee to study the Birth Limitation issue. The deal is, if I don't get you to stop advertising it, all hell is going to break loose. We've got to go about this cautiously and thoughtfully, Martha."

"Can't make it today. Sorry. But look, I don't think you understand why I'm calling this meeting. As I see it, if we don't develop some kind of public forum about this we're going to find ourselves merely reacting to things other people are organizing. I'm thinking of the culties, Geneva. And I don't think reacting is a good way of going about formulating a community policy."

"I agree, Martha, we definitely don't want to react. You know I've been active in reproductive rights issues for years. Well I don't think you realize how emotional a subject this will be for people. Or how complicated it is."

"I'm getting a sense of that just fine," Martha said drily. "And that's the reason I think we need a meeting as soon as possible."

"No, really, Martha. Listen to me. If you do it that way, you'll only be stirring up a hornet's nest. Let's get a private group together first, do some brainstorming, and then try to educate people into the subject as it emerges. That's the only approach that makes sense."

Martha sighed. "A backroom deal? Sorry, Geneva. Too many people already know about it. And of all things, I don't want rumors to start flying about the Co-op's clandestine conspiracy for assuming the Executive's control over reproductive rights."

There was a pause. Now Geneva sighed. "Okay, Martha. I know well enough by now that no one can stop you when you're really set on something. I just wish to the goddess you'd wait even as little as a month or so. Say until after the Steering Committee meeting. You realize that the Steering Committee meeting— if you go through with this crazy public debate you're planning— will be dominated by the issue. And you can bet it will draw some real psychos to it, too."

"We have to take those kinds of risks, Geneva. Or else we'll fall back into the same old traps and find ourselves in the role of rulers. You and me, I mean. I'm all for public political education. You *know* that. But what you're talking about is closer to executive-style management practices."

"Damn it, Martha!" Martha closed her engagement book and jammed it back into the rucksack. Was Geneva seriously angry with her? But after a couple of seconds Geneva said, her voice considerably cooler now, "I heard you and Louise split. Sorry."

Martha had met Geneva through Louise, but it had turned out that Martha and Geneva had more in common than Geneva and Louise, and so Geneva had come to seem more Martha's friend than Louise's. "It's probably for the best," Martha said awkwardly. "Uh, look, Geneva, we should get together sometime. I'd still like to talk about Birth Limitation with you. Just not before the meeting."

"Yeah," Geneva said. "I'll give you a call early next week. Okay?"

"Sure. Will I see you at the meeting on Sunday?"

Geneva sighed. "If you insist on going through with it, I suppose you will. Goodbye, Martha."

"Bye, Geneva." Martha finished snapping closed her rain parka and shouldered her rucksack. Of all things, she hated conflict with her friends. In her book, friends were supposed to support one another. But the fact was, sometimes conflict just couldn't be avoided.

[iv]

An hour later, her business in the newspaper's office finished, Martha descended the stairs in the Old Market Building, intent on stopping at an espresso cart for a cup of cappuccino. One flight before she reached street level, however, sounds of disorder disrupted the quiet, sounds she quickly distinguished as shouting, screaming, and the shattering of glass. Galvanized into action, Martha ran the rest of the way down and emerged into the south end of the open market area in time to see a man in olive tunic and trousers swing a bat into a fish vendor's refrigerated display cabinet. When the first blow cracked the glass without shattering it, the man drew the bat back and hammered it again. The glass shivered into shards and fragments that

flew in all directions, sprinkling the fish and bystanders. The men behind the counter, bellowing their rage, charged around the display case; long sharp filleting knives flashed in their hands. Another man in olive appeared, also brandishing a bat, and both men in olive— bats raised over their heads— faced the vendors.

There were other sounds of violence. At least half a dozen more men in olive had materialized on the concourse brandishing bats. Cabbages, onions, and apples rolled as the men overturned high stall after high stall. Vendors huddling in frightened knots watched the men smash and scatter the vegetables and fruit with wide vicious sweeps of their bats— except at one stall where a woman backed against the wall kept the men off with a pistol she held out from her body with both hands. Few customers were around, suggesting most had fled. Martha thought she heard the words *violence* and *men with bats* being shouted outside.

The fish vendors' confrontation continued in an apparent standoff. Martha hoped that the men with bats would back off the way cats did when they got into such situations, yet given their uniform-like garb thought it unlikely.

She began to consider how best to intervene.

A half-dozen women in the gray clothing of the Women's Patrol poured into the market concourse. Martha was at first relieved, but when she saw that the women held rifles, she grew alarmed. Escalation, she thought angrily, and wondered if the men with bats had more sophisticated weapons ready to draw when challenged by superior firepower.

"Drop your bats," one of the Women's Patrollers shouted. At the sound of that voice, Martha took a closer look at the woman who had spoken and found that she had not mistaken it. Fear for Louise's safety was now added to Martha's emotional amalgam.

"What's wrong, girls, can't take a little anarchy?" one of the men yelled at the Women's Patrol. "Thought you bitches claimed to be anarchists! Well we're just practicing here. What do you want to come on heavy with your police stuff for if you're the anarchists you claim to be?"

Martha gritted her teeth. Louise and her group had played right into their hands. The people directing these men had probably scripted to the last epithet exactly what was to be said in given situations. Martha stepped forward. "Everybody put down their weapons," she shouted. Out of the corner of her eye she glimpsed several bodies shifting. "Including you with the rifles! Unless you're interested in a bloodbath, there's no point to this scene. So everybody drop their weapons, and when you see that everyone else's weapons are down, back off. It's that simple."

One of the men in olive hooted and mimicked, "It's that simple. Boys! You know those nasty little boys will be boys!"

But after a good deal of uneasiness and excruciatingly tentative moves, they all followed Martha's suggestion, and the men in olive backed out of the market and took off, abandoning their bats on the concrete. After their antagonists' exodus, the vendors retrieved their knives and gun and the Women's Patrol their rifles.

The contingent of Women's Patrol approached Martha. "That was really bright," Martha said to Louise, "aiming rifles at the bastards. *Really* bright."

Louise glared at her. "Because of your damned interference we lost them, Martha. We would have taken them and found out who was organizing them and made sure they never set foot in the market again. As it is they'll probably be harassing people here again, as well as in other markets."

"You would have taken them," Martha said. "And then what? March them off to jail? Shit. Don't you see how you played into their hands, coming on with the heavy police action crap? What they're going to do now, probably, is go home and write up some propaganda analyzing what happened here. And a lot of people will listen to them. Some will wonder about our credibility. And others will begin to want a police force and a government and will look for caveman types to protect them. And all because you came on with your goddam rifles!" Standing eyeball to eyeball with Louise, Martha was only dimly aware of the other women circling them and of the bystanders surrounding the outer-ring of the Women's Patrol.

"Fuck, Martha, you don't know what you're talking about," Louise said in disgust. "The people who buy and sell in the market have a right to expect the Women's Patrol to protect them. And I intend to see to it that we do protect them. Whatever ideological garbage you mouth to the contrary." Louise turned from Martha. "Come on, women," she said. "Let's get out of here." And the six of them marched off.

Trembling, fighting tears, Martha went out into the rain. It was as though she and Louise had never been friends, much less lovers. She turned her face to the sky and let the rain slip down her cheeks. It hurt. It hurt terribly.

[v]

Lying in the hot bath she had drawn as soon as she and Dana had arrived at the Edmonds house, Allison scrubbed three days' accumulation of odor and dirt from her body and cosmetics from her face. She knew Elizabeth had insisted on Allison's attending the weekly conferences of the CAT's executives only because she wanted Allison to be able to report on them to her. Yet deep down she believed that Elizabeth had understood her need for occasional escape from her deep-cover immersion in service-tech life. With her new story of having found a lover in Seattle, Allison could now plausibly get away often from her cover situation without raising suspicions. She would be able to make a habit of spending Friday nights and perhaps even Saturdays (depending on developments requiring her attention in Seattle) in the comfortable Edmonds enclave. Everything seemed set now that she had a job and the means of easily getting away to make her reports. And she had the feeling that with the new job she would learn a great deal more about the Free Zone's political organization.

Only when her skin began to wrinkle did Allison drag herself out of the tub. It gave her great pleasure to rub herself with a towel until her body flushed and glowed, perfume herself, and slip into the gown Elizabeth had given her (and which Dana had brought to Edmonds for her). She loved smoothing her fingers over the silk; she adored feeling it slide over her skin. The gown, which would always remind her of Elizabeth, was like having a bit of Elizabeth physically with her.

Discussion at dinner proved a great deal livelier than the previous time Allison had dined with the team. Lauder was less taciturn and perhaps less inebriated. And this time Hughes dined with them, perhaps because Goodwin and Lauder were pleased with the execution of a disruptive action by his agents in one of Seattle's public markets. About the Boston debacle no one spoke. Allison waited to see if it would be brought up during the conference. If it wasn't, she would ask. But of course it was possible Lauder had as yet received no information. Communications across the US remained primitive.

Hughes exited after dessert, and Dana cleared the table, leaving only bottles and glasses and an ashtray for Lauder's inevitable cigar. Goodwin addressed Allison as soon as Dana had closed the door after her. "We've looked over the flyer you brought with you, Bennett. I think you're essentially correct in considering this meeting significant. Not only is it the first sign of a development of possibly crippling divisiveness among the leaders, but we can assume some of the most important figures in their organization will make an appearance." Goodwin looked at Lauder. "I propose, Henry, that we send Hughes to the meeting. Not only to gather intelligence, but with an eye to making contact with one of the women. Some of them, at least, have a heterosexual orientation."

Lauder cackled. Allison could not help thinking of how little he lived up to the image she had had of "Mr. Clean." How could this dissolute wreck of a man, who when he laughed cackled like an old crone out of Macbeth, be the legendary personage who commanded the worldwide respect of all Company executives? On the surface at least he seemed no more in control than Mason Bennett, another drunk— but one who had a fittingly low position in of all things the Department of Agriculture, perhaps the least influential of all the Executive's agencies and departments.

"Sex," Lauder said juicily, pulling the unbroached bottle of scotch closer, "is about the most fortunate thing for executives ever invented." Lauder broke the seal and poured the golden liquor into the squat heavy crystal tumbler Dana had placed beside the bottle. "Its bestial pursuit devours more time and energy of the masses than any single other thing. Shall we drink to the convenience of sex?" Grinning, he raised his glass and downed at least a quarter of the four ounces Allison estimated he had poured into the glass.

Allison lowered her eyes as she always did when these sorts of comments were made (as they so often were) by male executives. Among the four executives sitting around the table, she alone had not been fixed and never would be. Every one of the men knew that and were probably at that very moment thinking something contemptuous about her because of it (excepting, perhaps, Morgan, if what Elizabeth had said about him was true). Contempt for executive females' intact sexual interest had been something she had had to live with all her life, something she had been schooled to accept without comment. But for a moment, thinking of her night with Elizabeth (and wearing her gown, how could she not be thinking of her almost all the time?), and of Elizabeth's distrust of Lauder and Goodwin, brought a flash of insight to her, that perhaps the female executives had the best of both worlds since it had always been the males who had been unable to control their sexuality and their sexual desires, growing irrational in its pursuit, melancholic at its absence, and— most significant of all— allowing themselves to be manipulated on its account, while women on the other hand had until very recently ignored their own sexual desire, maintaining a basically economic relationship to it— and to *male* sexual desire at that. Women had always exercised fine control over their own sexual desires... And so now she and Elizabeth— and other women executives— controlled yet sexual, could have it all.

This insight faded, however, as Allison wondered if Lauder had made his crack out of resentment at orders from above concerning herself— both her having been specified for contact with Headquarters as well as her inclusion in the CAT's weekly executive conferences.

"But you know, Henry," Goodwin continued in the same vein, "the general response since Zeldin told the world all is that we are the unfortunates." And at this, Goodwin and Lauder almost choked on their laughter.

"But perhaps they should ask our women, eh Bennett?" Lauder said, addressing Allison directly. "You could tell the story, *n'est ce pas?*"

As though he were a prize exemplar of control! Allison wanted to laugh. But she said easily, softly, "Yes, I suppose I could— if I had to. One would rather not discuss it, of course." This, Allison knew, she had said in the best executive style: her mother would have been proud of her, for her response showed only delicacy, deference, and the faintest trace of pride.

When Allison failed to rise to the bait, Goodwin resumed discussion of Hughes's possible recruitment of Free Zone cadre.

"Penetration, one might almost say." And Lauder giggled.

Goodwin grinned. "Not in the Company's sense of the word, Henry. But possibly one penetration could achieve another."

"Possibly, Mark, just possibly," Lauder said, manifestly pleased at Goodwin's success at redeeming his own feeble attempt at witticism. Allison sipped her wine and wondered about Lauder's lack of irritation at Goodwin for this. It was, she felt, another clue to what was going on in this CAT. Most controllers would have been annoyed to be shown up in this way by a subordinate. But obviously Lauder wasn't like most controllers. Perhaps she had been too quick to write him off as a drunken failure. Perhaps there was more to this setup than met the eye.

Allison drank little that night, the better to observe her colleagues— as closely, she reflected, as she observed Verna, Micki, and the others. Given Elizabeth's interest, the one task of observation might very well be as important as the other.

Chapter Twelve

[i]

While in Boulder Kay had the rare opportunity of attending a Sunday afternoon all-Beethoven symphony concert in the Veronica Astor Skeffington Performance Theater, which she knew to be acoustically one of the best concert halls in the country. Though designated as a "benefit" performance with the proceeds intended to assist the now crippled professional music community in the Boulder and Denver area, most of the people attending paid only nominal admission since they could not afford the extravagant sum being charged executives. The colleagues who had brought Kay to the concert explained that the musicians themselves had decided to hold concerts whether they were paid or not, and that it was hoped that the executives, thus reminded of the straits of the professional community, would prove generous. Glancing down at the mezzanine level, Kay predicted the strategy likely to succeed, for the boxes fairly teemed with executives.

The concert began with the first Egmont Overture, followed by the Violin Concerto. Immersed in the music, Kay forgot her surroundings and her reasons for being in Boulder. She had not heard a full symphony playing Beethoven since before the Blanket. And for a short while it was as though the Blanket and its aftermath had never been.

At intermission Kay accompanied her colleagues down to the lobby where they drank sparkling water and discussed the violinist's controversial cadenza. Kay gladly joined the tacit conspiracy to treat the occasion as nothing out of the ordinary. People rarely had the chance to forget all they had lost, and though it would not do to live in constant fantasy, outside the Free Zone especially one sometimes needed to escape the reality of post-Blanket life.

Correctly guessing that the lines of women waiting to use the toilets would be substantially diminished by that time, Kay waited to go down to the women's room until just before it was time to return to the hall. When she emerged from her stall, she found herself alone in the glittering white cavernous rest-room. She had, she thought, probably cut it too close. Anxious not to miss so much as a measure of the symphony promised for the second half, she paused only to brush her hands with a towel-wipe and then dashed out the door and toward the staircase.

Kay ran up the first flight of stairs. She heard a spatter of applause as she passed the lobby landing and put on speed, for she had two more flights to go. But rounding the curve on the mezzanine level— she could hear the orchestra playing the opening full A-major chord— her gaze ran straight into a particular, impossible pair of startled blue eyes. Shocked, she froze— until adrenalin spurted into her blood, spun her around, and sent her hurtling back down the stairs. Heart racing, she clattered out over the foyer's marble floor, sprinting for the front entrance, mightily resisting the urge to glance over her shoulder.

"Stop her!" she heard Weatherall shouting, presumably at the pair of Guard stationed in the lobby.

Breathless, flinging out her hand at the massive brass handle, Kay catapulted herself into the heavy glass door. Her body connected with the door, and it yielded to the force of her weight and velocity. Her speed hardly flagging, she careened out into the street, unsure of where to go, unfamiliar with the territory. Knowing that she had to keep on, Kay veered right, hoping for open public buildings she could attempt to hide herself in— presuming pursuit of her lagged.

But it did not. About twenty yards from the door, Weatherall herself leaped onto Kay from behind, knocking her to the ground. Kay struggled wildly to get up, but Weatherall's foot slammed into her diaphragm, knocking the wind out of her lungs. Gasping, Kay jack-knifed into a ball, tucking her chin and knees and head into her chest to protect her chest, belly, and face.

Hands grasped Kay's shoulders and forced her onto her back. She stared into her opponent's smiling face. "To think of all the trouble we've gone to for retrieving you, Zeldin, and by a stroke of luck you simply stroll straight into my arms. Life's jokes are choice, don't you think? And I'd even forgotten your passion for Beethoven. Isn't that funny, Zeldin?"

Kay did not answer.

Weatherall glanced up at the guards. "One of you fetch my escort from Box Eight, the other of you roust out my car and driver from the garage." Her voice was curt. "It's the only internal combustion car there. You'll recognize it." She smiled down at Kay, then looked up again at the guards. "Oh, and lend me a pair of cuffs, will you? We're not taking any chances of losing her again."

Both guards immediately held out a pair of cuffs then watched as Weatherall attached Kay's right wrist to her own left wrist. "It's safer if we stick together, don't you think?" she said, waving the guards away.

Gloating, the bloody bitch was *gloating.* I should have killed you both while I had the chance, Kay silently raged.

Weatherall hauled her to her feet and deliberately probed her rib-cage with long bony fingers. "It *is* your lucky day, Zeldin. I didn't break a single one of your ribs."

Kay stared down at her satchel lying on the pavement with its contents half-spilled out around it. Her gun. There was still her gun if she could get to the satchel. Kay bent as though to pick up the mess, but Weatherall jerked her cuffed wrist high. "Leave that," she said. "We'll let the help take care of it. That's what we pay them for."

Kay clamped her jaw tight to keep from retorting. One started silent in order to remain silent: she would do it right this time. She would maintain absolute silence, no matter how innocuous the gambit— and never cease to watch for opportunities to escape, handcuffs or not.

[ii]

Martha had estimated an attendance between twenty and thirty-five. But by seven o'clock the room had filled with perhaps seventy-five people, most of whom had to stand. Should she postpone the meeting so that they could assemble somewhere else? Or should she start and hope some people would leave— on the presumption that only those

intensely interested would stay under such conditions? "I didn't expect this kind of turnout," Martha said to the crowd. "Maybe we should put this off to another time so that we can meet in a larger room."

Silence.

"Does anyone have another suggestion to make?"

"Postponing the meeting is an excellent suggestion." Martha recognized Geneva's voice and scanned the crowd until she spotted her. "We couldn't possibly have a reasonable discussion under circumstances like these."

"Does anyone else have an opinion?" Martha asked irritably. "Or know of a room the appropriate size we could move to right now?" Martha wondered whether the lounge in the building housing the Co-op's offices would be large enough and whether anyone there would mind if they used it, but decided that the lounge was probably too small. What about the basement of the Denny Regrade Y? But the management of the Y would be perturbed at a group so large trooping in without advance notice. And it might already be in use.

Again, silence.

"Okay," Martha said, giving up. "Since there aren't any other suggestions, we'll have to postpone. I'll try to arrange something for tomorrow or Tuesday night, same time. Anyone interested can call me tomorrow. Say after noon. My number is 197-382-4664. Ask for Martha. I'm sorry for the hassle and hope I'll see you all when we try this again."

The no longer silent crowd shuffled out of the room past Geneva, who had lost no time positioning herself at the door to pass out literature. Trying to gauge the attendees and guess the character of their interest, it seemed to Martha that a good portion of them were obvious heterosexual couples. The room emptied quickly, except for Geneva at the door— talking to a couple who looked like fundamentalist Christians— and a man, dark-haired, bearded, dressed in shabby professional clothing, leaning against the wall. Martha slid her notepad into her briefcase and began considering the problem of finding a suitable meeting place at such short notice.

"Disappointing," the man said.

Martha gave him a quick look and guessed that his interest in the issue was not personal. "Sorry. But I never guessed there'd be this kind of turnout."

He moved a few feet closer. "Even apart from all the people who have wanted children and been denied them, there's bound to be a lot of interest in such an explosive issue."

Martha picked up her briefcase. "So what's your interest?" she asked.

He held his hands out, palms up. "It's rather complicated," he said. "Part of it is concern for the future of the Free Zone. Part of it is my scholarly interest in the relation between demographics and economy. There's been a great deal of study over the century on free reproductive practices in both historical and cross-cultural contexts."

Martha said, "Sounds as though you're well-informed on the subject. I'd be interested in talking to you sometime about it."

He grinned, his eyes, all friendly warmth, crinkled up at the corners. "Obviously I have some free time now. I'd be happy to go somewhere for a cup of coffee and give it the same quality attention I'd been hoping for from the public meeting."

His grin was infectious; Martha had to smile back. "It's true, now would be the obvious time. You have a place in mind?"

"I belong to a club, it's about eight blocks from here. We can talk as we walk."

"I'll have to wheel my bicycle along with."

"Ah, one of the lucky ones," he said as they moved to the door. At Martha's inquiring look, he elaborated. "Someone ripped mine off a couple of months ago, and I've been reduced to hoofing it ever since. By the way, my name's David Hughes." He extended his hand.

Martha shook it. "Martha Greenglass. I loathe being called Marty, so please don't." When they reached the door, Martha acknowledged Geneva, who had been effectively button-holed by a middle-aged heterosexual couple who apparently had a *lot* to tell her. "Nice work," she said.

Geneva raised her eyebrows at Martha, likely over her being accompanied by David Hughes. Martha hustled out into the hall. It

would serve Geneva right if she got stuck with the fundamentalists all night.

[iii]

Sitting across from one another at a table in a place she suspected still operated with plastic credit, Martha and David talked for several hours, first about Birth Limitation and the possible practical effects its abolition would have on the Free Zone, and then more personally. Although they started with coffee, after the first hour they switched to beer, which David ordered in pitchers. Each time they were served, David signed a book the server presented to him. Martha could not say exactly why she suspected the place of being money-based, only that something about the clientele, the server, and the book seemed different from the barter-based clubs Martha belonged to. Martha of course knew that some professionals still had credit in the International Banking System. Though she disapproved of the use of money, she strongly believed that private clubs or co-ops should not and could not be barred from using it if they so chose. It would, after all, be governmental for the Co-op to make and enforce such an interdiction. But as a matter of principle, she herself had never had anything to do with money since the Withdrawal.

This one niggling detail, though, hardly disturbed her pleasure in talking with him. His attentiveness, his intelligence, his warm responsiveness made her want to touch him. His eyes in particular fascinated and charmed her, at times flashing with concern, often twinkling with humor, occasionally responsive with sympathy. So Martha ended up going home with him to a bare, impersonal apartment in a tall complex near the Pike Place Market. She found it strange being with a man again— strange and, for brief moments, repulsive. But each time her repulsion vanished almost as soon as it appeared. He was different from Walt; playful and lighthearted, he made her laugh so much and so often that her throat filled with phlegm. Martha almost forgot he was a professional— and did, for a while, forget Louise.

Later, though, when after fucking they were lying quietly apart, Martha remembered. Silently she wept.

"What is it, Martha?"

Martha had thought him asleep. "Sorry." She dabbed her face with the sheet. "I guess I didn't expect this. I split from someone I cared a lot for only two weeks ago."

David put his arms around her. "I understand. It's awfully soon. But maybe this is for the best."

Martha sighed shakily. "I don't know. Maybe so. Sorry to be such a nuisance."

David squeezed her close and told her not to be silly.

Martha's heart ached. She wanted Louise, but Louise was gone forever. She would get past it, she knew. But it hurt so damned much. She knew she'd never get so over it that she'd ever be the same person she'd been with Louise.

[iv]

Entering the base that Weatherall and the others referred to as "the Rock" stripped Kay of all hope for escape. Never had she seen or imagined such a fortress— from the guards to the electronic sensors and barriers to the vast distances and confusing maze-like profusion of levels, roads, and corridors. She saw that save for destruction by massive thermonuclear attack, the base was impregnable— and inescapable. If this fortress was now Security's central headquarters, it had been well-chosen.

Weatherall's car parked soon after entering the base; her escort opened both of the back doors. Weatherall freed her own wrist from the handcuffs and bound Kay's hands behind her back and gave orders that she expected "the prisoner" to be delivered to Internal Security "in mint condition" under pain of finding themselves transferred to L.A. by the next shift. Then she took Kay's watch and satchel, climbed into a battery-powered one-seater, and zoomed off into the tunnel alone.

Weatherall's escort dragged Kay out of the car; cursing and deriding her, they thrust her into the back of a minivan. Kay became almost paralyzed with fear. To calm herself, she concentrated on Weatherall's explicit orders to them. Striving to ignore the taunts and graphic descriptions of what she "had coming to her," she kept silent and stared down at the floor of the van.

When the van stopped they pushed her out onto the cement. Conscious of how important it was to keep upright, though her side throbbed from Weatherall's kick, she struggled to her feet as quickly as she could. Of all things she did not want to present herself as a target for kicking or give them an excuse for dragging her. When she did succeed in getting to her feet— she saw that they had come to a loading dock— three of the men hustled her into a high-speed elevator that plummeted them to a level she knew must be far below the surface of the earth.

They emerged from the elevator into a maze of long wide fluorescent corridors controlled periodically by armed checkpoints. The vastness of the metal, plastic, and concrete sterility numbed her. Word of her capture apparently proceeded them, for before they had reached their final destination men and women began appearing in the corridor— to glare, to gape, to curse and jeer her. The book, Kay thought, all this hatred is because of the book. And because of Sedgewick... The solid mass of hatred she could feel directed at her threatened to engulf her; its power nauseated her. Kay kept her eyes focused on the gleaming linoleum floor. When finally they reached a large, low-ceilinged office holding at least twenty desks, she felt relieved to be out of the corridors— even if it did mean she was closer to an interrogation by Wedgewood or even Sedgewick himself. Here her captors uncuffed her, shoved her into a vinyl straight chair, re-cuffed both wrists to the bar under the seat— and left her.

No one questioned her, but for the entire time she sat cuffed to the chair, men came in groups to harass and revile her, spewing streams of obscene vituperation, spitting in her face, abusing her for her treachery, describing what they each of them would do to her, graphically detailing the instruments they would use to rape and otherwise torture her. Kay tried not to listen— by closing her eyes or staring into her lap, by trying to discover ways to ease the agonizing cramps in her arms and legs, shoulders and neck, by fighting claustrophobia— soon wanting only to collapse from the fatigue that soaked into her. Once she was taken to a toilet. But apart from that one short break she sat cuffed in that same position for time incalculable. Now and then she

nodded off, but each time the arrival of a new group come to taunt her would jerk her back into full consciousness of the nightmare.

After the first few hours Kay realized that although they abused her verbally none of them touched her, and she took hope from the realization— hope that they— she tried to avoid specifying to herself who the "they" were— might need her for something too important to risk her physical and mental well-being, suggesting that she might have something to bargain with. Many times she reminded herself that Goodwin's loquazene interrogation of her had been interrupted, but each time the possible implications of that occurred to her, Kay banished that area for concern to the darkest corners of her mind. Eventually the giddiness of dehydration and the psychological effects of fatigue set in, and Kay lost track of any thread of hope.

The man who had first taken control of her in the office left. When after a long time he returned again, Kay conjectured that possibly two shifts had passed during his absence. But she did not really know. Thirst and muscle-shaking fatigue so distorted her sense of reality that it could have been eight or eighteen hours she sat there— or twenty-four or thirty-six. She began to worry that she would be cuffed to the chair until she expired from filter-failure. It would be an extremely unpleasant way to die.

For that reason it might appeal to "them."

[v]

Wanting to arrive early for her first day on the job, Allison set out on Monday morning at 8:15. She had walked only a few yards from the house, though, when she spotted Dana sitting in a van parked near the corner. Allison wondered at the openness of the approach. If anything could blow her cover, this would. For all she knew, they could be seen from a second-floor window of the house. She decided she would walk by without offering any sign of recognition. Dana would, she was sure, follow her at a distance before making contact. But then Dana frankly beckoned, and Allison gave up all thought of discretion. Something must, she thought, be up.

Dana reported through the open window that Goodwin had ordered that Allison shut down the cover job and return at once to the

Edmonds enclave. She said that Goodwin had given her the instruction without explanation.

Allison crept back into the house and up the stairs, on tenterhooks lest she encounter anyone. Swiftly and stealthily she stuffed her things into her backpack and carried it out to the van. To her relief, she got away without encountering any of the house's residents, and Dana lost no time getting the van out of there. But she didn't realize the depth of her relief at escaping the assignment until the moment they accessed the interstate. It then crashed joyously over her: she was free, finally free of that place. Whatever they had in mind for her next must be better than this last assignment. She would be away from those service-techs and their tight little world, away from the grunginess of their daily existence. She hadn't realized how much she loathed eating out of biodegradable dishes, using chemical toilets and blue showers, and discussing politics from a service-tech point of view. The atmosphere in that house had been stifling.

When they arrived at the Edmonds house Goodwin called Allison into Lauder's office and informed her she had been transferred. Allison could see that Goodwin, never having really considered her a part of the team, was pleased. When Allison asked him where she was being sent, he shrugged. The orders had said nothing about her final destination, only that she was to be taken to the airport in Vancouver, where she would be met.

The orders said nothing about maintaining the service-tech cover, so Allison insisted on bathing and changing into her one decent set of clothes before leaving. Elizabeth, she thought as she bathed. This was Elizabeth's doing. Elizabeth had come up with an assignment that would allow them to see one another more often. That had to be it. Elizabeth must be missing her as much as she was missing Elizabeth. Allison's elation heightened. Elizabeth wanted her near her and had pulled strings to make it happen. She *knew*— she could feel it in her bones— she would be seeing Elizabeth soon— probably, in fact, that very night.

Allison dug out her Biretta, her plastic, and her Security ID and slipped them into her tunic pouch. She could be her executive self

now, for she was returning to the civilized world where being an executive was of all things most desirable.

Allison felt better than she had in weeks.

[vi]

Dazed and numbed, Kay hardly noticed when they removed her from the chair. As they half-dragged her through corridors, into and out of elevators and through more corridors, she made no attempt to study her surroundings, for she had become oblivious to everything but her need for sleep, her thirst, and the nausea, numbness, cramping, and shakiness of her body that made movement so intolerable. It seemed an eternity before they stopped to insert a strip of plastic into a slot above what looked like a thumb-lock plate. A few long seconds after the plastic was swallowed, the door slid open. They shoved her inside and the door slid closed. Stumbling from the shove, Kay crumpled to the floor in a faint.

When she came to she was at first aware only of the coldness of the concrete. Opening her eyes into cold blue light, a wave of nauseating dizziness swept over her. She closed her eyes again and drifted. Some time later a voice in her mind told her to get up, to explore her changed circumstances, to look for water. But she could not bring herself to make the effort and instead lay unmoving. Though shivering, she was glad to be recumbent, glad to be left alone in silence.

For a long time her mind remained empty, almost unconscious; she did not think much, except to long for darkness and warmth. Then, after a while, a distinct thought came to her, that she might almost be dead, because it was near to being dead to lie motionless, wanting nothing but to be quiet and left alone to lie like this. The image of famine victims in places the executive countries would not aid because of their refusal to practice Birth Limitation policies came into Kay's mind, the image of people so inert as they neared death that flies settled on them without hindrance. She, Kay, was almost as if dead, too. If a fly were to settle on her she might not lift her hand to brush it off. It seemed obvious she would die of filter-failure; she might be dying now, for she had no idea how long it had been since they had taken her.

These images disturbed Kay to the point of overpowering her inertia. She raised her head. Trembling and sweating from the strain, she pressed herself upwards until she was sitting on her knees. Waves of dizziness ebbed and flowed with the buzzing in her ears; she shook violently because the cold sweat lathering her skin made her even colder. Sitting propped against the door she could see everything there was to see. The floor she already knew. At one end of the narrow room she saw low to the ground what was probably a toilet, and above that a towel-wipe dispenser and a narrow slot in the wall, probably for disposing used towel-wipes, and, on the wall opposite the door, a platform cantilevered against the wall. Kay thought she saw a folded blanket on it, though as she stared at it she decided it might be something else and not a blanket at all. She could be imagining the blanket because she was so cold. And a table, in the middle of the room. And along the wall facing the platform to the right of the door, an enormous mirror. For seeing in, Kay warned herself. The mirror is for seeing into this room. Though she saw no source of water, she told herself she had to get to her feet and look and then she would also see whether that thing were really a blanket. She tilted her head back to stare up at the ceiling and discovered thick blue plastic panels— the reason for the blueness of the light— shielding the fluorescent source of the illumination. She scanned the walls, but found no light switch.

Promising herself that this would be the last great effort she would have to make, Kay struggled to her feet and staggered around the room examining it. The seat-less stainless steel toilet had a chemical flush, providing no water of any grade whatsoever. That disposed of her one hope. She again examined the walls for a light switch, but found none. Dizzy and trembling with exhaustion, she collapsed onto the waist-high platform of hard, molded plastic, pulled the thin synthetic blanket over her body, and curled into a ball. Her head hidden under the blanket, she drifted into sleep, half-hoping she would never wake again.

[vii]

Allison reached Elizabeth's office at around four-thirty Mountain Daylight Time. Simply getting from the base's entrance to Elizabeth's

office had taken them almost an hour, for since neither she nor her escorts were of the rank that allowed quick passage through all the guard posts and electronic barriers, they had had to stop at each and every barrier and insert their plastic into data slots and press their thumbs to thumb-plates and wait for guards to scrutinize the security badges they wore clipped to their clothing. "Now if you were a top-ranker," her escort had explained, "we'd be flying through here without ever having to stop. Their badges transmit a signal that triggers all the barriers as they approach. Of course they have to have it set up this way for security reasons. You'll note that the corridors can be easily sealed in segments when there's a security emergency. Only thing is, we have false alarms every so often. And it's damned inconvenient getting stuck for a couple of hours in a stretch of bare corridor." Though interested, Allison had said something snubbing: she could not after all have a male service-tech getting so chatty with her— even if the service-tech in question rated a security-clearance as high as her own. But then she could not help noticing that her own security rating was fairly low in comparison with that of many of the people she saw here.

Though underground, Elizabeth's suite of offices lacked none of the panoply one might expect of offices occupied by the Chief of Security Services and his most immediate staff. Allison's first view, of course, was of the outermost reception area and the service-tech assigned to attend it. "Let me tell Ms. Lennox you're here," the service-tech said when Allison told her she was here to report to Elizabeth.

Less than a minute after the service-tech had gone out of the room she returned and directed Allison to go past her desk and into the inner office. Entering the latter, Allison found an executive sitting at the only desk in the room, lowering a handset from her ear. She rose to her feet and held out her hand. "I'm Jacquelyn Lennox, Allison. Nice to meet you. Elizabeth has been expecting you." The most outstanding feature of Jacquelyn's appearance— besides her fiery hair cut in soft yet crisp-edged scallops and the luminous perfection of her complexion— was the four-inch wide band of gold she wore around her silk-swathed neck. Jacquelyn had Daughter of Wealthy Parent

stamped all over her. No PA of a PA would ever be able to afford that kind of decor on her executive salary alone.

Allison shook hands with her. Out of the corner of her eye she saw that the blue light on Jacquelyn's terminal was strobing, indicating com mode. After weeks in this country it seemed wonderful and marvelous to find the com mode in use. "You're Elizabeth's PA?" she asked with a glance at the rating— far superior to her own— on Jacquelyn's badge.

"Yes. I've let her know you're here, and she'd like to see you immediately. I'll take you in now."

Allison followed Jacquelyn down a long, broad hallway painted a sumptuous shade of burgundy. "Do you ski, Allison?"

Allison said, "Yes, of course. I was living in Austria until recently. I hadn't thought about it— but of course there's marvelous skiing around here— in the winter."

"It's wonderful," Jacquelyn said. "When, that is, things aren't too crazy and one can get away." They halted before a closed door, which Jacquelyn thumbed open. She went in, and Allison followed.

Elizabeth was seated behind an enormous desk littered with stacks of manila folders, flimsies, purples, and two terminals. "Welcome back to civilization, Allison," she said. The slightness of her smile put a knot in Allison's stomach. "It's a little late for getting you started here this afternoon, so I think it would be best if you got yourself settled in your apartment today and started work tomorrow." Elizabeth nodded at her PA. "Jacquelyn will help you with all that. She has a badge for you— considering your new job as my aide, we've seen fit to upgrade your security clearance. You'll be getting a salary increase of about fifteen percent, too. Any questions, ask Jacquelyn." Allison held the smile on her face and tried to put aside her disappointment at Elizabeth's briskness, a disappointment threatening to quench her excited burst of satisfaction that her new job would be as Elizabeth's aide. "I thought perhaps I might cook dinner for you tonight," Elizabeth went on— and the surge of warmth in her eyes banished Allison's misgivings and brought the joy flooding back over her. "Jacquelyn will give you my apartment number. It'll be just up-

stairs from yours— she's arranged a place for you in the same building I live in."

Allison beamed at Elizabeth. But Elizabeth's eyes moved to Jacquelyn. "You'll take care of all this, Jacq, won't you?" she said.

"It'll be smooth sailing, I promise," Jacquelyn said.

Elizabeth's gaze returned to Allison. "I'll give you a call when I get home." She gave Allison a measured smile, then returned her attention to one of the terminals on her desk.

Jacquelyn took Allison back to her office and handed her the new badge (with a rating still below Jacquelyn's though higher than most of the ratings she had seen on badges she had passed in the corridor) and explained about transportation from base to village, about housekeeping arrangements— that her apartment came with two hours' service-tech labor a day and that she should leave instructions about shopping and food preparation every morning— and about base security regulations and other matters of procedure. She did not, however, tell Allison about the nature of her new job, saying she had no idea what Elizabeth had in mind for her. It was almost five when she summoned a male service-tech to show Allison how to get to the main transfer point and where and how to access one-seaters for driving to the village and back.

By six Allison had taken possession of her new apartment. To her delight she found that Elizabeth had had her luggage sent on from Vivien's— and had left her gifts, besides: a gown with a card welcoming Allison and asking her to wear the gown when she came up to Elizabeth's for dinner; a case of the Margaux she had drunk at the admiral's (from his cellar? Allison wondered); a bottle of cognac; and a vase of white and yellow roses.

Allison unpacked and settled into the bathtub with a glass of wine to fantasize about the coming evening with Elizabeth. She could not remember having felt so happy in her life.

[viii]

"We will have to be very very clever to pull this off— but I think we can." Again Elizabeth pressed her lips to Allison's. "Not even Jacquelyn can know. I can't give her that kind of power over me, darling. We

must be absolutely discreet. Never can we say anything at all personal in my office." And again Elizabeth kissed Allison, drawing her deeper into sensual daze. Allison understood why Elizabeth had been so distant, though she still felt jealous of Jacquelyn. But she would not let Elizabeth know that. Sexual jealousy was an embarrassing development: anyone would laugh at her for it. Elizabeth drew a little away. "I think we can work together, but we will have to be careful. We don't want you resenting having to take orders from me."

"I'll love working for you," Allison assured Elizabeth.

Elizabeth pulled back far enough for Allison to look into her beautiful, sparkling eyes. "But I am something of a fanatic about work, sweetie. You see, I have the sense that executives— those like me, I mean— can rebuild the world. We must! Or the executive ways will die. You must know right from the start that I put my work ahead of everything. And I mean *everything*, Allison. You understand?"

"Of course. I feel the same as you. It makes me sick to see so many executives sinking under defeat. Drinking themselves unconscious!"

Elizabeth's fingers stroked Allison's cheek. "Yes. That's it precisely. Those of us who have not fallen apart must do everything we can to restore the world to what it was. I will work you hard, Allison. You must insist when it becomes necessary that I relent. Because I will get as much work out of you as I can. I'm that way." She half-smiled. "And I don't want to lose you. It may be hard to be lovers in such a situation."

"Not at all!" Allison cried. "We'll be fighting together! We'll be comrades in arms!"

Elizabeth laughed and kissed the tip of Allison's nose. "Let's go to bed, darling, shall we?"

They went into Elizabeth's bedroom and lay on the bed in the semi-dark stroking and kissing one another. After only a few minutes, though, the phone's buzz interrupted. Instantly Elizabeth detached herself and turning her naked back to Allison reached for the handset sitting on the bedside table. "Yes?" she said crisply. There followed a pause. "I see… No, you did well, Barton, you did very well. Goodnight." Elizabeth turned back to Allison. In the dim light diffused

from the living room Elizabeth's face looked excited and calculating. "That was the base. There's no time for you to get your clothes on and leave. You'll have to lie still, with the covers up to your ears— perhaps even partly over your head, and pretend to be passed out. Sedgewick has flown in. They've sent him over here, by chopper. For which I must be grateful, considering the alternative. But he must not find out who you are. I'll tell him you're passed out."

Sedgewick! The legendary Chief of Security! Coming *here*?

Allison watched Elizabeth slip back into her gown and smooth her hair. "He will know he has gotten me out of bed," Elizabeth said. "The important thing is making him believe I've a service-tech dead drunk in here." She bent and kissed Allison's forehead. "Play your part well, darling, or we're in the soup." Leaving the door to the bedroom half-open, Elizabeth went out into the living room. Allison heard her moving around out there, perhaps setting up some sort of scene to corroborate whatever impression she wanted to impart to Sedgewick. The handset buzzed again. Elizabeth spoke only a few syllables that Allison could make out. Less than a minute later the door buzzed. Allison strained to hear their voices. Sedgewick's voice was so low, though, that she found it difficult to distinguish his words.

"They just called me from the base and said you were on your way here," Elizabeth said.

Sedgewick rumbled something Allison could not at first make out, something that ended with the words, "... you've someone here? You'll have to get rid of her."

Elizabeth laughed. "I would, except that she's out cold. I'm afraid I overestimated her capacity for liquor."

"Really, Weatherall, your tastes are so low. How often does this happen to you?"

"Would you like some of this wine? There's half a bottle left." Allison knew that Elizabeth must mean the Margaux she had opened for her to drink with dinner.

"Good god, you gave this to your service-tech to drink? Are you mad? You might as well feed a squirrel the best grade of Russian caviar!"

Allison heard the clinking of glass. "I know she enjoyed it. I just gave her a bit more than she could handle," Elizabeth said. "Here you are. I hope it's up to your standards."

"Why throw it away on someone who probably couldn't tell the difference between that and ethanol swill?"

"I'm not about to buy something cheap for my lovers, Sedgewick. It would be simply too tacky for words. Why not give them a treat? It certainly makes *me* feel better seeing them drinking something I know on good authority to be excellent. Besides, I like to believe of my lovers that they all have impeccable taste."

They laughed. Allison burrowed further under the covers. Her cheeks flamed with embarrassment.

"And Maine?" Elizabeth said.

"The weather's been tempestuous. But shall we cut the crap now, Weatherall?"

"I suppose that means you want to discuss Zeldin."

"Why the hell did you appoint yourself her controller? You know damned well Wedgewood is the natural in this case. Unless your grudge exceeds his?"

There was a pause. "Wedgewood would just waste her," Elizabeth eventually said. "That's all he knows how to do, Sedgewick. And it's precisely because of my detachment that I think I'm the best person to control her. She could make all the difference in patching up our spat with Military. She could give us information about the aliens. And she could make all the difference in reassuring Booth."

"It's not worth it, Weatherall. You know how I feel about this."

"You're letting your emotions override what's best on the larger scale," Elizabeth said. "I promise you, you'll get satisfaction. What I am going to do with her... what I am going to do is reconstruct her."

"I want her dead, Weatherall. Is that so difficult to understand?"

"You came to do it yourself?"

"No."

"To watch?"

There was a long pause. Glass clinked. "No," Sedgewick finally said. "I don't want to watch. What I want is just to know she's dead. And to know she's dead I'll have to see her— afterwards."

"When I— when we have finished with her, Sedgewick, that can still happen."

"Don't be a fool, Weatherall. She's utterly uncontrollable. She won't control herself, and no one person can control her. You'll never do it. She may let you *think* you've succeeded, but she's the smoothest damned liar I've ever encountered. Short of lobotomizing her— oh fuck. The very idea is obscene. She's like a fast smart horse that won't accept a saddle. Gorgeous to watch, but destructive as hell. A rogue. The only thing to do with such animals is to put them down. Imagining lobotomizing Zeldin is as obscene as your pouring this stuff into your zombie cunts."

So even high-ranking males like Sedgewick indulged in the same general crudities about sex as the more common male executives, Allison mused.

"It's not lobotomy I had in mind," Elizabeth said, her voice creamy in comparison with his. "I'm going to make her love authority."

Sedgewick roared with laughter that careened frighteningly near hysteria. Allison shivered and was relieved when the raucous sound finally stopped. "Are we talking about the same bitch?" he said.

"Consider it an experiment," Elizabeth said. "You needn't know anything about it until I've either succeeded or given up on her. If the latter, I'll hand her over to Wedgewood, or take care of it myself. If the former, I'll hand her over to you."

"No. Not to me. I don't want to see her or talk to her again. Do you hear me, Weatherall? You know what a liar she is, what a traitor. She doesn't have a loyal cell in her body. She's a renegade. If you have a use for her, use her. But leave me out of it. All I want is to wipe her real existence out of my mind. Do you understand me, Weatherall?"

A long, long pause followed, disturbed only by the sound of clinking glass. "Yes, of course I understand," Elizabeth said belatedly. "But just supposing, Sedgewick, that I did rehabilitate her. Would you consider—"

"Didn't you fucking hear me, Weatherall?" Allison flinched at the violent sound of a crash and glass shattering. "I don't want anything to do with her! In any way, shape, or form. Clear, Weatherall?"

"Understood," Elizabeth said softly.

"Christ, Weatherall. Christ. All right. Do what you want. But if you lose her— if she escapes— I will hold you personally responsible."

"I understand that. But we've never lost a prisoner from The Rock."

"You've never had Zeldin there. What if her alien friends come looking for her?"

Elizabeth laughed. "Then we'd be ready. Believe me, we'd be ready."

There was a long silence. "Do you have another bottle of this somewhere?" Sedgewick asked. "I'd like to take it on the plane with me."

"You're going back then?"

"Immediately."

"I see," Elizabeth said.

But Allison didn't see, not at all. Why was the Chief of Security leaving when Central Headquarters was located here? Why, for that matter, was he so wrought up over Zeldin? And when and how was it that they had captured Zeldin? She hoped Sedgewick would leave soon. There was an edge to his voice, an instability that made her skin crawl. No wonder everything was such a wreck if the Chief of Security was himself such a wreck. Fortunately, Elizabeth seemed to have him under control. Which now that she thought about it did not seem so surprising.

Sedgewick murmured something too low for Allison to make out, and then she heard the front door close. After about a minute Elizabeth came in and stood near the bed. "I suppose you heard all that, Allison."

Allison sat up. "Most of it," she said.

"You are never to speak of it to anyone. Clear?"

"Understood."

Elizabeth sat down on Allison's side of the bed. "I'd like to celebrate. Now that I've gotten Sedgewick to consent to my keeping Zeldin alive, I'm reasonably assured that all my plans will work out."

"Does Zeldin matter so much?"

"On Zeldin hinges a great deal, darling. Once I was faced with the necessity to deal with her myself— after hearing about Lauder and after their bungling— I began to think seriously about how I could use her and about what I would have to do to make her at all usable. As Sedgewick says, she's not easily controllable. Once I started thinking about all these things, the whole picture came clear." Elizabeth smiled and stroked Allison's hair. "You will help me with it, sweetie. That's why I called you here."

"I want to help you, Elizabeth. It will involve Zeldin?"

Elizabeth nodded. "Sometimes indirectly, but she will be at the center of the plan. She is the key. I knew that before although I didn't see the big picture then. There's a far greater advantage to be won than merely what we can get out of her by interrogation. Why go for crumbs when we can have the whole pie?"

Allison reached up and put her arms around Elizabeth's neck. "Let's get on with the celebration," she urged, "and talk later."

Elizabeth let Allison pull her down. "To the victor, the spoils," she murmured. And Allison, feeling like a victor, took her spoils.

Elizabeth would tell her everything... afterwards.

Chapter Thirteen

[i]

Kay woke in tears, fleeing a dream about Susan Hoffman and the despicable Boltmann straight into the merciless blue light of the cell, re-encountering a reality she found less credible than but nearly as horrible as the dream. She closed her eyes against the light; she wrapped the thin, ugly blanket more tightly around herself. But she could not escape the particular physical details making her miserable: her body gnawed by the penetrating cold, her lips so parched they were cracked and scaly, her mouth so dry that her tongue felt swollen to unbearable proportions. Worst, though, were the thoughts obsessively revolving in her head. Kay knew she had to stop the thoughts, but could not.

As an antidote she concentrated on her physical surroundings. Though she had examined the details many times already, they provided an anchor to reality— if indeed this was reality and not hallucination or a dream (and the other dream simply a dream within a dream). The thick plastic platform measured perhaps six feet by three or four. It was featureless, except for the raised steel rings set into its perimeter. A wall of rough concrete blocks— painted the same chilly blue as the ceiling panels— bordered one side of the platform. Along the same wall near the ceiling of blue plastic panels ran a thin narrow strip of metal mesh. This, Kay had decided, must be for ventilation and heat (if they did in fact heat the cell, which she guessed must be at most 55 degrees Fahrenheit). The smooth plastic-coated wall a couple of feet from one end of the platform— the end she chose to lay her head on— had square white panels embedded in it, perhaps thumb-lock panels. A chair-less heavy gray steel table— excepting the blanket and individual towel-wipes, the only movable object in the cell— stood in the center of the room. Under the table where the floor troughed lay a drain of some sort. Perhaps they hosed the concrete to clean it. Or perhaps all the cells in this hellhole had drains in them because some of them were used for certain sorts of things. Or perhaps they always used this room for those sorts of things…

Kay jerked herself back from that train of thought to keep from being sucked down again into the terrible images.

And made herself go on.

The mirror across the room: she considered it again and reviewed the possibility she had earlier seen in it. If she were to shove the table into the mirror hard enough, it would break. What was on the other side wouldn't matter, because undoubtedly there would be no way out through the other side. They wouldn't be so careless. But a piece of glass would provide her with a weapon. With a piece of glass in her hand she could lie in wait for whoever might come through that door.

Since she had been brought to this cell Kay had half a dozen times fantasized an escape in which she used a sliver of glass as a weapon against her captors. Each replay of the fantasy had included more and sharper details. This time when she replayed it, though the fantasy had more details than in previous versions, it, too, disintegrated— as all the other run-throughs had— with her acknowledgment of physical debility. If she could hardly sit up, how could she ever make it out of this fortress, even supposing she somehow managed to escape the cell?

She knew, of course, that other things could be done with glass. One could use a piece of glass on one's own throat.

But another obstacle occurred to her, blocking out the ugly images flooding her thoughts: how, given her physical impotence, could she hope to have the strength to push the table with enough force to break the mirror? At this new admission of impotence, Kay broke down into sobs.

When her fit of self-pity had exhausted itself, Kay sat up and slid carefully off the platform until her feet were planted solidly on the floor. A wave of dizziness assaulted her, pressing her back against the

platform until her vision and hearing cleared of the dark sweaty buzz engulfing her. Slowly, then, she took the three steps to the table and pushing on it managed to move it a few inches. It was not as heavy as it looked. For someone in normal physical shape it would be trivial to slam the table into the mirror.

When the dizziness brought on by her test effort had passed, she took two steps back, then fell at an angle with all her weight onto the table, gliding it unresistingly over the concrete until it rammed into the mirror with a degree of force Kay felt certain must succeed in cracking it.

The mirror remained intact.

Fighting back tears of frustration, Kay examined the mirror. When her eyes encountered her own image, she recoiled in shock. Then, careful to avoid even the edges of her reflected image, she reached out and pressed her palm against the mirror, thinking that it might be best to use her body rather than the table— and discovered that a thick, solid sheet of Plexiglas covered the entire area of the mirror, raised perhaps half an inch away from it. She would never be able to crack it, no matter what her physical condition.

Kay returned to the platform. After wrapping herself in the blanket she lay on her side facing the mirror. So. Whoever had set this place up had expected that she might try such a thing, otherwise why cover the mirror with such an excessively thick layer of Plexiglas?

Sedgewick. Only he would think about her shattering any glass at hand.

Kay shivered; noticing the sweat chilling her nose and forehead, she realized she had worked herself into a lather. Without thinking she stuck her arm out of the blanket, slid up her tunic sleeve, and put her lips to her goose-fleshed arm. She regretted the loss of the water pouring out of her, and her helplessness to stop it frustrated her. Cold, she drew her arm back inside the blanket and flopped onto her back and stared up at the translucent blue plastic ceiling. She wished she could destroy the lighting. She would rather be perpetually in the dark. Even if it would mean…

Moving her eyes from the ceiling, Kay continued her survey. There was not much left: the toilet, the roll of toilet paper, the towel-wipe dispenser, the slit in the wall three fingers long and half an inch wide, probably for disposing the towel-wipes, and, of course, directly to the right of the mirror, the door.

Throughout her waking hours Kay's gaze continually gravitated to the door almost as reflexively as she blinked. For many reasons she dreaded the opening of the door, yet the tension of waiting, of not knowing, made her long for it, too. Part of the time she hoped she would be left to die from filter-failure. But inevitably the thought came to her that there might be some deeper plan than either letting her die or torturing and killing her, for why else had she been left physically untouched during the time she had sat cuffed to that chair? Yet what could they possibly want with her? In all the time she had been here, they had not even tried to interrogate her. What could be the point? Was Sedgewick on the other side of the mirror, hoping to watch her crack up before she died? Maybe hoping she would beg for his forgiveness in utter, degraded abjection?

Prying her thick, furry tongue from the roof of her mouth, Kay assured herself that she would go into filter-failure before she ever had a chance to crack up. She reviewed the symptoms she'd been taught to watch for: headache— which she had; tense, aching, and cramping muscles— which she had (though her muscle cramps could be attributed to the cold); patches of numbness spotting her scalp and body— no, though her feet and legs and hands did keep falling asleep; nausea— yes; painful, burning urination— no, but then she hadn't urinated since after the time she had first woken in this cell; pain in her kidneys— no; sweating, trembling and excessively rapid but erratic pulse— sometimes, yes...

And so Kay passed the time in the cell drifting into sleep and then jerking awake out of nightmare, fantasizing escape, worrying about her body, fearing and longing for the door to open— until finally it did open, and Weatherall walked in.

Weatherall's appearance stunned Kay. She looked so real, so *ordinary*. Yet here she was, studying Kay, smiling at the table shoved up

against the mirror, pushing the table back into its previous position... She was not a hallucination, Kay decided as Weatherall slipped a leather bag off her shoulder and set it on the table.

Silence, she reminded herself. *Absolute* silence. She knew too much about the Marq'ssan and the Free Zone that Security would love to get its hands on, most of which they'd never be able to get out of her by loquazene alone. So much could be lost if she betrayed what she had been helping to build.

Weatherall dug a liter-and-a-half bottle of water and a disposable cup out of the bag. Kay's throat tightened, and her pulse raced with desire for the water; her parched lips seemed sorer, her tongue and throat burning and desiccated. Tears welled up in her eyes when Weatherall broke the seal on the bottle and poured some of the water into the cup.

Weatherall seated herself on the table. "Good morning, Kay."

Was it morning, then? Kay wondered. She said nothing, only dragged her gaze from the water to stare at the hard blue eyes that never wavered or flickered in the room's loud silence. Inevitably, though, Kay's gaze fastened again on the water.

"Now you owe me an apology for your rudeness," Weatherall said. She extended her hand until the cup was less than two feet from the platform and with one flick of her wrist upended it. Kay watched the water in the cup fall in a thin stream to the floor. Only by the greatest exertion of will did she keep herself from looking over the edge of the platform to watch the water slide toward and down the drain. The thought came to Kay that if she flung herself off the platform she might at least touch her lips and tongue to the wet traces sliming the concrete.

Weatherall poured more water into the cup. "It's really very simple, Kay. Just say, 'I'm sorry, Elizabeth, for being so rude to you.' That would satisfy me— this time. I'm not asking you to get down on your knees and beg."

Unable to bear the sight a second time, Kay turned her head to the wall. After about half a minute she heard another stream of water splashing onto the floor. Tears threatened her stony composure. Silence, she commanded herself. Keep silence no matter what.

"I am to assume from your recalcitrance that you don't care if you ever drink another drop of water?"

Kay squeezed her eyes shut.

"Then perhaps," Weatherall said, "I should pour out the entire bottle at once." She paused for about ten seconds, during which Kay waited to hear the water gush onto the floor. But Weatherall said, "Let me explain what will happen if the entire bottle goes down the drain, Kay. I won't simply walk out of here and forget it. You're more dehydrated and far closer to filter-failure than you might imagine. I have no intention of letting you die. Therefore, if you continue recalcitrant, I will have you taken to the infirmary where a feeding tube will be inserted through your nostrils by which you will be fed and watered and then returned here. Force-feeding is not a pleasant experience, Kay. Some people would say it is both painful and humiliating. And intaking water through a feeding tube won't exactly refresh you. What it will do is keep you alive."

Kay opened her eyes and turned her head toward Weatherall. She damned herself for her weakness of will, but she could not bear the thought of an infinity of sessions of the sort described by Weatherall. Under such conditions she would break, sooner or later. And, she thought, completely demoralized, if they chose to they could get a lot out of her with loquazene, anyway...

Kay stared at the bottle of water Weatherall held in her hand. "I'm sorry Weatherall for being so rude to you," she said with difficulty, her tongue sticking to the roof of her mouth, her throat protesting at the imposition.

"That's not what I asked you to say, Kay. Try it again."

"I don't understand," Kay said in a voice the tremulousness of which made her writhe with mortification.

"'I'm sorry, Elizabeth, for being so rude to you.'"

Kay forced the words through her throat. "I'm sorry Elizabeth for being so rude to you."

Weatherall leaned forward and offered Kay the cup. Kay struggled to sit up. With shaking hands, she took it and held it to her lips and trickled the water into her mouth, where she held it a little before

letting it slide down her throat. She drank every drop in the cup, but her thirst raged all the more fiercely for the taste of water.

Weatherall took the cup from her. "You said it was morning," Kay said, "but which morning? I've lost track of the days."

"I didn't say it was morning," Weatherall said. "I said 'Good morning.' Which is how I shall greet you and you shall greet me on all my subsequent visits to you here."

Kay's gaze strayed to the bottle. She was determined not to ask for more. "I've lost all track of time," she said.

"Yes, I expect you have. That's your problem and one I don't intend discussing any further with you." Kay now noticed the watch on Weatherall's wrist. Perhaps she could snatch a good look at it, for it could probably tell her not only the time, but the date as well. Weatherall picked up the cup and poured more water into it. Leaning forward, she stretched to give the cup to Kay. Kay grasped it and closed her eyes to drink, this time savoring every drop. When she had drained the cup she opened her eyes and handed it back to Weatherall.

Weatherall set the cup down on the table beside the bottle and told Kay to remove all her clothing.

Kay stared at her. "But...it's freezing cold."

Weatherall stood up. "Do as I say, without arguing. Or the rest of the water will go down the drain all at once."

Fearful that she might actually cry, Kay let loose her rage. "You goddam bloody bitch! After years of being Sedgewick's perfect slave, 'Yes sir, No sir, Mr. Sedgewick sir,' it must be the thrill of your life to be dishing it out instead of taking it. Go ahead! Why not show me who's boss by dumping it. That's what you really want to see happen, isn't it?"

Weatherall's smile chased chills down Kay's spine. "For outbursts, Kay, the punishment is different. I will allow you this one loss of control. But the next time you indulge in verbal excess you can expect to be restricted." She moved forward until she was standing immediately beside the platform. "You see these rings set in the plastic?" Her finger tapped one of the annulations along the platform's perimeter. "They're for handcuffs. Each time you lose control you will be cuffed— with or without the extension of a chain, depending on the

circumstances. You will find that restrictions in your freedom will be applied in increments that when experienced will seem to be widely spaced, though you probably cannot realize that now. At any rate, it will be your choice to make. As for the water, I *will* pour it out if you aren't undressed one minute from now. And as for your method of addressing me, only one form of address is acceptable, and I've already told you what that is." Weatherall moved to the wall into which the white plastic squares that looked like thumb-locks were set. She pressed her thumb against one of the squares, and a panel slid open.

Conscious of the minute elapsing, Kay struggled with trembling fingers to get her clothes off. She could not remember hating anyone as much as she hated Weatherall at that moment. She had not hated even Sedgewick this intensely. When she had gotten her clothes off, she cringed at the cold air assailing her skin and drew the blanket over her rapidly rising gooseflesh.

Weatherall returned to the platform and held out her right hand. "Give me your clothing, Kay."

Kay gathered it all up and passed the bundle to Weatherall. Weatherall handed her a pile of blue nylon which Kay noticed matched Weatherall's eyes precisely. "You can wear these," she said.

Kay took the bundle and unfolding the blue nylon discovered a pair of tights and a leotard with a snap closure in the crotch. She looked at Weatherall in disbelief. "Tights?" she said.

"Just put them on, Kay. Consider: if anything should happen so that you somehow managed to get loose, you'd be easily visible in them."

Kay bit back her retort and stretched the tights and leotard over her shivering body.

Weatherall went back to the wall and bent down to another cupboard and put Kay's clothes in it. When she returned to the platform, she said, "Now hold out your wrist."

Warily Kay obeyed, and Weatherall circled Kay's wrist with a tubular piece of gray metal around which twined a thin strip of black metal, then slid the strip of metal into the tube where it somehow locked into place. "There," she said. "A further precaution. This will serve not only as a tracer, but to transmit a signal that will trigger any sensors you might pass in the corridors. Only by carrying a device

transmitting the correct frequency for jamming the signal can you get by any sensor on base." Kay attempted to force her finger between the band and her wrist but found it so tight it had not a millimeter of give in it.

Weatherall glanced at her watch (which Kay still had not succeeded in getting a look at). "My time's almost up." She dug into her bag and pulled out two tubes of food and a disposable bowl and spoon and set them on the table beside the water bottle and cup. She looked at Kay. "I won't tolerate insolence and I won't tolerate disobedience. But I won't torture or kill you, either." She picked up the leather bag and slid its strap over her shoulder. "Bon appétit," she said as she made for the door. She pressed her thumb on the square white plate. The door slid open, and then she was gone, and the room was silent and empty and bare. But on the table were water and food.

Kay seethed with such rage that she had an urge to throw the plastic water bottle at the door. She didn't, though. She was too thirsty to do anything but open it and pour most of its contents down her throat in one, desperate, go.

[ii]

To Allison's relief, she and Elizabeth started the trek back to Elizabeth's office as soon as Elizabeth had finished with Zeldin. How, Allison wondered, could Elizabeth look so pleased and excited? They paused at the end of the corridor for Elizabeth to press her thumb on the plate. "Isn't she splendid, Allison?" Elizabeth asked as the door opened, letting them out of the sector vacant but for Zeldin.

Splendid? Why would Elizabeth think a prisoner's insolence splendid? "The way she talked to you, Elizabeth! My hand was itching to slap her silly for it."

Elizabeth *laughed.* "But it was perhaps the best indication I could get that I was right about her," she said. "I'm so pleased."

"I don't understand." God how she hated being down here. The emptiness of the place was spooky. "What's so remarkable about a renegade taken prisoner being so hostile and insolent?"

"Come, Allison. Think of what she's been through in the last forty-eight hours. Her resilience is marvelously reassuring. Frankly, I had no idea what I was going to find when I went in there, especially considering the episode with the table and mirror. You see, most people in her situation would have reacted much more extremely in one of several directions. For instance, she could have been off in her own world, gaga. But Zeldin is very firmly rooted in her physical surroundings. Notice, the only questions she asked me— because obviously from her point of view asking questions of me at all cost her something— the only questions she asked me had to do with re-establishing her sense of time. It was far more important to her psychologically to know the time than to try to find out what we are going to do to her. It's some kind of survival instinct, don't you think? Something there is always clicking in that busy little brain of hers in sharp response to the world around her. Or she might, of course, have raged at me, out of control, the entire time. But she's too canny, too practical to let herself completely lose control. Or she could have collapsed in total despair. The kind of fear and disorientation we have induced in her often makes prisoners lose their grip. But confined as she is, limited as she now is, what little there is for her to have a grip on, she has a grip on."

Allison still didn't see why Elizabeth should be pleased at what she took to be signs of strength and tenacity. "But won't that prevent you from carrying out your plan? How will you ever break her if she's so resilient?"

They came to the end of the corridor and another door, which Elizabeth's thumb quickly opened. "Breaking her would sabotage all my plans, Allison. That's not what I'm trying to do. I need her to be strong and resilient. It was my sense of her flexibility and resilience that made me think I could use her in the first place." Elizabeth touched Allison's arm. "Let me take a crack, Allison, at analyzing what was going on with Zeldin when she had her outburst and speculate on what she will have learned from the way I responded to it. You might then begin to understand what it is I'm hoping to accomplish with her.

"First, the outburst came after her desire for the water caused her to give in to me. I'm sure that's how she thinks of it— as caving in. She'd probably decided not to talk at all— this is a guess, true, but

remember, she wouldn't speak at first. Of course she understands the psychological momentum of resistance that never breaking silence builds up. Even the most trivial conversation during hostile interrogations will weaken the prisoner's position psychologically. And she had at least some training when Sedgewick first ran her." Allison nodded. SIC officers routinely learned this elementary principle in their earliest training sessions.

"Now in the first few minutes I drew the lines that I made it clear I expect Zeldin to keep herself within, forcing her to deal with two sets of boundaries. The most obvious boundaries are the physical ones— namely her cell and her physical needs. But the set of boundaries that will be the key to my restructuring Zeldin is a construct that will come to exist both in her mind as well as in her relations with the world. I drew these boundaries indicating that if she did not observe them she would suffer physical consequences. She bowed to them when she said the words of apology I demanded, by talking to me, by listening to me— until I told her to take off her clothes, at which she balked. That this point should be the locus of her defiance is perfectly understandable. By her outburst she then violated the boundaries I had just finished drawing for her, letting me know she was willing to take the consequences.

"It could have been a simple loss of control, but I doubt it. Zeldin's much more complicated than that. Possibly she was angry at herself and needed to demonstrate that she did have alternatives and would take them and accept the consequences of taking them— perhaps she even wanted to punish herself for her earlier weakness. Or possibly she wanted to test me. But quite apart from all this, it's crystal clear that she in some way perceived the things she said in her outburst as the one way she could exercise power in her situation. I'm convinced she believed that what she was saying would upset me. Instead of merely railing at me, she reached for something with which to sting me, searching in her mind for the most potent weapon she could fling at me. Which proves, Allison, that she has her wits about her and that she's prepared to fight me to the death. She expected me to lash out at her— perhaps even to go out of control and hit her, or at the least to

immediately punish her by dumping the water and having her hauled off to the infirmary to be force-fed. If I had done either of those things she would have gotten some satisfaction, would have felt just a little bit powerful, because she'd have believed the retaliation came solely because she'd managed to score a hit against me."

They reached the elevator and Elizabeth took a strip of plastic from her pocket and inserted it into the slot by the up button on the express elevator— another perquisite Allison by herself was not privileged to access. "It was perfectly reasonable for Zeldin to believe that I resent Sedgewick. You are the only one who has ever heard me talking alone with him. Whenever anyone else is present, I do yessir him. Zeldin's not alone in seeing me as simply his appendage, incapable of independent thought or action." The elevator door slid open; they stepped in, and Elizabeth jabbed the button for level three.

The elevator took off like a rocket, causing Allison's stomach to drop. "But rather than giving her the illusion of power, I responded by drawing the boundaries with a slightly heavier line and by letting her see that violation of those boundaries will result in the constriction of her physical boundaries. Thus when in the future she defies me she will find that her freedom of movement has shrunk even further, her control over her circumstances even more diminished." Elizabeth paused. "Have you ever seen those handcuffs that tighten whenever the prisoner struggles against them? If the prisoner persists, the handcuffs can tighten to the point of cutting into the flesh all the way to the bone. Well, that's Zeldin's situation. Whenever she struggles, she'll be constricted. Fairly soon she will perceive the status quo— unfettered life in her cell, I mean— as relatively desirable. She will grow comfortable. And violation of the boundaries will become increasingly difficult for her." The elevator door slid open. "The tightness of those boundaries will not be readily apparent at first, since so far it is a matter of her treating me courteously, of obeying trivial commands, of keeping her anger to herself."

Elizabeth led the way around the corner down a little hallway ending in a door. She pressed her thumb to the plate, and the door slid open— admitting them to the hallway running through Elizabeth's

suite of offices. Allison exclaimed in surprise. "I don't care to walk through the front offices— god knows who might be trying to see me out there," Elizabeth said. She opened the door to her own office and gestured Allison in. "Actually, it helps me to discuss this with you, because the one thing that will be necessary in this experiment is thinking ahead. Zeldin's too smart to manage if I don't keep several steps ahead of her, anticipating every possible reaction and move she might make. Coffee?"

Elizabeth took two thin porcelain mugs from a cupboard behind her desk and poured coffee from the thermoflask on her desk. Allison saw that they were hand-painted with exquisitely detailed depictions of flowers, the mug Elizabeth handed to Allison with dahlias and the one Elizabeth kept for herself with delphiniums. "Let's see," Elizabeth said after taking a swallow of coffee. "Where was I..."

"So what you basically want to do to her is to make her obedient and deferential?" Allison asked. Why all the talk about boundaries and so on? Wasn't obedience what it came down to?

"No," Elizabeth said. "I want her to be obedient and deferential, yes, but that's only one part of it. Most people could probably find a way to make others obey them if they constantly supervised them from the position of absolute power that I'm currently exercising over Zeldin. But she won't be of use if her cooperation always requires such close supervision. I mean, if she can only be managed by being as constricted as she is now, then we could never use her outside of those conditions." Elizabeth sipped and swallowed. "What I want is to change the way Zeldin perceives and structures reality. I want to alter her relational structures. Oh, not what I think of as the infrastructures of her personality— those are set in lead— changing those would be impossible. It's precisely because she has such a solid infrastructure that I can even attempt this experiment."

Allison found Elizabeth's use of so many abstractions confusing. "I don't understand what you mean when you talk about these structures and reality and so on."

Elizabeth sighed. "I'm sure you'll see what I mean as the experiment proceeds. But let me try to explain. In the first place, the only source of a non-solipsistic reality for her while she is in that cell is me: I'm the only thing outside of herself that can assure her of her own existence. Therefore she is going to crave recognition from me. Approval, you may think of it, but it's something more than that. I'm going to tell her what sorts of things she cannot say to me. Do you see: when I prohibit her from using certain words or concepts when she talks to me, I'm setting up a situation in which she is eventually going to have to abandon even thinking them. At that point she will be able to explain, interpret, analyze, etc. reality— which she ordinarily does to the nth degree— only with the language and concepts I allow her. She will at first of course try to maintain one set of language and concepts for herself and another set for me. Because very soon now she's going to perceive what I'm doing— remember, she's extremely bright. But doing that won't work. She will change, therefore. The way she interprets reality will change. And the way she deals with me will change because of her need for recognition, which only I will be available to give her."

"But if she knows what you're doing, how can it possibly work?" Allison asked, more bewildered than before. The whole thing sounded so abstract and speculative it seemed doomed to failure. Still, Elizabeth was clever, and she seemed utterly confident.

Elizabeth laughed. "But you see, consciousness isn't everything. How long can it survive unscathed when I have such power over her and refuse to acknowledge that which I have thrown out of bounds? You see, she's going to be dying to talk to me. There will be the dependence on me for food and water, but there will be this other dependency, too. I don't think she will be able to sustain her old conceptual structures and values when I've so isolated and constricted her. It will take time. I realize that. But I'm as patient as Penelope." Elizabeth poured more coffee into her cup.

Allison refused more for herself. "What if it doesn't work?" she asked.

Elizabeth bit her lip. "If it doesn't work . . ." The lines around her mouth deepened, and her eyes grew grim. "If it doesn't work, it could be godawful, I admit. But. . . I would of course have to kill her. I am

determined Wedgewood shan't lay a finger on her. I won't let them put her through that."

It was so confusing: Elizabeth sounded disapproving of certain things, but perfectly willing to perpetrate others. Some people would call this kind of brainwashing psychological torture. Well, Zeldin had done terrible things. If anyone deserved it... But thinking about what Elizabeth said she was going to do, though she could not understand it, gave her the creeps. "I don't know, Elizabeth. It troubles me, what you're doing. I can't say why, but something about it frightens me." Wedgewood's methods were one thing, but...

Having said this, Allison wished she hadn't. Elizabeth would misunderstand and think she was soft.

But Elizabeth nodded. "I'm not surprised, Allison. I'm playing with another person's mind. The only people who exercise this degree of power over other individuals are parents over their children and psychiatrists over those patients they have locked away in an institution. The dynamics are pretty much the same."

Parents over their children!

"Oh dear, you look shocked," Elizabeth said. She ran her finger around the rim of her mug. "What is it you think our parents did to us— particularly our mothers— when raising us? Do you remember any of it, Allison? The parts I remember most vividly have to do with differences between what was allowed to boys and what was allowed to girls. You should watch sometime an interaction between an executive mother and daughter— it will fairly make your skin crawl."

Allison hardly knew what to say. She had always felt...but one never said these things out loud! Just as one never ever objected to what the men said about one's not being fixed.

Elizabeth was frowning. "I've said too much, haven't I. We must both get back to work. We can discuss this later, in more leisured circumstances." She stood. "Let's get you set up in the office across the hall, and I'll show you the procedure for hiding the Zeldin files from all the indexes. I made up the program years ago and know it to be foolproof."

Elizabeth started for the door. Allison of course got up and followed. "You do understand you aren't to discuss any of your work in any way with Jacquelyn?"

Allison nodded.

"Once I show you how to hide the file, you can get started inputting the first Zeldin transcript. When you've finished that, I'll make time for briefing you about the other confidential projects you'll be working on for me." She glanced at her watch and thumbed open the door. "I don't think you'll have time to go in to Denver today. Well, that's all right, another day won't matter. You should probably read some of the files first, anyway."

[iii]

Martha and Laura had been toiling over paperwork for about two hours when David Hughes walked into the office. "Hi," Martha said without enthusiasm— and immediately returned her attention to the monitor.

David approached Martha's desk. "Do you quit work at five, Martha?"

Martha laughed shortly. "I don't keep regular hours." Reluctantly she looked at him. "What time is it?"

"Five after five."

No wonder her headache had come back: she needed another boost of aspirin. She said without looking at him, "Then I guess I won't be quitting at five today. I've got at least another half hour of work here."

"When you're through would you have dinner with me?"

Martha rose and moved to the door. "Let's step out in the hall to talk," she said. "I'm sure we're disturbing Laura." Martha knew for a fact that Laura was following the conversation with interest.

David followed her out into the hall. "I already have plans for tonight," Martha said when she had closed the office door behind her. "But I don't think I'd have dinner with you even if I didn't."

David's eyes moved over her face. "Will you tell me why, Martha? I thought you enjoyed my company."

"It's nothing personal," Martha said. "But I feel it would be a mistake for me to go on seeing you." She stared past him at the heavily postered wall. "I'm not ready to get involved, even lightly, with anyone else yet."

"You didn't think that the other night."

Martha had been thinking of it as a one-night-stand that would be lost soon in the debris of ephemeral memory. But she could hardly tell *him* that. "I wasn't thinking at all," she said, trying not to sound exasperated. "It just happened. But since it did happen, I've realized I don't want to be close to anyone now." She made herself look at him and saw his eyebrows rising high into his furrowing forehead. "It sounds bad, I know. But that's how it is." She would *not* apologize. "I want to heal quietly by myself. Pain isn't something that can be shared, at least not this kind of pain, with someone one is going to bed with."

"What if we aren't going to bed together?" David said. "What if we just meet to talk or do things together? I respect your need for privacy, Martha. And I think I could help maintain that privacy when we see one another."

Martha rubbed her throbbing temple. She had had a headache all day. "I don't know, David. I don't have much time or energy for individual people these days. Some of my oldest friends are mad at me because I'm always so busy. I don't see how I can afford to take on a new friend."

David smiled. "You're a slippery character, Martha. But everyone has to eat, you know. Why not eat with me?"

"I told you, I already have plans for this evening!" Martha glared at him— and immediately felt ashamed of her display of temper.

"You were pissed last night at the meeting, too," David said.

"When someone you've been working with since the Blanket comes out selling all that Good Life crap to defend what she calls Modified Birth Limitation, it does tend to make you pissed." Martha sighed. "You think you know someone, and then they start spouting nonsense. It keeps happening lately— my finding out I was entirely mistaken about someone I thought I knew." Martha put her fist to her forehead. "Oh shit why am I standing here babbling when I should be in there working? I'm sorry, David. But at this stage it can't make that much difference to you. And anyway, it's better that we know where we are now than having things run along and break up further down the road."

He said, "It does matter to me, you know. I don't often meet someone I can talk to the way we did that night. But I can see why you're afraid, if you've had so many personal disappointments lately."

"Afraid! That's not it at all."

At his half-smile, Martha turned away. "Never mind. Let it go. I have to get back to work." And before he could say anything, Martha turned the doorknob and went back into the office.

Laura said, "All settled, Martha?"

Martha sat down at her terminal. "Yeah. It took some doing, but I did manage to get rid of him."

"And all because you and I are going to discuss what we're going to prepare when it's our week to do meals?"

Martha pressed her lips together. "A commitment is a commitment," she said. "And I told him I didn't want to see him anyway. I didn't use you as an excuse, Laura."

"I wouldn't care if you had, you know."

Snorting, Martha split the screen and called up two of the Rainbow Press files. What did she want with a male professional, anyway? After Louise, the thought was an absurdity.

After Louise.

Chapter Fourteen

[i]

On Friday Martha and Laura had breakfast alone on the porch so that they could discuss the prep session for the Steering Committee meeting. It wasn't Martha's turn to appear as her committee's representative at the meeting, but Laura thought that since the Birth Limitation issue needed to be discussed and she, Laura, did not feel competent to discuss it, and that since it was Martha's own project and not the committee's, Martha should represent the committee at the meeting. Because the introduction of the issue to the Steering Committee meeting worried her, Martha assented.

The paper carrier came by as they were finishing their yogurt and granola. "Oh good," Martha said. "I'm dying to get the latest scoop on Boston." Everyone she knew was avidly following the struggle between Security and Military forces. Schadenfreude was rife, focusing most especially on the interesting dilemma the executives faced of finding a way of fighting one another without destroying the very property (executive-owned, of course) that was a large part of what made Boston such an important place to control. Even more to the point, the conflict had become complicated by an escalation of revolutionary activity. Boston was all anyone had been talking about in Seattle for the last three days.

But when Martha opened the paper, she forgot about Boston. "Oh no oh no oh no!" she cried out. "They've killed her! The bastards have *killed* her!" Her voice broke, and tears streamed down her face.

"Who? Martha, for godsake, *who?*"

"Damn it, why wasn't she more careful? She *knew* they were after her!" Martha's stomach heaved; she dropped the paper and ran into the house to the toilet. On her knees, her hands clutching the cold porcelain rim, she retched up everything she'd just eaten, then sat on the floor and leaned her head against the wall and cried. Shutting off the thought of what they had probably put Kay through before killing her, Martha raged with the wish for Marq'ssan powers so that she could destroy every last one of the bastards.

Laura knocked on the door and came in. "Are you all right?"

Unable to speak, Martha nodded.

"I didn't realize you were so close to her. I, uh, somehow had got the idea you didn't like her."

Martha, still crying, said, "I didn't much *like* her, not really. But damn it...their killing her, it's like... I don't know. But I feel...I mean she may not have been like us, but she did so much, she... She saved my life! If it weren't for her... Oh Laura, I feel so sick. Why couldn't she have stayed here? She would have been safe here. We would have protected her if she'd let us. But she was so damned..." Martha's words were swallowed in her sobs. Laura knelt beside her and held her.

After crying herself out, Martha withdrew from Laura and said she would be all right. Mechanically she went through the motions of bathing her eyes and wiping her face, and went out to the kitchen to pack her lunch. The world felt different. Something horrible had managed to force its way into paradise, like a great bloody blot on the sun.

Martha could hardly bear it.

[ii]

Though Kay had no way of knowing whether Weatherall's visits came at consistent intervals, she decided that for the sake of establishing a way of measuring time she would assume that Weatherall visited her daily, in the mornings. There was really no way for her to tell whether this was the case, for the hours stretched so endlessly and the cell was so devoid of anything of the remotest interest that the time between visits seemed equally infinite. She had no sleeping rhythms: the cold as well as the constant presence of light in the cell prevented her from sleeping for long, thus maintaining her in a constant state of jagged exhaustion. She tried, under cover of the blanket,

to masturbate, thinking that orgasm would help relax her, but her erotic imagination lay beyond her reach, and her vulva remained as dry as a stone tumbling through the vacuum of cold, deep space. The sleeplessness in turn interfered with her digestive processes, which meant that she could not use the time it took to digest the tubefood as an increment by which to measure time. Weatherall's visits were the single break in continuity, the one concrete indication of time passed. Therefore, Kay decided, she would measure time by those visits. And she decided that she would assume she knew the days of the week, too. Calculating that Weatherall's first visit to her fell on Tuesday, she would thus assume the current day to be Saturday. And when— or if— Weatherall appeared again, the count on changing to six visits would mark the day as Sunday. It might not be accurate, but such a method enabled her to escape the infinitude of an otherwise unrelievedly subjective experience of time.

Though her body suffered from sleep deprivation, Kay regained some physical strength. She always felt hungry and thirsty, but the food and water Weatherall provided at least rid her of dizziness. In order to further strengthen— and warm— herself she began doing exercises, especially those she had learned at Farley's. The sense that she needed to prepare herself to face an ordeal lashed her nerves raw. She told herself that at the least she should prepare herself physically, not only to give her the strength for resisting whatever ordeal Weatherall had in store for her, but also so that she could take advantage of any opportunity for escape that might arise. She knew she should also be preparing herself psychologically, but she felt helpless even to attempt it until she got at least one solid "night's" sleep.

If only Weatherall weren't so damned big— Kay guessed she must be six four at least— and so obviously strong. She regretted not having heeded Louise's advice about getting in more practice. If she could in some way overpower Weatherall... Weatherall, after all, always came into the cell alone. Perhaps Weatherall carried some sort of weapon in the shoulder bag she set on the table during every visit... If so, and if Kay could get to it, she might have a fighting chance of getting out alive. Kay resolved to make a play for the bag once she

had made herself stronger. If she failed, they couldn't do much more to her than she knew they inevitably would do anyway.

Angrily Kay shook off thoughts of Wedgewood. Did Weatherall expect her to be grateful for her "protecting" her from him? Kay vividly remembered his viciousness, remembered the sorts of uses Sedgewick had put him to. And yet she resolved not to let Weatherall get to her through those kinds of manipulations. Weatherall was her enemy as much as any of them. Weatherall was no better than Sedgewick. Kay slammed her fist into the table. She hated Weatherall, hated her guts. She would find a way out, and if it required killing her, that would be fine. She had been a fool to let the two of them live.

Her exercises warmed her up and even made her sweaty, so that when she finished doing them she went to the towel-wipe dispenser and pulled out an envelope and tore it open. She wrinkled her nose. Both the leotard and the tights had begun to stink. Why was she being kept like this? She had still not been interrogated. And why was *Weatherall* handling her? Weatherall was only Sedgewick's personal lackey. She had no place in the chain of command. It made no sense that he had assigned her to handling a prisoner.

Kay squeezed the used towel-wipe through the narrow slot in the wall and returned to the table. She would allow herself a little water now. She had gotten into the habit of carefully conserving food and water, never knowing for how long she would need to stretch it. Weatherall had never yet taken away the small amounts still left at the time of her visits, had only set the new tubes and new bottle of water down on the table and taken away the completely empty containers.

Why were they not interrogating her? she wondered again, swallowing water. As always happened whenever she started asking herself such questions, Sedgewick snaked into her mind. Weatherall never did anything but execute Sedgewick's orders, usually as a whip to flick people into line. What was it he had said about Weatherall? That she was a "perfect tool" but incapable of making decisions or formulating any ideas of her own... For Weatherall to be doing all this, and so methodically, meant that Sedgewick must be closely involved.

Suddenly suspicious, Kay— avoiding the reflection of her haggard and disheveled blue nylon-clad self— stared at the mirror. Was Sedgewick behind it? Or a video camera? For years and years he had been in the habit of keeping her under close surveillance. Why not now? Maybe all this was for his amusement?

Kay slammed the table into the Plexiglas fronting the mirror. Turning her back on it she prowled the cell for a place that might be out of the range of vision of someone behind the mirror. But except for the door, there was no such place. Everything was open and exposed, and the mirror extended most of the height of the room. Her gaze roved the cell— and lighted on the blanket. She snatched it off the platform and carried it to the mirror. Privacy suddenly seemed more important than sleep or warmth. But holding the blanket up to the mirror's frame, she saw no way to drape it. The Plexiglas extended almost to the ceiling and was exactly flush with the strip of wall between the Plexiglas and ceiling. Disappointed, Kay stamped back to the platform, wrapped the blanket around herself and leaned back against the wall.

Sitting so quietly she began to watch the door and wish Weatherall would come. Except for the time she spent exercising and eating, she was always waiting for the door to open and Weatherall to walk in. She waited because of the food and water, of course. And now only one or two swallows remained in the bottle. What she really wanted was to be able to down at least half the bottle at once. Such small, rationed swallows never quenched her thirst.

She would pick up with the thirteenth century. Innocent III. The Hohenstaufen. The sacking of Constantinople by the Fourth Crusade. The Albigensian Crusade. The Fourth Lateran Council (1215). Magna Carta. Thomas Aquinas, Michael Scot, the Dominicans and Franciscans and Joachim da Fiore...The Ghibellines...the Guelfs...Giotto and Dante... Yes, think of Giotto and Dante, close your eyes, Kay, and think of Giotto's frescoes...

Kay was trying to perfect her visualization of a certain fresco in Santa Croce, trying to remember the yellows and browns and greens and the eloquently pained expressions in the eyes of the figures in the fresco, when the door opened. Keeping the blanket wrapped around her, Kay slid off the platform. She would stand. Standing would give her resolution and strength.

"Good morning, Kay," Weatherall said as she slung the leather bag onto the table.

"Good morning, Elizabeth." Kay moved away from the platform to stand near the toilet.

"You'll have to work on your inflection now that you have the words down pat," Weatherall said. She shoved the table away from the mirror and returned it to its usual place.

Kay watched tensely as Weatherall dug into her bag. She didn't realize she had been holding her breath until it exploded out of her when Weatherall pulled a bottle out of her bag and set it on the table.

Kay licked her lips and began to pace.

"You're a great deal livelier than you've been," Weatherall said. "You must be feeling better. The accommodations must be agreeing with you."

Kay clenched her fists around handfuls of the blanket and did not answer.

"By now," Weatherall said, "the news of your death will have reached Seattle. Do you think anyone will mind?"

Kay stood absolutely motionless, unable for several moments even to breathe. "News of my death?"

"Yes. Almost immediately after your apprehension we gave a press conference for the national and international media to announce the apprehension, court martial, and execution by lethal injection for treason of Kay Zeldin, the notorious counter-espionage agent, author, historian, and saboteur."

The blanket was not warm enough to stop Kay from shivering.

"As far as the rest of the world is concerned, you are dead," Weatherall said. "You will never leave this base— except perhaps to be transferred somewhere else, which I doubt will happen."

"Then why am I still alive?" Kay said with anguish. "To be tortured and interrogated?"

Weatherall picked up the bottle and held it absently in her hands as, leaning against the platform, she gazed intently at Kay's face. "No, I told you I've told Wedgewood he can't have you." Her smile, Kay thought, was full of pride and cruelty. "I don't see why I shouldn't tell you. The reason you're still alive and in this cell is that I'm experimenting on you. I have a bet on with Sedgewick over whether I can rehabilitate you. Or should I rather say, deprogram you? He says I can't, that you're completely intractable and should be shot as one shoots horses with broken legs, while I say that you can be reformed with the proper handling. Of course it's all academic, for we will never release you in any event. But since you are as good as dead, Sedgewick was perfectly willing to let you live a little longer for the sake of our bet."

Kay lifted her hands to her face— the blanket dropped around her ankles— and raked her cheeks with her fingernails. "I don't believe this, I don't believe this." Horror, terror, and rage so overwhelmed her that she spoke without thinking. "You're trying to brainwash me!"

Weatherall stepped away from the platform and set the bottle on the table, then dug into her leather bag. "You must learn to control your habit of using inflammatory and ideological speech, Kay." She pulled out a set of cuffs with a chain between them that was perhaps a foot long and held it dangling by one cuff before her. "I'm not going to let it pass this time. You knew when you used the word that I would object to it. You'll have to learn to control yourself."

Kay's chest heaved as she fought for breath.

Weatherall lifted a finger and crooked it, beckoning Kay over to the platform.

She would not let Weatherall cow her. She would not. "No!" Kay said hoarsely.

"That instance of disobedience just cost you your food ration, Kay."

Kay felt a rush of tears threatening and screwed up her mouth to hold them back. "I will not collaborate with you at my own abuse," she said, glaring defiantly at Weatherall.

"The word is punishment, Kay, and for that infraction you'll have to have a shorter chain." Weatherall dug into her bag and pulled out another set of cuffs and dropped the first set into the bag. The second set's chain was perhaps six inches long. "And if I have to fetch you," Weatherall said, "you'll wear a cuff without any chain at all."

Kay picked up the blanket and wondered if she could use it against her when Weatherall attacked. She would not go willingly. She might not have a chance against Weatherall, but she damned sure wasn't going to give her meek and craven obedience.

Weatherall said, "Your stubbornness is pointless, Kay. Very well. The chainless cuff it is." She pulled out a pair of handcuffs attached to one another by two steel links and dropped the second set into the bag. The cuffs, Kay saw, quailing, were already opened. Weatherall crossed the distance between them in three strides and grabbed Kay's wrist. With her free hand Kay aimed a blow at Weatherall's solar plexus, but the executive deflected the blow and twisted Kay's arm up behind her in an ordinary but painful hold Kay knew she could not break. When Weatherall pushed her toward the platform, Kay moved unresistingly, for she did not want her arm broken. She certainly did not put it past Weatherall to abandon her with a fracture just to make her point.

Soon Kay was lying supine with her right hand cuffed to one of the rings on the right-hand side of the platform. Weatherall took the bottle of water and placed it near the edge of the platform within reach of Kay's left hand, then packed up her bag and went to the door. As it slid open she said, "I hope you find it worth it." Then she left and the door slid shut.

Six visits, Kay said to herself. Which makes it Sunday. Which means it's been one week since Weatherall got me. One damned, long, godawful week.

[iii]

Since Elizabeth was lunching in Denver with Georgeanne Childress, the Secretary of Com & Trans' PA, and since the only other person she knew on base was Jacquelyn, Allison went by herself to the Executive Dining Room for a very late lunch. With the help of the 3x5 electronic directional card Jacquelyn had giver her, she had no

trouble locating it. It did not surprise her to find it so thinly patronized at two-thirty in the afternoon; she had hoped, in fact, that it would be nearly empty.

En route to a table on the far wall, she passed a couple of men drinking wine and recognized Roger Stevens, the head of ODS. Out of the corner of her eye she glimpsed a telltale transmission jammer. Allison wondered if they believed someone in the Rock might be bugging them. She seated herself two tables away from theirs. She didn't want them to think she was eavesdropping.

The service-tech came with the day's menu, but Allison waved it away and ordered a Niçoise Salad, French bread, and a glass of white Bordeaux, and then sat back to reflect on her long morning and the project she was assisting Elizabeth with. Was Elizabeth right? Was it true that if Cabinet people discovered what they were doing they wouldn't be condemned for it? Allison was not as sure as Elizabeth seemed to be. Perhaps if they hadn't been going to own the stock in the proprietary it would have been all right. And yet Elizabeth said that since it had always been done it would be all right. Allison didn't know how to point out that it was different when it was women doing the setting up and profiting. It looked like a conspiracy of the women against the men, for one thing. And the fact was that Elizabeth didn't know of any woman who had ever been given or allowed to buy stock in Company proprietaries. Elizabeth hadn't even tried to argue that the results of setting up this proprietary would be so beneficial to executive interests that no one would blame them— Elizabeth knew she wasn't *that* naive.

The service-tech brought the wine almost at once. Allison thought of how at that moment Elizabeth would be setting up some of the final details with both Georgeanne and an electronic contractor already working for Security. The contractor, Elizabeth said, would never know about the proprietary. Only the people at the top of the proprietary's management plus Georgeanne and a few of her people— all women— would know. Allison didn't like it. But Elizabeth insisted she knew what she was doing. And it was true, vid was immensely important. If they actually got that first satellite up by the end of the year, it would

make all the difference. And as Elizabeth pointed out, the aliens hadn't zapped the satellites the French recently launched or even the ones the Russians had boosted into orbit last spring— at least not yet.

"...but then you know the Man didn't even bother to see him while he was here and of course that bitch's office didn't let anyone know. She has absolute control over access to him." What point was there in using a signal-jamming device if one didn't bother to keep one's voice down? Allison had no choice but to listen.

"Why the birthing fuck is he letting her do it? That's what I can't fathom," the other man said.

"Oh, she's damned smooth. What this means is that he's selling Wedgewood down the river. As long as Zeldin's alive Wedgewood's looking at an end to any decent kind of career. Assuming, that is, the breach ever gets mended. But once it does, he's had it. *If* Zeldin's around to tell the tale."

"You think that's why she intervened?"

"Who knows the mind of a cunt? I wouldn't put it past her to be pulling that kind of power play. The way things are going around here anyone she hasn't been bringing along herself is going to find himself stashed away in dead-ends."

"Including you, Roger?"

"And including you, my friend."

"But I've been completely cooperative with her. I can't see why she wouldn't keep me where I'm at."

"Time will, as they say, tell." He paused, Allison supposed to drink. Then, "So you're going to put your money on her."

"I am. Especially after the other night. But shit, why the hell did the Man bother to come here if he wasn't intending to make any kind of appearance?"

"More wine, Leonard?"

"Nah. Got to get back to the office. With Weatherall running things I can't trust her not to give my bitch my job if I delegate too much. She's already done that to some, you know."

"Well frankly, I'm not missing the Man that much." He belched loudly. "It's a true puzzle. First he meddles in everything to the point

of driving us nuts. And now he ignores the entire damned organization. That's bullshit that she puts out, saying he's spending all his time touring bases and stations. If he were really active, he'd be here. This is where it's at."

"Maybe he's holed up somewhere reading reports and sending her instructions? I can't believe she can be running everything. Or that he'd let her. It's too big a job for a woman. She'd have cracked by now if she were making real decisions. Especially with this damned war dragging on. And she sure as hell isn't relying on anyone senior for direction, or we'd know about it."

The men left, and Allison tried to digest what she had heard. Were they a threat to Elizabeth? And was what they were saying about Sedgewick true? And was Elizabeth really running everything and keeping Zeldin alive as a way of squeezing out Wedgewood (who apparently was the one most likely to challenge her)?

The service-tech brought the salad and bread and butter. Allison dug in. She was ravenous.

[iv]

Late that night when Allison and Elizabeth were lounging together post-sex in Elizabeth's Jacuzzi, Allison described the conversation she had overheard in the Executive Dining Room that afternoon. "Roger Stevens and someone named Leonard," Elizabeth murmured when Allison had finished. "I can think of two Leonards, Leonard Longworth who is Director of Management and Services, and Vernon Leonard, who is Deputy Director of Clandestine Services… Longworth weighs about three hundred pounds and has thin silver hair and blue eyes and a round rubicund face. Vernon Leonard, though not slim, is considerably trimmer and has long brown hair and a mustache. Did you get a look at him?"

"Only a brief glance at the back of his head as I passed. I think it must be Longworth," Allison said.

"Interesting." Elizabeth leaned her head back against the wide ceramic rim and closed her eyes.

Allison reflected that she seemed to be turning into an informer. But surely, if it was for Elizabeth…

"It is probably useful that there's this perception about my winning a victory over Wedgewood," Elizabeth said, not opening her eyes. Allison gazed on the perfection of Elizabeth's stunning bone-structure, at Elizabeth's delicately flushed skin, at Elizabeth's sleek golden hair, and grew giddy at the fact of her relationship with her. "To tell the truth, I never gave Wedgewood's access to Sedgewick a thought— Sedgewick is so little likely to give anyone in Security his personal attention that it never occurred to me to make an effort to control access to him."

"I don't understand it at all," Allison said. "About Sedgewick, I mean."

Elizabeth opened her eyes and lifted her head to look at Allison. "What exactly don't you understand, Allison?"

Something in the way Elizabeth was looking at her made Allison uncomfortable. "Well everyone in Europe anyway was always saying that Sedgewick was the best thing that had ever happened to Security, that he'd really shaped us up, that his attention to detail and his constant intensive supervision— frequently showing up on the spot out of the blue, and so on— was what made Security so efficient and tightly run and powerful."

Elizabeth's gaze held steady. "That was a true enough assessment— perhaps giving Sedgewick himself rather exorbitantly exclusive credit, though of course Sedgewick always claims that choosing what to delegate to whom is the most critical responsibility of any Executive officer. But all that has changed. Sedgewick takes little interest in running Security these days. So I run it for him."

Though she had caught hints, Allison was not prepared for this shockingly bald statement. "*You* run it?" she said, frightened and uneasy. Elizabeth was clever, yes. But capable of running all of Security?

Elizabeth said, "I run it. I have his signature stamp and what amounts to a glorified power of attorney to act for him as his proxy, for matters relating to his capacity as Chief of Security as well as in his private affairs. Very occasionally he will ask for or accept a briefing from me, at which time I jet up to Maine to talk to him. Mostly, though, he keeps aloof."

Allison searched Elizabeth's face. "But *why*? Why would he do that?" And why allow Elizabeth to run everything? Why hadn't he appointed a successor if he wasn't interested in the job? Or made one of his senior men acting chief?

Elizabeth's eyes grew watchful and hard. "All of this of course is of the highest confidentiality, Allison. But what I am going to tell you next is not to be mentioned by you, ever. Don't even bring it up with *me*. Clear?"

"Understood," Allison said breathlessly.

"Only one other person besides myself is aware of this. The fact is that during the time we were marooned and isolated on his island in Maine, Sedgewick suffered a breakdown."

Allison's queasy stomach cramped. She didn't know what to say.

"Since I was absolutely in his confidence, when we finally managed to resume contact with Security, I had no problem taking over for him on the operational level. But the difficulty is that I cannot deal on the Cabinet level politically." Elizabeth, absently pinching her ear, paused. After a few moments of abstraction, she continued. "It is my understanding that if Sedgewick were functioning we would have been able to put an end to this debilitating and absurd civil war. He would have managed to arrange something by now. None of the other Cabinet members are strong enough, or have enough grasp of the situation— since they know little of what's going on, at least partly because Security is controlling things precisely on account of the war— to be capable of dealing with the Military faction. This is ironic, since some of the most powerful men in the Executive have become negligible in the larger scheme of things, while I am calling the shots for all Security-controlled territory."

Elizabeth looked critically at Allison, her eyebrows raised as though asking whether Allison understood what she was saying. "And the sooner we patch things up with Military the sooner we can get the country under control and rebuilt," Allison said.

Elizabeth smiled slightly. "That is my ultimate project. If I cannot deal directly with Cabinet-level people, I will deal indirectly and still manage to tap their power."

Allison raised her eyebrows to show she didn't understand.

"Oh darling, really it's perfectly obvious," Elizabeth said in an almost caressing tone of voice. "I'm dealing through their PAs for the most part."

Allison goggled at her. "But surely the other PAs don't have the kind of proxy authority you have!"

"Not the same degree, no, but you'd be surprised how very much gets left up to us. We all have signature stamps, you know. And let's face it, sweetie, not very many of *them* are standing up to the situation well. The only ones of them who aren't sliding into despair or apathy are the ones who are conducting the day-to-day fighting of the war. They have a sense of purpose, I suppose. I don't quite understand what it is about the situation, but so many of them are simply falling apart. Not generally to the extent that Sedgewick has, but of course he has special problems compounding his stress."

Allison had noticed and felt anxious about this demoralization, but had thought only that certain weak types had fallen under the pressure and strain of prolonged crisis.

"I've told you too much, haven't I sweetie," Elizabeth said, moving closer and sliding her arm around Allison's shoulder. She kissed Allison's cheek. "It must be an awful blow for you to learn all this at once. Instant disillusionment. But the one thing you must not do is worry. Some of us are sufficiently together that we're going to pull the whole mess out of the fire. I promise you, Allison. I'm going to see to it that the war is ended within a year from now. And I promise you that by the end of this calendar year— and that's not far from now— all sorts of things will have happened that will make people realize things can be patched up. You'll see. You must have faith in me, darling."

Allison gripped Elizabeth's hand.

"And you must promise to work hard for me."

Allison felt a lump rising in her throat. "I promise," she said.

"That's my sweetie." Elizabeth again kissed Allison's cheek. "But now I'm going to have to get out and dress."

"Dress?" Allison repeated blankly.

Elizabeth levered herself out of the tub and grabbed a towel. "I'm going back to the office. My driver and escort are downstairs waiting."

Allison got out of the tub, too. "It's the middle of the night, Elizabeth. Aren't you going to sleep?"

"Oh I can catch a couple of hours on the futon in that little room behind my office." Elizabeth finished rubbing herself dry and let the towel drop to the floor. "Among other things I want to look in on Zeldin. I'm curious as to how she's taking her punishment and what her response will be."

Zeldin again! This was the second time that Elizabeth had gone in the middle of the night to see her. Allison slipped on her robe. "I think you're enjoying your 'experiment.'"

Elizabeth, uncoiling her silky golden braid, smiled. "I'm enjoying it immensely. It's fascinating having that much power over another human being, especially one as responsive and intelligent as Zeldin. And then considering the intensity of her hatred for me and her intelligence, she is one of the greatest challenges I've ever taken on. It's quite exhilarating for me, darling." Vigorously she drew the brush through her long, thick hair.

"You know, Elizabeth," Allison said acidly, "in all the versions of the Pygmalion story I've ever heard, the creator always ends up falling in love with his creation."

Elizabeth's eyebrows soared. "Darling, aren't you clever! I never thought of the Pygmalion angle. You may be closer to the truth than you know. Except that I won't be falling in love with her, of course." Elizabeth's gaze met Allison's in the mirror. "You're not jealous, are you?"

"Should I be?" Allison asked— and instantly wished she could take back the words.

"Zeldin is the last person in the world you should be jealous of, Allison. I wouldn't be in her place for anything. And I venture to say neither would you."

Allison tried to smile. "I know," she said. But all the same she wished Elizabeth wouldn't be going off in the middle of the night to see Zeldin.

Having finished brushing and rebraiding her hair, Elizabeth began putting on fresh clothes. "My girl is going to be annoyed at me for missing our session in the morning. Taking care of my hair is a passion with her. Do you know she searches every morning for individual split ends which she then snips one at a time? I once contemplated cutting off my braid, or at least cutting my hair so that it would only reach my waist, and she started talking about quitting. Can you believe it?" Allison smiled wanly. Elizabeth went to her and stroked her cheek. "Stay as long as you want, darling. But do me a favor and leave a note for the girl saying I won't be seeing her until Sunday morning... And of course turn off the lights when you leave."

Allison would have protested that she had no desire to stay in Elizabeth's apartment when Elizabeth wasn't in it, but Elizabeth had slipped away and was out the door before she could speak. Allison glanced around the bathroom; she felt its emptiness without Elizabeth's presence. Seeing herself reflected in the room's many mirrors, she grew lonely and anxious.

After writing the note and turning out the lights, Allison went down to her own apartment where she poured herself a cognac before trying to sleep. She had a lot of new information to process, information that made a shambles of her old ideas of how things worked. She hoped Elizabeth knew what she was doing.

It would be comforting to know that somebody did.

Chapter Fifteen

[i]

Martha arrived at the Co-op's office building at eight, an hour before the meeting was scheduled to begin. She, Lenore, Denise, and Mata carried three cases of half-liter bottles of water into the lounge, made coffee, set out mugs, yellow pads, and pens, and rearranged the furniture so that people choosing to sit on it would all be able to see one another. Then Martha went to her committee's office to fetch the notes she needed for the meeting. She had just unlocked the door when she spotted Louise striding down the corridor toward her. Quickly Martha closed the door.

Martha went to her desk and began sorting the stack of files on it. She resolved not to think about Louise. But when a knock sounded and the door opened, she knew without turning to look that it was Louise.

"Martha," Louise said quietly.

"What is it," Martha said, staring down at her desktop. She could not remember now which files she wanted.

"It was terrible hearing about Kay Zeldin," Louise said. "It made me think, Martha. It made me realize that we can't let our political differences stand between us. We—"

Martha turned around. "Political differences!" she said. "That's how you think of it?" Martha wanted both to melt into Louise and to run from her.

"No question. It's *totally* a matter of politics."

Martha said, "I read in the paper this last week that another man was killed. There's no way I could live with you and go on reading in the morning paper about the deaths you cause."

"That's the condition, then?" Louise said evenly. "If I quit the Night Patrol, you'll come back to me?"

"I'm saying I couldn't live with you while knowing you're killing people, Louise. I don't know if that's a condition, but it's the only way I can be."

"And if I quit?"

Martha for the first time looked directly into Louise's face. "How would I ever know for sure that you had?"

Louise searched Martha's face for an uncomfortably long time. "You don't trust me to tell you the truth?"

"I don't know," Martha said.

Louise closed her eyes for a moment. When she had recovered herself, she said, "Martha, please. Please come back. When I heard about Kay I wanted to be with you, and I realized how absurd it is for us to be disintegrating like this without even trying to talk. Do you remember the night Sorben brought her to us, back at the beginning? Do you remember giving her the rainbow patch you had just sewn?"

Martha nodded through flowing tears.

"That was a time only a few of us share, and there was something so special about it, Martha, that when I heard—" Louise was crying, too. Mutely she held her arms open, and Martha crossed the room to her. Embracing Louise, feeling Louise's arms around her, Martha felt warmed and comforted. "There's something so terrible about hearing of the death of someone like her, so strong and active and gutsy," Louise said when Martha withdrew a little. "Maybe too independent. She was reluctant to let us help her. But death. It's so final, so empty, so..."

Martha, suddenly physically revolted at Louise's touch, pulled her hand away from Louise's. She backed away. "I can't talk to you, Louise. Please go. Anyway, I have a meeting. It must be almost nine."

She went to her desk and blindly snatched up some of the files she had been sorting before Louise had come in.

"I was offering to end my involvement, Martha. Doesn't that mean anything to you? Don't you care enough to—"

"Stop it, Louise. Leave me alone. I can't talk to you."

"I thought you cared."

Martha headed for the door without looking at Louise. "I'm late for the meeting," she said and went out into the corridor. Hurrying

back to the lounge, she heard Louise's footsteps behind her. How could she attend to business with all this emotional stuff going on in her head? Damn Louise for using Kay's death like that. Damn her.

In the lounge, the others were still pouring coffee and getting settled with their files and yellow pads and pens. Martha found a cushion on the floor and arranged her mug of coffee and files around her. When she looked up she saw that Louise had come in and was sitting in a chair on the other side of the room. Great, Martha thought. That meant that Louise was probably representing the Women's Patrol and would in all likelihood be her opponent on several points. She swallowed a healthy slug of coffee, but the acrid, sour taste in her mouth lingered.

The meeting started fifteen minutes late. For the first two hours each committee representative gave a brief synopsis of the reports they would be making at the Steering Committee Meeting, reports that fell under the rubric "Old Business." During the actual Steering Committee meeting this section of the agenda would take up most of the first day. Not only Seattle-area committees would be making reports, but representatives from other parts of the Free Zone would be doing so also. A few were present at this meeting, but most had sent synopses, which Lenore read out for them.

After Louise gave a synopsis of the Women's Patrol's report, Martha initiated a discussion of the Pike Place Market incident. Louise had not included the incident in her synopsis. "I think," Martha said after describing the incident, "that we are going to have to adopt a policy for handling these situations. There's no reason to believe there won't be more of them. I don't think confrontation by rifles is the answer. In fact, after having faced the Women's Patrol rifles last week, it's likely that these goon squads will start showing up with rifles themselves. Once we get that kind of escalation, we'll find these assholes much harder to deal with. We need to figure out ways of defusing these situations, as well as teach the Free Zone population at large how to deal with them. It's a public problem, not a matter for the Women's Patrol to use its machismo— sorry, machis*ma*— on."

"Pacifist theory is all very pretty," Louise said, "but it's an ugly reality we're dealing with here. Precisely because Martha interfered in our handling of the incident, those men will show up somewhere else to intimidate and terrorize the public. If we had taken them into custody and questioned them we would not now be waiting to see where they're going to strike next."

"We don't need a National Guard to keep public order," Martha said. Louise's relaxed posture, with her booted legs stretched easily before her, her face stubborn and confident, infuriated Martha. "Baseball bats we can handle. Storm troopers calling themselves Women's Patrol we can't."

Murmurs and whispers rustled through the room. Martha ground her teeth: they were probably all thinking this was spinning out from a "lover's quarrel."

"*Storm troopers*, Martha?" Louise said. "Next you'll be calling us fascists."

"Come on, Martha, name-calling isn't going to get us anywhere," Lenore Markov said.

"The point is," Martha said, "that if we have Women's Patrol going around with rifles to 'defend' or 'protect' the public, the very *image* of that will be enough to provoke violence from the men who are disgruntled. 'Why,' they will say, 'should we allow those bitches to go around armed like National Guard? Wasn't that what the Co-op was supposed to be abolishing?' Don't you see?" Martha said, moving her gaze from face to face. "If we introduce rifles into these confrontations, not only will the thugs also take up rifles, but the public will resent it and start wondering about our credibility. It's far better to give the public the means of community self-defense than to merely provide protection. There are ways of effectively handling that kind of violence without resorting to it ourselves."

"I agree," said Janice Corleone of the Committee for Housing. "Public perception is extremely important. And bringing on rifles etc. can only leave us open to whatever propaganda ploys they have prepared to use against us." Martha noticed other women nodding. "I would like to ask Louise something, though." Janice looked at Louise.

"What were you planning to do with these men once you had... I believe you used the expression 'taken them into custody'?" Janice was one of the few professionals in the room. She spoke so well that Martha was glad she was taking her side of the argument.

Louise's lips twisted; she didn't respond at once. Martha supposed she was framing her answer to be as acceptable as she could make it. "We would have questioned and then deported them," Louise finally said.

"Deported them? How?"

"Easy," Louise said drily. "Just drive them to the border and point a rifle at them and tell them to get the hell out and stay out."

"I see. That's the technique. Though there's no guarantee they won't come back," Janice said. "But I wonder at your use of the word 'deport,' Louise. I thought only governments had such powers."

Martha's head jerked up. She hadn't caught that, but it was true: Janice had hit the nail on the head.

Louise sighed impatiently. "I'm getting a little tired of worrying about semantics," she said.

Maria Ullman, a representative of the confederation of tribes in the Pacific Northwest Free Zone, suddenly spoke. "Louise, when I was listening to Martha's report on the incident in the Pike Place Market, a question came into my mind that I think only you can help me with."

Louise gestured Maria to continue. "Yes?"

"Tell me if I have this straight: when Martha interfered, the Women's Patrol were in a position of strength, right? I mean, you had these guys out-gunned, and everybody knew it. All you would've had to do was demonstrate your willingness to shoot just one of them, and they'd've surrendered. Do I have that right?"

Louise's cheeks grew rosy. "Yes, Maria. That was exactly the situation when Martha interfered."

Maria nodded. "Okay. Now here's the part that I don't really get. I understand why Martha 'interfered,' as you put it. What I *don't* understand is why you allowed her to do it. I mean, why didn't you-all just ignore her?"

Louise sat up straight with her shoulders squared and stared at Maria, apparently speechless.

Maria looked thoughtful. "Maybe she put herself between the goons and your rifles?"

Louise bit her lip. "No."

"So she wasn't really in your way. Then why didn't the Women's Patrol just ignore her?"

Louise shot Martha an angry look. "Hell. *I* don't know."

Maria nodded. "You don't suppose it was because everyone present instinctively knew she was right and were secretly grateful to her for giving everyone an easy exit out of a dangerous situation?"

"It was simple reflex! If I'd had my wits about me, I'd've—" Louise stopped herself and folded her arms over her chest.

"Then maybe it's lucky," Janice said, "that Martha was the only Co-op person present on the scene who *did* have her wits about her."

"There are dozens of the goons who killed Kay Zeldin running around loose in the Zone, acting with impunity." Louise turned her head to stare across the room at Martha. "Who do you think those goons in the market were, Martha? Who do you think put them up to their little acts of intimidation? Who do you think is orchestrating it all?" Louise's gaze swept the room. "The fact of the matter is we're under attack. Covert attack. Since we mostly can't prove it— except for such instances as Kay Zeldin's abduction a couple of weeks ago— the Marq'ssan can't legitimately retaliate against the Executive for any of the attacks. And speaking of self-protection, I'd also like to comment that we can't always rely on the Marq'ssan to protect us. We're dealing with some damned rough enemies. And pacifism isn't going to protect us against them, either."

"I think," Lenore said, "that we're not going to be able to decide about this matter here. Nor should we be the ones to do so." She looked at Martha. "I take it you intend to bring this up at the meeting."

Martha said, "It's too important to let pass. If we did let it pass the policy would be developed without the Co-op's having a chance to help decide it, and the Women's Patrol would be unilaterally determining the direction the Free Zone will be moving in. I think we can do better than that."

Lenore scribbled on her yellow pad. "So we can expect you to bring it up in the discussion and question session following the Women's Patrol's report." Martha nodded, and Lenore moved the meeting on to the next committee's report.

When they had finished the "Old Business" section of the meeting, they went straight into "New Business." Martha introduced the subject of organizing a memorial march and assembly for Kay Zeldin. "It's important that we publicly pay tribute to Kay's accomplishments on behalf of the Free Zone, that we not forget her. It's important that people realize what it means that the Executive murdered her. And it's important that we preserve and insist on our own history. Kay Zeldin is an important part of that history. We have to make sure she isn't forgotten."

There was a long moment of emotional silence before someone spoke to suggest that Martha organize the memorial events. Martha countered by asking that someone else do it since she was already so busy. When Louise volunteered, Martha did not look at her or say anything more about the memorial events.

Lenore moved the meeting on, and Martha brought up her second piece of "New Business," the Birth Limitation issue, and asked that Venn be allowed to speak on it preparatory to any discussion. "It might be best if we put off any substantive discussion until a committee has been formed to look into the matter— not just the political ramifications and the formulation of Co-op policy, but the medical technology and the social and economic issues involved, and so on. I think it's essential that we all be well-informed before making any decisions."

No one objected to Martha's suggestions, and Lenore added Venn's report to the agenda, and the meeting passed on to other items of "New Business." Martha spoke little during the remainder of the meeting. She had said what she had come to say. It was just such a damned shame it had to be Louise sitting in this meeting for the Women's Patrol. The tension between them was exhausting and mind-killing.

[ii]

To distract herself, Kay concentrated on remembering Scott's face. But a year-and-a-half was a long time, and Kay's mental image of him had grown fuzzy and uncertain.

More importantly, her general concentration was poor, for most of her attention had become fixed on her physical discomfort. The hand cuffed to the platform kept falling asleep, making it necessary for her to flex her fingers and rub and knead her arm with her free hand. Worse, try as she could to put it out of her mind, she was constantly aware of the pressure on her bladder and the fierce cramps caused by it, constantly fighting the temptation to seek relief by peeing in her pants, constantly aware of the unopened bottle of water beside her and her desire to drink it. If she were to drink it, she *would* wet her pants. All things considered, she would not be surprised if Weatherall were to refuse her another pair of tights. If so, the demoralizing humiliation of that particular loss of control would be followed by the choice between wearing urine-scented tights or going without.

Repeatedly she reviewed how, on her last visit, Weatherall had asked her whether she "had anything to say to her" and how her own response had been to assert that she, Kay, did not grant Weatherall the moral authority to punish her and that therefore lying cuffed to the platform was not punishment but abuse. Kay had not been surprised when Weatherall had condemned her to remaining on the platform, but she had not expected that Weatherall would make her access to the toilet contingent on an apology— while still requiring her to return to the platform to take "punishment" for the new "transgression." Kay had refused to apologize; without speaking, Weatherall had taken the bottle out of her bag and set it on the platform and departed. Miserable with the need to void her bladder, Kay had almost called after her that she would apologize. But she had held herself back, obeying her own decision that she not give in to Weatherall's tactics for any reason.

Penetrating cold exacerbated the discomfort, for Weatherall had not brought her the blanket from where it had fallen on the floor

during Kay's struggle with her, and so Kay shivered as well as suffered from unmediated exposure to the light and could not sleep at all.

Kay's rage had eventually given way to misery. In spite of her resolve to take her resistance to the wall, she knew now she could not do it. In her demoralization, she doubted her strength to withstand the more extreme tactics that would succeed this piece of abuse were she to continue her resistance.

She shed hot tears, bitter tears, too many tears. She held conversations in her head with Scott, with Sorben, with Magyyt, weeping self-pitying conversations, conversations explaining why she couldn't hold out, conversations asking them why they had deserted her when she needed them, conversations begging their comfort. But she held imaginary conversations with Weatherall, too— conversations explaining to Weatherall why she could not do this, why she *must* not do this, conversations reasoning with her, raging at her, pleading with her. Ashamed, Kay would pull back from her imagined pleadings, hating herself for her weakness, afraid that she *would* plead, afraid that Weatherall would succeed in brainwashing her, afraid Weatherall might actually hand her over to Wedgewood… And worst, she held conversations with Sedgewick, whom she often imagined behind the mirror. Only by great force of will did she keep herself from addressing him out loud, as though knowing beyond a doubt that he was there.

With her free hand she scratched her oily, itchy scalp. Her unwashed state offered another irritation— the filthiness of her hair and teeth, the smell of the leotard, the dried residue of tears on her face. Why why why? She hadn't come to this base seeking Scott— she hadn't even decided whether or not to go against Sorben's advice. How could she have run into Weatherall like that? A concert was the last place in the world she would have expected to see that woman.

She could not go on much longer without wetting her pants. Even when they had cuffed her to that chair they had let her up once to pee. Weatherall was counting on this to break her. Damn her. Damn her. Feeling the tears starting again, Kay cursed herself and her weakness and rubbed her hand hard over her face. Oh her aching muscles, even in her arms. Exercising so vigorously and then lying still for so long had made her horribly stiff.

At last the door slid open and Weatherall sauntered in. Kay stared dully at her. What would happen now? Would she give in to Weatherall? Or would Weatherall relent?

Looking at Weatherall, Kay knew she would never relent. She would always be inflexible, it was written in every line of her face and body. Kay almost turned away, toward the wall. She wanted to. But she couldn't.

Weatherall stood beside the platform. "Good morning, Kay," she said, smiling.

Kay hated her smile more than anything else about her. She licked her cracked lips and imagined what it would be like to be allowed to get up and go to the toilet and empty her bladder. "Good morning, Elizabeth," she whispered, knowing she was going to betray herself.

Weatherall stared down at her. "Have you anything new to say?"

Kay's lips trembled out of control. "I apologize," she said.

"You apologize. For what exactly do you apologize, Kay?"

Kay swallowed. Weatherall was going to make it as hard as she could. "I apologize for using ideological and inflammatory words, and for being rude to you."

"Let me see. What was it you said during my last visit about moral authority... Does this mean you grant me the moral authority to punish you?"

Kay hated her own stupidity in having supplied Weatherall with such ammunition. Weatherall's victory in this was much more sweeping than it would have been if she, Kay, hadn't put the idea of moral authority into her head.

"I'm waiting for your answer, Kay."

Kay closed her burning, watery eyes. "Yes. I admit you have the moral authority to punish me."

"Use the word *grant*, Kay. And say it again using my name."

She wanted only to get it over with, to be allowed to pee. "I grant you the moral authority to punish me Elizabeth."

Kay felt Weatherall's fingers brushing hair back from her forehead and tensed. How could Weatherall stand to touch her greasy filthy hair? "You are strong, Kay Zeldin," Weatherall said softly, "but even the strongest trees are destroyed by the wind during storms unless they bend." Kay opened her eyes. Weatherall was smiling again. "One more thing. I want you to give me your word you will not make a fuss the next time it is necessary for me to punish you. That you will obey me when you are being punished."

Already her concession about punishment and moral authority was being used against her.

"You understand," Weatherall said, "it is important that if you give me your word on something that I can trust you. If you should ever happen to break your word, you will lose the ability to negotiate with me. Clear?"

"Understood," Kay said weakly.

"Well?" Weatherall said when Kay said no more. "Do you give me your word?"

"All right," Kay sighed, "I give you my word that I will obey you when you are punishing me." She had already given away so much that she could not resist now when she was so close, must be so close to release.

Smiling, Weatherall leaned over Kay and unlocked the cuff binding her to the wall side of the platform. Slowly Kay sat up and swung her legs over the side. Her right arm was stiff and prickly, her legs shaky when she tried to stand on them. She almost collapsed when the wave of nauseating dizziness overwhelmed her, but she clung to the thought of the toilet and held herself upright. She ignored Weatherall's gaze as she tottered across the cell, unsnapped the leotard, tugged down the tights, and lowered herself onto the icy stainless steel rim. The relief was so great that her eyes overflowed.

Kay grabbed a handful of towel-wipes, retrieved the blanket, and returned to the platform. Weatherall handed her a cup of water. "You must be parched," she said. "You didn't even touch the second bottle."

Kay gulped the water and thought of how she had kept herself from opening it to rinse her mouth out, fearing she wouldn't be able to keep from swallowing, knowing that even one swallow more would exacerbate the pressure on her bladder. She hoped, though, that Weatherall would let her have both yesterday's bottle as well as today's. Today's... This, she realized, was Weatherall's eighth visit, so today must be Tuesday.

Weatherall took two tubes of food from her bag. "I'm pleased with you, Kay," she said. "And so I will give you something special this time." She handed Kay a pear.

Kay stared at it, astonished. Straightforward behavioral technique, she reminded herself. She looked up: Weatherall was waiting for her response. Afraid Weatherall would say something that would maneuver her into further disadvantage, Kay said quickly, "Thank you, Elizabeth."

Weatherall nodded. "My pleasure." She stood up. "And now I must go." She picked up her bag and went to the door. Kay saw that she had not left another bottle of water. The door slid open, and Weatherall left.

Tuesday, Kay repeated to herself. It's Tuesday and she's visited eight times now. She stared down at the pear and touched its soft smooth skin with her fingers, cupped its full roundness in her palm, then lifted it to her nose to smell. Perhaps she would save it a while to look at and smell and touch and wait before eating it. It was beautiful, behavioral tool or not.

[iii]

Following Elizabeth's instructions, Allison dressed in evening clothes and went down to the side-entrance where Elizabeth's immense internal-combustion car was waiting. Allison had learned through the base's grapevine that Elizabeth's car was the only internal-combustion ground vehicle allowed to operate in the territory. Elizabeth said she had grown accustomed to it during the early days of the Blanket and chose not to give it up since it was far more powerful, faster, and comfortable than even the largest battery-operated vehicles. It was of course one of the most visible signs of Elizabeth's power. As she waited, Allison wondered what Elizabeth had planned for the evening that they must dress in formal clothing out here in the boonies. Something personal? Or something to do with Elizabeth's projects?

Allison checked her watch. A quarter after five. Had she misunderstood the time? But wouldn't the driver have said something if she'd arrived terribly early?

Finally Elizabeth appeared, her tunic magnificent in its many overlapping layers of black and deep blue-violet silk— some of the layers patterned in those same colors, others solid black or solid violet-blue— both slashed-sleeved arms loaded with amethyst-studded silver bracelets, one heavy silver chain twined several times around her neck, her coroneted braids threaded with silver and amethyst strands, her feet shod in silver-embroidered black silk boots. Allison, making a comparison, saw that her own soft flowery streamered gauze and silk was uncomfortably frivolous. "Elizabeth," she said, "you take my breath away!"

Elizabeth's fingers brushed Allison's cheek. "Thank you, darling. You yourself are an absolutely delectable, appetite-stimulating sight." Instead of returning Elizabeth's smile, Allison grimaced. "Did I say something wrong, darling?"

Allison shook her head. "No. But it occurs to me that I haven't dressed as I should have. You didn't give me any hints about the occasion or what sort of thing I should wear."

"You are dressed perfectly, Allison, there's nothing to feel concerned about. Now I want you to sit back and relax and watch the scenery. Fall is coming on, you know. It's for your pleasure that I decided we'd take the car to Denver. We'll come back by chopper, of course, because it's simply too long a drive to make for no good reason. The car will come back without us. And while you're taking in the scenery we can talk. I'll explain about tonight presently, but first I'd like to discuss Zeldin with you."

Allison was beginning to hate discussing Zeldin. Bad enough that she had to input transcripts of Elizabeth's conversations with the woman, but the discussions she and Elizabeth had about those conversations invariably unsettled her— partly because she didn't understand half of what Elizabeth was talking about and partly because something in Elizabeth's role in Zeldin's rehabilitation struck her as distressingly ugly and disturbing.

"Let me ask you this," Elizabeth said. "When you were inputting the latest Zeldin transcript, what did you make of it?"

"You mean her capitulation?" Allison asked. Elizabeth nodded. "Well, it seemed to me that she was willing to say whatever she had to to get you to release her. I don't believe for a minute she was being sincere."

Elizabeth laughed. "It doesn't matter whether she's sincere, darling. Or at least not right now it doesn't. Sincerity will come later. But what do you think of the words I extracted from her?"

Elizabeth's eyes— because of the colors she wore, Allison thought, or maybe just the dimness of the car's interior— had gone such a dark purple they were almost black. "You mean all that stuff about moral authority?" Elizabeth nodded. "I don't quite see the point," Allison said. "If she didn't mean what she said then it's only a word game the two of you are playing."

"But don't you see where the word game must lead, Allison?"

Allison thought. "No," she said. "I can't say I do."

"In future situations Zeldin will be forced to consent to my having the right to punish her. She has given me the foundation on which to build an entire structure of authority."

"But if she didn't mean the words she won't buy that at all," Allison said.

"Don't you see, darling, by using words and entwining them with actual consequences and behavior, the words eventually become too weighty to be ignored."

"But if she believes she only uses the words because of your coercing her?"

"It doesn't matter, especially since Zeldin attempted to *resist* saying the words in the first place. Don't you see, she felt that saying the words *did* mean something. Otherwise she would have rattled them off the first chance I gave her. Words are all she has to fight me with. And because that is the case it makes them all the more significant. Moreover, what happens between Zeldin and me in these encounters is the only reality available to her apart from what goes on in her head. Ordinarily Zeldin is not at all solipsistic, Allison: she has to engage

with whatever reality is available. And that means that words spoken out loud, no matter how insincerely, mean something whether she wants them to or not."

"Oh!" Allison said. "You're saying that you think words will trap her, because in her situation they mean so much more than they usually do. Because they are more of her existence now than they would be if she were free."

"Something like that," Elizabeth said. She leaned forward and opened the car's small refrigerator. "Juice?" she asked, pouring what smelled like grapefruit juice into a tall glass.

"I'd prefer water, I think." Allison helped herself to a bottle.

The car had reached the summit of the steep grade they had been climbing. A spectacular view lay spread before them, especially beautiful in the late afternoon sun; some of the trees and shrubbery had begun to turn, and their foliage looked as if it had caught fire from the blaze of the sinking sun.

"And now, about this evening," Elizabeth said, pausing to sip her juice. "We're going to a party being hosted jointly by Georgeanne Childress and Vanessa Vesey. It's work, darling, under the guise of pleasure. Vanessa, like most of the women who will be there tonight, is not career-line and is enormously wealthy. If anyone can still be said to be wealthy. However. The other executives present will be key administrative people— key to my projects, that is. You will have to exercise great discretion, Allison. Very few of the people there will know much about my projects. I am hoping, however, to tap the wealth of maternal-line women and the assistance of those who are career-line. And I'm hoping you will be of use to me. I'll expect you to be watching me for signals and know when to accompany me and so on."

Elizabeth paused, and Allison assured her she would do her best.

"The party is being held at the most exclusive executive women's club in Denver. I've had you made a member." Before Allison could protest that she could not afford membership in that kind of club, Elizabeth said, "Since it is important to my projects that you have club membership, all the expenses of your membership and use of the club will be carried by Security."

Allison thanked Elizabeth for the membership and strove to subdue the sick dread already blooming in her: the party sounded like the sort of affair she would inevitably be out of place at. She had seldom mixed in those sorts of circles; doing so must always be an ordeal.

"But of course we must create the impression that it's purely for pleasure that we are going," Elizabeth said. "You should be prepared to do so in advance, Allison. There will be a pool of girls there, as is usual at these affairs. These parties are ostensibly at least partly for the purpose of making a wider variety of sexual partners available to us, you know. Not for pursuing business."

Allison sighed. She knew now *exactly* what kind of party it was going to be. She had never felt comfortable at such affairs, even those appropriate to her social status, and in fact seldom attended them. There was something degrading in knowing the girls had all been paid to be there and make themselves available. Granted it was not always easy for executive women to find suitable sexual partners. But the notion of paying for that availability repelled Allison. It was always better, anyway, to have one's sexual partner in love with one. But worse was the sick feeling that came to her when she thought of having sex now with someone other than Elizabeth, or thought of Elizabeth's having someone other than herself. Elizabeth, however, seemed unperturbed by the prospect. Allison carefully placed her empty water glass in its holder inside the small cabinet beside the refrigerator. "I think I'll pass on the sex," she said.

Elizabeth finished her juice and set her glass in the holder beside Allison's. "Don't be ridiculous." Elizabeth's eyes fixed on Allison's face. "We must appear to be at the party for the usual reasons. And besides, as I've already warned you, we must be extremely careful that the full extent of our relationship is not even suspected."

"I don't think I can go through with it," Allison said. "I'm just not in the mood for sex with anyone other than you."

Elizabeth's eyes flashed. "You worry me, Allison. I hope you aren't developing a sub-exec attitude toward sex? Executives do not confuse sex and love. Our affection for one another has nothing to do with our sexual relationship. And it must not."

Allison flushed. Elizabeth was warning her against one of the dangers that had made sex between executives such a forbidden thing, against the danger of one partner taking on sub-exec characteristics, of one partner debasing herself. Is that what Elizabeth thought was happening? Did Elizabeth already think of her as behaving like a sub-exec? "I'm not confusing love and sex, Elizabeth," Allison said very low. But she wondered: could one always make such a clear distinction? She felt toward Elizabeth as she had never felt toward a sub-exec lover. Often when they had sex she felt overpowered by a flood of feelings she thought of as love. True, she had always felt love for Elizabeth. And now her love was more intense. But was it substantially different from what it had been? Had Elizabeth correctly sensed something perverse in her?

"I hope not, Allison. But if that is so, I don't see what your objection to using the girls at the party could possibly be."

"I've never liked those kinds of parties," she said. "Where do they get those girls from, anyway?"

Elizabeth's face relaxed; apparently she was satisfied that her suspicions were unfounded. "Mostly they're employees who have been lovers of executive women in the area, and their friends. Of course now, when things are so bad, they especially appreciate picking up some extra credit. You mustn't feel sorry for them, Allison. Most of them are on the make for better situations, and it's at these sorts of events they have their best chances for finding new executive lovers. They are all experienced, of course."

They rode for a time in silence, and Allison stared sightlessly out at the scenery. "There are a couple of things I should warn you about," Elizabeth said after a while. "First, there will be alcohol there— but only the girls will be drinking it. You won't find any executives imbibing alcohol tonight. I suspect it's something to do with maintaining clear distinctions between the girls and the executives." Elizabeth smiled cynically. "I personally find this absurd, but you know how some executives are... So I advise you to abstain from alcohol. Second, your dealings with the women concerning my projects: you must be very, very careful. All the women there are extremely loyal to their

men— the maternal-line to their sons and fathers, the career-line to their superiors. The question in each case will be how that loyalty is interpreted. This is the sort of thing I will want you to be feeling out with certain women. It must be done delicately, subtly. At the slightest hint of having exposed yourself, pull back. Clear?"

"Understood," Allison said.

Elizabeth smiled and patted Allison's hand. "I'm sure you'll do splendidly, darling. And now, let's sit back and enjoy the rest of the drive until we get into Denver. It will be time enough then to think of business again."

Enjoy the rest of the drive? Allison thought. When she was sick with dread at the evening ahead? But she mustered a smile for Elizabeth and stared obediently out the window. It was what Elizabeth wanted her to do.

[iv]

Elizabeth swept Allison into the club, bestowing smiles and slight bows on everyone she met, brushing cheeks with the jewel-bedecked, transacting flirtatious exchanges with many of the girls they passed. Elizabeth burned like a flame around which all the rest of them— moths, executives, and service-techs alike— fluttered. She introduced Allison to everyone as her aide and the daughter of her "dearest school friend," each time bringing a moment of notice upon Allison followed by a virtual dismissal of her as every person to whom Allison had been introduced attempted to keep Elizabeth's so-desirable attention to herself.

Before long Georgeanne Childress and Vanessa Vesey had drawn a small circle around Elizabeth quite separate from the rest of the party. Allison did not expect that Elizabeth would put up with this for long, for she had the distinct impression that Elizabeth intended to circulate with a vengeance. Quietly, unobtrusively, Allison stood at the fringe of the circle looking around her and trying to follow Elizabeth's conversation, ever alert for her signals.

An "Indian motif" dominated the party's setting. Everything and everyone but the executives themselves had been forced into manifestations of this motif: batik-patterned Indian fabrics draped the walls

and ceilings and swathed a myriad cushions scattered over the floors, the heavy smell of sandalwood incense perfumed the air, small candles provided the only visible sources of light, the cuisine served— chiefly consisting of curries— was Indian, Indian-looking women played Indian music on Indian instruments, pots of tropical plants had been set around the rooms, and all the sub-exec girls wore clinging, rather sleazy versions of saris. Allison estimated the party's cost at a small fortune.

The executives knotted around Elizabeth gossiped, mostly about people Allison had never heard of. Allison soon grew bored. At one point an executive approached her and said, "I used to be Vivien's neighbor." Allison apologized for not remembering her name. The woman offered her name and began a long roundabout story about life in Big Sur and Carmel society and what a lovely garden Vivien had. Allison wondered if this woman had been one of those who had snubbed her mother because Vivien— for purely financial reasons— shared a house with another executive woman, or whether this woman was one of the few who had chosen to ignore the irregularity. Allison was relieved when the woman finally drifted away; it occurred to her that perhaps the woman's motive in talking to her was the hope that she might thereby worm her way into Elizabeth's circle.

After a respectable interval Elizabeth weaned herself from Georgeanne and Vanessa, promising that she would have "a little chat" with Vanessa later. "I'm in a lecherous mood," she said. This amused everyone and allowed Elizabeth to glide away— presumably in search of lechery. Allison trailed her at a distance. When Elizabeth stopped to talk to someone clearly career-line, Allison eased closer and paid attention. While Elizabeth talked, her gaze roamed the room; the other woman's eyes remained fixed on Elizabeth's face. And then Elizabeth's eyes stopped moving. Curious, Allison followed Elizabeth's gaze— and found a service-tech with red hair the exact shade of Elizabeth's PA's. Allison's chest tightened as she watched the service-tech's eyes make contact with Elizabeth's. Something in Elizabeth's face must have signaled the girl, for she came slinking across the room toward Elizabeth, her lavender sari swaying from the hips.

The girl stopped short just a foot from Elizabeth and threw her head back and smiled up into Elizabeth's face. Unable to make out what the girl was saying, Allison inched closer. "Call me Liz or Lizzie, whichever you prefer." Elizabeth fairly cooed. The girl replied so softly that Allison could not distinguish her words; whatever she said, though, drew a laugh from Elizabeth. Elizabeth lifted her hand and leaned forward. Allison's stomach hollowed as she watched the tip of Elizabeth's index finger trace the girl's jaw from ear to ear and disappear into the flaming hair. It was the publicness of it, Allison told herself. These women's clubs that Allison seldom entered... Elizabeth leaned even closer and bending her coroneted head whispered something into the girl's ear. The girl whispered something back, and then Elizabeth's hand was on the nape of the girl's neck and the two of them were moving toward one of the room's cloth-festooned doorways.

"It's hopeless, your wanting her."

Allison started, and turned to find a sari-clad woman standing beside her. "What do you mean?" she said coldly, upset that this sub-exec might have understood something about the way she was feeling about Elizabeth.

"That executive must be the most powerful woman here tonight or Genelle wouldn't have made such a beeline for her. I'd forget Genelle if I were you. It's power that attracts her. The word is that's the main reason she goes with women at all— not as a matter of sexual preference, but simply the only way she can get near executives."

Though sick-hearted, Allison almost laughed with relief. She grinned down into the delicately sweet, sepia face. "Don't worry, I won't pine." She checked the girl's name-tag. "I'm finding it a little too warm in here, Anne. Could I interest you in a stroll somewhere where there's breathing space?"

"What would you like me to call you?" Anne said.

Allison slid her arm around Anne's waist. "Call me Lise," she said, dropping her voice. "You'll have to show me the way, sweetheart. I've only become a member here recently... I'm a stranger to Denver."

Anne led the way to a dim, candlelit room that happened to be vacant. Allison unwrapped Anne's sari and was pleased to find that Anne

had bathed with scented soap and water and perfumed with something musky. Remembering her service-tech days in Seattle, Allison thought she could see a reason for service-techs' willingness to be a part of such pools of girls. The bath alone would be a strong motive. She stroked the hollow of Anne's throat, smoothing her fingers along the girl's prominent collarbone, and drew her down to the thickly pillowed carpet. Closing her eyes she sought pleasure in Anne's soft, rounded curves, in a body and smell and hair entirely different from Elizabeth's.

She had to forget Elizabeth, at least for this moment...or die of the pain.

[v]

It was around four o'clock in the morning when they boarded the helicopter for the return trip home. Numb with exhaustion, Allison slumped in her seat and closed her eyes, ignoring the others who had begged lifts from Elizabeth. A long depressing night was over: Elizabeth had successfully raised all the money she could possibly need for her current projects, and Allison had felt out many of the working executives of whose support Elizabeth wished to be assured. But the personal incidents of the night remained more vivid in her thoughts than the business transactions. How many times had her gaze knocked into the silver and amethyst bracelet Elizabeth must have slid over Genelle's wrist? And Anne's tears: weeping after coming, over her unrequited love for the executive she was secretary to, someone who had been at the party and had twice chosen other girls and never once looked Anne's way... Anne's pain had seemed so close to her own that she had almost let the girl's grieving devour them both. It shocked Allison that she could see a similarity between Anne's relationship with her boss and her own relationship with Elizabeth.

Now that it was all past (for surely Elizabeth would not seek out Genelle), Allison felt somewhat embarrassed for the intensity of her reaction to Elizabeth's taking a sexual interest in another woman. Elizabeth was right: executive women did not allow themselves to be jealous of service-techs nor adopt their easy emotionality and immature romanticism. It was the service-techs' emotional immatu-

rity— an aspect of their general lack of control— that made them so easy to manage. Using Anne tonight could only remind Allison of the differences between executives and service-techs. Perhaps there were aspects of her relationship with Elizabeth that were not good for her. Perhaps Elizabeth was right. Perhaps she should force herself to look up Anne— who conveniently worked on base— in the near future, simply to keep everything in perspective. Perspective was something her intense feelings for Elizabeth had deprived her of.

Allison opened her eyes and stared at Elizabeth's shadowed sleeping face. Elizabeth knew her so well. Far better than she would ever know Elizabeth.

Allison closed her eyes again— and slept.

Chapter Sixteen

[i]

Martha woke on Thursday morning in David Hughes' bed. A splitting headache and queasy stomach suggested she must have drunk so much that she had blacked out. Since she had never done such a thing before, the very suspicion that this had happened upset and frightened her. Believing David still asleep, she tried to ease herself out of bed without disturbing him.

He opened his eyes. "Good morning, lady."

Just her luck. "Do you have anything in your medicine cabinet for hangovers?"

He rolled closer and touched her cheek. "I'm not surprised you ask. Why don't you lie down and let me fetch it for you with a nice big liter of water. Water is what you need most, you know."

Martha lay back down and closed her eyes. "Yes. I suppose you're right," she said. She felt the bed shift as David got up and listened to his feet padding on the hardwood floor. How could she have been such a fool as to get so drunk? And with the Steering Committee meeting beginning that day, too. Of all times. So much depended on it. And now she wouldn't be in even decent— let alone top— form. Geneva would walk all over her. And Louise. Martha groaned. *Louise.* She recalled now that she had been half out of her mind about Louise...

David returned with the promised liter of water and a morning-after. Martha sucked the vile fluid from the morning-after until the tube was empty, then uncapped the water bottle and took a large swallow. But the first gulps made her mouth feel even more gluey and woolly. What the *hell* had she been drinking? She remembered running into him on Second Avenue and agreeing to have a drink with him at his club, and that she had drunk several glasses. But what the

fuck was she doing in David's bed? She had had no intention of ever sleeping with him again. Martha tried to think, tried to remember, but she remembered nothing after the first few glasses.

"I'm not surprised you're hung-over," David said. "The way you were knocking back the wine, it was inevitable. Especially since you're not what I'd call a seasoned drinker."

Martha said, "This is embarrassing to admit, but I don't even remember how I got here from your club."

"That sometimes happens."

Martha took another swig of water. "It's never happened to *me* before."

David sat on the edge of the bed. "You were upset about something but didn't want to talk about it. We were on the third bottle when you passed out. I had a hell of a time bringing you back here."

Martha flushed. "Oh, shit, I'm so sorry, David. What a drag for you."

David's smile filled his eyes with a warmth that felt to Martha like empathy. "Then don't give it another thought. We're all granted grace for at least one such experience in our lives."

He's so damned *nice*, Martha thought. Even though I'd given him the cold shoulder. Why did he have to be so understanding? If he were even faintly disapproving or making some kind of demand it would make it so much easier to get up and walk out of there without ever giving her obligation to him another thought.

Martha picked up her watch, which David had put on the bedside table. It was only six-thirty. She had plenty of time before the Steering Committee meeting began.

"I know food probably doesn't sound very good to you now, Martha, but I think it would help enormously to get your metabolism back on track. Let's face it, your body must have taken a beating. Let me fix you some breakfast before you rush off as I can see you're preparing to do."

He made her sound so rude in the face of his generosity. It was true, she had been planning to rush off— after offering a few words of gratitude and apology. Well, she owed him at least the courtesy of

eating breakfast with him. "That's nice of you, David. I don't know if I can get anything down, though."

"But you'll try, won't you, Martha?" He smiled engagingly at her, as though encouraging an invalid.

Martha laughed. "Okay. I'll try."

"Good. You go ahead and dress while I go out to the kitchen and rustle something up."

Martha watched him leave the bedroom, then got herself out of bed. Naked, she was completely naked. Well at least her clothes wouldn't be rumpled. Which was probably why he had undressed her.

He was just so fucking considerate, damn him.

[ii]

Waiting in the viewing room for Elizabeth to finish her session with Zeldin, Allison stared at the numerous bottles of water and tubes of food piled on the table. Would Zeldin consume them while Elizabeth was away, or would she try in Elizabeth's absence to force herself into filter-failure? Elizabeth argued that the previous weekend's punishment had "settled Zeldin down" somewhat. Allison hoped she was right. She had never had anything to do with prisoners before now and had no stomach for the routine tactics that came so easily to many Company people.

Ah, good. Elizabeth was slinging the bag over her shoulder and heading for the door. Allison switched off the recorder and carefully stowed it in her pouch. Elizabeth came in and dropped the bag on the table. "Well," she said, "What do you think of her now? You haven't seen her for over a week. Do you think she's changed at all?"

"She's a lot grungier," Allison said. "Christ she must stink. I can tell it just by looking at her. Her hair! At the very least you should dump her in a shower, Elizabeth. And those tights! They're disintegrating on her!"

Elizabeth, laughing, went back out into the corridor. Allison followed. "You and your fastidiousness, darling!" Elizabeth leaned against the corridor wall. "If you had any idea of what she would look like if Wedgewood had had her all this time you might not be so critical." Allison shivered. "Besides, one must dole out showers and such

with a sparing hand, or they won't be properly appreciated. Perhaps when I get back— if she's behaved while I'm away, of course— we might undertake something of the sort. But I wasn't talking about her hygiene or clothing, Allison. What did you think of her body language and tone of voice and such?"

Allison hadn't looked too closely at Zeldin— the sight of her was in some way too disturbing to take much of. "I think she's barely under control," Allison said. "She's so jumpy and tense."

"Yes," Elizabeth said thoughtfully, "she is a bit edgy, but that's probably due to lack of sleep. I think, though, that she's well under control. She's been toeing the line remarkably well. And her tone of voice is not as hostile."

Allison didn't see these differences. But then she wasn't paying such close attention, while Elizabeth was intently fixed on Zeldin. And yet couldn't it be that Elizabeth was seeing what she wanted to see?

Allison inched along the corridor, anxious to get out of the closed-off sector. "Wait a bit, darling," Elizabeth said, taking her arm. "I wanted you to come down here with me so that we could have a few private minutes. There's no other place in the Rock where we can be sure no one will overhear or interrupt us."

Glancing toward the ceiling, Allison wondered about the cameras monitoring the corridors all over the Rock. Surely if someone wanted to they could use the cameras to watch them?

Elizabeth followed Allison's glance. "Not to worry" she said, smiling. "As with everything else in this sector, I have exclusive control, exclusive data access. There's no way anyone in the Rock could access the cameras in this sector without going through me first. I keep the codes in my head. Only one copy of my most highly confidential access codes exists in hard-copy, and that's tucked away in the safe of one of Sedgewick's houses." Elizabeth's fingers combed through Allison's still-permed curls. The touch of Elizabeth's hand first on her neck and then on her lips flooded her with sensation, and she sagged back against the wall. Had Elizabeth brought her here for a daytime tryst? "I should be back Sunday or Monday," Elizabeth said tenderly. "I want to take the precaution of telling you something I should have told you

before. After all, accidents can happen anywhere. Though it was the potential dangers of the trip that brought this into my head."

The pleasurable sensations of desire morphed into the cramping and aching of anxiety. "You'll be in danger, Elizabeth?"

"I'll be in San Diego during part of my trip."

Allison's heartbeat accelerated. "But *why*? Can't you send someone else? It's too dangerous there, especially for someone as important to Security as you are!"

"Ssssh, don't be an alarmist, sweetie. No, I must go myself. The PA of the Southern California territory supervisor has been nurturing connections with a few people in Military. She has risked her neck to do so. If Security people there found out, you know what would happen. She's arranged for me to start talks. And what better place, after all, than Southern California for making a start?"

"Because Southern California is so violently torn up? Or because it's a crazy quilt of so many noncontiguous patches of Military and Security territory?" Allison asked, remembering the terrifying atmosphere at LAX.

"It's violently torn up because both sides have such heavy forces concentrated in the area, Allison. But the main reason is because this is the one place where I'll easily be able to make contact with a few Military people without calling attention to the fact. We must go slowly. This is only the first, tiny step. And I have to be the one to take it, Allison. The whole process will take months."

Allison wrapped her arms around Elizabeth and rising on her tiptoes, drew her close in a fierce hug. "I hate it, Elizabeth. How can I not worry? So many things could go wrong!"

"It's not *that* dangerous, sweetie! And as I say, it's only a beginning. But of course, that's my role, setting things up. And I'll have to nurse all my other projects along, too, for everything will have to mesh at precisely the right moment. Zeldin, unfortunately, is the most uncertain of these. Though I'm confident she'll be manageable by the time we need her. But to get back to what I was saying, Allison." Elizabeth stepped back to look down into Allison's face. "Two things. First, keep an eye on her, make sure she's intaking water and food. And if I'm

later getting back than Monday afternoon you take more water and food in there. You know where it's kept." Allison nodded. They had discussed this earlier. "The second thing is this: if anything should happen to me— and now I'm not talking about this trip only— I want you to make sure Zeldin doesn't fall into Wedgewood's hands."

Allison swallowed. How could she stand up to Wedgewood? Without Elizabeth, Allison was nothing in the Company.

"What I want you to promise me is this: if I should die, after verifying that I am indeed dead— and do be careful about verification— I want you to come down here and shoot Zeldin. I don't believe you would get in much trouble over it. You know as well as I do that Sedgewick himself would prefer it that way. Or at the least wouldn't mind. Only you and I can get in and out of this sector. So all it would require is your being careful. They have no reason to suspect that you even know where Zeldin is being held. Will you promise me?" Elizabeth's eyes demanded Allison's promise.

"Yes, I promise," Allison said reluctantly. "But may I ask why it matters that I do this?"

Elizabeth bit her lip. "I have an aversion to Wedgewood's predilections, darling. There are a number of people like him in the Company, as you probably know. That his chief sources of pleasure and affirmation derive from the debasing of other persons, from the deliberate annihilation of their humanity, is not only perverse, but in cold hard terms grossly inefficient. It's another form of loss of control in my opinion, though that's an opinion not generally shared around here. The prevailing attitude is that these methods accomplish things. Wedgewood's interest, however, isn't in accomplishing anything but the stripping of what is human from the body and destroying it, and in the process feeling powerful at the powerlessness of the prisoner to resist his doing so."

Elizabeth pursed her lips. "Far be it from me to criticize another for enjoying power. But the lengths Wedgewood has to go to do so— that is something else. It demeans all of us, Allison. And I don't want to have Zeldin on my conscience. One might argue that in such a circumstance I would already be dead and so it wouldn't matter.

But it matters to me a great deal now. And I believe that for you that would be enough. I would haunt your thoughts if you didn't keep your promise."

Allison's arms tightened around Elizabeth. "I don't like to hear you talking about your dying, Elizabeth. Please, now that I've promised can't we talk about something else?"

Elizabeth bent her head so they could kiss, and Allison felt a surge of positive feeling, reassurance perhaps, at Elizabeth's having said out loud to her what she thought about people like Wedgewood. Allison had never seriously considered the subject but had occasionally been queasily aware of it when non-Company people made sly or acerbic remarks about the Company's methods. It was something Company people did not talk about. But Elizabeth trusted her. And Elizabeth shared her repugnance for it.

"I'm going to have to be getting back, darling," Elizabeth said, disengaging. "I'm holding a meeting on the director and deputy-director level before I leave. I'm going to do a little squeezing of the directors this morning and see how they shape up under that kind of pressure. I want to begin to sort out who's who before I get things really rolling."

They began walking toward the sector door. "And where are you going first?" Allison asked.

"To Maine." Elizabeth pressed her thumb against the thumb-lock panel that controlled the door.

"To see Sedgewick?"

"To see Sedgewick."

Allison wondered, but instead asked about the other stops on Elizabeth's trip. If Elizabeth wanted her to know why she was seeing Sedgewick, she would have volunteered it. There was no point in asking questions that were likely to end in Elizabeth's refusing to answer them. Though Elizabeth would probably not be vexed by such an exchange, it would subtly spoil the warm feelings running high between them. It was much better to leave it to Elizabeth to volunteer confidences. Allison would feel much less left out and Elizabeth wouldn't have to assert her control. Allison was beginning to realize the extent of the delicacy required to assure the success of this sort of relationship. One constantly had to work hard at it to be comfortable.

But it was worth it.

[iii]

Martha arrived at the Assembly Hall fifteen minutes before the Steering Committee meeting was scheduled to begin. The place was in an uproar. Pickets, both men and women, marched in the plaza in front of the building, brandishing placards demanding male participation in the meeting and the abolition of Birth Limitation. A crowd of a size Martha judged to be over a thousand packed the street north of the building chanting what sounded like demands for the institution of elections, voting, and male participation. An impressive— armed— contingent of the Women's Patrol occupied the area directly in front of the building. And dividing the street south of the building was a crowd of perhaps two hundred demanding the disarming of the Women's Patrol and a larger, more vocal crowd demanding that Kay Zeldin's death be avenged. None of the previous meetings had been surrounded with this sort of atmosphere. Martha took it as an ominous sign of things to come, for she could feel a deep, intense anger emanating from the demonstrators.

The sight of the Women's Patrol carrying rifles among peaceful (albeit angry) protestors especially disquieted her. If provocateurs showed up armed as they had been the previous day, there might well be bloodshed. Even just another exchange of gunfire could throw the Co-op into a panic. The popular tendency to want to be controlled by government could become a large-scale desire if enough people panicked. And if Seattle resumed any sort of institutionalized government, the promise implicit in what the Co-op had been doing would be lost, probably forever. Once made, it was almost impossible to unmake government. People would want only to change or reform it once they had it, not abolish it. They would be too afraid, especially if the government had been established in response to public panic.

Inside, everything seemed normal— women bustling, laughing, chatting and hugging in the usual sociable atmosphere of Steering Committee meetings, for among the women attending, strong bonds

had been forged at the outset of the Co-op's existence, and many of them saw one another only at these meetings. That people from other areas of the Zone chose to attend paid tribute to a larger field of cooperation and interest extending beyond local communities and imparted the sense of a cohesiveness within the Zone that Martha knew was partly illusory. Illusory or not, this sense of cohesion mattered, for it made a certain level of cooperation possible and gave rise to dreams of what the Free Zone might someday manage to become.

Martha smiled and nodded whenever someone greeted her but did not stop to chat as she walked through the plush lobby into the Hall and toward the table she shared with other committee members. When planning the seating arrangements they had decided to put as many tables on the main floor as possible, with one mike and one terminal to a table, and chairs in the gallery extending along three sides of the Hall's perimeter. People who wanted to sit at tables reserved a space— assigned on a first-come, first-serve basis unless there were too many applicants, in which case the committees were assigned tables first, and the remaining seats assigned by lot. There were 350 such seats and at least as many seats in the gallery. So far this system had worked. But since attendance at Steering Committee meetings rose with each successive meeting, no one knew how long the arrangement would hold. Of course most people did not sit through the entire session, which usually lasted two or three days. Still, considering the intensity of the crowds outside, that might rapidly and radically change.

Martha found her committee's table and took the empty chair to Laura's left. "What a scene outside," she said.

Laura, busy with a file, looked up briefly. "Not encouraging," she said. "And Toni Farren has a table on the floor. You know what that means."

Martha groaned. "Yeah. We all know what that means. Madam Mayor is going to drag us through more arguments about male participation and democracy."

"Former Mayor," Laura said. At Martha's feeble smile Laura added, "You look terrible, Martha. You sure picked a strange time to go out on the town."

"Yeah," Martha said. "I know, I know. Which means I'm not going to be in top form, and considering the scene outside..." Martha pinched the bridge of her nose. *Just fucking concentrate, woman! Or we'll have Louise or even Farren calling the shots before you know what's hit you.* "To tell the truth, all this bullshit with the Women's Patrol has me worried."

Laura's mouth puckered, as though tasting something bitter. "After that incident yesterday... And the timing! When the hell did they decide to start using guns and shooting? That's what I'd like to know."

Martha shook her head. "I saw a few of them with rifles at that incident in the Pike Place Market last Friday. When I raised the issue at the meeting Saturday, I got a hot response from their rep. Which happened to be Louise."

"I bet that didn't help."

"I'm sure some people there thought it was an extension of a lovers' quarrel. And I probably wasn't very effective just because it was Louise. I hate having to face off against her in public."

"Well I'm sure other people will take up the cause today," Laura said grimly. "It's turned out to be the sleeper issue of them all. We might not even get to Birth Limitation this session."

Martha opened her briefcase and unloaded her personal processor, pen, yellow pad, and files. "Unless the meeting goes on for days and days."

"It can't," Laura said.

"I hope you're right." Martha glanced at the rostrum. "But my hopes aren't high. It's already ten after nine. Who's chair?"

"Ursula Martel."

Martha rolled her eyes. "Then we'll be here a week. It's a cinch. Maybe we need a permanent chair."

"So we can always have Lenore?"

Martha nodded.

"Sounds perilously close to government, Martha."

Martha laughed in spite of herself. "That's a low blow, Laura."

"But it got a laugh, didn't it?"

Judging by the way the day was going, a laugh was nothing to sneer at. Laura's feeble joke might be the only thing to laugh at through the whole Steering Committee meeting. Martha reached for one of the half-liter bottles set out on the table. The more water she drank, the sooner her hangover malaise would go away. And then maybe things wouldn't look quite so grim.

[iv]

The initially submerged dissension surfaced late Thursday afternoon when Janice Corleone raised questions about the Women's Patrol's recent tactics in dealing with incidents in which olive-clad men intimidated people in the markets. At first, Martha stayed on the sidelines. But Toni Farren's contingent chose the moment to introduce a demand that if a police force were going to be re-established, men should be allowed to participate in it. This had the effect of throwing the discussion into a roiling confusion of issues, thereby obscuring the one Martha considered most important.

Unable to sit silent, she stood up, was recognized, and put Janice's argument in more extreme terms, thinking to refocus the issue. Carried away by her own rhetorical excess, Martha said things that led to Ursula Martel's reminding her that everything said in the meeting would be transcribed and made universally available on demand, and would Martha Greenglass please bear the significance of that in mind…

Embarrassed, Martha sat down and let others make the argument. As she listened to the debate she realized that her basic problem was that she alone knew that some of the Women's Patrol were on the Night Patrol. She was certain that if other people knew what she knew, they would feel very much as she did. But she also understood that if the identity of the Night Patrol got out, the Co-op would be endangered. And the result of that could be the takeover of Seattle by Toni Farren or some other pro-government contingent. Exposing Louise would carry a high price. Too high a price.

When Ursula Martel adjourned Thursday's session at eight, nothing had been resolved but that discussion must be put off so that the rest of the reports under the rubric "Old Business" could be made. Many women at the meeting had traveled from other parts of the Zone and could not afford to spend a week or however long it would take to resolve the controversy. Martha had the distinct impression that Ursula considered the debate about whether or not the Women's Patrol should carry firearms an internal dispute that should be handled within the family and not aired publicly in that particular forum.

Friday afternoon saw the end of the reports and the beginning of "New Business." The first item on the agenda was Kay Zeldin's death. When Lori Jackson, one of the members of the Women's Patrol, took the floor and made a speech demanding vengeance, nearly everyone in the room fixed their gaze on the Marq'ssan in attendance. Martha realized that many women expected the Marq'ssan to avenge Kay's death— apparently associating previous retaliatory strikes against the Executive with vengeance. Though Martha did not get up to speak, Beatrice Sweetwater did, protesting the notion of vengeance and insisting that the Free Zone's response to Kay's death be constructive, not destructive. But Beatrice's statement made little impact on most of the people in the Hall. The appeal for vengeance had fired up their rage against the Executive and provided them with a focus— and by inference tied the olive-clad men to Kay Zeldin's death.

Martha grew depressed; she saw that with arrangements for memorial events in Louise's hands the vengeance theme would be played to the hilt. How was it that she hadn't seen any of this in Louise until after discovering her involvement in the Night Patrol? She must have been blind! Louise surely hadn't been concealing her attitudes all along. Or had she?

Martha wondered: had Louise's offer the previous Saturday to quit the Night Patrol if Martha would return to her been genuine? It didn't seem to make sense, especially considering the emergence of the Women's Patrol's violent attitudes and tactics into the open. Martha felt sunk in confusion. How would she ever disentangle her personal relations and feelings from the larger issue?

She slumped in her chair; she wished she could avoid speaking about Birth Limitation. The meeting was already overloaded with conflicts. But since Venn was scheduled to speak, she had no choice but to make a formal proposal that a new committee be formed. Unless she intended to abandon that responsibility altogether?

Fortunately Ursula adjourned the meeting before they got to Venn's report. Martha wearily shoved files into her briefcase. She would go home, eat, and go to bed early. Maybe a night's sleep would help her recover her energy and shake her depression.

"Martha, Sorben and Magyyt are having a meeting they'd like you to be in on."

Martha turned and found Beatrice behind her. "Beatrice, hey. That was a nice try you made. But I'm afraid the rabble-rouser did her damage."

Beatrice looked old, worn out, sad. But she always looked that way when she was away from Sweetwater, Martha reminded herself. "Name-calling doesn't help, Martha," Beatrice said sternly.

Martha bit her lip. "You're right. It doesn't. I guess I'm frustrated."

"Will you come along to the meeting?"

"Yeah. I'm exhausted, but I'll do that. I'd like to see something of Sorben, anyway."

"Meet me in the lobby. There are a few other people I need to check with." Beatrice plodded off, and Martha wondered about the meeting. To do with Kay Zeldin? Or a lecture on the evils of dissension? No, Martha thought, there would be no lecture. That wasn't how the Marq'ssan operated.

Martha waited in the lobby for ten minutes before Beatrice showed up with five other women. "Sorben suggested the lounge of the Co-op," Beatrice said, and the seven of them set off for the Co-op's building three blocks away. Martha was glad to see that Janice Corleone was part of the group. She was less happy, though, to see Toni Farren. It looked as though the Marq'ssan notwithstanding, the meeting in the lounge would probably turn into a more intense (because private) brawl along the lines begun Thursday afternoon.

When they arrived at the Co-op building, they found Sorben and Magyyt in the lounge with several other women who were attending the Steering Committee meeting, among whom numbered Geneva and Louise. Martha seated herself on the floor near Geneva, and they made small talk until Beatrice closed the lounge's door and took her seat.

Magyyt spoke first. "Considering everything we've heard and seen at the Steering Committee meeting over the last two days, it occurred to us that you need help. By now it's painfully clear what the major disagreements are among you. I won't bother to recapitulate them— if you want to do that in a while for yourselves, you can. But it seems to me that what you need now is to be reminded of what you agree on. Because that is where you need to start talking from. Which is not to quash dissent. But to allow it to be integrated into a constructive framework." Magyyt's dark gaze moved from face to face around the room. She brushed a fallen lock of heavy dark hair off her forehead. "Sorben and I will mediate for you— assuming you want our help."

Martha wondered why the Marq'ssan hadn't simply washed their hands of them: they must seem like squabbling children.

Magyyt waited. After a long silence, Martha said: "Some of us are glad for your help. I, for one."

After Martha, the other humans present also expressed acceptance of the Marq'ssan's mediation. Toni Farren, the last to speak, said, "I don't accept that the aliens have the right to interfere so directly in our business. Nevertheless, it is clear that since they've persuaded the rest of you to accept their interference, if my people are to have any representation in this process at all, I must accept it too. I object, but I will go along with it." By this Martha understood that Farren believed that the rest of them would cut a deal excluding her if she left the meeting now. Farren had no idea what the Marq'ssan's interest was, or even what they meant by "mediation."

"Now that that's settled," Magyyt said without commenting on Farren's animadversion on Marq'ssan involvement in the dispute, "I suggest we review exactly what goals and values all of you share in common. Such an articulation must be very general, even vague. I suggest that at this point we omit any discussion of the means each of us believes is the correct way to go about achieving those goals and values. We will undoubtedly get to a discussion of means and differences very shortly."

Martha wondered at this methodology: wouldn't they get into a philosophical dispute right from the start?

Beatrice began and Martha sat back, determined to concentrate. Were the others as hungry and tired as she was? It was probably going to be a long, grueling night. But better they argued here, she thought, than in the Steering Committee meeting, for the world to hear and for factions to be formed and polarized. Except that she knew that was likely to happen anyway. Louise had to be made to see how the tactics of her and her cohorts were threatening the very existence of the Co-op, and maybe even the Free Zone, and Martha had little hope of that, not even with the Marq'ssan helping them to talk together. Louise was incomprehensible. Louise was damned stubborn. Louise was Louise. And that was the truth they were stuck with.

Chapter Seventeen

[i]

As Kay worked through the bottles of water and tubes of food Weatherall had left her— during a period of time she could not characterize within her system for keeping track of time, leading her to consider counting bottles of water instead of visits from Weatherall— as she paced the cell, as she squirmed and shifted on the platform seeking the so-elusive sleep her body craved, she wrestled with questions she knew she must come to decisions about. She did not doubt that this extended period of absolute uninterrupted solitary confinement had as its purpose the furthering of Weatherall's brainwashing "experiment." About "the experiment" she would not think, for it was pointless to do so— though from time to time consciousness of the mirror brought rage bubbling up to the surface as she wondered whether Sedgewick or Weatherall or both were on the other side, watching her attempt to cope with this new situation.

And she determined she had to decide: (a) whether she should live or die; (b) whether she should resist Weatherall with all her strength, pretend to capitulate entirely, or engage in a semi-resistance that would allow a certain level of submission for survival purposes; and (c) if she chose to live, what she wished to do, or rather how she wished to live under the circumstances. Kay recognized that the third question was something of a conflation of the first two but nevertheless saw that the first two had to be considered before the third. That she had to make up her mind about these questions she never doubted: if she did not, she knew, she would never be able to live with the situation, for she would be reacting aimlessly as the moment dictated and would thereby fall into Weatherall's thinking. Whereas if she made rules for herself and was clear about what she intended, then she would have a base of strength— however feeble and minuscule— from which to act and accept whatever consequences her actions brought. While at times she sneered at herself for this rulemaking— since presumably she had enough rules with those imposed by Weatherall— she knew that rules would give her her own sense of authority, would give her some standard to live by that was not Weatherall's. To use the Marq'ssan's expression: she needed her own structures. Therefore she would consciously create them.

She must, or be lost.

Did she want to live? It might be that she would have no choice. Yet it seemed to her that if she wanted to suicide it would be possible. She could for instance surreptitiously dispose of her food and water rations and be in the throes of filter-failure before Weatherall even realized what she was doing. There might be other ways, too. But the point was: *did* she want to live? *Was* it worth living in these circumstances? Weatherall had told her that as far as the outside world was concerned she was dead. What did this mean for her? Plainly, she was living on death row. Plainly, she was isolated from the rest of the world. Plainly, she had not even the remotest hope of rescue.

Was this limited temporary existence worth living? Were there momentary pleasures that made it worthwhile? Kay thought of the pear and scorned herself: was she to be like a dog living for treats? But apart from the pear…

She had to admit that uncomfortable and miserable as she was, she did not want her existence to end. Not at least while she still enjoyed a reasonable level of mental activity. Her thoughts might run in circles, she might cry and pity herself and ache physically, yet there was still something there going on that was Kay Zeldin, that made her feel that Kay Zeldin existed. Still alive, she did not want to die. She wasn't that miserable, that defeated. And if she were to go crazy, it wouldn't matter to her. She would not think about that possibility, for there was nothing she could do, and there was no point in being humiliated by and grieved at possible futures.

Next she faced the question of how exactly she wanted to live under these circumstances. This was harder, not only because it did not offer the binary that a choice of living or dying entailed, but also because it involved thinking about Weatherall and Weatherall's intentions and about what she, Kay, could live with. One point recurred to her: Weatherall had indicated that when Kay had been successfully brainwashed she would have served Weatherall's purpose in keeping her alive and would then be killed. From that point of view resistance looked critical— though Kay also suspected that the experiment would not go on forever. They might lose interest and kill her anyway. And if they started introducing drugs into the experiment, she would lose whatever chance she had at resisting. Suppose she simply set herself to doing whatever she had to do to satisfy Weatherall. What then, especially if she made it clear in small ways that she was not by any means "deprogrammed?" If Kay decided in advance that she would do so, surely it would not mean that she was in fact giving in, would it?

But, Kay decided, it would. It was not possible to play by Weatherall's rules and keep possession of her own soul. She had been wrong to give Weatherall the words about punishment.

But if she were to resist completely, she would end up in such intolerable straits— enduring force-feeding and constant confinement to the platform— that her life would not be worth living. And so in that sense though asserting her will she would at the same time be losing to Weatherall. She might even in such straits lose her mind.

Some time after finishing the seventh bottle of water Kay concluded that she should adopt a strategy in which she would attempt not to challenge Weatherall, but when explicitly challenged by Weatherall to then abide by her own rules. That is, she would not refuse the obligatory greeting, nor use the word "brainwash" or other words she knew would give Weatherall the excuse to confine her more closely. Yet if Weatherall's commands in any way contradicted Kay's own rules, then Kay would stick by her rules and take the consequences.

All the way to force-feeding? she wondered. Once she was cuffed to the platform, the choices to be made changed. And she could not gauge the strength of her own will.

Staring at the eighth bottle of water, wanting to open it but afraid it might be her last for a long long time, Kay brooded about the extent

to which she should carry resistance once embarked upon. Impulsively she grabbed the bottle and uncapped it: she would drink the whole damned thing at once. If Weatherall wanted to keep her alive, she would not allow her to get to the point of filter-failure. Therefore it did not matter about conserving water.

Turning her back on the mirror, Kay leaned against the platform and stared at the blue cement blocks on the wall opposite. Once she resisted, she would have to carry her resistance all the way. Otherwise she would simply be vegetating, entirely dependent on Weatherall's whims, merely eating and drinking and getting through the interminable hours.

Kay finished the water and set the empty bottle down beside the seven others. So that was that. The food was gone; the water was gone. And now it was time to make her rules. She had to be prepared for Weatherall's next visit. She needed to decide where she was and what she was doing. Once she had decided that, she could then try to live by her decisions for as long as they allowed her.

[ii]

At around eleven o'clock Monday morning the door to Allison's office opened and Elizabeth filled the threshold. Allison leaped out of her chair. "Elizabeth! You're back!"

Elizabeth smiled and made a warning sign with her index finger. "Yes, I'm back. Just now. Will you bring over your report on Zeldin?"

Allison nodded, and Elizabeth vanished. Her report on Zeldin. And not a word about anything else. The first thing Elizabeth wanted after four days away on a danger-fraught trip was Allison's report on Zeldin. Allison pressed her lips tight and suppressed her anger. As she ordered a hard-copy from her terminal she searched for a reason to explain why Elizabeth had been so abrupt. It must, she thought, be because of Jacquelyn. Mustn't it?

When Allison took the flimsies across the hall to Elizabeth's office, Jacquelyn was there, answering Elizabeth's questions and receiving Elizabeth's flow of orders while Elizabeth stood behind her desk ripping open purples and glancing over files and stacks of paper. Finally Elizabeth concluded with one last order: "I want you to make an appointment for me with Wallace Maxwell for sometime this afternoon. And don't take no for an answer. Clear?" Wallace Maxwell: Allison thought he might be the Deputy Director of Science and Technology in charge of the Office of Electronics.

Jacquelyn uttered a crisp "Understood" and departed. Elizabeth looked at Allison and smiled. "It's nice to be home," she said. Allison, taking this as a discreetly worded lover's effusion, smiled back. Elizabeth sat down and gestured Allison to the chair in front of the desk.

Allison handed Elizabeth the flimsies. Elizabeth quickly read the three pages, then sat for an abstracted moment in frowning silence. She glanced at Allison. "There's something about this... I can't quite put my finger on it..." She stared at the flimsies, her eyes moving rapidly over each of the three pages. The she looked again at Allison. "You're sure about the water? She drank that last bottle down all at once yesterday?" Allison nodded. Elizabeth bit her lip. "I expected her to conserve the food and water the way she usually does and thus have a couple of bottles left by the time I returned... I could easily imagine her not having any notion of time elapsed. Four days is a long time. It's almost a quarter of the amount of time she's been here. But to drink down the entire bottle straight, all at once. You *saw* her do it?"

"Yes," Allison said. "I was surprised myself. She did it with her back to the window, too."

Elizabeth's brows lifted. "*Did* she... Well, well, well. The plot thickens. What is going on in that woman's head? I thought she'd be climbing the walls with anxiety for my return. No watching of the door, you say. Whereas before my trip she was constantly watching the door..." Elizabeth sighed. "I wish I had time to figure this out before going in to see her. I have the feeling I'm missing something."

"She's anxious," Allison said. "She's been pacing her cell like a caged beast. Back and forth, back and forth, for hours without stopping. Yesterday especially."

"She turned her back to the mirror and drank the whole bottle," Elizabeth said. Her eyes stared at Allison, but Allison doubted Elizabeth was actually *seeing* her. "I think I'll pay her a visit now," she said, rising to her feet. "Want to watch?"

Allison's heart beat faster. They would have some time alone together in the sector. Tonight was so very far away and Elizabeth had been gone for four, long days. That must be Elizabeth's reason for asking her to accompany her.

[iii]

Kay leaned miserably against the wall of blue concrete blocks. Another fit of sneezing seized her, and she knew without a doubt: she had a cold coming on. And she was out of water, had been out of water for a long long time.

She wiped her nose yet again on her leotard sleeve. At this rate her leotard would soon be a sodden mess. Bad enough being sweat-soaked, but being mucous-soaked was something else. There was no doubt she would go on sneezing and sniffling. And there was absolutely nothing in the room— beyond toilet paper, so precious little that she conserved it carefully— to use. She decided to remove her leotard and wrap herself in the blanket. The leotard didn't give much warmth, anyway. It merely allowed her to move about without always taking the blanket with her, as when she exercised.

Damn Weatherall. The only thing surprising about catching cold was that it hadn't happened before now. Her resistance was low from lack of sufficient sleep, food, and water, and the room was too cold for her ever to be comfortable except during vigorous physical exercise. She had been physically miserable enough without the cold; with it she was sinking fast into depression and apathy.

The irony was bitter. Just as she had begun to feel strong enough to cope with her situation and found a plan by which to live, this debilitation had sneaked up on her, threatening to sap her last ounce of strength. Kay knew her only source of energy now was anger at Weatherall. *That* she must hang on to.

A little while later, though, nodding awake from a doze, she wondered whether it mattered at all. She was so tired, so achy, so shaky. Maybe she had come down with something worse than the flu and would die from lack of fluids. Ailments that were normally trivial could be fatal in primitive circumstances. And surely these circumstances could be properly characterized as primitive.

Exhausted, dispirited, Kay lay back down and curled into a ball with the blanket covering her head, moving only to wipe her nose. She sank into a sort of stupor, not sleeping, but only minimally conscious. Every time she came close to dropping into actual sleep, her muscles jumped, forcing her awake.

Weatherall sang out, "Good morning, Kay." Kay shuddered. She had not heard the door open.

Kay debated not moving but wanted the water too badly to defy Weatherall with her apathy. And then she remembered her rules and sat up. This was not an occasion for challenging Weatherall. "Good morning Elizabeth," she said, her voice thick and nasal. She tried to clear her throat.

Weatherall busied herself with sweeping all the empty plastic containers off the table into a large plastic garbage sack. "Sounds like you have a cold," she said.

"Yes," Kay said— and censored a remark on the tip of her tongue about the inevitability of her getting sick given the conditions of her captivity.

Weatherall took a bottle of water and a fresh disposable cup from her bag. "I'm surprised you finished everything," she said, pouring water into the cup. "You're usually careful to stretch your rations between visits." She handed Kay the cup of water and perched on the edge of the table.

Kay downed the cup in a few fast, greedy gulps and handed the cup back to Weatherall, She saw that Weatherall was studying her and tried to make herself indifferent to the threat. Wearily she leaned back against the wall and waited. Weatherall usually did not stay long.

"I thought you'd be interested to know that the announcement of your death has precipitated a crisis among your friends. Do you remember David Hughes? He was with the team that apprehended you in Seattle."

One of the rules Kay had made for herself required that she not think about the world outside. She resented Weatherall's attempt to force such thoughts on her. "Yes, I remember him," Kay said. "An analyst, he called himself."

"An economist. It was thought you would find him sympathetic."

Kay half-smiled. "Oh yes. A veritable kindred spirit."

Weatherall's lips twitched. "Obviously a miscalculation on someone's part," she said. "But Hughes, it seems, has proven to be a kindred spirit for someone among the Free Zone cadre, for he's gotten tapes of all sorts of interesting confabulations, including sessions in which the aliens were present and speaking. Really, these tapes have given us our first chance to hear how they operate." Weatherall looked extremely pleased. "But as I was saying, they are in an uproar of which the announcement of your death was the catalyst. Some of them have taken to carrying rifles and shooting at assets our Covert Action Team has been recruiting and organizing. And that is not going over well with the public. Amazons running around armed and shooting, while the men are left out of the most important activities: how long do you think it will be before everything blows up in the Free Zone, Kay?"

Kay shrugged. "I have no idea."

Weatherall's eyebrows lifted. "I thought you'd be interested in all this. You sound as if you don't care."

"I don't," Kay said. "What is any of that to me? As you said, as far as the rest of the world is concerned, I'm dead. There's nothing I can do about any of it. The rest of the world might as well not exist as far as I'm concerned."

Was that true? Kay wondered. For it did matter to her that the Marq'ssan existed, that the Free Zone survive. It mattered whether she ever thought about them or not. But she didn't want to think about them precisely because there was nothing she could do. Thinking about the outside world could only frustrate her.

"You mean you wouldn't even like, out of ordinary vanity, to hear a tape of a speech made about your death and all your heroic contributions to the Free Zone?" Weatherall asked incredulously.

Kay, shaken by a paroxysm of sneezing, snatched for the leotard. When she had finished sneezing and wiping her nose she said, "I really don't care."

"Why have you taken off your leotard?"

Why didn't Weatherall just leave the food and water and go? Why was she hanging around talking? Was this some new phase of the experiment? Or was Weatherall hoping to provoke her into doing something she could punish her for? "I need something to wipe my nose on," Kay said. "The leotard was disgusting enough before I started doing that. You can imagine what it's like now."

"Nevertheless you will put it back on," Weatherall said.

Kay stared at her a moment before forcing herself to obey. This was not something for which to challenge Weatherall. But still it infuriated her. Kay slipped the blanket off her arms and shoulders and pulled the leotard over her head and torso, then snapped closed the crotch. Angry at feeling damp patches on her skin, she pulled the blanket around her and focused her stare on the bottle of water. Surely Weatherall must be going to leave soon. Now that she had forced her will on Kay she must have gotten the satisfaction she had been seeking.

Weatherall dug a roll of toilet paper from her bag and set it on the table. "Use this instead of your leotard. It's far more absorbent."

Kay bit down on her tongue and said nothing.

Finally Weatherall slipped off the table and removed two tubes of food from her bag and set them beside the roll of toilet paper and the bottle of water. "I'll bring you something to help with your cold, Kay," she said. "It's a pity you haven't made progress enough to move across the hall to a more comfortable cell already prepared for you."

Kay needed to wipe her nose. She eyed the roll of toilet paper, wishing Weatherall would leave. Weatherall, of course, was watching her for a reaction to her remark. Kay sniffed to keep the snot from dripping out of her nose. "What do you mean by progress?"

Weatherall shrugged. "That's rather intangible," she said. "But for one thing, you haven't worked on your tone of voice when you talk to me. It's a bit different today— petulant instead of hostile, but that's because of your cold. I'm looking for a change in attitude. It's too bad about your cold, but that's the way it goes." She picked up her bag and went to the door. "I'll be back shortly with some aspirin," she said as the door slid open.

When the door had closed after Weatherall, Kay slid off the platform and grabbed the bottle of water and the roll of toilet paper. In spite of her sickness, this round had gone to her. She felt sure of it. Her rules were going to work— until Weatherall changed the game. But she wouldn't do that for a while since it would take some time for her to grasp what was happening. Until that time, life would be bearable— if, that is, she ever got over the damned cold.

[iv]

"There's nothing like sex for stoking one's appetite," Elizabeth said. "Let's go see what we can find to eat in the kitchen."

Elizabeth was incredible. It must be two-thirty in the morning. Why did she have so much energy still? Allison was so relaxed and sleepy she wanted just to lie as they were, drifting in and out of sleep, and savor Elizabeth's nearness. But Elizabeth nudged Allison into removing her head, arm, and shoulder from Elizabeth's breast.

"What a sleepyhead you are," Elizabeth said. "You can stay here if you like. It's just that I'm all of a sudden famished."

"Hmmm," Allison said, forcing her eyes open. "I'll keep you company. My stomach has been growling too."

In the kitchen, Elizabeth opened the refrigerator and loaded a tray with mustard, butter, mayonnaise she had made the night before she left on her trip, goose liver paté, radishes, slices of cucumber and tomato, olives, pickles, Lorraine Swiss, Camembert, slices of baked ham and roast beef, potato salad, and a quart of milk. Allison gathered up plates, knives, forks, glasses, and napkins and a bag of French rolls, and followed Elizabeth out to the living room.

"We need a fire," Elizabeth said. "It's chilly enough for one, don't you think?"

Allison wanted to remind Elizabeth that it was two-thirty in the morning. Why make a fire when they were just going to go back to bed?

Elizabeth got the fire going while Allison arranged the food. At last they were settled on the floor with the fire roaring before them and a feast spread around them. "Hear anything interesting while I was away?" Elizabeth said casually as she split open a roll and spread butter and mustard on it.

Allison observed that the paté was studded with green peppercorns. "Could you explain something to me, Elizabeth?" Elizabeth raised her eyebrows. "Why is it that Zeldin's being alive is considered such a threat to Wedgewood?"

"Ah," Elizabeth said, piling ham and Lorraine Swiss onto her roll. "I'm surprised you haven't asked me that before now." She added a slice of tomato to the sandwich and closed it up. "The reason, my sweet," she said, picking up the sandwich in both hands, "is that as long as Zeldin's alive, Wedgewood is vulnerable to exposure of certain actions of his that, if known outside the Company, would result in his being indictable for treason. And that of course is a serious matter to him." Elizabeth bit into her sandwich.

Treason! "What does Zeldin have to do with it?" Allison asked. "Did she find out about it while she was working for us?"

Elizabeth finished chewing and swallowing before replying. "Not exactly. In sum, after Zeldin abducted me and Sedgewick, Wedgewood was left in an embarrassing situation. To wit, he had just spent hours torturing Turpin—" Allison gasped "—and naturally when Sedgewick and I went off with Zeldin he was left with this situation of being Turpin's controller and having no one around to tell him what to do about Turpin. And so he shot Turpin and had his body dumped in the Potomac."

"In the Potomac!"

Elizabeth nodded. "Incredible as it seems, he dumped Turpin's body in the Potomac. But to continue, the only non-Company person who can tie Wedgewood to Turpin's torture and death is Zeldin. Furthermore, the story has generally been that it was Zeldin who started the war against Military. And using that story it has been assumed that some of Zeldin's confederates were responsible for Turpin's torture and death— Zeldin's book to the contrary."

Fragments of Zeldin's version of Turpin's being forced to sign a paper granting emergency Executive control to Sedgewick began to come back to Allison. "Some people suspect that Zeldin was telling

the truth in her book," she said. As far as she recalled, Zeldin had written nothing about Turpin's being tortured.

"They may suspect it," Elizabeth said, "but they don't openly accuse Security of having done away with Turpin. But of course, these suspicions have made people nervous. The story *we* tell is that Zeldin took us hostage before all the shit came down. And that Turpin and Devito walked into Zeldin's trap and that Zeldin and her people were responsible for their deaths and forced our people— with three Cabinet members as hostages— to move in on the Pentagon and the Department of Science and Technology." Elizabeth took another bite of her sandwich.

Allison frowned. "But if that's the case, isn't Zeldin's death in your and Sedgewick's best interests, too?"

Elizabeth smiled. "It might seem so. As she is now, that's of course true. But you realize that only Zeldin herself can lay all the suspicions and rumors to rest."

"Oh! So that's it: you want to force Zeldin to make a confession! So that she can publicly take the rap!"

Elizabeth licked a dab of mustard from her lips. "Not exactly, darling. Any confession coming out of the Rock will be assumed to have been extracted and thus not worth the paper it's printed on. So a confession isn't quite good enough. She has to be natural and convincing."

Allison crunched into a radish. "But how are you going to get her to be convincing?"

"You'll see."

"Well at least now I have an idea of what you want Zeldin for," Allison said.

"That's certainly part of it, though not by any means all of it. This is wonderful potato salad, Allison. Try some."

"Your ways are mysterious, Elizabeth," Allison said, helping herself to a bite of potato salad.

"My ways are complex," Elizabeth said. "Unfortunately, so are Zeldin's. I can't make out this last visit at all. I offered her so much bait, and the only thing she even nibbled at was my reference to the cell across the corridor. I'd thought of playing the tapes for her to see her reaction. But I'm not sure now about that tack. She seemed actually uninterested, though that was probably an act. But why bother to pretend?"

Allison shook her head. "Maybe it's her cold. Maybe she's too miserable to care about anything else."

Elizabeth's eyebrows knit into a frown. "I think she has something up her sleeve."

"But how can that be? It's not as though she has a sleeve in which to hide anything."

"One would think that, wouldn't one," Elizabeth said. "Yet I may have underestimated her— again. I thought I was making allowances for everything. And I was so sure that she would be in a state after so much time alone. I don't understand her, Allison. I thought solitary was supposed to make people desperate, if not crazy."

"Maybe she is crazy,"

"No. Not at all. In spite of everything, Zeldin is completely in control of herself." Elizabeth poured milk into her glass. "And that worries me. It doesn't fit with the situation."

"You said you were pleased she was so strong."

"It's not necessarily strength. She's bending quite easily. Maybe even too easily— considering how she began." Elizabeth sighed. "I'll have to think about this before I visit her again. Perhaps reviewing the tape will give me a clue."

Always Zeldin, Allison thought, staring into the fire. Always Zeldin. It was like having ghostly competition: always present even when physically absent. Did Elizabeth realize how obsessed she was becoming?

"You're suddenly very quiet, darling," Elizabeth said. "Did you miss me at all while I was away? Or did you look for your little service-tech friend?"

"No," Allison said, "I didn't look for Anne. Why would I do that? It's you I missed, not just a warm body."

"You're angry at me, Allison?"

Allison moved her eyes from the fire to Elizabeth's face. "No, I'm not angry at you. Why should I be angry?"

Elizabeth's eyes were cool and watchful. "I have no idea why you might be angry, darling, but you *sound* angry."

Allison dropped her gaze to her plate and picked up a cucumber slice. "I'm not angry," she said quietly. And it was true: she wasn't angry; she was hurt. But she didn't know how to tell Elizabeth that, and she wasn't sure that if she knew how to tell her that she would.

Elizabeth set her plate aside and slid across the rug to Allison. "Then prove it," she said softly, touching her fingers to Allison's neck.

Allison slid her arms around Elizabeth and pressed her face into Elizabeth's shoulder. "I guess I'm just very tired," she said, hoping Elizabeth would be satisfied with that. Elizabeth's hand caressed her hair and Allison knew the moment of tension was nothing. It was all right, she told herself, it was all right.

But she was pleased that she did not cry.

Chapter Eighteen

[i]

After crossing the bridge at Deception Pass, Beatrice turned the car right, into the park. Remembering the last time she had stopped here, Martha sighed a little. She had been living with illusions then. Was that why she had been so happy? Was the truth inimical to happiness? Martha sighed again, this time with impatience at herself. Why did she keep thinking about such absurd notions as "happiness"? Because she was so miserable and the opposite of misery seemed to be happiness?

"You're sighing a lot this morning," Beatrice said when she had parked the two-seater. Her eyes looked out of her old, wrinkled face with matter-of-fact frankness. From their expression Martha expected a probing personal question, but Beatrice only said, "Want to take a walk down to the beach?"

They put on their rain gear and took a half-liter bottle of water each with them. They did not sit on the rocks but walked through the fine, thin drizzle along the beach, swigging water as they went. Every now and then Martha moodily dug her toe into the gravel, kicking it in the direction of the water. The screech of a circling gull irritated her so much she felt like screeching back at it.

After about ten minutes, Beatrice said, "Tell me what the hell happened between you and Louise. You're both almost unrecognizable these days."

Martha stopped walking, glanced at Beatrice, then out at the water. She knew she'd been acting like a spoiled kid. And she also realized she'd been wanting Beatrice to ask. She didn't really have anyone she could talk to about Louise, and Beatrice was about the safest confidant she could ever hope to have. "Louise has changed, I agree," she said.

"But I haven't. I'm just reacting to everything happening around me." She looked Beatrice in the eye. "I really dislike the change in Louise and her contingent, Beatrice. Their embrace of violent methods scares the hell out of me."

Beatrice's gaze remained steady. "You are so angry these days it's hard to talk to you. You weren't this angry after Sorben brought you out of that ODS cell. You weren't even this angry when the government was killing hundreds of people a week. Nor were you this angry when the government shot our friends in Boston. What the hell is going on with you, Martha?"

She had such a powerful urge to tell Beatrice about the Night Patrol she could hardly stop herself from spilling everything. To give herself time to think, Martha held her water bottle to her lips and took a long, slow swig. Careful not to meet Beatrice's eye, she said, "I can't tell you. I can only say that it has to do with Louise. And that if you knew, you would understand."

Beatrice made a *ch* sound that might be signaling disbelief, but might also be merely an expression of impatience. "Is that so? You're telling me that you do understand?"

"No. I don't understand," Martha said. "Not really. Maybe if I understood… No. If I understood, I wouldn't be myself."

Beatrice's brows pulled down sharply, and the creases around her mouth deepened. "Oh come on, Martha! What a ridiculous thing to say! Since when does understanding mean the corruption of somebody? That *is* what you meant to say, isn't it?"

Martha finished the half-liter and jammed the cap back onto the empty bottle. "You've seen what's happened to Louise," she said.

"I see what's happening to *you*," Beatrice said. "Louise is not my friend. You are. I never knew Louise very well, and frankly it doesn't surprise me that's she's become the leader of a militant group. She's always had a militant bent. It may be that the combination of the strikes made against us by the government with whatever has happened between you two has brought all this into the open in her. I don't know her well enough to say. And obviously I'm missing a critical piece of the story that you don't feel you can tell me. But that

it is eating away at you like this is something else. I've always been impressed with the way you can work things out in your head the way you so often do, Martha. I mean you're ordinarily steady-going and consistent. Suddenly you're so emotionally driven that not only can no one get near you, but you've lost your steadiness of purpose and clear-sightedness. It's freaky, Martha, seeing this happen to you. I don't think you realize the extent to which you're acting out of character. Or the extent to which this upsets people."

"Sorry," Martha said acidly. "Sorry to be upsetting people."

Beatrice stared out at the choppy gray water. "I didn't say that to load a guilt-trip on you or to pressure you in any way." She looked Martha in the eye. "I just want you to know that I think you can straighten out your head, that I know you have it in you, and that I am willing to support you if you need it."

If Beatrice knew, she wouldn't be coming down so hard on her. It was Beatrice who didn't understand. How else should she be reacting to all this mess, anyway? What was it Beatrice— and apparently others besides her— expected of her?

They resumed their walk along the beach and did not talk again. Out on the water a crowd of gulls screeched frantically, circling and diving in a small patch of water, thieving fish from sea lions, no doubt. Martha thought about what she had to do and whom she had to see during her stay on Whidbey Island. There was no point in brooding over Louise. It was time to move on.

[ii]

Kay tried to doze through her cold. The extra blanket Weatherall had given her allowed her to escape the light, but her nose was so stuffy that the reduction of oxygen made her feel as though she were suffocating. Her feverishness exacerbated this impression of suffocation, plaguing her with images of immurement as her mind intermittently conjured pictures of the Rock and of her cell buried deep below the earth surrounded by hundreds of walls and covered by thousands of feet of rock, of which the four walls, ceiling, and floor of her cell were only the nearest, only the most visible of those rings of walls and barriers that existed between her and the air, between her and the sun, while above her a million tons of rock pressed her down down into the earth. That she would never breathe the open air again became the most terrible thing of all, the most unbearable of everything forced on her. It was then that the silence imprisoned with her in this cell began to press on her, battering at her ears, nose, and mouth, trying to force itself inside her body. Each time she became aware of the pressure, struggling against it she would feel a scream rising in her throat to pierce it, until imagining the scream, she grew afraid of it, afraid to know for certain that the silence would swallow it up, that any sound she might make would be meaningless, that the outside was less real than the inside of her own head. Inside her head her words and screams existed, had meaning, imparted significance. But in the silence of her cell the scream would not be real. The vibrations of it would die, would be swallowed up; and then it would be as though the scream had never been. Kay's dawning realization of this terrified her.

And there was her rule, too. She had made a rule for herself that she would not speak or make outbursts in this cell, mostly because of the mirror. In her battle against them she would express nothing of her feelings to them. Nor would she recognize their presence on the other side of the mirror. If Sedgewick were concealed behind it, she did not wish to acknowledge her suspicion of it to him.

But the silence, pressing more and more inexorably upon her, finally drove her to consider alternatives. It occurred to her to engage in a non-personal mode of speech. She would imagine herself standing before a class, lecturing. She would deliver a lecture. Her mind would choose her words, would function as it did during a lecture, and she would be aware only of her comprehension, insights, and ideas as she spun out the lecture, her words filling the room, speaking of a reality too intricate, too well known, too long acknowledged, to be swallowed up by the silence, into the walls.

Infused with purpose, Kay got off the platform, swept the empty plastic containers off the table and shoved it against the mirror, spread the extra blanket on the floor to keep her feet from freezing, and faced the wall of blue concrete blocks supporting the platform. She chose as her topic "The Berlin Wall vis-à-vis the Relationship of the Divided Germanies during the First Cold War Years." She stood with the blanket wrapped around her, her arms folded, as though facing a sea of blank young faces. "On August 13, 1961," Kay said, "the government of the GDR erected a wall in the City of Berlin that physically divided the Soviet-held sector of Berlin from the Western-held sectors. The erection of this barrier proved to be perhaps the single most powerful act of symbolism of the entire period of the Cold War. Ironically, the power of this symbolic act affected international politics and the course of the Cold War to a far greater extent than it affected the people of Germany, East as well as West. Today we will examine the international context within which the Berlin Wall was erected and then consider the Berlin Wall and its effects upon the people of both Germanies as well as upon the relations between their governments."

Thus Kay launched her lecture, one she had given perhaps five or six times in the years preceding the Blanket. This time, however, her lecture did not proceed quite as it usually did. When she began talking about the Berlin Wall as a symbol, she found herself delving further into the question of symbols and their relation to reality than she had ever done before.

"Walls have traditionally been imbued with political significance. They enclose space and thus create territory. It is thought by some that walls originated as a way of enclosing holy space and thereby of containing the holy, and consequently containing the power of the holy. Thus the power of the holy belongs to those who enclose it and is in some way controllable, tappable, and containable, holding inside what might be either inaccessible or overwhelming outside in the world at large. The walls of homes have of course been understood as creating a possession— or territory— as well as offering shelter and privacy, to such an extent that Europeans developed a long tradition of believing that whatever happened within the walls of one's home was sacrosanct from outside interference, except of course in cases of parricide, which can be defined as the murder of the household's primary figure of authority. Likewise cities have had walls. Many old European cities still retain traces of their old walls, walls often constructed by the

Romans. City walls supposedly provided protection and above all kept out undesirable elements. Walls were conceived by the Romans to be barriers of defense, excluding the uninvited. Walls around cities may also be seen to be inclusive as well as exclusive, for it may be thought that by surrounding the city one fosters a sense of community, perhaps precisely because of its exclusiveness. In the middle ages textile workers camped outside city walls— thereby creating suburbs— excluded as unfit to be community members by the lights of the burghers who ran the city.

"On a larger scale are such historical relics as the Great Wall of China and Hadrian's Wall. In modern times such edifices would seem absurd as defenses. But their symbolism as a physical line drawn to keep out barbarism and the alien is still easily understood. Walls constitute more than physical barriers. Physical barriers, after all, are in the end vulnerable as such. Walls are statements, they are acts of psychological warfare, they are attempts to bridge the abstract with the physical, which is a very complex thing to do. For a long time paper and metal money served the function of bridging the abstract, for the very notion of money is extremely abstract though paper and metal coin seem quite physically tangible. It is surprising how easily people forget how abstract a thing is when it is granted a physical manifestation. When they forget the abstraction of which the physical object is at first only a symbol, and when they begin to treat with that physical object as though it were *only* physical, they become swallowed up in the abstraction itself.

"But of course there is another, very old use to which walls have been put: walls have been used to imprison, to contain. Not every society has constructed prisons, though most eventually have in the long run. The walls of the prison provide physical barriers that enclose that which offends against the authority of those whose power predominates in a society. For that reason the walls of the prison are most powerful as a physical manifestation of the symbol of that power and authority. Nothing symbolizes a regime as does its prisons. It is a symbol taught to children to inculcate them with respect for authority by frightening them with the physical existence of the walls of the

prison. There is no one who does not understand the threat of involuntary enclosure.

"To return to the Berlin Wall: this physical symbol in the end did not in itself as powerfully divide the people of East and West Germany as one might have predicted. It was real, of course. And it was only one of many barriers imposed between East and West Germany. But its larger significance was not to the people of the Germanies, but to the superpowers, completing, as it did, for instance, the construct— both physical and abstract— known as the Iron Curtain, always present in the minds of the people of the West during the time of the Cold War. Quite obviously ideas and relations and feelings permeated the Wall, passing between East and West Berlin in spite of the physical barrier. One of course talked of East Berlin and West Berlin and was forced to contend with the reality of the Wall and all that went with the Wall. Yet the Wall was not as impermeable for Germans as it was in the minds of Western Europeans and Americans. And thus its significance to the Germanies was quite different from its significance to both of the superpowers as well as to the international community as a whole. It is a lesson worth bearing in mind..."

Kay went on to deliver the portion of the lecture that she had given several times in the past. Half an hour later, after making a brief summary statement, Kay stared at the wall of blue concrete blocks and realized she had finished her lecture. She glanced at her wrist as though to ascertain that fifty minutes had passed— and saw with shock the metal band instead of her watch.

She knew, though, that her lecture had taken fifty minutes: that was one thing she could be certain of after so many years lecturing in fifty-minute increments. And the idea that she could, if she chose, demarcate time accurately, even if only in this very discrete way, filled her with joy.

Walls! she thought, picking up the blanket she had used as a rug and returning to the platform to drink the remaining water in the bottle— the last of the two bottles Weatherall had given her. In talking about the Berlin Wall she had said something that helped her, though she wasn't sure what it was. But she felt stronger, better able to

stand her immurement. Satisfied with her hour's labor, Kay curled up on the platform, draped the second blanket over her head, and went to sleep.

Lecturing had exhausted her.

[iii]

Elizabeth was explaining to Allison why some of the people whose dossiers Allison was reading should be considered as candidates for certain jobs precisely because of the spotty nature of their records. "Don't you see, Allison, that such people are easily controlled when one has something on them. We can't expect to draw people who will put their loyalty to me over their tendencies to want to exploit any possible vulnerabilities of mine they might— and surely would— encounter in their new positions in this proprietary."

"But Elizabeth," Allison said, "people like that will betray you the first chance they get! And surely they aren't *easily* controlled!"

Elizabeth yawned behind her hand. "You're so naive about some things! Listen to me. I've seen it work for years and years. How do you think Sedgewick had such a handle on areas outside Security? Even now we're getting weekly reports from people inside the Pentagon and other departments of the Executive. Even in the middle of a civil war those people are for the most part toeing the line, though they might reason we can't touch them now."

"But their hostility! How can you expect decent work from them?"

Elizabeth drummed her fingers on the desk. "First, their own advancement and well-being depend upon how they execute whatever job they hold. Second, some of them will I hope be motivated by their loyalty to the Executive System as a whole and will genuinely want to get things back under control. Third, our having a hold over them will matter only where the temptation to betray me personally is concerned. Otherwise they will be like any other executives in their zeal for or indifference to their jobs. We of course will want to pick the best people for the job. And then keep them up to snuff."

Allison stared down at her yellow pad. It seemed so degrading, so sleazy, to deal in what was in reality blackmail. Worse, Elizabeth seemed to expect her to be able to weigh these various factors when

choosing which people to interview and then select the right people and supervise them. All this was new to Allison, but Elizabeth expected her to pick it up instantly and effortlessly.

What if she were to fail Elizabeth? So much was riding on the success of the proprietary. And all this was on top of the other duties Elizabeth assigned her. Anything of a confidential nature that Elizabeth did not consider important enough to create the time for doing herself she assigned to Allison. Since getting back from her trip she and Elizabeth had been going home at around midnight while still rising at the usual early hour. And Elizabeth had warned that the pace would not let up, either.

"Do you see what it is I want you to weigh in your decisions?" Elizabeth said when Allison did not speak.

"I think so," Allison said reluctantly.

"Good. Now before you—" The phone chirped, and Elizabeth interrupted herself to answer it. She listened, then merely said, "Show him in in exactly three minutes." When she hung up she said to Allison, "I want you to stick around. It seems I have a surprise visitor. I'll want you to record our conversation and transcribe the tape afterwards. I may want a record of it."

Allison set up the recorder and checked the mikes and pulled a straight chair over to one side of Elizabeth's desk. Allison seated herself on the chair just as a knock sounded on the door and Jacquelyn ushered in a short stout man unpleasantly red-faced. "Mr. Bernard Grace to see you, Ms. Weatherall," Jacquelyn said.

Elizabeth stood up but did not move from behind her desk. "How do you do, Mr. Grace."

Grace did not come far into the room. "It's Sedgewick I want, Weatherall. Where is he?"

Elizabeth looked at Jacquelyn. "If I need anything I'll call you, Lennox." Jacquelyn left, closing the door after herself.

"Would you care to sit down, Mr. Grace?" Elizabeth asked politely.

"I'm not interested in talking to you, Weatherall. I want Sedgewick. Where the hell is he?"

Elizabeth sat down. "Mr. Grace, did you or did you not receive an affidavit and letter from Mr. Sedgewick some time ago instructing you that all matters pertaining to his personal affairs were to be referred to me?"

"I asked you a question, Weatherall. Where is Sedgewick?"

Elizabeth leaned back in her chair. "That, Mr. Grace, is none of your business."

"I insist on seeing him personally. These latest orders— issued by you, Weatherall— are preposterous. Before I sell—" he broke off and stared pointedly at Allison. "Get that bitch out of here. What I have to discuss with you is confidential."

"My aide stays, Mr. Grace. There is nothing you can't say before her."

"I insist on seeing Sedgewick himself."

"Let me put it this way, Mr. Grace. If my personal assistant had the poor judgment to make known my whereabouts to someone when I'd given her explicit instructions not to, I would terminate her without another moment's consideration. And I venture to suggest that you would do the same. I've been Mr. Sedgewick's personal assistant for nearly a decade and a half. If I had *ever* taken it upon myself to disobey his very explicit orders, I would not be his personal assistant today."

Grace stepped closer to the desk. "I don't give a damn about that, Weatherall. If you don't produce Sedgewick, I'll have an investigation started. I haven't seen him in well over eighteen months. Nor talked to him on the phone, nor indeed had any communication with him other than the affidavit and letter you just mentioned. That is suspicious in itself. And I'm quite certain other people will see it that way." He folded his arms and stood in the challenge stance.

Elizabeth remained unruffled. "Do you recall that we are in a state of war, Mr. Grace?" she asked very softly. "Mr. Sedgewick is Chief of Security, which at this time is perhaps the most important position in this country. That being so, it amazes me that you have the audacity to demand that he account for his time and whereabouts to you, whose connection to him is decidedly marginal. We are talking about National Security, Mr. Grace. It is nearly treasonous of you even to suggest you have a right to Mr. Sedgewick's attention. As for searching for him! I assure you that that would be a most foolhardy undertaking."

"I'm not impressed with your theatrics, Weatherall."

Elizabeth smiled. "No? Then I'll speak in a blunter, cruder language, Mr. Grace." Her soft, easygoing tone and smile made Allison marvel: this was control! "If you don't follow my instructions and keep your nose out of what Mr. Sedgewick doesn't intend you to concern yourself with, I will see to it that certain details in connection with the Barneshoff Merger of 2073 are leaked to your Wall Street colleagues as well as to Mr. Booth and other Cabinet-level men. Do you understand me, Mr. Grace?"

Grace's stance deflated; his face went gray. "You know about that?"

"I have a complete dossier in my possession. There are details of other dealings as well that I feel certain you would not wish to leak out. Unlike you, Mr. Grace, I am entirely in Mr. Sedgewick's confidence."

"*He* knows about the Barneshoff Merger?"

"Certainly. And now, Mr. Grace, I must ask you to allow me to return to more pressing matters. Oh. One more thing. I wish to make clear to you that I am displeased that you delayed to carry out my orders. In future if you do not carry out, as specified, and immediately, the orders I send you, I will move Mr. Sedgewick's entire portfolio to another firm. Be assured of that." Elizabeth looked at Allison. "Escort Mr. Grace to the outer office, Bennett."

Allison went to the door and held it open. Grace said, "Good day, Ms. Weatherall," to Elizabeth and went with Allison out into the hall. Allison wordlessly led him to Jacquelyn and then returned to Elizabeth.

"You see, Allison," Elizabeth said, "how useful it was for me to have that ammunition at hand. I waited and gave him a chance to shape up, and when he continued to resist being controlled, I brought out some of my heavy artillery. You can bet he won't give me another moment of trouble. Ever."

"He certainly did fall into line when you mentioned whatever it was you have on him," Allison said.

"It's one of Sedgewick's methods. I've learned well from him. I think this lesson will be useful for you in your selection process— and later, when you're handling the people we ultimately choose."

Allison swallowed. "Yes," she said, deeply uncomfortable. "I'd better get back to it now." Allison turned toward the door.

"Just a minute, Allison." Allison looked over her shoulder. "If you think you can spare a few minutes, I'd like you to look in on Zeldin."

Allison pivoted to face Elizabeth. "What is it you'd like me to look for or do?"

"Just look and see if she's drunk all her water and so on."

Allison frowned. "I'm pretty busy, Elizabeth. I'm not sure I understand..."

"She's sick, Allison."

"She has a cold," Allison said. "Not pneumonia."

Elizabeth shrugged. "All right. It's not important. It's just that I haven't been down there since seven-thirty this morning."

"I don't understand." This was crazy! "Is it possible you're feeling guilty about her having caught a cold?"

"Not at all. I suppose I find something pathetic about it."

"Oh Christ Elizabeth. It's not like she's in some camp in Siberia!"

"I'm so glad you pointed that out to me, Allison," Elizabeth said coldly. "And now instead of standing here psychoanalyzing me, I suggest you get back to your work."

Allison flushed. She shouldn't have said anything. Who was she to talk to Elizabeth that way? Damn Zeldin. She was nothing but trouble. But Elizabeth didn't seem to realize it, even if everyone else did. What was it with Zeldin, anyway? Her famous brains? Or simply that she was there under Elizabeth's absolute control? Whatever it was, Allison had to figure it out. Because at this rate she would lose Elizabeth.

That was clear.

[iv]

With the help of the aspirin, Kay nodded in and out of dreams. All too quickly after finishing the second of the two bottles of water

Weatherall had left her, she began wanting more. She had been schooling herself to feel indifference about her water supply, insisting to herself that it was Weatherall's responsibility and that she must not let her dependence on Weatherall for water foster a continual anxiety about it. So she consciously directed her thoughts to Weatherall's apparent attitudinal change as implied by her furnishing Kay with an extra blanket, a half-liter of fresh-squeezed orange juice (a luxury Kay had seldom in her life imbibed), aspirin, and an extra liter-and-a-half of water.

Kay told herself she must be on guard against Weatherall's attempt to appear sympathetic, for whatever Weatherall did must spring from her strategy for "deprogramming" her. She would not refuse anything that would make life in the cell easier. That would be foolish. But neither would she allow herself to feel grateful for it. Weatherall's attitude in furnishing these things was that of a benefactor bestowing gifts or privileges on an inferior. That Weatherall was not obliged to furnish these things made it all too easy to regard them as favors granted. But Kay knew that if she accepted that version of Weatherall's behavior she would in some way be granting legitimacy to Weatherall's power over her circumstances, would in some way be admitting Weatherall's right to keep her here like this. It was as though the very fact that Weatherall had it in her power to give or not give her them granted her a moral position which necessarily manipulated Kay's perception of these things as well as her emotional response to them and to Weatherall herself. But even when seeing this, she found it difficult not to fall into the trap of thinking of these things as favors and not simply as neutral or due her. And she realized that if she thought of them as due her she would begin thinking of everything else that was due her— thereby making her situation all the more intolerable. Thinking of them as neutral, however, was difficult, for they signified so much to her, the blanket especially. And the extra blanket was something, unlike the completely consumed aspirin, juice, and extra water, that could and probably would be taken from her.

Having firmed up her resolution to understand the psychological stratagems lying behind her being given these "extras," Kay deliberately shifted her thoughts back to the lecture. She sensed there a resource.

But instead of thinking of the content of the lecture, she visualized what she must have looked like delivering it: a professor with a rat's nest of unwashed hair dressed in ragged electric blue leotards and tights wrapped in a blanket, holding forth to an otherwise empty cell...and the image tickled her. As a professor of history she had always held forth with the utmost dignity, dressed in professorial corduroys, striding about the dais in large lecture halls and between the desk and the first row of students in small classrooms, hands behind her back, the calm, self-assured distiller of facts and insights and theories, never a hair out of place, impeccable, well-organized, authoritative. But to project the attitudes of that professorial image onto her present physical self offered an absurdity that made her first giggle, then chortle, and finally hoot with laughter. Laughing for the first time since her capture, she threw herself into amusement for the sheer pleasure of laughing and literally rolled around on the platform with it.

She was so absorbed in her laughter that she did not hear Weatherall come in. Weatherall's "Well, well, well," stilled her hilarity. Clad in a mauve and gray tunic and solid gray trousers, Weatherall stood with her feet planted about a foot and a half apart, her arms folded across her chest, the leather bag swinging from her right shoulder, looking exceedingly tall and real. "Is this hysteria or genuine amusement?" she asked, scrutinizing Kay with her hard (though not her hardest) frosty blue gaze.

Kay sat up and hunched the blankets more closely around herself. "Not hysteria," she said.

Weatherall nodded. "I'm glad of that. Then tell me what amused you so. I'm curious."

Kay resolved not to tell Weatherall. But she must not seem to refuse to tell her or Weatherall might choose to take it as a challenge and force the issue one way or another, and this was not a situation warranting Kay's challenging her. Her frightened thoughts scurried in search of a way out of the dilemma.

After ten seconds of silence Weatherall said, "Answer my question, Kay."

"Not amusement, either," Kay said, grasping at a fleeting thought.

"Not amusement and not hysteria," Weatherall said. "So then why were you laughing?"

The darkness and coldness of the world, shrinking sharply after that brilliant, expansive moment of laughter, frightened her, made her shiver. "I was laughing at myself," Kay said. "Laughing at the absurdity of my appearance." A partial truth: missing the essential kernel she would not let Weatherall have.

Weatherall said, "I see." Kay sensed she only half-believed it. "It is interesting that you retain a sense of the ridiculous." She looked at the table shoved up against the mirror and at the plastic containers scattered over the floor. "It is less interesting that you are making a mess of your cell. Considering how little there is to make a mess with. Get up and put the table back where it belongs and pick up the plastic. Now."

All this was said in such a chilling tone of voice that Kay moved quickly to shove the table back to its place and to pick up the half-dozen or so plastic containers. One of them lay a few inches from Weatherall's soft mauve ankle boots; as Kay bent to retrieve it she reeled from a flash of nausea that she knew was in some way connected with Weatherall's towering above her, inches away. The memory of Weatherall's foot smashing into her ribs seared her; and she recalled the occasions on which she herself had worn soft cloth boots like Weatherall's. When she straightened up with the empty bottles, her head swam; she gripped the edge of the table and stood for a moment waiting for the wave of dizzy nausea to pass. Then she returned to the platform to watch Weatherall unpack her bag.

Weatherall was setting out a bottle of water when she said, "Good morning, Kay," as though remembering that the ritual greeting had not been attended to.

This struck Kay as ridiculous. "Good morning, Elizabeth," she said, a bit of her dry amusement seeping through into her inflection.

Weatherall's eyes narrowed. "Yes, Kay?"

Fear threw a punch to the pit of Kay's stomach. "Sorry," she whispered.

"Share the joke with me."

Kay bit her lip. "I don't know exactly," she said helplessly. "It just seemed funny that you said it now after having been here for a while. As though a formula had been forgotten and must be said no matter its irrelevance."

"It is a formula," Weatherall said. "Your euphoria is remarkable." She moved to the platform. Kay flinched as she put her hand out and touched Kay's forehead. "You aren't feverish." She resumed her seat on the table. "You are afraid of me, Kay?"

Kay broke into gooseflesh; she pulled the blanket all the way up to her chin. This was a dangerous, frightening, conversation. If she weren't careful she would end up in restraint before the end of Weatherall's visit. "Yes, I'm afraid of you," she said warily.

"Physically afraid of me, I mean."

Kay swallowed. "Yes, that too."

"But why? I've made it clear I won't do you physical violence."

Kay stared down at her blanket-covered knees.

"Haven't I made it clear?"

Kay said, "You've said you won't torture me."

"Well then?"

Kay had no idea what to say, so she said nothing.

"I'm talking to you, Kay." Weatherall's voice had grown sharp.

Kay looked up to meet her gaze, remembering how annoyed Sedgewick used to get with her for not looking at him. "What is it you want me to say?" she asked faintly.

"Tell me the source of your irrational physical fear of me."

"I don't know what it is. It is just there."

"Hypothesize, then. It is your specialty, hypothesizing."

Kay's mouth went dry. She was bound to say something that would give Weatherall an excuse to "punish" her. But if she did not answer,

Weatherall would say she was disobedient. She felt a terrible pressure to choose every word with care, yet had no idea what it was safe to say. It was as though Weatherall were backing her into a corner, steadily, inevitably. Unless she could change course, the next few steps in this conversation would put her on the borderline and leave her no way of moving without going outside the bounds of what was acceptable to Weatherall. "Perhaps it is because you can chain me to this platform, at will, which may seem an act not physically violent to you but seems so to me," Kay finally said into the tense silence.

"Violent?" Weatherall sounded incredulous.

"It is an irrational fear, you said so yourself," Kay said quickly.

"It is unnecessary. I won't strike you unless driven to it."

Kay laced her fingers together and clasped them tightly over her knees.

"Do you believe me, Kay?"

"Yes," Kay said evenly.

"Your cold must be better."

"The fluids and warmth have helped."

"I've brought you an extra bottle of water this time, too," Weatherall said, unloading the other containers of food and water she had brought. She stood up. "I suggest you think about this physical fear you have of me, Kay. I think it's a good idea that we get to the bottom of it." Kay watched Weatherall, thinking she would go to the door. But after a few seconds Weatherall said, "Did you hear me, Kay?"

"Yes."

"I expect our conversations to be two-way. When I say something, you reply. Clear?"

"Understood."

"Well?"

"I will do as you wish and think about it," Kay said mechanically.

Weatherall picked up her bag and went out into the corridor without saying another word.

Kay got off the platform and tore the cap off the water bottle. She was parched.

Chapter Nineteen

[i]

On Saturday, Martha's last day at Sweetwater, she took advantage of Sweetwater's relatively plentiful supply of wash water to launder her underwear, tunic, and pants. She was happy for the chance because washing was so much of a hassle in the city. As she hand-scrubbed her clothes on a washboard in a tub of hot soapy water in the barn, Beatrice chatted with her. "I think it's wonderful that John Doyle has been persuaded to send a woman to represent his group on the Birth Limitation committee," Beatrice said.

Martha smirked. "He knew it was his only shot at direct involvement in the committee. Though we'll have some men on the committee, there's no way I was going to tell him *he* could be on it. It would be impossible to function with someone like him on the committee."

Beatrice brushed loose gray strands out of her eyes. "What happens when his representative finds out there *are* men on the committee? Won't she tell him so he can raise hell with you?"

Martha wrung out the pair of pants, satisfied she'd scrubbed them enough. "I don't give a damn what kind of hell he raises. He's not sitting on that committee. And when I've talked to all the other committee members— once the committee is actually established— they'll agree with me."

"You're so sure."

Martha plunged the tunic into the suds. "I know how these things work. And I know some of the people on the committee. In this case I'm perfectly willing to throw around what weight I have to keep him off." She smiled at Beatrice. "I know that this means-end argument is not in character, sometimes..."

"Sometimes one must be flexible," Beatrice said.

Martha found this pointed and looked up from the suds in quick suspicion. Beatrice's face gave nothing away. "You don't think I'm always flexible," Martha said.

"My theory— and it is only a theory, and you may be angry with me for stating it— is that your real anger at Louise is for not living up to your image of her. Whatever it is she's done, and obviously something set you off, your relationship with Louise was always problematical."

Martha flushed. "What is that supposed to mean? In what way was it always problematical?" She and Louise had never had problems. Which was why it was so terrible to discover how thoroughly corrupted and evil Louise really was.

"I mean that your relationship with her was more like a relationship you might have had with a man," Beatrice said flatly.

Martha's head jerked up, and she dropped the sleeve she had been scrubbing. "That's ridiculous!"

Beatrice shook her head. "From what I could see— and of course any outsider to a couple can't know everything going on. But from what I saw, it seemed to me that you were treating Louise like some kind of hero-figure, some kind of authority. Not quite a parent or mentor. But in the way women often relate to men. Louise was always strong, Louise always knew what she was doing. Louise somehow replaced Sorben for you."

Martha stared at Beatrice and saw that Beatrice believed what she was saying. She picked up the tunic and scrubbed like mad.

"You never ever had anything negative to say about Louise," Beatrice said. "Everything was always wonderful. You didn't like what she was doing, training women in handling firearms, but it was still all right because Louise was doing it and Louise must know best. When did you ever argue with her?"

"We were compatible!" Martha said. "We had no *reason* for arguing! And teaching and knowing how to use firearms is different from using them for intimidation!"

"In a year and a half you had no reason to argue," Beatrice said. "That's very interesting, Martha. You think it's the sign of perfection?"

Martha worked on the collar. "I don't know anything about perfection, but—" Martha broke off as her fingers puzzled over a lump. She bent down for a closer look. Yes, there was definitely a lump there, a very hard lump that had not been there the last time she had washed the tunic. "That's odd." Martha glanced at Beatrice. "There's a lump in this collar that was never there before."

"Maybe the sizing got bunched up?"

"It's denim. There isn't any sizing. Besides, it's hard, like glass or metal or plastic." She worked at the lump. "And it slides around in the collar when I work it sideways."

Beatrice sat up on her knees. "May I?" She took the tunic and moved her fingers over the collar. "It feels as though something's been sewn into it. Maybe it's a coin." Beatrice handed the tunic back to Martha.

"It's too thick."

"Maybe a bunch of coins wrapped in something to keep them together?"

"But how could a bunch of coins get in my collar? Is there a scissors or knife around here?"

Martha let Beatrice rip out one of the collar's seams, and a small plastic disk fell out, into the soapy water. Martha fished in the tub for the plastic. "What in the world?" Martha stared at the object lying in the palm of her hand.

"It's a bug, Martha."

Martha's gaze met Beatrice's. "Who could have put it in my tunic? And why bother to do that? And how?" She felt a sick, hollow feeling in the pit of her stomach.

"Those are questions it would be wise to answer," Beatrice said. "Do you have any ideas?"

Mute, Martha shook her head.

"It's probably someone you know. When was the last time you remember feeling your collar and can be sure the thing wasn't in it?"

Martha stared at Beatrice. Strange and scary thoughts flowed through her mind. She bit her lip and struggled to focus. "I'm not sure. I didn't start wearing this tunic much until the weather got cooler.

Though I wore it some of the time on my trip, when I was in the mountains. I think I last washed it up in Colville. That was almost two months ago."

"That's a long time to have been carrying a bug."

"Well we don't *know* it has been there since Colville. How do these things work, anyway? How far does it transmit?"

"Not very far," Beatrice said. "Probably not more than a mile. But I don't know much about these things, I'm just guessing. I suggest you talk with someone who does."

Martha sighed heavily. "Do you know, Beatrice, if this had happened a few weeks ago, I would have picked Kay Zeldin as the person to ask about it. But I can't now, can I."

"Louise will know someone who knows about such things," Beatrice said drily.

"Do you think it's working now?" Martha asked, wondering if the water had disabled it.

"I doubt it. But just to be on the safe side, I'd wrap something tightly around it and put it in a box. And then find someone who knows about electronic surveillance equipment."

Martha threw the bug onto the barn floor and picked up the tunic to continue her scrubbing. This was the sort of thing she had expected in the old days when ODS was around to contend with. But in the Free Zone? Who would want to bug her? And have had the opportunity to sew something into her collar? The two questions seemed to require answers in total contradiction to one another.

"Go easy, Martha, or you'll scrub your collar away."

Martha looked up from her work. "Is everything going to hell, Beatrice?"

"I've been getting along in this world a long time, Martha. I even managed to live in this world halfway contentedly without the Free Zone. That's something to consider."

Martha glared at Beatrice, then looked down at the tub and wrung out the tunic. There were some things that Beatrice just did not understand. Many things, in fact. And that that was so at this moment made Martha unbearably sad and lonely.

[ii]

With the dwindling of her cold into a post-nasal drip, Kay, growing restless, resumed exercising and pacing her cell. And when the silence pressed on her past bearing, she delivered another lecture, this one on the nuclear disarmament movement in Europe in the 1970s and '80s. This time, however, on finishing her lecture Kay moved the table back into its usual position and retrieved the plastic containers and set them back on the table. Weatherall had lately begun the nerve-wracking practice of questioning Kay's behavior, reactions, and feelings— or a perceived lack thereof that she thought she detected in Kay. Kay did not know how to handle such questioning, for most of the time there was no clear answer that she could be certain would satisfy Weatherall and at the same time preserve her own sense of privacy. Weatherall made evasion difficult.

At what point should she openly refuse to answer the questions put to her? Eventually she would say something that would end in "punishment"; Kay considered it only a matter of time. Wouldn't it thus be better to refuse altogether and hence be certain of giving away nothing at all? But if she refused once, she would have to continue refusing, which would be difficult in the face of the likely escalation of the course of "punishment" that would result from refusal to answer. There could be no doubt now that Weatherall was pressing her further and further, perhaps to locate her point of resistance. But would Weatherall reason that way? Would she imagine there might be a point of resistance? Kay decided she would. Perhaps she should regard this phase of her captivity as in some sense a testing out of limits.

Weatherall's mood swings— from cold and watchful, waiting to pounce on anything that could be construed to be the slightest challenge of her control on one day, to easy and expansive and generous (with objects for Kay's consumption) on the next: this strategy was far more recognizable to Kay, though no less dangerous. She began to doubt whether it would be possible to keep at arm's length from Weatherall in spite of her understanding the various tactics being used to manage her. Weatherall and Sedgewick would not overlook the well-documented Stockholm Syndrome (which indeed they must have seen at work a myriad times) that almost inevitably crept over prisoners held in isolation. Though they might have reasoned that frequent exposure to Wedgewood-types might advance the tendency for identification and sympathy with Weatherall, obviously they had decided this exclusive exposure to Weatherall would work more effectively on her and believed a less violent approach more efficacious because of what they comprehended of her personality.

These considerations worried her, for she did not know how to interpret them. She was supposed to grow psychologically dependent on Weatherall, clearly. But did they really believe they could force such a dependence on her merely by the circumstances of her isolation and her dependence for food and water on Weatherall? No. They couldn't believe that. This pressing on her of intrusive questions must form an integral part of their general strategy. And for that reason it was critical that she draw the line, that she keep herself emotionally balanced, falling neither into passionate hostility nor grateful dependence. Each were opposite sides of the same coin. She somehow had to keep her distance. It might not be possible to do that if she again found herself cuffed to the platform. Her one experience of that sufficed to demonstrate the psychological hazards of close restraint, for while under restraint she had spent a large part of the time talking in her head to Weatherall. And that was something she must not do again, ever. She wasn't certain *why* talking in her head to either Weatherall or Sedgewick was so dangerous. She only knew, intuitively, that it was.

Kay was pacing the cell puzzling over these things when Weatherall arrived for one of her visits (number twenty-one, which for purposes of calculation Kay added to the eight bottles of water Weatherall had left during that long hiatus). "Drop your blankets, Kay, and come with me," Weatherall said from the open doorway.

Kay let the blanket fall to the floor and went to the doorway. Facing the open door, she had the thought that the cell was likely the safest place of the entire base she could be. She hesitated, but Weatherall gripped her arm at the elbow and propelled her through the doorway. In its blindingly white light, the corridor looked strangely long, empty, and threatening. Kay had not realized the relative dimness of

the constant light in her cell. She blinked, and her eyes watered; and Weatherall steered her into a room diagonally across the corridor from her cell.

Inside, Weatherall pressed a small plate near the door, and the room filled with light. When the door slid shut behind them, Weatherall dropped her arm. Kay received a quick blurred impression of a room that looked something like an ordinary bedroom (albeit windowless) a professional might have in an apartment. "This way, Kay," Weatherall said briskly as she made for a door at one end of the room.

On the other side of the door lay a small bathroom. Weatherall entered it and pressed a thumb-lock plate beside another door on the far wall, and that door slid open, revealing a shower. "Voilà," Weatherall said. "Out of your tights and leotard, Kay, and into the shower with you. There's soap and shampoo on the ledge. Enjoy." She left Kay alone in the bathroom.

Joyfully, Kay stripped off the disgusting nylon. A wave of emotion overwhelmed her, and she fought to repress her excitement and pleasure at the sensation of hot, needle-sharp water cascading down her body, the slippery cleanness of soap against her skin, the relief of scrubbing her scalp and lathering her greasy matted hair. She told herself she must not worry about its significance now, she must simply *use* it, enjoy it, but without the degree of emotion now tightening her throat and wetting her eyes.

After she had thoroughly scrubbed her hair and body two or three times over, she reluctantly turned off the water. Better, she thought, that she decide when to stop than to have Weatherall order her to.

When she stepped out of the stall Weatherall was waiting with a towel. Her gaze ran over Kay's body. "I can see I'm going to have to increase your food ration." She handed Kay the towel. "You're fading into fleshly insubstantiality." Kay rubbed the towel over her skin until it tingled. "I've laid out a comb and fresh clothing for you," Weatherall said. And then she left.

When Kay had dried her body and toweled her hair, she went out into the bathroom and found the comb as well as a toothbrush and toothpaste, body lotion, and a new set of tights and leotard. Body lotion? A water shower? Anxiety gnawed at her stomach. All this comfort must be a trap. Wasn't there some way she could enjoy it while avoiding falling into the trap? Her hair combed out soft and fluffy, the lotion spread silky smooth over her dry, rough skin, the vigorous bristling of the brush against her teeth, gums, and tongue, though it drew blood, felt wonderful. She regretted only the new set of blue leotard and tights.

When she had finished grooming herself, Kay felt energetic, stimulated, ready for battle. Weatherall was wrong if she thought these comforts would demoralize her, for they had the effect not of soft, cushy seduction, but of making her blood sing, making her more her old self. She faced the door to the outer room; stoically she left the bathroom and all its objects behind, resolved not to think about them again.

Weatherall was seated in the desk's upholstered armchair, turned to face the bed. She smiled at Kay. "Good morning, Kay."

Kay was taken by surprise. "Good morning, Elizabeth," she said—and immediately felt troubled. She was on unfamiliar ground now.

"You look much more comfortable. Did you enjoy your shower?"

"Yes, very much," Kay said warily.

"I thought you would. Choose a piece of fruit and sit." She gestured at the basket of fruit on the desk and then at the bed.

Kay distrusted the setup. Should she refuse the fruit? She sensed that doing so would not be construed as a punishable offense. What would be the point of refusing? She had after all decided she was to consume whatever was offered to her on the clear understanding that anything that came her way was her due no matter the manner in which it was offered.

"It isn't poisoned, Kay." Weatherall looked amused.

Kay took a banana and sat on the edge of the bed. What an odd thing a bed looked to her now. After how long? More than a month? She held the banana in her lap, letting her fingers surreptitiously stroke its skin, the texture of which was like nothing in her cell. Weatherall took an apple from the basket and, staring straight at Kay, crunched into it. And Kay understood: Weatherall intended them to sit here in

this comfortable room and eat fruit together and chat. As though this were a social occasion. Kay determined not to eat the banana while Weatherall was eating her apple. She would not eat with her. If she had to make a point to refrain from doing so, she would. This was a line Kay understood it essential to draw.

"Aren't you going to eat your banana?" Weatherall asked.

"In a while," Kay said. "I like to make these things last as long as possible."

Weatherall's eyes narrowed. "Then why have you been drinking your water ration so quickly these days?"

Kay started. So they *had* been watching her: this confirmed it.

"Well?"

"I've been very thirsty. And the darkness of my urine made me worry about skirting too close to filter-failure."

Weatherall chewed and swallowed another bite. "That's not a satisfactory answer."

Yes, there it was at last— open tension and Weatherall's clear assertion of authority: this was easier (though less pleasant) to deal with than the executive's slippery amiability with its hidden pitfalls. "Then I guess I don't understand what you're asking," Kay said.

"You were very thirsty— perhaps more thirsty— when you were first brought here," Weatherall said. "And no doubt your urine was as dark then as later. But you conserved your water anyway."

"Yes, that's true. I suppose I was afraid that each bottle might be my last."

"Whereas now you are quite sure I'll bring you your usual ration."

"Not positive," Kay said. "But I have decided that since there's little I can do about it there's no point in my taking any responsibility in the matter myself."

Weatherall's smile was malicious. "And so now you're simply carefree about your survival."

"No," Kay said seriously. "I could never be carefree about my survival here. But one must find ways to live with the situation. If you intend me to run out of water, I will run out of water. If you intend me to have enough water to live, then I will. I have accepted this as a fact of life."

"Fascinating," Weatherall said. "With such a philosophical approach it must not matter much to you where you are or what your circumstances are."

"I don't make that claim," Kay said.

"Do you like this room?"

"It's all a matter of context, isn't it."

"Your shower has certainly perked you up. Admit you'd prefer this cell to the one you must go back to."

"Is it important for me to admit to?"

"No, not at all," Weatherall said. "But I thought you'd be interested to know that this cell like the one across the corridor has been prepared solely for you. It will be yours when I've decided you've made sufficient progress."

A shiver snaked up Kay's spine. "Then I suppose I must hope I am never kept here," she said— and instantly feared reprisal.

But Weatherall laughed. "Only you, Kay Zeldin, would make an improvement of circumstances a reason for lamentation. Very well. Then you won't in the least mind returning now to your current circumstances." Weatherall stood up, went to Kay, and took the banana from her. "You should have eaten it while you had the chance," she said, placing it with the remaining fruit in the basket.

Weatherall returned Kay to her cell. A bottle of water and three tubes of food and disposable bowl and cup had been placed on the table. The floor and tabletop were wet. The two blankets she had had were gone, and a single blanket lay folded on the platform. The room felt different for having been cleaned, perhaps because of the faint scent of chemical in the air, perhaps because the blanket was different, perhaps because of her exposure to the cell across the corridor. Feeling suddenly empty and depressed, Kay climbed onto the platform, sat against the blue concrete bricks, pulled the blanket over her, and clasped her arms around her legs. Resting her head on her knees, she wept.

[iii]

In order to expedite the transfer to the new proprietary of an employee they had interviewed and chosen to be the proprietary's senior comptroller, Allison found it necessary to go in person to the Office of Finance. The person they had chosen for this position, a professional named Milton Hewett, had a great deal of experience setting up the books and payroll systems for Company proprietaries; he also had a sufficient number of skeletons in his closet to guarantee his discretion. To sweeten the deal, Elizabeth had issued him shares in the proprietary. But there remained the problem of extricating him from his current position in the Office of Finance. Thus Allison herself had to run over to Finance to have a private chat with the PA of the Deputy Director in charge of the Office of Finance. The prospect did not thrill her, for she knew in advance the person she would be talking to was the boss that Anne, the girl she had used at the party, was in love with. Allison had met Alice Warner at the party. And she had talked to her on the phone earlier in the day. She disliked mixing up her association with Anne with business. Though Elizabeth did such things all the time, Allison did not. It struck her as messy.

As she entered the sector of the base allocated to Management and Services, Allison recalled the conversation that she had overheard in the Executive Dining Room between the Director of M & S and the head of ODS. Everything was so much trickier here than in stations located in embassies in Europe. It was like moving from a village of fifty people to a city of twelve million without transition.

Allison cleared the Office of Finance guardpost, pulled open the thick glass doors, and entered Finance's outer office. Anne looked up from her terminal and smiled. "Lise," she said softly.

Allison smiled back. "Alice is expecting me, I think."

Anne nodded. "You can go right in."

Alice Warner gave her a cup of coffee. "What's on your mind?" she said bluntly.

"Elizabeth Weatherall has a project she wants Milton Hewett for." Allison matched bluntness with bluntness.

"Yes, I recall we got some paperwork the other day from you on that," Alice said.

"Elizabeth wants him to start tomorrow."

Alice looked incredulous. "Impossible! You'll have to give us at least two weeks to arrange his departure, Allison. By the time the paperwork is processed we'll be able to handle his going."

"Sorry. Elizabeth is very clear on his starting tomorrow," Allison said apologetically.

"That's too bad." Alice's tone indicated that the subject was closed.

"Hewett isn't indispensable to anything you've got running now. We've checked that out already."

"Maybe not, but you can't just pull somebody like Hewett and not create havoc. And Elizabeth knows it, too."

Allison put her cup down on Alice's desk. "Am I supposed to go back to Elizabeth and tell her you think she has miscalculated and is going to create havoc in your department because of one single dislocation?" Allison shook her head. "I think she's going to wonder what's going on in the Office of Finance if I tell her that. But I don't think you want to start anything. Do you?"

Alice's eyes hardened. "You certainly are the perfect aide for her," she said in an unpleasantly grating voice. "Though you don't really look the part. But then Elizabeth has always known how to pick her own."

Allison's lips tightened. "Just have Hewett report to us on Monday morning," she said. "I was forgetting that tomorrow is Sunday." She stalked out into the reception area.

"Goodbye, Lise," Anne called after her.

Allison fumed all the way back to her office. She had better things to do than worry about Alice Warner's opinion of Elizabeth. It was probably just envy, anyway. No one in Security could touch Elizabeth on any ground, and that was a fact. It must make dried-up sour types like Alice Warner writhe with jealousy. What Allison could not figure was Anne's attachment to the woman.

One simply could not account for tastes.

[iv]

Absorbed in her work, Allison lost all track of time. She was sending out a memo when Elizabeth opened the door and came in. "So you *are* still here," Elizabeth said. "You needn't have stayed so late, Allison. You make me feel a regular Simon Legree."

A little dazed, Allison glanced at her watch. "It's eleven! I had no idea! Where did all the time go?"

"And have you even bothered eating?"

Allison realized she was ravenous. "No," she said. "I forgot."

"Well so did I. Let's go home, darling."

"I'm waiting to get my memo through," Allison said, eying the blue light. When the light blinked off, she said, "I'm all set." She locked the terminal. "I've finished arranging the most important meetings for early next week," she said proudly. She opened her attaché case and slipped a few files into it. If she rode in with Elizabeth in the morning— as she had been doing the last few days— she would want to have some work with her. Elizabeth always worked in the car in the mornings.

Because of Elizabeth's priority status, the two of them zipped by the security barriers and guardposts with a minimum of fuss and were soon comfortably ensconced in the back of Elizabeth's car. "Would you like some cognac?" Elizabeth asked. "It's the only alcohol I have in the car."

"I'd love some," Allison said, leaning back against the cushions, aware now of the stiffness in her neck, the ache in her shoulders.

Elizabeth handed her a small snifter and poured juice for herself. "Ah," Elizabeth sighed, sipping her juice. "So I am to take it that you may actually manage to keep to my schedule?"

Surprised, Allison peered through the dark at Elizabeth. "Of course I'll keep to your schedule."

Elizabeth chuckled. "I didn't think you had it in you. I was sure there would be delays of up to two weeks before you got things moving."

"But why? I'm not lazy," Allison said, trying not to sound indignant.

"No, you're not at all lazy, my sweet. But I sense a tendency in you to let people walk all over you. I knew you'd have to be pushy to meet my schedule. And so I doubted you could do it."

Allison sipped the cognac in silent consternation.

Elizabeth's hand touched her knee and slipped up her thigh. "It must mean you managed to wrest that comptroller away from Finance."

"Yes, I did," Allison said, trying to keep her voice steady as waves of sexual sensation washed over her.

"It couldn't have been easy," Elizabeth said. "Alice Warner can be nasty to tangle with."

"Yes," Allison said breathlessly. "She was horrible."

"But you dealt with her?"

"Yes. Why does she dislike you so?"

"She and I have had many run-ins." Elizabeth turned her head, and her mouth was only inches from Allison's ear. "And when Sedgewick first came out of the field and into the upper echelons of Central, she and I were competitors for the job of being his PA. I was chosen, she was not. And of course she disapproves of my current position. She buys the line that women can't handle that much responsibility and power." Elizabeth laughed softly. "I have yet to figure out a way to smooth over that little contradiction. I wish I could. A lot of people would feel much less anxious if I could let them keep their opinions about sexuality while still being so visibly in control. I used to try to foster the idea that Sedgewick was directing my every move, but of course that is becoming rather too obviously lame."

While Elizabeth talked, her fingers continued to move over Allison's silk-clad flesh, creeping under the tunic, brushing between Allison's slightly parted thighs. "Do you know," Elizabeth said after a while, "there's something you could do for me that would be very useful."

"What is it?" Allison whispered.

"I would like to keep a weather eye on Alice Warner. You could do that for me by occasionally taking her service-tech to the club. It wouldn't have to be an intense sort of thing, darling, just an occasional evening, to see what she has to say."

Allison battled the hot tears that sprang into her eyes.

"You did say you get along with her, darling. You don't find her repulsive, do you?"

"No," Allison said hoarsely. "I don't find her repulsive. But the whole thing, seeing her just to pump her, that repulses me."

"You mustn't be so squeamish, Allison. It's too important. We're talking about something much more important than individuals."

"I know," Allison said miserably. "But she's in love with Alice. I told you that?"

"Yes, you told me that. I don't think that need necessarily get in the way, unless Alice warns her off you, or unless Alice begins consciously to move against me. I don't think she'll do that, or that if she does she'll inform the girl of it."

Allison sighed. What was the point of cultivating Anne for so little?

"Will you do that for me, Allison?"

Allison swallowed the rest of her cognac to wash the bitter taste out of her mouth. "Yes, Elizabeth. I'll do that for you," she said. She wanted to tell Elizabeth that doing so might kill something in her, something important, that it was no trivial matter to her. But she did not. Elizabeth would probably misunderstand. And if there was one thing Allison dreaded, it was Elizabeth's misunderstanding.

The car pulled up before their apartment complex, and Elizabeth chuckled. "Just in time. I don't think I could have waited much longer. I am going crazy with wanting you."

Allison said nothing. Elizabeth knew exactly how she was feeling down to the most minute quiver and ripple. Of that Allison had not the slightest doubt.

Chapter Twenty

[i]

After leaving Whidbey Island, Martha traveled around western Washington State for nearly two weeks before returning to Seattle. She spent ten days of that on the Olympic Peninsula. Although most of the lumber companies had been taken over by their employees after the Withdrawal, some of the companies remained under the control of their executive owners (who were, Martha guessed, living mostly outside the Free Zone). And although the plastic money system was mostly useless in the Free Zone, some of the people Martha saw had contracted to supply wood and wood products (paper, especially) to executive companies outside the area. She suspected that the people making such arrangements were intending to use their credit to buy goods for importing into the Free Zone to barter or even sell at exorbitant prices. This was nothing new, of course. The previous winter profiteers had imported some of the first available batteries and battery-chargers, for which people all over the Free Zone had been willing to barter almost anything in exchange. The only way of eliminating such profiteering was by flooding the market, and that always took time to accomplish. The Co-op, however, had eventually arranged for a wider availability of batteries and battery chargers, and prices had fallen sharply. Eliminating plastic did not necessarily eliminate market unfairness. But it did give one a fighting chance.

In the case of the lumber companies, the Co-op's leverage was significant. The Blanket had wiped out all but the most antiquated of the companies' equipment. If there was one thing people everywhere were anxious for, it was electronic hardware, which was why the largest and most ambitious of Martha's current projects were directed toward making such hardware available. In addition, not much of the heavily forested area was crop-cultivated. That meant that people in the lumber industry had to import most of their food.

But these business matters receded from her mind as she rode the express bus from Aberdeen to Seattle. The need to talk to Louise about the bug she and Beatrice had found in her tunic collar pressed on her. She hated to suspect anyone she knew. But it seemed indisputable that someone had gone into her room to plant the bug in her collar. She had never kept her room locked. Nor was the house kept locked. People— mainly Co-op people— flowed in and out of the house all the time. And because she was so busy she used her room only to sleep. It had never occurred to her to keep her room locked.

When the bus stopped in Tacoma for its fifteen-minute layover, Martha used a data kiosk in the station to call the Women's Patrol office in Seattle. A part of her was relieved to be told that Louise wasn't in the office. She left a message saying that she would be in Seattle by two and would Louise please call her at either Laura's or her committee's office.

Martha tried not to think about how difficult it would be talking to Louise. She couldn't let the bug pass and pretend she hadn't found it. And brooding about her personal problems with Louise was pointless. She just wished Kay Zeldin were still alive to help her.

[ii]

As time passed, Kay grew more restless and depressed. She stuck by her "rules" but often found it difficult to articulate to herself precisely why it mattered that she follow them. Sometimes, especially at certain moments during her encounters with Weatherall, she would experience a diamond-hard sense of the point to her resistance. But at other times the logic of her resistance grew fuzzy, bringing her to question why anything mattered when clearly nothing mattered but finding a way to keep her sanity. Sometimes she would search for the elusive something that would bring the reason for her sense of purpose into her mind. The word "brainwash" most often reminded her, for drifting vaguely through her thoughts, the word evoked the vivid memory of Weatherall's cuffing her to the platform and recalled to

her consciousness the reasons for her rules, flooding her mind with the fears and ideas that lay behind the making of them.

But depression increased her vulnerability. Hours spent in brooding, aching misery— dozing off, never stirring from the platform— fed her depression, making her sluggish and dull. At such times she did not use her mind much, for shutting out thoughts of the outside world— in obedience to her own rules— and refusing memories left her empty.

Weatherall's visits, however, jostled her out of this vegetable state. At times the visits would have an abrasive effect, stimulating her mind, provoking resistance. But at other times— when Weatherall held out the lure of sympathy and she was tired, discouraged, dull— Kay, though clinging to her rules, would wonder why she should not simply sink into Weatherall's soft, soothing embrace. In her sharpest moments Kay knew the hours alone were taking their toll on her. But she did not know how to rouse herself and wasn't even sure she wanted to. It was less painful to be a vegetable than a constantly thinking, feeling, frustrated creature. If she had control of the light in her cell she would probably choose to do nothing but sleep in a long eternity of hibernation. She wondered if she were more dead than alive. Certainly she was dead as far as the world was concerned: perhaps she was dead in all but fact? What, she queried in one of her lucid spells, was the definition of "alive"? Was there not a social definition of life that must be superimposed over the biological?

She was lying down with her eyes closed when Weatherall made a visit that jarred her out of one such phase of semi-hibernation. She heard the door slide open and Weatherall say "Good morning, Kay," but did not move or even open her eyes.

"Good morning Elizabeth," Kay said, hoping Weatherall would simply leave the food and water and go (though she almost never did).

"Get up."

Kay opened her eyes and effortfully sat up and propped her body against the concrete-block wall.

"Did you hear me, Kay? If you're not off that platform in five seconds I'll chain you to it."

Kay slid off the platform and leaned against it, waiting.

"Your apathy isn't at all amusing. In fact, it's downright boring." Weatherall tilted her head to one side and watched Kay through narrowed eyes. "We'll have to do something about it. You look so sleepy we'll first have to wake you up. About fifty jumping-jacks should accomplish that. Count loud enough while you're doing them so that I can hear." When Kay merely stared at her, she commanded: "Get moving, woman. NOW!"

By the time Kay had done the calisthenics she was sweating and angry.

"Very good," Weatherall said, pouring water from the fresh bottle into Kay's cup. Kay accepted the water without speaking, drained the cup, and slammed it down on the table. "At least you're awake now," Weatherall said. "You were beginning to let yourself go, Kay. You're not here for vegetation, you know."

"No," Kay said. "Obviously I'm here to amuse you."

Weatherall smiled. "That's partially true. And you haven't been at all amusing lately."

"I'm so very sorry."

"Oh, you needn't be. I don't require you to be sorry for that." Kay walked to the wall dotted with thumb-locks and leaning against it watched Weatherall dig into her bag and pull out a leather-bound book. "We're going to start something new," Weatherall said. "I want you to do some writing for me."

Kay choked out a short, sharp bark of a laugh. "Writing? I don't think I remember how."

"Oh, it will come back to you. I have complete confidence in your capability. Now come over here and pay attention. I'm only going to explain the rules once."

Reluctant but curious, Kay went to the table. Whatever Weatherall had up her sleeve, it was undoubtedly some new phase of her brainwashing strategy.

Weatherall opened the book, revealing ruled pages entirely blank except for numerals heavily inked at the top of each page. "Note, Kay, that all the pages are numbered. If you tear one out I will know.

Which means that if you use the paper in this book for any purpose other than the ones I designate to you, I will know it and punish you for it. Clear?"

"Understood," Kay said, afraid she did understand.

"Excellent. Now the way we will work it is that I will assign a topic to you, and you will write on that topic. And then I will read what you have written and probably require further elaborations on it." She lifted her gaze from the book to look at Kay. "I'm not giving you any choice in this matter. I probably will not be very tolerant with any evasiveness you might try to get by with. Clear?"

"Understood."

It was starting. This was the interrogation she had feared on her arrival here. They must have decided she'd been sufficiently softened up.

"You can sit down now, Kay."

Kay went to the platform and sat cross-legged with her back against the concrete blocks.

"It's time for us to go back a year and a half," Weatherall said. "To your time working for— and against— the Company." Kay waited apprehensively through a long pause. "Do you remember cuffing and gagging me?"

Suddenly cold, Kay wrapped the blanket around herself. "Yes, I remember," she said. She had actually forgotten about cuffing and gagging Weatherall— and holding a gun on her.

"I feel it is necessary to ask because your memory is known to be highly selective," Weatherall said.

Kay's mouth went dry.

"The interesting thing, Kay, is that I don't hold any of that against you. You look skeptical."

"It's a little hard to believe."

Weatherall smiled. "But you could have made life very difficult for me. In fact I was sure you would do so. Because of your influence over Sedgewick. It seemed incredible to me, that day when I realized you were actually going to throw all that power away. I still don't understand it, you know. Except that it wasn't a simple thing. And I

suspect you yourself have little idea about it. But don't worry, we'll get to the bottom of it."

Kay's teeth clenched. It was none of Weatherall's business.

"So I want you to start thinking about Sedgewick."

Kay said nothing.

"Your first assignment won't be terribly introspective— we'll ease into it, I think. You will explain at what point you decided to go renegade, and at what point you made arrangements with the enemy. I'd also like you to write a bit about your conscious motives in coming to such a decision. You needn't delve deep; simply give me the factors and context surrounding your decision." Weatherall set the book and pen down on the table beside the water and food. "Have it ready for me by my next visit." She slid the thick leather strap of the bag over her shoulder. "If you omit any of what I've specified I will surely punish you," she said. "Do you have any questions?"

Kay shook her head.

"Good." Weatherall strode to the door and pressed her thumb against the access plate. "I'm sure you'll do your best to amuse me."

The door slid shut, and Kay was alone again— with her chagrin, her anger, and her fear.

[iii]

On Thursday afternoon, Allison took Anne to Denver. Anne got off work at three on Tuesdays and Thursdays (because she worked all day on Saturdays). Allison could do this only because Elizabeth had ordered a helicopter placed at her disposal. Anne was astonished. "I didn't realize," she said to Allison. "Not even Alice has the use of helicopters for trips to Denver!" Allison tried to explain that Elizabeth was simply doing her a favor, but Anne shook her head as though dismissing undue modesty in Allison and said, "You know, Lise, if you still want Genelle—"

"Let's forget Genelle," Allison said a little sharply.

They arrived at the club before four. Allison signed in and took Anne along to the salon where the hairdresser Jacquelyn had recommended was to meet Allison. Allison had at last gotten it together to do something about the curly-perm, to eradicate the final traces of

her few weeks as a service-tech. Anne chatted with her and watched as the hairdresser razored away most of the perm, creating a cap of short dark brown meringue-like waves. Allison grimaced at the mirror. "This hairstyle would be wonderful on someone with a decently proportioned face," she said. "It's at times like these that I wish I'd ignored all the advice I got as an adolescent against having my nose fixed."

"Oh no, Madame," the hairdresser said. "Your nose is *très très distingué.* So truly aristocratic!"

"Yes, that's what they said to me then," Allison said. "I think I'd rather have an ordinary nose. It would make it easier to carry off this sort of affair." She waved at the mirror.

Both Anne and the hairdresser assured her— at length— that she looked "ravishing" in the new hairstyle. But Allison knew very well that Anne would probably say that no matter what and that the hairdresser, apart from his interest in her tip, wanted her future custom and recommendation.

It was Elizabeth's reaction that would signify.

Next, under the pretext that they needed it to work the day's stiffness out of their backs and shoulders, Allison took Anne into the Jacuzzi she had reserved. The truth was, however, that Allison could not relax with Anne until the chemical smell had been washed off Anne's skin. Her aversion to the odor had lately grown to almost unmanageable proportions. Both she and Anne donned caps to protect their hair. Flirtatiously Allison soaped Anne's body and let Anne soap hers— and discovered a giggly, infectious side of Anne she could not help responding to. Anne like this was very different from the quiet, melancholy, and occasionally cynical girl of the party. Allison stopped worrying about the outfit she had chosen as a present for Anne. She had wondered if it might be completely out of character for someone so quiet and subdued.

After they had gotten out of the tub and dried themselves, Allison gave her the present and asked her to put it on. Anne shyly thanked her, then dressed in the leather-trimmed, close-fitting bodice and pants of the sort service-techs wore dancing. "Oh!" she said when she stroked the leather. "This is real leather, isn't it!"

Allison gave a final twitch to the linen bodice. "Of course it's real leather! It looks wonderful on you, Anne." Allison adjusted the lay of Anne's bodice at the neck and shoulders. "The contrast with your skin— I guess I lucked out on the tones, didn't I. And your boots are just right with it, too. But you need some kind of splashy scarf or something else to brighten it up, don't you…" These dancing outfits were supposed to be flashy. Most of them were shiny sequin-covered productions (which Allison just could not see buying).

Anne, looking critically into the mirror, said, "A hat. That's what it needs. Maybe broad-brimmed leather, with a scarf wrapped around the crown?" She smiled at Allison. "I don't go in for gaudy stuff, Lise. It's just not my style. This I like very much."

Allison stood behind Anne and slid her arms around her. "So do I. It's *most* attractive on you."

Anne's gaze met Allison's in the mirror. "You really shouldn't think badly of your nose, Lise," she said. "I like your face just the way it is."

Allison ducked a kiss on the now sweet-smelling neck. "I made an early reservation for dinner. Are you hungry?"

"Sure."

"We can have something to drink first. And then have our dinner. Do you like wine?"

Anne nodded.

"Well so do I." Anne's eyes widened. "Some of us do drink, you know," Allison said drily. "Though so few do that mostly I drink alone. Which is very lonely. It'll be fun drinking wine with you." And Allison realized it was true: she was looking forward to her evening with Anne, in spite of everything. Anne was easy to be with.

Though she wasn't Elizabeth.

[iv]

Martha had agreed to meet Louise at her apartment at around four. The alternatives were Laura's house and the office. Since Martha had not yet decided whom she would tell about the bug, the privacy of Louise's apartment seemed preferable. Yet as she knocked on Louise's door it occurred to her that Louise was probably assuming that she

wanted to talk either about personal matters or about the issue of an armed Women's Patrol. Martha hoped neither of these things would come into their conversation. She was determined to be as terse and businesslike as possible.

When Louise opened the door and invited Martha in, Martha stepped in and said before Louise had even gotten the door closed, "I'm hoping you can refer me to someone who can give me some advice about this." She held out the small box containing the bug.

"Sit down, Martha," Louise said. She took the box. "Would you like water or anything else to drink?"

The way Louise was watching her made Martha's face and neck tense. "It was sewn into my denim tunic collar," Martha said. She sat down in the only chair and concentrated on the box, brushing away the memories the room evoked.

Louise sat on the couch. "What was sewn into your collar?"

"The thing in that box," Martha said, wishing that humans had different languages to speak in for different modes of relation the way the Marq'ssan did.

Louise's gaze dropped to the box. Her fingers removed the rubber band and lifted the lid. Slowly she peeled away the layers of cotton fluff that Beatrice had packed around it. "Well," Louise said, taking the plastic disk in her fingers. She looked at Martha. "You found this sewn into your collar?"

Martha nodded.

"When?"

"I was washing the tunic at Sweetwater the Saturday before last and felt a lump. I opened the seam, and there it was."

"Do you have any idea how long it could have been there?"

"The last time I washed it was in Colville. About two months ago. I have no idea when it could have been inserted, or where. I didn't wear that tunic much in August, it was too hot. But I can't remember specifically handling the collar, so I suppose that doesn't say much."

"The important questions are who and why you," Louise said. "And what about opportunity?"

"Easy opportunity— I never lock my room in Laura's house. Anyone could have gone into that house and gotten into my room."

"Not just anyone," Louise said. "Someone who looked out of place at Laura's probably wouldn't have felt like waltzing in there. And how would such a person know the room was left unlocked?"

"Then you think it's someone I know. One of us."

A faint smile curved Louise's lips. "So you're still saying 'us,' Martha? After all that hullabaloo at the Steering Committee meeting?"

Martha flushed. "You know what I mean, Louise."

"Sure. I know what you mean. I just wanted to point out the obvious. But as for whether I think it's one of us… I don't know. It would have to be someone who would know you would be wearing that tunic at some appropriate time. Presumably you don't have bugs in all your clothes. You did check, didn't you?"

Martha's mouth dropped open. "Why, no. I didn't think of that!"

"Well you'd better check. But to get back to my point. This thing has to be used with a receiver— possibly with a data-recorder, maybe with just a set of earphones, and at reasonably close range. So if you don't have bugs in all your clothes, there'd have to be the idea you would be wearing this tunic at the time that person expected to be able to bug you— being nearby and ready to pick up from the bug— and at a time they knew they wanted to be able to bug you."

Martha frowned. "You mean you don't think this was for a sort of general eavesdropping, but that it was intended to eavesdrop on a particular occasion?"

"That's my guess."

"But that's crazy! How would anyone know when I'd be wearing this tunic?"

"It's just a theory. It doesn't seem to make sense, I agree. Any ideas why someone would want to eavesdrop on you? Could it have to do with your arrangements for a particular project, do you think?"

"Oh!" Martha said. "I hadn't thought of that."

"What was it you were thinking of?"

"I don't know… Maybe the ODS types that got Kay Zeldin."

"Well that's possible. But in that case they'd have to be one of us. Unless... you didn't leave your tunic somewhere for any reason, did you?"

Martha shook her head. "No. I thought about that. But Louise, if someone I do business with wanted to bug me, how would they get hold of the technology? This isn't the kind of stuff that's lying around easily available."

"I know. That's a problem."

Martha bit her lip. "If Kay Zeldin were alive, I'd ask her what to do about it. But she's not. Can you think of anyone else who might be able to advise me?"

Louise shook her head. "Sorry. You'll have to do some detective work, as well as take preventive measures. Go through all your clothes and check for bugs. Start locking your door. And try to keep your ears open to see if anyone says something you know they should know nothing about. I don't know what else you can do, Martha. Except be careful. Some of those Birth Limitation people are real nuts."

Martha said, "Yeah. I thought of them too. But somehow, Louise, I think it must be ODS agents."

"Or the agents of other governments," Louise said. "There are all sorts of things going on in the Zone that you seem to be barely aware of. I don't think you realize—"

"Oh please, Louise, don't get into that now. I'm too tired tonight to argue with you."

"Do you want me to do anything? Would you like the Women's Patrol to keep an eye on you? Do you think you could be in danger?"

Martha said, "No. All my instincts tell me there's no threat to me personally."

Louise gave her a look. "Your *instincts*. What the fuck does that mean?" Louise dug her fingers into her head and closed her eyes— a mannerism Martha knew meant she was having a hard time keeping her temper. When Martha got to her feet to go, Louise opened her eyes. "I'm not about to force help on you," she said in a carefully level voice. "But if anything new develops, keep me posted. We need to be open about these things. Kay Zeldin wasn't. Which is why they managed to snatch her from the University campus in August and then recapture and kill her in September." Louise's eyes were grim.

"I know," Martha said. "I know. Really. But I haven't gotten any threats."

Louise held up the bug. "And this, Martha? What do you call this?"

Martha's throat got tight; the intensity of Louise's concern made her want to cry. "I'd better go now. Thanks. And of course I'll let you know if I find any more of the things." She went to the door.

Louise sprang up from the couch. "Be careful," she said.

"I will." Martha went out into the hall and closed the door after her. As she walked away from what had once been her home, her eyes filled with tears. Her life, she thought, had gone totally out of her control.

[v]

Allison and Anne dined at the club. The walls of their circular banquette gave them almost total privacy from the rest of the dining room, a privacy the girl serving them hardly seemed to intrude upon as she came and went. They ordered two of the day's three choices in dinners and— seated side by side— fed each other from their very different plates, and Anne's pleasure in the meal delighted Allison. It surprised her, though, when Anne said that since the Blanket she seldom ate anything other than tubefood. Curious, Allison began asking personal questions and discovered that Anne was not a Colorado native as she had thought. Alice Warner, she learned, had brought Anne out of DC at the time of the Executive's collapse. Anne described the final days in DC with great emotion. "Hardly any service-techs were brought here," she said, "but Alice helped me, Alice insisted that I come. I felt terrible leaving my family and friends behind, but…I couldn't stay, I had to go with Alice! I sometimes lie awake at nights unable to stop thinking about DC, going crazy wondering what has happened to all my people… But Alice. Alice cared enough to bring me here." Reaching for her wine glass, Anne almost knocked over Allison's water goblet. "We are so lucky here. Look at Denver— Denver is almost a real live city like there used to be everywhere! They have some public transportation, you see the mass auto-system working, there's no

one going around setting bombs or shooting out of windows at people walking in the streets..." Her wavering voice halted.

"It will change in the other places too," Allison said, trying to put hope into her voice, trying to believe that what Elizabeth had been telling her would happen would happen. "And then you'll be able to return to DC."

Allison's heart wrenched at the pain she saw in Anne's eyes. "How can you even think that, Lise? It's better not to hope for so much. It's better just to keep going and not think about what might or might not be."

It was perfectly clear now how Anne could be in love with Alice. And it *was* remarkable that Alice had brought Anne out of DC: especially if there was nothing now nor ever had been anything sexual between them, as Anne insisted.

They were subdued for the remainder of the meal. When they had finished, Allison said, "What shall we do now? We've several options. We can have coffee and cognac or more wine in the lounge— there's some kind of band in there, I think, for dancing and listening to, or we can go for a walk, or we can go upstairs to the room I've reserved and possibly drink another bottle of wine there..." She smiled at Anne. "You decide. I'd be happy doing any of them."

Anne's eyes widened, and Allison wondered what sorts of dates Anne was used to. "*I* must decide?"

Allison laughed. "You don't have to if you don't want to. But I thought you might like to choose."

Anne's smile was simultaneously shy and sly. "Then I'd like to go upstairs. And drink more wine with you." She slipped her hand into Allison's, and Allison lifted and kissed it. Anne was so easy to be with, so easily pleased, so eager to please, that Allison had to struggle against fleeting twinges of guilt at her deliberate management of the girl. Did Elizabeth understand what she was asking of her?

They went to the room; while they were waiting for the wine, Allison went into the bathroom and changed into the lounging gown she had brought. When she came out of the bathroom, she found Anne lying naked under the sheet. "This is what I choose," she said to

Allison, patting the bed beside her. Smiling, Allison went to the bed, pulled back the sheet, and sat on the edge, one foot braced on the floor, facing Anne. Anne lifted her arms, encircled Allison's neck, and drew Allison's head down to kiss her.

The arrival of the wine interrupted them. Allison took the tray and set it on the dresser, then dimmed the lights and returned to bed. She devoted herself to rousing and teasing Anne, stroking, kissing, licking, nibbling, and as Elizabeth sometimes did with her, several times bringing Anne to the verge of orgasm and then withdrawing just enough for Anne to miss climax yet hover near the edge until Anne was begging her to make her come. After Anne's long, long series of orgasms, Allison lay down beside her and held her to her breast. Though her body was fuller than Elizabeth's, Anne seemed terribly fragile, perhaps by contrast to Elizabeth's hard muscular body. "That was so good, Lise," Anne whispered. "It was so much I didn't think I could stand it."

"And now you'll probably go to sleep on me," Allison said softly. She knew what it was like. Though she seemed not to be able to do it for Elizabeth, she had done it for Anne.

"No, no, not at all," Anne said. "Though I'm so very relaxed. It was better than the Jacuzzi."

Allison laughed. "Thanks," she retorted, and Anne laughed, and then they were quiet for a little while. Allison wished she had put the wine on the bedside table instead of on the dresser across the room. She could not get to it without disturbing Anne. She decided to wait. "Why, sweetheart," she asked curiously after a long silence— not sure whether Anne had indeed fallen asleep on her— "do you always straighten your hair?"

Anne shifted slightly. "Alice asked me to," she said. "She prefers it that way."

Allison snorted. But of course, if Alice requested something personal of Anne, Anne would never hesitate. It would be like her, Allison, hesitating to do something Elizabeth— but Allison stopped the thought before she had finished it. There were no comparisons to be made. Alice and Anne were different in every way from herself and Elizabeth.

Anne lifted her head and slid her fingers under the neck of Allison's lounging gown. "Let me make love to you now," she said. Her eyes were shining. She didn't look at all sleepy.

Allison extricated herself from Anne and got up to fetch the wine. "Let's have some wine," she said, pouring them each a glass. She had not removed her clothes when she had gone with Anne at the party, nor had she let Anne make love to her. As for tonight, she had decided in advance that she would not let Anne pleasure her. She knew she would only fantasize Elizabeth, and Anne would not be at all like Elizabeth. Allison handed Anne one of the glasses, then sat down cross-legged beside her on the bed. "You must tell me," Allison said, "if you want to go home early or not. We can sleep here if we like, or we can leave at any time. All I need to do is call Buckley and let them know and they'll have the chopper ready to go by the time we get there."

Anne's eyes were grave now. "You can decide," she said. "I don't need to be home at any special time. And if you want to sleep here that's all right, too, as long as I get home early enough to get to work on time."

"Do you like sleeping with another person in the same bed?" Allison asked curiously. "Or do you prefer sleeping alone?"

"What do you like?"

Allison sighed. Obviously Anne wanted to defer to her wishes. Or was it that she wanted to hear what Allison wanted before admitting to what she herself wanted? Allison shrugged. "Let's see how we feel. We don't have to decide at all, you know. In which case we'll end up staying all night." She took a large swallow of wine. Didn't Elizabeth understand that with someone like Anne things soon stopped being casual? As though goaded by remembering the reason Elizabeth had given her for going out with Anne, Allison said, "Does Alice Warner know you're out with me?"

Anne's face became very still. "Why should I tell her that?" she asked.

Allison smiled cynically. "She wouldn't like it."

Anne frowned. "Why not?"

"Because she disapproves of me."

"Because of the fuss over the transfer?" Anne looked troubled.

"Yes. She was very angry about that."

"I know nothing about it," Anne said quickly. "I'm not in Alice's confidence that way... And anyway, I don't believe Alice would care who I went out with. Probably the only reason she knows I go out with women and not men is because we're sometimes at the same parties."

That, Allison thought, sounded bitter. But the truth was that Alice *would* know; Alice would know more about Anne than Anne knew there was to know. How little the service-techs ever suspected... For a moment Allison hated herself, but then she thought: no, there *is* a difference between how Alice and I use you. For because of me, you laugh, while because of her, you cry. Allison put her arm around Anne's shoulder. "It must hurt you, working for her," she said gently.

"No! I *love* working for her!"

"Yes, I suppose you do," Allison said, knowing that the hurt would seem preferable to no contact whatsoever. "Never mind. I was just wondering. I don't want you to have trouble with Alice on my account."

"She's not like some bosses," Anne said. "She's really fair."

"I'm glad of that." Allison leaned forward and kissed Anne's cheek.

Sipping at her wine, Allison watched Anne stare down into her glass for a long time. She could feel tension in Anne and waited, wondering if she was going to talk more about Alice. But when she finally looked up and met Allison's eyes, it was to ask in a carefully level voice, "Why don't you want me to make love to you? Is there something wrong?"

The question Anne was really asking, Allison thought, was *is there something wrong with* me? "There's nothing at all wrong," Allison said. "I'm enjoying being with you very much. Can't you tell?"

"Usually it's the other way around," Anne said with constraint. "Usually they... usually they want to be made love to and aren't much interested in *me*. It seems strange, Lise..." She broke off and stared down again into her glass.

They, Allison thought, referred to executives. There was something horrible about this. And Anne looked not only confused, but as

though she felt rejected at Allison's not letting her caress her or see her naked. "You aren't too sleepy?" Allison asked weakly.

"Sleepy!"

It was a ridiculous question, Allison had to agree, since they had been sitting up and chatting about Alice. "Your pleasure gives me pleasure," Allison said.

"And you don't think that the reverse can be true, too?" Anne took Allison's glass and set it beside her own on the bedside table. Allison let Anne unfasten her gown and helped slip it over her head and allowed Anne to arrange her body with a pillow slid under her hips. She closed her eyes and surrendered herself to Anne's caresses. But instead of imagining it was Elizabeth making love to her, she imagined herself making love to Elizabeth. When Anne knelt over her to put her mouth to her vulva and slid her tongue between her labia, it was as though she herself were doing the things Anne was doing, and she imagined the smell of Elizabeth's cunt filling her, she imagined the taste of Elizabeth's smegma in her mouth— and the feeling in her chest of adoration for Elizabeth, choking and elating her... Allison finished coming and opened her eyes. Anne lifted her head, and their gaze met in one shocking naked moment that made Allison, recoiling, squeeze shut her eyes. Anne lay down beside her. "Should I turn off the light?" she asked. "Do you want to sleep?"

"Yes," Allison said. "Turn off the light." They needed the dark now. And if Anne could sleep, so much the better. For Allison there would be no sleep. It would be best if they were to go back now and she were to return to the office and work. But she couldn't yet face the thought of the trip back— involving the necessity of talking to and looking at Anne and the others. She needed to be invisible for a while.

And then it would be all right, later.

Chapter Twenty-one

[i]

So many reasons presented themselves to Kay for why she must disobey Weatherall's orders for writing in the leather book that she knew she had reached her point of resistance. Weatherall's questions threatened her small interior realm of privacy and intruded into a likely painful area of her memory. She did not want to think about those days; she did not want to think about Sedgewick at all. Also, she suspected that these orders marked a new phase in the brainwashing project. Certainly they were a form of interrogation.

Perhaps most crucially, however, what Weatherall demanded of her would require her writing in some way *for* Weatherall—which was only a more emphatic, more visible version of talking to Weatherall in her head. By writing to Weatherall's specifications in that book she would be opening herself to what would probably become a series of attempts to explain herself to Weatherall. This, she suspected, would imbue Weatherall with a certain moral authority she must not under any circumstances admit to in her own mind. It was one thing to pay lip-service to Weatherall's authority, but quite another to begin to feel that authority within her own self. Kay suspected she understood only a small part of the dangers involved in talking to an absent or imagined Weatherall; but what she did understand offered warning enough for her to prevent herself from slipping into such ghostly communication.

Deciding, finally, to write something in the book so as to put off the day of reckoning, Kay quoted as closely to verbatim as she could remember a passage from her most recently published book, describing how her alliance with the Marq'ssan had come about. She had said little about the explosion (beyond mentioning it to account for her concussion when discussing how Leleynl had healed her head injury) and nothing about regaining memory of past events involving Sedgewick, for she had considered such details irrelevant to the book's subject.

Kay next contemplated what her attitude and manner should be when "punishment" inevitably ensued. She could not stand to think much about it but nevertheless felt she must formulate more "rules" for herself, rules that would be her chief authority in determining how she should behave and react, supplying her with an internally constructed authority to counter Weatherall's assumed, arbitrarily imposed authority.

After lengthy consideration, Kay decided she must react as calmly and unemotionally as possible— keeping her anger under control, for instance, as she had not done the first time she was "punished." She would give Weatherall no reason— apart from her refusal to write to her specifications— for further abuse. Calmness and firmness must be her weapons in such a situation. She must at least feign calmness even if she were angry and afraid.

Excited, fearful, and ready for confrontation, Kay did nothing but wait for Weatherall's arrival. Too hyper to sleep, she paced the cell, back and forth, back and forth, reviewing her rules of engagement as though donning a full suit of body armor.

Finally, Weatherall arrived. Even before removing water and food from her bag, she seized the leather book and opened it. Weatherall's eagerness made Kay realize that they had embarked on a new phase of their relationship. And the realization did not sit well with her stomach.

It did not take Weatherall long to read the entry. When she finished, she slammed the book shut and set it down on the table. Then she dug into her leather bag. Kay expected her to pull out a fresh bottle of water; instead, Weatherall pulled out a pair of cuffs connected by a long chain. Kay had assumed she would be given another chance before punishment. Still, she had thought she was prepared for the moment. But dismay and fear streaked through her. "Please, Elizabeth," she cried, "please don't!"

Weatherall moved to the platform. "Your left hand, Kay." Kay saw from her eyes that there was no chance she would relent. She reminded herself that she must at least *seem* calm. Mutely she held out her hand. Weatherall snapped one of the cuffs around her wrist, then leaned forward and attached the other cuff to a ring midway along the length of the platform on the side abutting the concrete block wall. Kay was stunned. Cuffed this way, she would not be able to stretch out full length on the platform. Having recovered enough to hold herself to her rules, however, she said nothing.

"This was intentional disobedience," Weatherall said. "You knew when you wrote this that it wasn't what I wanted." Kay did not deny it. "You will have to do better than that." Weatherall laid the book and pen on the platform. "First, you will not refer to yourself in the third person. Second, you will not quote from your book. Third, you will answer all the questions I posed in the first place. If you don't abide by these conditions, you will forfeit your freedom to move about this room as you wish."

Weatherall removed from her bag a bottle of water and three tubes of food and put them on the platform beside the book. She smiled. "It may be better this way, Kay. It will show you with marvelous clarity that you have a choice in the matter. So that when you do choose to cooperate with me you will not be able to say to yourself that you did not."

Kay said nothing. Still smiling, Weatherall slung the leather bag over her shoulder and left.

Kay stared at the objects on the platform for a long time. Then, using her foot, she deliberately and bleakly pushed them off the edge of the platform: first the water, then the food and disposable cup and bowl; and last— and most importantly— the book and pen. Even if her will to resist weakened, she would be unable to capitulate.

She wrapped herself in the blanket and lay down as best she could. She would be uncomfortable, far more uncomfortable than she had been the first time she had been cuffed, even though there was a chain between the cuffs. But she could live with the discomfort.

She had to, now.

[ii]

At around three-thirty Elizabeth came into Allison's office and said she was going home for a few hours before coming back to work late. When she asked Allison whether she would like to do the same, Allison naturally said she would. Elizabeth suggested that they work out together, then bathe and eat and nap "or something," and commented that doing so would make them fresh and ready for several more hours of work. Allison hoped she was right, for she had felt dragged out all day, probably because of her night with Anne.

In the car traveling from base to village Elizabeth asked Allison how things had "worked out with your little service-tech." Allison delivered an abbreviated report and added, "I don't think there's any point in my seeing Anne again. There's nothing for me to learn from her. Alice Warner tells her nothing. And she's rather naive about Security politics."

"Don't be so hasty, darling," Elizabeth said. "I think you should maintain contact with her. You can never tell when it might be useful. She does like you, doesn't she?"

Allison laughed shortly. "Oh, she likes me all right. The whole thing is disgusting."

Elizabeth's brows knit. "Disgusting? What are you talking about?"

"This management of her emotions. I hate it! She may be wild about Alice Warner, but that doesn't mean she's not susceptible to me. If it were for something specific and obviously important, I might be able to see it. But as it is it's ugly and unnecessary!"

Elizabeth shook her head. "I don't like to hear you talking this way, Allison. Just how is this different from any other relationships you've had with service-techs— sexual and nonsexual? It's only a matter of degree. You talk about management? Well it's all management, from start to finish. One can't get around that fact. And for good reason! They can't manage themselves! Do you think she minds? Did she seem at all uncomfortable with your managing her, Allison?"

Allison swallowed. "I don't think that's the point, Elizabeth. If they knew, they would feel betrayed. That girl trusts me!"

"Yes, and with good reason. You haven't betrayed her, and you aren't going to. Last night you gave her a delicious meal, a lovely bath, good sex— that much I can be sure of— and a gift of clothing. What exactly is it you feel badly about? The fact that you deliberately took her to bed because I asked you to? Is that it?"

"I don't know. I'm a little confused," Allison said. The coldness in Elizabeth's eyes upset and flustered her.

The car pulled up before the apartment complex. "Yes," Elizabeth said, "you *are* confused. You'd better get yourself straightened out, Allison. This kind of ambivalence is dangerous mush. We can't afford to indulge in mush. If you can't articulate what you object to, I think you must seriously question the nature of your objection."

Elizabeth's escort opened her door, and Elizabeth got out. Blindly Allison followed. She should not have said anything. Obviously Elizabeth did not understand. But then, Allison thought, why should she, when she clearly did not understand herself?

[iii]

Weatherall came into the cell. "Good morning, Kay."

"Good morning, Elizabeth."

She dumped her bag on the table and took a step toward the platform. Frowning, she looked down at the floor, then knelt to retrieve the items Kay had knocked off the platform. "You're not being very bright, Kay," she said, setting the water and food on the table. She opened the book and thumbed over the first few pages. "At least we're clear about this. This is defiance, not misunderstanding." She moved close to the platform. "Sit up, and hold out your left wrist as far as you can." Kay obeyed both orders, and Weatherall leaned forward and unlocked it, and then unlocked the other cuff from the ring. "Now hold out your right hand." Kay obeyed, and Weatherall snapped one cuff around Kay's right hand and the other to a ring on the right side of Kay's body. Then she turned to the table and dug into her bag and pulled out a set of cuffs with no chain between them. "These are for your left hand," she said. And she cuffed Kay's left hand to the platform.

"You said you wouldn't torture me," Kay said. "Prolonged forced immobility is a well-known method of torture."

Weatherall transferred the items she had taken from the floor from the table to the platform. "You knew the possibilities for punishment when you chose to defy me," Weatherall said. "Don't whine about it now. You would be better employed reconsidering your position."

In line with her rules of engagement, Kay censored her retort.

Weatherall leaned against the platform and rested her arm along the edge. "Do you remember what I said during my first visit about intaking food and water, Kay?"

Kay nodded.

"I meant it. If you don't drink your water and eat your food, I'll have you force-fed the next time I come. I'm not putting up with hunger strikes or any other nonsense." Her icy blue gaze bored into Kay's. "As far as I'm concerned, you're behaving like a child who holds its breath trying to blackmail its adult caretaker. The only conclusion to such tantrums is a headache on your part. It's nothing to me. Clear?"

Kay did not answer.

"That, too?"

"I apparently have nothing to lose now," Kay said.

The blue eyes flashed. "Don't be too sure of that, Kay." She picked up the bag and stalked to the door. "I've left you just enough slack to use your right hand for writing. I advise you to take advantage of it. Otherwise it will be your last chance for some time."

Kay stared at the door sliding shut. She could of course find a way to spill the water onto the floor if she were able to maneuver sufficiently. And presumably it would go down the drain and all traces evaporate before the next visit. But what to do with the food? Anyway, did she really want to precipitate filter-failure? Wouldn't it be better to endure force-feeding? Must she decide afresh whether she wanted to live now that she was caught in this bind? But she realized she was certain she wanted to live. She didn't know why. For though in certain respects it was as though she weren't living, she somehow felt alive in making this resistance, horrible as it was and horrible as it would increasingly be.

With difficulty, Kay nudged everything off the platform. The pressure on her bladder already seemed intolerable. But it was, so far

at least, manageable, as long as she did not move or think much about it. But forced to sit in one position, for how long would that be true?

Kay bent her mind toward reconstructing early modern French history and its historiography. It was something she was rusty at, which meant she needed considerable concentration to call it to memory. She would pretend she had to give a course in it for graduate students. If such an exercise couldn't take her mind off her physical situation, nothing could.

[iv]

An unknown number of hours later— an infinity, it seemed to Kay— Weatherall made the visit Kay both longed for and dreaded. She longed for it because she felt constantly as though she couldn't bear another second of restraint, of hunger and thirst, of cramping and numbness, of pressure on her bladder. She dreaded it because she knew Weatherall would carry out her threat of having her force-fed. Kay did not bother to return Weatherall's greeting, did not speak at all. Weatherall unlocked the cuffs from the rings set into the platform and pulled Kay off the platform and onto her feet. Kay reeled with dizziness; her stomach heaved. Weatherall used the close pair of cuffs to bind Kay's hands behind her back, gripped Kay's arm, and propelled her out into the corridor.

Squinting against the harsh glare of the lights, Kay staggered along, her mind empty of all but her awareness of her weakness and discomfort and fear that she would collapse from the stress. She hardly noticed the twists and turns through the corridors or the number of the floor the elevator jetted them to, and in fact saw little in the painful fluorescent glare until they began passing people. Appalled, frightened, suddenly conscious of her appearance— filthy tights and leotard, dirty hair, dry cracked skin and lips, handcuffs— Kay longed to retreat to her cell. But Weatherall pushed her on, kept her going, on and on and on until they came to a place even more glaring— all white and chrome-glinting sterility— where she was fastened into a clinic chair and tilted horizontal— though knowing she must be flat, feeling as though her head sloped towards the floor— facing nightmare medical equipment. When it was over, when they— never once speaking to her— had wiped from her face the slimy slop that had come out of her nose along with the tube, Weatherall took her back through the corridors to the cell. Her stomach heaved; she thought she would vomit, but only bile surged into her aching raw and parched throat. The physical mess that she had become disgusted her. Never had she experienced such a surfeit of her own bodily excretions, a hatred of her bodily weakness, while Weatherall, strong, vigorous, almost superhumanly pristine, towered over her, detached, as though none of it mattered to her enough even to disgust her, as though she could not see or smell any of it.

Back in the cell, Weatherall took Kay directly to the platform. Kay forced herself to try: "Please Elizabeth let me use the toilet."

Weatherall unlocked the left-hand cuff and turned Kay around to face her. "You'll write in the book now?"

Kay shook her head.

"Then get up onto the platform, Kay."

"It isn't fair," Kay pleaded.

"You cannot judge what is fair," Weatherall said. "They are my rules. I decide what is fair. Get onto the platform."

Weatherall made Kay lie on her back and tightly fastened Kay's right wrist to the platform. She then turned her back to the platform, and Kay heard the sound of paper tearing and other noises she could not identify. When Weatherall turned around she held a hypodermic syringe in one hand and a cotton swab in the other. To Kay's horror, Weatherall pushed up Kay's leotard sleeve and brushed a spot on her left arm with the wet cotton swab— from the smell and fast evaporation Kay knew it must be rubbing alcohol— and jabbed the needle into the arm. Before she even had time to wonder what Weatherall was injecting her with, she experienced the same panic and paralysis that had overwhelmed her when they had shot her with a drugged dart in Seattle.

Kay heard the rustle of Weatherall's clothing, then perceived that Weatherall was perched on the platform beside her. Weatherall turned Kay's head so that she had to look at her. "Do you see, Kay, how far I'm prepared to go? I want you to think carefully while you're under

the control of the paralytic. I don't know your reasons for refusing to write for me as I require of you. But I have to wonder what's going on in your head when you prefer to go through this to complying with my orders. You're flying in the face of reality." Weatherall's fingers stroked Kay's face. "The reality is that you are here in this situation and must deal with me. There's no getting around it. That's the physical fact of your life. You aren't the transcending or masochistic type, so I don't think you're escaping reality in either of those directions. You know that what you do has no bearing on what happens in the other world. Don't you? You do know that, I believe you do. Why should it matter to you so very much as to bring you to go through this? It will go on and on, you know, and just get worse— unless you come to terms with the situation, come to terms with me. I have no choice but to force the issue now. You've made such a point of it... But the reality is that you're here, and at this moment you are so far confined that you can't even blink your eyes. What can be worth that degree of loss of freedom? For that's what you're doing, you're losing what little freedom you had left to lose. While if you cooperate with me, you will *gain* freedom. You will move across the corridor."

Kay became aware of warmth and wet trickling out between her legs. She realized she had lost control of her bladder.

"Think of that cell, Kay, waiting for you. You'd have control of the lighting— giving you night and day— you'd have a bed, a desk, regular water showers, pen, paper, perhaps even something to read, a sink, comb, toothbrush, an unlimited, accessible supply of water... I would even let you have a watch and clothing I know you'd prefer to your current attire. Why this defiance? It doesn't make sense."

Tears trickled out of the corners of Kay's eyes. When would Weatherall leave, leave her alone in her sodden mess?

Weatherall sighed. "You have made up something in your head, haven't you Kay. Something that seems— god knows how, considering how extreme your physical circumstances are— but it's something that seems more real to you than the true reality. If you force me to continue escalating your punishment, everything will eventually shatter, you know. I don't want that to happen. But you see I can't allow you to get away with this. In making this choice you've left *me* no choice."

Kay, her head still turned to one side, watched Weatherall slip off the platform and go out the door. This time she did not take the leather bag with her.

[v]

Possessed by the fear that she would vomit and strangle because of her lack of control over the muscles of her stomach, esophagus, and throat, Kay was vastly relieved when the paralytic wore off, though the relief dissipated as she grew accustomed to having the use of her muscles and increasingly aware of her damp tights and leotard, the wet blanket, and the smell of urine. She tried not to think about giving in, tried not to think of what Weatherall might do to her next, tried not to think of how long it could go on. She tried not to think at all.

Weatherall returned some time after the paralytic wore off. "Good morning, Kay."

Kay croaked out the words. "Good morning, Elizabeth."

"Have you reconsidered?"

Kay watched Weatherall's hard blue eyes. "I can't do it. I just can't do it."

Weatherall sighed. "Not *can't.* Let's be clear about that. The word is *won't.*" She leaned against the edge of the platform. "I'm not enjoying this, Kay. I don't like what's happening, not at all. I wish you would get hold of yourself and try to think rationally. Do you understand what will happen to you if you continue like this? How your self-image will change? How you will weaken yourself?" She picked up Kay's free hand and stroked it. "Think what it will be like when I take you to be force-fed the next time."

Kay bit her lip to stop it from trembling. "Please, Elizabeth. You are the one with power over me. Not me over you. If you don't like it then stop it."

"Listen to you! You're whining! You're losing all control over yourself. Don't you see that? You've lost control of your bodily functions, including those that are voluntary; you're losing control over your emotions. And for what? Why are you doing this? It's not as though I'm asking you to betray anyone. What is it that's so important for you not to discuss this thing with me?"

Kay turned her head to the wall. She shouldn't have tried to talk. But something in Weatherall's attitude had made her hope that she might relent.

"You intend to push this until you break, Kay? Is that what you want?"

Kay did not answer.

Weatherall unlocked the cuff that was fastened to the ring in the platform. "Get up."

Kay assumed she was being taken to another force-feeding and began to dread the humiliation of encountering other people in her noisome, sodden state. But they did not go far along the corridor from the cell before Weatherall stopped her and thumbed open a door. It was a small empty closet, perhaps two feet by three. "Your last chance, Kay," Weatherall said.

When Kay did not reply, Weatherall pushed her into the closet and shut the door. Kay stumbled to her knees and tried leaning back against the wall. She could not find a comfortable position, however, because her hands were cuffed and the walls were made of cold rough concrete blocks pressed too closely around her to allow her to extend her legs while sitting. What was Weatherall doing to her? Was she planning to keep her in here when she wasn't being force-fed? How would she bear it?

Kay laughed at the irony: finally she had dark. But now she was in no position to sleep, or do much of anything but feel miserable. She tried to think of seventeenth-century France, but that only led her to wonder whether incarceration in the Bastille had been as horrible as her own was fast becoming.

[vi]

On Saturday evening, Elizabeth prepared dinner for Allison. Thinking they would have all evening and night together, Allison happily drank and ate and chattered to Elizabeth about her work and offered anecdotes she had picked up in her peregrinations around the base. Elizabeth, she noticed, seemed preoccupied. Toward the end of the meal Allison caught Elizabeth checking her watch for the fifth or sixth time. Driven by concern that they wouldn't have the evening

together after all, she asked pointblank, "Do you have an appointment tonight?"

Elizabeth pushed her plate away. "Not an appointment in the formal sense of the word," she said. "But I must go back to the base. God knows what is happening with Zeldin now."

Allison bit her lip.

"I never imagined she would take it this far," Elizabeth said slowly. "I thought she was more flexible than that, I thought her more firmly rooted in her physical circumstances. If this goes much farther she will crack on me. No one can be locked up in a closet for very long and remain stable and sane." She sighed. "I got so exasperated with her earlier today that I almost slapped her."

"Maybe that's what is required," Allison said.

"You still don't understand anything about this, do you, Allison."

Allison stared down at her half-eaten crème-caramel. "No, I guess I don't," she said. "I've been inputting those transcripts, yet I haven't seen most of what you say is going on in your conversations with her. Except that now she has for some reason decided to defy you."

"Yes. She certainly has done that," Elizabeth said dryly. "Do you care to join me in an espresso."

"No thanks, Elizabeth. I think I'll stick with wine."

Elizabeth rose from the table and took her plate out to the kitchen. Allison sat looking at her half-eaten dessert. Then she, too, got up and carried her plate out to the kitchen. She found Elizabeth standing at the counter, staring blankly at the espresso maker. "I'll be out very shortly, it's almost done," Elizabeth said without turning.

Allison went into the living room and plumped down on the sofa. Though she hadn't paid much heed to it, Elizabeth had been distant all through the meal. In fact, she had been distant all day, though that was often the case when they were at the base working. Allison sipped her wine and wondered if her work was in some way not up to Elizabeth's standards. Now that she thought about it, she sensed in Elizabeth some sort of dissatisfaction with her. She was trying hard to handle all the responsibility Elizabeth had thrust on her, but she knew she was inadequate. She had never done these sorts of things

before. Perhaps Elizabeth had at last come to realize this and was intending to tell her so tonight.

Elizabeth came in carrying a demitasse cup and sat at the other end of the sofa. She sipped the coffee, then replaced the cup in the saucer and turned to Allison. "There's something we must discuss, Allison."

Allison's pulse raced. "Yes, Elizabeth?" Her voice came out high and thin.

"I realize that I must bear the major responsibility for what has happened, for misjudging, for letting my personal inclinations overrule my common sense." Allison's gaze fixed on Elizabeth's face and watched Elizabeth's eyes as they stared a little to the side of Allison's face and then flicked to meet Allison's. "I'm disturbed, very disturbed, at what I'm sensing in you. Our sexual relationship has, I think, had a disastrous effect on you. I can't quite put my finger on what it is, but I know that that part of our relationship must stop. Your reactions to the little service-tech, for instance. This is not the Allison I have known for years."

Allison tried hard to hold her face steady, to keep herself still. How could Elizabeth be saying this to her? How could this be happening?

"What we were doing was dangerous. And we both knew it. There are always reasons for taboos, Allison." She set her coffee cup onto the low table and took Allison's limp hand in her strong, warm fingers. "The expression on your face, Allison...that is enough to tell me what a mistake this has been. We must stop. Don't you see?"

Allison shook her head. "I don't understand. You don't want me now? You're already—"

Elizabeth interrupted. "That isn't the point. Of course I still want you. But that doesn't mean I can't act responsibly toward you, either. Better late than never," she said bitterly. "Listen to me, Allison. Nothing else will change. We will be as close as we have been." She half-smiled. "What would I do without you? I need you in so many ways. You are my confidante. I've never before had the relief of being able to talk to another person as I can to you. We will see one another as much as before. With only one difference. A difference that would be minor, if everything were well."

"I see." Allison pressed her lips together and stared down into her wine. "Are you angry with me, Elizabeth?"

"No, no, darling, I'm not at all angry. You must try to understand!" She squeezed Allison's hand. "Come, darling, come over here for a minute. Let me hug you. You look terrible. You mustn't be hurt by this. Come Allison, come to me..."

Swallowing back her tears, Allison set her glass of wine down and moved to sit beside Elizabeth. Elizabeth put her arms around her. "You are something of a baby," she said softly, her hand rubbing and patting Allison's back. "But I know you're strong and sensible. You're an executive, Allison. Remember that. You *must* remember that. You're an executive."

Allison pulled away. "I won't disappoint you, Elizabeth." She looked into Elizabeth's face, and the pain of seeing in Elizabeth's eyes that she meant what she said felt like a fist jabbing her in the gut.

Elizabeth's smile was warm. "I know that, darling. I know that very well." She picked up her cup and drank the rest of her coffee. "I really must go back to the base now. If you like, we can talk later, when I get back..." Allison schooled her face to blankness. "Would you like to wait here for me? You could have a fire, or use the Jacuzzi—"

Was Elizabeth trying to placate her with the privileges and objects life with her afforded? "No," she said. "I think I'll go downstairs. This will be my first chance in a long time to sit down with a book. We've been so busy..."

Elizabeth nodded. "I understand. Perhaps you would like a bit more time to yourself."

Allison did not want Elizabeth to know how little she wanted more time alone, so she said nothing, only got up to go.

Elizabeth stood, too. "One last kiss, Allison?" Her voice was caressing.

Shivering with tension, Allison closed her eyes while Elizabeth—giving her tongue— lingeringly kissed her. And then it was over and Allison was in the elevator going down and walking into her apartment and throwing herself on her cold lonely bed and sobbing and

screaming into the pillow, screaming that she couldn't bear this, sobbing for another chance.

[vii]

The darkness and silence engulfed Kay, suffocated her, negated her. For a long time she repeated over and over to herself that she was in a closet, only in a closet, simply in a closet. And for a while this worked. She visualized where she was in relation to her cell, visualized the corridor outside, and visualized slipping out into the corridor, moving in some ghostly way through the door as though it could not confine her. But the nothingness, the emptiness, grew harder and harder to push away. She struggled to hold back the words and the scream, to keep them tight in her throat and contained. She dragged herself to the door and put her face up against it, trying to feel it as a door, as a confirmation of there being an outside. But horror bubbled up, inexorable, powerful, wild, until finally she was screaming. Hearing her own screams dying in the nothingness, she shrieked "Elizabeth" over and over and over until the word lost meaning and hysteria swallowed her up.

Later, thoughts came into her mind— empty for a time after her exhausted collapse— and she could not keep from whispering them aloud. "My rules my rules my rules keep me upright, rigid, inflexible, resistant. But what are they but something in my head they can't save me from nonexistence? Are they even real if I am not? I'm dying, I'm killing myself, bit by bit... She's right to say I will be destroyed, shattered...and then what will be left but my rules and my consciousness of my rules and if I am the only one in this void in this vacuum in this emptiness what will my rules matter to me...

"...like all those wars. People dying for some principle...and they eventually forget what it was and then more people die to justify the deaths of those already dead and on and on and on, every damned time, the fools never know when to stop, never can cut their losses... I am like that, going further and further, destroying myself in the process, and now I don't remember why, at least not clearly, only thinking I must go on as I've begun, must obey my rules when I can't even

think of what was behind the rules to know if there is any sense in this now...

"...while in this closet I become an hysteric...and earlier, when I was hysterical, I forgot. I forgot everything, just everything, even my name; I forgot there is a closet— though even now I'm not sure I am in a closet not sure I am not drifting alone in a coma in space or even am Descartes' brain in the jar does it matter that the name Descartes comes into my mind? Does it mean I exist? That I am thinking like this: can that assure me that I think as it did Descartes, if indeed there ever was a Descartes who formulated the cogito...

"...the truth is, Elizabeth is the only one who knows I am here, that I even exist... For I might as well be dead she said, and it is only the two of us, only Elizabeth and me..."

And then horror again crept over her, and there were no words, only the shuddering, ugly terror of being crushed in vacuum...

Kay alternated between a state of partial lucidity and inarticulate dread and horror until nothing any longer existed for her but the dark emptiness and her consciousness. Not her words, not her body, not her screams the darkness and silence always swallowed up.

After a nameless, null infinity Elizabeth opened the door and the light flooded painfully into Kay's eyes. Kay sobbed Elizabeth's name. Elizabeth knelt beside Kay. "Tell me, Kay," she urged.

"I will do anything you want me to do, please, Elizabeth, please take me out of here."

"Of course I will, of course I will, Kay," Elizabeth said and held Kay in her arms. "Everything will be all right now. But you must give me your word, Kay. Give me your word you will cooperate."

"I give you my word I will cooperate," Kay said hoarsely.

"You shall have a shower and anything you'd like now. And then sleep. Come, let's get up. I'll help you." Elizabeth uncuffed Kay's wrists and pulled her to her feet and putting her arm around Kay's shoulders led her to a door in the corridor, which opened when she pressed the thumb-plate. The room was dark. Frightened, Kay pulled back. But Elizabeth pressed a switch and the lights came on.

"Let's peel off your horrible clothes, love, there, that's better. Now you may have your shower." She led Kay into the bathroom, opened the door to the shower, and turned on the water. "All set, in you go." Afraid of the small empty space, Kay shook with the effort it cost her to force herself into the shower and tried to think only of how wonderful it would feel.

When she came out Elizabeth toweled her dry and slipped a white cotton nightshirt over her head. The table in the bedroom held water and fruit and cheese and bread. "Help yourself," Elizabeth said, and Kay chugged most of a bottle of water. "You may have as much as you want, Kay. You see that cabinet over there?" Kay looked where Elizabeth pointed. "It's full of water, and I won't keep it locked, either." Kay sat on the bed and chewed on a piece of the thick, tough bread. "Tomorrow," Elizabeth said, "when you wake up, then you can write for me. You must be exhausted. Tonight you can sleep."

"It's night?"

"Yes. It's around midnight."

Kay nodded. Around midnight. She knew the time. It was around midnight.

"You'll be all right now, Kay." Kay looked at Elizabeth. "I'm going now. You can have the light on or off. You can decide for yourself. I'll see you in the morning." Elizabeth moved to the door.

Kay was engulfed by a wave of panic. "Wait! Please don't go!"

Elizabeth's eyebrows lifted. "What is it? Is there something else? Or something you want to say?"

Inarticulate, Kay shook her head. She did not know what she wanted.

"Then good-night, Kay."

"Good-night, Elizabeth."

Elizabeth went out into the corridor; the door slid shut. Kay glanced around the room— and was afraid. She got up and put the hunk of bread she had not finished eating on the table, then returned to the bed and got in under the covers. She took the pillow from under her head and held it to her breast. She would sleep with the light on. She could not be in the dark. Not now.

Chapter Twenty-two

[i]

"After this session we'll rotate the chair," Martha said, "so that no one person structurally controls our meetings, and so that each of us will share the responsibility for making things work." Isabelle, the woman John Doyle's group had sent, looked distinctly uneasy. "One important aspect of Co-op committees— for those of you unfamiliar with the way the Co-op functions— is providing a forum for diverse voices and viewpoints. And I don't think anyone can deny that this committee is about as diverse in its viewpoints as it's possible to imagine." Martha paused for the uncomfortable laughter most of them consented to produce, then said, "In this first meeting, our first order of business must be to find a name for the committee. I'm sure we can all agree that we don't want to call ourselves The Birth Limitation Committee, since finding a satisfactory way of loosening or even undoing the Department of Health's control is the ultimate reason for this committee's existence." Martha glanced at a couple of the people at the other end of the table and thought that perhaps that was stretching it. Some people *did* like the idea of Birth Limitation. They only wanted to take control over the selection process themselves. "In any event," Martha said hastily, "it would be better if we could find a more politically neutral name for ourselves."

"Politically neutral?" Geneva said. "I'm surprised to hear you suggest that such a thing is possible, Martha."

Martha bit her lip. "All right. I take that back. I should have said more politically acceptable."

"Care to let the rest of us in on this discussion?" David Hughes said, looking back and forth between Martha and Geneva.

"Geneva was merely pointing out to me that I don't believe anything put into language is politically neutral," Martha said. "So I corrected myself."

David smiled broadly.

Martha looked away from him. "So. Suggestions, anyone?"

"How about, The Committee for the Abolition of Birth Limitation?" Jackson Fellowes said.

"No!" several people said simultaneously.

"I think it should be something less negative-sounding," Geneva said. "Something to do with restoring reproductive rights."

"Restoring?" Martha said. "I'm not sure restoring is the way I'd put it. And what do you mean by *rights*? Don't you think 'reproductive freedom' is more appropriate? Your reference to reproductive rights is anachronistic." From what Venn had told her, "rights" might have been a meaningful term seventy years ago, but it really didn't apply now.

"But we *are* talking about rights," Olivia Friedman.

"Isn't *rights* a specifically political word?" David said. "I doubt if we're going to come to an agreement about it if we insist on using the word *rights*. Then we'd have to discuss who we think should have reproductive rights, whatever that means."

"And besides, if we talk about *rights*," Martha said, "then we'd have to assume some authority was granting them. And since we don't have a government, I don't think that's appropriate."

Many of the committee members sighed. Not all those present were devoted anarchists. Martha reckoned that at least one-third of them would be pleased to see a government in place.

"Okay," Geneva said. "What about The Committee for the Facilitation of Responsible Reproductive Freedom."

Responsible? Martha fretted a little over the use of such a qualifier. But the ensuing discussion made it clear that certain elements on the committee would not accept "freedom" without "responsible," and no one offered serious objections to "responsible." To most of them it seemed a "harmless enough word," as David put it. How could anyone object to "responsible?" Martha could not find an argument to articulate and support her objection, so she kept her qualms to herself, and the group agreed on the name. Marveling at the relative painlessness of the naming (for she had assumed it would take hours of acrimonious wrangling), Martha moved the discussion on to the projects and subcommittees and inquiries and reports their committee would be organizing. Perhaps this committee wouldn't be as difficult as she had thought, perhaps the issue would not prove as explosive as it had first seemed. The CFRRF, Martha thought: it had a symmetrical ring to it, though it did sound horribly bureaucratic and not at all anarchistic. But it would just have to do.

[ii]

For days and days— and she knew the measure of time now, for Elizabeth had given her a small flat screen that showed the time and date— Kay sought to assess her new position, to assess the extent of the damage, and to find some way to cope in spite of it. She never doubted that she had simply been shifted from one circle of hell to another. And though Dante might have been able to designate hell's circles along a continuum of horror and pain, Kay could not make such distinctions in her own experience, even if the physical comforts of her new cell might seem to suggest a lessening of discomfort and an increase in freedom. The comforts of the new cell confused her and did nothing to mitigate a new aspect of her torment— viz., overwhelming anxiety.

She recognized her symptoms, and she comprehended her anxiety's sources. But her intellectual understanding provided no escape. She could no longer, for instance, sleep in the dark. Elizabeth had— astonishingly it seemed to Kay— upon simple request and with no comment whatsoever brought her a night light so that she did not have to sleep with the lights on. (Not that she slept that well with the night light, either.) At times claustrophobia kept her from going into the bathroom— though her new compulsion to wash constantly impelled her presence there. These symptoms she knew to be a reaction to the trauma she had suffered in the closet. But another cluster of symptoms plagued her even more fiercely. Everything in the cell had to be just-so and spotless. The sheets and blankets, even while she was

under them in bed, had to be arranged perfectly. The desk chair had to be precisely lined up in relation to the desk. She brushed her teeth and washed her body a dozen times a day (at the sink, for Elizabeth controlled her use of the shower), and though she was at first dismayed at Elizabeth's bringing in a service-tech to crop her hair with a razor, she was soon pleased to have it neat and clean.

Kay located the key to this obsessive fastidiousness— completely out of line with her previous habits and personality— in the extreme disgust for her own urine she now experienced every time she peed. The very smell of it made her anxious to wash. Even worse, she often imagined she could smell it while lying in bed or sitting at the desk or pacing the cell. When this happened, as it did several times a day, the only way she could rid herself of what she knew was a wholly imagined odor was by washing. Though she chided herself for humoring these compulsions, though she rehearsed the psychological reason for her obsessiveness, she still fell prey to the symptoms.

But the overhanging anxiety eating away at her hour after hour she was less able to diagnose or understand. Her current level of fearfulness made her previous state of apprehension seem by comparison like nonchalance. On the one hand, she was substantially more afraid of Elizabeth than she had been before the closet trauma. Merely brushing up against the thought of the closet made Kay break into a cold sweat. And whenever Elizabeth came into the cell, every fiber of her being fairly quivered with the knowledge of the closet and Elizabeth's power to shut her up in it. It was a potentiality that Kay felt lay unspoken but palpable between them, making Kay careful not to risk even annoying Elizabeth.

On the other hand, because she had abandoned her rules, because she wrote in the leather book for Elizabeth, because she had been moved to this cell— presumably as the promised reward for "progress"— Kay worried that she had lost her grip, that Weatherall was succeeding in brainwashing her, that she was being managed in ways she only vaguely sensed. She understood well enough her ambivalence toward Elizabeth: but she determined to fight it, determined to keep herself clear about Weatherall, determined to find a clarity as strong as that she had achieved while inhabiting the other cell.

She imagined using the pen for jotting down notes on toilet paper but could not nerve herself to do so, fearing she might be seen through the mirror, fearing that even if no one were watching from the other side of it no matter how well she hid anything she wrote it could easily be found, and knowing that if it were found she might have to pay a price higher than she could afford. Kay judged she had lost her nerve. And along with her nerve the moral authority of her resistance vanished. Had she any resistance remaining, beyond her repeating inside her head— never aloud— her recognition of what Weatherall was up to, her determination to keep for herself the word "brainwash," her insistence that what she wrote in the book was meaningless? Was she fooling herself? Was she fooling herself the way Glen Boren, her colleague in Champaign-Urbana, had been fooling himself?

Sometimes she hoped that if she rested up, if she waxed physically stronger, she would be able to resume open struggle against Weatherall. But though she slept more than she had in the other cell— mostly at night, for with the watch she tried to make herself keep "ordinary" hours, absurd as it was, isolated deep under the earth, never to see the world again— she still felt tired, drowsy, languid, as though her physical strength were draining away. As though sleeping in a bed in near dark and dreaming were leeching her lifeblood...

Dreaming: that posed another problem. In the other cell, her dreams had been short, blurred, jaggedly fragmented, usually to do with food and water. But in the new cell her dreams were varied and vivid. Almost every night now she dreamed she was wandering around the base, the metal bracelet on her wrist for some reason not setting off the alarms, the doors almost magically opening to the press of her thumb. She was searching for Scott; she knew she could escape but wanted to find Scott first. So she opened door after door, looking for him. After opening countless doors she would open one to find Sedgewick waiting for her in a room that was the room at the top of his Gothic island house. And then she would wake, her heart galloping in fear. The dream varied only in the sorts of things she saw in

the rooms she peered into; the feelings were always the same, and the encounter with Sedgewick in that room always came at the end of the dream. She also dreamed about Seattle and her own funeral, and about Elizabeth in various situations (not in a cell, not as a jailer, but out in the world).

And then there were erotic dreams— mostly featuring David Hughes— from which she would wake with slickly wet thighs and damp nightshirt, her genital smell in her nostrils, driving her to get up to wash herself and change the nightshirt and to wash the nightshirt she had been wearing. She deemed her sexuality an intrusion where she lacked privacy; she wanted to keep that part of herself locked away, separate, so that it could not be touched by the terrible things she was living or somehow used against her. That it was David Hughes she dreamed about particularly galled her. These nocturnal disturbances could only contribute to her turmoil and confusion.

The proof of her weakness and confusion seemed to be sealed by the difference in her reaction now to one of Elizabeth's absences. A few days after Elizabeth had brought her to the new cell she had announced to Kay that she would be away for a few days. Kay knew there was a large supply of water and tubefood in the cell's cupboards readily accessible to her. Elizabeth had left her free of a writing assignment, taking the book with her when she had left. Instead of feeling liberated by the looming reprieve from pressure, she felt panic at Elizabeth's announcement. The silence of the new cell seemed absolute and somehow more suffocating with its rug and other soft absorbers of sound than that of the old cell. Here Kay was unable to stand at the table and look out at the room and deliver a lecture, for something in the room muted her. Instead of lecturing, she would get up and wash herself, then return to bed and slip between the sheets, obsessively straightening and smoothing the covers over her body. Or she would begin a conversation to Elizabeth in her head, only to break off when she realized what she was doing and switch to reviewing past conversations with Elizabeth— searching for clues to the problem she sensed she needed to solve, a problem she could neither name nor define but felt almost palpably engulfing her. She needed to believe that if she thought enough about it she might eventually name

and define the problem as well as find its solution, perhaps all in one single, brilliant insight.

Elizabeth's absence stretched into a week. Kay decided that the watch made time pass more torturously but did not care to put it away where she would not see it, telling herself that the watch was her only link with objective reality— a reality independent of Elizabeth Weatherall. Except, she admitted to herself, that Elizabeth could have reprogrammed the clock— though why would she bother? What would it matter to her that Kay knew whether it was day or night?

On the second Friday of Elizabeth's absence, Kay turned on her night light, turned off the indirect ceiling lights, and "went to bed" (as she thought of it) at ten p.m. She then tossed and turned, brooding over the explication she had written in the leather book of her betrayal of Sedgewick. Elizabeth claimed that in her published book Kay had not written the "whole truth" about what had happened— not because it was irrelevant, but because she hadn't wanted to think seriously about it and hadn't wanted any of her Free Zone associates to know "the whole truth." When Kay had pointed out that she had told the whole story to some of the Free Zone people and to three of the Marq'ssan, Elizabeth had said she didn't believe that Kay had admitted even to herself, much less to anyone else, the "whole truth." When Kay had asked her to be more specific, Elizabeth had said that Kay herself would have to be the one to "find the truth." Kay fretted constantly about this, especially while lying in bed in the semi-dark; she often wondered if the key to the brainwashing would be in this "finding" of "the truth" that Elizabeth intended to foist upon her. Through what lie was she to implicate herself in telling? How could she resist Elizabeth's pressure yet keep from being immured in the closet?

Kay checked the clock by the glow of the night light and saw that only two hours had passed. She rolled onto her side and hugged the pillow (which she never used under her head) close to her breast. Perhaps she could remember what it was like to sleep beside Scott... But no, she berated herself a few minutes later when the tears began: she was not to think about Scott. She knew she could not bear it if she were to

let herself think about him, for she'd soon be thinking about everything else and loathing her current existence all the more intensely.

After some time, Kay heard the door slide open. She lifted her head and saw Elizabeth outlined against the bright corridor lighting, framed by the doorway. "*Bon soir*, Kay."

That soft voice floating out into the shadowy room evoked an eeriness that shot prickles along Kay's spine. Elizabeth stepped forward and the door slid shut. The night light provided the room's only illumination, which Elizabeth's silver laminate tunic caught and reflected. The dully gleaming tunic hinted at thirteenth-century armor. Elizabeth sat on the side of the bed. Kay inched closer to the wall. "Aren't you going to greet me?" Elizabeth said, slipping the leather strap off her shoulder.

The bag hit the carpeted floor with a thud. "*Bon soir*, Elizabeth," she whispered.

Elizabeth's eyes, though shiny, seemed of a dark indeterminate color, creating a bizarre effect in combination with the silver threaded through her coronet of braids and the glint of her tunic. "I've just finished with a very dull dinner party at which, apart from the mostly silent hostess, I was the only woman. Executive men are rather boring creatures taken collectively, don't you think? You must remember the things you attended with Sedgewick."

"The executive attitude toward women is absurd," Kay said boldly. "It's more than a century out of date."

"But there's good enough reason for it," Elizabeth said. "The sort of responsibilities professionals are charged with can safely be entrusted to fully sexual persons. But for the more important jobs...in general, it is true that people are made vulnerable by their sexuality."

"You can say that about yourself?" Kay asked curiously.

Elizabeth smiled. "Ah, but I am an exception. I use my sexuality to manage others, rather than allowing others to manipulate me through my sexuality. But that is seldom the case with most fully sexual people. You and I can both think of someone who has paid heavily in this."

Kay knew Elizabeth referred to Sedgewick. She found it astonishing that they were having this conversation.

"But perhaps the dullness is due to jet-lag. As soon as my plane landed I had to rush off to the dinner-party... How very odd being here, deep underground, when only hours ago I was in Paris."

Paris? What had Elizabeth Weatherall been doing in Paris? How could she be traveling when Sedgewick— but no. Obviously some things had changed. After all, Weatherall's being Kay's controller was sign enough that not everything had remained the same.

"I have a couple of presents and one *devoir* for you." Elizabeth bent to reach into the leather bag. She dumped several items onto the bed. "First, I thought you'd like to read this—" Elizabeth held up a print newspaper for Kay to see. "It's one of the rags they put out in Seattle, all about the memorial speeches that were made in your honor."

Kay shivered. She had no wish to read about people talking about her death.

"I thought you'd be amused to see how you've achieved revolutionary martyrdom. And here is some scented powder I've brought you from Paris...and last but not least, the book. It's time for you to do more writing for me." When Kay said nothing, Elizabeth continued. "I've carefully gone over everything you've written, and it seems clear to me that you're missing something important. What I want you to do for tomorrow— I'll come by sometime in the evening, so have it ready for then— is to explain why you continued with your plan to betray the Executive even after Sedgewick took you to his island. After all, you must have realized that day that you had nothing to fear from him. Why stick with the plan to betray him?" Elizabeth held her hand up to keep Kay from speaking. "I don't believe it's because you had some sort of ideological conversion. You aren't the type to experience conversions. I would even go so far as to guess that if it hadn't been Sedgewick controlling you, you never would have gone renegade. And, as you have already written, you in fact didn't even think of doing that until after your memory partially returned."

Partially returned?

"So perhaps," Elizabeth said, "you should write on two questions. First, whether you would have gone renegade if your controller had been someone other than Sedgewick. And second, why you did not choose to put your loyalty back on track after Sedgewick came out into the open with you. Be careful, Kay: I don't want to read any nonsense about your getting in too deep with the other side to back down, because you and I both know you could have explained everything to Sedgewick and that we could have made use of your involvement with the other side to good effect."

Kay's stomach twisted. This was definitely the worst of the "writing assignments." What could she write that wouldn't infuriate Elizabeth? Yet that would satisfy her?

Elizabeth picked up her bag and rose to her feet. "Have it ready for me by evening, Kay." She moved to the door and opened it. "Good night," she said as she stepped out into the corridor.

Kay decided she might as well turn on the lights. It was unlikely she would be able to sleep that night.

[iii]

Saturday afternoon, when Elizabeth was in Allison's office discussing the week's developments concerning the vid project, news came that Security personnel and troops had to evacuate from Boston. The Marq'ssan's tardy response to the announcement of Kay Zeldin's apprehension and execution had been the final blow giving Military the advantage.

Allison felt sick at the news. "Is she really worth it, Elizabeth?" she asked bitterly.

Elizabeth's eyebrows lifted. "Whether she had actually been executed or not, the Marq'ssan would have done the same thing. Are you asking whether her apprehension was worth it?"

Allison averted her eyes from Elizabeth's penetrating blue gaze. People like Lauder and Wedgewood would of course think a dead Zeldin worth losing Boston over. They were that irrational. But what about those lacking such an intense emotional investment in avenging treachery?

"There was no choice about her apprehension, you know," Elizabeth said softly. "She was simply too flagrant."

"But couldn't all that have waited? Until things were back under control?"

Elizabeth laughed. "You seem to forget that *she* came to *us*, Allison. She literally ran straight into me. Are you suggesting I should have let her go?"

"Maybe you shouldn't have had her death announced."

Elizabeth shook her head. "No, no, the main reason I did that was so that the Marq'ssan would take one shot at us and then leave us alone. If they thought we had her alive they might very well have tried to get us to give her up to them. You see?"

"Oh," Allison said. She hadn't thought of any of that. Obviously, though, Elizabeth had been thinking of it all along.

"Yes," Elizabeth said, "oh." Her lips curved in a faint smile. "Now that she's writing in the book for me it's only a matter of time. And from my point of view, at least, what will be accomplished will be worth losing Boston for. Not that 'losing Boston' will matter at all in the long-run: the war will be over soon."

Elizabeth sounded so confident. Had something definite come out of her trip? "You'll be seeing Zeldin today?" Allison asked. "Will you want me to get out the book for you?"

"I took it to her last night," Elizabeth said.

Last night! It must have been very late... and obviously Elizabeth had forgotten to retrieve the disk from the data recorder. "Do you want me to run down now and get the data disk, or is it all right for me to wait to update the transcript with the next one?"

"I didn't turn the recorder on," Elizabeth said carelessly. "So there's nothing to input."

Allison stared at her. Elizabeth never neglected to record her conversations with Zeldin, even the most fleeting. "Then do you want me to input your notes?" Allison asked.

"I didn't make notes." Elizabeth put her yellow pad and pen down on the table at her elbow. "All right, Allison. What is it that's got you so disturbed?"

"Nothing. I mean, I'm not *disturbed.* It's just that it's...unusual...for you not to record or make notes of conversation with Zeldin."

"Don't worry about it. Nothing important was said."

Allison stared down at her desktop. It had been Elizabeth who had told her that even the most trivial things taken in the whole could form a pattern of significance, that completeness in their record-keeping might at some point prove invaluable.

Elizabeth resumed discussion of the proprietary, made several suggestions that Allison jotted down, and left. Allison stared for a few minutes at the closed door and thought about how empty her life now seemed. She had hoped Elizabeth would suggest they spend some time together in the evening, but now that hope was dashed: Elizabeth obviously intended to spend most of the evening and night working.

After a few minutes' thought, Allison picked up her handset and keyed in Anne's extension. Anne, it turned out, would be delighted to have dinner with Allison. Because Allison would be working later than Anne, she would pick up Anne at her home.

Allison simply could not face another night alone. And Elizabeth, it seemed, no longer cared to spend her evenings with Allison, not even after a week away. For a moment Allison thought of asking Elizabeth for a transfer. But as soon as she conceived the idea she knew it was impossible, for if she did request a transfer, Elizabeth would realize the extent of her pain, the depth of her feelings, and would disapprove of her for it and condemn her for putting her feelings ahead of their work. She must try to forget Elizabeth, try to shut herself off from those feelings. Perhaps that's what Elizabeth wanted, perhaps that was why Elizabeth had become so casual— even cavalier— toward her in a way she had not been before this last trip.

Allison tried to settle down to work, but the most disturbing element of her session with Elizabeth persisted in obtruding. What reason had Elizabeth had for neither taping nor taking notes about her late-night meeting with Zeldin? Allison could imagine only one thing, and she knew she must be wrong, for if it were that, Elizabeth would not care if Allison knew. She vowed to listen with special care

to the next recordings— if, that is, there were any... Who knew what Elizabeth might do, now that she had violated her own protocol?

[iv]

At around seven Allison left the base in a two-seater. As she had expected, the auto's terminal was able to provide her with a map and directions to the prefab settlement Anne lived in. She had noticed it many times in passing from village to base and knew that high-skilled service-techs and the lowest echelon of professionals— all people imported from outside the area to work at the base— lived there. Security's policy was to discourage fraternization with locals. All persons working at the base had thoroughly-researched security clearances. Security thought it prudent to encourage a separation (which would be natural in any case) from local people (or indeed from all the other outsiders who had somehow filtered into the area). Accordingly, the settlement had its own security system, as Allison discovered when she pulled onto the service road and found herself stopped at a guardpost.

Following the directions to Anne's unit that the guard provided, Allison's free-wheeling vehicle bounced along a rutted gravel road through the dark. An occasional light revealed the square ugly buildings and the gravel and sand surrounding them. Allison tried not to let the sterility and desolation of the place touch her. She thought of Anne, working by day at the base— underground, airless, bleak— coming home to this. But, Allison reminded herself, Anne might very well not mind, for she probably didn't know much else, and even if she did she counted herself lucky to be here and not in DC— to be here working a paying job, in an atmosphere of order. And for scenery there was always the mountains...

Allison parked in front of the unit numbered 884. Through a curtainless window Allison glimpsed a brightly-lit room in which four women sat around a table playing cards. Anne was one of the women. Allison debated honking the horn but decided for some reason she could not name to herself to go to the door.

Anne opened to Allison's knock; she looked surprised. "Lise! Just a minute, I have my coat right here." She did not invite Allison in but

darted out of sight, said something to the others, and then came out into the night. "You should have honked," she said.

Allison drove into the village and parked near a casual, moderately priced restaurant patronized primarily by professionals. Before getting out of the car Allison asked Anne how she was.

"I didn't think I would be hearing from you again," Anne said.

Allison winced at this candor. "I've been frantically busy. This was my first real chance to get out." A lie, but Anne wouldn't know.

Anne said, "I'm glad you called me."

Allison brushed a light kiss over Anne's lips, and they went into the restaurant, which was pleasantly redolent with the fragrances of garlic, olive oil, cheese, and bread. After a quick look at the menu, they agreed to order red wine, antipasto, and a small Venetian-style pizza. "We were listening to reports about Boston on the radio when you came to pick me up," Anne said.

Allison groaned. "I don't even want to think about it."

"It seems like Military has taken almost every eastern city now."

"Not New York," Allison said.

Anne shuddered. "Yes, but can Security really talk about holding New York? Think about what most of it must be like!"

"Let's *not* think about it," Allison said. "Do you listen to the radio much?"

"Sure. Everybody does. It may not be vid, but it's better than nothing."

For a moment Allison remembered the service-techs she had lived with in Seattle and their breakfast-table reading of the newspaper and their discussions. What sorts of things did Anne and her unit-mates talk about when they heard the carefully controlled stuff that got broadcast as "news" on the radio? Some of it was obvious— about how awful it was that Military held most of the eastern seaboard... but if the others came from DC— Allison had no idea whether they did or not— it was probably understandable: they would be homesick. Homesick! Allison could not imagine what that might be like. She missed different places at different times and for different reasons. But there was really no one place she ever thought of as "home."

Executives who as children went away to school and as adults moved continually from place to place mostly didn't. "Do you get homesick, Anne?" Allison asked.

Their server set the obligatory swallow of the bardolino before Allison, and she tasted it. She nodded, and he filled first Allison's glass and then Anne's. When he had gone Anne said, "Sometimes being here gives me the creeps. There's something so separate about it, so dead. Sometimes I feel like a ghost, like all of us here are ghosts wandering about the base. As though the mountains don't even acknowledge we're here, contemptuous at us for having scooped out one of their own and made it an emptiness."

Anne's sensitivity startled Allison. "You feel that too?" Allison sipped her wine. She had only started feeling it herself since Elizabeth had broken with her. She had noticed nothing about her surroundings before then. "It is desolate," Allison said. "And the base— so much of it is empty, and echoey, and hollow. I sometimes feel we could all be swallowed up in it, just all that space and the electronic tech, which exists seemingly independent from the rest of the world."

"It *must* have been independent, since the Blanket didn't affect it."

Allison frowned. "How do you know that?" That was supposed to be classified information.

"Everybody knows that," Anne said, her eyes suddenly very careful of Allison.

Allison glanced around at the tables nearest them. "That may be true, but it's still best to be discreet. Maybe everybody knows it because too many people were free with the information." She herself had known nothing until Elizabeth had explained it to her.

The service-tech brought an antipasto platter, plates, forks, and paper napkins. Allison bit into a sizzling sausage-stuffed mushroom. She found it liberally laced with cayenne and juicy. "Oh, what a good idea to do this," she said, smiling at Anne.

Anne returned the smile and popped a basil leaf- and olive oil-garnished chunk of fresh mozzarella into her mouth. "Do you come here often?" she asked Allison.

Unable to answer because she had just taken another bite, Allison shook her head. "No, this is my first time," she said when she had gotten her mouth clear. "Mostly I just eat at the base or fix a sandwich at home. Contrary to what you might think, I don't get to Denver that often." Forking some of the giardinera, Allison suddenly felt tactless: Anne probably lived on tubefood and never got to Denver except in the company of an executive lover… But that thought led in an uncomfortable direction, so she dropped it and said, "Do you ski, Anne?"

Anne's eyes widened. "*Me*? Last year here was the first time I'd ever been in any mountains at all."

And of course she couldn't afford to ski unless someone took her. "Well maybe I can talk you into trying it this year," Allison said, trying not to feel nettled by all her conversational blunders. "It could be fun, you know, once you got started."

Anne looked doubtful. "I'm pretty much of a klutz," she said.

"Well, even if you don't want to ski, it might be fun just getting away from here for weekends."

Anne looked wistful. "I have to work every weekend. Though it sounds wonderful."

"Maybe Alice would be willing to arrange something," Allison said, hiding her own skepticism about that. If Alice Warner knew Anne was seeing Allison she would undoubtedly be as uncooperative as possible.

Allison was relieved when the pizza was served and they could eat in unstrained silence. Probably both of them were simply too tired and for various reasons feeling awkward with one another. Things would improve, Allison told herself. Anne liked her, and she liked Anne. It was all a matter of timing.

[v]

Kay leaned against the wall by the desk, her cheek pressed against the smooth cool wallpaper, and stared down at the book lying open on the desk. She wondered if Elizabeth would be coming soon, or if she would be coming at all that night. Evening, she had said. By Kay's watch it was now past eight-thirty. She stared at the newspaper pre-

cisely folded and positioned in diagonal relation to the book. So far she had not even glanced at the picture on the front page, had not read the inky text (though the headline— **Twenty Thousand Pay Tribute to Zeldin**— could not escape her notice). She refused to be seduced into losing what little perspective remained to her. Again and again she told herself that she must not read the paper though she had not had anything to read for as long as she had been here, and words... well, words were after all words. For someone who had spent most of her life producing and consuming words, the presence of the newspaper offered Kay the ultimate in temptation.

Also on the desk— unopened— sat the ivory box of powder bearing the inlaid lapis lazuli monogram entwining an F with an R. Why had Elizabeth given this to her? Kay intended to leave it there, unopened; she hoped Elizabeth would take it away (as she had once taken from Kay the banana Kay had not immediately eaten). Like everything else, it could be only a snare. But Kay found these snares difficult to decipher. The sharp outlines she had perceived before being moved to this cell had vanished, leaving only fuzzy, amorphous anxiety and the fearful recognition that Elizabeth was succeeding in forcing her to think about Sedgewick because she, Kay, was afraid to disobey Elizabeth openly. Elizabeth's reasons or even a plausibly connected picture of what was happening or what Elizabeth wished to happen eluded her. She was going through a stupid period at a time when her very survival depended upon her being sharp.

As she stared down at the book the word "coward" repeated itself in her head in endless litany. *Coward, coward, coward, coward*... Yes it was true, Kay fretted, but it did not help to dwell on it when what she needed to do was to think. To think about what was happening, to think about what she needed to do to keep from being swallowed up in this abyss. Surely it was not already too late?

Coward... Not only did she write for Elizabeth. But she wrote so carefully, took such pains to phrase what she had to say as obliquely as possible... fearful of saying openly that after the visit to the island she had grown even more afraid of Sedgewick than she had already been, fearful of saying his madness had terrified her, fearful of saying

she hadn't been able to stand being around him, fearful of saying her hatred had increased after the island confrontation, had increased the more he had pressed himself on her. Instead, Kay wrote with near detachment, almost coldly, about Sedgewick's refusal to believe that there were aliens, about his mismanagement of the crisis, about her disagreement with his policies, especially those affecting Seattle… In short, she wrote as a political historian, not as one interested in the psychological motives of those identified as key actors in events. Elizabeth would not be satisfied. But as Kay saw it she was caught in a double bind, since if she wrote about her psychological motivations Elizabeth would probably punish her for using the terms necessary for describing her own state of mind. Kay wondered whether Elizabeth had forced her into the double bind deliberately, knowing she would be unable to find a way out of the dilemma. The thought chilled her and intensified her anxiety.

When at around quarter after nine Kay's eyes strayed to the clock, she realized she had been standing motionless for more than half an hour. Thirsty, she went to the table, poured herself a cup of water, and drank it. Then she got into bed, imagining herself a child as she slipped under the covers, smoothing the cotton night shirt down the length of her body, pulling taut the sheets and blankets. For a little while it seemed to her that she had been jettisoned into a sort of childhood. I'm as powerless as a child, she thought, as an unloved orphan child who is locked in the closet for punishment…

But I'm *not* a child, Kay said to herself after a few minutes' singing that riff. I have a powerful mind, there must be a difference, the metaphor must break down somewhere… At ten Kay got up to pee. On her way back to bed the door opened and Elizabeth entered, carrying a cup of coffee, the smell of which awakened desire in Kay. Oh coffee! she thought with longing. If she could only drink some coffee perhaps her mind might actually wake up. Elizabeth set her cup on the desk and turned the chair around to face the bed. "Good morning, Kay."

Between the coffee and the greeting, Kay for a moment wondered if it might actually *be* morning. There was no way she could know for sure. "Good morning, Elizabeth."

Elizabeth looked tired. "Did you enjoy reading about your martyrdom?" she asked, Kay thought only half-ironically.

"Oh, but I didn't read about it," Kay said in the same tone of voice Elizabeth had used.

Weatherall's eyes narrowed. "How very uncharacteristic," she said. When Kay said nothing, she asked, "Any particular reason why you did not read it?"

Kay answered without hesitation. "I don't have many choices allowed to me. You didn't tell me I *had* to read the paper. Therefore I assumed it was my choice."

"Yes, that's true, it was your choice. But I still don't see why you *chose* not to read the newspaper."

Kay stared up at the white-plastic ceiling. "Precisely because it was a choice. If I had read it I would have been doing the expected. Therefore I chose not to read it."

"Ah," Weatherall said, and Kay wished she had made up some story about being upset at the thought of people talking about her as though she were dead. For all she knew, she had just given Weatherall information that could be used against her.

Weatherall sipped her coffee and turned around in her chair to pick up the book. Waiting to see if the new entry would pass muster was the most nerve-wracking moment of the "writing assignments." Out of the corner of her eye Kay watched her read the new entry straight through without stopping to question Kay as she sometimes did.

When she had finished reading, Weatherall set her cup down, got up, and crossed to the bed and sat down on it. Kay shifted toward the wall and struggled into a sitting position, wary for what might come next. "This entry is disingenuous, Kay," Elizabeth said, tapping the book in her lap with her long, bony index finger.

"It is all true, Elizabeth. All of it." Even if she could not keep herself from so much fear, Kay wished she could at least keep it out of her voice.

"No. Each sentence taken singly might be true, but taken as a whole the thing is a lie."

"I don't understand," Kay said.

"You can't tell me with a straight face that because you didn't like Sedgewick's policies you decided that rationally speaking it made more sense to throw your lot in with anarchists! You were as appalled by them as anyone. The only reason you went over to them in the first place— at least according to what you have already written for me— was because of your fear after the partial return of your memory that Sedgewick was going to kill you. I don't buy this, Kay. You try to make it sound very rational, but it doesn't hang together. You didn't like Operation Scapegoat, in fact you were angry about it. I remember that very clearly. Yet I'd swear you never had a thought of going over to the enemy on that account. Correct?"

"But when I knew that it was aliens we were dealing with— for god's sake, they healed my skull injury!— and I saw Sedgewick refusing to come to terms with it! I knew nothing would ever work out his way!"

Elizabeth shook her head. "This is all nonsense, Kay. And I can see by your face that you're holding back." She smiled. "I'm getting to know you very well. I can tell when you're lying."

Kay's throat went dry, and in the silence, her pulse pounded loudly in her ears. "I was still afraid of him. Maybe more afraid of him than I had been before going to the island."

Elizabeth closed the book and laid it down on the bed beside her. "When it comes to your reactions to Sedgewick, I feel I know you even better than he from all that he talked and talked and talked about you, and better than you know yourself, for you have never been honest with yourself about him. I do know about this, Kay. That you ran away from him all those years ago... is perfectly comprehensible. You did it out of your so strongly developed sense of self-preservation. But that you not only fled but also betrayed Sedgewick later, that is something else. If you were afraid, it wasn't of him per se. You knew you had nothing to fear from him after the past came out into the open. What an easy time you had manipulating him! I know, I watched you

doing it, and I knew you'd get better and better and bolder and bolder. He was putty in your hands."

"No! That's not true!"

"If there was fear, it was not of Sedgewick, but of yourself. A fear of what so much power would do to you. But of course, you were angry, too. What was it you said to him about how you would take pleasure in killing him if he gave you an excuse? I think part of the reason you betrayed him was because you hated him."

Kay pressed her lips together to keep from speaking that hate.

"But of course you never bothered to ask yourself *why* you hated him so much, did you."

A surge of anger swept aside Kay's fear. Weatherall was baiting her, looking for an excuse to hurt her. "What is it you're trying to make me say?" she said, barely keeping her voice from betraying the rage that was close to physically consuming her.

"It's not so much what I'm trying to make you say, Kay, as trying to get you to be honest about this."

"You seem to have all the answers." Kay's teeth were clenched so hard that she felt as though she were choking on all the words she knew she must not say. "So you tell me the answer you're dying to hear."

"If I tell you, you'll simply deny it. It's better that you figure it out for yourself."

"Oh, I see. You have privileged information about the inside of my head."

"You're not being very cooperative."

The tone of warning in Weatherall's voice put Kay's body on high alert. Adrenalized with the consciousness of pushing Weatherall to the very border of what she would tolerate, Kay said, "I'll say whatever you want, I'll agree with whatever you say, but of course you first have to tell me what it is you want me to say. Or what it is I'm supposed to admit to."

Kay thought she saw the muscles around Weatherall's eyes and mouth tighten. Though she had annoyed Weatherall, she could see that the executive was not even close to losing control. "There are

times when that superficial level of cooperation is acceptable to me," Weatherall said evenly, "but this is not one of them."

She stood up and went to the desk and put her coffee cup to her lips. She swallowed, then walked with the cup into the bathroom. Kay heard the water running. And then Weatherall returned, the coffee cup dangling from her fingers. "What are the reasons people have for hating?" she asked conversationally.

Being locked up and badgered, Kay thought: that's reason enough. A wave of fatigue washed over her. She just wanted to put the pillow over her head and zone out. Barely able to muster the energy to speak, she said, "People hate others for hurting them, for making their lives a misery, for threatening them, for hurting others, for endangering them physically, existentially, ontologically."

"And?"

Kay sighed. "There is no 'and.' I've been as complete as I can be. I don't know that much about hate. It's not something I sit around thinking about."

"Well you'd better think about it now," Weatherall said tartly. "In fact, that will be your next assignment. But in the meantime, let us consider your suggestion that you were still afraid of Sedgewick even after you knew his state of mind where you were concerned. Tell me about that."

"His state of mind," Kay said, seizing on the phrase. "That's exactly what frightened me."

Elizabeth walked over to the bed. "Go on," she said. "What about his state of mind frightened you?"

"You know as well as I do that it's not safe to be around someone in that state of mind, especially if one is the obsessive object in question."

"I know as well as you do...?" Elizabeth said. "What is it that you seem to think we both 'know'?"

Kay trembled. Frantically she searched for words that would not offer Elizabeth an excuse to punish her. "He was volatile," she said. "At any moment he might have changed his mind about me. I couldn't believe anything he said!"

"Volatile," Elizabeth said, staring down at her. "A curious sort of word to use for Sedgewick. Considering how constant he was toward you over so many years. I can't agree with you there. You are saying you didn't trust him?"

Kay nodded. Perhaps that would be enough.

"Why didn't you trust him?" When Kay did not answer, Elizabeth said, "Had he ever given you reason to think he was a liar?"

Kay licked her very dry lips. "No," she whispered.

"So you didn't think he was lying to you. Therefore you thought he might change his mind about you?"

Terrified to speak, Kay could only nod.

"But why should he? If he wasn't lying? And if his feelings toward you had been so consistent?"

"He hated me even though he never said so."

"Then you *are* saying he was a liar."

Kay couldn't take her eyes off Elizabeth's face, which she had never before seen looking so *intense*. "Not exactly a liar. Maybe he didn't admit it to himself."

"Oh, you mean he had your problem," Elizabeth said drily. "But of course you know that isn't true. If he hated you— even unconsciously— he would have raped you that last night. But he didn't, did he. You admit he *could* have, if he had wanted to."

Kay rubbed a piece of the sheet between her fingers. Elizabeth was closing in on her; Kay could feel herself being maneuvered into a corner.

"Do you know *why* he left you alone when you asked him to?"

Kay swallowed. "No," she said. "Except that he had some ulterior motive."

Elizabeth snorted. "You're not being very bright about this, Kay."

"Maybe not," Kay said, very low. "But your question was about what I was thinking then, not about what I might think now as I talk to you. If you are looking for the reasons— past reasons— for why I did what I did." Kay realized she might even go so far as to say now that at the time she had thought Sedgewick psychotic and perhaps get away with it.

"You are clever, Kay, and very slippery. I think we will take a new approach now. For your next writing assignment I want you to describe— in detail— the beginning of your sexual relationship with Sedgewick."

Kay's stomach hollowed. "But I can't remember," she said. "It's been more than twenty-five years!"

"You'll remember— if you have to." Elizabeth moved to the desk to fetch her bag and coffee cup.

"It doesn't work that way, Elizabeth!"

Elizabeth went to the door. "I know all the details myself." She pressed her thumb into the thumb-lock plate. "And if I know them, you should be able to recall at least some of them. I'll expect it to be done by noon. Good night, Kay." Kay slumped down on the bed. There was no doubt about it. Elizabeth was far worse to deal with than Sedgewick and at least as shrewd. She would have made a brilliant Jesuit in the early modern days of international Jesuit intrigue.

Chapter Twenty-three

[i]

Minutes after Elizabeth's stereo had arrived, she invited Allison to spend a few hours in the evening listening. And that evening, Allison went upstairs to listen to it. The EMP had wiped out almost every stereo system in existence, though fortunately not the laserdisks themselves, so that anyone with the clout and money to have a new stereo system made could use the compact disks that were everywhere lying around in disuse. Elizabeth had not had any CDs to hand (since she had nothing in Colorado that had been hers in DC) but had easily acquired them since almost no one in the Denver area had any use for them.

Lying on the floor beside Elizabeth, listening to Chopin's E-minor piano concerto and staring into the fire, Allison almost forgot the fact that the Marq'ssan had zapped everything. But when the concerto was over, Elizabeth shattered the illusion. "Alice Warner called me this afternoon. Her service-tech was badly beaten and raped last night. I of course will find out who— I gather the attackers were Security service-techs, from what Alice got out of the unit-mates who were present at the onset of the attack. And when I find out, they must be punished."

Allison, now sitting up, stared down at Elizabeth's cold, taut face. "Anne? You're talking about Anne?"

"Is that her name? Yes, the one you have been seeing."

"Is she all right?"

"She's in the infirmary. There are broken bones and some internal injuries, but of course she'll recover— physically, at least. Every time this happens—" Elizabeth broke off with a sound of disgust.

"I don't understand how it could have happened— or why," Allison said. She was so full of anger she could hardly think. "How could Anne have let herself be raped? Or her unit-mates allowed it?"

Elizabeth sighed. "What do you mean, *let*, Allison? I doubt she has any inclination for men. The proof of that is in the injuries she sustained. As for her unit-mates, they were undoubtedly too frightened to do anything when these men dragged her off. I gather resentment has been growing toward the girls who won't go with men. There are more men than girls at the Rock, and we've put the locals off-limits. The girls who aren't heterosexual keep to themselves, and the men get angry. Add to that her being black… I suppose they thought they'd make this girl an example."

"Damn it, why didn't they fight? It burns me up that service-tech men think they can have any service-tech girl they want!"

Elizabeth sat up and leveled her steady blue gaze at Allison. "You know very well why they didn't fight. Don't be coy about this, Allison. They didn't fight because they are socialized to be vulnerable."

"Well I think they should at least be taught how to defend themselves! It's not fair that they can be beaten and raped and intimidated. And the idea of these men thinking—"

Elizabeth interrupted. "For the birthing fuck, Allison, the better I get to know you the more convinced I become that Vivien did an incredibly sloppy job of raising you! Where do you get ideas like *fair*?" She shook her head. "No, don't tell me, I already know. From novel-reading." She snorted. "It's all right to read that stuff for understanding professional and service-tech culture and values, Allison. But to be uncritically adopting concepts like *fair*?" She shook her head again. "I wish you'd think a little more clearly about things. Nothing in nature is *fair*. You won't find a single instance of justice or fairness in nature. Survival is what determines how things work. The best we can hope for is to make things as livable as possible while we go about preserving culture and maintaining stability. But forget *fairness*. That's one of those anachronistic idealisms we leave to professionals so self-righteously to mouth."

"But if I taught Anne just a few things— purely defensive things, Elizabeth—"

"No," Elizabeth said, "you're not to teach her anything. Soon she'd be learning other things on her own and then teaching her unit-mates who would in turn teach others..."

"But all this heterosexual nonsense!" Allison cried. "Every time I hear of one of our girls getting pressured or picked on or raped and beaten— as though they're the ones who are wrong, when everyone knows heterosexuality is loathsome and perverse—"

Elizabeth got up and went to the stereo and punched in a new selection. "You know what unfixed males are like. They're uncontrolled beasts. Why do you think *our* males have themselves fixed? Heterosexuality for service-techs is absolutely essential, Allison. There's no point in your talking about getting rid of it. What in the hell would we do with all those men and their aggressions and frustrations at being powerless if their energies couldn't be channeled onto women? Just let it be. A simple demonstration of what happens to service-tech males who interfere with our girls will ensure that this will not happen again for a long time— among base people, anyway."

Allison poured more wine into her glass. "I want to be included in this, Elizabeth," she said through her teeth. "I want to be one of the ones to deal with the males who attacked Anne."

"Fine, Allison. As soon as I get a report from the people I've got investigating it, you'll be among the first to know."

Allison had to be satisfied with that. She lay back down again and closed her eyes to listen to the Beethoven piano sonata that had already started, but she heard little of the music. She could not stop thinking about Anne and Anne's victimization. Whatever Elizabeth said, it wasn't fair, and "fair" *did* mean something in certain contexts, whatever the wider political consequences.

[ii]

When in the morning Allison went to the infirmary to visit Anne, she found a service-tech sitting beside Anne's bed, holding her hand. Allison, standing just inside the door, asked: "Should I come back later?"

Anne's gaze moved from the girl's face to Allison's. "Lise!" Quickly she held her hands up to her face. "You shouldn't see me like this," she said in obvious embarrassment. "It's very ugly."

The other woman stood up. "I'll come back during my lunch break, Annie."

Anne took her hands from her face. "Thanks, Rosa. You're so good to me."

"Don't talk nonsense." She leaned over the bed and planted a kiss on Anne's mouth.

Were they lovers? Allison wondered with some pain and shock. It had never occurred to her that service-tech girls might be one another's lovers— she had always assumed— unconsciously— that the only sexual relationships between women were between executive-service-tech pairs...as though service-techs observed the same taboo executive women observed. But, Allison realized, that assumption was absurd, considering how little alike executives and service-techs were in general.

Allison waited until Rosa was almost to the door before approaching the bed. Anne looked fragile and small, her dark self swallowed up by the white sheets and bandages. "You mustn't think about your looks now, love." Allison smiled. "The important thing is your getting well." She sat on the chair the girl had vacated and took Anne's hand. "I've brought you something." She laid the gift-wrapped package on the bed.

"Would you open it for me?" Anne asked. One of her arms was in a cast from wrist to shoulder.

Allison tore off the wrapping, opened the box, and held up the purple- and black-flowered cotton nightgown. "It's got lots of Velcro fastenings— to make it easy for you to get on and off," Allison said. "I'm sure it will be a lot more comfortable than that thing you're wearing."

"That's nice of you, Lise," Anne said.

"Are you in much pain, love? You look dreadfully uncomfortable."

Anne smiled effortfully; so much of her face was swollen that Allison wondered if it hurt her to smile. "They're feeding me codeine, so it's not too bad." Was the liquid dullness of Anne's eyes an effect of the drug?

"If there's anything you want, or anything I can do, you make them call me, Anne. Even if it's the middle of the night and you just need to talk."

"Did you make your deadline the other night?"

Allison's mind went blank; it took her a few seconds to recollect that the last time she had been with Anne she had been scrambling to get a report finished. "Just in time. I was up most of the night, though," Allison said. "I feel so stupid when I end up doing things like that in a rush, racing the clock. But there just doesn't seem to be enough hours in the day."

"You work so hard, Lise," Anne said. "It makes me feel lucky to have only my scheduled hours."

"Alice never asks you to stay late?"

"Hardly ever. But our office is much calmer than the Chief's office."

Silence fell, and Allison felt that the only thing they could say was being said by their hands, still clasped. "We are going to find your attackers, Anne," she said after a while.

Anne's lips trembled visibly. "Some people came by with a data base that had hundreds of photos of base employees. I've already identified them."

"They will pay," Allison said, her throat choking up as she saw that Anne's eyes had gone glassy.

Anne pulled her hand away; looking down at it, Allison saw that it had clenched into a fist. Anne said in a voice that seethed with emotion that seemed all the more intense for being very low, "They're beasts!" Tears overflowed her eyes. "I've never hated anyone the way I hate them."

"We can't undo what has happened, but we can at least punish them," Allison said.

"We had all just gotten off the bus," Anne whispered. "Those of us who don't go with men were together, as usual. Earlier, while waiting at the base for a large enough group to form for the bus to

leave, a couple of guys who've hit on us before came over and started hassling us. But we hung tight together, and since it was on base and there were lots of guards around, they eventually left us alone. But when the bus let us off at the guardpost and we started off toward our units, there were only three of us walking together to our end of the settlement. It was dark, you know, there aren't many outside lights in the settlement. I think those guys were following us, stealthy-like, because we didn't notice them until we'd gotten far in. And then they ran at us, and when I tripped, they grabbed me. Jeanette and Sherry kept on running and got away. I couldn't get loose. I thought I was going to suffocate. One of them stuffed his jacket over my mouth and nose. They dragged me part way across the settlement— I couldn't say where now— and into a unit…" Anne gasped. "It was horrible."

Allison barely held onto her temper. "How many were there, love?"

"Three." Tears streamed down Anne's face. "I didn't have a chance." But, Allison thought, if Anne and her friends had had even a smattering of self-defense skills they could at the very least have run them off, if not fought them in earnest.

Allison stood up. "I have to go now, but I'll drop by later. And of course I'll come this evening. Remember what I said. If you need anything I can get or arrange for you, or if you need me, you tell them to call me. I'll tell them, too. Okay, sweetheart?"

Anne, still tearful, nodded. "I'm glad you came, even if I am a mess."

"You are beautiful, and nothing those bastards did can change that," Allison said. She bent to kiss Anne's hand. "See you later."

After talking to the head nurse and giving her instructions about calling her, Allison headed for her office. Elizabeth would have the names of the attackers now and be ready to discuss what they should do to them. Allison would have liked to drop them into a vat of boiling oil. But she would settle for beating the shit out of them.

[iii]

When she got home from work Martha found Ariadne Sweetwater curled up on the couch in the living room. "It's my turn to attend the

Steering Committee meeting," Ariadne said after hugging Martha. "Poor Beatrice was always getting stuck with it, but she's got a bad cold now and should stay in bed, especially at her age. I haven't been in Seattle for months, so I don't mind— much."

Martha flopped down onto the other end of the couch. She was exhausted. "When did you get in?"

"A little before noon. I walked around a lot this afternoon. Things sure are different."

"How so?" Martha asked, curious.

"Tense," Ariadne said, her face scrunching up in concentration. "And all the flyers and pamphlets people kept giving me to read! Downtown, I couldn't walk half a block before being leafleted. What's all this about *elections*, anyway?"

Martha grimaced. "There's a Committee for the Establishment of Government— COMEG, for short, that's meeting while the Steering Committee meeting is in session. A sort of counter-Co-op movement. They're trying to get enough organization to hold citywide elections and form some kind of government. So now we're locked into a kind of coalition scramble. COMEG is trying to splinter the Co-op, and the Co-op's trying to woo those COMEG people who aren't completely set on government but who are dissatisfied with the way the Co-op's handling things."

Ariadne shook her fuzzy head. "We haven't heard anything about this at Sweetwater. Sounds serious."

"It could be," Martha admitted. "At first we didn't pay much attention to it. But Toni Farren has joined up with COMEG, and she's been getting a growing amount of support among what people around here like to call the 'moderates.'" At Ariadne's raised eyebrows, Martha snorted. "Yes, 'moderates,'" she said. "We now have leftists— that's us anarchists, and rightists— COMEG and the strong-government types, and moderates— Toni Farren and anyone leaning towards government who has so far been in any way communicating with us." Martha sighed. "I don't know what's going to happen, Ari. Armed guards have sprung up all around the city; the merchants hire them. And there are daily demonstrations by pro-election types,

there's the Reproductive Rights issue, and to top it off, some of the foreign people we've been trading with are caving in to some kind of pressure from executive governments to refuse to do business with us except in hard currency."

"You sound depressed, Martha."

"And you sound surprised that I could be depressed about all this," Martha said.

"Well, I am. In the past you've always been so upbeat whenever there have been seemingly insuperable problems..." Ariadne slanted a narrow look at Martha. "How's your private life these days?"

Martha rolled her eyes and folded her arms over her chest. "It's nonexistent, Ariadne, if it's my love-life you're talking about."

Ariadne stared at her, then smiled gently. "How quaint. Your 'love-life.' What about friendship? Or sex?"

Martha lifted her feet onto the coffee table and slid down in her chair to stretch her spine. "My friends are still as wonderful as always. Though I don't seem to see people much outside of working with them. As for sex? Nonexistent is the most accurate way to put it."

Ariadne shook her head. "Shame on you, Martha. You should know better. How can you be surprised that things are getting you down when you're treating yourself so badly? There's more to life than work."

Martha raised her eyebrows. Dinner would be ready in about twenty minutes, she thought.

"I suppose this is all because of your breaking up with Louise."

Martha stared at Ariadne. *What the fuck?* "Has Beatrice been talking about me?"

"Of course not!" Ariadne sounded indignant. "But certain things are pretty damned obvious, Martha Greenglass. So I take it you're giving up on ever getting involved in a sexual relationship again?"

Martha's stare became a glare. "With a woman, you mean?"

Ariadne frowned. "I suppose that's what I mean. I meant that in particular. Why, do you think you can't have sexual relationships with women? And that the reason you broke up with Louise was because she was a woman?"

"No, that's not the reason we broke up," Martha said irritably. "I wish people would stop trying to figure out why I broke up with Louise. The fact that I did is enough. It's been three months now. I think that makes it clear that it's for good."

"I didn't mean to pry," Ariadne said. "I was just wondering if you wanted to talk. Since Louise was your first woman..."

Martha moved her feet off the table and stood up. "I think I'll go wash. See you at dinner."

Martha trudged up the stairs. Sweetwater women were too used to knowing everything about everybody, too into taking care of one another: only that could explain why they thought they could act the same with non-Sweetwater friends. They probably didn't realize how intrusive this seemed to somebody not in their family. Martha knew she would go nuts living at Sweetwater. She needed her privacy to keep herself sane.

Especially now.

[iv]

Allison stripped, then stuffed every article of clothing she had been wearing— including her soft boots— into the trash bin. Before getting in the tub to soak she stood under a hot shower with her eyes closed, visualizing filth sloughing off her skin, washed down the drain by the steaming needle-sharp water. When she felt sufficiently cleansed, she got out of the shower, poured herself a large cognac, and climbed into the hot bath. She could not have stood going into the Jacuzzi with Elizabeth as Elizabeth had suggested. She needed this time alone to get hold of herself.

The deadness, the exhaustion, the failure to slake her anger weighed on her along with this new knowledge of herself. Her world had cracked open— her anger over the assault on Anne having elicited an unreasoning savagery she hadn't known lay hidden under her own skin, lying in wait ready to emerge given the catalyst of certain circumstances. She hadn't even noticed Elizabeth or Alice until the moment they pulled her away from that beast she had marked out as her own target (telling Elizabeth and Alice, "*Him* I will take, *he* did the worst things, *he* is *mine*"), she had not even seen Alice and

Elizabeth taking on the other two, had not been aware of anything except the meting out of justice and the exertion of her rage.

Elizabeth's car and the van accompanying them for the arrest that would follow had drawn the attention of most of the settlement. Enough people had seen the state the men were in when they were put into the van for word to spread through the settlement. And after tomorrow, when word of the castration surgery got out, everyone on base would know. The example made would, Allison was willing to bet, be highly effective.

But Anne would still have to live with it. Lying in the tub with her eyes closed, Allison swore to herself that she would try in some way to make up for it to her. She could not get out of her mind how defenseless Anne was— and defenseless for the sake of preserving the executive system. Anne was a casualty of the system Allison helped run. Undoubtedly Elizabeth was correct about how the overall benefits outweighed such casualties, yet guilt wrenched at Allison's guts, made her sick and nauseated, grieved her. It would have been far better if Anne could have defended herself. No matter how much she thought about it, it always came down to that. But she knew she must keep this conclusion to herself. And so her sense of guilt took on the pale fervid secrecy of some disgusting slimy maggot wriggling and crawling beneath a rock.

The cognac burned her empty, heaving stomach; the hot bathwater scathed her scraped raw knuckles. She could not put off getting out much longer, or Elizabeth would be calling, wondering what was taking her so long. She really didn't want to see her. The three of them riding the rest of the way to the village in the back of Elizabeth's car had not spoken to one another, nor even looked at one another's dishevelment. There had been only the heavy sound of their gradually slowing breathing in the dark among them, until Alice had gotten out at her apartment complex. En route to Elizabeth and Allison's complex, Elizabeth had suggested Allison use her Jacuzzi and warned that she would be sore if she did not. Allison had demurred, saying she wanted a shower first. Of course Elizabeth's bathroom also had a shower, but Elizabeth must have understood Allison needed to be

alone, for she said only "Fine. Why don't you come up when you've finished bathing and I'll prepare something light for us to eat." Allison hadn't been able to think of an excuse for declining and thus had assented. But what she really wanted was an evening sitting in the dark drinking herself into a stupor.

Elizabeth greeted Allison with a smile and a glass of wine. "My fiercest of warriors," she said, handing Allison the wine glass. "You were magnificent. Even taking Alice's and my adrenaline rushes into account, you were a positive fury!"

Elizabeth's approval ran over Allison like a shockwave, leaving her shaken. "I was so angry," she said.

"And that was the first time you ever went after someone intending injury, wasn't it."

Allison nodded dumbly and sipped the wine. The unreality of the moment seemed intensified by the crackling fast fire and the crisp Brandenburg Concerto on the stereo.

"Some sort of territorial instinct, I believe," Elizabeth said, leading the way out to the kitchen.

Allison wanted to protest: she felt no territorial claim to Anne whatsoever! If this had happened to any woman she knew and in any way cared for, she would have felt the same. Elizabeth *didn't* understand this. Sitting on a stool at the long woodblock worktable, Allison watched Elizabeth make their omelet and knew she would not be able to eat it, or that if she did eat it she wouldn't be able to keep it down.

"I've arranged," Elizabeth said, pouring the egg mixture into foaming butter, "to have their wages garnished for the next five years— by five percent each, with that amount to be paid to your Anne. And I will make it clear to those animals that if they leave their jobs with Security within that time-period they'll never get another job, anywhere. Bar the Free Zone, of course."

Allison remembered Elizabeth's last words to the men as they were being put into the van, words she must have known would carry to the crowd watching from a safe distance: *We won't tolerate anyone interfering with our girls. Let this be a warning to anyone who thinks he can get away with it.*

Elizabeth slid the omelet onto the hot platter she had taken from the warming oven, poured the sauce over the omelet, and garnished it with sprigs of herbs and slices of fruit. "Crab and cheese inside, avocado and lime sauce outside, Allison. Have you ever had that combination before?"

"Never."

"I think you'll want white wine with it. There's a half-bottle of Sauvignon Blanc in the refrigerator chilling for you."

Allison took the wine from the refrigerator and followed Elizabeth into the dining room. "I don't think I can eat, Elizabeth," Allison said when Elizabeth began to serve her a portion of the omelet.

Elizabeth glanced at her; Allison saw sympathy in her eyes, now a lustrous deep blue. "I know how it is, you probably have a wildly upset stomach. But I think it would be a good idea for you to try to eat something. I'll give you a wee portion, and you can chew on a roll— bread is easy on the digestion— and see if your stomach doesn't settle after all."

Allison poured wine into the fresh glass already sitting beside her plate. "Let's not talk about it any more tonight," she said. "I'm sick of the whole thing."

"I'm glad to hear you're interested in talking about something else. Frankly, I wanted to pour out my woes to you. I'm feeling rather depressed lately. There are so many problems cropping up, and faster than I seem able to cope with them."

Elizabeth didn't sound particularly worried, Allison thought. She said, "Well at least the proprietary's reports are good so far. And it's reassuring to know that it's setting off an economic chain reaction because of all the things we need to be produced to make the project go. It's as though every component requires the production of dozens of other materials."

"But you see," Elizabeth said, buttering a roll, "part of the reason it's so hard getting everything started again is the intense interconnectedness of it all. It's just that we're pushing so hard, organizing things from the outside. And we don't know yet that some little link in the chain won't hang us up in a catastrophic way."

Since when had Elizabeth become a pessimist? Allison tore a piece off the roll she had taken and held it for a moment in her fingers. "If it's not the proprietary that's worrying you, what is?"

Elizabeth swallowed a bite of omelet. "Several things," she said. "Several things are worrying me. I've gotten a report that makes it clear that the cleanup projects Science & Technology promised to execute haven't yet gotten off the ground."

Allison raised her eyebrows. She had no idea what Elizabeth was talking about.

"At the time of the EMP, we had partial meltdowns at most online nuclear power plants," Elizabeth said.

Partial melt-down? Jesus! Civil war or not, how had the remnants of the Executive managed to keep *that* quiet?

Elizabeth continued. "The Acting Secretary of Sci & Tech swore he would get the cleanup accomplished within a reasonable timeframe. But he hasn't done shit. Which means that not only do we still have godawful disasters sitting around, but we're far from the point of being able to resurrect the plants. If indeed we want to, that is. When I think of how the Free Zone has already cleaned up— and permanently shut down— all *their* nuclear plants..." Elizabeth paused to eat another bite. "The problem is that I can't turn the screws to make that idiot get off his ass. I need Sedgewick to do that. And it won't be easy getting Sedgewick to stir himself. Second, I need Sedgewick to meet with his Military counterpart— we're almost to the point of setting up a secret top-level meeting. I was hoping I'd be able to use Zeldin to assist me with Sedgewick, but—" Elizabeth shook her head and doggedly swallowed another bite. "You must have noticed from the tapes that I have in some way lost control of *that* situation."

Baffled, Allison asked, "What do you mean, Elizabeth, about getting Zeldin to assist you— ?"

Elizabeth put her napkin to her lips. Her eyes looked thoughtfully into Allison's. "The only way I'm going to succeed in getting Sedgewick out of this goddam funk he's in is through Zeldin."

"But... but doesn't he want her dead?" Allison asked in bewilderment, recalling how Sedgewick had thrown his glass against the wall after Elizabeth had said something to him about using Zeldin.

"He *thinks* he does." Elizabeth's tone was scornful. "But if I had allowed Wedgewood to off Zeldin, Sedgewick would have gone entirely down the tubes. Why the hell do you think he's in this state to begin with? Because of his thing about her, and her having betrayed him! She— or rather I should say his obsession with her, which I admit are two distinctly different things— has been a sort of *raison d'être* with him for years and years. While the world was falling apart before our very eyes he was thrown into a state of wild excitement, mixing fantasy with reality." Allison sent Elizabeth a look of confused inquiry. "Because he finally managed to get Zeldin working for him again," Elizabeth said patiently. "But when it didn't work out, everything came crashing down around his ears. And he spent the next year and a half obsessing over her apprehension and wanting her dead." Elizabeth sopped up the remaining sauce on her plate with her roll. "But does he *really* want her dead? No. Of course he doesn't. What he wants is a reinstatement of his fantasy. But he's suspicious and doesn't actually believe it *can* be reinstated. He's been terribly hurt, he doesn't want to risk hoping. That's why once I've finished rehabilitating Zeldin he will resist a little— but not a lot. He will be afraid of getting burned again. But he won't be able to resist the temptation."

Though Allison like everyone else working in Security had always been curious about the Chief, she hated to hear Elizabeth talk about him this way; it really gave her the shivers. "But I thought... I thought you wanted her to take the rap for starting the civil war? How can that happen and the other—" Allison didn't know what to call the plan Elizabeth had just revealed— "thing happen too?" Did Elizabeth actually intend to manipulate Sedgewick to that extent? This was the Chief of Security she was talking about!

"If I can get Zeldin in shape and use her to get Sedgewick in shape, none of the other stuff will matter in the least," Elizabeth said. "Especially if Sedgewick pulls off— with my assistance—" Elizabeth grinned— "the stunning coup of ending this damned war with Military."

"So then Wedgewood would take the rap."

"I refuse to concern myself with those details right now. The real problem is Zeldin. Everything was going so promisingly, and now..." Elizabeth's eyes clouded. "I may be losing her. It's that simple. I'm trying to rethink my strategy. I've miscalculated, yet again, the depth of her interior resources. If I continue in this direction she will crack on me. In fact, she's very close to the edge now. It's clear I can't continue these bouts of punishing her as I've been doing. She's terrified of being punished— the way she pleads with me and cries is proof enough of that— yet she simply will not cooperate with me. As though what I want her to do is far more horrible to her than the punishment."

"She certainly does sound miserable on the tapes," Allison said. "As though she doesn't really want to defy you, but can't help herself."

"Are you going to join me in a cup of coffee?" Elizabeth asked.

"No thanks." As if she weren't already wired.

"Then I'll meet you in the living room. Just leave everything. The girl can clean this up in the morning." Elizabeth swished out to the kitchen. Allison looked down at her plate: she had eaten only a small piece of the roll and one tiny bite of the omelet. She poured the rest of the wine into her glass and carried it out to the living room, where she sat on a cushion by the fire, leaning forward to poke the half-burned smoldering logs into flame. She still could not bring herself to sit on Elizabeth's sofa again. The memory of the night they had sat there and Elizabeth had broken it off was still painful.

When Elizabeth came in she sat on the sofa. Allison wondered if Elizabeth habitually drank an after-dinner cup of coffee there. "The last time I pulled her out of the closet," Elizabeth said, "I had to stay most of the night with her. Until I finally injected her with a sedative. She got hysterical at the sight of the syringe— I suppose she thought it was a paralytic... She couldn't even form coherent sentences that night. Since then she's been very withdrawn and what I'm tempted to

call paranoid." Elizabeth sipped from the demitasse, then set the cup down on the low table and tucked her legs up under her gown.

Allison listened to the fire crackle and burn, aware of its warmth on her back. "I need a new approach, Allison," Elizabeth said after a long pause. "I wish I didn't feel under so much pressure about Zeldin. I thought I would have a longer grace period before I needed to start worrying. If I can't get things straight with Sedgewick, everything might explode in my face. All it would take would be a little concern among certain Cabinet men, and that would be it." She sighed. "Do you know that Booth has never even acknowledged my existence? After all this time?"

Allison hugged her knees to her chest. "Sometimes with them it's as though we aren't there," she said. "But for this to happen with you, Elizabeth...seems incredible to me."

Elizabeth's smile was a wry spasm twitching her mouth. "Why? Because I have so much power? It's all officially nonexistent, you know. Much of it hinges on Sedgewick's never failing to rubber-stamp me, though practically speaking it's taken me years to build up my own network of power. But you see, though they all know I exist—and have for years: Sedgewick often relayed to me his peers' attitudes about me— that unofficial recognition is far from acceptance. They put up with my exercise of power because they have no choice. And they put up with it with poor grace because they don't want to see someone outside their very close ranks ever penetrate again. And so in a sense I haven't penetrated, for my penetration is invisible. But though my exercise of power is for the most part invisible, sometimes it's necessary to be visible. And in such instances..." Elizabeth choked out a sort of laugh. "It's so absurd, Allison. Think of how someone like Wedgewood sees the world: he imagines that to be powerful means to forcefully assault and lay waste everything around him. But the truth of the matter is that by using open aggression he only demonstrates how truly feeble is his control, how weak his power. One resorts to force only when one has otherwise lost control." Elizabeth shook her head. "As I obviously have with Zeldin," she said ruefully.

Allison once again found Elizabeth's astuteness and insight into their world breathtaking. What she said about physical force was true, so obviously true! It was the sort of thing one never thought of oneself— and the sort of thing that would never be said openly, even by people who knew it, for it was likely to be considered heretical. Unless, of course, in higher circles— Sedgewick's, for instance— such things were commonly known and understood? Had she missed all this during her university days? So much that she had learned since her transfer to this base seemed new yet elementary. It was as though she had been walking in a muzzy, naive fog for years and years. If she were to return to Vienna now, would she see everything differently? "You seem very worried about Zeldin," Allison said in her most sympathetic voice.

"I am," Elizabeth said. "I had the idea that if I could force a breakthrough on her— a breakthrough into her memory and her misperceptions about herself and her past relationship with Sedgewick— that the rest would be easy. Making her see herself, question her more recent perceptions and judgments, and come to terms with it in a way directed by me. But I can't seem to force the breakthrough. Which means I have to give up that idea for now and think of another way of—" Elizabeth frowned. "Hmmm," she said after a while. "There's some vague idea chasing around in my head... Maybe I'll be able to get hold of it later. I think though that for now I should try to leave it."

Elizabeth sprang off the sofa and went to the stereo. Allison watched her key in her choice. She had always known Elizabeth lived in a different world, at a different level, than herself. But until recently she hadn't known how significant the differences were. Elizabeth knew and understood so much, she was so solid, so rocklike in her very being. The complexities that Elizabeth comprehended without even consciously thinking about them meant that she operated at a level of experience and understanding far beyond what Allison could appreciate even when certain aspects and connections were spelled out to her. Elizabeth was, in short, an awesome human being. Now Elizabeth turned away from the stereo, and Allison added to herself

that Elizabeth was beautiful, graceful, controlled. That this one woman embodied so much took her breath away.

Elizabeth did not return to the sofa but knelt beside Allison. Allison's immediate response was to feel a desire to move away. She did not want to have to go through the painful and frustrating emotions being physically near Elizabeth educed. Awkwardly Allison began to rise, thinking she would use her empty wine glass as an excuse. But Elizabeth put her hand on Allison's arm, stopping her. Discomfited by a surge of feelings and the need to conceal those feelings from Elizabeth, Allison stared down at Elizabeth's hand. "Don't desert me," Elizabeth said softly.

Allison had trouble controlling her laugh. "I'm only going to get more wine," she said unsteadily.

Elizabeth's fingers pressed into Allison's flesh. "You are always avoiding me, Allison. Do you think I haven't noticed?"

Allison's face burned. "Please, Elizabeth," she said, unsure of what it was she wanted to ask of Elizabeth, still staring down at Elizabeth's hand.

Elizabeth's other hand lifted and turned Allison's face toward her own. Allison looked at her through the blur of tears welling up in her eyes. "Please what?" Elizabeth said. "You won't let me near you, Allison. It hurts me. I think you're angry at me. After all these years, to have you build a wall between us...and especially now, when I need you so much."

"I have to protect myself," Allison whispered. "I've never wanted to hurt you. But I have to protect myself!"

"Protect yourself against what?" When Allison didn't answer, Elizabeth pressed her. "Against me?"

Allison shook her head. She couldn't talk, her throat was too tight for words to pass.

"Why are you crying, darling?"

"It's been a long day," Allison said, her voice ragged. "Maybe if I went and washed my face—" She again tried to get up.

"All evening I've been wanting to kiss you, Allison," Elizabeth said.

Allison's gaze returned to Elizabeth's face. "Why are you doing this, Elizabeth? Can't we just please..." Allison's voice trailed off, for she didn't want to say that they should forget their affair, or pretend it hadn't happened, for both those were impossible, and if it weren't impossible doing so would only degrade them. What she wanted was for Elizabeth to be careful of her feelings. But she wasn't supposed to have those feelings in the first place, so she couldn't openly demand this of Elizabeth. What she wanted was for Elizabeth to understand and be careful without their explicitly acknowledging that that was what was happening. Elizabeth *must* know. Mustn't she?

Elizabeth took her hand from Allison's arm. "You are angry," she said, "or you wouldn't be rejecting me. Unless you've already lost interest? Are you that attached to your little service-tech?"

Allison let the wine glass fall from her fingers onto the carpet. "You know that's not true," she said very low. "You said, you said we couldn't..."

"I know what I said, darling. But I'm afraid I'm very selfish. It's too difficult working with you and seeing you and talking with you and not being able to make love to you, it distracts me, wanting you so and knowing I can't have you. Well we've tried. Let's simply admit that it's no good."

Allison dug her fingernails into her palm. She should be happy that Elizabeth still wanted her, but instead she felt torn apart. There had already been so much pain... She should tell Elizabeth that they must not start again, that she didn't want that now, that she had been growing a callous and with a little more time would be insensitive to much of the pain.

Elizabeth's arm slid around her waist and pulled her close. Allison kept very stiff and still, trying to keep herself from responding to Elizabeth's long, slow kiss. But her sexual self overrode the warnings clamoring in her head, and she let Elizabeth lay her down on the rug and open her gown.

Afterwards, when they lay quietly catching their breaths, Allison buried her face in her arms to hide her tears. She had thought when imagining such a scene that she would feel ecstatically happy. But

she had imagined wrong, for she felt lost. For a moment she hated Elizabeth for having hurt her so needlessly. But after a while the hatred ebbed and she felt merely sad and depressed.

Her thoughts returned, then, to Anne lying alone with her injuries in the infirmary.

Chapter Twenty-four

[i]

Kay lay curled on her side with the pillow clutched to her chest, staring at the colors in the thin Indian cotton bedspread. No matter how much she dozed— for she seldom managed to sustain deep sleep— she could not seem to shake her exhaustion. She hardly got out of bed now at all, except to drink water, urinate, and wash. Because several days had passed since the last time Elizabeth had let her out of the closet, Kay began dreading the next round of punishment. Elizabeth had asked nothing of her since then, had only dropped in— she said— to "visit." The book sat on the desk, but Elizabeth had said nothing more about Kay's being required to write in it. She had not asked Kay to promise anything when letting her out of the closet. But Kay knew another confrontation over the book was inevitable.

How long could this go on? If there were any way of killing herself quickly she would do it now. Her mind and emotions were deteriorating. She could not stop remembering how when Elizabeth had opened the door to the shower she had clung to the front of Elizabeth's tunic shrieking in panic at the thought of being made to go into that small dark space. "Think of how nice you'll feel after," Elizabeth had said, as though reasoning with a child. Finally Elizabeth had taken off her own clothes and gone into the shower with her, washing Kay's body and hair as if she were an idiot or a child unable to care for herself. Drying her, she had scolded Kay about not eating enough and had opened the box of scented powder and dusted her body with it. The smell had evoked a memory she could not put a name or place to... Sometimes Kay got out of bed and went to the box, opened it, and sniffed. Where had she smelled this particular scent before? The sense of familiarity haunted, disturbed, eluded her.

Perhaps she had not tried hard enough to find a way out of the maze. But now she was too weary, too worn down, too dull. Perhaps this was the state into which Elizabeth had from the first been hoping to get her? Unable to hold onto the thought long enough to explore it, she drifted into a daze half-despair, half-sleepiness.

Elizabeth, dazzling in pale yellow wool, came to see her at four. "Good morning, Kay."

"Good morning, Elizabeth." It was always the same, except when she was in the closet.

Elizabeth stood by the side of the bed and stared down at her. "What have you eaten today?"

Kay tried to remember, but nothing came to mind. It was all the same. "The usual," she said. "Tubefood."

"One tube? Two? Three? And what in particular?"

Kay shook her head. "I don't remember. All that stuff's the same. I eat as much as I can stomach, and then stop."

"You don't remember what you ate in the last eight hours?" The blue eyes were skeptical.

"No. All the days spent in this cell are the same. The food is the same. There's no particular reason to remember."

"From now on you're going to write down what you eat as you eat it," Elizabeth said. "And there will be other measures taken. Now get up. We're going to the infirmary."

"The infirmary! Please, Elizabeth, I haven't refused to eat, there's no reason—" Kay's heart raced so hard it seemed about to break through her chest wall.

"Don't argue with me, Kay. Just get up."

"Please, it's not necessary, I'll eat whatever you like right now!"

"Stop whining and do as I say." Elizabeth's tone brooked no dispute. Kay got out of bed and stood on shaky legs. She was not surprised when Elizabeth handcuffed her wrists together. At least this time she was not wearing electric blue leotard and tights as she had always been wearing on previous trips to the infirmary, though now her feet and legs were naked, and her appearance was still odd enough to attract attention. But she felt less ridiculous and less exposed in the

nightshirt, though by the time they reached the infirmary her feet and ankles were icy cold and she almost wished for the tights.

As they passed the guards at the infirmary entrance Elizabeth instructed them that they were to be sure Kay did not leave the infirmary without Elizabeth's "direct and personal" orders. Inside, Elizabeth steered Kay to a different room from the one they had on the other occasions gone into. A nurse already in the room nodded at Elizabeth and told Kay to step on the scale. Kay obeyed and stared at the reading in LEDs: according to this scale, she weighed eighty-nine pounds. Which *had* to be wrong. Next the nurse extended the metal rule from the scale and measured her height. While the nurse was keying the data into the desk terminal, the door opened and a doctor came in. Kay recognized him, and a wave of panic engulfed her.

"Madam," he said, nodding to Elizabeth. His gaze wandered around the room and came to rest on Kay. "This is the prisoner we discussed this morning?"

"Yes," Elizabeth said.

He was still looking at Kay. "Then let's get on with it, shall we? Nurse, you have her current weight and height?"

"Weight eighty-nine point five pounds, height sixty-six inches," the nurse said.

The doctor gestured Kay to sit on the clinic couch. Horrified, she shrank back against the wall.

"Kay, go sit on the couch," Elizabeth said sternly.

Kay tore her gaze from the doctor to look at Elizabeth. "You *promised*, Elizabeth," she choked out. "You promised me. But you lied, didn't you!" Kay grew so faint and shaky that she could hardly stand, even with the wall at her back.

Elizabeth stared at her for a moment, then turned to the doctor. "Both of you wait outside until further notice."

The doctor and the nurse left the room and Elizabeth and Kay were alone together. "What did I promise, Kay?" Elizabeth asked softly.

Kay's eyes filled with tears. "You promised I wouldn't be tortured. Several times you promised."

"Yes, I did. Of what relevance is that to your refusing to cooperate with the doctor?"

Kay turned away, put her face against the wall, and broke into despairing sobs. She was destroyed now. There was no hope.

Elizabeth pulled her away from the wall, and Kay put her cuffed hands to her face. She heard the squeak of the stool, and then Elizabeth was pulling Kay down into her lap, pressing Kay's head against her breast, stroking Kay's back. "Calm yourself, Kay, there's no need for all this hysteria, calm yourself." Elizabeth crooned the words into Kay's ear. When Kay's sobs subsided, Elizabeth said, "Now tell me why you're so upset. I didn't lie to you, you know. What does Dr. Gordon have to do with my promise not to torture you?"

"That's what he does, I recognized him, and I know his name. He tortures people."

"Gordon? How do you know that?"

"I saw him. I saw him. Sedgewick made me watch him do it."

"Oh, yes, I remember now," Elizabeth said. "Sedgewick was terribly annoyed with you because you weren't keeping yourself enough under control. He so dislikes people being out of control... But listen to me, Kay." Elizabeth shifted Kay so that she had to sit up straight. Kay met Elizabeth's gaze. "Gordon is only going to examine you. I have no intention of letting him hurt you. I won't break my promise to you." Elizabeth stroked Kay's hair. "Your hair is growing so fast. Do you believe me, Kay? About Gordon?"

Kay swallowed. "Yes. I believe you."

"Good. Let's wash your face and let them get on with this. I don't much like infirmaries myself, you know." Elizabeth shifted Kay off her lap, stood up, and went to the sink where she wet a napkin. "Here," she said, handing it to Kay.

Kay listlessly swabbed her face. The hollow feeling and headache would be with her all day. If only she were left alone in this room there would be plenty of means at hand for suicide. She could not go through much more. The way she had collapsed against Elizabeth, the way she had let Elizabeth soothe her, meant she was lost. For a moment she had actually felt safe sitting clasped to Elizabeth's breast

like a child, though she knew that was absurd, for Elizabeth was the enemy. How could she have felt safe from Elizabeth in Elizabeth's own embrace? Yet for a moment, she had.

Elizabeth let Gordon and the nurse back into the room. Kay went docilely to the clinic couch and submitted to the physical examination while Elizabeth looked on. She half-hoped Gordon would discover she had some incurable disease. She was too tired to go on like this much longer, and she had run out of even the most covert resistance.

Elizabeth had finally defeated her.

[ii]

That week Martha and Ariadne shared the task of cleaning the cookware used to prepare dinner. On the third evening of Ariadne's visit, by the time they had gotten to the pots and pans they were well-launched into the issue of reproductive freedom, which was on Martha's mind, since the CFRRF would be making its first report to the Steering Committee in the morning. In the course of their discussion, Ariadne said, "The way I look at it, Martha, it's a problem of balance, which may in fact be the same problem the Co-op is having on a larger scale over the general question of government."

Martha was scrubbing a pot bottom with an abrasive chemical and steel-wool. "The problems are philosophically similar," she said. "But the way I see it, either you allow and encourage the expression of a great many voices, or you control expression— usually by silencing dissent, whether through the tyranny of a majority that claims its experience is the universal experience, or through the tyranny of a minority that claims it knows best. The former tyranny in this country during the twentieth century resulted in the latter tyranny as exercised by executives. You can think of reproduction as in some way like expression— either you limit it according to the dictates of a tyranny— whether of the majority or a minority— or you don't. It's that simple."

Ariadne put aside the pot she had been scrubbing and took up another. "But it's *not* that simple, Martha. Think of John Doyle and his cult! They want to use reproduction as a means of control and power for their own ends, and they don't give a flying fuck what happens to

the rest of the world. For them the world is only themselves. If you allow them to, they will become a tyranny."

Martha put what her mother called "elbow grease" into her fingers, where the beans had burned to the bottom of the pan. "You believe that? You think they could do that, merely by reproducing to their fullest capacity?"

"Everything I've heard about those people makes me think they're power-mongers. And the way they treat the women among them! Martha, those women would be turned into breeding machines! And other people would see it and copy them. Think of how having children has become such a power-related thing! It's not only status, but something else, too. I don't really get it, because I don't know many people who have a child. And now you're saying we should just throw this very politically and emotionally significant thing up for grabs?"

"Then you think there should be standards by which to judge who should be allowed to reproduce? Think, Ariadne: who decides what the standards are? It's tyranny again!"

"Not *standards*, Martha," Ariadne said. "But *limits*. Say on the number of children you can have. Something like that. Though I think I wish there were some way to limit the thing to people who are fit, I'm enough of a realist to know that there would be no way of avoiding political judgments and that therefore one has to let that be. But if John Doyle, for instance, could father only two children, the force of his power would be checked. Don't you see?"

Martha sighed. "I don't know. I suppose so. It's just that I worry about imposing things on people. I guess I just wish people would be socially and politically conscious enough to impose upon themselves."

"There, that's the last of these wretched pots. Are we ready for making up a rinse water?"

Martha checked all the pots, pans, lids, and implements to see that they had been scrubbed clean. "Yep. All set."

As they watched the water rise in the tub, Martha said wistfully, "You know that in restaurants and in houses where people can afford such things there are lots of dishwashers that combine heat, chemicals, and water to be extremely efficient, thereby using the least amount of water necessary for washing dishes. You can't have real dishes unless you have the most efficient of systems for cleaning them... Wouldn't it be nice if everyone could have such a dishwasher?"

Ariadne laughed. "Sure. But who can afford it?"

"In a world without an executive class? Maybe everyone could. I keep wishing we could get the ones abandoned at the time of the Withdrawal to work."

"They don't work because they're processor-operated?"

"Yeah. And there are too many more important things to fix before we can even think about such luxuries."

Carefully they dipped each item, saving the most chemically saturated until last.

"But of course," Ariadne said, "if the water situation weren't so bad you wouldn't even have to think about processor-run washers. I can't imagine what it was like even a century ago, when there was still plenty of uncontaminated ground water... Oh hey. Take the rapid pollution of ground water: now there's a fine example of what people will do when they aren't *imposed* upon, as you put it."

After they had dried all the cookware and put it away, they drew themselves beer from the keg in the pantry. Finding a heated political argument in progress in the living room, they went up to Martha's room to drink. There they sat cross-legged on the floor-level mattress Martha slept on and for a while discussed the "Counter-Steering Committee meeting" the COMEG people were holding each day the Steering Committee met.

"If the Marq'ssan weren't still on this planet, the Co-op would long ago have been finished," Martha said glumly. "People seem to be incurably brainwashed about needing to give institutional power to one small group of people."

"That's the way it is, Martha. You didn't really think that getting rid of government would change people's need for authoritarian structures, did you? It's a little like throwing a declawed house cat who has never known anything but life in the house out into the jungle. Such an animal would probably spend its entire life trying to find its way back to the house."

Martha set her empty cup down on the floor. "Yeah. But I'm hoping that since people have greater powers of reasoning and comprehension than cats the analogy has to break down. If the cat could *think*, don't you think it would gradually come to terms with its situation?"

Ariadne whooped with laughter. "Who says most people think, Martha?" she said when she had managed to stop laughing enough to be able to talk.

Martha slumped, resting her elbows on her knees and making a chin-rest of her clasped hands. "You don't seem overly troubled by any of this. It must be your sense of isolation on Whidbey."

"Hardly." Ariadne smiled. "Whidbey isn't an island paradise, you know. We have John Doyle, and then we have a lot of people in Oak Harbor who hate us and long to have the Navy back... Some of their sons are in the Navy or Guard, you know. Can you imagine how they feel, knowing that and living in the Free Zone? There must be lots of Seattle people in the same situation."

"In other words, the government was so entangled in people's lives that even without it in the Free Zone many people are still in its toils."

"Try to think of it from their point of view sometimes, Martha. It doesn't do any good to get mad at them. I know it's frustrating, but you have to consider how they're feeling and thinking— doing so is the only way we're going to be able to help them to see differently."

"Maybe," Martha said grudgingly.

They sat quietly for a time. Somewhere below a door slammed. Martha sighed. The person slamming out of the house was probably Laura's acquaintance Fred, an old-time socialist whom Laura thought must be nearly a hundred. Since he was a professional you couldn't really tell, because professionals generally could afford the longevity drugs and treatments... Martha thought of Beatrice. Why should professionals be allowed to live longer lives in better health than the rest of them? Instead of worrying about restoring fertility, maybe people should be concentrating on extending longevity to everyone. A thought occurred to Martha. "I've just realized something, Ariadne," she said out loud. "We don't have longevity drugs and treatments

in the Free Zone. Which means that all the professionals still living here won't be able to get them... Do you think they'll all start leaving when they realize that?"

"I never thought of that," Ariadne said slowly. "But then, why should we think of such a thing when we assume people start falling apart at sixty without fail... Look at Beatrice. But you're right..."

They relapsed into gloomy silence until Ariadne went downstairs to fetch another round. When she had returned, handed Martha her cup, and reseated herself, she said, "I know you don't like talking about your personal life. But there's something that I'd like to know. Before Louise, was your only sexual experience with that guy you met in high-school?"

"You mean Walt?" Martha asked. Ariadne nodded. "Yeah. Walt and only Walt. I was young. And once I started living with him and became a part of his organization it seemed unthinkable to even look at anyone else. That's the kind of scene it was."

Ariadne shook her head. "That's bad, Martha. It's makes sex so dull and serious, to always regard it as a kind of monogamy thing. Maybe what you need is to have a few flings. To be lighthearted about sex."

Martha stared at her. "Lighthearted? If you aren't that way to start with, how do you become that way? It's a little weird talking about *trying* to be lighthearted."

Ariadne laughed; her eyes sparkled. "Just an idea. I doubt you're interested in having a serious relationship right now, anyway. Or are you?" Martha shook her head. "Well then, there you go."

Martha sighed. "That may be easy for you to say, Ari, considering how you live at Sweetwater where such attitudes about these things predominate. I mean, you have a big group of like-minded women to choose partners from. But here...you never know what people have in mind about sex. I could find myself getting involved before I even realized it— or else find the other person is serious when I'm not. It's too easy to get hurt. Maybe celibacy is the best policy for someone like me."

"Martha! You talk like you're fifty years old!"

"Well."

"Have a fling with me," Ariadne said with a smile and a toss of her head. "I'm going back to Sweetwater in a week, so you'd know it can't be serious. Just for *fun*, Martha."

Shy and dubious, Martha looked over at Ariadne and found herself feeling very awkward. Could you simply say "let's have a fling" and do it? How would they start?

"Unless you're not in the least attracted to me," Ariadne said, still smiling.

Martha cleared her throat. "It's not that. I *am* attracted to you. But it seems sort of, well, a little cold, to decide to do it before doing it."

"Cold! Thanks, woman! Thanks a lot!"

Martha guessed Ariadne wasn't really affronted, though she wasn't entirely sure.

"What have we got to lose?" Ariadne asked softly.

Our friendship, Martha thought. And peace of mind. She shrugged. "Okay, I guess we could try it."

"Such enthusiasm," Ariadne said drily. "Let's not."

Martha swallowed a large mouthful of beer. She wondered what it was like to have a "fling." Is that what she had had with David Hughes? If so, flings weren't as lighthearted as Ariadne made them out to be. Maybe she just wasn't the fling type. Maybe Walt had been her speed, after all.

[iii]

Allison and Elizabeth did not get away from the base that night until well after ten. Because Elizabeth had been involved for most of the evening in an emergency meeting with the top people in Clandestine Services, Allison had not had a chance to give her a verbal report on her trip that day to Goodland, Kansas. And so on the drive home Elizabeth asked her if she had successfully negotiated arrangements for the meeting they hoped to hold there with Military people.

"I made the arrangements with the man you suggested to me," Allison said, "but I'm not sure that it's wise to hold the meeting there. On our way back to the base, near the border between Colorado and

Kansas, we encountered ground-fire." Allison shivered. "Have you ever been shot at in a helicopter, Elizabeth?"

"As a matter of fact I have."

"It felt like we were sitting ducks," Allison said, a little defensive at Elizabeth's matter-of-fact tone.

"It would take a lot to damage one of those birds," Elizabeth said drily. "They're as armored as most tanks. I hope the pilot reported this to Buckley?"

"I'm sure he has. It's standard operating procedure, he said. He theorized that the ground-fire wasn't necessarily Military's, but that a Security helicopter passing first once and then a second time might raise some hackles among the locals around there. If that's the case, Elizabeth, are you sure you want to risk having the meeting at Goodland? If any of your Military people turn up as casualties it could mean the end of any chance for resolution."

"I think that's a minor consideration," Elizabeth said. "Southern California is the alternative, and it's a damned sight riskier from that point of view. Not everyone will have adequate escort— keeping clear within the agreed upon radius, of course— so that any possible danger from ground-fire will be minimized. My only concern was that Pritchardt wouldn't come through."

"It always surprises me how coming up with the correct connections works," Allison said, thinking of how Pritchardt's attitude had changed when she had identified herself as the daughter of his third cousin three times removed.

Elizabeth laughed. "I don't think you have any notion of how important bloodlines are to them, darling. Especially now that people no longer have *that* many relatives. And of course it helped that you have a somewhat prestigious position with Security with which to impress him."

"Yeah," Allison said bitterly, "so it didn't matter that much that he probably wouldn't give Mason Bennett the time of day."

"You mustn't dwell on such things, darling. If I had brooded about my father's failure I would never have made it to where I am now."

Yes, but Elizabeth's father had killed himself, Allison thought callously, while her own father was still around to tell the tale. "It's curious, Elizabeth," Allison said, "that so many of the women we know in the career-line have fathers that are failures and wrecks."

Elizabeth snorted. "Darling! Consider who it is who is allowed to birth males. When there are girls birthed in one-child executive families, you can generally assume the father is a failure. And of course in such families the girls almost always *have* to take the career-line, unless they want to perpetuate the situation and contract with men like their fathers. It's almost impossible to arrange a decent maternity contract unless you have your own money to start with."

"That's why the maternal-line are so snobbish, I suppose," Allison said. When Elizabeth talked about such curiosities they always seemed to fall into place and become aspects of a larger pattern. Whereas Allison only noticed isolated instances that she could not make much sense of. How had Elizabeth figured so much of this out? Was it something that most people knew, but that Allison was too dense to pick up from social chitchat or learn for herself?

"The reason the maternal-line are snobbish, darling, is because they don't have enough to do and consequently feel on the outside of everything of importance," Elizabeth said. "They have all the leisure and wealth they could possibly want. But the bottom line is that someone like me has a great deal more power, even lacking the money and background. It must gall and frustrate them. And on top of that, they have to put up with the fathers of their children laying down most of the conditions for how they do the one thing that they do do— namely raise their children."

The car pulled into the garage of their apartment complex. "You make them sound pathetic," Allison said.

"Hardly pathetic, darling. I wouldn't feel sorry for them if I were you. I do think though that something must be done to tap their energy. Not only are they a resource we've been underutilizing, but the sorts of discontent that sometimes brew in such situations can be dangerous."

The car doors were opened and Allison and Elizabeth got out. Allison went up with Elizabeth in Elizabeth's elevator; she had left a gown in Elizabeth's apartment so that she wouldn't have to detour to her own apartment first.

After getting themselves drinks— wine for Allison and fruit juice for Elizabeth— they went straight into the Jacuzzi. Elizabeth stretched out and laid her head back on the rim of the tub.

"You look terribly tired," Allison said, noticing for the first time the dark circles under Elizabeth's eyes. "You've been working too hard."

"I have to," Elizabeth said. "I sent a request to Sedgewick that he come out here and handle this crisis himself, but this afternoon I got a purple from him saying that he's sure that with the assistance of Operations I can handle it myself." She sighed. "And I had put off the damned emergency meeting until the evening on the off-chance that he might respond to the urgency and fly in this afternoon and handle the meeting himself."

"There's a crisis, Elizabeth?" Allison carefully asked.

Elizabeth did not open her eyes. "Yes. Keep this to yourself. The indications are that the Russians might be preparing some kind of move on Eastern Europe. And since Military and Security aren't cooperating, we have one hell of a mess over there. US forces stationed in Europe are run by Military, while most intelligence operations— except Military's of course, which aren't really up to *our* standards— and all the NATO connections and most of our embassies are run by Security. It's a hell of a mess. If war should come..." Elizabeth sighed. "If I could only get Sedgewick to exert himself! He could handle all those fools at State...and this sort of thing isn't something I'm certain I'm capable of handling... I can't rely on Vernon Leonard to be making the major decisions... Frankly, the Executive should be handling this crisis, but there is nothing one can even *call* the Executive any more."

Russia moving in on Europe? How could Sedgewick and the other Cabinet members simply stand by twiddling their thumbs? It was insane! "But what about Mr. Booth?" Allison asked, grasping at straws.

Elizabeth opened her eyes. "Yes, what about him," she said quietly. "If I bring him into this now all sorts of undesirable things would likely happen. I have little doubt that if he got his foot in the door

here and thoroughly understood what is going on in Security— and he probably already has an idea, but for some reason hesitates to interfere— but if he were openly brought in, Sedgewick would probably be permanently retired and his position taken by someone else, probably an outsider. And then the shakeup in Security would start…" Elizabeth fell silent. Allison watched Elizabeth stretch her arms to hold her hands out against the powered streams of water shooting out of the nearest nozzle. "I'll go to Booth if I have to. But only if the situation is desperate."

Desperate? What did *that* mean? Allison said slowly, "The nuclear umbrella is dismantled, and we are engaged in our own civil war…and we've lost so much status because of the aliens…"

"Yes. And in fact most of our allies— or how long our allies, Allison?— most of *them* are far ahead of us in recovering from the EMP. And *China*… Some of the intelligence reports coming in make me very uneasy. If this goes on much longer we'll come to be considered utterly negligible geopolitically."

"The US always loses when there's rebellion in the ranks. Every cycle of rebellion among our allies always leaves the US a little weaker, a little more hated, even by countries operating on the executive system.

"Oh hell, I don't want to talk about this now," Elizabeth said. "Let's talk instead about today's breakthrough with Zeldin." Elizabeth smiled, and her eyes came to life. "I must be careful not to rush this, though I'm so anxious to get Sedgewick functioning. But with today's breakthrough I'm almost positive everything will work out with Zeldin."

What was Elizabeth talking about?

"You *did* have time to input today's recording, didn't you darling?"

"Yes," Allison said, "but I'm a little puzzled about why you think there was a breakthrough…?"

Elizabeth shook her head. "Really, Allison, you are totally without a clue when it comes to psychology, aren't you. You'd never be able to manage an interrogation, that's clear!"

Allison bit her lip. "Well explain it to me then. I'd like to understand."

"You recall Zeldin's reaction to Gordon?"

"Yes. She was terrified of him."

"Her response was to turn to me and remind me of my promise to her. The significance of her doing that struck me immediately. In short, Zeldin was in the first place admitting to me that she had trusted me, at least in this one thing. She could instead have flung a nasty sarcastic remark at me about how she had been right never to trust me, but since she didn't do that it is quite clear that in some very fundamental sense communication has been established between us."

"But I'm sure she *wanted*, even *needed* to believe that you had been telling her the truth about not torturing her," Allison said. "Why should it be so surprising that she felt let down and lied to when she thought you weren't keeping your promise?"

"It doesn't matter that she wanted and needed to believe me, darling. What matters is that deep down she did. Which means she on some important level trusts me. It's the trust factor with her that's so absolutely critical. She is very suspicious of me in general. But when it came to something important, it turned out she does trust me. And because that is so, I can be certain that she is relating more and more to me in an unalienated way. You see, in order to remain sane, Zeldin *must* relate to me at least part of the time as though there is the modicum of trust between us." Elizabeth boosted herself onto the rim and reached for the soap. "I had an idea last night for my new approach. With this breakthrough I'm more confident than ever that this new strategy will prove effective." Elizabeth lathered her arms, breasts, and belly with the soap.

Allison joined Elizabeth on the rim and reached for her own soap. "What is your idea?" she asked. Whatever Elizabeth said about Zeldin, Allison could not see it as she did. Zeldin was breaking down, true. But as far as Allison could see that wasn't due to this "trust" thing so much as it was to do with spending so much time in restraint.

"I think it's time to provide a social atmosphere for Zeldin. She should by now be susceptible to certain sorts of social pressures she would have ignored or refused to heed earlier. I think we must have a few small parties— not really parties, just little get-togethers— bringing Zeldin upstairs into one of the small lounges. You, me, and

maybe one or two other executive women. I have someone in particular in mind, but it will take a little managing. I'm frankly not certain including her won't tilt Zeldin off the deep end— she's someone Zeldin has known and been attracted to." Elizabeth returned the soap back to its dish and slid down into the tub to rinse.

"It sounds a little strange, Elizabeth. What exactly is it you have in mind?" Allison went back into the tub as Elizabeth came out.

"I'm not sure. But I feel certain that being part of a social gathering, adding a new dimension to Zeldin's reality, will force her to adjust herself to us and our values. It's the question of whether or not to add the complication of Felice Raines that I'm debating." Elizabeth dropped the towel she had been drying herself with and stepped into a lounging gown.

"Felice Raines? Who's Felice Raines?" Allison asked, climbing out of the tub.

"Who is Felice Raines!" Elizabeth picked up Allison's towel. "Really, darling!" She rubbed Allison's back and arms with the towel. "Felice Raines is the woman with whom Sedgewick has a maternity contract. She is also Varley Raines's daughter!" Elizabeth finished drying her.

"Oh," Allison said, properly awed.

Elizabeth laughed and handed Allison her lounging gown.

"But she doesn't live in Denver," Allison said, certain she would know if such a person did live in Denver.

"No, but I'm handling Sedgewick's affairs. *All* of his affairs. Which means Felice will be anxious to cooperate with me. Not that she will be thrilled at seeing Zeldin— she had quite a harrowing time getting herself and Sedgewick's children out of DC, you know, and she's most grateful to Wedgewood for services rendered."

"Then she's Zeldin's enemy," Allison said.

"Maybe, maybe not," Elizabeth said, leading the way to the kitchen. "There should be a Niçoise salad in the refrigerator. Are you hungry?"

"Not especially," Allison said. What she wanted was another glass of wine. "Do you think Zeldin's trying to starve herself?" she asked curiously, recalling Elizabeth's new rules for Zeldin about eating and a weekly weighing-in.

Elizabeth brought an enormous plastic-covered platter out of the refrigerator. Allison saw at once that it was a true *Salade à la Niçoise* (unlike the ones called by the same name that they served in the Rock's Executive Dining Room). "I don't know what she thinks she's doing," Elizabeth said. "Maybe it's simply boredom. It could even be an unconscious method of slow suicide. But she must have known I would eventually notice."

Allison helped carry plates and forks and bread and butter out to the living room. When they were settled on the floor before the fireplace, Allison said, "You know why I think you're wrong about Zeldin, Elizabeth?"

Elizabeth, frowning, looked up from her plate to meet Allison's gaze. "No, Allison. Why do you think I'm wrong?"

"Because you have given up trying to get her to write in that book. She won that round from you."

"But at what cost," Elizabeth said softly. "She's not herself now. She's weakened. I could afford to let her win that round. Because there are so many to come. You must look at it that way, Allison. You have to know when to bend, when to stop beating your head against the wall. I don't consider that a defeat, you know. And in a way, I have to admire Zeldin for holding on like that. But it was a mistake for her. Because now she's almost entirely defenseless. And when I ask her to write in the book again, as I'll soon be doing, she'll have no choice but to comply." Elizabeth speared three green beans and a potato slice with her fork. "It's necessary to take the long view, Allison. Time is not on Zeldin's side." Elizabeth lifted the fork to her mouth.

"But it's not on yours, either," Allison said, thinking about Sedgewick.

Elizabeth nodded. "I know, darling, I know. But Zeldin doesn't."

How did Elizabeth stand it? She was literally living on the edge of a precipice. One strong gust of wind would blow her over the edge. It was nerve-racking even to watch. And then Allison realized: if Elizabeth went over the edge, she, Allison would probably follow.

Was it treason, what Elizabeth was doing? Was it treason, what she herself was doing with the proprietary and setting up peace-seeking meetings with Military?

Almost Allison wished she were back in Vienna at her dull but safe low-level job. Almost. But she knew she wouldn't want it now. Not with everything she had here with Elizabeth.

For that, every bit of the risk was worth taking.

Chapter Twenty-five

[i]

Her memory, Kay thought, was seriously warping. Whether she was in this cell or the one across the hall, the days blurred without distinction. The clock in this cell furnished her with the time of day and the day of the week, but such data did not seem to help her organize her place in time in any meaningful way. After Gordon's examination of her, she had begun to keep a log noting down everything she ate and when she ate it, but when she looked at the log, the notations connected with nothing in her memory. She could not even recall how long it had been since she had last been in the other cell, or even in the closet. Trying to recall all the individual infractions for which Elizabeth had punished her and all the occasions on which she had been taken to be force-fed was like trying to remember at five o'clock in the afternoon every dream one had had the night before.

She even lacked a clear sense of when she had started writing in the book for Elizabeth again, except that it had been the day after the scene in the infirmary, an occasion that stood out in her memory as prominently as her first experience of the closet, disjunct and unique. Each writing assignment entailed the same terrible struggle, each confrontation with Elizabeth the same terrible tension. Some of them ended with a new assignment, others with a stint of being chained to the platform in the cell across the hall. The struggle and tension had worn her out. And yet though she could not in retrospect remember making any particular entry, only an assignment from Elizabeth put its mark briefly on the elapsing of the days and nights, for time then assumed the shape that anxiety dictated, anticipating, always, the moment in which Elizabeth read the assignment.

Now, sitting on the bed with her knees tucked under her chin, Kay watched Elizabeth read the latest entry in the book. Elizabeth had told her to write about what she had been doing in the area in general and Boulder in particular on the day Elizabeth had apprehended her. Though she could find no reason not to mention either her search for Scott or her attempts at recruiting scientists for the Free Zone, Kay did so reluctantly. She did not, however, mention her discussion with Nadine Morris in Ann Arbor, or her travels talking to people whose friends and spouses were missing. She counted on Elizabeth's inference that Scott had been the sole object of her search and that her reason for being in the area was her memory of a reference to the base in one of the files she had seen in Sedgewick's office.

It made her uneasy to write about what she had been doing just before capture. Such writing and discussion enhanced the likelihood of Elizabeth's questioning her about things she must not discuss—things to do with the Free Zone, things to do with her travels, things to do with the Marq'ssan.

It seemed to Kay that Elizabeth was looking almost haggard with exhaustion. Sedgewick, she thought, must be working her even harder than usual.

Finally Elizabeth closed the book and set it down on the desk. "What were you doing in Ann Arbor?" Her eyes focused sharply on Kay's face.

Kay's mouth dropped open. "Ann Arbor?" she said, stalling. How did Elizabeth know she had been to Ann Arbor?

"Yes, Ann Arbor," Elizabeth said. "Don't deny you were there. I would like to know why you didn't include your conversation with Nadine Morris in your writing."

Almost deafened by the loud beating of blood in her ears, Kay stared stupidly at Elizabeth.

"I'm losing patience with you, Kay. You lie to me so often that I begin to wonder whether there's anything you say that I can reasonably believe."

Kay lowered her eyes to the bedspread. What did Elizabeth expect? Why shouldn't a prisoner lie, especially when someone else's safety

might be in question? What did it matter that she lied? Elizabeth's hypocrisy... The only thing that mattered was that she had been caught in the lie and would probably be hauled across the hall again to be chained to the platform.

"You have nothing to say?" Elizabeth said.

Kay did not answer.

"I am disappointed. Consider, Kay, how fair and honest I've been with you. How *respectful* of you I've been."

Kay looked up in disbelief to stare at Elizabeth's face. "Respectful!"

"Yes. Respectful. Never once have I demeaned you in any way, though there have been a myriad occasions for it. I've been very careful of your dignity, very careful not to use intrinsically humiliating situations to embarrass or degrade you. If you think about it, you will realize that."

Kay's face burned. It was true that Elizabeth was always matter-of-fact about her symptoms of claustrophobia, about her unavoidable incontinence during punishment, about the many small, humiliating details of this existence. The mockery Elizabeth employed against her was always directed at some point of resistance, never at the humiliating details springing from her captivity or punishment. Other controllers would have exacerbated the humiliations. Kay wondered now why Elizabeth had not.

"Ah, so you do see," Elizabeth said drily, her mouth— but not her eyes— half-smiling. "And you know that within the framework I've explained to you I've been scrupulously fair, never arbitrary, never gratuitously cruel. *I've* told *you* the truth, Kay. Yet you lie to me whenever you think you can get away with it. Why should I believe anything you tell me?"

"Perhaps you shouldn't," Kay said.

Elizabeth's mouth tightened. After a moment she said, "Perhaps I shouldn't play fair with you. If you won't play fair with me, why should I play fair with you?"

"Fair!" Kay cried. "You think that what you are doing to me is *fair*? You make the rules. Of course you can afford to follow your own rules! Why pretend to all this communication nonsense when it's all

merely a matter of control? Control isn't communication. All that's happening here is that you're handling me." Her sense of injustice brought Kay close to tears. "Why do we have to go through all this bullshit? Why don't you just chain me to the damned platform now and get it over with?"

When Elizabeth stood up Kay waited for the expected order. But Elizabeth walked over to the bed and sat down near Kay. "It's almost easy for you now, isn't it— contemplating punishment, I mean. Shuttling back and forth between this cell and the other one. This time you've gone way over the line. And in doing so you've made it clear to me that it's time for a change."

Kay tightly laced her fingers together to conceal the trembling in her hands. She could see anger in Elizabeth's posture, in the tension of the muscles around her eyes and mouth. But of course Elizabeth would never so lose control as to let her see more than these small, almost invisible signs. She watched Elizabeth's mouth, dreading her next words.

"It is time to bring Scott Moore into the picture," Elizabeth said.

Kay's heart contracted. "Scott Moore!"

"Yes, Scott Moore. Surely you knew we had him? Did you think we'd say we did when we didn't?"

"Is he..." But Kay could not ask.

"He's on base," Elizabeth said. "We've left him alone— until now. But henceforth what goes on here between you and me will concern him."

A wave of dizziness washed over Kay, nauseating her.

"It will work like this," Elizabeth said. "When I get back to my office I'll order him picked up for interrogation, using the connection between you and Nadine Morris and Nadine Morris and him as the pretext for suspicion of disloyalty. After a sufficiently lengthy interrogation he will be taken to a cell like the one across the hall. And then he will be punished as you would have been punished. I will not be his direct controller. I'll leave that to one of Wedgewood's people. I will merely issue orders to whomever is assigned to be Scott Moore's controller."

"I don't believe you," Kay said hoarsely. "You don't have him!"

"You will see for yourself, Kay. I'll take you for a viewing tomorrow."

"Not even you can claim that this is fair," Kay said bitterly.

"I'll chalk that up, too," Elizabeth said. "Whatever I choose to do is fair, and it's not for you to say otherwise."

Kay pressed her lips together to stop herself from saying anything more that might be used as an excuse to harm Scott.

"But that is for tomorrow," Elizabeth said. "The more immediate matter is a social occasion which you will be attending this evening."

Kay stared at Elizabeth. Was she *mad*?

"You don't believe me? But it's true. You are going to dine with me and a couple of other executives tonight."

Mindful of the threat against Scott, Kay held back her objections. What was it Elizabeth was trying to do to her? "I don't understand," she said faintly.

"It's very simple. I've decided it would be good for you to get out of your cell and have a bit more contact with the real world. You look suspicious, Kay. What is it you think will happen?"

"I'd rather be alone," Kay said carefully, hesitantly.

"A very unhealthy attitude for someone who has been solitary for as long as you have," Elizabeth said. "Yes, I think it's high time you were exposed to other people. It has become easy for you, to be so entirely self-centered, self-absorbed, self-focused. You've become exceedingly egocentric. It's time we did something about that."

All these things happening at once were confusing— and obviously part of some new tactic. "You don't expect me to believe that?" Kay asked.

"It's as good a reason as any. I don't have to explain anything to you. The fact is that you'll do as I say."

Elizabeth got up and went to the door.

"Don't forget, tomorrow is the day you are weighed. I'm sure you don't want to spend the next week being force-fed. From what I've seen of the log you've been keeping, you haven't been eating nearly enough. Consider it fortunate that you'll be given such a palatable meal tonight."

Elizabeth went out into the corridor and the door shut. Kay pulled the covers up to her chin. Elizabeth, she thought, was the scariest person she knew. If Wedgewood had been controlling her, she would have been dead by now without ever having had to face whatever horrors Elizabeth had in store for her.

[ii]

Allison felt especially pressed for time that Thursday morning because she knew she would have to copter into Denver to meet Felice Raines's plane at three and then take her to the club and squire her around Denver until it was time to bring her back to the base. Elizabeth insisted that no one else could be detailed to see to Felice; the reason for Felice's visit was such a confidential one that Elizabeth was concerned that no outsider should even speculate about it. Elizabeth had arranged for Felice to stay in the area— mostly at Aspen, where many of her friends spent part of the winter— on call as needed for Elizabeth's plans. Elizabeth had told Allison that she had used the combination of a bribe (a fat chunk of stock to be transferred from Sedgewick's portfolio if all went well) and a threat (of changing Sedgewick's son's prep school to Wilton, which Sedgewick preferred, but which Felice had earlier persuaded Elizabeth against) to "bring Felice into line."

All morning Allison's thoughts kept straying from her work to dwell on intriguing comments Elizabeth had made about Felice. Of a wealthy family, Felice was maternal-line with two children. According to Elizabeth, though wealthier than most executives, Felice was always greedy for more. "Nothing is ever enough for her," Elizabeth had said. That sort of valuation Allison could understand. But she found mystifying Elizabeth's saying she hoped that Felice would have a service-tech with her, for finding one who would suit her sexually would be very difficult. "She has tiresomely exacting taste," Elizabeth had said. "She prefers service-techs that are excessively overeducated— intense types that understand more of what's going on around them than they're capable of handling, emotional and intelligent with some exotic factor in their backgrounds. I doubt if anyone we had at the party at the club would have been up to *her*

standards." That had been enough to pique Allison's curiosity. But Elizabeth had also said that Felice was "like a barracuda disguised as a dolphin": charming, even sweet in her appearance and manner, but with a voraciously bloodthirsty appetite and teeth like newly sharpened saws. "She's out for blood. No, I take that back. Barracuda is an overly generous comparison. Try bloodsucker. There's nothing clean about her kills. Her method is slow and slimy." At Allison's reaction, Elizabeth had added, "Try to keep some distance from her, darling. Or she'll eat you for breakfast. Though if she does, you'll of course thank her for the honor and only afterwards understand what happened... So please, please be careful with her. Permit her to be charming, but don't fall for it."

What was Allison to make of such comments? She had never heard Elizabeth talk about another woman that way before. Lurid as her fascination was, Allison both dreaded and anticipated meeting Felice. Someone like her had a vulgar allure— being of that kind of executive family, moving in those circles, living in very private glamour and luxury....

At a few minutes after ten Anne phoned and asked Allison if she could meet with her some time during the day, to talk. "Must it be today, Anne?" Allison said. "My schedule is murder. Can't it wait until tonight— or better yet, tomorrow, since most of my evening is going to be taken up with work?"

Anne hesitated, then said, "Yes, of course it can wait until tomorrow, Lise. Sorry to bother you." And hung up.

Allison tried to get back to work, but an uneasiness about Anne dogged her. This was the first time Anne had ever phoned her: in fact, Allison realized, it was the first time Anne had ever initiated contact of any sort with her. Would Anne even have "bothered" her during working hours if it weren't important? Anne's voice had sounded strained and depressed.

Allison picked up her handset and called Anne back. "It's Lise, Anne. I find I can get away for a few minutes— can you take a break now?"

"Thank you, Lise. But if it's inconvenient for you—"

"It's no problem, love. When can you take a break?"

"I can get away in about ten minutes," Anne said.

"Good. I'll meet you at Central 3530. It's a small lounge that will give us some privacy. See you there in about fifteen minutes?"

"Yes. Thanks again, Lise."

Allison checked her watch. What she needed was a service-tech she could trust with the drudgery she got stuck with because Elizabeth wouldn't trust the drudgery to anyone else. She had so much to do before taking off for Denver. And there was another Zeldin transcript to clean up. How wonderful it would be if Elizabeth were to decide they could trust a service-tech to clean up the data recorder files. But of course she never would. Now that Allison had some idea of Elizabeth's ultimate goals in "rehabilitating" Zeldin, she understood very well why everything to do with Zeldin had to be kept absolutely secret.

Twelve minutes after talking to Anne on the phone, Allison set off for the lounge— only three minutes' walk from her own office but about twice as long from Anne's. Allison found Anne already outside the room, leaning against the wall, her crutches propped beside her. Allison quickly put her thumb to the access plate; inside she urged Anne to sit. The cumbersome casts on Anne's right leg and left arm gave her the appearance of being uncomfortable standing or walking.

"It's not as bad as it looks," Anne said. "I'm getting used to it."

Allison knew she should hug Anne, but her aversion to the chemical smell prevented her from getting close, for she feared revealing her aversion, which would be horrid for both of them. "You're looking frazzled, sweetheart," Allison said. "Do you think maybe you should have waited a bit longer before going back to work? I'm sure Alice would understand if you decided you'd come back too soon."

"No, it's better this way." Anne sighed and stared down at the floor.

"Is something wrong, Anne?" Allison felt sure that there was. Anne looked as though she were trying to pluck up the courage to say or ask something.

"I know this may be impossible, but you are, you do have... I mean, the channels you go through aren't the same that most people..." Anne swallowed and lifted her head to look at Allison.

"I have some connections, you mean," Allison said gently.

"Yes, I guess that's what I mean."

"And you need me to help you in some way. If I can I will, Anne. What is it you need for me to do?"

Anne drew a deep breath. "I can't stay here, Lise. I just can't." Her eyes filled with tears. "If you could help me get a transfer... I know service-techs like me aren't usually transferred. But unless I get transferred I have no way of leaving here. And I *have* to get away from here." To Allison's dismay, Anne's tears spilled over; first one, then another and another formed and rolled down her cheeks.

Allison went to Anne and knelt beside her chair. "Why do you have to leave?" Allison clasped Anne's hands between her own. "I don't understand."

"Ever since...ever since I left the infirmary, things have been happening...and now I know I can't stay here. I guess I'm a coward. But I can't go on like this. And my unit-mates are getting upset and scared, too. It's not fair to them, my putting them in danger, their getting hassled just because they live with me."

"What things, Anne? You never said anything about this before. Explain it to me. What danger?"

"I'm so easily identifiable," Anne said. "How many black women live and work around here, anyway? And with these casts— everyone knows about what happened. And now they know where I live. So they're retaliating. Sherry thinks it's because they're scared and mad and want to take it out on me. That because it was unarmed women who beat up the rapists a lot of guys are really upset. So they leave creepy threatening notes and do other things. Like hanging out in the dark and yelling things at me as we pass on our way home. And last night at one in the morning they bashed in the door to our unit and dumped excrement inside." Anne averted her gaze.

"You should have told me about these things right away, sweetheart! We can do something about it."

Anne shook her head. "It's no use. It'll only make them madder. Don't you see, they can't take it out on you and Alice and Ms.

Weatherall, so they take it out on me. And on Sherry and Jennifer and Nell."

"Who, Anne? Who is 'they'?"

"I don't know. Men. Men who are like the men who..."

"I don't want you to leave. And I know you don't really want to go somewhere where you will be without anyone you know. And I know you don't want to leave Alice."

"I can't stay here, you know what they'll do to me. All they have to do is keep their faces hidden and they'll know nothing will happen to them."

"I want you to move into my place," Allison said. "You'll be safe there."

"You won't help me, Lise?"

Damn them! And damn the system for making Anne so needlessly vulnerable! "Yes, I'll help you," Allison said quietly. "But I don't think you need to run away. First, come and stay at my place for a while. You can tell anyone who asks that you're doing it only until you're completely recovered, that it will be much more convenient for you with all your casts and everything to live in my apartment. And that will be true. No one would dare touch you at my complex. And you won't find any male service-techs there. As for when you're on base, a little elementary caution will be protection enough, though if you like I can have a guard assigned to escort you around."

Anne swallowed. "That would help for now. But I can't do that forever, Lise. If I could stay with you until a transfer was arranged... If you could do that, I mean..."

Allison looked deep into Anne's glazed brown eyes. "When you've recovered, Anne, I promise you I'll show you how to deal with creeps like that. I know plenty of women who are as small as you who can more than defend themselves." She paused. "There are ways. And I can teach them to you. Only you have to promise me something."

"What's that?"

"That you won't tell anyone, not even your best friends or your unit-mates or Alice, about whatever I teach you. It has to be a secret. Clear?"

"Understood," Anne responded, puzzled. "But you will see about the transfer?"

"If you want me to, I will. But can we wait a bit, first? To try what I just told you about?"

Anne sighed. "Whatever you think is best, Lise."

Allison leaned forward and kissed Anne lightly on the lips. "I promise I won't let you down, Anne." Anne nodded, slowly, sadly, but trustingly. "Now," Allison said, becoming brisk, "the thing to do is to arrange this move. Although I can't personally help you do it, maybe it would be best if you moved tonight considering what happened last night. I'll have a car take you home and wait for you while you get your things, and then take you to my place. And I'll arrange to have your thumbprint put into my household processor so you won't have trouble getting in the door. Okay?"

Anne nodded.

"Good. Maybe you could come back with me to my office for a minute while I access my household processor. It would be easier to do it with you directly giving me your thumbprint than by my calling up your personnel file."

Allison helped Anne up, and they returned to Allison's office. Not only would this arrangement complicate Allison's life (especially when it came to her relations with Elizabeth), but it could potentially get her into trouble for subversion. Still, Anne was discreet; Allison knew she could be counted on to act responsibly and to keep quiet. Until Elizabeth had told her it was wrong, Allison hadn't known so. Only Elizabeth knew that she knew it was wrong. If worse came to worst, she could count on Elizabeth's keeping quiet about her knowledge that it was wrong. Anyway, what could anyone do to her besides disapprove and suspect her of renegade tendencies? Whatever could be done to her for it could not weigh significantly against what was owed to Anne. Not by a long-shot. Whatever Elizabeth might say, Allison believed that sometimes it was necessary to think in terms of fairness. And not even Elizabeth would ever be able to convince her otherwise.

[iii]

The jet's rear hatch swung open and the ground crew wheeled a ramp into place. A small, elegant woman descended. Allison moved forward and offered her hand. "Felice Raines? I'm Allison Bennett, Elizabeth's aide. I hope you had a smooth flight?"

Felice's hand clasped hers firmly and warmly. "I hate these little planes," she said in a lyrical voice unexpectedly high in pitch, though not unpleasantly so.

"I've got the car right here." Allison indicated the large internal combustion vehicle Elizabeth had put at Felice's disposal. Would Felice realize that besides Elizabeth she was the only other person in the area allowed such a luxury? Should Allison mention it, to impress her with the lengths to which Elizabeth was going to please her? "As soon as they've unloaded your luggage, we can go. The red-tape has already been seen to."

"Thank god," Felice said. "I've had some dreadful experiences over the last year. You simply can't imagine— ah, there you are, Marianne. I was wondering what had happened to you."

Allison watched a luggage-burdened service-tech struggle down the steps— and restrained herself from going to help. A *faux pas* like that so soon after meeting Felice would indelibly mark Felice's future attitude toward her. Behind Marianne, another service-tech— one who probably went with the plane— followed, with yet more baggage. Evidently Felice Raines did not travel light. Or could she be intending to stay the winter? Elizabeth had been vague about the length of Felice's visit.

While Marianne and the driver loaded the luggage into the trunk, Allison asked Felice whether she had brought her own escort. "Since Elizabeth wasn't sure, she provisionally assigned Karnes to you." Allison pointed to the burly service-tech leaning casually against the car, cradling an automatic weapon in his arms.

Felice's upper lip curled; she tossed her glossy chestnut hair. "I left my gorilla in Atlanta. Frankly, I'm sick to death of having to deal with these men. The fool *shot* someone two weeks ago, can you believe that, he actually shot someone! Needlessly! At that rate one doesn't feel very safe. I or Marianne could be next!"

Allison bit her lip to suppress the laugh threatening to bubble out of her throat. This woman was practically a caricature, though of what Allison could not be sure. She was stagy, but as though every word and gesture had been studied for an effect known only to herself. The flashing green eyes continually widened and narrowed to punctuate her speech, and from one moment to the next the chin pushed forward, tucked in, tilted. She stood with one hand dug into her hip pocket, her leg thrust forward with its foot sometimes tapping, sometimes pointing or angling up from the heel. Trying to take it all in was exhausting and confusing. Felice Raines's body-language seemed— on first sight, at least— indecipherable.

In the car, though, her body-language grew clear enough. Her heavily jeweled hand rested on the nape of Marianne's neck. "You are a wonder, Marianne, an angel. The way you handled the luggage! What would I do without you?"

Marianne's smile was enigmatic. "Oh, it's nothing, Felice."

Felice looked at Allison. "*And* she is modest, too, my Marianne."

Allison's stomach fluttered. Something in all this disturbed her, reminded her of things she could not put her finger on. What did Marianne feel about it? she wondered. Elizabeth would probably say she enjoyed it. But what if she, Allison, were to behave in such a way to Anne... What would Anne feel? But Anne was not in love with her. Probably Marianne... Allison made an effort to clear her mind of so much garbage. "We'll check you in at the club first," she said to Felice. "There will be perhaps two and a half hours then before we need to copter to the base. You must tell me how you'd like to spend that time, or if there's anything in particular you'd like me to arrange."

Felice smiled. "Naturally I'd like a bath first, and then I thought I'd get in touch with a few friends whom I know to be in town... Let's not arrange anything, shall we? I hate any kind of rush and bustle."

Good. Allison could take an hour to drop into Com & Trans. And then if she had any time left over she'd see if she couldn't find some little thing that Anne might like. It could be a sort of housewarming present. Maybe if she made her feel welcome enough, Anne would be more inclined to forget her desperate idea of a transfer.

[iv]

For a large part of the day Kay paced her cell, inveighing in rage against Elizabeth— but silently, too afraid of the consequences to whisper much less shout her hatred of her controller. At one point she looked around the room for something to destroy. Her eye lighted on the box of powder sitting on the desk. She snatched it up, hefted it, and studied the ivory and lapis lazuli as she considered dashing it to the floor. But glaring down at the carpet she knew that if the powder spilled it would get into the nap and scent the cell for days to come. Instead, Kay carried it over to the wall of cupboards and opened the door that concealed the waste slot. But she hesitated. If she threw the entire box away, Elizabeth would immediately notice it was missing: how much better simply to empty all the powder into the garbage and replace the empty box on the desk. It would be a private rebellion, but a rebellion nonetheless. And if— when— Elizabeth found the box to be empty, she would know what Kay had done though Kay would say she must have used it all up. Elizabeth would then accuse her of lying. But at least Elizabeth would not know when she had done it.

Kay awkwardly jammed the box against the slot. The powder got into her nose and hair as she poured it out, and the room smelled of it. It was so damned familiar. Who, Kay again asked herself, had worn this scent?

By late afternoon her anger had exhausted her. She collapsed onto the bed in dull misery, and her thoughts turned to Scott. That she would at last be seeing him only to see him abused, was the bitterest irony. What should she do? Did her sporadic and feeble rebellions matter to the extent that Scott be dragged into it? When the situation had been between herself and Elizabeth it was one thing. When another person was involved— and that a person she loved— the politics and ethics of the situation altered. Did it matter, these rebellions? She submitted in almost every way to Elizabeth's decrees. What did these small resistances matter if she behaved meekly and obediently and submissively the rest of the time?

No, Kay realized, that was not right. Anent the resistances, she didn't know what they were exactly, only that they prevented something from happening between her and Elizabeth. She could sense Elizabeth pushing her inexorably toward some unknown point or position or confinement. And Elizabeth wouldn't be dragging Scott into this if she weren't in some way frustrated by Kay's resistances.

Kay sat bolt upright as it struck her: why would Weatherall bring *Scott* into this if it were merely an academic experiment? Would she really have the authority to abuse someone of demonstrable use— surely even executives would consider an electrical engineer in times like these to be an invaluable resource— purely to shore up the seemingly losing side of a frivolous bet? She supposed it was *possible*: she had no idea to what lengths the pair of them would go in their amusements. And it was always possible they were doing this to her not as an experiment, but merely to torment her. It was not difficult to imagine Sedgewick going to great lengths to torment her before killing her. And if that were the case, then Scott's appearance on the scene would have been inevitable and nothing she did or did not do would substantially matter in the way he was treated. But if the other thing were true, if there were some other motive— if, that is, they still planned to get some use out of her (but of what use could she possibly be that would justify the time, energy, and money this brainwashing project must be costing?), then their bringing Scott into the picture must be a sign of frustration. Elizabeth seemed to think she could not take much more of close restraint and the closet. And for some reason they did not apparently want her to suffer a full-scale mental breakdown...

The door opened and Elizabeth walked in. "Good morning, Kay," Elizabeth said as she dumped the leather bag on the table.

Kay stiffly mumbled the correct response.

Elizabeth pulled something made of a patterned brown and lavender cloth out of the bag and draped it over the back of the chair. "Into the bathroom with you," she said. "You're to have a shower in honor of your first evening out."

A shower. Anxiety sank its claws into Kay. "I'm perfectly clean," Kay said, trying to keep the importance of the matter out of her voice. "Can't we skip the shower?"

"Don't be silly," Elizabeth said. "You'll feel so much better. You always do feel bright and invigorated after your showers."

Not always, Kay thought as she shuffled into the bathroom. Not those she took immediately following her releases from the closet.

When Kay emerged from the shower Elizabeth handed her a towel. "You have some explaining to do, Kay."

So what else is new? Kay rubbed herself dry. "What is it?"

Elizabeth pointed to the powder box now sitting on the vanity.

Kay glanced at Elizabeth's eyes and then away. "I threw it into the garbage," she said. "This afternoon." Kay looked around for her nightshirt but did not find it where she had left it. She looked at Elizabeth. "I assumed it was like the newspaper. Mine to use or not. I decided not to use it."

"But you didn't throw the box away, I notice."

Kay wrapped the towel more securely around herself.

"And why is that, Kay?"

"I don't know. I suppose I thought you might want the box back."

"Another lie. Because you knew you were doing wrong, you hoped to conceal it. Admit it."

"I'll admit anything you like," Kay said, smiling bitterly. "I knew I was doing wrong so I hoped to conceal it."

"Dry your hair," Elizabeth said and stalked into the other room.

Kay looked in the mirror for the first time in a long time. She hardly recognized what she saw: pale bony face, the hair perhaps half an inch long, her eyes— now enormous— both frightened and frightening, sharp new lines around her mouth and between her eyes, her arms like toothpicks, her collarbone painfully prominent. She turned away and lifted the towel to her head.

"We don't have all night."

Kay went back into the bedroom and Elizabeth handed her a fresh nightshirt. Kay reluctantly dropped the towel, took the nightshirt, and slipped it over her head. "For this evening you can wear these socks and this robe." Elizabeth pointed to the things on the table. Kay pulled on the long wool socks and slipped the soft woolen robe on over her nightshirt. It had a belt and fell nearly to the floor. "I was concerned, you see, for your physical and psychological comfort," Elizabeth said ironically. "I hardly know why."

Kay stood awkwardly with her arms folded over her chest, waiting for Elizabeth's next order (which she expected to concern handcuffs). Elizabeth seemed to be waiting for something, but what it was Kay could not imagine. After about a minute Elizabeth sighed. "Come over here and sit down. We're going to talk before we go upstairs." Kay went to the bed and sat on the edge; Elizabeth sat down beside her. "I realize you're upset about Scott Moore," Elizabeth said. Her hand moved toward Kay's head, but Kay ducked to avoid the touch. "But you brought it on yourself," Elizabeth said in a very much harder voice. "You are going to have to learn to control yourself. I told you that the first time I saw you in your cell across the corridor. I will repeat it now: you must control yourself. Second, you must stop lying. Third, you must obey me. You've known these things all along, yet you persist in your defiance. Therefore, until you accept these terms, you can expect to watch Scott Moore being punished in your stead. Are you listening to me, Kay?"

"Yes, I'm listening."

"Look at me when I'm speaking to you."

Kay turned her head and looked at Elizabeth. "And I know *you've* been lying to *me*," Kay said. "About your reasons for keeping me alive. It's obvious now that you want me to do something. Otherwise you wouldn't have brought Scott Moore into this. Electrical engineers with his experience and expertise don't grow on trees. If you will just tell me what it is I will do it. And then once and for all we can stop this bullshit game you insist we play."

Elizabeth's eyes flashed. "Do you understand what effect you're having on Scott Moore's existence when you drop your control like this?" Elizabeth's voice was harsh. She looked furious, more furious than Kay had ever seen her look.

But Kay was furious, too. "What is it you want from me?" she said through her teeth.

"What I want from you is the reasonable behavior I just described. You are regressing minute by minute. If it weren't for this dinner party I would take you across the corridor right now."

"I would rather go there than to your party," Kay said.

"Enjoy yourself now. You'll regret it after your first few sessions watching your beloved spouse." Elizabeth stood, went to the table, and dug a pair of handcuffs from the leather bag. "Behind your back," she said.

Kay stood and held her hands behind her back. Usually Elizabeth let her keep her hands in front of her body, a far more comfortable position than having them bound behind.

Elizabeth snapped the cuffs on Kay's wrists and roughly gripped her arm. "Let's go. We're already late." They went out into the corridor and Kay wondered why it mattered so much that she attend this "party." Who was going to be there? Sedgewick? Kay shrank at the idea and trembled. She did not think she could stand to see Sedgewick, not now. Not with her defenses so stripped. "I expect you to be civil and courteous to everyone you see tonight," Elizabeth said as they walked.

The elevator took them almost to the top floor marked on the control panel. Then they walked a considerable distance. At each barrier at which a guard was posted Elizabeth instructed the guard that Kay was not to be allowed to pass without her, Elizabeth's, direct and explicit permission. Finally they halted before a door where Elizabeth spoke to the guard posted there before thumbing open the door and moving Kay inside. On her mettle, Kay quickly swept her eyes around the room and took in a confused impression of a large rectangular space filled with armchairs and sofas at one end and a dining table set with china, crystal, linen, and flowers at the other. A door at the dining room end led into another room.

Two executive women watched them come into the room. Kay recognized one of them and immediately connected her with the scent of the powder. She turned and looked at Elizabeth, half-hoping to read an answer on her face for why she would bring Kay into contact with Felice Raines. Felice had nothing to do with Security. Why should she be here, at this base? Not for love of Sedgewick, that was certain.

Elizabeth removed the handcuffs and carelessly laid them beside a large crystal bowl of floating gardenias on the table near the door. "Felice, you remember Kay Zeldin, I'm sure. Allison, meet Kay Zeldin. Kay, this is Allison Bennett." Elizabeth gave Kay a little push in the direction of the women. "Sit down and be sociable, Kay."

Her teeth clenched, Kay picked out a chair and— keeping her gaze fixed solely on it— went straight to it. She felt the others watching her. This was probably simply a new form of punishment, she told herself. Elizabeth must know how difficult it would be for someone kept for so long in isolation to have any kind of encounter with another person, much less with people like these dressed in street clothes while she wore a bathrobe. No doubt she'd soon learn the point painfully, awkwardly as these people watched. When she reached the chair she sank into it without looking at the women sitting nearby. Then she chose a picture on the wall to stare at and folded her hands in her lap, careful to pull the robe's sleeve over the strip of metal banding her wrist. At the periphery of her vision she glimpsed Felice's gleaming hair.

"You know, Elizabeth—" Kay recognized Felice's smooth round voice— "when I heard that she had been apprehended and executed I was quite frankly delighted. No one likes to be made a fool of, and god knows she made fools of all of us. Then you tell me you're keeping her alive. But now that I see her, it looks as though that's only a half-truth. Is it simply death by starvation? A new form of capital punishment?"

Kay felt sick to her stomach. It was one thing to know that everyone thought her dead, but yet another to hear someone talking about their pleasure in having thought so.

"No, Felice, I'm not starving her," Elizabeth, standing directly behind Kay, replied. Her hand dropped onto Kay's shoulder. "She was starving herself until I caught on. But perhaps we can tempt her palate at dinner." Felice snorted. "You see, Kay, Felice isn't very happy with your trickery and deceit. Not only were you a guest in her house under false pretenses, but you left her and her children in a dangerous situation."

A silence fell. Kay listened to the rattling of a cup in a saucer and the sound of cloth rustling. She wished Elizabeth would take her hand off her shoulder.

"Has anyone been skiing yet this season?" Felice asked.

This gambit nearly launched Kay into hysteria. She imagined herself saying brightly, "Oh dear me no I've been simply too tied up to get out." Pressing her lips together, she fought down the laughter shaking her diaphragm.

"I've been out once," the woman Kay did not know said. "We're so busy, though, that it's been difficult to get away. You'll find the pack is rather decent already."

"It must be about the only thing to do around here for amusement," Felice said.

Aside from torturing prisoners, Kay barely managed to refrain from retorting aloud.

"My impression," the woman called Allison said, "is that there's very little amusement to be had anywhere in this country the way things are now."

"Depends on what you want," Felice said.

"You know you are *so* right," Kay surprised herself by saying. She forced her gaze onto Felice's face. "Amusement is such a very personal matter, don't you think?" Elizabeth dropped her other hand onto Kay's other shoulder. A warning. But what did anything matter now? She might as well be hung for a sheep as a lamb.

Felice turned to the other woman. "Kay is so clever that one can never be sure precisely what she is saying. Apart from her general deceitfulness, I mean."

Elizabeth's fingers tightened their grip on Kay's shoulders. "We're working on the deceitfulness, Felice. Aren't we, Kay."

"Well," Kay said blithely, "you know what they say: once a liar, always a liar."

"Madame is served," a voice said from the other side of the room.

"Shall we, ladies?" Elizabeth said, lifting her hands from Kay's shoulders.

Elizabeth directed them so that Felice sat at the foot of the table and Elizabeth at the head with Allison on Elizabeth's right, across from Kay. Two service-techs waited on them, one serving steaming bowls of soup, the other filling their water glasses. Kay saw that she and Allison (unlike Felice and Elizabeth) had been given three wine glasses. When the service-tech finished pouring the water she brought out a bottle of white wine and poured some into the first of Allison's wine glasses. "On second thought," Elizabeth said, "I think it would be unwise for you to drink wine, Kay. Shelly, remove Ms. Zeldin's wine glasses from the table."

Something in the way Elizabeth said this brought a flush to Kay's face. She stared down at the creamy white soup. It looked and smelled like potato and leek soup and made her hungry in spite of her nausea. While Shelly removed the wine glasses from Kay's place setting, the other service-tech went around the table with a basket of rolls. Kay took one and lavishly buttered it. She would intake as many calories as she could, for tomorrow she would be weighed. And if Elizabeth carried out her threat about Scott, she would probably be unable to eat.

Kay grew increasingly uncomfortable during dinner. As they ate, the executives chatted about the special problems for raising children that had been created by the Civil War. The sleeve of Kay's robe, long for her arm, continually threatened to drag or flop into the soup. The conversation ranged so far outside Kay's current experience of reality that several times she felt as though she could not understand the English words they were speaking. Images of Scott interpolated a discussion of the impingement of the Civil War on executive boys' schools. Scott would be taken entirely by surprise...had it happened already? Had they already "arrested" him? Or was that yet to come? Was he still moving about freely, unaware that at any second a nightmare would be descending upon him?

"And Alexandra is still with your mother?" Elizabeth was inquiring of Felice.

Kay put down her spoon. If she ate another bite of soup she would be unable to eat any of the entrée.

"Frankly I'm so nervous about all these assassinations and so on that I suggested to Mother that she take Alexandra to some nice quiet island in the Caribbean. So Mother took her to Barbados— for the

duration, she says. There's quite a colony of women and children there now— from both sides, and so far neither side seems inclined to bother them." Felice sighed. "Not that it's always easy to know who is on which side. After all, Daddy's connections are mainly with Military."

Elizabeth smiled. "But Felice, dear, you know which side you are on." Thinking that sounded a little like a threat, Kay darted a look at Felice's face.

"Of course, Elizabeth," Felice said sweetly. "I have no doubts. Nor do my children."

Sedgewick's children, Kay thought. No one would ever have any doubts about which side they were on.

The service-techs cleared the soup plates and set delicate gold-rimmed dinner plates before them. Then they went around the table, one of them offering a platter of roast lamb and vegetables, the other pouring more water and wine. Kay took the smallest slice of lamb on the platter and one each of the small glazed potatoes and carrots.

"A roaring appetite, Kay?" Elizabeth said, calling everyone's attention to her plate.

Anger gripped Kay as she thought about what was or would be happening to Scott, as she thought about her own looming force-feedings, as she thought about the kind of lives these women took for granted. "Somehow," Kay said clearly, "my appetite fails me when I think about what my future feedings will be like." Kay turned her head to the left and smiled at Felice. "Imagine, they insert a tube down one's nose and—"

"Kay," Elizabeth said.

Kay looked at Elizabeth: what could Elizabeth do apart from sending her away? Everything she could do to punish Kay she was already intending to do. "I especially find the removal of the tube distasteful, particularly the way it trails god knows what slimy shit all over one's face." Kay stared defiantly into Elizabeth's eyes, daring her to take her from the table.

"Is she always this childish?" Felice asked before Kay could continue.

Elizabeth sighed. "She's not used to polite society. Too many tube-food meals taken alone."

Allison giggled.

"Too bad we can't send her to my mother," Felice said. "She's doing a wonderful job with Alexandra."

Outflanked, Kay dropped her gaze to her plate and sipped water. Whatever she did or said now would not make them the slightest bit uncomfortable. And that Felice, who was not particularly bright, had been the one to disarm her made it a doubly disgusting defeat. Trapped with these women and their silks and linen and crystal, Kay hated Elizabeth with all her mind, body, and soul.

[v]

After seeing Felice off to the waiting copter, Allison returned to Elizabeth's office but found that Elizabeth had not returned yet from taking Zeldin back to her cell. Allison fetched her coat from her own office and paced up and down the length of Elizabeth's. What was keeping her so long? Allison glanced at her watch and found that it was ten o'clock. Had Anne gotten settled in? It was a pity she couldn't have gotten home early to make it nicer for her. But it had been impossible with Elizabeth's insistence on this damned dinner with Zeldin. And the thing had been a fiasco from start to finish. Zeldin certainly had a sharp tongue— three months in solitary had apparently not even begun to dull it. It surprised Allison, for Zeldin seldom talked that way to Elizabeth when they were alone together. Had it been Felice's presence? Or something to do with the flare-up that morning?

Elizabeth finally appeared; she stood leaning against the door after it had closed. Alarmed, Allison went to her. "Are you all right, Elizabeth? What is it?"

Elizabeth looked at her; the bleakness in those knowing blue eyes chilled and frightened Allison. "I'm all right, darling. Come." She held open her arms and clasped Allison tightly to her. "What a miserable mess things have gotten into. Maybe I'm just tired. I haven't been bothering to sleep much lately. Maybe that's my problem."

"What is it?" Allison whispered.

Elizabeth heaved a great sigh. "I've completely fucked up with Zeldin. And I don't know if it's irretrievable or not. She's gone completely out of control."

Elizabeth disengaged from Allison and walked over to her desk. Allison watched Elizabeth's hands move restlessly through the papers on it. "What do you mean about Zeldin, Elizabeth?"

"What a disaster. That in one day— one day, Allison!— I could have completely sabotaged all my hard work with her. I lost my temper this morning, she made me so damned furious, that I leaped before thinking. And damned if she didn't figure *something* out— I'm not sure what, but enough to give her a new sense of confidence in herself. Look at the way she behaved tonight! Bringing Felice into it, even having Zeldin up at all was a mistake, too. Just now when I took her back to her old cell, to additionally punish her, she had the nerve to tell me she preferred it there, tights and all. She knows I'm riled, so she's riding me." Elizabeth shook her head. "By bringing Scott Moore into this I somehow tipped my hand to her. She no longer considers this merely a contest between herself and me, but suspects something more is involved." Elizabeth put her hands to her face and rubbed her eyes. "Now that she suspects that, I doubt if I'll be able to do anything with her. The whole game may be lost, Allison."

"Why don't you try talking to her about what is at stake?" Allison asked, thinking about the probability of the Russians starting a war. "Maybe with Scott Moore as a point of coercion she'd be willing to help you with Sedgewick without going through all this rehabilitation stuff."

"Tell Zeldin?" Elizabeth cried. "Are you mad? If Sedgewick saw her the way she is now— no matter what kind of words I could manage to put in her mouth, supposing I could— which I don't suppose for a minute: if Sedgewick saw her now, he'd hand me his Colt and tell me to do it on the spot! Don't you understand, Allison? The reason Sedgewick lost it is not because he's pining away in love with Zeldin, it's because he couldn't control her! Why the *fuck* do you think he fetishized her in the first damned place? It's because in his mind he's made her into a goddam fucking symbol of sexuality— male or female, I don't know, maybe both— it's all mixed up with his bizarre response to getting fixed— and all those years fetishizing her made her safe! Then after the Blanket when he finally got near her, she was completely out of control, more so than ever before. Christ, Allison! If *I* can't control her, there's no way *he's* going to feel safe around her! Which means that if he saw Zeldin now, he'd continue to wallow in his goddam depression— or worse." Elizabeth's head dropped into her hands. "I don't know what to do about her. I've blown it. She's beyond me. Maybe she *is* completely uncontrollable, just like Sedgewick said."

Allison went to Elizabeth and put her arms around her. "I think you're tired, love. If you could just get a night's sleep, I'm sure you'll see this more clearly in the morning. There's still time to reconsider about Scott Moore, you know." Allison softly stroked Elizabeth's face and wished passionately that Elizabeth would snap out of this despair. It was so uncharacteristic of her— and so untimely.

"Maybe you're right, darling. Maybe we should go home, dip in the Jacuzzi, and go to bed." She sighed. "I don't know, Allison. If I can't manage Zeldin I don't see how all the things we are doing will work out. I can't see Sedgewick simply coming out of it on his own. And god knows Security has enemies enough who'd like nothing better than watching us all go down to ignominious defeat..."

Allison thought about Anne waiting for her at home and wondered how to tell Elizabeth that she would have to go to her own apartment, at least for a while, to make sure Anne was okay. She felt that with Elizabeth so depressed she must stay the night with her.

"Get my coat for me, will you darling?" Elizabeth said. "And then we'll get the hell out of here."

Allison went to the closet and pulled out Elizabeth's lovely sable. "I like your sable so much better than Felice's damned pretentious baby seal," Allison said. "She was so full of 'Daddy gave me this don't you think it's lovely?' that I thought I'd puke. I can't stand the Daddy stuff those maternal-line types simply *ooze*." She held the coat for Elizabeth to slip into. Slowly Elizabeth put her right arm into the right sleeve. "How did you acquire your sable, Elizabeth?" Allison asked, suddenly curious. "Did you buy it for yourself, or was it a gift?"

Wearily, Elizabeth smiled. "No, of course I didn't buy it for myself, darling. Sedgewick gave it to me on the tenth anniversary of his being made Chief of Security. Felice's nose was out of joint that whole winter, as I recall."

Allison laughed. "Good. So of course she had to one-up you, via Daddy. What a bitch she is."

"Oh darling, you don't like her. I'm so glad."

Allison slipped into her own coat— merely fur-trimmed cashmere. "Does anybody like Felice Raines?" she asked.

"Now that's not nice, Allison. That's not nice at all. Let's go home, shall we?"

All the way home Allison worried about her dilemma. She would have to rely on Anne's understanding. Elizabeth needed her tonight, needed her badly. She would make an excuse to run down to her apartment so that she could explain to Anne. But she would wait until tomorrow before telling Elizabeth about her. This was no time to be bothering Elizabeth with petty details, not considering the responsibilities weighing Elizabeth down now. The scale of events Elizabeth had to deal with made Anne's problems seem trivial by comparison.

Anne's problems would just have to wait.

Chapter Twenty-six

[i]

"I can't tell you how much I appreciate this," Martha said to Gina. "This report will tell us almost everything we need to know about the medical end of implementation, including wider implications. Taken with Venn's report on the history of reproductive politics, we should be able to provide enough information so that people can think intelligently about the issue."

Gina removed the filter from the coffee carafe and poured its steaming black contents into the waiting pottery cups. "I doubt if they will think intelligently about it," she said. "No matter how much information you give people, they'll persist in deciding things for reasons mostly invisible to themselves. Neurophysiology refers to these as 'somatic markers.' They're the primary force in every exercise of choice or judgment. Which is why I'm afraid this whole thing could be a disaster." Gina sat down across from Martha.

Gloomily they stared into their coffee cups, and Martha listened to the rain pattering in discrete drops onto the roof and against the windows. "Gina," she said suddenly. "There's something I've been thinking about. That I wanted to ask you about."

Gina fingered the handle of her mug. "Yeah? So ask away."

"It's about longevity treatments."

Gina looked surprised.

"Is there any way we could make them widely available in the Free Zone?"

Gina looked thoughtful. "An important question. Frankly, I was surprised the reproductive issue came up before the longevity issue. But yes. We could do it. Practically speaking it would be easier to do than universally restoring fertility and taking the consequences. But

we couldn't do both at the same time. It's a question of medical resources. A longevity treatment is just a very intensive cleanout of the blood and the monitoring and correction of DNA transcription. And of course a replacement of any organs that are wearing out or malfunctioning. But doing longevity treatments would almost certainly preclude fertility restoration as far as resources go."

"In fact," Martha said dreamily, "longevity might be better than free fertility."

Gina's face grew cautious. "What are you thinking, Martha?"

Martha tilted her head and raised her eyebrows. "That maybe we could tie the two things together? To deflect the issue from its current political position?"

"Whoa. That's some idea. You mean offering people a choice, either one or the other but not both? Would you do this individually or on the level of the whole population? But no, you couldn't do it at all, at least not yet, because our facilities couldn't handle both, at least not now."

"I've been thinking and thinking about this," Martha said.

"Have you shared this idea with anyone else?"

"No," Martha said. "I wanted to talk to you first to see about whether or not it was practical."

"It's practical. But you realize it's potentially explosive?"

"Why hasn't anyone else brought it up?"

"That's easy," Gina said. "People who never had it available to them probably don't give it a thought as something possible. And the people who did— people like me, Martha— have been guiltily and secretly worrying about what they're going to do as the time comes and goes for their five-year cleanouts. They of course don't want to bring up the subject because they know that most people have never had them. There's something in the atmosphere in the Zone that keeps professionals from talking about it."

"I'm surprised they're not all leaving then." Martha heard the unexpectedly sharp edge to her tone; she struggled to suppress a fresh surge of the resentment she often felt for professionals.

Gina shrugged. "Maybe those of us who have stayed or specially immigrated here have stronger reasons for wanting to be here than the reward of longevity we'd presumably earn by sticking with the executives."

Martha swallowed the remaining coffee in her cup. "Of course," she said quietly. "I didn't mean to denigrate professionals."

Gina smiled. "I know. But you must have some resentments. Right?"

Martha half-smiled. "I suppose so."

They exchanged a long, friendly look, rueful on both sides. "Are you spending the holidays on Whidbey?"

"At Sweetwater? Yes. I've heard they have a beautiful Winter Solstice celebration— a tradition with them." She had missed the last one because she had spent Christmas with her parents. She had done it because her mother had begged her to try to "make it up" with her father. The visit had been short and bitter: her father considered Martha a traitor to his country, which he felt was now lost to him because of her and her "commie pals."

"They've invited all of us from the Science Center to join them, you know. Which is really generous of them."

Martha grinned. "They appreciate you as the wonderful neighbors you are. Needless to say they didn't invite the Doyle crowd. Are any of you going?"

"Maybe. I think I will. But some of the men are not entirely comfortable with the idea. They get a little strange around the Sweetwater people. Even Max, who's ordinarily so sensible and unselfconscious."

"Change of subject: how's the clinic doing?"

Gina's face lit up. "I've been using a lot of the things I learned during my six months in Africa with Leleynl. I tell you, the Marq'ssan influence could revolutionize medicine. Make it cheaper, too. Naturally there's a lot of resistance, but I often work some of her techniques into the usual procedures, which make them seem less radical. Some of the other staff are still skeptical, of course. But a few of them are familiar with similar techniques that have been used by non-establishment practitioners for a long long time. At any rate, the clinic has gotten

on its feet. And no small thanks to you, either, for all the equipment and supplies you've acquired for us. We never would have been able to manage on our own, Martha."

Martha glanced at her watch. "I have to be going. Not that I want to: Isabelle— the woman from Doyle's group who's on the CFRRF— is my next appointment." Martha sighed. "Which I fully expect to turn into a confrontation with Doyle."

"Are you going to give her my report?"

"Not yet. I have to have copies made so we can give everyone on the committee a copy. Actually, I'm dreading your report falling into Doyle's hands— he'll probably start pushing all the harder once he knows that the thing *can* be done."

Gina sniffed. "I doubt he can push hard enough to overcome so many obstacles without the concerted efforts of a lot of people. Otherwise he would have found a way to get what he wants without working through the Co-op."

Martha donned her rain outfit. "I hope I'll see you at Sweetwater, Gina."

"On this longevity stuff, Martha? Go carefully. It may be more emotionally fraught than you know."

Martha thought about this as she tramped toward Doyle Territory. And she thought about Beatrice lying under heavy quilts and eider-down, her aging body racked with bronchitis. She felt as though she were carrying an important secret around with her. A secret big and warm and powerful. A secret that could change the world.

[ii]

Allison lingered in the corridor outside Zeldin's cell, bracing herself to go in. She loathed, hated, and detested handling Zeldin for Elizabeth. Allison understood that she was the only one Elizabeth could trust to have unsupervised contact with her. Still, she hated it, though she thought that perhaps it might be best that it was she rather than Elizabeth seeing Zeldin, considering how unbalanced Elizabeth had been getting about her.

Elizabeth had taken to spending hours studying transcriptions of the recordings, as though searching for a solution she believed to exist.

And then there was the matter of her anger. Allison was astonished to realize that Elizabeth was angry at Zeldin for her lack of gratitude! It seemed almost a kind of madness that Elizabeth should expect Zeldin to feel anything but hatred and resentment for her. Allison tried talking to her about it, but each time Elizabeth turned prickly and defensive and shut off the discussion by saying that Allison understood nothing about Zeldin. Perhaps it was true, Allison thought, but she did understand some things about Elizabeth. She knew, for instance, that Elizabeth's emotional involvement had clouded her judgment— even to the point of Elizabeth's denying emotional involvement. According to Elizabeth, it was all a matter of Zeldin's importance for shaping up Sedgewick and nothing at all to do with her personal expectations about her dealings with Zeldin.

Allison nerved herself to press her thumb against the plate. Not that Zeldin was that difficult for her to deal with: Zeldin hardly spoke to her. It was almost as though she did not see Allison. Even when Allison took her to view Moore she had little to say. Everything in that woman remained locked inside— the fury, the despair, the frustration Allison could sense lurking behind Zeldin's gaze. It wasn't necessarily that Zeldin was holding it inside through fear so much as that Allison hardly existed for her. To Zeldin she was simply a courier who existed solely to pass messages between principals.

Zeldin, sitting on the platform with her back to the wall, huddled under the blanket with her knees tucked under her chin, looked up when Allison came in, then away. "Good morning, Kay," Allison said. It made Allison feel silly, but Elizabeth insisted on this.

"Good morning Allison," Kay droned back.

"I'm taking you back to the other cell now," Allison said.

Zeldin looked at her. "No. I don't want to go back there."

Allison sighed. "That's crazy. You can't even sleep properly in this place! And look at you— you're filthy and smelly in those tights and leotard. You can't be comfortable in here!"

"I won't go," Zeldin said. "If you take me over there I'll just do something that will make you bring me back here."

Allison shook her head. "Elizabeth thought you might say something like that. Something to do with guilt and solidarity of suffering? Nothing you do will end in your coming back here. The only result will be increased suffering for Moore. Increased time spent in the closet, most likely."

Zeldin closed her eyes. Allison hoped she wasn't going to cry. It was bad enough without that.

"Come on, Kay, let's get it over with."

Zeldin opened her eyes and stared at Allison. "Are you..."— she hesitated, perhaps to force the words— "Are you my controller now?"

"No. I'm just handling you for Elizabeth. Come on, Kay. Get off the platform."

"I want to talk to Elizabeth. If she's still my controller—"

"Get off the goddam platform. Now. Or I'll call somebody to help me with you. And if I have to do that you can be sure Moore will suffer for it. Don't make this harder than it has to be." Allison went to the door and waited. She would give Zeldin ten seconds. And then she would bring down a couple of warders to deal with Zeldin for her.

Zeldin acquiesced, dropping the blanket on the floor, dispiritedly crossing the corridor. Everything was ready in the other cell— Allison had even opened the shower cubicle and laid a clean nightshirt out on the bed. She told Zeldin to take off the tights and leotards, to get into the shower. But Zeldin balked.

"Do you have any idea what you smell like?" Allison said. "Stop arguing with me and do as I say. You know there's no use disobeying. Everything will go the way Elizabeth ordered, sooner or later. We both know that."

Wordlessly Zeldin stripped off the ugly blue nylon and moved slowly toward the shower. According to Elizabeth, Zeldin suffered from claustrophobia.

Ten minutes later when Zeldin— bathed and dressed in her nightshirt— was sitting on the bed drinking water, Allison relayed Elizabeth's offer: "Do the writing for Elizabeth that you refused to do before, and Scott Moore will be released and given transport to the location of his choice. It's that simple."

"What writing?"

"Elizabeth said you would know what she meant. You've spent a lot of time in the closet because of your refusal to write about your early relationship with Sedgewick. If you write fully enough to satisfy Elizabeth, Moore will go free."

Zeldin's gaze stabbed into Allison's. "Why can't I talk to Elizabeth?"

Allison found it difficult to keep her eyes on Zeldin's. Those freaky blue eyes— strange, frightening, accusing, no matter whether according to mood they were dull or burning— deeply disturbed her. "You know I can't tell you anything. I follow orders. I do what Elizabeth tells me to do."

Zeldin's gaze dropped to her knees. Such a cantankerous, obstreperous, creepy professional: Allison could not imagine her involved in any connection with the Sedgewick whose portrait hung in the executive conference room in the Chief's suite. Nor even with the man whose voice she had heard that first night in Elizabeth's apartment.

Allison got up to go. There was little point in sitting there. "I'll come by in the evening to take you for another viewing."

Zeldin looked up. "Tell Elizabeth. Tell her I want to talk to her."

Allison went to the door. "Why should she care that you want to talk to her?" Allison said, her hand hovering over the access plate.

"Just tell her. Please, Allison." Zeldin's eyes demanded rather than begged.

"I'll tell her. The book is on the desk, Kay. You can settle everything for Moore whenever you're ready." Allison thumbed open the door and went out into the corridor. Elizabeth would be pleased at Zeldin's wanting to talk to her, for whatever reason. But Allison doubted it would be for the right reason. Zeldin was probably hoping to talk Elizabeth out of punishing Moore. Zeldin seemed to be almost as off-the-wall about Elizabeth as Elizabeth was about Zeldin.

Allison trekked back to the office. When would Elizabeth realize how hopeless the whole project was? It had been crazy, Elizabeth's idea. It would have been better for her to have tried to deal with Booth and the others than to pursue this long-shot with Sedgewick.

But it was too late now; Elizabeth was right about that. They had no choice but to press on. And as Elizabeth had pointed out, that tended to be true for all the others— the men— too, especially the men in Security, and of those especially the ones being used to deal with the other departments of the Executive. All of them knew they had too much to lose in a revolt against Elizabeth. Sedgewick had exclusively handled the Executive himself, Elizabeth had explained, with the result that none of the others had any experience dealing with Cabinet-level men, and none had the connections necessary to save their own skins should Security be shaken down from the outside. They were all in this together.

The thought did not console Allison.

[iii]

When Martha got back to Sweetwater and she entered, as usual, through the kitchen, Ariadne asked her if David Hughes wanted to be invited to dinner and possibly to stay the night. The look of speculation on her face pricked Martha. "David! I had no idea he was coming," she said brusquely— then sighed. "I suppose giving him dinner would be the decent thing to do. Can I ask him, if it seems appropriate?"

"Sure," Ariadne said. "He can stay the night, too, if that's what you want."

Martha gave her a look of smoldering rebuke, then stamped off to the living room to face David. She found him sitting in the corner, staring down at the wood carving— one of Lee's wild mountain-women— he held in his hands. "Hello, David. This is a surprise," she said to him.

David smiled at her. "I had to get out of the city," he said. "I knew you were here. I thought I'd stop by and see if I could get you to go camping with me."

"It's a little wet." Martha sat down on the couch.

"You sound annoyed to see me."

Martha shrugged. "I can't just go off with you. I have things to do. Even over the holidays."

"Such as?"

"I have visits I need to make for my other committee," Martha said. "I'm going up to the Bellingham area, for one thing."

His smile got warmer— too warm for Martha's comfort, and she stared down at her hands and picked at a bit of dirt beneath the nail of her right ring finger. His tone became gently mocking. "And this work can't be put off for a few days?"

"I'm not punching a clock, David." She glanced at him. "But since everything that happens in the Free Zone depends on the initiative of individuals, it's necessary to be self-disciplined about such things. And since there are now a number of foreign trade agents operating out of Seattle, it's all the more critical that I keep myself up to the mark. The Zone isn't exactly on its feet yet. You should know that, economist that you are."

"What, you can't take a couple of days off now and then without the entire Zone going to pieces?"

Martha shot him a Look. "That's not what I'm saying. As you very well know, damn you."

"Let me go with you then on your trip to Bellingham."

"No way. It just wouldn't work. Anyway, though you can stay here at Sweetwater one night, you sure as hell can't stay here as many nights as I'll be staying. This is generally a women-only environment."

"I wouldn't have to stay here. I have my camping gear with me."

"You're making me feel hounded, David."

There was a silence. After about a minute he said, "I didn't intend to hound you, Martha. I only thought it would be fun for us to spend a little time together away from Seattle. But if you're feeling hounded, I'll leave in the morning."

Martha stared down at her folded, twisting hands. It occurred to her that David's reason probably had something to do with his not wanting to spend the holidays alone. But why was he so alone? Wasn't there anyone else in his life besides her? She looked at him and realized that he *never* mentioned friends or colleagues, even in the most casual, unconscious way. Was he really that much of a loner? It was hard to believe, considering how easily he handled social situations. "Never mind," she said. "Maybe we can work something out— for

a couple of days, anyway. As for a place to sleep tomorrow night, you could always stay at the Science Center. I'm sure they'd find a bed for you there."

David's eyes glowed. "I promise not to be a nuisance, Martha."

He looked like a little boy who'd just been promised a special treat. Martha's mouth curled into a smile. "I'm sure," she said. She glanced at her watch. "We have about an hour and a half before dinner. We could run over to Deception Pass and walk on the beach for a bit if you'd like."

David sprang out of his chair, went to the couch, and held his hand down to Martha. "The battery in my car should be recharged by now." His smiled widened into a grin. "Let's go."

Martha took his hand and levered herself to her feet. David held onto her hand. "We'll have to stop in the kitchen and let them know you'll be staying," she said, hoping she wouldn't regret having acted on impulse. She couldn't help musing on how Ariadne— and the others— would probably interpret all this. But that was one of the hazards of Sweetwater.

[iv]

Kay agonized over what to do. It seemed to her there were two distinct and opposing ways to view what was happening. On the one hand she could regard the situation as one in which some larger concern than her own personal survival lay at stake. In that case, Scott's having been brought into it must be taken as an attempt to bring additional pressure to bear on her, to push her into a direction she had been (mostly unconsciously) resisting. The demand that she write in the book might be seen either as pushing her another step along some determined route, or as a source of leverage to be used at a later time, or as intrinsically providing some sort of evidence that they wanted— though considering the subject matter in question Kay could not fathom how the book could be used except indirectly. If that were the case then she must at all costs avoid writing anything more in it. But *at all costs* posed a rather grim absolute.

Yet if she looked at it from the other perspective, holding out— at the expense of Scott's sanity— would be a horrendous, tragic mistake,

especially if they genuinely intended to release him upon her acquiescence. For whatever it might cost her personally, if this situation really were a matter strictly between her and Elizabeth and Sedgewick, then any casualty besides herself would be not only unnecessary but unforgivable. She would find it painful to obey, and frightening, but however bad it might be, the sacrifice of Scott— who might still belong to the land of the living— would be too high a price to pay merely to preserve herself from pain.

Kay had no way of assessing which perspective was the correct one. She mistrusted her own judgment, for she knew she could no longer be emotionally balanced enough to sift through the little that she did know, and even worse understood that what she did know was what they had allowed her to know and that she could no longer judge what they might or might not do under certain circumstances. After all, that Sedgewick had had her watched all those years meant he certainly would not stick at any degree of effort in exacting vengeance if that was what he had in mind. Thus she could not assume unproblematically that simply because they had dragged Scott into this there must be some larger issue at stake than her own torment. In short, she could not dismiss the second possibility merely on grounds of paranoia. In fact, it seemed more likely that she should dismiss the first possibility on the grounds that it depended upon seeing herself as an important player— or pawn— in some larger game. It was hard to imagine Sedgewick thinking her connections with the Free Zone and the Marq'ssan worth so much bother, worth keeping her alive, worth preserving her from Wedgewood. Considering Sedgewick's longtime obsession, the second possibility seemed much more likely the longer she thought about it.

She sat with the book in her lap and the pen in her fingers and considered. What would it cost her, really?

She sighed. What if they were trying to get *Scott* to do something? That was a third possibility. What if they intended to show him— but no. That made no sense. She knew from those interrogations of Scott she had been forced to watch that he believed she was dead. He had read her book, and he knew now that she had a past. What he thought

of her treason wasn't at all clear. Weary and exhausted as he had been (they had kept him up for thirty-six hours at a time with successive teams questioning him without respite), he had said very simply the same few things over and over again, baffled that they were doing this to him, puzzled at their seeing something insidious in his having known Nadine Morris, never really saying anything about her, Kay, though he might reasonably have denounced her now that he believed she was dead.

Kay went to the bathroom for tissue to wipe her eyes. No, it wasn't Scott they were after. They wouldn't have gone about it like that. She was the target, she could not doubt it.

Kay filled the sink with water, to wash. She thought she smelled urine on her body.

She needed to talk to Elizabeth. She had this feeling that it wasn't even the book so much as Elizabeth's anger that was behind this abuse of Scott. Elizabeth had not come to see her since that night when she had gotten so furious. Instead Allison came with instructions from Elizabeth, and Allison took her to view Scott. There was nothing to be gained talking to Allison. Allison knew nothing and was powerless. Whereas Elizabeth... Perhaps she could persuade Elizabeth to relent. Elizabeth wanted more than the entries in the book. Her anger had come not from anything to do with the book but because Kay— when Elizabeth had caught her in a lie— had refused to pretend there was communication between them, and also because she had thrown away the powder. What if she apologized and promised not to lie again and helped Elizabeth promote the illusion that what they said to one another mattered? Would that induce her to relent? For Scott Kay could do that, for Scott's release it seemed little enough to do.

But Allison's words: write what Elizabeth wants you to write in the book and Scott Moore will be released... Kay finished washing and returned to bed. She picked up the book, opened it, and took the pen in her fingers. Leaning back against the wall she forced herself to remember that first time with Sedgewick. There had been a debriefing. She had met him to report after returning to Frankfurt from the conference in Milan, where most of the European branches of Green

Force International had met to plan the next year's strategy. She had been surprised to find him, an executive, debriefing her (by that time he had sloughed off most of his professional background and appeared to the casual observer a born executive); always before she had been debriefed by a professional. She had had no idea that he was head of the Western Europe division. If she had known that she would have wondered at his dealing with her at all. He was exotic enough being an executive, one of the few she had ever had contact with. She had exercised caution because she had heard stories about how nasty executives could be. But he hadn't been in the least disagreeable: a little cool, at first; but she had had the feeling that he was waiting, giving her a chance to prove herself. So she had been as competent and witty and self-assured as she could manage, as determined to show well as she had ever been with her professors as a student. Now that she forced herself to think about it, she could remember the encounter very clearly.

Sunday afternoon in late fall... they had gone to a wine-bar where she had made her report and answered questions, which she knew he was recording. He had been serious. He hadn't smiled much in those days, either. But there hadn't been that hardness to his face yet, and when he did smile a certain charm and magnetism had drawn her. They'd finished the bottle of wine, and he'd casually asked her if she were interested in drinking something "quite a bit better" at his place. She found him attractive. It would be a one-time thing, and being the sort of person he was there would be no awkwardness later. More interestingly, for the first time the debriefing process had been amusing, even stimulating as he elicited her analyses (which her previous controller had never bothered to do). So she accepted his invitation easily, almost unthinkingly. He drove her to his apartment in a four-seater with diplomatic plates— the first time she'd ever ridden in a free-wheeler. When she asked him about the plates he said his cover billed him as the cultural attaché at the embassy in Bonn. So you live in Bonn? she'd asked. Part of the time, he'd responded. And then he'd begun asking her questions about her research.

His personal style was entirely new to her. He prepared a meal for them while she bathed in his clear-water shower. So young, she was so young then. Not that she'd thought so at the time: she'd had plenty of sexual experience— with professionals. But not enough, apparently, to prepare her for someone like Sedgewick. How thoughtful, how charming, she'd thought, his sending her off to get comfortable while he cooked. Wearing one of his silk robes (the first time she'd felt silk against her skin), eating his wonderful food (in her single room she ate nothing but tubefood, having only a microwave for heating tubefood and boiling water for coffee and tea, consuming "real" food only when eating out, usually sandwiches), drinking the wine that was far beyond her experience to appreciate, and all this so pleasantly, without hurry, while he drew details of her life from her. She'd sensed she could leave the arrangements of the evening in her partner's hands for a change— she would let him lead the way, let him get them into bed. He used speech, body language, his eyes to intensify the sexual tension between them long before they even touched. What a pleasure being with someone so smooth and self-confident, rendering everything so effortless. Is this, she wondered, what being around executives was like? Why then did people accustomed to being around them talk about executives the way they did?

Afterwards, late in the evening, he dropped her off outside her building: "Next time I won't be so easy on you," were the words he left her with. Intriguing, yes, but what she chiefly heard was "next time." After a week, however, she had stopped waiting to hear from him. Some sort of parting line, she thought. She fleetingly considered calling him, but his number and address were nowhere to be found, and she was not sure that if she had the number that she would really care to risk the snub. Tracking him to the embassy was of course unthinkable. So she went about her work determined to forget him, at least until her next scheduled debriefing when it was possible he might again be her contact.

Thinking back, Kay calculated that the next encounter had been about three weeks later, on a Thursday night when he had met her getting off the train from Mannheim, where she had gone for the day to work in the archives there. How had he known she would be getting off that train? She had wondered but hadn't asked. Rather than be concerned about it she had been flattered and amazed, ready to speculate privately and to romanticize. But the second time hadn't been like the first. She hadn't known how to deal with him and had crept out of his apartment at two-thirty in the morning (while he slept) humiliated and resentful. He liked to play games? She didn't, she couldn't, she wouldn't. And she hoped she wouldn't see him at her next debriefing. Awkwardness wouldn't begin to describe how she would feel if she did.

But of course he had been the one to appear for her next debriefing. He was businesslike at first, sliding into charming: "You're wasted on this, Zeldin, we could use you for more important things. Though we still need you placed as you are in this organization..." She'd taken the bait and also let him draw her into another sexual encounter even more equivocal than the previous one. Power, she thought afterwards lying sleepless beside him: that's all he cares about, it's his only interest in sex. Never again. This time she stayed the night in his bed and in the morning coldly drank his coffee and feigned indifference as she sauntered out the door ostensibly off to a long day's work in the state archives.

On the fourth occasion— this time initiated by a phone call: "Want to come over and play?"— she'd turned the tables on him...at first out of anger, through her teeth, but then, when she'd realized he was playing along and enjoying it, caught up in a strange vertigo of elation, that this highly controlled and controlling executive allowed her— for the night— absolute sexual control over him. Remembering, it seemed to her now that that had permanently changed the nature of their encounters.

She had never refused to see him. The rules became clear: he would call her (she did not even have his number), always using the same formula ("want to come over and play?"); most of the time he assumed control, allowing her control about one-fourth of the time. At all times there was a clear sense of one or the other of them being in control. Nothing "simply happened" between them as might happen

spontaneously— innocently— between people unconcerned about power and control. Kay recalled now that they had once discussed this, and Sedgewick had commented that they could be freer, more daring by making such an obvious structural division in their sexual roles... Her memory of their encounters blurred past the fourth one. She could not, for instance, recall when they had introduced violence into their sex-play. She only knew that it had happened at some point after they had begun using handcuffs, and that it had not been one-sided. Did the violence start because they had grown so intense, or did they become so intense because of the violence? They saw one another more and more frequently. And she began doing other jobs for the Company. He would take her with him to other cities where she would sit in on debriefings and other meetings and then write analytic reports for him afterwards. Somewhere along the way she had discovered who he was and that there were other women. She grew increasingly involved with him and with the Company, and he talked to her about becoming permanent and brought her into more and more operations. When they had finally shut down Green Force International a little more than three years after the conference in Milan, Kay had been on one of the interrogation teams. Remembering it now, it seemed neither real nor possible: she had been so wrapped up in Sedgewick that she had moved through it all as through a dream. That, she had thought then, was real life— unlike her other existence spent patiently and meticulously reading documents in state archives and libraries. Doing the same kind of patient, meticulous reading and analyses for the Company had seemed different from working in the archives.

"Good morning, Kay."

Kay started. She had not heard Allison come in. Looking afresh at Allison she was again reminded of a hawk: the deeply hooded, thick-fringed eyes watching and waiting, the nose and chin jutting sharply out, belying the soft curves of the cheeks, the fluffy roundness of the hair and head. "Good morning, Allison," Kay said. "I've written in the book for Elizabeth. Will you let him go now?"

"Have you?" Allison sounded surprised. "You know she'll have to read it first." She held out her hand, and Kay gave her the book. "But you'll still have to go for the viewing."

Kay got up from the bed, and even though she remembered to do so slowly, she still had to cope with dizziness. "Did you tell Elizabeth I want to talk to her?"

Allison slipped the book into the leather bag. "She said she's surprised you asked to talk to her. Because you said that there could be no communication between her and you since she's controlling you. And so she wonders why you would want to talk to her, why you can't simply pass along whatever it is you want to say through me."

Kay dug her toes into the rug; the dizziness had passed. "Tell her I want to apologize to her."

Allison went to the desk and picked up Kay's intake log. "Did you forget to enter today's food on this?"

Kay sat down on the edge of the bed. "No. I didn't forget. I couldn't eat today."

Allison replaced the log on the desk. "Why are you doing this to yourself?"

"I've been too upset about Scott," Kay said. "Believe me, I'd eat if I could. I've tried to force myself, but…"

"Look, Kay. If you don't make the minimum weight Elizabeth has specified, she'll order force-feedings. Twice a day for the whole week. Wouldn't it be better to force yourself?"

"I'd just vomit it up," Kay said. "That's what happened both times I tried yesterday. And now I can't swallow that stuff. I would if I could."

Sighing, Allison pulled a pair of handcuffs from the leather bag. "Hold out your wrists, Kay." Kay stood and held her hands out for Allison to cuff her. It was a curious thing, but she could tell that Allison hated these trips to "view" Scott almost as much as she herself did. For a few seconds she wondered what kind of a person Allison was, but soon her thoughts strayed to speculation on whether Elizabeth would be satisfied with what she had written in the book. She hoped this would be the last time she would be "viewing" Scott— even if it

meant it would be the last time in her life she would ever lay eyes on him. If she could be sure he was safe and free, this hellish existence would not matter so much, for deep inside she would know some part of her self had survived and gone free.

And that was the very best she could hope for now.

[v]

Allison arrived home at about nine-thirty, dead tired. She had been going since six that morning and had had nothing to eat but a sandwich in the early afternoon. She found Anne lying on the sofa reading a novel, her left arm's cast propped up on a stack of cushions pushed up against the sofa. Allison laughed. "So you've finally figured out a way to deal with your encumbrances."

Anne made a droll face. "I get pretty tired of having that cast lying on my body. Sometimes I have the urge to saw the arm off, just to be rid of it. It's so clumsy!" The worst of it, Allison thought, was that the med-techs couldn't predict how long it would take for Anne's bones to regenerate. Tissue growth-rates varied widely from individual to individual.

Allison went into the kitchen. As she made herself a sandwich she thought about how a simple thing like food had (like so many other trivial matters) proved to be an excruciatingly complicated issue when Anne had moved in. The day after Anne had moved in Allison had discovered food tubes in the kitchen. On asking Anne about them she had come up against a stubbornness in Anne that took the form of not wanting Allison to pay any expenses directly incurred by her. The sight of the tubes had upset Allison, and at Anne's balking she had shouted at Anne that she wouldn't have them in her kitchen and that she paid no living expenses here, that Security was paying for her food and rent because she was technically on temporary loan from Vienna and what did Anne take her for anyway...

Instead of shouting back at her, Anne had begun packing. Allison had apologized. They had talked tearfully for a long time and at last come to an understanding. But though Anne ate the food Allison's service-tech kept the kitchen stocked with, she had so little experience with non-tubefood that she did not quite know how to prepare it or in what forms to eat it, which meant that unless Allison was there to cook for them, Anne ate bizarre makeshift meals out of whatever foodstuffs she thought it was proper for her to eat. (She worried, Allison knew, about eating extravagantly expensive things.) The subject of meals was now a hypersensitive one, something they skirted in conversation.

Another issue had been the sleeping arrangements. It seemed obvious to Allison that because of her casts Anne should sleep— alone— in Allison's bed. Nothing else made sense to Allison, and she at first insisted she would sleep on the couch. But that Anne would not accept. Finally Allison had realized that the issue could conveniently be used to explain her sleeping upstairs in Elizabeth's apartment, so she told Anne that Elizabeth had an extra bedroom that she, Allison, would use until Anne's casts came off. For the time being, then, Anne's presence in Allison's apartment did not disturb her relationship with Elizabeth.

Not that Elizabeth had approved of Anne's moving into Allison's apartment. On the contrary: Elizabeth could not understand what possible reason Allison could have for having invited Anne in the first place, and in the second place was inclined to see it as a nuisance now and a potential threat to their privacy later. She issued warnings about the inevitable problems having a service-tech living with one entailed. She herself had done that once, thirty years past, and had found the resulting messiness intolerable. And she warned Allison that if Anne found out about the sexual aspect of her and Allison's relationship, they would be vulnerable to blackmail... No amount of discussion could change Elizabeth's mind about Anne. Allison finally gave up trying to do so and did her best to keep the subject of Anne out of their conversation. Sometimes she worried about what would happen when Anne's casts came off, and about Anne's future. But so many other concerns crowded her mind that her worry about Anne never became very specific or focused.

Allison carried her sandwich and glass of wine into the living room. Anne, smiling, set her book aside. "It's so nice having such a big selection of books to read," she said.

"You should see all the books I have in my apartment in Vienna," Allison said. "I guess I'm something of a bookworm. I've never been that much into social life. The books I have here are just things I've picked up at book dealers on my few trips to Denver." Allison bit into the sandwich.

"I had to leave most of my books behind in DC, too," Anne said sadly. "And not many of the girls here are into reading. And now that books are so scarce they're terribly expensive."

"I'm glad you like to read. Otherwise it would be pretty dull living here— no company to speak of, since I'm away most of the time, and nothing to do. It must seem *too* quiet after having lived the last year and a half with three other people in the same unit." Allison took another bite of her sandwich and felt mustard oozing down her chin.

"I don't miss the company so much as I miss the radio. I'm surprised you don't have one, Lise."

Allison suppressed a sigh. Anne's illusions about radio broadcasts drove her nuts. "If you really want a radio I can easily get hold of one for you," she said. "I didn't realize you missed it so badly." Of course, besides the news there was music and soap operas and other entertainment standing in for vid these days.

Before Allison had finished eating her sandwich, her handset beeped. She knew even before picking up that it was Elizabeth. "Can you come upstairs, Allison?" Elizabeth said. "I have several things to discuss with you."

Allison wolfed down the rest of the sandwich and said good-night to Anne. Upstairs she found Elizabeth in a state of agitation, pacing her living room to the rhythms of the Schubert symphony filling the room. "What do you think, Allison? Tell me how Zeldin seemed to you. That she's finally started writing in the damned book! And her wanting to talk to me. Maybe my strategy didn't misfire after all. Tell me what you think, darling!"

"I think she's feeling desperate. I think the idea of Moore's being freed if she writes for you worked powerfully on her."

"But her wanting to talk to me? Don't you think that means something? And that she wants to apologize to me? Maybe my getting angry was the best thing that could have happened. Maybe my staying away from her made her rethink her situation."

"Are you satisfied with what she wrote?" Allison asked.

"Let's get into the tub, darling. I'm wound up so tight I'm about to jump out of my skin." Without waiting for Allison's response, Elizabeth strode into the bedroom. Allison followed more sedately, fretting at Elizabeth's hyper state. She had never seen her like this before.

When they were both sitting in the Jacuzzi Elizabeth returned to Allison's question. "What she wrote is a start, but it's not enough. Still, it is an honest start. That she wrote what she has means she's had to admit a few things to herself that she's covered over for years. It's all a matter now of how I work with this material on her. And some of that depends largely on her receptivity to me. I wish I knew..."

"If you let Moore go and find a way to assure her of it I think she'll be likely to cooperate," Allison said. "It obviously means a lot to her. Things are so bad with her that she hasn't been eating, even though she knows she's going to be getting on the scale three days from now. She'll be under, Elizabeth." Allison paused. "It will make things difficult, you know. I don't see how you can expect to work on her except through coercion if you're having her force-fed twice a day."

Elizabeth sighed. "You're right about that. Damn. I'll have to think about what to do. Whatever it is, I suspect you'll be handling her for me. Obviously playing hard-to-get is proving effective."

Allison's heart sank. She hated handling Zeldin. Never had she been so aware of the fragility of human dignity. Every moment spent with Zeldin forced her into an awareness of how hard the other woman had to struggle for her personal dignity.

"Whenever I don't think things out thoroughly in advance where Zeldin is concerned," Elizabeth was saying ruefully, "I get into trouble. Do I suspend my own rules? Or do I go through with it just because I made a rule about it? Do I fuss over her to reward her for finally coming through? I don't know, Allison. I simply don't have the time now to be thinking about Zeldin. Though I'm delegating almost everything to do with the possibility of war, I'm finding it essential to keep the coordinating in my own hands— suddenly our morale problem

is disappearing and people are waking up: they're actually snapping to— which means I may be in for challenges from the director level." Elizabeth laid her head back and closed her eyes. "Maybe the Russians have the right idea, creating such a visible and obvious enemy. It sure beats fighting other executives and dealing with the mess the aliens left us in." Elizabeth opened her eyes and shifted her body so that a powerful jet of water could pummel her neck. "Ah... that little spot of tension must have been the source of my headache."

"So you think the war could be a good thing?" Allison asked doubtfully.

Elizabeth grimaced. "Maybe a temporary shot in the arm, but ultimately a dead loss," she said. "It may get some of our economy moving, but in the long run I'm sure we'll lose by it. Some people, however, don't see it that way. They have a big problem, though, when they start jabbering about unity and so on: we're still fighting a civil war... I have a feeling the time's ripe for settling that. I'm going to try again to talk to Sedgewick about it. Perhaps the reports about the Russians' invasion preparations will help me get through to him."

Allison closed her eyes. Again she wondered why Elizabeth didn't simply ask Zeldin outright to handle Sedgewick for her. Why not be overt about it? What was it Elizabeth thought she had to do to Zeldin to "prepare" her?

"Did you read the new entry in Zeldin's book yourself?" Elizabeth asked.

Allison opened her eyes to find Elizabeth watching her. "It's horrible," she said. The notion of a mature executive male unfixed— that alone was hard to think about. But to go into the details of an intrinsically violent heterosexuality was nauseating. "I find it so hard to imagine those sub-exec women letting themselves be used like that. The whole idea of hetero fucking is so inherently perverse—" Allison shuddered— "and then to take it even further, the way Zeldin did. How can they find it pleasurable? Do you think they're all deluding themselves, Elizabeth? Or is it something to do with the sub-exec mentality, a kind of masochism?"

Elizabeth laughed. "More of your fastidiousness, darling? I couldn't really characterize Zeldin as a masochist, could you?"

Allison brushed the sweat out of her eyes. "I don't know anything about Zeldin," she said crossly. The only thing she knew about Zeldin was that she felt sorry for her. This thought surprised her, for before she had begun handling Zeldin she had resented Elizabeth's absorption in her and could only think of her as someone who had gone renegade in the worst possible way. In spite of her pity, though, Allison found Zeldin frightening. The watchfulness in her eyes, the look of someone who knows a great deal that others would rather not know, sometimes made Allison's flesh crawl. How could Elizabeth seriously think that Sedgewick could respond positively to someone like the person Zeldin had become? Did Elizabeth not see the change in her?

They soaped, rinsed, and got out of the tub. Allison, drying Elizabeth, let her hands linger over the curves of Elizabeth's breasts. Desire swept over her; slowly she trailed her fingers through Elizabeth's pubic hair, needing to make Elizabeth want her, now, this minute.

They did not bother to put on their robes, but went straight to bed. Some things at least remained simple and clear enough to make words between them unnecessary, notwithstanding whatever else might be happening around them.

Chapter Twenty-seven

The dream from which Kay woke choking in horror permeated her consciousness for the entire day. She remembered nothing of it but the image that inspired the horror that woke her, of herself lying like an infant in Elizabeth's arms, suckling her breast. The moment of horror in the dream had come when she became fully conscious of what she was doing. The image imprinted itself indelibly on her mind.

And so began the day's despair.

She knew that that day she would be weighed and found below the required weight. That this would happen was inevitable, as inevitable as anything in her existence could be. She knew, too, what consequences would follow on fourteen occasions over the next seven days. The passages down which the tubes would be forced had already grown raw in anticipation.

Her ebullience of the day before at Allison's telling her that Scott would be released had vanished. How could she believe what they told her? Why should she believe them? If she had caved in this time, why would they not keep Scott around to pressure her another time? She lacked the power to make Elizabeth keep her promises. Why would Elizabeth do what she was not required to do? As she had said to Kay, she made the rules of the game. They both knew no one was there to hold her to any of them.

And if she had given in for nothing, but out of weakness? What little peace of mind she had eked out for herself had been wrecked now that she had wrenched open the floodgates of memory. Details from those years with Sedgewick continually flowed out from the dark corners of her mind, making her question all she had ever thought about herself, making her doubt the patterns by which she had learned to understand her life, making her writhe with retrospective torment and shame. And now Elizabeth knew some of these things about her. But Elizabeth, Kay reminded herself, had always known some version of them through Sedgewick, had known of this vulnerable area Kay had blinded herself to.

Elizabeth must have some idea of using it. Even an overt reference to it would be painful for Kay. But Elizabeth would not confine herself to a bare mention. How to shut the door on the subject once Elizabeth had gotten her foot inside? No, Kay decided, she did not want to speak to Elizabeth now after all. In ordinary life, by this point in any game she would have long since conceded and ended the boring, painful certainty of loss. In this game she did not have the option to concede, but was required to play it out— limping, humiliated, wounded— until the very end. Her hatred for Elizabeth flared anew, for a few minutes overriding despair, until, exhausted, Kay sank into the closest approximation of apathy she could achieve.

At one in the afternoon when Kay saw Allison and not Elizabeth coming through the door, she felt both relief and disappointment. She rose from the bed and ignoring her dizziness held out her wrists to be cuffed before Allison even greeted her. She would try to be indifferent about it, try to feel nothing. She would think herself into robotdom.

"You're in a hurry, Kay," Allison said, apparently forgetting the greeting.

Kay's vision cleared; she watched Allison rummage inside the leather bag. "Why put off the inevitable? You know as well as I do that I won't make the weight Elizabeth set for this week." As she had many times before, Kay looked at those soft brown eyes and wondered how someone who looked like Allison could be involved in such obscenity. It seemed so foreign to this woman, so unaccustomed. Several times at difficult moments Kay had thought she had seen Allison flinch— out of a sensibility someone in her position should not still have.

Allison did not meet her gaze, but snapped the cuffs around Kay's wrists and opened the door. "Did I ever mention to you that I once took a couple of graduate-level courses with you?" she asked as they walked.

Kay stared at her. "At the UW?"

"Yes. It was more than ten years ago, of course. I took my masters there in history. Did my undergraduate work at Stanford. Anyway, one of my minors was twentieth-century Europe."

"How did you do?" Kay asked curiously.

"Both times you gave me an A-minus," Allison said.

"Not bad," Kay said. "Maybe if I think about it I'll eventually remember." She cringed as she recognized the irony of her using such an expression.

"There's no reason for you to remember me," Allison said. "I was quiet and spoke as little as possible. I never talked much— still don't, actually— except around other executive women."

"I often wondered why executive women students were so shy about participating in discussion," Kay said.

They stepped into the elevator. To Kay's surprise, Allison punched the button not for the infirmary floor, nor for the floor they had gotten off on when going to "view" Scott, but for the top floor of the elevator's range. The unexpected disturbed Kay: she preferred to know what was happening to her, no matter how inevitably disagreeable. Deviation threw her off balance, made her quiver with anxiety. In her situation innovation usually meant the introduction of a new source of pain and anxiety. She stared hard at Allison's face, searching for a clue. But the perfectly guileless face showed nothing.

Elizabeth— like Sedgewick— knew well how to pick her tools.

Allison led her to a room that might or might not be the same room to which she had been brought to dine. She spoke briefly to the guard posted outside the door, then thumbed open the door. As she unlocked the cuffs she told Kay to sit. Kay glanced around the room and saw that the table had been set for two. After a minute or two the door opened and Elizabeth came in.

"Good morning, Kay," Elizabeth said from the doorway.

Kay's heart thumped with a spurt of fear. "Good morning, Elizabeth." This was the first time she'd seen Elizabeth in more than a week.

Elizabeth came into the room and stood a few feet from Kay. Waiting. For the apology Kay had told Allison she would make? Kay cleared her throat and swallowed hard. Elizabeth's substantiality, her hardness, the vividness of her excessive presence brushed painfully against newly exposed nerves. The cell, Allison, even she herself seemed shadowy by comparison, of dubious materiality. Kay had forgotten about Elizabeth's not-to-be-evaded solidity. Elizabeth watched her, waiting, while Kay held her face still and sought— without finding— a reason to hold herself defiantly apart. She could not do so now without appearing to be merely indulging a fit of petulant temper, for she'd made her bargain with Elizabeth, had sold for Scott's release the one thing that Elizabeth wanted of her. It would all break down now anyway with only a few words from Elizabeth. How had it happened that instead of growing a thick protective callous she'd helped locate the old half-concealed seams that made it possible to peel back the epidermal layers in a few easy tugs at the strategic spots? This apology should be nothing to her, a meaningless formula. That it was so difficult granted it an importance that exacerbated the pain. She told herself to simply say the words, say them and get them over with... "I apologize, Elizabeth, for losing control." Kay said the words while staring at the neck of Elizabeth's rose silk and white wool tunic.

Elizabeth glided forward and perched on the arm of Kay's chair. Kay stared down at her hands lying limp in the lap of the nightshirt. "And the lies?" Elizabeth said. "If you still maintain that what you say to me is of no significance...then of course there would be no point in our talking."

"You know I was telling the truth this time when I wrote in the book," Kay said.

Elizabeth's hand settled on Kay's head to stroke her hair. Kay steeled herself to accept the galling humiliation of the touch. Elizabeth was having it all her own way, and Kay found nothing but anger for response. She knew how useless anger was without careful reasoning, without recourse to carefully formulated rules, without an internal authority directing an expression of anger she could recognize as correct. Overwhelmed by emotion, Kay felt more powerless than she had ever felt while chained to the platform or even while lying motionless under the influence of a paralytic injection. She needed to think,

needed to find a way through the anger— but she had not been able to bring herself to think clearly about recent developments precisely because she had not yet been able to reconcile herself to memory, to accepting any of these new memories as part of herself— while knowing all the time that they were, their importance looming impossibly large because she had kept them buried and denied their reality for so many years. And this reluctance to face the significance of what she now remembered constituted the very ground of her vulnerability to Elizabeth: it wasn't so much that she had "caved in" as that being unable to face something in herself deprived her of her own authority. Kay half-recognized this as she floundered in resentment and humiliation. She had lost conviction, lost faith, lost both solidity and backbone: hence her amorphous, quivering anger.

"But do you realize now how important it is to tell me the truth? How impossible it is for us to deal together if you lie whenever and as you please?" Elizabeth's hand slid under Kay's chin and forced her face up. Kay held every nerve and muscle in her face rigidly immobile, from tightly pressed lips to deliberate blankness of eyes and forehead. "You wanted to speak to me," Elizabeth reminded Kay. "But I won't waste my time on you if you want only to return to your old attitude. There's always Allison, you see."

Why had she wanted to see Elizabeth? Because of Scott? Or for some other reason?

Elizabeth stood up. "Come, let's have lunch."

Kay wondered: would Elizabeth not be pressing this further? She followed Elizabeth to the table and sat at the place setting arranged to Elizabeth's right. Quiche, salad, and bread had been laid out on the table. "It's Christmas Eve, Kay," Elizabeth said as she served Kay quiche.

Late December? Then she must have been here for more than three months. So long? But instantly she revised this: *only* three months? Was that all? It seemed an eternity. Kay buttered a hunk of bread. This mark of time meant nothing, could mean nothing to her. She did not exist in the calendar world. She did not exist "out there." What did it matter how long it had been by that world's count? Here time did not exist except in the tiniest of increments— and the largest: viz the rest of her life, however long that was.

It was the largest increment of time she found imaginable now.

Kay held her quiche-laden fork to her lips. Glimpsing Elizabeth's movements out of the corner of her eye, she recalled her earlier determination never to eat with her. Accepting into her mouth the sliver of quiche, she experienced a response of her taste-buds acute nearly to the point of pain. How incredible, that food could taste like this, that she could savor such pleasure... She distinguished salmon among the melange of flavors... Could she manage to stuff herself— without later vomiting— to the point of making up the pounds lacking for the day's reckoning?

"And since it is Christmas," Elizabeth said, as though continuing her earlier dropped remark, "and since I'm generally pleased with you, I've decided to excuse you from seeing Dr. Gordon this week."

Kay looked up from her plate to stare at Elizabeth. *Reprieve!* A crushing tension she had not acknowledged released its grip on her heart; she suddenly breathed more easily. But Elizabeth— smiling approvingly, benevolently at her star pupil— was waiting for an acknowledgment of her generosity. "Thank you, Elizabeth," Kay quickly got out, trying to believe the saying of the words effortless, the significance of the words negligible. She poured water from the liter decanter into her glass and drank, concentrating her whole being on her thirst and its assuagement.

"As usual it's snowing today," Elizabeth said between bites. "Even in times like these the ski resorts do well."

Kay ate with her eyes bent on her food. Outside was inconceivable: what were snow and skiing to her? The clear sharp sight of a shadow— while any sort of shadow was achievable in her cell only with the night light, since one could not cast shadows under the indifferent glare of indirect lighting— was the closest resonance with the natural world accessible to her.

"It's your turn, Kay," Elizabeth said. Kay glanced up to signal her query: her turn for what? "To make conversation."

"Have you let Scott Moore go?" Kay said baldly. Though she did not like to ask Elizabeth questions, this was one Kay had determined to put to her.

Elizabeth drank from her water glass. "Oh yes. The day before yesterday. He is in San Jose now. We offered him a choice of several possible jobs, and he chose the one located there. He knows he is completely in the clear and that the job comes without strings attached." Elizabeth ate another bite of quiche. "You see, Kay, I keep my promises."

Kay didn't know whether to believe her or not. Scott could still be here buried in this pile of rock and she would have no way of knowing.

"I will arrange to have him photographed in such a way that you can see for yourself," Elizabeth said. "Salad?" she asked, piling a large serving on one of the waiting plates.

Kay enjoyed the crispness of the lettuce in her mouth and took notice of its long forgotten texture. The uniformity of the texture of tubefood was its worst aspect; no matter how many different flavorings they used the textures roughly remained the same, with differences only in the relative smoothness or chalkiness or grittiness or chunkiness of the paste. The uniqueness of this thin green fiber smooth yet crisp struck Kay for the first time. Bits of red onion crunched between her teeth, releasing a sweet yet sharp aroma that brought tears to her eyes. "Lettuce is quite remarkable when you think about it," Kay said out loud. (Her contribution to the conversation: surely innocuous.)

But the immense gratification visible in Elizabeth's eyes dashed Kay's moment of pleasure, transforming her remark into naive collaboration. Kay laid down her fork, unable to eat another bite.

"That's all you're going to eat of the quiche?" Elizabeth asked.

"I'm not used to this kind of food. It's too rich." The cream and eggs and cheese in the quiche had already begun making her queasy.

"Dessert, then." Elizabeth went through the door into what Kay guessed was a kitchen and returned with a plate of cheese cake in one hand and a bowl of sliced fruit in the other. "The cheesecake is for you," Elizabeth said, setting the plate before Kay. "You need the calories."

Kay picked a slice of kiwi off the top and ate it. Enviously she watched Elizabeth eat the sliced fruit.

"At least try it," Elizabeth said, a trace of annoyance creeping into her voice.

Kay obediently inserted a sliver of the cheesecake into her mouth, chewed it, and swallowed. This was the worst possible combination of food she could have eaten— too heavy and rich for her, too much at once.

"If you eat a bit more of that I'll let you have a cup of coffee," Elizabeth said.

The consummate bribe. With caffeine in her veins her brain might clear, her apathy might vanish. Determined to earn the coffee, Kay ate two more bites before laying her napkin beside her plate.

When Elizabeth finished the fruit she stood up, opened a drawer of the buffet, and removed a gift-wrapped package. "Let's sit over there," she said. Kay left the table and returned to the chair she had earlier sat in. Elizabeth dropped the package into Kay's lap and took the chair opposite. "Your Christmas present, Kay."

Kay set the green foil-wrapped box on the low table between them. "No," she said, struggling for control of her emotions. This was the worst yet, it was an outrage, Elizabeth's imposing this on her. She could not regard it as she had the other objects Elizabeth had bestowed on her— the fruit, the powder, the newspaper... The roles Elizabeth was attempting to establish here today would hopelessly entangle her if she did not keep their true relations sharp and clear and open between them. Elizabeth's forcing a "gift" upon her now was far more humiliating than the caress she had earlier bestowed.

"Oh but I insist." Elizabeth, smiling, watched Kay.

The nausea worsened. "I think I'm going to be sick. I need the bathroom," Kay gasped, clapping a hand to her mouth as she struggled to her feet.

Elizabeth took her by the arm and propelled her through the kitchen to a small room with a toilet and sink. Kay barely made it to the toilet in time. When she had finished vomiting and was washing the slime from her mouth and hands, Elizabeth said: "You did that

on purpose." Kay sensed anger seething beneath the cool matter-of-fact tone.

Kay said, "I couldn't help myself. The food was too much for me. I'm not used to it."

"Unconsciously you wanted to vomit. Do you think I don't know what you're doing?" Elizabeth's eyes were implacable.

Kay leaned against the wall and wondered if she were going to be sick again. But she felt relief that their enmity again stood starkly naked between them.

They returned to their chairs. "Open the gift, Kay," Elizabeth said.

Kay obeyed the order. Inside the box she found several pairs of long wool socks. Elizabeth bent forward and pointed to a pair patterned in burgundy, rose, and blue diamonds. "Put these on now." Kay pulled them up over her icy feet and legs. "Do you like them?" Elizabeth asked.

Kay looked at her. "Is it necessary that I like them?"

Elizabeth's eyes of glittering blue flint chilled her. "It isn't *necessary* that you like *anything*. Your pleasure and amusement are superfluous."

"Yes." Kay noticed that Elizabeth's hands had clenched into fists; the observation made her breath come faster. "That's what I thought. I just wanted to be clear about it."

The corridor door slid open and a service-tech carried in a tray she set down beside the box of socks. Elizabeth waved her away, then poured coffee out of the thermoflask into both cups. "You've cheated, but I'll let you have the coffee anyway." Elizabeth handed her one of the cups. "Help yourself to cream and sugar if you like."

Kay held the cup under her nose and inhaled the coffee's aroma. It would be hell on her stomach, but she couldn't resist. She sipped and while the full flavor of the coffee was still in her mouth felt the scalding hot liquid blaze a trail of heat all the way down her esophagus.

"And now, to business," Elizabeth said briskly. "It's time we discussed your latest entry in the book."

In spite of the coffee Kay could still taste the acrid residue of vomit in her mouth. Now. It was to be *now.*

"You wrote," Elizabeth said, "that you were on one of the teams that interrogated the Green Force International prisoners." At Elizabeth's pause, Kay nodded. The tension in her face and neck were already starting to make her head ache. "But you hadn't been trained in interrogation techniques and protocols, had you."

"No."

"Then why were you assigned to it?"

What did Elizabeth know or think she knew about it? What lay behind this particular question? Kay drew a deep breath and strove to keep her voice steady. "Because of what I knew, and what the prisoners knew I knew, and because of what I suspected, it was obvious that I could be useful during interrogations. The interrogations were directed toward two objectives— collecting implicating statements and exploring further the areas that I myself in my dealings with GFI had not been party to. I never made it into the very highest circles. But I knew enough to piece a lot of it together. It was necessary to tie the other European leaders to the Frankfurt group. We were using what we had on the Frankfurt group as a springboard for getting the others." Kay had not thought about any of this for years. But days of remembering and now actually putting it into words for another person brought a myriad details flooding back into her mind. How strange the ways of memory, that she could have forgotten everything for years yet now suddenly begun remembering so much detail.

"But I don't see why that should have been reason enough for your inclusion in the interrogation process. It's not quite usual. And you were inexperienced?" Was Elizabeth being ironic? Or was she testing her to see if she would lie? Or could it be she was asking about things of which she knew nothing?

"I'd watched several interrogations." Kay's face heated up. "And as I watched I wrote on a yellow pad suggestions for questions, suggestions for new lines of approach. Sedgewick told me I had a knack for leaping ahead, for seeing openings for what they were. So he began to

use me as backup in interrogations. I'd let whoever partnered me run the interrogation and then write my suggestions."

"It's not usual for infiltrators to participate in interrogations, especially of the groups they've infiltrated," Elizabeth said. "No matter how clever and astute and intuitive they might be."

Kay lowered her eyes and smoothed her nightshirt over her knees. "I requested that I be included." She spoke the words in a mumble. Why had she done it? She could remember her excitement when the three-and-a-half year project came to fruition, she could remember her need to nail every one of them, most especially Peter Adler. During all those months putting up with Adler's arrogance and petty cruelties she had used the image of his future incarceration to sustain her. How she'd despised him. When she had told him and a few of the others about methods of terrorism common in the late twentieth and early twenty-first century, he had gobbled it up, had grown obsessed with visions of chasing NATO and US forces out of Europe (thus in his words ending "a century of foreign occupation"). His attempts at implementing some of those methods had been GFI's ultimate downfall.

Elizabeth's voice cut through Kay's memories. "You requested the assignment? So you undertook the assignment willingly."

Kay knew Elizabeth referred to Kay's more recent insistence to Sedgewick that she would not and could not interrogate a prisoner. "Yes," Kay said. "I did it willingly."

"Look at me while we are talking like this," Elizabeth said. Kay forced herself to look at Elizabeth's face. "So how did it work, these interrogations?"

Kay swallowed. She needed water; her throat was horribly dry. "The usual intensive method. Usual at that time, I mean. I don't know what is usual now. Solitary confinement interrupted only by interrogations. The interrogation sessions at thirty-six hour stretches, with three teams of two people each taking it in four hour shifts. Exactly the way it was done with Scott Moore, excepting your innovations with the closet and so on." Kay's mouth twisted. "The usual conditions. Small brightly lit room with a table and two chairs for the interrogators. The prisoner standing between the table and the wall with

two guards behind the prisoner, usually leaning against the wall." The guards were there to use the necessary force to keep the prisoner standing upright and to take the prisoner, when necessary, to be immersed in a tub of cold water. A picture of a trembling, gray-faced Peter Adler, his clothes soaking wet, water dripping from his hair and neck, flashed into Kay's mind. She had gone after him ruthlessly, as though it were a personal duel between them, indifferent to anything but winning the contest. In the end it had been she who had tripped him up and extracted enough details from him to lead to the arrests of everyone they had hoped to get and to the confiscation of their bomb factory in Amsterdam. She'd been so zealous, all the time needing to prove herself to Sedgewick, to impress him, to show everyone that Kay Zeldin was more than an academic who happened to be able to write good reports and had short-term eidetic memory, more than a good fuck. She had needed to prove that he wasn't talking about making her permanent merely because he wanted to keep her around for personal reasons. She had postponed returning home several times... For him? Or for this new work?

"How did it feel, Kay?" Elizabeth asked softly.

Kay stared at her. "You know how it feels," she finally said. She knew by the spread of heat over her flesh that color was creeping up her neck, into her face. Elizabeth interrogating her, Elizabeth controlling her... What was it like? She could hardly remember or imagine... Yet fragments came to her...the sense of being on one's mettle, of driving hard, of having the power to say "a five-minute break"— words that meant momentary release to someone at the end of his or her tether— or, obversely, to say "he's falling asleep on his feet: take him for a dip"...and then when it was over, the exhilaration of having won and the temptation to pity the loser— a temptation that lasted only while the loser was a flesh and blood person still within one's sight, a temptation that quickly faded once one had left the interrogation room knowing it was all on the record, all the loose ends neatly tidied.

"Do you imagine we are so similar as that?" A smile curved Elizabeth's lips. "You don't consider your situation here different from that of those whom you interrogated?" Elizabeth waved her hand, indicating the amenities surrounding them.

"You think any of your niceties— your presents"— Kay sneered "— make a damned bit of difference? It just makes it a bit more comfortable for you, sitting here in your armchair instead of in one of the hard-seated straight chairs in an interrogation room, away from the stench such places always have, away from the dreariness. But it's always there in the room with us, the same old thing, from the knowledge on the one hand that the closet and the rings on the platform are there at your disposal— along with me— to the simple fact that if I want a sip of water or need to urinate I'm not free to do so without your permission. That every word I speak has to be carefully censored while at the same time every order and gesture and question of yours is calculated toward some ulterior end involving my management."

"Nevertheless you are privileged for what you are. Unless you are telling me you would just as soon be turned over to Wedgewood as continue with me?"

"That's different," Kay said. She was sweating, not just under her arms, but between her breasts and behind her knees. "Wedgewood is different."

Elizabeth smiled as though Kay had walked into her trap. "Wedgewood is different? Then these small matters of degree signify, you think? But tell me, Kay, isn't it true that Sedgewick sometimes used you in assisted interrogations?"

Kay put her shaking hands to her face, as though to stop it from going out of control. Pictures flooded her mind of even more terrible things she had forgotten.

"Sedgewick found it hard to believe you didn't remember that, even after he had you watch Gordon assisting with that interrogation of the woman who had been doubling on us. Your reaction shocked him, I think. The woman of steel falls apart. After twenty years of being an academic."

Was Elizabeth laughing at her? "I hated it," Kay said to counter Elizabeth's unspoken accusation. "I hated it. But I didn't feel I had any choice by then. There was something I had to prove… I had to show Sedgewick that I wasn't..." Kay could hardly speak for the tears choking her throat. "That he couldn't...that... I don't know what. I can't remember. But I couldn't stand thinking that he thought..." She hadn't been able to stand the thought that he might despise her, that he might think he was using her because she was weak; she had had to show him...always this need to show him, to shatter his ideas about her, to hurt him if she could, she had wanted him to think that she was using him as much as he was using her...

"It had something to do with your dominance and submission sex games?"

Kay stared at her. "Your contempt," she said— and stopped. There was nothing she could say that would be worth the consequences of saying. Or that would even matter.

Elizabeth shook her head. "Not contempt. Do you think any of that matters to me? I'm the last person to care what others do sexually. It's only play, after all. But the other stuff, Kay— that was the real thing. What I'm asking is whether you were simply dragging feelings about your sexual relationship with Sedgewick that you couldn't cope with into the work. That's what I'm asking. You *couldn't* cope, isn't that right?"

"I need water." Kay felt as trapped as she had after Elizabeth had injected the paralytic into her arm and sat beside her talking.

"Help yourself," Elizabeth said. "It's on the dining table." She leaned forward and poured herself another cup of coffee. Kay went to the table and poured water into her glass; she stood for a few seconds there sipping. "Bring your water over here," Elizabeth called over her shoulder.

Kay topped up the glass and returned with it to her chair. At least she had had reasonable motives in the sorts of questions she had put to prisoners. Elizabeth's motives were at best voyeurism and at worst malice. "Are you doing this to me because I vomited? Or because I didn't want to accept your gift?" Kay did not dare accuse Elizabeth of voyeurism.

Elizabeth set her coffee cup down on the table. "You were about to tell me how you felt about your relationship— your *sexual* relationship, that is— with Sedgewick."

"You will have to find another way to punish me," Kay said very low.

"I don't consider this punishment, Kay," Elizabeth said evenly. "On the contrary, it's part of the bargain we struck over releasing Scott Moore."

Kay gulped more water. "I understood I was to write in the book. Nothing was said about this kind of harassment."

"Inflammatory language," Elizabeth said wearily. "I have no doubt you're hoping I'll stop this discussion to punish you for it. But we will leave the question of punishment until later. The fact is that you're quibbling. When a witness agrees to testify in court, the witness consents not only to the testimony itself but to submitting to cross-examination as well."

"I don't know what to say. All this took place more than twenty years ago, and most of what I've remembered I've only remembered in the last few days." *Or the last few moments.*

"Were you happy with that sexual relationship?"

"I haven't had another like it. So that must mean I wasn't. Don't you think?"

"But you wanted to please Sedgewick?"

"I wanted to prove something to him. I don't know. I think I must have hated him."

Elizabeth, smiling, shook her head. "That's too easy. You stayed with him. Even after he got himself fixed."

"Fixed?"

A frown of annoyance flitted over Elizabeth's face. "*Fixed* is how we— executive women— refer to the surgery the men have. Don't repeat the word again."

Fixed! Like cats being neutered! Only of course it wasn't quite the same thing. But didn't it suggest contempt among executive women if they used such an expression?

"Why did you stay with him?"

A terrible lethargy stole over Kay as she recalled the night he told her what he was going to have done and asked her to stay with him in spite of all the problems they would have. Kay sighed. "He asked me. And... maybe I thought I cared about him. It was a delusion. Obviously I was ambivalent. Maybe I liked the idea of doing him a favor..."

"But it didn't work, did it. You wanted to leave less than six months after he'd had it done. At least that's when you sent your resignation to headquarters in Washington."

"It was hell," Kay whispered. "He was angry at me most of the time. It was as though he had undergone a major personality change. And the sexual relationship fell apart because his surgery left me powerless. His desire was no longer sexual. All he wanted was to control me, to keep me there with him. I had to get away from him."

"You mean he wasn't playing anymore," Elizabeth said.

"He wanted to hurt me, *really* hurt me. So I left without telling him, and then he caught me at Calais. You know the rest."

Elizabeth drank the remaining coffee in her cup and set the empty cup down on the table. "To backtrack. Before the surgery. You wanted to prove something to Sedgewick, you said. How did the other Company people you came into contact with feel about you, treat you?"

"Oh," Kay said, remembering. "At first they ignored me. Later on, though, they loathed me. I once heard someone sneering to another person about Sedgewick's background, 'once a professional always a professional.' Then the other person made a remark about me, and the first person said, 'like to like.' Though a few people of course toadied up to me because they thought it would help them."

"'Like to like,'" Elizabeth repeated. "That's what *he* thought, you know. He thought you were just like him. You were the first to respond to him in kind. And I suppose your professional background appealed to him. There's some truth in looking at a man's background. He wasn't raised by service-techs the way executives are. And he too had something to prove— which gave him a lot of drive." Elizabeth smiled. "Yes, on the whole I think I agree with him that the two of you are very similar. You just happen to be stronger than he is, probably

because you escaped the stress of the executive life, and perhaps because your sexuality is intact."

"I'm nothing like him," Kay said through her teeth. "*Nothing* like him. The way I lived my life after leaving him is proof enough of that."

Elizabeth leaned forward. "The reason you hate him, Kay, is because you see the things you hate in yourself in him. You have no real grievance against him. But you know he was right about you. He's the only person who has really seen deep into your psyche. And you know it."

Kay hugged herself to try to stop the trembling. "Hate," she said hoarsely. "What I want to know where hate is concerned is why you hate me so much."

Elizabeth got up and moved to sit on the arm of Kay's chair. "No, love, you've got it wrong. I like you a great deal." Elizabeth smiled and took Kay's hand. "That's why I'd have to say you're wrong in thinking that I in controlling you am similar to Kay Zeldin interrogating Green Force International prisoners. I don't think of you as my enemy, you know. I admire your strength. And I think I may be able to understand you better than anyone else ever could. I admit to finding it pleasurable wielding so much power over another human being. But I don't think of it the way you described it for yourself. While we've been talking, a part of me has been trying to think of what to do about your use of inflammatory language a while back, trying to find a way out of having to chain you to the platform." She sighed. "But I don't see what else I can do. I think you came in here determined to be punished. Perhaps to assuage the guilt you feel over Scott Moore? Or perhaps to prove to yourself that you aren't really making peace with me?" She dropped Kay's hand and stood. "I want you to eat a bit more now. Before you go back to your cell. To compensate for your having vomited." Elizabeth went to the dining table and gestured to Kay. "Come, Kay, you can manage a few more bites, I'm sure."

"You know I don't eat when I'm chained to the platform," Kay said.

"I haven't decided yet how to punish you," Elizabeth said. "Come over here."

Kay sat down at the table. She hated Elizabeth. Elizabeth was like a wicked stepmother harassing abusing persecuting the hapless child thrown into her control. All the while those blue eyes watched her she could see behind them the platform, the tights and leotard, the chain. What a fine way to spend Christmas Eve.

For a moment Kay remembered the previous year's festivities at Sweetwater. They had finally accepted her among them, all those women. But if they knew what Elizabeth knew, they would despise her. Of course they never would know because everyone thought her dead. Which she might as well be. This was not life, it was an obscenity. An obscenity of Elizabeth's and Sedgewick's invention.

Seeing the threat of the closet lurking in Elizabeth's eyes, Kay picked up her fork and ate a bite of quiche. Almost anything was preferable to the closet and its aftereffects, which included the infantile behavior that had followed the last few instances. And Elizabeth knew it.

Chapter Twenty-eight

[i]

Allison leaned over and unlocked the cuff from the ring it was attached to. Kay slid stiffly off the platform and, moving blindly as the usual wave of dizziness attacked her, went straight to the toilet. Elizabeth for undisclosed reasons was allowing her to use the toilet during this bout of punishment. When Allison (how long ago? time now stretched endlessly before and behind the present moment) had first told her about this dispensation, Kay had sneered, "What a warm and generous heart that woman has." Allison had looked at her and said, very quietly, "Please, Kay, be careful. You know as well as I what is acceptable." Allison seemed to have little taste for the role of warder. The tightness of her face, the stiltedness of her movements all seemed to suggest that she performed the role reluctantly, perhaps even under protest.

Now as Kay stood by the wall beside the toilet delaying her return to the platform as long as she could, she watched Allison squeeze the contents of the tube of food into the bowl. When she had emptied the tube she looked at Kay. "You may eat this standing up— if you promise to eat every bit of it."

Kay looked at the bowl; her stomach tensed and her throat choked up. How could she eat such disgusting stuff? A few bites, yes, but all of it? "I don't know if I can eat *all* of it." Kay looked at Allison. "I promise to eat as much as I can."

Allison shook her head. "That isn't good enough. If you don't eat it all I'll have to take you to be force-fed." Allison's eyes pleaded with Kay. "Please, Kay. Don't let's have to go through that again."

Kay cleaned her hands with a towel-wipe, then went to Allison and took the bowl. She scooped the pasty stuff into the plastic spoon, stuck the spoon into her mouth, and gagged; but she made herself swallow. "Do you know what an oubliette is?" she asked conversationally between loathsome spoonfuls.

Allison shook her head. "No. It sounds French?"

"Yes, it's French. From the verb *oublier.*" Kay dug the spoon into the mess.

"To forget?"

Kay swallowed another pasty bite. "Yes." She ran her tongue over her palate and the back of her teeth to dislodge the pasty gunk that clung so disgustingly to her mouth. "To forget. And *s'oublier*, to be forgotten. An oubliette is a dungeon. Usually a trapdoor dungeon. You know, where one's standing in a perfectly ordinary-seeming place and the floor suddenly goes out from under one, and falling one finds oneself closed into a dungeon." Allison's eyes widened. "A lot of French chateaux had such conveniences. But I suppose though technically other dungeons might not be referred to as oubliettes, one might justify calling them oubliettes— considering all the manacled skeletons found chained to dungeon walls. Poor souls simply left to starve and rot. Forgotten about." Kay stared into the bowl and wondered if she could swallow any more of the vile stuff. She looked at Allison. "This place is an oubliette, don't you think? Here I am starving and rotting, forgotten. If she chooses, Elizabeth can simply forget me... in this oubliette, deep under ground." Allison stared at Kay as though petrified. "How does it feel, Allison, coming down here into this place? Does it ever prickle your spine? Do you ever wonder what it would be like? No, probably not. When I worked for the Company it never crossed my mind it could ever be me. Even when I was doubling I doubt I really believed it could be me. They made me watch a woman who had doubled being tortured, Allison." Kay leaned forward, and Allison recoiled backward into the table. "Even then I don't think I believed it could happen to me."

"I'm not a traitor," Allison said tremulously. "Elizabeth wouldn't lock up just anyone, you know."

Kay sighed. "I don't even remember how that kind of thinking goes, it eludes me. Words like *traitor* don't mean very much to me.

Traitor to what? Traitor to whom? Who is truly a traitor? The concept's a little elusive and vague, don't you think?"

"No, I don't," Allison said with an emphatic shake of her head. "Most people know what a traitor is. You have a problem." Allison's hand clutched her throat. "Finish your food, Kay. Or I'll take you to the infirmary."

Kay estimated there were three more spoonfuls in the bowl. Somehow she got them down, and Allison rechained her to the platform, left the liter bottle of water near Kay's hand, and hurried out of the cell. She's afraid of me, Kay realized. If she hadn't grown so physically weak she could have tried to overpower Allison and escape.

Kay knew that was fantasy, and a fantasy that could only give her pain. But there was almost nothing in her mind now that did not give her pain. She wished she could stop thinking, wished she could forget everything that Elizabeth had made her remember. How ironic, she acknowledged, that in this oubliette she was forced to remember all that she most wished to be lost to oblivion.

But Scott was free: she had seen the pictures and she believed them. That was what mattered, for *he* still existed. Life did go on...somewhere.

[ii]

It was after eleven by the time Allison and Elizabeth got away from the base. In the car, Elizabeth poured Allison a cognac, which she drank in great gulps. A gravelly spot in the pit of her stomach and the late December cold made her shiver. As they sped through the dark, Allison kept imagining Zeldin's eyes staring at her, staring through her, staring past her. Finally, Allison spoke. "Elizabeth." Allison's teeth were chattering. "It can't go on like this with Zeldin. I'm telling you, it's impossible."

"What is impossible?" Elizabeth asked softly.

"Tonight I asked her, as you suggested, what she cared for. She looked at me a good long while before answering. And something in her eyes just gave me the creeps. The same way that this morning her talk about oubliettes gave me the creeps." The eeriness, the spookiness of knowing Zeldin was going to speak and not knowing what she was

going to say was like perceiving that a ghost had entered the room and would presently be manifesting itself, making its presence felt. "And when she did speak, she said, 'I don't care about anything. The dead don't care.'" A frisson like the one she had experienced at the moment Zeldin had said it unpleasantly thrilled her. "Don't you see, Elizabeth, that if she doesn't care— and you know, I believe her, I entirely believe her— if she doesn't care, then simply keeping her alive will take more effort than we'll be able to supply. She'll wear us out, Elizabeth. Going down there is like... I don't know. I can't tell you how much I hate it. Each time I hate it more. And taking her to the infirmary! Pulling her along knowing she's dreading the force-feeding, pulling her along to her cell, knowing she's dreading the platform. Her face, Elizabeth, the way she endures what she loathes!" Allison stopped because the tears were hot in her eyes and she did not want Elizabeth to hear them in her voice.

Elizabeth's gloved hand held Allison's. "You sound upset, darling. It's too much for you?"

"She doesn't *say* anything, Elizabeth," Allison said, somehow managing to keep her voice steady. "I don't think she's going to ask me. She just gives me a look when I order her back onto the platform— and says nothing. *Nothing*. If you were to go down there she would apologize, I know she would. She's not defiant. It's not that at all."

"She will come around," Elizabeth said.

"You know what I think? I think that even if you make her do everything your way, once you have her outside of such close restraint she'll just kill herself the first chance she gets. If you aren't there to make her eat, then she'll simply not eat. That's what I think. It's spooky, Elizabeth."

"She wants me, Allison. She wouldn't have talked about oubliettes if that weren't so. Let her ask for me."

If only someone else could be sent down there to see to Zeldin. She was starting to dream about the woman, and this afternoon in the middle of the day sitting at her desk in her office she'd gotten gooseflesh while cleaning up the transcription of the morning's session.

"At least give her something to care about, Elizabeth," Allison said. "Unless something changes you'll get nowhere." Allison drank off the rest of the cognac and set the empty glass in its niche. She laughed bitterly. "It would even be preferable to have Zeldin fall in love with you. Why don't you make her infatuated with you, Elizabeth? You could do that, god knows. She'd care then all you'd want." It would be easily done. Elizabeth was so beautiful, and she was already the only thing or person Zeldin saw when Elizabeth was in the room with her, and she had been celibate for months... it would take only a little flirting on Elizabeth's part, making Zeldin sexually self-conscious, flattering her... Elizabeth knew how to do that so well. Allison had seen her do it almost without thinking.

"You aren't thinking *clearly*, darling." The lightness and dryness of Elizabeth's voice dismissed Allison's anxieties as if they were bits of lint she was dusting off her sleeve. "This is just a little demoralization because of what she's remembering. I have to help her come to terms with it. My doing that will make her dependent on my approval— or at least that's what I'm hoping. But there must never be anything sexual between Zeldin and me, except at an unconscious level, because being who and what she is Zeldin would only resent me for engaging her sexually. I'd be forcing her into ambivalence. While now there's still a chance for her to change her attitude toward me. Because of the extreme power differential between us, she'd always know I was using her and would get terribly caught up in fearing my contempt, in fearing abandonment— much more of the same things she felt about Sedgewick all those years ago. She would feel even more so now than then that she'd have no choice, that I could make demands on her that she would not be free to make on me. You see?"

"May I have more cognac?" Allison asked.

"But surely." Elizabeth passed Allison the bottle.

"We have sexual relations with service-techs all the time, and there's a great difference in power between us and them. Maybe even greater than between you and Zeldin, considering what kind of person she is." Allison wondered how much cognac she'd gotten into the glass; it was too dark to see.

"The analogy isn't apt," Elizabeth said thoughtfully. "In the first place, the power differences with service-techs are partially masked and in any event are far from absolute— as with Zeldin and me. Service-techs are socialized to those power differences. There are all sorts of things that mediate them, make them palatable. And then in our sexual relationships with them we offer them flattery, gifts, and the illusions of emotional parity and sexual equality. Second, service-techs tend to be masochistic. They like the balance of power the way it is. Which is why it is so easy for them to fall in love with us. They eroticize authority figures. I don't think there has been a service-tech working for me who hasn't wanted me to make love to her."

Allison's heart was pounding so hard she could scarcely breathe. "And you think that's because they've all been masochists?" Allison breathlessly asked.

"Mmmm," Elizabeth said absently. She sighed. "The important thing is for Zeldin to snap out of this state she's in and come to terms with herself. That's the real problem, you know, not her imprisonment. If these memories weren't so appalling for her she wouldn't have repressed them. My only worry is that I've been wrong in thinking that what makes her so strong isn't the thing that keeps her from being controllable. I have faith in her survival instinct, Allison. She *will* pull through this."

Did Elizabeth think *her* a masochist? She worked for Elizabeth. Did Elizabeth think she wanted her sexually because she was so powerful?

After half a minute or so of silence Elizabeth spoke again. "About her caring for nothing: I've just had an insight. Do you see, I've stripped from her almost everything. And her final defense against me has been to stop caring. For Zeldin it may be that to care for anything whatsoever would give me power over her— the power to deprive her of that thing she might care about. But in fact, by depriving herself of caring she is left more vulnerable to me because in some way, I think, she cares about *me*, though she doesn't yet admit it to herself. She *can't* yet admit it to herself! And the longer she goes on like this, the more she will come to care."

The car pulled around to the side entrance this time. "I think I'll sleep downstairs tonight, Elizabeth," Allison said before the escort had gotten the doors open.

The doors opened, and in the wash of the building's exterior floodlights Allison could see Elizabeth watching her. "But you'll come up for a Jacuzzi," Elizabeth said, not asking.

Allison got out of the car. She could find no reason to refuse that would not attract Elizabeth's attention. It was late, but the Jacuzzi would make her sleep better: she could almost hear Elizabeth saying it. "A quick one," Allison said. "I'm dead tired and tomorrow will be another long day." She thought of how she would have to be at Zeldin's cell by six a.m. and shivered. Maybe tomorrow Zeldin would break down and ask for Elizabeth. She hoped so, for she knew she couldn't take much more of it— even if Elizabeth and Zeldin could.

The truth was she wasn't like them, not at all.

[iii]

The sky cleared enough in the morning for the sun and a few patches of blue to appear and for Martha and David to be able to make out the coast of Vancouver Island to the north. They had awakened early, and while Martha lay snug in her sleeping bag listening to the soft patter of the rain on the roof of the tent, David braved the drizzle and the chill, damp air to make them coffee. He reported that he could see some clearing to the west, that the front— one of the many fronts that seemed to pass daily, on the northwest edge of the continent— was blowing over. So Martha dressed and they walked on the beach for as far as they could go before being cut off by rock and water, their eyes fixed on the gray and silver waves. Three times they encountered others, people who probably lived in the woods on the bluff above the beach. "When the tide goes out we'll be able to see all sorts of wonderful things," Martha shouted at David over the roar of the surf. He had never been on the Olympic Peninsula before, or even camped within sight and sound of the ocean. When they had arrived late the previous afternoon after having tramped several miles through ankle-deep mud in the rain from the Neah Bay village where they had been allowed to park their vehicle, David— his gaze in thrall

to the ocean— had expressed amazement that such a wonderful place could exist without attracting the crowds of people or development typical of most coastal areas in the US. "The Pacific Northwest is different," Martha said, then added, "especially now that it's the Free Zone." But the fact was, she well knew, that the Olympic Peninsula had never been able to sustain development. David hadn't exactly enjoyed pitching camp in the rain, of course, but he hadn't complained, either. She had, after all, warned him.

After their walk, they drank hot chocolate and ate multi-grain cereal cooked with powdered milk and honey. "The sun's coming out," David said.

Martha smiled knowingly. "But for how long? It will come and go all day, if today's at all typical. Still, it'll be nice. If we just keep an umbrella handy and dry out our clothes every chance we get, we'll be fine."

After breakfast the sun shone down on them. Martha chose a large flat rock and stretched out on it and closed her eyes to listen to the surf. After a while she heard David settling down beside her. A few thoughts that had come into her mind during the drive resurfaced. She considered, then ventured: "David?"

"Mmmm . . . yes, Martha?"

"Have you taken longevity treatments?"

She heard him stir. "Yes," he said cautiously. "Why do you ask?"

The red light beneath her eyelids seemed to intensify, as though the sun had grown stronger. "Are you going to go outside the Zone to get the treatments when you need them again?"

He laughed— uneasily, Martha thought. "I don't know, Martha. I mean, that's still a couple of years away for me."

"How long do people go without them before their bodies start to be affected?"

He sighed. Martha didn't have to see his face to know he didn't want to talk about this. "Nobody's certain. People like me, who don't have tons of credit to spend, get them about every five years, at least in the younger years. But I've heard that some executives get them every six months. As insurance, I guess. It's not clear how long the

aging process will be delayed because of them. Some people believe indefinitely, but most don't. Those who can afford it get the maximum medical attention. And eat right and all that."

"I hardly know anyone who can afford them even at five-year intervals," Martha said. The sun was so warm that she opened her jacket. "You know Beatrice Sweetwater? She was around part of the time on Saturday— in spite of having bronchitis. She's only seventy, David. But she was never able to afford treatments. Her body is deteriorating. It's horrible. And that is true for most people. Because most people can't afford any of it."

"What can I say, Martha?" Martha detected a note of defensive vexation in his voice. She turned her head toward him and opened her eyes and automatically shielded them with her hand. "Money has always made a difference in the allocation of resources."

"I don't see why everyone shouldn't have the treatments," Martha said.

"It would be a disaster. The demographics would be simply catastrophic. I don't think you understand the implications of wishing nice things for everybody. The end of implementing something that sounds nice wouldn't necessarily be nice."

Martha closed her eyes again. Always she came up against this sort of dismissal in him. He refused to think about the possibility of things being other than they already were. It was a limitation in him that she had to ignore to get along with him. He was almost as sensitive and considerate in bed as Louise (though the orgasms he gave her, unlike Louise's, seldom surpassed the pleasure of the ones she gave herself), and he could somehow make himself fit in at Sweetwater— she had been surprised at how easy his being there had been for everyone— yet inevitably she ran up against this barrier.

A few sprinkles feathered Martha's face. She opened her eyes and squinted up at the sky: a bank of dark clouds had massed overhead. "I'd better rescue the stuff hanging up to dry," she said. "It looks like we're in for a shower." She scrambled to her feet and ran for the clothes they had draped over the rope they'd stretched between two trees and got them into the tent just as the sprinkles thickened to a

drizzle. Straightening up after having zipped the tent shut, she found David behind her. He put his hands on her waist, and they kissed. And before long they decided to join the clothes in the tent.

It seemed the logical thing to do.

[iv]

Kay at last brought herself to make an effort to think. Through hours of physical misery she had avoided thinking because thinking implicitly required an acknowledgment of the things she had said to Elizabeth and because more than anything else she desired to forget those things. But though she had consciously avoided thinking about them, still they tormented her— fragments of memory, of words spoken to Elizabeth constantly presenting themselves separate from the whole... Indeed, her life now seemed to be made up of disjointed fragments, none of which fit together. Lying trapped in restraint, she fell into the abyss of alternately accusing herself and addressing Elizabeth to justify herself. But why justify herself to *Elizabeth* of all people? And yet she felt compelled to do so. She did not know how to compare what Elizabeth had been doing to her with her own past actions. And it seemed to her that whatever Elizabeth did to her might have some ultimate justification in it because of what she, Kay, had done to Elizabeth in the past... Whereas by her own admission, what she had participated in some twenty-odd years ago seemed to be horrid examples of inhuman indifference to the existence of others.

When she began consciously to think, to seek an understanding of her new situation, unexpected ideas came to her. For one thing, she could no longer believe that Sedgewick was very closely involved in whatever project Elizabeth had mounted against her: never would Elizabeth have been able to take the attitudes she so easily expressed if that were so. *Fixed*, she had said without self-consciousness. Kay remembered other times when Elizabeth had made matter-of-fact references to Kay's having been able in the past to manipulate Sedgewick. This way of talking about him intimated a certain detachment from him. So Kay had to wonder what was going on. Could she have been wrong to give in to Elizabeth for Scott's sake? Could there be some larger issue involved here? Was there some significant purpose to

which Elizabeth intended to put her? And just what *was* Sedgewick's involvement— if any?

Once these doubts and questions sprang into Kay's mind, she began posing questions that had never occurred to her before. She could be deluding herself, but it seemed to her that there *must* be something going on. Those memories seemed to be the corner into which Elizabeth had been backing her all along... But why? If she were to suppose that Sedgewick were not directing Elizabeth's handling of her...if she were to suppose Elizabeth had sole control over her...what sort of things would be likely to be true? Just supposing?

But it was difficult to make that leap: doing so would be to presume that either Elizabeth was doing this behind Sedgewick's back (but how, considering Kay's being openly paraded through the base's corridors?), or that Sedgewick was indifferent and had simply allowed Elizabeth to do as she pleased about Kay. But no, Kay thought. It was not possible for him to be *that* indifferent: considering his rage at her in the past, for what she had done this time he would want to kill her. Apart from all the damage she had done, she had put him in an impossibly embarrassing position— to have one's protégée not only go over to the enemy but abduct one, to be found to be that blinded to what a subordinate was up to... And then the way he had looked at her when she had left him handcuffed on the island, stranded with Elizabeth... Could something have happened between Sedgewick and Elizabeth? Could Elizabeth in some way have... *No.* The notion was preposterous.

So she would assume that Elizabeth was working behind Sedgewick's back, though it seemed impossible. But then Elizabeth was an unknown quantity: her on-the-spot-quickness, her superb control were nothing Kay had expected to find in her. There was much more to Elizabeth than she had suspected back in the days when she had thought of Elizabeth as merely a tool deploying Sedgewick's orders. Could she be hoping to use Kay *against* Sedgewick in some way, for some gain? But what could Elizabeth possibly have to gain working against Sedgewick, unless she'd defected to another executive, or even perhaps to someone in Military? Could Elizabeth be secretly working

against Security for Military? Could that be it? Could it be that she was trying to find a new angle for manipulating Sedgewick by picking at Kay's memories?

Kay bent her knees, desperate to take the weight off her aching back. With both wrists restrained, she could never lie on her stomach or her side and was always trapped on her back. At times claustrophobia would overcome her, and she would break into a sweat, fearful she would suffocate if she could not get loose, only by arduous effort suppressing the scream lurking in her throat. Except for the endless presence of light it was very much like being in the closet, even though this cell had space in it and there was the table, the mirror, the blue concrete blocks, the plastic food and water containers to look at. Yet the emptiness the silence the enforced immobility pressed upon her, threatening to nullify her mind no matter how tightly she held to her certainty that Allison would eventually walk through the door, threatening to nullify her belief that the images and memories and strands of thought in her mind were something real, something that defied the emptiness.

She tried to ignore the restraint, tried to concentrate on forming a plan, a new map for getting by. She defined her problem: since that first time in the closet she had been vagulating, aimless, reacting without any fixed standards for guidance. She needed a map, a plan, a new set of rules of engagement. Otherwise, she reminded herself, she had no alternative to Elizabeth's rules. Surely there must be a way for her even now to retrieve something while she waited.

Waited?

For what was she waiting?

Kay knew, but would not let the words form in her mind. She pushed the thought away, pushed it down deep.

So hard to think, so very hard. But she had to. Just in case there was a point to it all... Dissimulation: she finally accepted that that was her chief weapon to hand. She must manipulate Elizabeth by dissimulating. But it came to her that for more than three months she had been doing her very best *not* to manipulate Elizabeth: holding herself in, trying to remain always aware of the barriers between them, striving

to keep everything as visibly raw and bloody as possible so that she, Kay, would not be all the more easily handled by Elizabeth, so that she, Kay could maintain her own authority... But her own authority was gone. What did she have to lose? No, she wouldn't think about that. There was a great deal to lose, even now. But she could not go on like this, she had to feel she was doing *something*. So she would dissimulate, pretending to be feeling and reacting as Elizabeth wished, in order to glimpse the place into which Elizabeth was trying to herd her...while remaining at least partially free of whatever it was by which Elizabeth hoped to be psychologically hobbling her once she got her there.

What sort of responses did Elizabeth want of her? Some of it Kay felt she knew already: Elizabeth had been displeased at the way Kay had refused her gift. She enjoyed Kay's falls into dependency that always followed time spent in the closet or that had occurred at other times of severe distress. She wanted Kay to play along with her social formulas... It would be hard, but Kay would perform as Elizabeth wished her to. It would not be as easy deceiving Elizabeth as it had been deceiving Sedgewick. Sedgewick had wanted it so badly, and he'd had no reason to distrust her. While Elizabeth knew of her having deceived Sedgewick... Yet Elizabeth had expectations, too. And she did sometimes respond emotionally, however much she tried to conceal it from Kay. Therefore Elizabeth, too, was susceptible to manipulation.

But it would be dangerous for Kay, because in manipulating Elizabeth she would be opening herself to further involvement, would grow more emotionally entangled with Elizabeth. That horrible dream image flashed into her mind, and fear tingled along her limbs, tightened around her heart. She had to do this. She had to see how far she could manipulate Elizabeth and how far Elizabeth intended to go with her. The only alternative was to continue lying here in restraint, and she did not think she could do that for much longer without completely breaking down. Recalling the last time she had been in the closet, Kay wriggled the blanket up over her face and let herself cry. Allison will come, she told herself, and then I'll ask for

Elizabeth. That is what will happen. I can bear this a little longer. Just a little longer, Kay.

And then it will be over.

[v]

Because Elizabeth was holding a meeting for one of the projects she wished to keep secret from Jacquelyn, Allison went into the executive conference room in the Chief's suite to make the usual preparations: setting out the necessary accouterments on the table, checking the recorders and mikes, making fresh coffee, checking the controls at the head of the table, making sure all the terminals in the room functioned. It seemed to Allison ridiculous that she should have to spend her time doing this when a service-tech could be doing it without compromising the secrecy of the meeting. But Elizabeth insisted on certain routine "precautions" as she called them. She wanted no one allowed access to the room and its electronics between the time Allison had checked everything out and the meeting began.

Once the meeting began, moreover, Allison was to work in the small room behind this one, on call for anything Elizabeth might need, half-monitoring the proceedings. ("Just in case" Elizabeth always said, though Allison had never been sure what "just in case" referred to.) As she set out water glasses, Elizabeth's passing comment about service-techs came into her mind (as it had done so many times since the night before): *gifts, flattery, seeming emotional parity and sexual equality*— the things executive women used to manage their service-techs... Allison could not vanquish the terrible suspicion that perhaps Elizabeth was using these things to manage *her*— though manifestly she was not a service-tech. Yet in some ways she used her as one: to tend to these details, to serve during her secret meetings, running her errands, typing for her. (*Word-processing* for her!) Moving Zeldin around. So many menial tasks: and of course their sexual relationship, of a sort unknown to occur between executive women.

Was Elizabeth beginning to take her for a service-tech?

Once articulated, the question would not be dismissed. Glaring at the oil portraits on the wall— all the past chiefs of Security: Sedgewick and his two predecessors— Allison cursed herself for her foolishness.

How could she think that of Elizabeth? Elizabeth had known her all her life. She wouldn't be that contemptuous of her, not considering all she had done for her. She was childish to be so suspicious of Elizabeth and was misreading a complex relationship she clearly did not understand. It must be her own sense of inadequacy at fault: frequently she found it hard to believe that Elizabeth could want her or care for her. That sense of being undeserving of Elizabeth's attention and affection was misleading her into disparaging Elizabeth.

A few minutes before the meeting was scheduled to begin, Elizabeth came into the room. Suddenly overwrought, Allison fussed over the thermoflasks of coffee. Elizabeth came up behind her and put her hand on Allison's arm. (Allison immediately understood it as a gesture no one coming into the room would wonder about.) "Everything arranged for dinner, darling?" Elizabeth said softly into her ear.

Allison swallowed. That, too: she had had to supervise arrangements for Elizabeth's dinner with Zeldin this evening. "Yes. I'll have to check on things just before I go down to her, but everything's basically set."

"Wonderful. You've become most efficient, Allison. I don't know what I would do without you."

Allison recalled Felice's saying that about her personal servicetech. She flushed.

"I wish I knew… I don't know whether to put off going to Maine or not, to get the go-ahead for this cease-fire arrangement. We've worked everything out as far as we can, short of the involvement of Cabinet men in the negotiations… Dare I risk putting pressure on Sedgewick now, or do I wait, hoping Zeldin is really coming around?" She sighed. "What did you think about her attitude, Allison?"

Allison moved away from Elizabeth and the side table and ran her eye over the conference table as though double-checking the arrangements. "I don't know, Elizabeth. She was very emotional. I don't know what it means. Probably because I don't know what it is you're hoping for. I don't understand any of it."

Elizabeth again came up to her. "Is something wrong?"

Allison looked at Elizabeth's face, at the strong yet delicate bone-structure, at the translucent pearl and rose complexion, at the long dark lashes fringing her light blue eyes. "Nothing is wrong," she said, turning to go into the room she would be staying in during the meeting.

Elizabeth caught her wrist. "Don't be coy, Allison. No games. No manipulation. Not between us. There's some kind of problem. That being so, it is only fair that you speak about it plainly." Her gaze held Allison's.

Allison's cheeks burned with resentment. "Sometimes it seems that you take me for a service-tech."

Elizabeth's eyes flew wide. "What!" she exclaimed in disbelief.

"This kind of stuff," she said, waving her hand at the table. "Why do you have me doing such menial things for you?"

Elizabeth's eyes grew cold. "*Menial*? Let me tell you, Allison, that I did this sort of thing all the time I worked as Sedgewick's PA. In fact, I did much more of it than you or Jacquelyn *combined* do for me. He couldn't stand having service-techs around him— I even had to bring him his coffee and meals, no one else was acceptable to him. And certainly for a meeting of this caliber, if it weren't absolutely secret Jacquelyn would be doing what you do. Do you think she wonders if *she* is being taken for a service-tech?"

Allison averted her eyes from Elizabeth's. What the fuck was the matter with her, blurting it out like that?

"What I find truly remarkable, Allison, is that you could say this to *me*, whom you know so well: that, given the nature of our relationship, you could doubt me so. It's happened, hasn't it. You resent working for me."

Allison shook her head. "No," she whispered. "I don't resent working for you."

Allison heard the door slide open and saw that people were coming into the room. "We'll discuss this later," Elizabeth said, dropping Allison's wrist.

Allison fled through the door at the back of the room. What had she done? Would Elizabeth forgive her? Allison sank into the chair and flipped the terminal into com mode, then remembered to plug

the earphone into her ear so that she could monitor the meeting. For a moment an image flashed before her eyes— an image of herself on the witness stand in court, answering questions about conspiracy with Elizabeth. No, she whispered to herself. They would never do that. They've let her alone this long, they won't object now. But a second voice in her head retorted: no, not unless everything becomes even more screwed up than it already is and they need a scapegoat. Conspiracy, treason, unlawful usurpation of authority…

And now she had alienated Elizabeth.

[vi]

As they entered the lounge, Kay spotted Elizabeth lying supine on the long sofa. Silently Allison removed the handcuffs from Kay's wrists and left. Still standing near the door, suddenly nervous at the deception she must pull off, Kay watched Elizabeth sit up. It looked as though she had been napping. Kay crossed the room and stood near the sofa. Elizabeth looked at her face, then down at the socks she wore, then back up at her face. "*Bon soir*, Kay."

"*Bon soir*, Elizabeth." Kay took a deep breath. "I apologize for saying you were harassing me. I was upset because of what we were talking about, and I knew it would annoy you."

"Come," Elizabeth said, patting the sofa cushion beside her.

Kay sat down beside Elizabeth and steeled herself to be seemingly receptive to Elizabeth's overtures.

"If you would learn to control yourself your life would be a lot easier, Kay. All that time spent in restraint was unnecessary. How much satisfaction did you get out of that split-second of verbiage? Could it really have been worth it?"

Kay made herself look at Elizabeth. She produced a wry smile. "Of course it wasn't worth it," she said tremulously. "I can't take much more. I thought I would feel better after Scott was released, but…" She shook her head.

"But you are upset about what you've started remembering," Elizabeth said. Kay thought she detected satisfaction in Elizabeth's voice— satisfaction at her confiding so much. "Which is hardly surprising. I know it is difficult for you. But I also think it needn't be as bad as it is."

Kay knew that Elizabeth knew she was not stupid. She must be careful not to overdo it. So she would display a measured amount of shrewdness. "What does making me remember have to do with my rehabilitation?" she said hesitantly.

"Your rehabilitation?" Elizabeth's voice took on an edge.

Kay framed her answer with care. "At the beginning you said you intended to rehabilitate me." Kay thought of the word she had used to Elizabeth at the time: *brainwash.* "Since you went to some trouble to make me remember, I assume it has something to do with your chief intention where I'm concerned."

Elizabeth nodded. "You are always thinking, aren't you, Kay. You never stop. Never."

Kay stared down at her nightshirt. "Much of the time now I don't think at all," she said very low. Unfortunately, that was the truth. "I can't think very well anymore. Which may be why I don't quite understand what my memory has to do with your rehabilitation project for me."

"You speak so coolly about it."

Kay looked up so that Elizabeth would see the tears in her eyes. "You think so? Strange things happen to people in strange circumstances."

Elizabeth took her hand and stroked it. "We'll talk more after dinner, while we're having coffee. There are some things I want to say to you, but they can wait."

While they dined Kay haltingly sustained conversation with Elizabeth, a difficult task since there were many subjects that were off-limits or impossible to talk about because of Kay's loss of touch with the outside world. Once Elizabeth casually asked her to describe what the aliens were like, and Kay cautiously attempted to suggest a profile of what she imagined to be Marq'ssan by detailing certain personality traits common to all the Marq'ssan that she had ever met. Elizabeth in turn informed Kay that a movement to provide unlimited access to fertility was afoot in the Free Zone. Although Kay did not want

to think about the Free Zone, she forced herself to respond to this and Elizabeth's other conversational gambits. Elizabeth would never believe she had undergone a change in attitude unless she seemed in every way conciliatory and eager to please.

Kay managed to eat almost half a breast of chicken in addition to a few spoonfuls of soup and a small serving of cauliflower. To her relief, Elizabeth did not force dessert on her, but said only that they might have some later.

They moved to the pair of chairs with the table between them for coffee. The service-tech set the tray down on the table and left; Elizabeth poured out coffee for Kay as well as for herself. "You remember how when I first gave you the book I asked you to write about why you betrayed Sedgewick?" Elizabeth said.

Startled, Kay looked at Elizabeth. "Yes, I remember."

"I was dissatisfied with what you wrote for me," Elizabeth said. "I think, though, that now that you have achieved a more balanced look at your early relations with Sedgewick it has become possible to construct a new picture of what was going on in your head when you betrayed him." She sipped her coffee. "Fear was very much involved, with that I agree, but not the fear you would like to believe in."

Kay's fingers twisted together. How much more difficult it was to play a role when forced into such an emotionally loaded landscape. If only she could remain detached, could stand outside herself watching this exchange, could pretend it wasn't her own feelings, her own past experiences they were talking about.

"You don't seem eager to hear my theory."

"You know how difficult I find this," Kay said.

Elizabeth nodded. "What you did— doubling in that situation— might seem audacious and even courageous to some people. But as I see it, it was the easiest thing for you to do. It let you off the hook, and it allowed you to tell yourself a story about yourself that you wanted to hear." Elizabeth paused as though expecting Kay to protest. The blood rushed in her ears as Kay remained silent and waited for the accusation. Yet Elizabeth did not immediately elaborate. "Tell me,

Kay," she asked instead, "when you were considering what to do at that point, what did you calculate your options to be?"

Kay cleared her throat and kept her eyes fixed on Elizabeth's face, willing them limpid, clear, wide. "I saw two alternatives. And only two. One was to do as I did. The other was to have the Marq'ssan hide me. In fact, that's what I first asked of them— for I did want to run and hide. But when I began thinking about it I realized that if I did that I would not only endanger Scott and others I cared for, but also that I'd be spending my whole life running and hiding, afraid of being found by Sedgewick, always aware that I would be endangering anyone who in any way became involved with me, never able to live as a professional, never again able to teach or do research. What would be the point of such a life for someone like me? On the other hand, if I brought down Security in general and Sedgewick in particular, I would not only be helping those who were working to clear Seattle of Security forces, but I would also be freeing myself to live as I would like. I didn't have to think very hard about which alternative to choose."

"You didn't feel, then, that you had any responsibility for doing what you could to undo all the havoc the aliens had wrecked on this country?" Elizabeth's voice grew harsh. "You didn't feel that as someone with ability and access to power you should be doing more than merely saving your own skin?"

Kay stared at her, shocked. The accusation, unlike anything she could have imagined Elizabeth leveling at her, first stung and then left her nauseated and shaking with anxiety. "I don't know what you mean," she said. "I believed that's what I *was* doing. I believed Sedgewick and Security were the worst thing for this country."

"That's bullshit," Elizabeth said. "And you know it. You believed implicitly in the executive system at that time, didn't you."

Kay focused on the mammoth jet and amber pendant hanging from a gold chain around Elizabeth's neck. It was true. At that time she did believe the executive system was necessary, that though it might have problems it did work and was in fact the only possibility for feasibly running such a complex society. Back then she *had*

believed in it. There was so much she hadn't understood. "There was nothing I could have done within the system. There was no room for someone like me," Kay said, her voice low and hoarse.

"Not true," Elizabeth said. "If you'd had the guts to work with Sedgewick and accept power from him and had been willing to exert yourself to influence him, things would have turned out quite a bit differently. Not only would there not have been a civil war— which would have meant getting civilization restored and the economy back on its feet by now— but you probably could have made important changes, considering the extraordinary formal and informal power the signing of that emergency order granted him. A lot could have been done. Instead everything fell to pieces. Because of you, Kay."

"You can't blame that on me!" Kay cried. "You know what he was like those last days! He wasn't about to listen to me. When I made my suggestions to him for Seattle he wouldn't even consider them! There was no way for me to do anything but walk a tightrope with him!"

"That's what you want to believe now." Elizabeth leaned forward. "I read that report you made on Seattle, Kay. I thought it was brilliant. The sort of measures you were suggesting would have been our best shot, not only in Seattle but in many of the other cities we were having trouble with. In time you would have been able to work on him, would have gotten him to see it your way— once Turpin had been dealt with. It was all a matter of timing. He was adrenalized by the power struggle he was engaged in at the time. Once we'd gotten here— this base was the destination, you know— everything would have been different. But you were too scared of yourself even to try. You didn't think seriously about it at all, did you: you as much as said so a minute ago when you said you saw only two alternatives." Elizabeth paused. "You know what you were really scared of— besides the usual fear of failure, I mean?"

Kay shook her head.

"You were scared of reacting the way you did when you worked for Sedgewick all those years ago. That's what really frightened you— unconsciously, of course, since you weren't even admitting to yourself any of that. You were afraid to take responsibility, afraid you wouldn't

be able to be that powerful and at one and the same time the decent responsible professional you saw yourself as. So you abdicated responsibility. And you thought of yourself as a victim. You, Kay Zeldin, a victim! It's laughable!"

Violently shivering, Kay wrapped her arms around her body and longed for a blanket. It sounded so plausible. And it made her, Kay, sound like a hypocritical, self-deluding ass.

"The world was falling apart around you and all you could think about was escaping," Elizabeth said. "But you couldn't even leave it to executives to take care of things— instead you left the Executive nearly totally destroyed, divided against itself, and withdrew the one force able to accomplish anything. You created a power vacuum at the worst of times. All because you were too afraid to face yourself."

It wasn't true that she could have done anything, Kay insisted to herself. Elizabeth was trying to upset her, trying to twist her thinking for unstated purposes by misrepresenting what Sedgewick had been like and by overestimating what one professional woman in a world run by male executives could do. The problem of hierarchy, she thought, grasping at a straw. The problem of hierarchy... One couldn't work things out while inside that kind of power structure. But as Elizabeth had unwittingly pointed out, she hadn't understood about that at the time. She hadn't understood then about external structures of authority. She hadn't understood about responsibility. That was before she had learned about such things working with the Marq'ssan, working in the Free Zone.

"Kay." Elizabeth abruptly broke into the painful whirl of Kay's thoughts. "I have to pee. Either you can come to the bathroom with me or I can cuff you."

Kay stared blankly at Elizabeth. "There's a guard outside. I couldn't possibly escape."

Elizabeth smiled slightly. "I wasn't thinking of escape. With that band on your wrist you couldn't get far, anyway. No, I was thinking about other possibilities. You are known for your resourcefulness. Left alone in this room..." Elizabeth shrugged. "Especially now that you have become so self-destructive. What is your choice?"

Elizabeth thought she might kill herself?

It felt strange accompanying Elizabeth to the bathroom, watching as Elizabeth pulled down her trousers and sat on the toilet seat. Kay could remember— very distantly— past occasions when she had been so intensely involved in conversation with someone that the conversation had moved into the bathroom when she or her interlocutor had had to pee.

Kay took her turn on the toilet, and they returned to the other room. "You think you know me better than I know myself, don't you," Kay said.

Elizabeth settled into her chair almost sideways and stretched out her long legs at an angle to the chair. "Not better, Kay. That wouldn't be possible. One person can't know another person better than that person knows herself. I know you *differently* than you know yourself. And therefore I can see some things that you can't. I've been studying you for years— because you were so important for my understanding Sedgewick." She smiled. "To be effective and useful, I had to know Sedgewick as well as I could. You were part of it. So I also devoted myself to studying you. You must admit that for a long time I've known many things that you seemed not to have known about yourself— because of your massive repression. So perhaps I can claim to know some parts of you better than you do." Elizabeth gave Kay a quizzical look. "But you are sidetracking, aren't you."

"Things don't work as simply as you imply they do." Kay felt a pressing need to articulate what was wrong in Elizabeth's reasoning. "Implicit in the executive system is an externalization of authority that makes it extremely unlikely that people in subordinate positions will feel a sense of responsibility much less assume any responsibility except that of obedience to a superior. Take the formula in which a superior, usually to emphasize a point, says 'Clear?' to which the subordinate invariably responds 'Understood.' The very use of this formula blatantly states the given power relation and forces the subordinate to acknowledge herself or himself hierarchically inferior to the superior who has invoked the formula. I'm sure it's often invoked precisely to do that more than for emphasizing the point being made. Authority

is thus always vested in others— those above one— never in oneself. How can someone operating in such a system ever feel responsible for anything but enacting his or her obedience? Whereas among the Marq'ssan and among certain people in the Free Zone, authority is considered to rest within every individual, never in a superior— for among them there are no superiors— and therefore responsibility, too, rests with every individual. More precisely, every individual must find within herself authority and a sense of responsibility. That doesn't mean taking on the burdens of the world, only that each person must define for herself authority and responsibility. As long as I was a part of a system that allocated power and responsibility hierarchically, there was no chance that I would feel the degree of responsibility you are rebuking me for not having assumed. No one could have. Why should I have been any different?"

"But of course most people shirk responsibility," Elizabeth said. "Your anarchy cannot work for that reason. A bureaucracy mechanizes the process. By and large people like being told what to do. Because you do not— and I think you've made that aspect of yourself crystal clear— it would seem to me likely that you would be ready to assume responsibility: if, that is, you did not have such deep-seated fears about power. Most of us who *do* assume responsibility— which is to say most executives, since it is our function to bear responsibility and provide authority for the comfort and protection of the rest of this society— most executives, I would say, stand in hierarchical subordination to *some*one. And we find a way to accept our subordination even as we retain a larger sense of our function in the world. Being subordinate to another does not stop us from being responsible. It has never served as an excuse to keep me from doing so, for instance."

Kay did not buy this line of argument. She felt a need to say something in order to hold on to the clarity she had felt a moment earlier and groped for the words she needed to elaborate.

"Naturally you are upset," Elizabeth said. "The most shocking and painful moments are those when one finds one's image of oneself not according with reality. You need to find a way out of having to face what you've been concealing from yourself. But making excuses

will not help you come to terms with it, Kay." She paused. "Perhaps it's too soon for us to be trying to talk about it...you do look very upset." Elizabeth smiled— broadly, warmly. "Come, Kay. Come over here." She patted the side of her chair and indicated the floor beside it.

Heat suffused Kay's face: did Elizabeth expect her to kneel or sit by her chair? Was that what her gesture meant? Everything had gotten out of control. Elizabeth was pulling and pushing her every which way. And now she wanted Kay to adopt a servile position at her feet? How could she bring herself do it? But if she didn't, Elizabeth would not be convinced that she had undergone a change of attitude.

Elizabeth shook her head slightly. "It is a mistake to make things more important than they need to be, Kay. Now you make me feel as though I must insist."

Kay swallowed. Avoiding Elizabeth's gaze, she awkwardly got up and knelt as directed.

"There's nothing to be so upset about," Elizabeth said, putting her hand on Kay's head. "Why are you so afraid of this? It is fear that's making you tremble, isn't it?" She stroked Kay's hair.

"I'm very tired," Kay managed to say. "I hardly slept the whole time I was in restraint."

"I'll let you go soon, then. It is curious how difficult certain things are for you. Do you know I learned a long long time ago— as a child, actually, for all executive girls are taught this— that it is best when acquiescing to another's authority to do so as lightly and easily as possible— so as almost not to notice it. To trivialize its significance. I would never have lasted as Sedgewick's PA if I hadn't known how to do that. He hardly ever noticed any difference between his will and my own, you know. So it was never necessary for me to feel the sort of humiliation you just evoked for yourself."

"You must have resented him then," Kay said, too tired to be careful.

Elizabeth's hand continued stroking. "Not very much, Kay. His interests and mine were nearly identical."

Were? Kay realized that all this about Sedgewick was phrased in the past tense. She determined to keep the realization to herself, to keep Elizabeth from knowing she had caught her slip.

"Look at the time." Elizabeth shifted in her chair to reach the handset on a table nearby. Kay listened to her tap in the number. After a few seconds Elizabeth set down the handset without speaking. "I'll take you down myself," she said.

Kay rose to her feet and held out her wrists for the cuffs.

"I may be away tomorrow, Kay. I'm not certain yet. If I am, I want you to do something."

No matter how many times Kay felt the steel closing around her wrists, she still experienced shrinking dismay and the threat of claustrophobia each time she was cuffed. She looked up at Elizabeth, looming so very far above her. "What is it?" she asked wearily, thinking Elizabeth would require more writing in the book.

"I want you to think about how difficult you made things for Felice and her household, and to think about your having been her guest at the time you abducted Sedgewick. It would please me very much if you were to see Felice and apologize to her."

Kay stared at Elizabeth in disbelief. Apologize to Felice Raines?

"Don't look so disgusted, Kay. If you consider it from her point of view, you'll realize you owe her an apology. If you do decide to apologize to her, ask Allison to arrange for you to see her. It is that simple." Elizabeth reached out and pressed her thumb to the plate beside the door.

Kay moved through the corridors in a daze. She hardly knew what had happened, hardly remembered what had been said, and had no idea what the implications were for her situation. But she did have a new clue about Sedgewick. She would think about it after a night's sleep (if, for a change, she could obtain one). Maybe she could make sense of its possible significance then.

Chapter Twenty-nine

[i]

The eruption of sustained mental activity— now unaccustomed— drove Kay into a frenzy of nervous energy. She flung herself into fits of exercise and pacing, hardly able to sit or lie at rest without experiencing the perception of her self fragmenting and flying off wildly in all directions: better to keep in physical motion so as to preserve the illusion of an inner concentration of mental effort, of boring her way in single-mindedness without losing whatever direction (if direction it could be called) that she felt herself grappling flailing processing in. The sudden access to so much information overwhelmed her. Extracting that information, however, required sifting through Elizabeth's words, questions, inflections, ellipses, which in turn required that she, Kay, cut through the painful emotional welter threatening to submerse her. She was so used to thinking of herself as coiled tightly inward in opposition to Elizabeth that her initial venture to unwind and expose herself to Elizabeth— in a posture of submission, yet— frightened and appalled her. She sensed it as a terrible risk (provoking her to query what it was she thought she had left to risk) and intermittently it seemed to her that she had simply given up, given in, given out... in a form suitably disguised for palatability. And yet Kay recognized that in that one long session with Elizabeth she had learned and intuited enough to goad her into not hope, precisely (for there was none: the physical weight of the Rock pressing eternally down on her had stifled all notions of ever laying eyes on sky or earth, of ever feeling the sun on her flesh, of ever breathing air that had not been infinitely circulated and filtered before reaching her cell), but into desire: the driving response of something she *could* do, namely seek comprehension. Her mind for the first time since her arrival there functioned on edge and self-sharpening, questing boldly, erratically along any wild tendril shooting out from that amorphous welter through which she had constantly to nerve herself to search relentlessly and without squeamishness.

Her first clue: Elizabeth spoke as though her working under Sedgewick lay in the past. Now that Kay reflected on it, she realized that most of the times Elizabeth had spoken of Sedgewick she had used the past tense. An image flashed into Kay's mind of Elizabeth issuing orders with easy authority to the men at the mouth of the base then speeding off into the tunnel apart from and ahead of them all. Elizabeth's badge boasted the highest grade of clearance, Kay realized with shock, recalling Elizabeth in the car pulling the badge from her tunic pouch and fastening it to her tunic. Kay had seen that badge dozens of times since then but had never once noticed its rating, at least not consciously.

What else had she been missing?

So Elizabeth's security clearance had been upgraded to the highest level— to Sedgewick's level. Did that mean that Elizabeth had taken over Sedgewick's position? Or some other Cabinet-level post? The notion seemed preposterous. She knew how the top-level executive men thought of women...

Now Kay remembered another occasion: Elizabeth dressed in silver evening clothes, sitting on the bed in this cell, talking about being the only woman (besides the hostess) at the (boring) dinner party she had just attended... Elizabeth explaining how her sexuality did not interfere with her executive functioning...

No, Elizabeth had not been made a Cabinet member: it simply wasn't possible. Perhaps Sedgewick had promoted her into some specially created position? But doubt crept in when she recalled an occasion in the past when Sedgewick had insisted that Elizabeth Weatherall was most effectively deployed as his personal assistant... Well, people often changed when situations changed, and the circumstances under which Security operated had changed drastically since that day Kay had stranded them on the island.

But clues to Elizabeth's attitude towards Sedgewick further complicated Kay's speculations about Elizabeth's position vis-à-vis both Security and Sedgewick. Her casual use of the term *fixed* suggested a general contempt towards executive men that considering the context in which it had been used must in some way extend to Sedgewick himself. And then Elizabeth's insistence on discussing Kay's past relations with Sedgewick, seemingly without hesitation, without self-consciousness: what faithful tool (as Sedgewick had once explicitly designated Elizabeth Weatherall to Kay) could carry on such discussions so easily without having a sense either of the absurdity of the human weakness of one who had fashioned his experience as Sedgewick had or else of a general faltering in comprehension? Elizabeth did not seem to doubt her own ability to understand anything that had happened between Kay and Sedgewick, or even any of the folly and self-delusion in which Sedgewick had indulged to the detriment of the Executive. Did she then perceive the full extent of Sedgewick's weakness? From everything she could glean from her many conversations with Elizabeth, Kay concluded that Elizabeth did perceive this weakness and considered it a given of the situation. Could it be that accepting it (as Elizabeth must have done for as many years as Sedgewick had been Chief) Elizabeth in some way exploited it, consciously, shrewdly, and without embarrassment?

Now that Kay pursued such a line of thinking, that Elizabeth had always done this seemed obvious. It had been Sedgewick's representation of Elizabeth that Kay had uncritically assumed not only in those last days in Security Central, but during her imprisonment as well. She saw that this had been an error, one that had prevented her from making important observations. On the basis of that one constellation of assumptions about Elizabeth, Kay had formed some of her most important judgments and speculations. The answer of what Elizabeth was up to might very well be plain and obvious.

Kay had known this for weeks, though she had not consciously acknowledged it. For the most part she had stopped thinking of "them" (Sedgewick and Elizabeth) as controlling her existence and thought simply of Elizabeth. In all Elizabeth's dealings with her Kay could not in retrospect discern the slightest trace of Sedgewick's direction. In fact, Kay realized, since her capture Sedgewick had existed chiefly as a subject of discussion between her and Elizabeth, or as a ghostly presence whose observation had been invoked by Elizabeth from that single mention of a bet between her and Sedgewick concerning the experiment attempting Kay's "rehabilitation." From this Kay had extrapolated unduly; she saw that now. That one reference might merely signify that Sedgewick had handed her over to Elizabeth. Kay could imagine all sorts of contingencies surrounding such a disposal, but she understood now that such contingencies could not be read from anything Elizabeth had said or done. In sum, Sedgewick might know nothing of what Elizabeth had done with her. It didn't seem likely, considering the intensity of his past interest in her and his general taste for vengeance (with which she had extensive firsthand acquaintance), but it was possible...especially when taken with Elizabeth's seeming detachment from Sedgewick when speaking about him.

Kay put these speculations aside in order to follow another direction. At that last meeting Elizabeth had remarked about Felice that "It would please me very much if you would...," indicating that Elizabeth now assumed that Kay wished to please her...probably because Kay had voluntarily exposed herself, had played the role Elizabeth seemed to want her to play. Thus Elizabeth was feeling successful now in maneuvering her toward the end she had had in mind all along. (And Kay now assumed there was such an end, that Elizabeth's handling of her figured in some larger plan outside an interest in Kay herself.)

What were the things Kay had spoken that imparted so much confidence to Elizabeth? They all had to do with Sedgewick and with laying guilt on her, Kay, for irresponsibility in the recent past and ruthlessness, cruelty, and calculation in the remote past. Elizabeth ardently wished her to feel remorse for not having attempted to stay with Sedgewick and work through the system. It was clear that Elizabeth did not believe that Kay seriously dissented from executive political philosophy: her reasoning being, she supposed, that Kay had been satisfied with it before the Marq'ssan came, that Kay was not the type to have a "conversion" experience, that therefore she would

automatically continue to hold notions of political philosophy roughly the same as those she had held before going over to the Marq'ssan. Kay understood Elizabeth's thinking about this: that executive political philosophy was pragmatic and commonsensical, that Kay's problems with Sedgewick's handling of things had been disagreements about efficiency. Executives unquestioningly assumed they were eminently logical and utilitarian in their methods. As for morality, Elizabeth assumed (correctly) that Kay had notions of public responsibility, enough to make her vulnerable to charges of irresponsibility (as well as to reminders of Kay's less than sterling behavior twenty-five years past).

She could see clearly now that Elizabeth intended to run her for some large purpose. In fact, Elizabeth *did* believe she could "rehabilitate" Kay. She hadn't been satisfied with what might have been extracted from her through the usual methods of interrogation; what they might have learned from her about the Marq'ssan and the Free Zone had been sacrificed for something else. Likewise by announcing her summary execution, they had given up the opportunity for a public trial at which they could have pilloried a perfect scapegoat for their entire mess. It was obvious, so very obvious: they wanted to use her for some hidden purpose. *They?* She must not jump to conclusions: Elizabeth might well be planning to use her for her own particular ends.

In the midst of these cogitations Kay asked Allison to arrange a meeting with Felice. It seemed little enough to do to confirm Elizabeth's belief that she desired to please her. Elizabeth would presume it difficult for Kay to apologize to Felice; and Kay would describe it with constraint should Elizabeth later ask her for an account of it. But Kay took Felice so lightly that she felt she could easily manage to act the role required. Adopting a posture of humiliation before Felice would not produce the wrenching feelings that doing so before Elizabeth had overwhelmed her with. However much she reminded herself that she was playing a role, where Elizabeth was concerned the role inflicted pain. Part of this she knew to be due to the long struggle she had waged against Elizabeth; but another part of it pertained to Elizabeth's

knowledge of her. It flicked at her, irritating raw nerve endings just as images physically configuring Elizabeth's domination of her did: Kay clinging to Elizabeth in Gordon's office, Elizabeth undressing and going into the shower with her, Elizabeth sitting beside her most of the night as she blubbered after a bout in the closet, Elizabeth stroking her hair while Kay knelt at the side of her chair. She knew it essential that she overcome the shame her vulnerability exposed her to, just as she knew she had to renew in herself a belief in her own authority— a far more serious problem than sloughing off her sense of shame. She had an idea of how the Marq'ssan would deal with unacceptable revelations from their own pasts— or even revelations of things they might discover about themselves in the present— but she, Kay, lacked that bedrock conviction and that ineluctable strength that permeated the Marq'ssan's very being. To her such notions were relatively new. They had taught her to overcome her diffidence, had taught her to be patient with herself. But though she searched for a voice in her mind that would speak as they might speak, the potential power of any such voice seemed inadequate for confronting the enormity of her shame and guilt. She could not stop herself from asking who was she, Kay Zeldin, that she could pretend to be guided and formed by a moral imperative superior to Elizabeth Weatherall's.

Thus she uncovered another, more disagreeable secret: that what Elizabeth had been doing to her might be justified. She, Kay, probably deserved it. And as Elizabeth had taken pains to point out— and as Kay on some level believed— she had never treated Kay capriciously or with disrespect for her humanity as a feeling and thinking creature. Kay might argue that what Elizabeth did to her was abusive and that many definitions of torture might include some of Elizabeth's treatment of her within that rubric, but deep down there lurked terrible suspicions that she deserved it. And if that weren't enough, she always had the example of Wedgewood as a measure of contrast by which to consider Elizabeth's methods.

But a reminder to herself that Elizabeth was up to something pulled her out of the quagmire of considering moral questions and making moral comparisons. What did Elizabeth hope to gain by forcing

her into admissions of guilt? And what did these admissions have to do with Sedgewick? These questions, Kay concluded, formed the crux of the matter. If she could find answers to them she might be able to piece together a larger picture (if larger picture there were). She would continue to let Elizabeth think she wanted to please her (which was to say she would continue to do her best to please Elizabeth). All information must come from Elizabeth, there was no other source accessible to her.

And if she did discover what Elizabeth was up to?

Kay refused to allow herself to think about that question. For the moment it was enough to seek comprehension. What happened on the other side of comprehension did not now concern her, could not now concern her, and must not now concern her.

[ii]

Allison had not seen Elizabeth privately since their confrontation in the executive conference room on Tuesday. To avoid a one-on-one encounter, Allison had gone home that evening after delivering Zeldin to the lounge. On Wednesday, Elizabeth had gone to Maine. And on the two occasions on Thursday morning that Allison had seen Elizabeth, other people had been present. Allison felt both embarrassed and angry— at Elizabeth as well as at herself. She wasn't sure why she was angry at Elizabeth. But she did know one thing: she did not in any way measure up to Elizabeth. Never had she felt so inadequate. For the first time in her life she felt as though she did not deserve to be an executive, that she was an impostor. She believed that Elizabeth knew that— or would soon discover it. To be in the same room with Elizabeth was, now, to feel annihilated. Elizabeth despised weakness. Weakness was there to be managed, to be soothed, to be exploited and even protected— when it was found in service-techs. But when found in executives? What did Elizabeth think of the Henry Lauders who fell apart after years of defining by his very existence the meaning of the word *tough*? Allison of course could not count herself among such exalted company— she had always been weak. She was not simply falling apart now...for there was nothing there *to* fall apart.

On Tuesday night Allison had made love to Anne for the first time since the attack. Anne had been ecstatically happy, confessing to Allison that she had begun to think she no longer wanted her because of her having been raped. Allison suspected that Anne was in love with her. The night before when she had slept with Anne for the second night in a row she had seen in Anne's face a dawning belief that something special was happening between them. And Allison had fallen into despair: despair for herself, despair for Anne, despair at the things making service-tech-executive relations what they were. They could not escape from these things, even if Anne didn't understand or recognize their presence in their relationship, in their lives. (Would Anne begin to understand this when Allison started teaching her to physically defend herself? Would she begin to question the status quo? Would it occur to her that things were not what they might be, that certain evils were not inevitable?)

Late Thursday afternoon when Allison's phone beeped she picked it up expecting it to be Georgeanne Childress returning her call. But "Allison?" Elizabeth's voice said.

Allison's stomach fluttered, and her heart lurched into a gallop. "Yes, Elizabeth?" she said as steadily as she could.

"Have you arranged a meeting between Zeldin and Felice?"

"Yes. Felice said she would come tomorrow afternoon."

"You've been avoiding me, Allison?"

Allison swallowed on a very dry throat. "You were out of town yesterday."

"We are going to have to talk. Tonight, I think?"

Allison could not speak.

"Is this really necessary, Allison?"

"I'm sorry. I didn't mean—"

"I'll call you when I get home," Elizabeth said— and disconnected.

Allison put her shaking hands to her burning face. She couldn't continue like this. She would ask Elizabeth for a transfer. If Elizabeth cared at all for her she would allow it. Maybe she would even send her back to Vienna. But even if she couldn't go back to Vienna, she needed to get away. Anywhere at all.

[iii]

Allison found Elizabeth curled up before the fire, drinking coffee. She'd obviously bathed and dined before phoning down to Allison. Because of her nervousness, Allison was not breathing properly, which was probably why waves of lightheadedness were washing over her, half-disorienting her. Ill-at-ease, she settled on a cushion several feet from Elizabeth and stared into the fire.

"Talk to me, Allison," Elizabeth said into the silence.

Allison's cheeks flared into a burn. "I don't know what to say."

"For godsake, you're not a child that I should have to coax and pull it out of you!" Allison turned her head slightly to look sidelong at Elizabeth's face. "You're acting like a—" Elizabeth broke off, pressing her lips together.

Allison wondered what Elizabeth had been going to say. That she was acting like a service-tech? "I think," Allison said carefully, her eyes again on the fire, "you were right when you said I couldn't handle this sexual relationship. Please, Elizabeth. Will you have me transferred? Back to Vienna?"

"Transferred to Vienna?" Elizabeth's voice was harsh. "What can you be *thinking*? There's probably going to be a war fought in that part of the world!"

"Oh," Allison said. "I hadn't thought of that."

Elizabeth was staring at her. "So you want to leave me entirely? Is that it?"

Allison pulled her knees up and laid her head on them. "It's not that I want... I mean, it's just that... oh christ, Elizabeth. It's different for me than it is for you. My other lovers have never been anything like you. I've only had service-techs. This is completely different from anything I've known before. But for you— it's simply another of your affairs. You've made it plain what you think of your service-tech lovers. And this affair with me, it's simply another version of your usual thing. So of course you treat me as you'd treat one of them. Don't think I don't see how that has happened. I'm not blaming you. But it doesn't stop there. I... It's messing me up, Elizabeth. I can't think straight about myself anymore. I don't know what I'm doing. No, I don't *want* to leave you. But I can't go on like this. I simply can't." The deluge of words tapered into a trickle and then into a silence that thundered so loudly in Allison's ears she did not even hear the crackle and hiss of the fire she was staring at.

"I am trying to understand, Allison," Elizabeth said after a while. "From what I can make out you're telling me that you think that I have been using you, degrading you. Do I have that right?"

"That's not what I said!"

"Then I don't think I understand, or that I heard properly. The other thing of course is quite clear: you know that I need you particularly, and very particularly now, and that you will not only hurt me by leaving, but will put me in a difficult position with Sedgewick, Security, and the Executive. I trusted you, Allison. And I believed that you trusted me. All that was a sham?"

Hot tears slipped down Allison's cheeks. "Not a sham," Allison said. "And I don't want to leave you in a difficult position. If any of that matters— and I don't see how it could, I mostly do menial things that anyone could do— I of course would want to stay. But it's tearing me apart. You told me the night of that party at the club that I wasn't thinking or acting like an executive. Maybe that's the point. Maybe I can't be an executive and your lover at the same time. When I tried to tell you how I felt about you, you turned it aside, making it clear that I wasn't supposed to feel that way. But I don't know how to control those kinds of feelings, Elizabeth, not once they've been let loose. I don't know what they are, but they're there, and they're strong. I can control the way I look and act and talk, but I can't control how I feel. Believe me, I've tried. I know you can only despise me for it. I've told myself that since the night of the party. But somehow that hasn't helped stop the feelings." Allison swallowed with difficulty, then continued in a near-whisper. "And anyway, I suppose if there's any question of your using me it's all because I behaved in such a way that induced you unconsciously to treat me as a service-tech. I know perfectly well it's all my own fault."

Elizabeth irritably tapped her demitasse with a restless fingernail. "You think that you are the only one of us with feelings, Allison?

I don't know how you could come to think I'm indifferent and untouched by emotions. If you were correct about my regarding you as a service-tech I would have so thoroughly managed you that you would never have questioned my being madly infatuated with you. Instead I have treated you like the woman you are, have assumed a maturity...and assumed, too, that if you had problems with our relationship you would have brought them up before they'd become so magnified. I've had little time to think about anything personal. You do have some idea of the kind of pressures I'm working under. It never occurred to me that you found our relationship such a hell. I was so pleased to have you there at my side, giving me love and support. And as for the position of trust you've held in my work!" Elizabeth's eyes flashed. "The confidence I've placed in you, the sensitive information I've made you privy to... I'm terribly disturbed that you could take that so lightly. You think I would ever entrust any of it to a *service-tech*? What do you take me for, Allison?"

"I'm sorry," Allison said, "I didn't mean, I didn't think—"

Elizabeth rose to her feet. "If you want to leave, then it must be so. I only ask you to wait a while for the transfer. I really think this threat of war must make certain claims on your loyalty just now that must outweigh your personal needs and desires. I'm sorry you hate working for me. But I do beg you to stick it out for a while longer."

Miserably Allison stood, too. "I don't hate working for you," she said. "You aren't being fair. What I said—"

"What you said is that you want to leave, that you want a transfer," Elizabeth said sharply.

Allison stared down at the floor. "I'll be happy to stay for as long as you need me," she said.

"Then we'll hold off on the transfer. As for the other— you can rest assured I won't force myself on you."

Allison's throat was too tight to speak.

"If there's nothing else," Elizabeth said, "you're free to go."

"Good night," Allison whispered.

"Good night," Elizabeth said.

Elizabeth went into the bedroom. Allison pressed the thumb plate and stepped into the elevator. This was much worse than the time Elizabeth had broken it off between them. This was total exile. She could feel it already freezing the air around her. And she wouldn't even be able to cry herself out this time, for Anne was down there, waiting for her.

And Anne must never know.

[iv]

To wake in what must be the middle of the night to find someone in her cell evoked submerged feelings of terror Kay had never before consciously felt. That which the pressures of diurnal reasoning kept banished and concealed lurked in the recesses of her mind, emerging only when her defenses were down, revealed itself in one fulgurative moment as powerful, menacing, real. At that one instant of opening her eyes and seeing Elizabeth's tall shadowed figure blotting out the room's only illumination— that issuing from the night light resting on the desk— a terrible fear shook Kay: she did not really know Elizabeth, and down here in this oubliette anything could happen and no one would know, or if they knew, would not care.

Elizabeth stared down at Kay for a long time without speaking. Kay's breath caught in her throat. She could not see Elizabeth's face, for Elizabeth stood with her back to the light. Elizabeth's stillness and her uncharacteristic silence struck cold deep into her bones. Her mind consciously articulated what for a few shivering seconds she had been feeling. Elizabeth could, if she chose, kill her. It could happen right now. Elizabeth was strong enough to strangle her. And of course she could be carrying a gun under the long coat she was wearing. Was it her death that Elizabeth contemplated as she stood silently staring down at her?

"*Bon soir*, Kay," Elizabeth said softly.

"*Bon soir*, Elizabeth," Kay returned, unable to keep the tremor out of her voice.

"Scoot over," Elizabeth said. Without taking her eyes off Elizabeth, Kay slid sideways until her right arm was touching the wall. To her surprise, Elizabeth took off her coat and lay down on top of the

bedclothes, covering herself with the coat. "I had insomnia. So I came back to the base to work, and then decided I wanted to talk to you for a while first."

Any strangeness in her situation, any deviation from routine frightened Kay. She had no way of predicting or understanding what was going to happen or how she should react. Elizabeth was lying seemingly relaxed, staring up at the ceiling, aware of Kay but not focused on her the way she ordinarily was during each of their meetings no matter how insignificant the encounter might be. For the first time, Elizabeth wasn't watching her face, wasn't projecting the intensity and alertness of a hunter poised to pounce on her prey. This wild shift unsettled Kay and worried her. She did not know this Elizabeth lying beside her, inhaling and exhaling in the stillness.

"You're surprised I'm here, you don't quite know why, and that makes you a little afraid, I think." Elizabeth's voice was low, only slightly above a whisper. "Well, you needn't be afraid, Kay." Her eyes slewed sideways at Kay for a moment, then turned up again toward the ceiling. "I'm indulging myself, you see. There's a very great temptation you present people with, Kay Zeldin." She sighed. "One could of course dismiss Sedgewick's weakness to give in to that temptation because of its grounding in his peculiar sexual pathology. I have no such excuse. Lying in bed tonight, having wakened for the third time, I found myself talking to you. Extensively. Wishing to discuss things with you that I know I must never trust to you. One wants to trust you, Kay Zeldin. And for me, knowing so much of your past experiences, the temptation is all the stronger— there's the feeling that you will be able to understand what others cannot, that you are experienced, or have at least at some time understood something about it that would make talking to you wonderfully reassuring. It's probably wistful nonsense. You aren't exactly sympathetic, are you... and of course you aren't sympathetic to me in particular. But I mean in general. You aren't a sympathetic sort of person who will sit down and listen to others' confessions, jeremiads, lamentations, recitations, or even boastings of accomplishments. And you are very different from me. In so many ways. Yet again there's this wistful notion that you and I might actu-

ally share a great deal in common if only we enjoyed mutual trust. An alluring prospect...but wholly false." Elizabeth turned her head to stare at Kay. "You look astonished. Shall I tell you? Every time I prepare to encounter you I force myself to remember how Sedgewick trusted you and how you deceived him. I have to remind myself of that over and over again. I have such a strong urge to talk to you garrulously, freely, trustingly..."

Kay did not know what to say. At first taken aback, then irresistibly flattered, she admonished herself that this was probably a ruse.

"But intelligent people confident of their own intelligence are always attracted to the extremely intelligent," Elizabeth said. "Naturally you know that very well. It is only those unsure of themselves who hate and fear intelligence. There is something insidiously flattering to a person of intelligence when he or she is able to communicate with the very intelligent. But it is more than that, of course."

Kay laughed a little. "Am I to understand that you think me one of the very intelligent?"

"Surely you have no doubts?"

"I am here, aren't I," Kay said very low. "As far as I can see that's proof enough that I'm in some way deficient."

"Yes," Elizabeth said. "In some way you are deficient. That's what I've been trying to make you see. You turned your back on real power, you turned your back on the possibilities of a constructive response to your situation and instead did something wild and erratic and irrational. But I think we both understand now the roots of that deficiency."

Kay kept quiet. She had to let Elizabeth think she agreed with that assessment. She might then— especially while Elizabeth was in this peculiar mood— learn something.

"But to change the subject slightly," Elizabeth said. "I have for my own reasons been contemplating structural inequalities between sexual partners. You are something of an expert on this on the basis of your experience with Sedgewick. Particularly considering what a truly bizarre balance you managed to strike with him."

"Balance?" Kay said. "I can't imagine what you mean."

"Balance in several respects. For one thing, Sedgewick controlled your working relationship while you controlled your emotional and sexual relationship."

Kay snorted. "That's nonsense. He said that to me that day on the island, but it wasn't true."

"I think it was true. It was you who set the limits. It was you who made innovations in your games. And in another respect, the fact that you sometimes switched roles with him further suggests balance of the sort that is usually impossible in ordinary heterosexual relationships."

"I didn't want any of it," Kay said very low, shivering with cold and tension. "He decided. I wanted him to stop. I asked him repeatedly."

"Just how did he force you to go on?" Elizabeth asked ironically.

She would ask him sometimes over the phone, please, please, couldn't they simply go to bed together, without all the game-playing. But each time she put down the phone she knew she would be going to him anyway. Sometimes while they were playing she would beg him to stop, but of course such pleading was supposed to be part of the game and was always to be ignored.

"Once," Elizabeth said, "when Sedgewick was very drunk he told me something that he said made it clear to him that you, not he, were in overall control, that you were setting the limits. One evening, he said, you came over and assumed the controlling role. You handcuffed his hands behind his back and made him sprawl in the dry, empty bathtub. Then you squatted down over his chest and pissed on him. That impressed him, I assure you. Years later he was still impressed. He said he would never have done such a thing to you if you hadn't done it first to him. And that it was that way with almost everything that passed between the two of you. Always you escalated things. And because he came to believe you were indestructible— unlike his other lovers, whose destructibility always came either to bore or frighten him to the point of having to drop them, when they weren't the ones first frightened off— because of your willingness to take the other role, and your constant challenge to him to go further, because of all these things you assumed impossibly large proportions in his psychic landscape, even before he was fixed. Surely you must agree with this."

Kay shrank from the memory, but it flooded her consciousness. After one particularly brutal session she had fantasized pissing on him. As had so often happened she had been lying awake reliving humiliating details that at the time of their perpetration had escaped her attention, seething with anger at him, wanting to lash out at him, knowing that merely physical violence would not substantially touch him. So she had sought for a sure means of humiliating him, and the image of herself pissing on him (on his face, not his chest) came into her mind and would not go. When his next phone call came she went to him without even thinking of it. But as he opened his door to her she remembered the fantasy and wished she dared to do it, and perhaps because of it assumed the attitude of control and began giving him orders. Once the fantasy had come into her mind she had not been able to think of anything else. Still, she had not really believed she would do it. Even as she made him lie in the bottom of the tub she didn't believe she would go through with it. He'd had no idea of it as she climbed into the tub and crouched over him. Staring at his face, though, a wildness had seized her, her consciousness narrowing to an awareness only of his face and of the fantasy and of her power to do it. The urine flowed out, first in a trickle, and then in a stream, spraying him, spattering her legs, his neck, even his face. Never taking her eyes off his, she drank in his reaction. She had, she could see, truly shocked him. In their game of chicken she'd one-upped him in a way he would never be able to top. Yet even as she was doing it, even as she drank in the shock in his eyes, she knew he would in the future do it to her, and that he might make it even more degrading for her than she was making it for him.

"I wanted him to stop it," Kay tried to explain to Elizabeth. "I thought that he would come to his senses, he would know we couldn't keep going like that. I couldn't believe it when he didn't even protest at my making him lie there in my piss for almost an hour. But not only did he not try to stop it, he *enjoyed* it!"

"And did you enjoy doing it to him?"

Kay remembered how she had felt when he in his turn had stood over her— a few sessions later— and done it to her.

"You don't want to answer that, do you," Elizabeth said. "You're not being completely honest even now."

"It was insanity," Kay said. "Do people ask schizophrenics if they enjoy doing bizarre meaningless things that at the time seemed to make sense to them?"

"So in the end you resented him," Elizabeth said. "Because you worked for him? What if he hadn't been your controller? Would you have felt the same way? Wouldn't you have been more likely to see your sexual relationship from a more realistic perspective?" When Kay said nothing, Elizabeth continued. "Have you ever been in the reverse situation, Kay? Have you ever had a lover who has come to resent you for the power you wielded outside the sexual aspect of the relationship?"

Elizabeth must be having problems with one of her service-tech lovers, Kay thought, remembering the so obviously managed Mimi. "No," Kay said. "I never have. I always tried to avoid relationships susceptible to manipulation. People hate being managed."

Elizabeth sighed. "No. That's not what they hate. They like being managed. What they dislike is consciousness of being managed. To be cleverly enough managed so that one needn't be aware of it allows one to shirk responsibility. And it's your record in that regard that I think binds us closer together than you might think, Kay Zeldin."

"I don't understand."

"You refused to be managed by Sedgewick when he brought you back into the Company. Over and over again you challenged him. And of course what happened finally was that you manipulated him in the most spectacular example of treachery that I can think of. You knew just how to handle him, Kay, without his even being aware of it."

"That's what you do?" Kay said, not believing Elizabeth would answer her.

"Of course that's what I do," Elizabeth said. "It hasn't always been that way. I only started doing it when it became necessary."

"Letting him think he was completely in control," Kay said.

"Perhaps. I don't know."

"And does this make you feel completely in control?" Kay asked curiously.

"What do you mean?"

Kay's fingers pressed against the wall. "That one can never really be in control when one is doing it by manipulation. You refer to my having manipulated Sedgewick when I was trying to bring down Security. Never once did I feel in control— not until I held a gun in my hand and had the two of you tied to chairs and gagged. *Then* I felt in control. But not when I was surreptitiously trying to manipulate Sedgewick."

"That's because you didn't attempt anything of significance to you."

Kay remembered leading Sedgewick to believe that Torricelli was betraying him. She would not admit to Elizabeth having done that, of course. But perhaps at that moment when she had realized he had accepted her assessment without question, she had felt some spark of satisfaction— no, triumph. Triumph at his having been gulled by her.

Kay wished Elizabeth would go.

"We would make a wonderful team, Kay Zeldin. In spite of the blind, foolish men of the Executive. But you would take me to the cleaners, too— if I let you." There was silence except for the sound of their breathing. "That sense of your being indestructible— of course you and I know that you aren't, but that is only speaking of the most extreme circumstances—" Kay trembled at this oblique reference to the closet— "but that ever fighting, pulsing core that one can sense in you underneath the external layers of your personality— one would like to be able to tap that. To borrow some of it, yes, but also to be aware of it as a source of reassurance that there exists in some people a strength that can withstand almost anything... the sort of thing that until one grows up one imagines to exist in one's parents... Growing up is, I suppose, first recognizing and then coming to terms with the idiocy, silliness, and weakness of our parents. Some of us never can forgive them. Your parents died before you saw that in them I suppose."

"I was nineteen," Kay said.

"To lose both of them at once," Elizabeth said. "Were you able always to preserve your illusions about them?"

"No. Of course not." She would not talk to Elizabeth about that.

"You want to go to sleep," Elizabeth said. "Though you don't sound at all sleepy. But you want me to leave you in peace. And so I will go. It is not possible for us to be equals, and therefore it is necessary that you subordinate yourself to me. But there's no need to make you resent me for small things like my forcing myself on you in the middle of the night." Elizabeth swung her legs off the bed, stood up, and draped her coat over her arm. "We will have a less whimsical talk soon. Perhaps after you see Felice." She moved to the door and it slid open. "Good night, Kay," she said, going out into the corridor. The door slid shut.

After a long minute of straining her hearing and waiting— as though to be sure Elizabeth had really gone and was not returning— Kay got up to wash her hands and fetch a bottle of water. She peered at the clock and saw that it was three twenty-five a.m. Shivering, she went back to bed. She would not think about any of it now, not at this hour of the night. Yet as she dozed off she wondered as she had been doing constantly lately what Elizabeth was up to. Sooner or later she would know— presuming she survived. It would make a big difference, however, whether it was sooner rather than later. Knowing later what it was might not matter at all, because then it would be too late. Whatever "it" was.

Chapter Thirty

[i]

Offering her mea culpa to Felice Raines proved more trying than Kay had expected. Allison brought her to the lounge where she occasionally took meals with Elizabeth and left her with Felice and the service-tech attending her, both of them seated on the rug drinking what Kay guessed to be tea. "Do sit down, Kay," Felice said without smiling. "Standing there towering over us, you look as though you're about to attack."

That was an idea. Taking Felice hostage would probably be enough to get her out of the Rock alive. Or would it? They probably had some sort of gassing system built into the walls so that even if she could find something to use as a weapon she would not get far. She lowered herself carefully to the floor and tried to look conciliatory. "I asked Elizabeth if I could apologize to you for all the trouble I caused," she said. Felice's delicate eyebrows rose. "What you said the other night made me think about it from your perspective. I never imagined that you personally would have problems because of what I did to Sedgewick. And I did very greatly appreciate your kindness when I was ill."

Felice's green eyes lit up, making Kay think of polished jade. "DC went mad," she said. "Fortunately Wedgewood was sharp enough to evacuate almost everyone connected with Security. We had no idea where the hell Sedgewick had disappeared to...or why...no one *saw* anything, there were no vehicles visible anywhere near the building, and no intruders... It was at first believed that Sedgewick, Elizabeth, and you had all been spirited away by disloyal Security insiders working for Military. And suddenly it was open season on high-level Military and Security executives— people were actually being assassinated!

Wedgewood could do nothing but get us out of there. I was terrified for Daniel's safety especially. If it hadn't been for Wedgewood, we probably would have been killed. All of us." Felice glared at Kay. "And it would have been your fault. You have no sense of loyalty whatsoever. Not loyalty to the country, not loyalty to Security, not loyalty to Sedgewick, not loyalty to me, who welcomed you unreservedly into my home. I'll tell you this much, I will never again trust a professional. You people are consistently treacherous. You're never satisfied with all that you've got." Felice poured more tea into her cup. "More for you, dear?" she asked the service-tech.

The service-tech dragged her gaze from Kay's face to look at Felice and shook her head.

"I don't understand why Sedgewick didn't advise you to leave before everything broke," Kay said— then stopped herself from continuing. If she weren't careful she would endanger everything she was hoping to achieve with this apology. Kay again caught the service-tech's wide, rather horrified eyes watching her— and the service-tech recoiled. Kay looked at Felice. "Still, I do apologize for everything."

"You're blaming Sedgewick?"

Kay dropped her gaze to the carpet. "No, not at all," she said. "I'm sure he would have taken care of you if I hadn't interfered with his plans." Kay heard the door slide open; looking over her shoulder she saw Allison coming back into the room. "I do hope you can forgive me," Kay said, wondering at Allison's timing.

Allison held out the handcuffs. "You have an appointment at the infirmary," she said.

Kay got to her feet. Her head swam with dizziness. "May I have some water first?" she asked Allison as she waited for her vision to return. Every ounce would help.

Allison stared at her as though to let Kay know she knew Kay was stalling, then crossed the room, took a half-liter bottle from the buffet, and brought it to Kay.

Kay broke the seal and drank from the bottle.

"Kindness always does seem to leave one open to being made a fool of or betrayed," Felice said. "Do you know, Allison, I sat at this woman's bedside for *hours* while she was suffering from concussion. And not only that, I risked Sedgewick's anger for her in certain things, too."

Kay finished the bottle and set it down on the table beside the tea tray. "I assure you, Felice, that I fully appreciated all that. But it wasn't to hurt you that I abducted Sedgewick." What else could she say? Clearly the woman was not to be mollified.

But Felice surprised her. She stood and put her hand on Kay's arm. "Do you know, dear, I think I believe you. But there is something very wrong with you professionals." Her gaze moved to Allison's face. "They are lacking in common decency and loyalty. They have no sense of where their true interests lie. I assumed she was a part of *us*, the way Elizabeth has always been. I let down my guard because Sedgewick made it clear she was to be considered one of us." She shook her head. "But they simply don't understand, they simply don't think and feel as we do." She sighed. "I suppose that is why professionals are always calling themselves 'individualists.' I tell you, Allison, I will never take another one of them into my confidence again. They are pathological."

Little as Kay wanted to rush to the infirmary, she wished Allison would insist they must go now.

"But you are punished enough without my holding a grudge against you, Kay," Felice said in a sickeningly sympathetic voice. "I can see you are suffering. And I feel sorry for you."

When Allison didn't speak, Kay forced herself to say, "I'm glad you can forgive me, Felice. It's very kind of you." Never had Kay thought Felice such a bitch as she did now.

Felice, smiling, squeezed Kay's arm. Allison again displayed the handcuffs, and Kay held out her wrists.

En route to the infirmary she consoled herself with the thought that she would have felt worse if Elizabeth had ordered her to apologize to Felice instead of suggesting it. Or would she? Kay found it confusing trying to disentangle implications and wins and losses once frank manipulation was brought into the picture. She was gambling her small resistances on some larger resistance whose shape and very ground remained as yet unknown. She was counting on sabotaging Elizabeth's larger plan. Would the gamble be worth it?

"Here we are," Allison said as they approached the entrance to the infirmary.

When Kay got on the scale, the l.e.d.s read eighty and a quarter pounds. The nurse entered the new datum, then said to Allison, "I'll fetch Dr. Gordon. She's so far under that he will want to examine her."

Kay looked at Allison but knew there was no point in asking her to intervene. "Maybe the scale is wrong," she said.

Allison said, "I don't see why if you hate this so much that you don't just start eating more, Kay."

The door opened and Gordon came in with the nurse. Kay submitted, trembling uncontrollably, to the same procedures Gordon had put her through each time he had previously seen her— extracting blood, taking her blood pressure and an EKG, listening to her lungs, and ordering urinalysis. Except for curt commands to her for facilitating the examination, neither Gordon nor the nurse ever spoke directly to Kay but addressed their remarks only to Allison. Kay felt as though she were something between a robot and an experimental lab animal. She understood that to the people she had seen in the infirmary on her past visits there she appeared to be merely a body without personality or sentience. She especially hated that attitude when she was being force-fed far more than she minded the discomfort.

She was not surprised when Allison took her to be force-fed before returning her to the cell. She would, she informed Kay, be taking her from her cell twice a day for the next week to have it done. Kay wished she knew how to put herself in a trance to avoid consciousness of the procedure. No matter how many times it was done to her she would never get used to it.

[ii]

When early that evening the door to Kay's cell slid open, Kay expected it to be Allison. But instead Elizabeth came in, pushing a cart. Kay, trying to quickly think herself into her role, sat up. "*Bon soir*, Kay," Elizabeth said, beaming at her.

Kay sat up and leaned back against the wall. "*Bon soir*, Elizabeth."

Elizabeth came and stood by the bed with her hands on her hips. "Don't tell me you're depressed?" Elizabeth sighed. "I forbid you to be depressed tonight, Kay. I won't have it!"

Did Elizabeth imagine she could order Kay's moods? "What kind of person would be happy about being force-fed?" Kay said petulantly.

Elizabeth shook her head. "You know that is none of my doing. Be reasonable. I can't make you eat enough to avoid the feedings."

Kay stared down at her nightshirt, appalled at the quick rush of self-pity overwhelming her. If she weren't careful she would soon be losing control of herself and angering Elizabeth.

"At any rate, there's no need for you to think about that tonight," Elizabeth said. Kay looked up. So Elizabeth hadn't come to take her to the infirmary? But then that was Allison's job now: Elizabeth hadn't taken her since introducing Allison to Kay. "We're having a party tonight. It's New Year's Eve, Kay." Elizabeth smiled. "We'll see the New Year in together."

"Please, Elizabeth," Kay said. "Please don't make me go to another one of those things."

"Shame on you. You should be glad to be getting out of your cell—and glad to be missing a feeding: I'm going to trust you to eat with us tonight. Now get up, the occasion calls for a shower." Elizabeth took something from the cart. "Here," she said, turning back to Kay and dumping three gift-wrapped boxes in Kay's lap. "These are for you."

More "gifts." Kay hated the psychological pressure Elizabeth's "gifts" exerted. No matter how often she reminded herself of her analyses of what these objects represented in her relations with Elizabeth, because of the words she and Elizabeth used and the attitudes they adopted, her understanding never quite dispelled the effect Elizabeth undoubtedly intended. Because Elizabeth was watching, she made herself open them. In the largest box she found a gown of red and black silk. Kay stared at it and then up at Elizabeth. "It's lovely," she said, knowing Elizabeth expected appreciative comment. The second box held a pair of black silk slippers and the third box perfume. "These are for tonight?" Kay asked.

"For tonight especially, yes, but also to keep. You may wear them when you please."

Except while restrained to the platform or confined in the closet, Kay thought.

They went into the bathroom, and she asked Elizabeth to keep the door to the shower room open, and Elizabeth agreed. Kay sensed that though Elizabeth was not angry at her, she was disappointed at her lack of enthusiasm for the "gifts."

When Kay came out of the shower, Elizabeth stood waiting with a towel. Surprised, Kay submitted to Elizabeth's rubbing and patting her dry and spraying her with perfume. Elizabeth was so much taller and larger than she that Elizabeth's ministrations made her feel like a child. Slipping into the gown, Kay admitted to herself how pleasurable she found the feel of the silk against her skin. Elizabeth then brushed Kay's hair and commented as she always did about how fast it was growing out.

Emerging from the bathroom, Kay saw that a large basket of fresh fruit and several plastic bottles of fruit juice had been arranged on the table. "And I've brought you a few things to read," Elizabeth said.

Kay stared at her. "Why?" she asked baldly.

"Because I'm so pleased with you, Kay. I'm most pleased that you apologized to Felice without my ordering you to do so. We are beginning to understand one another, aren't we."

Kay could not pretend to being happy at Elizabeth's pleasure in these signs of weakness, so she chose another way toward satisfying Elizabeth's expectations. She turned her back; staring at the rug she said, "You make me ashamed, Elizabeth."

"For what, Kay? For choosing to please me?" Elizabeth moved to Kay and put her arm around Kay's shoulder.

Kay chose her words carefully, aware of how tricky constructing this role was. "You reward me when I show weakness," she said very low.

"That way of describing what has happened here comes out of a very twisted, even perverse perspective, Kay. That pleasing me must be automatically interpreted as weakness is simplistic. For instance, if I said that it would please me for you to gain forty pounds, would you

consider doing so weakness, when clearly it would benefit you more than it would me? I can't see that apologizing to Felice is weakness: you know as well as I that you did endanger her and her children's lives. And that is by any standard something to apologize for." Elizabeth moved a few steps away. "Do you agree?"

Kay looked up at her. "I see your point," she said.

"You think too much in terms of behaving to defy me," Elizabeth said. She went to the cart, dug into the leather bag, and pulled out a pair of cuffs. Kay held out her wrists, and Elizabeth cuffed them. Elizabeth slung the bag over her shoulder and pushed the cart to the door. In the corridor she abandoned the cart, then adjusted the lay of the gown's sleeve. "There, we're all set. *Avanti*!"

For the first time Kay suffered almost no self-consciousness while traveling the corridors. Only the handcuffs and her lack of a security badge visibly marked her as a prisoner. No one passing even glanced at her as they greeted Elizabeth. And when Allison met them outside the lounge, Kay observed Allison do a double-take. Her eyes widened and questioned Elizabeth. Kay thought she detected a slight blush. "They called and said Felice's chopper would be landing in five minutes," Allison told Elizabeth. "I'm on my way to meet them now."

Elizabeth pressed her thumb to the access plate and moved Kay over the threshold. When the door closed Elizabeth unlocked the cuffs and invited Kay to sit where she pleased. Kay took the armchair she usually sat in when talking to Elizabeth. "And help yourself to the food," Elizabeth said sternly. "We aren't having anything particularly rich tonight, on your account. So there are no excuses."

Felice and Allison would be there. And someone else? Didn't Allison say "them?" Or was that merely a general reference to the helicopter? Kay leaned forward and chose a plain boiled shrimp. It tasted sweet and juicy in her mouth.

Elizabeth sat on the sofa. "So you're going to be antisocial?"

Food had been set out on the low table between the pair of chairs. Elizabeth *had* told Kay to sit where she pleased. "Do you want me to move?" Kay asked.

"I told you to sit where you liked."

The implication being that she should move without Elizabeth telling her to? Kay decided she would stay where she was, at least for the time being.

When the door next opened three women came in— Allison, Felice, and the service-tech who had been in this room with Felice earlier. The service-tech, however, had changed into an antique dress— short with a low neckline and bare arms, without trousers. Kay had heard that people— usually college students— sometimes wore antique clothing to parties. And of course one saw such things in movies. Still, it struck her as extremely odd— perverse, even— to see someone dressed that way when everyone else (but herself, of course) was wearing conventional clothing.

"But how charming!" Cooing over the service-tech, Elizabeth got up and went over to inspect her. "What a splendid idea, it's absolutely perfect on you, darling!"

Kay detected consternation not on the service-tech's face, but on Allison and Felice's. The service-tech looked *flattered.*

"We found it in a little antique shop in Denver this afternoon," Felice said. "As soon as I saw it I knew Marianne must try it on. So she did, and we couldn't resist it."

Allison crossed the room to the buffet; she poured herself wine from a bottle already opened. "Marianne, do you want wine?" she called over her shoulder.

Marianne looked at Felice.

"Go ahead, dear," Felice said. "There's no reason not to."

"Yes, please." Marianne went to take the glass from Allison.

Felice noticed Kay. "So you're joining us tonight, Kay?"

Kay bit back the caustic comment that sprang to her lips. "Yes," she said. But so many sarcastic remarks came into her head that she could find nothing acceptable to add to the "yes."

"Oh," Felice cried, and moved closer. "Look at that silk, it's stunning!" She reached out and took a piece of Kay's gown in her hand. "Jouissance, isn't it?" She turned and looked at Elizabeth. "You dress your prisoners in Jouissance?"

Jouissance? It sounded, Kay thought, like the name of a sleazy perfume.

"I thought so too," Allison said. "Look at her, she doesn't even know what Jouissance is." She snorted. "What a waste."

"Now Allison," Elizabeth said. "One doesn't need to know the names of things to appreciate them."

Felice released Kay's gown and settled on the floor nearby. "In case you don't know, Kay, Jouissance is a specially designed silk that is fabulously expensive. It does seem a little much, Elizabeth. Though far be it from me to begrudge Kay her little pleasures." She slid Elizabeth a sly look that made Kay's cheeks burn. Did Felice think that she and Elizabeth...?

Allison sat on the far end of the sofa, Elizabeth on the near end, and Marianne on the floor near Felice. Elizabeth engaged Felice in a conversation about whom she had seen in Denver that afternoon, ostensibly seeking gossip. Felice, munching on shrimp and raw vegetables and other tidbits, easily complied, going into great detail about who had said what and supplying enough background for Elizabeth to understand what Felice believed the significance of every remark and gesture had been. But while Felice chattered, Elizabeth amused herself flirting with Marianne, nudging and stroking the thigh nearest her with her outstretched soft leather-shod foot. While Kay could see this because she was sitting above and at an angle to Marianne and Felice, Felice herself could not. Kay suspected Allison could see it, too, for Allison's face as she sipped grew almost rigid. All the while Elizabeth nodded and smiled at Felice, prompting her with questions at the correct moments, her foot was sliding along Marianne's thigh. Marianne stared down into her wine, never once turning her head to look at Elizabeth. Kay found the scene nerve-wracking; she was relieved when a service-tech opened the swing door into the kitchen and announced that dinner was served.

At the table Elizabeth directed Marianne to share Kay's side, placing Marianne at her, Elizabeth's, left. Kay wondered if Elizabeth would be continuing her games under the table, though she knew it made sense for Marianne to sit next to Kay, for otherwise Allison would be

crowded. (Kay and Marianne were, after all, the only non-executives in the party.) Yet it would seem more appropriate for Marianne to be sitting on Kay's left, near Felice… Kay ate most of the soup she was served— a clear chicken broth with thinly julienned vegetables— but paid little attention to the conversation, which seemed to be mostly about Felice and Sedgewick's daughter Alexandra and how differently she behaved when living away from her brother and father. Instead she mused on Elizabeth's having given her such an expensive gown, wondering if Elizabeth had intended for her to discover its costliness through Felice and Allison's reactions, and wondering also what motive (apart from the obvious positive reinforcement any gift might be expected to effect) lay behind it. And as she ate she grew physically uncomfortable. The people in the infirmary must have scraped her esophagus, for the passage of food irritated it. It would be worse, she reminded herself, a few days down the line. Twice daily on a consistent basis would generate cumulatively more discomfort.

"Ka-ay," Elizabeth's voice snapped Kay out of reverie. Kay, blinking, looked at Elizabeth. "So you are there," Elizabeth said drily. "It's very rude of you to prefer your solitary thoughts to our company, you know."

The others were all watching her. "I'm sorry, Elizabeth." Kay stared down at her nearly empty soup plate.

"You do see what I mean?" Felice said. "An executive woman would never allow herself to go off into fits of abstraction like that. It simply wouldn't happen."

"Not even if she had been accustomed to isolation for three months?" Elizabeth asked. "Be a little generous, Felice. I'd wager that Kay in ordinary circumstances is almost as well-behaved as the rest of us. *Almost.* Her control has always been bad. But I don't recall any instances of rudeness specially attributed to her. Really, Felice, I think you are much too hard on the professional class."

Kay gritted her teeth. What could be ruder than their talking about her like this? She reached for her water glass— and barely caught herself from dragging her sleeve in her soup. Aware of Felice's eyes on her, she suddenly became self-conscious about her table deportment. She could easily imagine Felice bemoaning the entrusting of Jouissance silk to a professional who couldn't even keep her sleeves out of her soup.

The service-techs took away their soup plates and brought out the next course, steamed bass with a thin wine, scallion, and ginger sauce. Kay felt clumsy when the service-tech stood beside her and held out the platter from which she was to serve herself. It was true she was not used to being served this way, which had nothing to do with three months of tubefood and everything to do with not being raised an executive. How did Marianne feel, sitting at the table with them? Had she grown used to this sort of service? Remembering Marie, Kay doubted it. When the service-tech moved to Marianne's side, Kay watched and was surprised to see Elizabeth herself serving Marianne from the platter. Embarrassed, Kay stared down at her plate and hoped Marianne hadn't noticed her attention. Elizabeth was treating Marianne like a child, as though she couldn't be trusted to fill her own plate. She supposed she should be grateful Elizabeth hadn't treated her similarly.

The meal dragged on. Kay ate as much as she could, knowing that though Elizabeth did not seem to be paying much attention to her she probably knew to the bite how much she was eating. Allison said little and steadily worked her way through her second bottle. Elizabeth and Felice maintained conversation into which the former persistently drew Kay, all the while flirting (or so Kay suspected) with Marianne.

At last Elizabeth released them from the table, and they drifted back to the other side of the room. This time, however, Allison sat where Kay had been sitting, and Kay took Allison's place on the sofa. A service-tech served them coffee. Felice gazed up at Allison and asked about her mother. Kay wondered whether executive women together ever talked about anything besides their mothers, their daughters, and other executive women. Could anything be more boring than Felice's conversation (or lack thereof)?

"I've told you about Vivien Whittier," Elizabeth said, interrupting Felice's interrogation of Allison. "She and I went to school together. Boarding school *and* college. A splendid woman. Unfortunately her

father did not fare too well during the transition to the executive system, and so she wound up contracting with someone not especially well off."

Kay glanced at Allison to see how she took this description of her parents, but Allison seemed unperturbed. "My father," Allison said, as though coming out with it before Felice inevitably asked, "holds a midlevel post with the Department of Agriculture. He's currently stationed in Arkansas."

"Mothers have the greatest influence on daughters," Elizabeth said. "After all, Felice, consider how much contact Sedgewick has ever had with Alexandra."

Felice sighed. "It really is a pity, too. She hasn't seen him in more than—"

"You know, Felice," Elizabeth said sharply, "I think it's best that we leave Sedgewick out of this conversation."

Felice stared at her. "May I point out that you introduced him into the conversation yourself, my dear."

"Have you been skiing, Felice?" Allison surprisingly bestirred herself to ask.

Kay looked from Allison to Felice to Elizabeth— and wondered. Had Elizabeth stopped Felice from saying something about Sedgewick because she, Kay, was there? Allison hadn't shown that kind of interest or energy all night. While Allison and Felice discussed skiing, Kay noticed that Elizabeth had resumed her foot games with Marianne. And Marianne was responding, too, touching Elizabeth's soft-boot with her fingers and then actually stroking it— all out of Felice's line of vision.

Kay began to feel the pressing need to pee. That was another problem: she was not allowed to go through the kitchen to the bathroom by herself. And in spite of everything, she was embarrassed to ask Elizabeth to take her. Why? Because of Felice and Marianne? It couldn't be because of Allison, since she had already been through so many embarrassing things with Allison. Or was there some lingering voodoo to this sort of occasion to which she was still susceptible, even now?

When Allison got up to get more wine, Kay followed her to the buffet. "Will you take me to the bathroom, Allison?" she whispered in Allison's ear.

"Right now?"

Allison led the way through the kitchen and into the bathroom. "I have to pee too, anyway," Allison said. Kay sank down onto the toilet seat. "Isn't this party wonderful fun?" Allison asked.

"I don't suppose I should answer that," Kay said.

"Have you noticed how Marianne is fascinated by you but can't quite bring herself to look into your eyes?"

Kay got up from the toilet and while Allison peed wiped her hands. "What do you mean? Because I'm so thin?"

Allison laughed. "Look in the mirror at yourself. Besides, I doubt if she's ever been around a real honest-to-god maximum security extraordinary political prisoner before, either."

"Is that what I am?"

"You like the sound of that? It makes you sound dangerous, doesn't it." Allison pulled her trousers up and took a towel wipe. "Well, back to the salt mines," she droned, gesturing Kay before her.

Kay opened the door and froze on the threshold. Less than a yard away, Elizabeth was leaning down into Marianne, whose back was to the wall, kissing her neck. Marianne's eyes were closed and she was breathing very fast. "Oh christ," Allison said, pushing Kay out into the room. As they passed, Kay saw that Elizabeth's hand was under Marianne's dress and that Marianne's feet were inches above the floor. She hurried out into the main room. Things were getting too heavy to handle. What was with these people? And why did she have to watch?

"Did Elizabeth manage to find the citrus press?" Felice asked when Allison and Kay returned to their places.

Allison slanted a sardonic look at Felice. "The citrus press?"

"Yes. Marianne went into the kitchen to squeeze us some juice. And then it occurred to Elizabeth that Marianne might not be able to find the press herself, so she went in there to find it for her."

"Oh," Allison said. "I see."

Felice frowned. "Damn it, if Elizabeth is—" she broke off as Elizabeth emerged from the kitchen.

Elizabeth's cheeks were flushed, her eyes gleaming. "She's so charming, Felice. I was wondering—"

"Did you find the citrus press?" Felice asked ironically.

"Yes. Our juice is being squeezed at this very moment. But Felice, about Marianne."

Felice bared her teeth. "That girl is under contract to me, Elizabeth."

"I've never understood why you do that."

"Because of all the travel I do," Felice said. "And because it also keeps off predators like you."

Elizabeth tilted her head to one side and smiled warmly at Felice. "Let me take her home for the night. I'll see she gets back bright and early in the morning."

"You have some gall," Felice said. "You could have decently arranged this with me somewhere private instead of pulling this stunt in front of Allison. There's such a thing as face, Elizabeth."

"This is all in the family," Elizabeth said. "Allison knows exactly how I am."

"Still," Felice said. After a pause she said, "I suppose she wants it?"

Elizabeth laughed low in her throat. "Need you ask, Felice?"

"You're an insufferable bitch, Elizabeth."

"That's a well-known fact. Then it's settled? I can take her home for the night?"

"Yes, it's settled," Felice said.

Kay's gaze moved from Elizabeth's face to Allison's. Allison appeared to be more upset by the incident than Felice, who looked comfortably resigned to the arrangement.

It seemed to Kay that for the rest of the time stretching to midnight everyone in the party waited impatiently for release from the enforced grouping. Elizabeth and Marianne were obviously anxious to get off alone together; Allison seemed to find the situation intolerable and made several acid remarks Kay conjectured to be out of character; and Felice, Kay sensed, preferred not to be around Elizabeth and Marianne in their current state of anticipation.

A few minutes before midnight two service-techs brought in an ice-bucket holding a bottle of champagne, tall fluted glasses, and a covered soup tureen. When Elizabeth declared it to be midnight, the service-techs served the champagne— with everyone, not just Marianne and Allison, taking a glass. "To 2078, the year in which the Civil War will end and everything will turn around," Elizabeth said, smiling. When Kay hesitated, Elizabeth told her that she must at least have a sip to honor the toast. And that, Kay realized, was an order. If she refused it her refusal would be taken as defiance. So she drank.

Next Elizabeth had the service-tech carry the tureen around: everyone was to eat at least one of the tortellini floating in broth. They might not be able to open the windows and throw furniture and dishes into the street, but they could at least eat pasta.

Allison fairly snarled. "For godsake, Elizabeth, we're not in Rome."

"This is an occasion, Allison. Don't ruin it."

As if anything anyone did or said now could matter!

They all obediently ate the pasta. Elizabeth smiled. "You'll all see, it will be a splendid year," she promised.

A splendid year for whom? Kay wondered, more and more depressed.

"What I suggest," Elizabeth said, "is that I take Kay back to her cell— since Allison is not really up to it— and that Allison and Marianne accompany you, Felice, to your chopper and then meet me at my car."

"I'll drive myself," Allison said through her teeth.

Elizabeth frowned at her. "Certainly not. You're in no condition to be controlling a car. Why do you think I'm taking Kay down myself?"

Allison glared at Elizabeth. "I will drive myself, Elizabeth." Elizabeth took two swift strides to the nearest handset. "I have no intention of..." But Allison's voice trailed off at Elizabeth's obvious lack of attention.

"This is Weatherall," Elizabeth said into the phone. "I would like you to be sure that Ms. Bennett does not take a car out tonight. If she

shows up, tell her she is to ride back to the village with me." Elizabeth turned and faced Allison. "Clear, Allison?"

Allison's face had turned fiery red. "That wasn't necessary, Elizabeth."

"Oh no? When you're throwing a tantrum of the sort executive boys throw?"

"For godsake, Elizabeth," Felice said. "That's hardly fair."

Elizabeth turned on Felice. "You stay out of this!" She turned back to Allison. "I asked you if that was clear, Allison," she said coldly.

Allison stared past Elizabeth. "Perfectly understood," she said expressionlessly.

"Excellent."Elizabeth snatched the handcuffs from the table where she had dropped them earlier. "Kay?"

Kay stepped forward into the tense silence and offered her wrists. Elizabeth snapped the cuffs on them, slipped the leather bag over her shoulder, and led Kay out into the corridor. "You did well, Kay. Albeit you were dreadfully bored with the conversation."

"I'm terribly tired," Kay said.

Elizabeth slipped a strip of plastic into the access slot and the elevator opened. "But you were bored. I would have been, too, if I hadn't found my own amusement." She keyed in the floor number and grinned down at Kay. "Women like Felice are inevitably and excruciatingly boring. But I'm sure you would find other executive women— those of the career-line— much more amusing to talk to."

Kay leaned against the wall, bracing herself against the lurch she knew was coming. "I know nothing of the world executive women live in." What was it Sedgewick had once said to her about her ignorance of executive women? He had warned her, and she had mistaken the nature of his warning.

The elevator jolted to a stop, and the doors slid open. Elizabeth took Kay's arm and moved her into the corridor. "I thought it a pity, Kay, that I couldn't offer you to Felice. But security is security."

Kay halted. "What the hell do you mean by that?"

"Don't let's dawdle, Kay," Elizabeth said, pulling on her arm.

Kay threw her head back to examine Elizabeth's face, then obediently began walking again.

"You know what I mean. Don't pretend you don't have a sexual interest in Felice."

"That's a lie," Kay cried, forgetting to watch her language to Elizabeth.

Elizabeth pressed her thumb to the plate to open the door barring their passage. "Don't be coy, Kay. Sedgewick told me all about it." The door slid open.

"All about *what*?"

"Lying to yourself again?" Elizabeth queried. "Or another memory gap?"

So Sedgewick had even told Elizabeth about the dream. Was there nothing he hadn't told this woman? "Just because I had a dream," Kay said bitterly, "doesn't mean that's how I feel. And anyway that was almost two years ago. I don't have a sexual attraction to women in general, and I certainly don't have an attraction of any sort to Felice Raines. But I suppose you told her I did, anyway. You're all quite a little circle."

Elizabeth opened another door. "I told her nothing, Kay. You still don't trust me, do you."

Kay began to laugh, but quickly stifled herself. Elizabeth had not yet punished her for laughing, but it was not out of the realm of possibility for her to do so now.

The cart still stood in the corridor outside Kay's cell. Elizabeth opened the door and Kay went in. "Good night, Kay," Elizabeth said, not coming in.

"Wait, Elizabeth!"

Elizabeth paused. "What is it, Kay?"

Kay held up her cuffed wrists.

Elizabeth saw, and came in. "Sorry, I forgot. It must be your gown. You look so ordinary wearing it." She found the key in her tunic pouch, unlocked the cuffs, and took them from Kay. "I'm not quite with it tonight." She smiled. "You might even say I'm distracted. There's nothing else I've forgotten?"

Kay shook her head.

"Then good night."

Slowly Kay walked from one end of her cell to the other, looking at everything in it, listening to the silence. For the first time it felt almost peaceful. Those people were horrible. Getting away from them was a relief. She stared at the gown in the mirror and ran her fingers over the fabric. It was beautiful, whatever its significance to people like Allison and Felice. But she must be careful. It was its significance to Elizabeth that she needed most to find out and beware of.

She removed the gown and resumed the cotton nightshirt. She had seen a different side of Elizabeth that evening, a side she could not have guessed at, a sort of roguishness that seemed alien to the cool perfection she had always shown Kay. Had Elizabeth deliberately revealed that side to Kay tonight, or had she simply casually disregarded Kay's presence as she acted her usual "social self"? Felice had seemed to think that behavior characteristic of Elizabeth. But Allison…Allison had been disturbed, even angry at Elizabeth for it. Another mystery…but one she would not solve tonight.

She switched on the night light, turned off the ceiling light, and slipped into bed. She was exhausted, too exhausted even to look at what Elizabeth had brought for her to read. Kay pulled the pillow to her breast. She dropped into sleep almost instantly.

Chapter Thirty-one

[i]

Jacquelyn was already at her desk when Allison arrived at the office at seven-forty-five on Monday morning. "Good morning, Allison," Jacquelyn said. "She wants to see you first thing."

Allison tensed. Conscious of Jacquelyn's gaze, she said, "Thanks. I'll go straight in." Of course. Elizabeth was going to haul her onto the carpet. All weekend she had been expecting a call from Elizabeth to do just that. Still, considering how badly Elizabeth herself had behaved... Allison dropped her coat off in her own office and checked her appearance in the mirror. Then she drew a deep breath, crossed the hall, knocked on Elizabeth's door, and entered. Elizabeth, dressed in severe black wool, was reading a sheaf of flimsies piled on the desk before her. "Good morning, Elizabeth," Allison said quietly.

Elizabeth looked up. "Sit down, Allison."

Allison sat in one of the two armchairs positioned to face the desk.

"Coffee?" Elizabeth asked, pouring from the thermoflask into the cup placed near the flimsies.

"No thanks." Allison folded her hands in her lap.

Elizabeth sipped before speaking. "Before we get down to work I think it in order for me to say a few words about the other night." Elizabeth's gaze was somber. "I do not on general principle absolutely oppose women executives intaking alcohol. I do oppose debilitating excess. You have seen as well as I what alcohol can do to executive competence. You might think of your father in this regard, since it's the example closest to home for you. Or think of Henry Lauder if you like. In any case, do, Allison, think of it seriously."

Elizabeth paused, perhaps for Allison's response. "You are right, Elizabeth," Allison said. "My control was very bad Friday night. I will in future be much more careful of my drinking."

"I do grant you did well in thinking so quickly to help me block Felice's carelessness around Zeldin. That was well done, Allison."

Allison swallowed. "Thank you."

Elizabeth took another sip of coffee and leaned back in her chair. "Unfortunately I've had disturbing news that might concern Zeldin." Allison raised her brows in query. "Dawson reports from San Jose that Scott Moore has disappeared. He somehow lost his surveillance team and has vanished without a trace. So far there's no record of his having used his plastic since Friday, which was the last time he was seen."

"What do you think happened?" Allison asked. "Do you think he's gone up to the Free Zone?"

"Perhaps. If it were only a matter of his changing sides, I wouldn't give a damn. But there's always the possibility that he smelled a rat in his interrogation. Once I began thinking about it I found it conceivable that he might start to wonder why we arrested him when we did— why we didn't go after him immediately after apprehending Zeldin, why we waited so long— and then simply let him go."

"You mean," Allison said, "that Moore might have asked himself why he was arrested more than two months after Zeldin's apprehension and execution, and finding no plausible explanation begun thinking that perhaps Zeldin hadn't been killed and had perhaps said something implicating him and Nadine Morris during interrogation two months later?"

"Something like that. Or perhaps he wondered why we simply let him go and set him up with a new job, saying we were satisfied with his story holding up under questioning. After all, none of it made much sense taken apart from Zeldin. But somehow it didn't seem important to me at the time for it to make sense to Moore, since he was a tangential player. Which was obviously a serious oversight on my part. Another possibility, of course, is that he was concerned that he might eventually be brought back here. The focus of *my* concern, of course, is the possibility of his contacting the aliens."

"You think he might go to the Free Zone and tell the aliens Zeldin might still be alive?" Allison whispered.

"It's certainly a possibility. Christ, Allison, I really screwed up when I decided to bring Moore into it. And the only reason I did that was because I was at my wits' end with Zeldin."

"But there's no way the aliens— or Moore, for that matter— can *know* Zeldin's alive."

"True. But even if they're not likely to target us on the mere suspicion, they might try something else. And it's conceivable they could give us trouble over the other scientists on base."

"But I thought you said the Rock was ready for them?"

Elizabeth frowned. "Yes. We are ready for them. But..." She picked up her coffee cup and took several swallows. "Needless to say I've ordered Lauder's crew to keep their eyes and ears open. And I've put out a priority-one Spot and Apprehend in Northern and Southern California." Elizabeth set her cup down. "But now for the projects you're working on for me. I want you to arrange a new meeting with Military, preferably for some time next week..."

[ii]

"It's only a slight change in plans," Martha said. "I'm just running over there and back."

Something in David's gaze made her uncomfortable. She needed to let him think she was going on account of Sweetwater business, which was the closest to lying Martha liked to come. But David seemed anxious to go along— and almost suspicious of her making an unplanned visit so soon after her last. Gina's note had been plain enough: no one, absolutely no one was to know Martha was going to the Science Center, much less accompany her. His apparent assumption that they had become joined at the hip clanged through her body like an alarm. The man was getting downright proprietarial! "I hope you don't think we're supposed to spend every sleeping and waking moment together?" Martha said sharply.

David's face closed down. "That wasn't the idea." He sounded *annoyed.* Martha stared at him. He managed an unhappy grin. "Hey," he said, "it's just that I like Whidbey Island so much, and I know you're

going off on one of your long trips soon, so I thought it would be pleasant for both of us." He produced a chuckle that sounded forced. "But I can see you think I'm being a nuisance."

Martha set her coffee cup on the side of the bed. "Why do you put it like that? There's no reason in the world for you to accuse me of considering you a nuisance. This trip is no big deal. But I *do* want to go over there alone. Considering what Sweetwater is, I don't think it's possible for me to continue the personal relations I've had with people there if you're always with me when I visit. I was glad that you fit in during your visit there. But that doesn't mean I don't want to see old friends by myself, either. And for you to feel hurt about it seems selfish to me. I might point out that I haven't met a single one of your friends!"

"All right, Martha, I get the message," he said— grudgingly. "I apologize for what you feel was an attempt by me to lay a guilt-trip on you. That is what you're saying, isn't it?"

Martha stared at him for a few seconds, then got out of bed and started dressing. Why was he so uptight about a single day and night away? Was this possessiveness— if that's what it was— the sort of thing she could expect from him simply because she had been spending so much time with him lately?

When Martha had finished dressing and was gathering up her things into her rucksack, David got out of bed and put on his robe. "I'm sorry for being such an asshole. Don't go away angry at me, okay?"

"I'm not angry." Martha slipped into her rucksack. "I'm just a little confused. I didn't expect this kind of possessiveness from you. I don't know how to handle it. Neither Walt nor Louise ever got into that kind of deal."

David held his hands out palm-up. "I hardly recognize myself. We've been pretty intense for the last week...and I guess it just seems like an end to a very special period in our relationship. Maybe I was holding on a little too hard to something I didn't want to end."

Martha went to David and hugged him. "Maybe it's time, then. You know we're not always going to be as intense as we've been this last week. Anyway, I can't keep putting off my obligations. You know how important my work is to me." She brushed a quick kiss on his lips and stepped back.

"Drive carefully, Martha."

She smiled. "I'll probably see you tomorrow, but if I don't, don't worry about me."

Setting off on her bicycle for the nearest available Co-op flex car, Martha at once lapsed into speculation about the urgency and secrecy of Gina's note. She had of course burned it as Gina had requested, but she knew its wording by heart. Could it have to do with longevity treatments? Or was it something to do with the fertility project? Pushing hard to make progress uphill, Martha told herself speculation was of no use. She would know when she got there and not before. Whatever it was, it was too sensitive to put in the note or to divulge to any third party. And that was all she would know until she saw Gina.

[iii]

Kay paced. And as she paced she stared constantly at the red and black silk gown draped over the arms and back of the desk chair. She had arranged it there to afford her the distraction of visual pleasure, but the sight of it raised doubts and questions and anxious guilt-feelings more than it brought pleasure to her. All day Saturday and Sunday she had avoided thinking by dividing her time between sleeping and reading. The things Elizabeth had brought her to read had proved irresistible: not only newspapers, but an anthology of hypermodern poetry, a revisionist account of the Executive Transformation of 2041, and a volume of Plato's dialogues. On Saturday, without thinking much about it, Kay had made the excuse to herself that she must take advantage of these riches because if she did not Elizabeth would know she was resisting. And on Sunday Kay had discovered the photograph of Scott— taken, according to the inscription on the reverse, in San Jose on December 29— secreted between the pages of the *New York Times*. She had stared at it for hours and hours— studying the anxiety etched into the lines of his face and the haggardness haunting his eyes, all the while the feelings, memories, and questions she had for three months dammed up overwhelmed her. Why, she asked herself, had Security rounded up him and other scientists as

they had, given that the Department of Defense had always been the chief government employer of scientists for defense-related projects? And what had Scott heard of her abduction of Sedgewick, and what had he thought of what he had heard she had done?

Imprinted in her mind, nearly canceling out all other memories of him, were the images of his abuse. Horror overwhelmed her whenever she thought about what he would think or feel if he knew what lay behind that abuse. She could only imagine that if he were to discover any of that past that she had hidden from herself for so many years he would despise her and want nothing to do with her. It was difficult to believe that he was actually living in the world outside, free of the mess— and ignorant of it and of her own existence. But the photograph seemed genuine.

Finally Kay buried the photograph under the stack of nightshirts in the cupboard. But on waking Monday morning, Kay's first thought was that Scott had not been kept in the Rock for nearly two years solely on her account. Though it was possible Sedgewick had decided for personal reasons to include Scott in the original group of scientists rounded up, he might have been included in that group anyway. What, she wondered, had been the purpose for there being such a group in the first place?

Kay had not gotten far with that question before she gave up. And then Allison arrived to haul her off to the infirmary. At Allison's glance at the silk gown, Kay debated asking her why Elizabeth had given her something so expensive. Allison, she guessed, would probably not tell her; but Kay thought she might at least learn something from her reaction. When she asked her, though, Allison, gave her a hard look and said merely that Kay should ask Elizabeth for herself. Kay recalled, then, the scene with Elizabeth over Allison's drinking and wondered whether Allison resented Kay's having witnessed it.

Throughout the afternoon Kay tried to concentrate on specific areas of speculation: what Sedgewick had to do with Elizabeth's plans for Kay, what the issues from Kay's past that Elizabeth had forced out into the open had to do with these plans, and what Elizabeth's motives for these "parties" with Felice and Allison might be. As she paced and thought, however, the gown continually caught her eye. Apart from the force-feedings, Elizabeth seemed to be attempting to mitigate her living conditions. Some of this she could ascribe to behavioral rewards for her new attitude of submission. Yet it seemed overkill, especially the silk gown and the reading materials. Could there be an intention to corrupt her through these things that by comparison with her previous conditions felt like luxury? But in what way corrupt her? To lull her? Perhaps. Though lull her from what? To make her feel gratitude (however grudging)? Probably. To give her something she would want to hang on to, something she would try to avoid losing (i.e., to give her something to lose)?

Kay felt she had stumbled onto something important.

And, Kay saw, Elizabeth might hope to muddy the emotional waters. For Kay did feel confused by the sudden introduction of these material objects. But *Sedgewick*. Surely Sedgewick figured somewhere. What was it Felice had been about to say that Elizabeth and Allison had needed to censor? There had been talk about Alexandra, and Felice had been saying that Alexandra hadn't seen Sedgewick for— yes, that was it. They hadn't wanted her to hear how long it had been since Alexandra had seen Sedgewick. It had been important enough to make Allison snap to attention. But why? What was so important about how long it had been since he had seen his daughter?

Kay paced and paced and paced. If it hadn't been for months that he had seen her...but what difference would that make? Alexandra was presumably in Barbados with her grandmother, safely tucked away from the Civil War. Why would it matter that Kay know he hadn't visited his daughter in Barbados? Surely, given his running Security during this Civil War, it would not seem at all out of the ordinary for him not to have the time to travel to Barbados simply to see his daughter. He was, after all, an executive. And male executives seemed to take little intimate interest in their children. Of what possible significance could that be?

Sedgewick, Sedgewick—there was something mysterious about Sedgewick's place in all this. It was strange that Elizabeth was forcing her to see Felice: she couldn't imagine Sedgewick approving of it.

And why would Felice be here at the Rock, anyway? If Alexandra was in Barbados and Daniel away at some obnoxious school, for what possible reason could Felice be coming to the Rock? Not to see Sedgewick, that was certain. As Felice had once put it to Kay, she and Sedgewick couldn't stand one another's company for more than twenty minutes at a stretch. And Elizabeth and Felice were hardly bosom buddies.

Kay halted mid-step as Elizabeth's intimation that she, Kay, was sexually attracted to Felice came into her mind: could Elizabeth have been hoping for some particular response in Kay that she could then exploit? But what could that have to do with Sedgewick? Or was Felice's connection with Sedgewick merely incidental to the purpose Elizabeth intended to use her for?

This line of thinking seemed to confuse more than it clarified. Kay dropped it. Instead she thought about how much more tightly she felt Elizabeth's restrictions on what she could openly communicate since deciding to pretend to submission. When the time came to act, would she be too psychologically bound by these restrictions? Or more to the immediate point, perhaps, would her morale effectively deteriorate because she was playing the game whereby Elizabeth rather than explicitly commanding her expressed a desire that Kay do such-and-such? Though she was aware of pretending, could she justify playing the role solely on the grounds of some possibly imaginary scheme she ultimately intended to frustrate? Or was it more truly the case that she was breaking down and disguising the truth from herself? Her fear of confinement was real enough. That she might find a way of rationalizing giving in to the fear in such a complicated way would be typical of the way her mind worked.

Kay opened a bottle of water. She could not escape admitting it: she no longer had any idea of what was real and what was not. Elizabeth did not allow her reference to anything outside of what she wanted her to know. Therefore Elizabeth could be playing her in the most fabulous ways, and Kay would have no way of knowing it. Further, she herself continually behaved as though the things she pulled out of her own mind were real. But how could someone who had lived as she had for the last three months (if indeed that

was how long it had been) be judged in any way sane or of reasonable mind? Her paranoia, her claustrophobia, her anal compulsiveness were signals to her. These deep neuroses had to be seen for what they were. And apart from these, she was slowly starving herself, though not with conscious intent. At this very moment she could not even be sure that they had done to Scott what they had said they had done: she could easily dream up scenarios in which someone made up to look like Scott would for her benefit act out the scenes she had "viewed." Also troubling was that memories from twenty and twenty-five years ago had become more distinct than memories of three years ago. She could hardly remember her many years with Scott, while those five and a half years with Sedgewick had grown almost more vivid than the experience of her current existence.

Kay finished the water and pushed the empty bottle through the disposal chute. She fought a wave of panic rising up in her and felt her grip on reality slipping away when she realized she did not know if Sedgewick even knew she was here. It came to her that she *knew* only one concrete fact: that Elizabeth was controlling her. One fact. No, make that two: she also knew that her life here boiled down to a series of binaries. She was in the closet or she was not, depending upon Elizabeth's will. She was in this cell or she was not. She submitted to Elizabeth or she did not. (Though right now she didn't know whether she was submitting or slyly resisting: not even that much did she know about her own self.) The more she looked at herself the more she understood how little control she exercised over any of her circumstances. Whether she was cuffed to the platform or in the closet, or whether she was in this cell wearing a comfortable nightshirt and allowed access to wash water, she was constricted.

Kay threw herself onto the bed and pressed her face into the pillow to stifle the scream she could no longer hold back. Elizabeth was choking maiming deforming her, suffocating whatever was left of her self. For the first time she saw that she was dying— slowly, bit by bit, dying. And Elizabeth was making her watch it happen.

That was what Elizabeth must have been talking about that night when she said that she, Elizabeth, knew that Kay was not indestructible, and that Kay knew it too.

Elizabeth's sadism far surpassed Sedgewick's.

[iv]

At three-thirty Allison came to take Kay to the infirmary. Worn out with crying, her face dry and stretched, her nasal membranes swollen, Kay shrank from the prospect of another force-feeding. "It's early," she said to Allison. "Why does it have to be now? Why can't it be in the evening? Please, can't we wait?" She hated the sound of her own pleading, but she could not stop herself from trying. Sometimes she sensed that Allison might in the small things left to her discretion try making things more bearable for her.

But Allison insisted. "You're having dinner with Elizabeth this evening," she said in an unusually brusque tone of voice. "You are to wear your new gown; you are to be ready for seven-thirty."

Kay held out her hands for the cuffs. "That was Elizabeth's order?" she asked bleakly.

Allison's smile was sardonic. "Oh no, that wasn't an *order*, dear. That was one of Elizabeth's requests. Does it matter to you?"

Kay did not attempt further conversation with Allison.

They had entered the infirmary and were passing through the outer lobby when Allison stopped. "Wait here," she said to Kay, then in several swift strides crossed into the waiting room to talk to a service-tech with plaster casts on her limbs. Kay's mind raced. What if she could get hold of some sort of sharp instrument or drug? If she held Allison hostage in such a way that no one but Allison knew what she was doing, she might have a chance— the slimmest chance, but a chance, the first she had ever gotten— of getting out of the Rock. She needed Allison for opening all the doors and getting her past the checkposts and sensors. The executive was standing with her back to her. If she could just slip into an examination room and then out again before Allison even noticed her absence ... She *had* to try it. It was the first chance she had had, and it would probably her only chance.

Kay moved quickly up the hallway, knowing that at least one examination room lay around the corner only a few steps away, but as she reached the cross-hallway and rounded the corner a high-pitched pulse shrilled through the air at one second intervals followed by half-second pauses. Uniformed guards appeared, confronting her with weapons drawn. And then Allison was slamming her against the wall, and her vision darkened with dizziness.

"She's under control, thanks," Allison said through her teeth.

The guards withdrew.

Allison, her breath coming in hard, short gasps, glared at Kay. Her grip on Kay's arm was brutally tight. "What in the birthing *fuck* did you think you were doing, Zeldin? I wouldn't be at all surprised if she put you in the closet for this." Her eyes had become enormous hating wells of rage.

"Please, Allison, can't we not tell her?" Kay begged, sick at the thought of the closet.

"Do you think I'd give a damn if she locked you in the closet and threw away the key?"

Shocked, Kay saw that Allison hated her. Allison *wanted* her to be punished. Kay groped through what she dimly sensed without clearly understanding: "But you must not want her to know, either. She wouldn't be pleased at your lack of attention." The scene New Year's Eve in which Elizabeth had slapped Allison down rose vividly in her mind.

Allison's nostrils flared. "You have some gall, Zeldin. Do you have any idea of how sick to the teeth I am of every day having to drag around a corpse? It's ruining my life. You don't think I have better things to do with my time? I'm sick of it and sick of you! You disgust me!"

Kay's hand and forearm had gone prickly from the tightness of Allison's grip. "I didn't know," she whispered, appalled. "I didn't know you hated me."

"No, of course not," Allison said bitterly. "To you I'm Elizabeth's robot, someone who gets between you and her. Why should you imagine I have feelings?"

"I'm sorry," Kay said. And then, "It's not my fault. You know it's not my fault." To her dismay, for the second time that day she lost control of herself and broke down into sobs.

Allison shook her. "Stop it! Stop it! You're going to your feeding, Zeldin, now! Control yourself!"

Kay raised her wrists and wiped her nose and eyes on her sleeve. What did it matter how they saw her, anyway? To them she was only a body to be tormented with tubes and whatever horrible stuff they forced through the tubes.

Without looking at her again Allison led Kay to the room where the force-feeding was always done. A corpse, Kay thought, lying down on the clinic couch. Allison thinks of me as corpse. No wonder she hates me.

[v]

At seven-fifteen Kay was still anxiously debating whether or not to wear the silk gown. If Elizabeth punished her, she would be made to change into the tights and leotard, in which case wearing the gown would not only be irrelevant but would make the rituals of punishment all the uglier. Yet not wearing the gown might exacerbate Elizabeth's anger and make a harsher punishment more likely.

Kay decided to wear it.

If Elizabeth knew she had thrown up after Allison had brought her back from her force-feeding, she would be even angrier. But perhaps she would not know. Kay had wiped all traces of vomit from the rim of the toilet and had washed her face and hands and repeatedly rinsed her mouth out. But she had no way of telling the extent of their surveillance. She knew only that sometimes she was watched.

Though she could wash away the traces of her vomiting she could not wipe from her face the ravages caused by hours of crying, and she could not control the physical manifestations of her anxiety. She tried to order herself into stillness, but her hands especially seemed to have a will of their own, twisting in her lap, picking at her hair, worrying at the gown. A vision-distorting twitch had sprung up in the lower lid of her right eye. And the tension in her limbs caused her to break out sporadically in tremors. She felt as though she were falling apart.

Was this all because she feared punishment? Had she broken down to that extent?

When the door slid open and Allison appeared, Kay started in near-panic.

"I'm sorry for the way I behaved to you this afternoon, Kay," Allison said. "What I said was horribly cruel, and I'm sorry for it."

Kay looked away from Allison's eyes. "I'm sorry, too. I hadn't thought about you. That this is merely a job for you. A disagreeable job. I don't know how you stand it."

"Don't be absurd." Allison's voice grew harsh. "You're supposed to be such an intelligent person. What are you doing, apologizing for your existence? Just accept my apology and try to forget what I said to you. I was appalled at myself when I got myself back under control. You threw such a scare in me that I lost my head." She held out the handcuffs. "Let's go."

Kay submitted to the cuffing. "I do understand, now that I've thought about it," she said. "But you were wrong about one thing: I do think of you as a person. Even if it seems as though I don't. It's these force-feedings, they're tearing me apart."

Allison propelled Kay out into the corridor. "Let's not talk about it now," she said shortly.

As they walked Kay felt relief that Allison had stopped her, for without thinking she had volunteered her feelings for Allison's inspection, had been surrendering her precious privacy. And for what? Why should it matter to Kay what Allison thought or felt about her?

Upstairs they found Elizabeth seated in an upholstered armchair, her long legs stretched out before her. Allison did not unlock Kay's cuffs but merely handed the key to Elizabeth and left. That was ominous enough. But Elizabeth ordered her to stand in front of her, which she had never done before. It immediately reminded Kay of interrogation, which she surmised was what Elizabeth intended. Kay waited silently, her eyes focused on the far wall at the other end of the room. Still, she glimpsed Elizabeth's face and body, and saw how absolutely motionless and nearly monochrome they were. Today Elizabeth wore clothing of unrelieved black.

After about half a minute of silence Elizabeth said, "What did you think you were doing, Kay?" Her voice was almost nude of inflection.

Kay drew a deep breath; gazing into Elizabeth's eyes, she answered as she had prepared: "I was looking for the bathroom."

Elizabeth's stare was frigid. "Do you remember what happened the last time I caught you in a lie?"

"Yes," Kay said very low.

"Tell me what you thought you were doing fleeing Allison in the infirmary."

"I wasn't fleeing Allison," Kay said.

"Tell me what you thought you were doing, Kay."

Kay stared down at Elizabeth's boots and shifted her weight from one leg to the other.

After an extended, charged silence, Elizabeth said, "What did you think you were doing, Kay?"

Kay tried to think of a better answer. Elizabeth would not accept an answer about finding a bathroom. But she could not admit to the truth, for then she would be the most severely punished. Yet if Elizabeth decided she was lying every time she answered, the end result might be the closet anyway. She must find some other answer that Elizabeth could accept.

"Did I ask you a question, Kay?" Elizabeth finally said.

Kay lifted her gaze from Elizabeth's boots to her face. "Yes, Elizabeth." Her legs were already beginning to tremble from the strain. She had no stamina at all.

"Why is it, do you think, that I even bother to ask you questions, Kay?"

Kay cleared her throat. "Because you expect me to answer them."

"I will ask you once more, Kay. What did you think you were doing?"

Kay concentrated on staring at Elizabeth's nose in the hope that Elizabeth would think she was meeting her gaze. There was a slight chance Elizabeth would believe this tack: "I wanted to find an examination room. Because I wanted to find a drug or a sharp instrument. To use on myself."

Kay heard Elizabeth's breath hissing in. She could not tell if Elizabeth believed her or not. Her legs were cramping. "Do you remember when I told you that I would not allow that, Kay?"

Kay now recollected several occasions on which Elizabeth had expressed the belief that she might try to kill herself.

"I meant it. I will not allow it. And you were certainly a fool to think you could walk more than a few yards away from Allison without setting off the alarm system. No more would I let you loose in any environment that hasn't been specially prepared for you."

After another long silence, Kay found herself yielding to her compulsion to ask: "My punishment... will you tell me now?"

Elizabeth rose, seized Kay's cuffs, and unlocked them. "I haven't decided yet. First we will eat." She put her hand on Kay's back and pushed her toward the table, then opened the door to the kitchen and announced they were ready to be served. Kay seated herself and spread the napkin in her lap. This meal would be almost as much a torture as the force-feedings. She hoped she wouldn't vomit afterwards. She didn't think she could bear the consequences if she did.

[vi]

Martha knew this man was who he said he was— Gina had assured her some of the others could vouch for him. Even so, she found the story he told incredible, the speculations he raised fantastic. He spoke in such a mumble, and his eyes shifted restlessly about, constantly straying to the window as though to snatch a look at what he said he still had not gotten used to: the outdoors, after nearly two years living inside a mountain. From his pallor he looked as though he could have been inside a mountain for that long. And she could believe that they had kept him there, she knew how Security could treat those they deemed enemies. But that Kay Zeldin was still alive? She wanted to believe it but found herself thinking that if he were who he said he was he might simply be indulging a fantasy that he was for psychological reasons foisting on others.

Because of his paranoia, she was to be the only one in the Co-op to be told. And she was to tell no one except the Marq'ssan.

"You see," he said in his soft, hesitant voice, his eyes not quite meeting Martha's, "the problem is that I don't know if she is still alive, and since that is so and any attempt to do anything concerning the Rock would be terribly dangerous, one would naturally tend to be cautious." He brushed a long lock of lank brown hair out of his eyes. "Yet if she is alive one would want to use all haste to rescue her. Because we don't know how long they will keep her alive, or what might be happening to her while she is alive."

"Let me review what you want me to tell the Marq'ssan," Martha said patiently. It could be a trap: he had worked for Security for two years; he could be attempting to entrap the Marq'ssan with the possibility of Kay's being alive as bait. "You want me to ask them to help facilitate a rescue plan involving the people who work in that place but live outside it. How do you know these people you mention will cooperate? If they voluntarily work in that place, why would they take the risk? Why don't you think they'd simply tell their superiors and help trap a rescue party?"

Scott shrugged. "I don't know. But there are a couple of people I think would do it. Some of the people working with the scientists were significantly disturbed about Security's keeping us there. One of them was my lover, and I trust her. Unless, of course, they've gotten to her because of her connection with me... but we kept our affair secret. Fraternization between the scientists and those who live outside isn't encouraged."

"All right. So you make contact with people who can go in, people who can possibly help get her out. Then what? How do you find out if she's even there, or where they're keeping her? From your description, it's a honking big place."

He stared down at his hands folded on top of the table. "Couldn't they— the Marq'ssan— help?"

Martha shook her head. "No. They can't survive in places that heavily shielded. Sorben told me that when Kay was taken."

Gina briefly touched Scott's hands. "Martha, perhaps it would be best to talk first to the Marq'ssan and see what they have to suggest. They may think of some other way— not involving physical rescue—

for dealing with the situation. Or they may have other ideas. I think you can see that Scott is pretty bent out of shape just now... But he's right about the time element. We can't afford to be leisurely in making our plans."

"I second the motion," Otto Fenichel, the scientist who had brought Scott here from Seattle, said. "And of course, in addition to Kay, there are the rest of the people she was looking for when they took her. Scott says that most of those on Kay's list were there where he was." Otto's spouse, Gina had told Martha, was among those scientists being kept in the mountain fortress.

"All right," Martha said. "And maybe by that time some of you will have come up with new ideas." But there was this leaden feeling in her breast that prevented her from hoping. Scott hadn't once laid eyes on Kay; his argument that he had been arrested and then released as a part of pressure tactics being used against Kay was sheer conjecture. He believed that the bizarreness of Security's behavior could not be explained otherwise. But Martha knew very well how bizarre those people could be. She didn't think it possible to reason appropriately from a manifestation of that bizarreness.

She remembered her own capture by ODS. If Kay were alive, there was no telling what those people might have done to her. Scott seemed ready to face that. And his stand was clear: until he absolutely knew, he could not let it rest— as Kay had not let it rest in his case. Martha could not argue with that. And she could not help remembering that without Kay, she herself would never have escaped ODS.

[vii]

After dinner Elizabeth made Kay sit on the sofa beside her. "Frankly, Kay, I'm not sure what to do with you," she said, sipping her coffee. Kay was not allowed coffee tonight. Elizabeth said caffeine would only aggravate Kay's "obviously upset state." "Your desire for self-destruction is defiant; but unfortunately punishing you won't rid you of it, either. I'm tempted to have Gordon prescribe tranquilizers for you. But there are problems with that approach, too. You might after all not care very much about controlling yourself if you are always drugged."

Kay's neck prickled. Elizabeth's matter-of-fact discussion of such strategies for controlling her seemed colder and crueler than anything she had yet done to her.

"Can you really be so miserable?" Elizabeth asked— seriously, Kay thought, astonished. She stroked Kay's cheek. "I've been trying to make things bearable for you, you know. Trying to relieve your solitariness, trying to pique your interest in things, taking care for your dignity. Yet you profess indifference to anything I do for you. Short of freeing you, what more could I possibly do, Kay?"

Could she be serious? Kay pressed back her anger, to keep it controlled and hidden, for she dare not speak it now of all times.

"Talk to me, Kay," Elizabeth said sharply.

Kay strove to keep her voice even. "There is nothing, Elizabeth. What more could I possibly want than this gown I am wearing?" She hadn't been able to stop herself, after all. Though she had spoken without a sarcastic inflection, though she had used no forbidden words, Elizabeth now had what she needed to confirm the decision to punish her. Worse: in a few words Kay had thrown away everything she thought she had accomplished with Elizabeth.

Elizabeth did not explode or remonstrate as Kay had expected. Instead, she set her cup down on the side table and rose to her feet, then stood for a moment with her back to Kay. Kay stared at the long golden braid that fell well past Elizabeth's waist. When Elizabeth turned around she was smiling. "You are hoping to anger me, aren't you."

Kay grew uneasy. "Why would I do that?"

"You are upset that you are not entirely alienated from me. I think you weren't thinking of killing yourself; nor thinking of escaping, since common sense would tell you it is impossible to escape from the Rock. I think you fled Allison precisely to anger me. You may not even have thought of it at the time, you may not even have understood why you did it. But that is why. A part of you is panicking at the new relationship developing between us."

New relationship? Kay could hardly believe that Elizabeth had cooked up such a wild theory. Could she want that badly to believe that Kay was beginning to accept whatever it was she was trying to foist on her?

"That doesn't make sense," Kay said. "You must know how afraid I am of being punished. If I made you angry you would punish me horribly. Therefore I couldn't possibly want to make you angry." She hoped Elizabeth would decide that this was mere rationalization and would hold fast to her crack-brained notion.

Elizabeth sat down beside her and took Kay's hand from her lap. "But of course a part of you undoubtedly thinks you should be punished for your change in attitude," Elizabeth said, stroking Kay's fingers. "Believe me, love, it all makes sense to me, even if you can't see it just now. And in addition there're all the guilt feelings you've got bottled up inside you. Really it's no wonder you can't eat properly... But in time, all this will be healed. You'll see."

Kay could find nothing with which to reply. Elizabeth apparently believed she had gotten through some critical stage in the brainwashing and could now "heal" everything she imagined she had lacerated and divided. Why was Elizabeth deceiving herself like this? (Why had Sedgewick deceived himself?) Rather than believe she had been trying to escape or kill herself, Elizabeth wanted to believe she was resisting some kind of perverse attachment to her. And she believed it for no other reason than that she wanted it to be true.

Unless this were some new mind-game?

No. For the moment Kay felt she had a grip on this...and that against all odds she had a stronger grip on reality than Elizabeth had. But considering the extent to which she relied on Elizabeth as her major source of reality, that was a devastatingly disturbing belief. If Elizabeth was crazy, she must be crazy. And for the moment at least, Kay did believe Elizabeth was crazy.

Chapter Thirty-two

[i]

Summoned to Elizabeth's office, Allison braced herself for another attack on the subject of Anne. She could see that the flimsies Elizabeth had spread out over her desktop were Zeldin transcripts. Elizabeth asked her if she wanted coffee. Allison declined, then took the plunge while she had the guts to do it: "That was some line you were feeding Zeldin last night."

"What do you mean, feeding her a line?"

Oh god. Elizabeth actually *believed* what she had said to Zeldin? "About her stunt in the infirmary being merely a provocation for punishment," Allison said levelly.

"I take it you don't agree with my analysis," Elizabeth said drily.

"For godsake, Elizabeth! That woman is notorious for her manipulative abilities! You're playing right into her hands! You know as well as I do there were only two possible reasons for what she did yesterday. As she told you, she hoped to get a weapon. The only real question is whether she intended to use it on me or on herself."

Elizabeth's smile was coolly scornful. "My dear Allison, your insight into Zeldin has all along been markedly inadequate. It comes as no surprise to me that you cannot now understand the complex things going on between Zeldin and me."

"And you do?"

Elizabeth said, "Naturally you are angry at her for showing up your sloppiness."

They had been through all that yesterday afternoon. Elizabeth had claimed that Allison was being ruined by too great intimacy with Anne, that she wouldn't otherwise have been "derelict in her duty," that living with Anne was corrupting her, that if she were maternal-line that might be all right, but for someone in her position it was damnable. Elizabeth had stopped just short of ordering her to get rid of Anne. But she had then launched into a tirade about Marianne, about how not only executives were ruined by extensive intimacy with service-techs, but that the service-techs themselves, if at all intelligent or with slightly too much education, could be corrupted, that Marianne clearly was on the verge of rebellion because she "saw too much," and that anyway living with an executive exposed service-techs to a standard of living that by comparison with service-tech existence must begin to provoke resentments and questions about the system.

"I am not angry at Zeldin," Allison said. "Merely realistic about what she is. You are the one who has always warned how important it is not to underestimate her."

"It is you who underestimate her when you attribute such superficial motives to her. She's deeper than you can fathom, Allison." It was hopeless. Elizabeth had made up her mind, and nothing short of cataclysm would change it. "But one of the reasons I called you in here," Elizabeth said, "was to ask you about this transcript." She tapped the flimsy with her finger. "It's incomplete, Allison."

Allison stared at Elizabeth. How had she figured that out?

And as though knowing the question in Allison's mind, Elizabeth said: "I especially wanted to hear what Zeldin had to say right after you caught her. So I very carefully studied the transcript at that point. And I simply don't believe that's everything. I want the recording, Allison."

Allison flushed. Elizabeth's tone suggested she no longer trusted her.

"The recording was garbled," Allison said defensively. "So I tried to reconstruct it from memory."

"I want it, Allison."

Allison swallowed. "The file has been erased from the disk," she said.

Elizabeth's gaze pinned her. "And why is that, may I ask? Isn't it standard operating procedure to wait until I tell you which recordings to erase?"

Allison stared down at the flimsies. "Yes, Elizabeth, that is the standard operating procedure. But since it was so garbled, I assumed I should just go ahead and erase it."

Elizabeth sat back in her chair. "I don't believe you," she said softly.

Allison's face went up in flames. "Why would I lie to you?"

"There's a very simple solution to this. I will ask Zeldin to write out what she remembers of the conversation."

Allison's stomach dropped. And now Elizabeth was using Zeldin against her?

"Come, Allison. Don't force me to go to Zeldin. Simply tell me— in full— what was said that you saw fit to omit."

Allison found it hard to believe this was happening. She swallowed a few times to work some saliva into her mouth. "I lost control, Elizabeth. And I didn't want you to know."

"Yes. All right. Go on."

"I was furious with her. I said something to her about how I wouldn't be surprised if you put her in the closet for it. That upset her. She flashed out with something about my not telling you, that after all I would get in trouble for what had happened, too."

Elizabeth *laughed*, actually *laughed*. "Yes, that sounds like Zeldin. Even in crisis she keeps her wits about her."

"Her saying that," Allison said, "drove me into a rage. I said I hoped you did punish her, and something about how I hated her, how I hated having to spend my time dragging a corpse around." Ashamed, Allison averted her eyes. "It was a terrible thing to say. Later I apologized to her, when I came to bring her upstairs. I omitted that from the transcript, too."

"Did that upset her, your saying you hated her, your referring to her as a corpse?"

Allison met Elizabeth's gaze. "I'm sure it did. It was probably that more than the pending punishment that she cried over."

Elizabeth sighed. "She is too much for you, Allison. But I do wish you hadn't said that to her. This depression of hers is severe enough as it is." She paused. "It's on account of her depression that I've decided to take the extraordinary step of arranging an outing for Zeldin. I'm going to take her out for a drive."

Allison gaped at Elizabeth. "Take her out of the Rock? But Elizabeth! There can be no security tight enough for doing that!"

"It will be sphincter-tight, believe me. I have an experienced crew working on it now. They'll set up roadblocks and supply air-support and extensive reconnaissance. There'll be little risk with such precautions taken."

It would cost a fortune, such a setup. And all because Zeldin was depressed?

"I'm going to begin talking to Sedgewick about her," Elizabeth went on. "I will mention to him Zeldin's voluntarily apologizing to Felice. And I may begin talking to Zeldin about Sedgewick. I don't know. I want to feel out the terrain a bit more. But I think she's close to ready."

Allison felt sick. Elizabeth was risking more necks than her own. They could all be brought down by Zeldin. Any little thing gone wrong could be catastrophic for Security. Certainly Sedgewick was in no position to avert disaster. What was it about Zeldin that caused people like Elizabeth and Sedgewick to go off the deep end? Here Elizabeth had Zeldin locked away in the deepest security possible, and still Zeldin was threatening to screw everything up! Elizabeth must be besotted with her, thoroughly and unequivocally besotted.

"It is possible— but not likely— that I can persuade Sedgewick to attend the upcoming negotiations with Military. If he does agree to attend, we will have to move fast to get his Military counterpart there at the same time. Now that we have some of our satellites almost ready for launch it seems more urgent than ever to mend the breach, for we can't launch without the cooperation of the Air Force."

After extensive discussion of the details for the upcoming meeting, Elizabeth dismissed Allison with a warning. "From now on, Allison, do not under any circumstances erase Zeldin's audio files until I tell you to do so. Clear?"

Allison, flushing, said, "Understood." Elizabeth no longer trusted her. Elizabeth might conceivably sacrifice her to Zeldin. She had,

after all, given Zeldin a gown worth two and a half weeks of Allison's pay, a gift of far greater value and beauty than anything she had ever given Allison.

Returning to her office, Allison realized she could hardly remember what it had been like being Elizabeth's lover. All that seemed buried in the remote past and quite, quite dead.

[ii]

Under a brilliant sky, buffeted by a fresh but bitter wind, Martha walked up and down the beach at Deception Pass as she waited for a Marq'ssan to answer her call. She had never sent out a call of this degree of urgency before— the *come as soon as possible* call, second only to the emergency signal in its priority rating— so she had no idea how quickly any of them would answer or who it would be. She hoped for Sorben, of course. She never felt as comfortable with the others as she did with Sorben.

It was Magyyt who appeared less than an hour after Martha had set the signal. "How can I help you?" Magyyt asked Martha after greeting her.

Martha looked into Magyyt's dark brown eyes. Magyyt had been known to Sweetwater well before the Blanket; but often when Martha saw her she had the suspicion that Magyyt was judging her and finding her wanting. "It's complicated, Magyyt, and I'm not sure what is really going on. But Scott Moore, Kay Zeldin's spouse, showed up on Whidbey the day before yesterday, telling a strange tale. He said he'd been kept with hundreds of other scientists and technologists in an underground base in Colorado. By Security, since shortly after the Blanket. You remember how Kay was out looking for him and other missing scientists when she was captured by Security?"

"Yes. I remember."

"Well Scott says he thinks Kay is still alive. I don't know what to think. There's every reason to believe he truly is Scott Moore. But past that, it's not possible to be sure of anything he says. According to him, Security released him just before Christmas, after having interrogated and tortured him... He says that after his release he was in a daze, that he had to get used to freedom, had to get used to having access to the outdoors, but that once his head started clearing he began asking himself questions. He doesn't know why they released him. To me, that's the most suspicious part. And he says he can't understand why they would ask him questions about Kay unless she was still alive. Why, he wonders, if they extracted information from her before they killed her, didn't they immediately arrest and interrogate him? That's the baffling part, he says, that nothing makes sense unless you assume Kay is alive. And then he further reasons that his arrest and interrogation had no point to it in itself, that if there was a point it concerned a third undisclosed party. Which he believes must be Kay. He thinks they may have been using him to pressure Kay, and that they released him as part of some deal they worked with her."

"Shall we walk?" Magyyt asked.

Martha laughed. "Definitely. It's the only thing to do to keep half-way warm when you're out in this kind of wind." And the two of them headed south along the beach.

"Did he say these people are being kept against their will?"

For the first time, that aspect of the situation fully struck Martha. "He says none of them have any choice. They've let a few people go, but they don't give the scientists any choice about staying and don't trust them outside on their own."

"And why does he think some people have been allowed to go?"

Before answering, Martha thought over what had been said the night before. "Scott thinks that Security needs specialists to work on projects outside, like the one they placed him on in San Jose— that's where they took him when they released him. But he says he slipped the surveillance that had been detailed to him and worked his way north. Then, once he crossed into the Free Zone, it was easy for him. He's really worried, though, about keeping his whereabouts secret."

Magyyt stopped walking, shifted her body to avoid the full blast of the wind in her face, and stared out at the water. "He asked you to contact us?"

"Yes. He has some idea that with your help we can find out if Kay is alive, and if she is, rescue her. I warned him that you wouldn't go into such a heavily shielded place."

"But we could help in other ways," she said.

They resumed walking along the beach. "It could be a trap," Martha said.

"Yes." They stopped again, this time to watch a ferry passing in the distance, its windows flashing with light. "But I think we can render assistance in certain ways without endangering ourselves. They have tried to trap us before now, you know."

"I keep wondering why they would let him go like that. They must have known he would speculate about it. And that he would be alienated from them by their treatment of him. Why release him at all? If everything he said is true, you would think they'd send someone else if they needed an electrical engineer that badly in San Jose. It's such a crazy story, Magyyt."

They began moving again. "I'd like to talk to him myself. You see, Martha, the very craziness of his story inclines me to believe it. He's intelligent. He could have thought up something a great deal more plausible with which to trap us if he put his mind to it."

"I see what you mean. But I've got to warn you, he has some risky-sounding ideas about rescue."

"We'll see when I've talked to him. But even if Kay is not alive— and there is this, Martha, we never saw her body, never received proof of her death, there was only their announcement that they had 'executed' her, and it occurs to me that they would want us to think she was dead to avoid the pressures we might have put on them to release her— but even if she is not alive, there are all those others being kept there to consider. There might be ways other than heroic ones to help those people, though not for rescuing Kay, I fear. If she's alive she's another matter altogether."

"I'm afraid to believe him," Martha said. "I don't think I can go through losing her twice."

Magyyt stopped. "Shall we go talk to him now?" The sun slanted into Magyyt's eyes, turning them dark gold.

"Yes. But please, Magyyt. Please be very careful. I couldn't stand any of the Marq'ssan being caught in a trap."

Magyyt said, "We're careful creatures, we Marq'ssan. We know our limits."

Which was more, Martha thought, than could ever have been said for Kay Zeldin.

[iii]

The night was slipping away. Allison listened to Anne's steady, rhythmic breathing and told herself she should give herself the suggestion and go to sleep. Yet for some reason she could not articulate, she resisted trancing herself with the simple string of syllables she had used since childhood and persisted in lying awake with the executive version of insomnia. The scene at the swimming pool remained too vivid in her mind to dismiss easily, and the ironies of that scene struck her so forcibly that for the first time she felt she saw clearly many of the intricacies of the Zeldin morass. Never had the nature of her relationship to Zeldin been more sharply apparent to her— and probably, Allison thought, to Zeldin as well. Zeldin's awareness since Monday afternoon of Allison's loathing for the role of warder had invested every exchange since with tension, pain, and vexation. Allison could feel Zeldin's awareness of her dislike, could perceive Zeldin attempting simultaneously to efface herself and demonstrate her recognition of Allison as a person. Zeldin had actually taken to asking her how she was, as though she were a social acquaintance.

This change in attitude irritated Allison, for it emphasized the meanness she sensed in herself where Zeldin was concerned. When she was out of Zeldin's presence her anger turned on Elizabeth for forcing the role of warder upon her. But while in Zeldin's presence, Allison seethed with hostility and resentment of Zeldin and felt a shrinking in herself from things Zeldin might say to upset her. Worse, Zeldin's eyes sufficiently disturbed her to make that extra weight of dread all the more horrible. She particularly hated Zeldin for having elicited from her that appalling reference to her as a corpse. One part of her knew her fury at Zeldin was unfair and that her rage about the Jouissance silk was childish (since she suspected Elizabeth's gift of the silk had been as much to slight and pique her as it had been to pamper Zeldin). It was not entirely Zeldin's fault that she, Allison, had

to drag her to force-feedings, chain her to platforms, and otherwise herd her from place to place. But another part of her insisted that Zeldin was not entirely blameless, since Zeldin's present circumstances derived from her past treachery and further, Zeldin, if she chose to, could avoid the force-feedings. But Zeldin's new attitude toward her rubbed salt in the wound. It dawned on her that Zeldin's reaction to her outburst demonstrated that Zeldin did not hold any of what she did against her personally. But then Allison's thoughts shifted again. What she had suspected all along was probably true: Zeldin undoubtedly thought of her as Elizabeth's tool and as therefore not responsible for her actions.

Zeldin might even feel sorry for her.

Allison revolted at the thought. The irony was intolerable. And the other ironies? That Elizabeth should have that swimming pool and all the gyms and locker rooms connected with it cleared out so that Zeldin could swim— to stimulate her appetite, to cheer her up— only for Zeldin, faced with the order to strip and dive into the pool, to regard it as persecution. "I'm not strong enough to swim," Zeldin had protested. Staring at Zeldin's emaciated body, Allison had found it hard not to agree. (And the emaciation seemed all the worse for the bruise on Zeldin's arm caused by her furious grip on it in the infirmary hallway.) "But Elizabeth wishes it," Allison had said and then advised Zeldin to get in the water and at least "paddle around." So much trouble, and what had it accomplished? But Elizabeth's response when Allison reported back to her had been that "in the long run" it would be favorable to Zeldin, and Zeldin "would appreciate it." *In the long run? Would appreciate it?* What *could* Elizabeth be thinking?

And when Allison wasn't brooding about Zeldin, she was brooding about Elizabeth. Did Elizabeth despise her after two fuck-ups in close succession? But her drinking too much on Friday night, that had been because of Elizabeth. Elizabeth must know that. Allison felt certain Elizabeth had toyed with Marianne chiefly for her, Allison's benefit, just as she believed Elizabeth had given Zeldin the Jouissance silk mostly to sting her (since whatever Elizabeth said Allison could not believe Zeldin would know the difference between Jouissance and quite ordinary silk). But if all this were for her benefit, to punish her for breaking with Elizabeth, why must she feel so terrible, as though she herself were to blame, as though she were so vastly inferior to Elizabeth? She *did* feel ashamed for her fuck-ups and by Elizabeth's rebukes on account of them. But she knew Elizabeth would not have treated her as she had if she were still sleeping with her. And therein lay the unfairness.

Justice, fairness: Elizabeth herself had declared she had no time for such concepts... What if she were to return to Elizabeth's bed? Elizabeth would make her crawl, of course, but would then (probably) welcome her back. Returning to Elizabeth's bed she would again be privy to what was going on; only since their split had Allison come to realize just how much Elizabeth had been telling her. Returning to Elizabeth's bed, she would undoubtedly be restored to Elizabeth's good graces. Returning to Elizabeth's bed, she might even be able to check this madness over Zeldin.

Or was that possible now? And would Elizabeth then press her all the harder to get rid of Anne?

And that was another thing: Anne. Anne's casts would be coming off soon. Since Anne had been faithfully performing physical therapy, the transition to activity should not be difficult. When that happened, Allison would begin working with her. It would be difficult having to work out in the apartment, but Allison would not chance using more public facilities. The risk of problems with Elizabeth would increase, however. Allison knew that. But what could she do?

Allison rolled onto her stomach. Though she loved Elizabeth, she hated her. (More than she loved her?) She could not live with that ambivalence, could not live being treated as Elizabeth had been treating her. To survive she must keep her distance and hope that Elizabeth would, after sufficiently punishing her, be fair. She would not go through that other hell again. Ever.

Allison rolled onto her back and subvocalized the trancing syllables. Instantly, she dropped into sleep.

[iv]

Elizabeth took the plain wool cloak from the service-tech, draped it over Kay's shoulders, and fastened it at the neck. Then she took the fur and wrapped it around herself. Kay stared down at the badge pinned to the cloak she now wore. Her name was not on the badge; where it should have been was the word **DAHLIA**. And in place of the security rating were two large letters with a slash between them: **Y/E**. **Y**, Kay knew, meant no access of any sort. She thought she could make out on the status line the word "prisoner." But the **E**? Kay looked at Elizabeth. "What does the '**E**' on this badge mean?" she asked.

"**E** is for extraordinary, Kay. It means that if you should happen to escape no effort or expense is to be spared for your capture, and that you are to be kept alive at all costs."

Kay was nonplused. Her gaze swept over the fluorescent-lit area and came to rest on what she thought must be the access to the tunnel. She could not remember if this was the access-area through which she had passed when she had been brought here.

Elizabeth had explained nothing, had only made Kay shower and dress in the gown and slippers and then brought her here. Elizabeth spoke to one of the men with radios and took Kay's arm. "Come, Kay." Elizabeth steered her to the freewheeling two-seater parked nearby, helped her into the right-hand seat, got into the driver's seat, and took off into the tunnel. "We don't bring internal combustion vehicles into the tunnel if we can avoid it," Elizabeth said. Kay sat quite still, trying not to wonder what Elizabeth had planned for her. Things had changed so much in the past few days that she felt only mildly surprised at this new deviation.

They emerged from the tunnel and parked; then Elizabeth helped her out of the two-seater and into the back of the car in which Elizabeth had brought Kay from Boulder. The interior of the car was warm. As they left the garage at the mouth of the tunnel and emerged into the blinding daylight, Kay could see that several vehicles accompanied them. She blinked as her eyes struggled to adjust. Even with the smoked glass between her and the dazzle, the light pained her eyes.

"Relax, Kay." Elizabeth smiled at her.

Kay said, "You haven't mentioned where you are taking me." Was she being transferred to another prison? Or was she being taken to see someone in particular?

"Nowhere, I'm taking you nowhere. We're just out for the pleasure of the drive, Kay."

So Elizabeth did not intend to tell her. Whatever was to happen was to be a surprise. Kay turned her head and stared out the window. Hard to believe all this existed...the sun, the blue sky, the icily glittering snow-covered mountains surrounding them. She hadn't thought she would ever see the outside again. The beauty and the freedom of the world on the other side of the windows clutched her throat.

After a minute or two outside the tunnel, Kay grew aware of the drone of helicopters. Whatever this operation was, it was large-scale— helicopters, ground escort, and their risking bringing her outside. Could it have to do with the Free Zone or the Marq'ssan? What else would justify Elizabeth's bringing her out? Was there something she was supposed to see? Or what if— no. Stupid Kay for even dreaming of such a thing. They wouldn't be bringing her as a hostage or an exchange prisoner. No one knew her to be alive.

After about twenty minutes the car pulled off the road into a turnout, one placed for the view. A snow-blanketed valley lay spread below them with mountains rearing up on every side. "Shall we get out for a few minutes, Kay?" Elizabeth said. "I know your slippers aren't designed for outdoor wear, but you can at least stand outside for a minute or so and breathe the fresh air."

Kay got awkwardly out of the car, holding the edges of the cloak together as best she could with her cuffed hands. The cold bit at her face like flecks of iron; the icy mountain air shocked her nostrils and lungs. Elizabeth took her arm and walked her to the stone ledge. "This is a treat for me, too, Kay. I seldom get out into the daylight myself. It's a hardship working below ground, even though it's safer."

Kay glanced around. The escort that had accompanied them remained at a distance. She looked up at the pair of helicopters hovering without showing any sign of landing. What sort of operation could this be? She gazed out at the silent white and blue world, at the frozen

river below, and savored the smart of the wind on her cheeks and the glare of daylight stabbing into her eyes. The world still existed. It had gone on without her. It all still existed. There was beauty in the world; there was life. In spite of everything.

Elizabeth put her arm around Kay. "You're shivering. You're already getting chilled. Tell me when you're ready to get back into the car."

That there must be pretense, even out here, pained Kay. It made this world that for a few precious minutes she could see and feel even more inaccessible, more of a fairy-tale.

"Your teeth are chattering, Kay," Elizabeth said after a while. "I'm sorry, but we must go in. You're not suitably dressed to stay out longer." Elizabeth moved Kay back to the car. "I've brought us a thermoflask of hot apple juice," she said, opening the back door. Kay got in and slid over the seat to the other side. Elizabeth spoke to one of the men standing against the car, then climbed in and closed the door. "Even from the car it's pleasant to look at, don't you think?"

"It's breathtaking," Kay said, struggling against the tears pressing her eyes and throat.

Elizabeth poured the hot juice into two heavy earthenware cups and handed one to Kay. Kay let the steam rise into her face; she savored the rich, cinnamon fragrance. "It's time for us to talk more about Sedgewick, Kay," Elizabeth said.

Kay, still staring out the window, strained to see Elizabeth's face at the periphery of her vision. So Sedgewick was somehow involved in this operation?

"I talked with him yesterday about you, for the first time since your apprehension."

Now Kay looked directly at Elizabeth.

"You look surprised. Or is it skeptical?" Elizabeth asked.

Kay stated the obvious. "I'm completely in the dark."

"Sedgewick has had no hand in your management," Elizabeth said. "It has all been my doing."

So much information, all at once. Kay strove to keep calm.

"Does this surprise you?"

Kay kept her face blank. "I'm not sure. I don't know what I thought."

"I told him you'd apologized to Felice. That piqued his curiosity, I think."

Kay thought of the few times Felice and Sedgewick and she had intersected. But she knew all that was irrelevant. She needed her wits about her.

"I think it's possible he may be willing to see you when he is next in the area."

Willing to see her! What did *that* mean? And did this mean he was not in the area at all? That he was not often here?

"No questions, Kay?"

"I understand nothing," Kay said.

"But the issue is whether you are ready to see him."

Kay shivered. Was this the object of Elizabeth's brainwashing? Being made ready to see Sedgewick? But why, for what possible reason? "You mean my rehabilitation?" Kay said, when it seemed to her Elizabeth was waiting for her to speak.

"It won't be like seeing Felice, you know," Elizabeth said softly, and she drank from her cup.

Kay tried to think. "I'm to apologize?"

"I'm not sure that's quite the way to think of it. Can you imagine Sedgewick caring very much for an apology?"

"Why if he doesn't want to see me am I to see him?" Kay finally asked. What was it Elizabeth wanted her to say to him? What was it Elizabeth hoped to achieve? For this surely was what all Elizabeth's maneuverings had been leading to. She finished the apple juice and began fiddling with the empty cup.

Elizabeth took the cup from Kay and fitted it into a small compartment built into the partition between the front and back seats. "It's a long and complicated story, Kay. But to put it as briefly as I can, Sedgewick has been depressed, very badly depressed, since you stranded us on his island. He takes little interest in Security or indeed in any Executive business. Which is your fault. I believe that with your help he will recover from his malaise."

Kay gasped. Elizabeth thought she would help her? *Voluntarily* help her? "I don't see what I could do," Kay said.

"You are the key to Sedgewick's psychological state," Elizabeth said. "One question is whether or not you can help him snap out of it. The other question is whether I can trust you to do just that." Elizabeth's gaze probed Kay's. "*He* won't be likely to trust you at all, you know. Which makes the first question tricky. As for the second question…we both know how little trustworthy you are. So superficially, at any rate, the answer would seem to be that using you to bring Sedgewick around is a hopeless enterprise. However." Elizabeth smiled. "However. On the first score I have great faith in your ability to manipulate Sedgewick."

Kay's eyes widened. "To manipulate him? You *want* me to manipulate him?"

"Oh yes. For good purposes. A positive sort of manipulation, if you will. Under my direction."

That Elizabeth would openly talk to her like this, that Elizabeth could even imagine managing Kay to manipulate Sedgewick… "As for the other question," Elizabeth said, her smile fading, "there are two elements to be considered. On the one hand, the unpleasant. On the other hand, what you have to gain." Elizabeth paused. "How do you like coming out here, Kay, into the open air?"

Was it possible all the security support around them existed merely to make this outing possible, merely to remind her of the freedom she had lost?

"You won't admit your pleasure? No matter. I can see it in your face. If, say, you were able to bring Sedgewick around, it is possible that it could be arranged for you to live a relatively free life. Never an unsupervised life, never a return to your previous activities, but a relatively free life. For instance, living on Sedgewick's island. Security is quite manageable there, you know. And if Sedgewick snaps out of it you would have the island almost entirely to yourself. Wouldn't you prefer that to the life you are living now, Kay?"

Kay struggled to keep steady: Elizabeth offered temptation, dazzling temptation to someone in great deprivation. But she needed to think, needed to keep from being swept away by the temptation, which in all probability was chimeric. How could a prisoner dependent upon her captor for information believe anything told to her?

"You say that you think it is my fault Sedgewick is... depressed." Kay stared out at the mountains. "And you further indicate that you haven't spoken to Sedgewick about me since my capture and say something about his perhaps being 'willing' now to see me. That suggests to me it is unlikely that his reception of me would be friendly, much less make him amenable to manipulation." She looked at Elizabeth. "It sounds as though what I choose to do has little bearing on the outcome you find desirable."

Elizabeth shook her head. "Don't underestimate your influence on Sedgewick, Kay. The only question I have is about you. I think you finally understand the extent to which I can determine the quality of your life. I am not like the others, who would revenge themselves on you for your treason. I'm first of all practical; and second, I frankly admit to liking you. You do see the choice I'm presenting you with?"

On one level, Kay *could* see the choice: the choice to live as a special prisoner in supervised luxury or to continue the living death below ground within the confines of her cell. But on another level, the terms of the choice had not been made explicit. What exactly did Elizabeth expect her to do, and how was she to go about doing it? Did it involve becoming something to Sedgewick she could not bring herself to put a name to? Did it mean allowing herself to be used for bolstering the system she detested? Did it mean, in effect, selling whatever shred of integrity she had remaining for the bribe?

"Kay," Elizabeth said, taking her hand. Kay pulled her eyes away from the sky and mountains to look at Elizabeth. "Let me put it very simply. You can choose to please me, or to displease me." Elizabeth's eyes glowed the deepest most intense blue, the most celestial azure of the sky as it pressed in against the snowy peaks. "Once and for all. It has been that all along, you know. A chain of simple binary choices. Of which this is the final one."

"I'm afraid of Sedgewick," Kay said.

"But now that you've remembered, you know you don't have to be."

Kay shook her head. "Not so. He and I aren't the people we were then. And I betrayed him."

"He is depressed, not angry," Elizabeth said. "It would be a mistake for you to be abject. That is part of the reason, you know, that I have avoided humiliating you. You must measure up to your old self. Yet you must also show him that you've changed in certain significant ways, that you are now what he wanted to believe you were when you came back to work for him. You will avoid challenging him. You will respond to him, you will understand him. And you will show him you regret your treachery. It's very simple, you know. It will be a matter of playing to his lead— of course all the while subtly guiding him. I know you can do it, Kay."

"Not if he hates me," Kay said.

"He doesn't hate you," Elizabeth said. "If he hated you he would have killed you himself. Or handed you over to Wedgewood. The only reason he hasn't wanted anything personally to do with you since your capture is that he considered you hopeless. Remember, you thought he hated you once before, and you were wrong. You've told me you were afraid of him when you were doubling, but you managed to overcome your fear and manipulate him all the same." Elizabeth lowered the window and beckoned one of the men to her. When he stepped up to the car, Elizabeth instructed him to start the return back to base.

Kay watched the window rise, then said, "You want me to pretend I'm not hopeless?"

"Don't be perverse with me, Kay. You know very well what I'm talking about. I think you know what he would like from you better than anyone else. Better than he, even."

So this was the point of the brainwashing? Taming her for Sedgewick? But could this really be all, was there not something beyond this that Elizabeth was not yet revealing? There must be. "But what," Kay said, "if he insists on . . . a sexual relationship, for instance? It would be horrible, I couldn't endure it. Or what if he behaves as he did after his surgery, out of frustration? You don't think he will be frustrated?"

Their car and the cars all around them began moving. Elizabeth took some time before addressing Kay's question. "He's much more controlled now, Kay. I don't think you need to worry about any of that. Anyway, I fully expect that once he sees you are under control and responsive to him he will turn most of his attention to taking back his power and resuming his responsibilities."

Kay stared at Elizabeth. What could she mean, *taking back his power*?

"My guess is that Sedgewick has given so much of his attention to you over the years precisely because he thought you were the key to what he lacked. He even came to believe it. Which may be why your betrayal was so devastating to him. When he no longer has any reason to brood over you his thoughts will naturally turn back to the wider sphere. He is a man accustomed to exercising power, a hard-driving man. I can't see him hanging around you on the island for very long. He will leave you mostly alone, Kay. He will like knowing you are there. You can expect occasional visits. But that will be it since he knows he can't use you in the Company, since he knows your security must always be painstakingly attended to."

If Elizabeth were correct about Sedgewick, and if Elizabeth were telling her the truth about her plans, then she did not intend to kill Kay once Kay had done whatever it was Elizabeth wanted her to do. But could she bear to serve this function for Sedgewick, even for the reward Elizabeth dangled before her? What if Sedgewick instead kept her in her cell? What if Elizabeth was wrong about the intensity and immediacy of Sedgewick's interest in her waning once he "had" her?

"You still haven't told me what your answer is to be, Kay," Elizabeth said after a while.

Kay, staring out at the scenery passing by all too fast, clasped her hands tightly in her lap. "You don't give me much of a choice, Elizabeth." Thoughts of how Elizabeth would punish her if she refused

to cooperate overwhelmed her. This time if she resisted, Elizabeth would probably not relent before breaking her.

"I would also remind you that at any time I deem necessary Scott Moore can be picked up and returned to the Rock," Elizabeth said.

Kay turned her head to stare at Elizabeth. "So that's why you were willing to release him."

"I haven't broken my promise about him, Kay. But I think you should be aware that any substantive regression on your part could ultimately affect him."

The car passed the final checkpoint before reaching the mouth of the tunnel. Her heart pounding, Kay twisted to stare out the back window so as to see the sky for as long as she could. And then it was gone, and they were pulling into the fluorescent ugliness of the garage. Glancing at Elizabeth, Kay understood that Elizabeth had intended the outing as a reminder of all that she was deprived of living down in that cell under the mountain— and as a taste of what she could have living out her captivity on the island instead.

"No answer for me, Kay?"

"May I sleep on it?"

Elizabeth laughed. "You want to think about it? Seriously? It's never before taken you so long to decide whether you want to obey or defy me."

Elizabeth saw this as simply one more step along the way. As the final step, perhaps, but still one of a long series of binaries to which she had subjected Kay. The image depressed Kay, for it suggested a weight of defeat pulling her down, down to an inevitable response. "I do need to think," Kay said.

"Think all you like. I've nothing against it. You've until tomorrow morning."

They got out of the car, transferred to the two-seater waiting nearby, and Elizabeth drove them into the tunnel.

Chapter Thirty-three

[i]

By Thursday morning Kay thought she understood a great deal, even as she recognized that she could not think with certainty about most things since she so heavily depended on Elizabeth as a source of information. She understood, for instance, how useful the "dinner parties" had been in checking her rebellion. Considering how every obedience made to Elizabeth had until recently been coerced from her and accompanied by visible expressions of hostility, Kay now saw the extent to which Elizabeth had brought her to control herself without substantial prompting. At the beginning of her captivity she had declared she would not collaborate at her own abuse and had forced Elizabeth to work hard even to chain her to the platform. Now Kay held out her hands to be cuffed as a matter of routine, went docilely wherever she was led, sat or stood as instructed, and even made conversation as required. Elizabeth had removed the open hostility and alienation from her speech and tone of voice. She could now be presented to Sedgewick without Elizabeth's having to worry about visible manifestations of hostility creeping out unchecked. On the previous Friday night Kay had even sunk so low as to worry about what they were thinking about her table manners. Her table manners! That she could even be concerned about such a thing! And she had been embarrassed about the necessity to ask to be taken to the bathroom to pee. Somehow she had begun to care what they were thinking of her— no, that wasn't right: she had begun caring about being seen to adhere gracefully to certain rules and formulas. Worrying about her table manners amounted to concern for knowing how to gracefully arrange the submission she had learned.

What Elizabeth said about Sedgewick fit with the other pieces Kay had been collecting, allowing her nearly to complete a puzzle that seemed to accord with the general tone and attitude Kay had been hearing in Elizabeth's references to Sedgewick. It also explained Elizabeth's emphasis on Kay's past relations with Sedgewick, as well as her insistence on Kay's ability to manipulate him. It all seemed too, too clear. Whatever Sedgewick's current state, "snapping him out of it" (to Elizabeth at least) apparently claimed a higher priority than any information they might have extracted from Kay about the Free Zone and the Marq'ssan. Kay suffered deep humiliation in realizing that all Elizabeth's efforts in brainwashing her had been directed toward an exploitation of Sedgewick's personal feelings about her. Elizabeth obviously took little interest in her as an actor and thinker of political significance; to Elizabeth she was merely the tangible object of Sedgewick's obsessions. And she perceived that Elizabeth had been careful not to break her or unduly degrade her strictly out of fear of damaging the object that she saw Kay could be. That was what the suspected "larger purpose" boiled down to, that and nothing more. The realization left Kay cold and sick. The image of Marianne sitting among those executive women flashed into her mind, and she thought she saw something of that in what Elizabeth had chosen to make of her.

On long, hard consideration, Kay concluded she had no choice but to continue to play along with Elizabeth— this time in the hope that she could somehow, with the sphere of her existence widening, find a way out. If she agreed to see Sedgewick and then behaved so rebelliously that he would never again consent to see her, her potential usefulness to Elizabeth would be over, and Elizabeth would be angry. The punishment then, when Elizabeth would have no practical need to spare her, Kay could not allow herself to imagine— unless Elizabeth killed her. But if she did handle Sedgewick and did end up on his island...she might be able to find a way to live. But could she stand playing the role Elizabeth had assigned her? Could she stand it long enough to find a way to revenge herself on Elizabeth— through

Sedgewick? But no. He would never again allow her to manipulate him in that way. It would be madness to think he would.

At this point in her ruminations the cell door slid open. Kay looked up, thinking Allison had come to take her to the infirmary— and saw Elizabeth.

"Good morning, Kay."

"Good morning, Elizabeth."

Elizabeth came over to the bed. "Are you ready to talk?"

Kay nodded.

Elizabeth sat on the bed. "And your decision?"

"I'll do as you wish," Kay said.

Elizabeth smiled.

"May I ask some questions about it?"

"Surely." Elizabeth looked immensely pleased.

"Yesterday you used the word 'manipulate.' But that's not what you mean, is it? All your earlier talk about my having had the responsibility to manipulate Sedgewick, that's not what you mean here. What you mean is never challenging him, always 'responding' as you put it."

"That is yet to be determined," Elizabeth said, looking surprised. "It depends on how he reacts to you, what role he creates for you. If there is room in that role for manipulation, then you would take direction from me." Elizabeth's eyes narrowed. "You do realize that at any point it would be a simple matter for me to regain custody of you. Though he will want to deceive himself on superficial levels, deep down Sedgewick will always be extremely leery about your loyalty and veracity."

"You admit, then, that this is all a charade. Yet you talk as though you've successfully rehabilitated me."

Elizabeth leaned forward and patted Kay's cheek. "I've made you safe, Kay. I've civilized you. That's as far as it's possible to rehabilitate you without taking more drastic— and in this case undesirable— measures."

Kay tried to stop the tears welling up in her eyes. "Do you know what I feel like right now, Elizabeth?" she asked bitterly. "I feel as

though I am a tree that has been pruned nearly to death, nearly to nonexistence, every branch stripped from its trunk, left with only roots and trunk and the illusory hope of being allowed to sprout new branches, new leaves. Illusory because I know that at the first sign of green any growth will be torn away. How long do you think trees last under such treatment?" Would Elizabeth punish her for saying this out loud?

"Stop feeling sorry for yourself," Elizabeth said lightly. "On that island you will live a life most people in the world would envy. You will eat and drink splendidly, you will have the sea all around you; and there will be Sedgewick's art collection, his library, even musical recordings, something very few people have access to now. The price you will have to pay for The Good Life will be relatively low. You should be thankful you are still alive... and intact."

Intact?

"Sedgewick will be flying out here tomorrow. I think it likely he will want to talk to you then— probably in the evening. If all goes well you could be on his island tomorrow night, Kay."

That fast? Kay got a rush of panic. "I don't know what I can say to him, Elizabeth."

Elizabeth's fingers ruffled Kay's hair. "We'll have to get something done with your hair, I think. You mustn't worry. We'll rehearse tonight. You will tell him how frightened you were of yourself and of him and that you didn't remember the most important details of your past relationship. You will tell him what he wants to hear, namely that your betrayal was for personal reasons, most of which were a misunderstanding on your part. It will be easy, for he will probably do most of the talking. Sedgewick loves to talk, Kay. I imagine that once everything is settled most of what you will have to do with him is listen and make intelligent and sympathetic comments." Elizabeth stood up. "You can expect people attending to your hair and so on today. Fittings for clothes. And of course your usual routines with Allison. I'll send for you tonight, and after we dine we'll do some rehearsing."

Wordlessly Kay watched Elizabeth stride in triumph to the door. She listened to the door slide open and shut, then pulled the covers over her head and gave way to shrieking, clenched-fisted grief. Allison had been correct, she told herself, Allison had been correct in calling her a corpse. There was really no other word for what she had become— even if Elizabeth had no intention of letting her rest in peace like one.

[ii]

Since Kay slept at most an hour or two on Thursday night, she faced the morning with trembling muscles and burning eyes. In the early hours she crouched over the toilet retching bile, feeling as though her insides were being torn out. Another forgotten memory came to her then, of an occasion on which Sedgewick had injected her with an emetic and had knelt beside her by the toilet holding her hair while she first vomited and then, when there was nothing left in her stomach, retched in helpless, debilitating spasms. This had so excited him that he had fucked her on the bathroom floor. Kay quailed at this memory, quailed at all the unknown possibilities. She wished she could sleep more, for she knew she would need a clear head and a slightly less wracked body to carry off her role that evening. But when she closed her eyes the melange of painful thoughts and feelings only crowded more thickly into her mind.

She brooded more over Elizabeth and their last evening together than about the future with Sedgewick. She did not know why it hurt so much to find how contemptuously Elizabeth thought of her. What should it matter to her to what purpose Elizabeth had chosen to use her— the fact that she chose to use her at all should be all that mattered. She thought of all the sly flattery Elizabeth had heaped on her and how in some way she had unconsciously succumbed to it— all the while Elizabeth had simply been preparing her for Sedgewick. Who she was had not mattered at all, only what she represented for him. As for her doubling, Elizabeth presented a picture in which what Kay had done had not been done for political reasons but for personal, emotional reasons. And Elizabeth insisted that Kay was to reinforce that version for Sedgewick…as though nothing of who she had been and what she had been about had any significance at all. Elizabeth had effectively rewritten Kay's history. In doing so she had virtually

excised Kay Zeldin's very identity. Kay felt her self vanishing, even to her own perception. What had been inside had gradually etiolated, dried up, and shriveled into dust, leaving only an empty shell. There remained only the roles Elizabeth allowed to her.

Kay stared at the ceiling. The early days in the blue cell, even when chained to the platform, seemed rich, sane times for her by comparison with how she was now. Giving those lectures! She had still been alive then. It had happened so gradually she hardly knew when she had ceased to be herself. It wasn't so much her lack of resistance now: she still had the strength to resist; she could if she chose force Elizabeth to break her. But what would be the point of it? She saw nothing left to salvage. She no longer believed in the integrity of her own being, even supposing she could start over, keeping mute as she had at the beginning. The threats Elizabeth had used at the beginning seemed child's play to her: she now underwent force-feedings as routines of her day. She could make Elizabeth physically work to move her around, she could refuse to walk, refuse to cooperate when being cuffed, and so on. But even supposing she did: what would be the point? She couldn't quite see what it was that had pushed her to her small resistances, couldn't see what it was that had got her to lecturing in that cell. All that eluded her, though she knew that at the time she had had strong feelings, strong reasons for resistance. As she saw it now, whatever she did, whether in cooperation or through violent coercion, she was still the same object being disposed of by Elizabeth. And Elizabeth would know she knew.

Would they force-feed her if she were taken to the island? Perhaps once she had made this final submission it would not matter to them whether she continued on or not.

When after hours of rumination the door slid open, Kay assumed it was Allison, come to take her to the infirmary or for the final fittings of her new clothing. She did not turn to look, but waited for the greeting.

"Well, Kay?"

Shocked, Kay turned her head and saw him standing a few feet away, blocking the scanty illumination of the night light. She made

an effort to unfreeze; she reminded herself that it would be like talking to Elizabeth— being careful of every word she spoke. "Robert. I didn't think... I wasn't expecting..." She hardly knew what to say. Elizabeth had told her she would be seeing him in the evening, and upstairs.

"They don't allow you proper light in here?" he asked. "I can hardly make you out."

"There's a switch near the door," Kay said.

He moved to the door, found the switch, and flicked it on. Kay blinked in the sudden brightness. Starting toward the bed, Sedgewick halted— obviously because the red and black silk gown had caught his eye. After a moment, he detoured to the desk and took a piece of the gown in his fingers. He glanced over his shoulder at her, dropped the cloth, and came over to the bed and sat on the edge. Kay tried not to flinch under his scrutiny. After about a minute he said, "Weatherall didn't tell me you've been ill."

Kay said, very carefully, "I haven't been ill. I've just had a couple of bad nights. I haven't been sleeping well." She didn't add that he himself looked like death warmed over.

His eyebrow quirked. "Weatherall tells me you have repented the error of your ways."

Kay took a deep breath. "She could have been a shrink, Robert. She made me remember everything about our past relationship— you see, I hardly remembered anything from the time before your surgery. She forced me to think about why I did what I did in light of everything I'd forgotten. It has been terrible, discovering I had distorted everything I didn't want to face in myself."

His eyes made her think of icy, straight-edged razors. "For instance?"

Kay made herself hold his gaze. "I wanted to believe I was your victim rather than your partner. Blotting out most of what happened between us before your surgery allowed me to convince myself of that. And I remembered almost nothing of the things I did for the Company. None of that would have matched up with my image of myself at the time of the Blanket. Nothing upset me as much as your

saying we were alike. As Elizabeth helped me see, I needed to prove to myself that I wasn't like you, and I needed to get away from you so that I could avoid finding out everything I was hiding from myself."

"You call her Elizabeth."

Kay had forgotten Elizabeth's warning to use only last names when referring to her and Allison, had forgotten Elizabeth's little lecture on the usages appropriate among executive women as distinguished from those appropriate for use with executive men. "That," Kay said carefully, "along with certain rituals, is a part of my discipline. Perhaps precisely because I called her 'Weatherall' at the beginning."

Sedgewick's gaze was intense. "When you told me that day on the island that you remembered, I thought you meant that you remembered everything about us."

"That is why I misunderstood everything. I was terribly afraid of you."

His eyes seemed to grow even bleaker. "I thought that day that everything was finally working out. When we returned to D.C., I felt certain... But you were already plotting against me then, weren't you."

"Yes," Kay said very low.

He sighed. "What shall I do with you? You are a misfit. A maverick gone too far out of control to be allowed loose."

"You don't wish me dead?"

Sedgewick shrugged. "I thought when you were captured it would be best if you were dead. But if you mean do I hate you, the answer is that I do not. I told you that day on the island that I could imagine killing you in only one circumstance. You remember your thinking I wanted to kill you that day?"

"And since then I've done the thing you imagined you could kill me for."

He frowned. "I don't understand."

"I've betrayed you," Kay said, puzzled.

Sedgewick snorted. "Another faulty memory, Kay? That's certainly not what I said." His gaze bored into hers. "Weatherall thinks you'd like to stay on the island with me. Is that true?"

Weatherall had told him that? "The question I think is whether you'd have me," Kay said.

"You would like to leave your cozy little cell?" he said sarcastically. "Though it really is a cut above anything I've seen anywhere, you know... Your motives would be perfectly comprehensible to me. But answer my question."

Kay flushed. At least she wouldn't have to pretend— at first, anyway— to wanting to go there to be with *him*. "Yes, I would like it," she said quietly.

He gave her one of his long, hard stares. "All right. We'll try it. I can always ship you back to Weatherall if for any reason it doesn't work out." Kay could hardly believe it could be so simple. What was going through his head? What did he think she was agreeing to? He rose to his feet. "I've something to attend to. When that's finished we'll leave. I'm certainly not about to spend the night in this hole." He glanced around the cell and chuckled. "Do you know you are the only person on this entire floor? They are ventilating on this level solely because you are being kept here. This base is immense, more immense than you might guess. It was intended to house an enormous number of executives should thermonuclear or biological war occur... And here you are, on the deepest occupied level, isolated several floors below the next occupied level...and with so many comforts. It's really rather bizarre."

Kay watched Sedgewick go to the door and press his thumb to the access plate. "Until later, Kay." And he went out into the corridor.

Kay got out of bed to get a bottle of water. She had done it. She had done what Elizabeth had asked her to do. Sedgewick hadn't smiled once, nor had he touched her. She wished she knew how to interpret that.

[iii]

For the last time Elizabeth toweled Kay dry and perfumed her. When Elizabeth handed her underwear, Kay looked at it curiously before putting it on. Underwear and street clothes had become as strange to her as the sun and sky and open air. She looked at Elizabeth. "It was all decided before he even spoke to me, wasn't it." She fought dizziness as she bent forward to step into the underpants.

Elizabeth smiled. "Not quite, love. But I think he had pretty much made up his mind, contingent upon your being neither lobotomized nor obstreperous."

Kay wondered what Elizabeth had said to persuade him.

"He thinks you're ill," Elizabeth said, handing Kay the burgundy wool trousers. "I even went so far as to show him Gordon's reports, but I don't think he trusts Gordon's judgment. Perhaps he would like you to be ill?"

Kay shivered. "He might," she said in a low voice. "Did you tell him you thought me suicidal?"

Elizabeth's smile vanished. "Of course. What do you take me for? Lift your arms, love."

Kay raised her arms and Elizabeth slipped the burgundy tunic over her head. Elizabeth's hands pulled at the tunic, twitched at the drape, smoothed the collar. "There. Nicely becoming, Kay." She bent down and kissed Kay's forehead. "You did very well this morning. I couldn't have written a better script myself. His mood is improved already, you know."

Unable to help herself, Kay burst into tears. She turned away from Elizabeth, put her hands to her face, and pressed herself into the wall by the desk.

"Kay, love, what is all this?" Elizabeth pulled Kay into her arms. "It's probably nerves. You mustn't be so upset. Just think how wonderful it will be living in the most princely style in that lovely old house surrounded by the sea..." Elizabeth's fingers combed through Kay's newly fluffy hair. "You will be able to do just as you wish, with the one exception of leaving. Exile, yes, but think what your life has been here."

Kay wiped her eyes and broke out of Elizabeth's embrace. "You are so pleased, so ecstatic," she said, staring into those excited blue eyes. "Does your successful destruction of me make you so happy?" Had Elizabeth only thought of it as a contest between the two of them? Had she never thought even once of what she was doing to another human being?

"You are not destroyed, Kay," Elizabeth said. "I've restrained you, yes. But not destroyed you. Otherwise we would not be talking this way." Elizabeth half-smiled. "Sedgewick thinks I'm infatuated with you. Did you know that? He saw the Jouissance silk and added that to the way I had been talking about you to him, and decided I've fallen in love with you." She paused, then added thoughtfully, "And I don't want you dispelling that impression in him. It's best he think that, for it will supply him with an explanation for why I was so anxious for him to see you, to appreciate the changes I've made in you."

"Oh god," Kay said, feeling sick. "It's all lies, everything about you is lies and deviousness."

Elizabeth laid her hand on the nape of Kay's neck. "Careful, Kay. I want you always to remember that if anything goes wrong in your handling of Sedgewick, either he will send you back here himself— for me or Wedgewood to deal with— or else I will take you from him. If I see the slightest sign of mischief in you, I will tell him something that will make him eager for me to take you back into my custody. And I promise you, if that happens, I really will destroy you."

The cold in Elizabeth's eyes promised terrible things.

"Clear?" Elizabeth asked.

"Understood," Kay responded bleakly.

Elizabeth nodded. "Good. Go bathe your eyes. And then we will go up. He will be waiting."

Kay went into the bathroom for the last time and flushed her eyes with cold water. "Do you want to take anything personal with you?" Elizabeth asked. "If so we can take it upstairs and put it in your bag."

Kay patted her eyes dry. "What do you mean, personal?" There was nothing here that was hers. "Unless you mean my satchel, the things I had with me when you captured me?"

Elizabeth shook her head. "None of that is yours now, Kay. I mean things in this cell. Your picture of Scott Moore, for instance, or the books I gave you."

Kay stared at Elizabeth's seeming seriousness. Could it be she understood nothing, nothing at all of what she had done to her? "There's nothing here I want," Kay said, putting the towel down.

"Then let's go," Elizabeth said— again smiling her pleasure.

Kay held out her hands for the cuffs. When they left the cell she did not look behind. There was nothing of her there.

There hadn't been for a long, long time.

[iv]

Anxious to make an end to all the work that had to do with Zeldin, Allison worked long past midnight. At last, at last the Zeldin project was over (if, that is, Zeldin wasn't at some future moment returned to Elizabeth's custody); at last she would be free of the horrible feelings it had evoked in her. The miracle was that Elizabeth's plan seemed to have worked: Sedgewick had gone to the meeting with the Acting Secretary of Defense (with Elizabeth at his side whispering in his ear, of course) and had agreed to deal with the Cabinet in the coming week. Elizabeth said this was all because of Zeldin. Yet if it were true he was snapping out of it, why was it that he had not expressed interest in anything else? He hadn't, for instance, asked to see any of the latest reports on the Russians' war preparations.

Elizabeth's delight...Allison could understand. But the things that had been said between Elizabeth and Zeldin over the last two days had made Allison's heart sink. Was it as simple as Elizabeth's handing a submissive woman over to Sedgewick for his personal use? The thought that Sedgewick, fixed though he was, might force sexual attentions on Zeldin sickened Allison. She had asked Elizabeth about it, but Elizabeth seemed to doubt that would happen. "He's too afraid of losing control," Elizabeth had said. "He knows what happened when he tried it after he was fixed. Zeldin's safe from that sort of thing." Even if that were the case, Zeldin seemed to have been devastated by the arrangement. Allison could not quite get a handle on what it was that upset Zeldin so much. She thought it had to do with Elizabeth more than with Sedgewick.

Letting herself into her apartment, Allison moved on tiptoe to avoid waking Anne. She got out the cognac, stripped off her clothes, and slipped into a gown; then she drank until she was too drunk to think any more about either Zeldin or Elizabeth. The last thought that occurred to her before passing out on the rug was that maybe now Elizabeth would let her go.

[v]

Early Sunday morning Martha, Scott Moore, and Otto Fenichel flew with Sorben and Magyyt to Colorado. As the pod hovered high above the clouds, Sorben brought the image of the mountain below, displayed on the pod's screen, into high resolution. They could see that part of the peak had been cut away and hollowed out, providing a shelter for a well-camouflaged helicopter hanger. "This is the area in which Kay thought the mountain base must be," Sorben said. "What do you think, Scott?"

"I think this is it," he said hoarsely. "Over there, in that direction, there should be a village."

They had chosen to come on Sunday precisely because it was the one day most service-techs at the base had off. About a minute later the screen changed to show a village below. "Shall I land?" Sorben asked.

"Yes," Scott said. "The compound lies between the village and the base."

The plan was that Martha would enter the compound where Scott's lover lived and find her. It was assumed that Martha would have a better chance of staying out of trouble because of her non-descript service-tech appearance. She would carry orange plastic faked by the Marq'ssan and would claim to be a local if challenged by the guard at the compound's security checkpoint. If Scott's lover agreed to see Scott, Sorben would come back for her in the evening and bring her out. Martha expected it to be difficult convincing her, however, since she would have no reason to believe her story. Worse, it was possible the woman had been contacted by security people at the base and would be prepared to betray Scott. For that reason it was considered best for one of the Marq'ssan to bring her out. Afterwards, depending on the woman's degree of cooperation, other plans could be made. Sorben had assured them that if they gave her a security badge she could easily duplicate it down to the arrangement of every last proton. As a last resort, they were prepared to use fake badges to get them inside the base.

"Are you ready, Martha?" Sorben said.

Martha nodded.

"Keep your transmitter open so that we can listen to you. If you get into trouble, remember we will find a way to keep them from taking you to the base. We can always intercept their vehicles if necessary."

Martha drew a deep breath and left the pod. She glanced around to take her bearings, then set off west along the shoulder of the road, walking away from the village toward the compound. After about twenty minutes, she caught sight of the compound and the heavy security surrounding it, and her stomach fluttered; it reminded her of a prison. At the compound entrance the guards demanded her plastic. She tendered it, and they inserted it into a data slot. The guards let her pass without question.

The difficulty lay in finding where exactly Jalna lived. Scott did not know the unit number; there had never been any reason for him to know it since he had never been allowed out of the base. Preferring not to call attention to herself by being seen knocking on too many doors, Martha decided to knock on a door every other row on the assumption that sequestered people who had been living in one place for two years would pretty much know the names of their neighbors.

Martha had to knock on only one door. The woman who opened it was friendly and invited Martha in, saying that though she herself did not know Jalna Perrine, Martha should ask her unit-mates, who very well might. It turned out that one of the unit-mates was an organizer of social activities in the compound and happened to have a list of the names and addresses of everyone living there. She looked up Jalna's name and gave Martha the unit number as well as directions for finding it.

Martha found Jalna Perrine at home. Jalna had a worn but still fine-complexioned face with straw-pale blonde hair and sad, faded blue eyes. When Martha told her that she wanted to talk to her about Scott Moore, Jalna quickly grabbed a coat, stepped outside, and suggested they go for a walk. Martha's hopes rose at this sign of savvy. As they walked, she considered how to begin, aware of how tricky the situation was for both of them. "Scott would like to meet with you. If you're willing," Martha said.

Jalna waited for a pair of men to pass before speaking. "We were told he had left the area to work outside."

"He's nearby now," Martha said.

"I've been given a number to call if he contacts me."

"They told you they expected he would do that?"

Jalna hesitated. "They told me they knew he and I were lovers. And that he has disappeared. They said they are concerned for his safety. But it's more than that, isn't it. If he's here."

"Yes," Martha said. "There may be a danger in your meeting him... Do you think they're watching you?"

Jalna shook her head. "No, why should they be? We're all locked inside the compound and only go out on passes. For our own protection, they say." She sounded bitter. "But then that's what they tell the scientists they keep inside the base."

"There is a way for you to get out without a pass and without having to deal with the guard. I can't tell you how it works, I can only ask that you go along with it. If you're willing, someone will come for you after dark, bring you out, and take you to Scott. It's for you to say if you want to do it, and when."

"He needs my help?"

Martha hesitated. "Yes, but not because his life is threatened. You mustn't be under that illusion. He himself is perfectly safe."

Jalna's brow furrowed. "There's something else?"

"I would rather leave it to Scott to explain."

Jalna stopped walking and faced Martha. "All right. I can live with that. Whoever it is who comes for me can come around midnight. My unit-mates will probably be asleep by then, since tomorrow's a work day."

"Where should she wait for you?"

At Jalna's suggestion they turned back the way they had come. "I'll show you when we come to it," she said. Two rows from her unit she stopped near a little shed. "Here by the laundry house. It's very badly lit, and the laundry is never open past ten-thirty. This will be a

nice unobtrusive place to wait. I'll try to be here as close to midnight as I can. If I'm late, it'll be because my unit-mates haven't all fallen asleep yet, not because I'm not coming. I absolutely will come."

They parted, and Martha walked quickly to get out of the compound and return to the pod. Such places made her nervous and depressed her. And this one most definitely reminded her of jail.

Chapter Thirty-four

[i]

On Sunday night Jalna returned with them to the Whidbey Science Center. Martha was terribly depressed and knew the others were, too. They spoke little during the flight, and Magyyt and Sorben left immediately after the humans had debarked from the pod. Martha knew her disappointment made no sense. She had never really believed that Kay was still alive, for she had never really believed it possible. But the emptiness of their return and the thought of all those people being forced to live inside the mountain pressed on her. She told herself that she shouldn't be feeling as bad as she did: though it would be hard work forcing Security to free those people, the Marq'ssan's commitment to the project would ensure its success.

Gina and Max wrested the details of the venture from them and welcomed Jalna with open arms. Jalna would fit in well, Martha thought, for she was apparently highly skilled in electronic technology in general and processor hardware in particular. From things Scott and Jalna had let fall, she gathered that Jalna had picked up most of her skills on the job and through independent study and by talking to the scientists she assisted. Scott claimed that Jalna's underemployment was a perfect example of executive inefficiency: they could not see her as other than a service-tech because of her education and background, yet if she were given only the duties appropriate to a service-tech with her function title (advanced tech assistant), her skills and experience would be wasted. Jalna, Scott assured the Whidbey scientists sitting at the table with them, was more an engineer than a tech assistant.

"You look totally wiped, Martha," Gina said. "Will you sleep over?"

Martha tried to smile. "Yes, thanks. I'm too tired to drive back tonight." She sighed. She would have to deal with David when she got back, too. She hadn't told him she was going away for the weekend but had simply left him a note saying she would be away for a few days. She would have to make up some kind of story, for it was still too soon to tell anyone about the project. Before long, everyone would know about the scientists, of course. But that would be soon enough to explain to David.

If, that is, they were still seeing one another.

[ii]

Kay lay on the padded plush lounge in the Small Study, listening to the lyrical (and to her almost unbearably poignant) notes of a Beethoven Bagatelle. She had been on the island five nights; this was her fifth day— and the very first time she had had to herself. She was finding it a strain after months of isolation to be almost constantly in the presence of another person. And of course that other person was Sedgewick; even when they weren't talking, she felt a pressure deep within her, a pressure that made her watch herself as well as Sedgewick. It was as though Elizabeth were always invisibly present. When she spoke to Sedgewick, it was as though she were speaking for Elizabeth's ears. She even experienced physical contact from Sedgewick as though Elizabeth's hands, not Sedgewick's, touched her, though she was aware of Sedgewick solidly, materially there— aware of his gaze, his voice, his touch, his scent— while pervading Kay's mind were Elizabeth's gaze, voice, touch, scent. Sedgewick did not suspect Elizabeth's presence in the room with them. His tension came not from any awareness of Elizabeth Weatherall, but from waiting. For he was waiting, Kay knew: he was waiting for her to challenge him, to lose control, or to refuse him in any way.

At first he had hardly touched her and had made conversation only when necessary. They had dined Friday night almost immediately after their arrival; and by the time they had gotten up from the table a suite of rooms had been prepared for her. He had told her she could ask for anything she liked in that house, that she would be treated as any executive guest would be treated. But then he had wanted her to sit up with him and drink wine. She told him that she could not drink wine and that she was exhausted. He had been annoyed at

this, and Kay had ironically reflected that Elizabeth had missed something in her training. It had apparently not occurred to Elizabeth that Sedgewick had always considered Kay a preferred drinking partner. And if it had occurred to her, what could have been done, anyway, considering Kay's physical condition? Disappointed, he had reluctantly allowed Kay to go to bed.

Kay soon found that though she could go where she liked in the house, an unobtrusive watch was kept on her. But more to the point, Sedgewick allowed her little time alone. Early that morning, however, long before she had gotten up, he had flown out, saying he would return in time for dinner. Waking up and staring out at the sea while she drank coffee and nibbled at a croissant, Kay felt a weight lift from her chest and realized that since Elizabeth had given her into Sedgewick's custody she had never for even a second been free of strain. She dressed, excited at the prospect of free time. She would go for her first walk outside. It would be cold and windy but magnificent.

Once outside and striking out for the beach, she grew dizzy and weak; she broke into a cold sweat and sank to her knees. Almost at once a service-tech appeared, asked her if she was all right, and helped her back to the house. Of course they would watch her outside especially, Kay thought. She took off her outdoor clothing and went into the Small Study to listen to music. She felt like a Victorian invalid, lying on Victorian furniture in a Victorian patriarch's stiflingly Victorian house.

Had Elizabeth been correct in predicting that Sedgewick would for the most part be leaving her alone here? Would it be like this most of the time, with Sedgewick off attending to Security business? Last night as she lay in his arms he'd begun talking about Weatherall and about the negotiations with Military. "Weatherall has certainly worked hard. And I see now that I underestimated the range of her capabilities. She has initiative, and ambition... and guts. She not only kept Security running in my name, but has come up with a settlement that both sides are likely to accept. I'll be flying out to Denver tomorrow to meet with the Executive and possibly to make final arrangements with Military. The Civil War will be over, Kay." He had spoken about this with surprising detachment, as though he had little stake in it. Yet he apparently was doing as Elizabeth had hoped. Was this the beginning of his reinvolvement in Security, or only a temporary participation?

If it were the beginning of his reinvolvement then she might have most of the time here to herself. But did that matter? After all, here she lay listening to music— something she had longed to do for two years, and she otherwise had available here what Elizabeth had described as The Good Life. But she could not seem to respond to the music, or even respond much to the sight of the sea, except to feel intensely depressed and sad, choked with anxious emotion. When two days before Kay had wondered out loud to Sedgewick what to do with herself, how to handle idleness, he had looked at her with astonishment. You may do anything you like, he had said. You could return to your scholarship if you liked. If there isn't a book or journal here that you want, I'll have them get it for you. You could even write books here, Kay... She had thought about that and knew it was not true. If she were free she would want to write a book, true. But she was not free. Such a book as she might write would not be something Elizabeth would tolerate. Kay further wondered whether she would even know how to write truthfully now, so distorted had her relation to language become...always taking care to avoid "inflammatory language," always careful not to challenge. How could a person so maimed write a book that was meaningful? No, she would not stoop to that. It would be like continuing her conversations with Elizabeth.

Kay stared out the window. Elizabeth, it seemed, was with her even when Sedgewick was not. She could not seem to elude her.

What was she to do? She could see the shape of what her life here would be, the only variables being whether Sedgewick would be here and what the limits of his physical contact with her would be. She would not, for instance, be surprised if tonight he initiated genital contact of some sort. The previous night he had kissed her and nuzzled at her breasts. He had explained that though he had no genital sexual sensations he did enjoy a more generalized sensual pleasure from his physical contact with her. You have done this to me, Elizabeth,

Kay thought again and again. You've made my self irrelevant, passive, functionally nonexistent. While Sedgewick had been handling her, Kay had reviewed Elizabeth's indifference to her feelings and desires. *It is a mistake to make things more important than they need to be, Kay... it is best when acquiescing to another's authority to do so as lightly and easily as possible— so as almost not to notice it. To trivialize its significance...*

Kay's stomach heaved. She sprang off the chaise lounge and began running— her hand pressed over her mouth— for the nearest bathroom. She hoped she made it to the toilet in time. She certainly did not want to make a mess in a house like this, run by service-techs who were likely bored out of their skulls and probably already always talking about her anyway.

[iii]

After dinner they went as usual into the Small Study— Sedgewick's favorite room— to listen to music— this time Brahms' First Symphony. Sedgewick stretched out on the long leather sofa while Kay— obeying his request that she do so— sat on the rug with her back against the sofa. The music, thundering around them, caused the floor and sofa to vibrate. Kay stared at the gas flames illumining the room, but was all the time acutely aware of Sedgewick— his hand constantly touching her head, neck, shoulders— gazing at the Turner hanging on the wall straight before him, sipping cognac.

When the symphony ended, Sedgewick said into the silence: "I'm enjoying having you here so much, Kay. I didn't believe it was possible, but it's like a new beginning for us." His fingers brushed over the nape of her neck.

A new beginning? Could he seriously believe that? Was he aware of nothing outside of himself? Over dinner he had given her a blow-by-blow description of the Cabinet meeting, telling her about the statement he had pre-taped to be released when Wayne Stoddard announced the treaty, referring to his clearing up what she, Kay Zeldin, had begun. She wondered how he could believe the Civil War had been her fault. Sedgewick, if anyone did, knew exactly how it had begun. But she dutifully acted the role of appreciative audience and

agreed that Weatherall was really quite shrewd and clever. Unlike Elizabeth, Sedgewick did not seem to notice what she ate or did not eat and never commented on it. It must be, Kay thought, that he saw what he wanted to see.

"How did you spend your day, Kay?"

Surely someone had reported to him all her physical movements during his absence. "I spent the day thinking," she said.

He left that alone. Then, after a while, he said: "I'd like to lie in bed with you, Kay. Could we do that?"

"Now?" she asked after a moment.

"Please, Kay."

Please. As though that word could mean anything when spoken to her by anybody. She was not a being to whom the word *please* would be used to mean anything honest.

They went into his bedroom and lay down as they were dressed, Kay in one of the gowns that had been provided for her, Sedgewick in a long robe. His hands moved gently over her breasts, diaphragm, belly as he kissed her. "You're so thin, so fragile," he murmured. "You're wasting away."

It's called going into a decline, Kay thought but did not say.

"Do you feel anything?" he asked her after a few minutes, his fingers moving over the silk between her legs.

"Don't ask me that, Robert," Kay whispered.

"I want to give you pleasure, Kay."

"That's not possible now," Kay said. "Don't you understand, I have been eviscerated, there's nothing left inside me but raw nerve endings that can give me only pain." Suddenly she felt Elizabeth's eyes on her and realized that for a moment she had forgotten. "Oh no," she cried, weeping, "I shouldn't have said that… I shouldn't have said that. I made a mistake."

Sedgewick put his arms around her. "Why 'eviscerated,' Kay?"

"Can't you see that I'm dead, Robert? Not too long ago someone said I was a corpse. She wasn't far out. It occurred to me today that now I am something like you, that my insides have been scooped out, the way your surgery killed off most of you years ago. You were pre-

pared to live that way, Robert. But I'm not." Kay wiped the tears from her eyes and propped herself up on her elbow so she could look into Sedgewick's face. "I want you to do something for me, Robert."

"I've told you, Kay, I'll do anything that I can for you— within the given limits."

Kay stared into his eyes, which were gleaming. "I would like," she said, her throat so choked she could hardly speak, "I would like you some time in the next twenty-four hours to take out one of your guns, come up behind me, put it to my temple, and shoot me." Sedgewick's face paled, and his eyes, now dull and dilated, fairly pierced her. Kay swallowed and blinked back her tears. "That's what I would like more than anything, Robert. If you would do that for me."

"You are talking out of your depression, Kay. You haven't yet gotten used to your freedom. You don't have a feel for the possibilities yet. What you need is a project," he urged. "Writing a new book, something like that."

Kay shook her head. "No, Robert. I'm through writing books."

He hesitated. "There's another possibility, too. I thought we might have a child, you and I."

Her stomach hollowed with horror. She have a child by Sedgewick? How could he even suggest such a thing? "But they would never allow that. Birth Limitation," Kay said haltingly, certain she had never heard of anyone with more than two children.

"Something could be worked out. And there is now a need to raise the executive birthrate a bit, after the losses of the last two years and other factors we are now forecasting."

"The idea appalls me," Kay said very low.

"I would never force you to have a child, Kay." The way he would never force her to lie like this in bed with him? "I only thought it might be good for you, that it would give you a more positive outlook on the future."

"I would like you to finish what was begun with my capture," Kay said. "It is the only decent thing to do. If you at all care for me you will do this for me."

"What did that bitch do to you to make you feel this way?"

A small surge of anger rippled over her. "I'm sure you have enough of an idea, Robert." How did he think she had become so tractable?

He closed his eyes. After perhaps a minute he said, "I wanted to believe it would work out. I still believe that if only you'd stick it out for a bit longer you'd throw off your depression. Your prison experience was bound to leave you depressed."

"Please, Robert." She could of course kill herself in some awkward, desperate way, unless he began resorting to Elizabeth's methods. And even then there was the matter of her inability to keep food down. He must realize these things...

He opened his eyes and looked at her. "I don't want to be alone."

She touched his face. "Oh, Robert. You are alone. You've been alone for years and years. At least since your surgery, if not before. You've chosen to be alone. Isn't that what being an executive is all about?"

He closed his eyes. After a long silence he opened them again to look at her. "All right, Kay. But can we at least have this night?"

"Thank you, Robert," Kay whispered. And lying back down beside him, she let him wrap his arms around her and lay his head on her breast.

They didn't sleep through the night but lay quietly, hardly talking at all. When in the morning the thin gray light filtered into the room, Kay asked him if he would do it then.

They went downstairs to the Small Study. Kay stood at the French doors and stared out at the sun rising from the ocean. She heard a drawer being opened and then the sound of an ammunition clip sliding out then in and finally snapping shut. She heard Sedgewick's footsteps approaching and drew a deep breath. Now, this was it. He was standing behind her, and he was putting one hand on her shoulder. She felt the trembling of his body, heard the raggedness of his breath. Then she felt the barrel of the gun against her temple. Kay stared at the waves and waited.

"Do you still want this, Kay? Can't you wait a bit longer? You might change your mind."

"I want it," Kay said.

"How strange it is, Kay. I'm feeling again. I can feel this."

"Please, Robert."

"There is something about this... But this time, it's final. This time we will not be able to switch roles. I wish..."

Kay watched a gull wheel and swoop. She remembered the tone of voice and the words to use to him. "Do it now," she ordered, never taking her eyes off the water.

"Yes, Kay," Sedgewick said, and he did it.

[iv]

Allison went in to the office Saturday morning with the intention of asking Elizabeth for a transfer for herself and Anne. The last of Anne's casts was coming off that day; more importantly, however, the end of the Civil War and the reconstitution of the Executive had been publicly announced. Allison had finished the special progress reports she had written for Elizabeth, complete with suggestions for organizing the work that she would be leaving behind if she were transferred. She was determined to make Elizabeth see that only personal reasons could lie behind a denial of a transfer.

But Jacquelyn, when asked if Elizabeth were available, told Allison that Elizabeth had left town the night before and hadn't yet returned, and that Elizabeth was scheduled to attend a high-level meeting on her arrival. Allison sensed that Jacquelyn knew a great deal that she wasn't telling. Her manner was grave in contrast with the gaiety she and everyone else on the base had indulged in the day and night before to celebrate the end of the Civil War. Allison went to her desk utterly dashed, conscious she wouldn't feel quite so confident when she faced Elizabeth later in the day.

At around noon Elizabeth came into Allison's office. "I've brought Sedgewick back with me from Maine," she said without preamble. "The Russians invaded Poland, Austria, and the Czech and Slovak republics yesterday. I'm fairly confident that Sedgewick intends to direct all the intelligence and covert-ops to do with the war himself."

They were at war! *Austria* invaded? Which meant that Vienna... "Then things must have worked out with Zeldin," Allison said.

Elizabeth closed the door and leaned against it. "In one sense, yes. In another sense, no. Zeldin is dead."

The blood rushed in Allison's ears. "I don't understand." Zeldin had been starving herself, but surely she hadn't been that close to death. "How could she be dead?"

"She asked him to kill her, and he did it." Elizabeth's eyes were stark. "Can you believe that? He did it because she asked him to! That's all he'll say. That was on Thursday morning. He buried her on the island. When I went last night to tell him about the invasion, he was sitting in his study, drunk as a lord, fingering a lock of hair he had cut from her head. It gave me the creeps, Allison. He said he cut the lock of hair when she was dead because he wanted something to remember her by and she had nothing personal with her. To *remember* her by, Allison. As though he has trouble remembering her, as though all his old photographs and slides and video recordings of her aren't enough. When I saw him like that I was sure he would be hopeless, that he would grow worse, maybe as bad as he was when Zeldin first dumped us on that island. But after I sat talking to him for a while I finally managed to bring up the subject of the invasion. He agreed to return with me without argument. And when I woke this morning, he was already up and dressed, drinking coffee and reading through the reports I'd left on his desk."

"So it's all over." Allison felt sick. And then before she knew what she was saying, the words burst out of her. "Oh god, Elizabeth, I'm glad she's dead. I'd like to forget Zeldin ever existed!"

Elizabeth gave her a strange look. "She really upset you, didn't she," Elizabeth said slowly. "Well I'm sorry she's dead. Not only for what it might do to Sedgewick. But because…" She looked away. "Never mind." She pressed her lips together and looked back at Allison. "I want to take you in to meet him now, Allison. He wants to hear all about the vid project. We've already begun talking about the possibilities for your managing— in liaison with Com & Tran— a big public education campaign for the war."

Allison stared at Elizabeth. If Elizabeth had already brought her to Sedgewick's attention, her chances of getting away had sunk to zero.

"Well?" Elizabeth said. "Shall we?"

Allison got up from her desk and followed Elizabeth out the door. What else could she do?

[v]

Martha and Sorben walked along the four-mile-long waterfront pedestrian park, occasionally stopping to watch the loading of cargo onto ships docked in Elliott Bay, and basking in the mild February sun as Martha tried to explain to the Marq'ssan her thoughts about longevity treatments. For a long while Martha talked to Sorben as though she were human, as though Sorben were one of them. But it struck her: Sorben was *not* human. And not only that, but Martha had no idea of the average lifespan of Marq'ssan. "How old are you, Sorben?" Martha said baldly, interrupting herself.

Sorben looked startled. "In earth terms?" She stared out at the water for a few seconds. "Somewhere in the neighborhood of two hundred years old."

Martha was shocked. "Two *hundred*?"

Sorben nodded. "Tyln, though, is much younger. Magyyt is a little older than I. And Leleynl— well, Leleynl is very old. Maybe close to four hundred years. I don't think I know anyone as old as Leleynl is."

Martha tried to conceal the strange nasty feeling taking hold of her. "How old do you think Leleynl will live to be?" she asked uneasily.

Sorben smiled. "I think Leleynl will live to be very very old. Much older than she is now. You see, everything has changed with us Marq'ssan in the last two hundred years. Because of our more sophisticated understanding of chiastics we can now expect to live— barring accidents and mayhem— well, forever. If we choose."

"But that is nothing like our longevity treatments."

"No, nothing like them at all."

"We must seem like some vastly inferior species to Marq'ssan. We breed excessively and then die young— you probably look on us the way humans look on rabbits."

"No, Martha. What I see is that humans have yet to come to terms with their biology. And obviously you have been struggling to do so for some time. And now here in the Free Zone, the concern has become

widespread— not simply a matter for your rulers to dictate to you. Now *that* is promising."

Martha leaned against the rough stone railing. A suction arm whined and wailed out over the water; a ship was unloading grain that Martha had reason to know had come from Argentina. "You keep talking about getting started and about things being promising," Martha said, "but all I can see is everything collapsing around me. Not only has World War Three broken out and become physically present on this continent, the Free Zone is disintegrating into armed bands of men bullying most of the Zone outside of Seattle." Martha looked at Sorben. "Why did you abandon us like this, Sorben?" she asked passionately, for the first time admitting to herself that she was angry and disappointed by the Marq'ssan's detachment from the Free Zone. "Everything we had going here was so fragile, we weren't ready to be left to cope by ourselves. We have so many problems, and most people are helpless to do anything but what they're told. Why, Sorben? Why have you stayed away?" A gull settled on one of the boulders that topped the small, choppy waves.

"You say abandoned," Sorben said slowly. "That suggests to me that you feel there is an obligation— perhaps parental?— on the part of the Marq'ssan, an obligation you feel we've fallen down on."

"You helped us hatch," Martha said, "and then pushed us out of the nest before our eyes were fully opened, before we had any notion of how to fly. All you gave us was limited glimpses of adult birds flying, glimpses circumscribed by the near-blindness of the newborn. We don't know what we're doing. And so now we're failing."

"You aren't failing, Martha. You haven't given up, which means you aren't failing. But I thought we'd explained why we weren't taking a more active role here? We have to be wary about direct interference. It would be so easy for us to tell humans what to do. And that we must not do. We are not colonialists. We help you when you ask us to. For instance in trying to free those scientists being held in that mountain in Colorado. But if we were to help you beyond a certain point, we would be forcing things on you that you wouldn't even be

aware of. No, it must be left up to humans to find their own way. As we found our own way."

"But Sorben!" Martha's palm slapped the rough concrete. "You Marq'ssan *did* directly interfere when you stopped everything two years ago! You did interfere by helping to create the Free Zones! Don't you see, we weren't at all ready for such a large step, and we need help coping with it! You talk about Marq'ssan's changes— well that was something that evolved indigenously. But here— you Marq'ssan were the catalyst! Don't you see?"

Sorben's eyes were sad. "Of course I see. Don't you think we Marq'ssan discussed this thoroughly when we prepared to stop everything, as you put it? But that doesn't mean— "

"It's not going to work!" Martha shouted.

Sorben's light gray eyes regarded her somberly. "You believe that, don't you."

Appalled, Martha realized she did. Never in her life had she lived without hope of achieving something better than the prevailing system. Until now. Now all she saw was a slide downward from that exciting exuberant time in which the Pacific Northwest Free Zone had been born.

They began walking again. After several minutes had passed Sorben said to Martha, "Maybe you're right. Maybe we should take a more active role in what is happening here in this Free Zone. Perhaps... perhaps the risk is necessary. Perhaps we have no choice, perhaps the necessity was inherent in the original decision to halt humans' hostile technology..." Sorben stopped and stared out at the massively snow-burdened Olympic mountains standing out against the deep blue horizon.

After several minutes of silence, Sorben said, "I'll talk to Magyyt and the others."

Martha also stared at the Olympics. With that she would have to rest content. She wouldn't hope, yet. Though now there was the possibility of hope. And that was something she could hold onto... for a while.

[vi]

Excerpt from the

Annual Report on the State of the Earth

(June, 2078, Earth dating)

...While cooperative socioeconomic and political structures and the habits of negotiation have been flourishing in the Free Zones in Southern Mexico, Western Australia, Korea, New Brazil, and Little Kenya, the situation of the North American Pacific Northwest Free Zone is another matter entirely. Unlike the other Free Zones, the Pacific Northwest Free Zone began life handicapped by its humans' lack of experience in either thinking or acting cooperatively and also, very markedly, by their susceptibility to executive-system propaganda (which, for reasons thoroughly discussed before the Intervention, has always been considerably greater for the inhabitants of the United States than for populations elsewhere).

The few activist groups that existed at the time of the formation of this Free Zone have hardened into political factions that see themselves as engaged in ideologically-framed struggles for position and influence. Any reflection and analysis they bring to bear on their problems tends to take the form of ad hoc problem-solving— at best— or, more typically, a determination of what specific individuals and groups may have to win or lose through various outcomes. (See the appendix to this report titled *The Dominance of the Game Paradigm in Intermural Interactions in the Pacific Northwest Free Zone.*) As resources of every type become more plentiful, these factions squabble ever more jealously over their allocation. The ideological perspective of capitalism is so deeply ingrained in those born and raised in the United States that few are able to conceive of resources as produced, owned, and maintained by the community. Thus even those persons most consciously dedicated to developing cooperative socioeconomic and political structures are unable to see beyond immediate personal potential outcomes when considering the allocation of resources previously distributed as privileges accruing to those favored by the executive system. Although they can see the long view in theory, they have so little sense of personal stake or interest in it that it never enters collective considerations or negotiations.

One possible approach to introducing this Zone to the long-term collective perspective would be to encourage more contact between this Zone and the Southern Mexico and Korea Free Zones. Unfortunately, the unconscious assumption of the US-born that individuals and organizations sited in non-European sections of the world are necessarily inferior makes this move, at least for the time being, a questionable tactic, since individuals in the Pacific Northwest Free Zone would likely find it difficult even to notice that they have much to learn from these non-Europeans.

Of more immediate concern is a sharp decline in morale in the Pacific Northwest Free Zone. Although morale revived following the difficult winter of 2077, it declined sharply when the US Executive's covert penetrations into a variety of paramilitary organizations throughout the Zone began to threaten many areas of the Zone with violence and disorder. The Executive's capture and murder of Kay Zeldin, who had been a hero in the Zone from its formation, contributed to the decline, although it appears to have exercised an artificially unifying effect through creating a martyr. Throughout human history martyrdoms have often spawned cults, religions, and mindsets at complete odds with the principles the martyr actually espoused in life. We have said nothing about this danger to our closest contacts in the Zone but intend to monitor the posthumous reification of Kay Zeldin closely. The symbolism of the destruction of the person who is perceived as responsible for having caused the Executive's Civil War has provoked emotional turmoil and expressions of despair out of all proportion to the event's strategic significance (and seemingly without regard for individuals' personal relations with Kay Zeldin when she was alive).

One of the Zone's leading organizers, Martha Greenglass, requested that we provide stronger guidance to herself and other organizers. Because of our concern about morale in the Free Zone, we have decided to increase our visibility there and adopt a more ostentatiously responsive face. Although our basic stance of observing, offering reflective and responsive dialogue, and providing support and resources will not be altered, we believe that an increase in our visibility and a more frequent engagement in dialogue with the organizers will bolster their confidence in their

own abilities and help stimulate the thoughtfulness and reflection that are still lacking in this Free Zone's individuals and groups.

Despite the slowness of change in the Pacific Northwest Free Zone, we are in no way discouraged. In the relative inexperience of its organizers (in comparison with the extensive experience of the groups working in effective, negotiated coalition in the other Free Zones), the Pacific Northwest Free Zone resembles most of the rest of the world. The mere fact that it is managing to survive (and even thrive) absent the domination of executives offers a powerful object lesson to its neighbors and will undoubtedly, with the passage of time, stimulate new, previously unthinkable ideas about human political, social, and economic organization. Shedding the dogmatic ideological blinders a society has worn for more than a century takes time. This was one of the lessons learned on *s'sbeyl*— and one we are in no danger of forgetting any time soon.

New Orleans
December 1984 – April 1985
revised June 1996

Acknowledgments

Although everything about Security Services, a fictional government agency of the equally fictitious Executive, is a product of my imagination, I found three books of great assistance in structuring my creation of this fictional institution: Philip Agee's *Inside the Company: CIA Diary;* Victor Marchetti's *The CIA and the Cult of Intelligence;* and John Stockwell's *In Search of Enemies: A CIA Story.*

It gives me great pleasure to thank the numerous individuals who, over the course of the two decades since I first drafted *Renegade*, read the novel in ms and offered me usefully frank comments on it. Among these I would especially like to thank Tom Duchamp, Professor Ann Hibner Koblitz (to whom I owe a particular debt for proof-reading), Shira Broschat (now Professor), Elizabeth Walter, Ken Hankinson, Dr. Joan Haran, and Dr. Joshua B. Lukin. The critiques they offered were a labor of love, and I will always be grateful to them for their engagement with my work.

The person to whom I owe the greatest debt is Kathryn Wilham. I sent packets of chapters to her twice (or more) a week during the first three months in 1985 when I wrote the novel, and she not only persuaded me to substantially rewrite the last four chapters but also offered sympathy and moral support via long middle-of-the-night phone conversations when I contemplated scrapping most of the book—going back to Chapter Thirteen and writing an entirely different story. She immediately saw why the narrative had to go where it did and never once reproached me for an ending that had to be. Throughout, her confidence in my vision for the Marq'ssan Cycle was vital.

Praise for *Alanya to Alanya*

Alanya to Alanya is SF on a broader scale, with *The War of the Worlds* as one inspiration, but its metaphors apply to a very human tangle of loyalty and betrayal, politics and idealism—Wells and Orwell updated for the end of the 20th century.

—*Locus*, June 2005

Responding to Earth's determination to focus on space travel, a group of aliens calling themselves the Marq'ssan shut down the planet's technological capacity and call for representatives from all nations, specifically asking for women. Professor Kay Zeldin, a former covert operative and currently a history professor, is recalled to duty to act as one of the ambassadors to the alien "terrorists." Presenting a contemporary tale of alien invasion and feminist revisionism, Duchamp's (*Love's Body*) series opener examines the issues of sex and power that still exist despite efforts to mandate equality. Politically savvy and philosophically relevant, this title puts a human face on today's problems. A good choice for readers who prefer a heavy dose of social science with their sf.

—*Library Journal*, June 15, 2005

Readers who still prefer their feminist science fiction in the radical dystopian/utopian mode,...readers who still appreciate the anger and surety of those early works can take heart at the publication of L. Timmel Duchamp's *Alanya to Alanya*... [T]hose with a serious interest in dystopias and particularly the feminist version thereof should find L. Timmel Duchamp's Marq'ssan Cycle a rewarding experience.

—Michael Levy, *New York Review of Science Fiction*, December 2005

Alanya to Alanya is not so much an exploration of the way humanity responds to an alien presence as an illustration of how a world under siege from its own governments finally revolts; the invaders are simply the catalyst for change. The main emphasis is on the silent majority finding its power, and even more so on the feminist revolution among that majority.

—*The Seattle Times*, July 3, 2005

Alanya to Alanya is an intriguing mixture of SF genres and styles: It has utopian and dystopian elements, a strong splash of the political thriller, a good mystery subplot in Kay's amnesia, a hint of the sense of discovery that imbues first-contact novels and plenty to say about the current state of the real world. The first of a five-novel Marq'ssan cycle, it offers no easy answers to either its readers or its characters—though Kay ultimately works out where her loyalties lie, the aliens find themselves seriously challenged by humanity's intransigence.

—*Science Fiction Weekly*, June 27, 2005

Duchamp's novel, both her first and the first in a five part series, works as political theory wrapped inside a thriller and tucked neatly into a package of science fiction. In lesser hands, attempting to blend these very different facets could result in a huge mess but Duchamp handles them smoothly. Her political world building has a level of detail and believability that rivals Bruce Sterling at his best, and her pacing is much better than most other books driven so heavily by political concepts, such as Ayn Rand's *Atlas Shrugged* or Sheri S. Tepper's *The Gate to Women's Country*.

...Much of the politics and concepts descend directly from feminist science fiction of the 1970s, most notably the work of Alice B. Sheldon, a.k.a. James Tiptree Jr. Duchamp's near future Earth sits very close to our own, and her story can be easily viewed as criticism of the status quo. It's not so difficult to imagine any nation, even our own, taking such drastic steps when faced with such overwhelming circumstances. Martial law, curfews, random arrests, gassing the public to keep them calm—all these tactics seem frighteningly close to reality, and *Alanya to Alanya* has some thoughtful things to say about the current direction of politics in this country.

—*Strange Horizons*, November 30, 2005

About the Author

L. Timmel Duchamp is the author of a collection of short fiction (*Love's Body, Dancing in Time*), a collection of essays (*The Grand Conversation*), three novels (*Alanya to Alanya, Renegade*, and *The Red Rose Rages (Bleeding)*), and dozens of short stories.. She has been a finalist for the Nebula and Sturgeon awards and has been shortlisted for the Tiptree Award several times. A selection of her essays and fiction can be found at http://ltimmel.home.mindspring.com.

The Marq'ssan Cycle

by L. Timmel Duchamp

Book 1: *Alanya to Alanya*
Book 2: *Renegade*

Forthcoming

Book 3: Tsunami, Fall 2006
Book 4: Blood in the Fruit, Spring 2007
Book 5: Stretto, Fall 2007